CW00501062

Anonymous

Public Acts and Joint and Concurrent Resolutions of the Legislature of the State of Michigan

Anonymous

Public Acts and Joint and Concurrent Resolutions of the Legislature of the State of Michigan

Reprint of the original, first published in 1875.

1st Edition 2024 | ISBN: 978-3-38538-425-5

Verlag (Publisher): Outlook Verlag GmbH, Zeilweg 44, 60439 Frankfurt, Deutschland
Vertretungsberechtigt (Authorized to represent): E. Roepke, Zeilweg 44, 60439 Frankfurt, Deutschland
Druck (Print): Books on Demand GmbH, In de Tarpen 42, 22848 Norderstedt, Deutschland

PUBLIC ACTS

AND

JOINT AND CONCURRENT RESOLUTIONS

OF

THE LEGISLATURE

OF THE

STATE OF MICHIGAN,

PASSED AT THE

REGULAR SESSION OF 1875,

WITH AN APPENDIX.

BY AUTHORITY.

LANSING:
W. S. GEORGE & CO., STATE PRINTERS AND BINDERS.
1875.

LIST OF ACTS

PASSED BY THE LEGISLATURE OF 1875.

three, one thousand two hundred and four, one thousand two hundred and five, one thousand two hundred and seven, one thousand two hundred and eight, one thousand two hundred and nine, one thousand two hundred and ten, one thousand two hundred and twelve, one thousand two hundred and fourteen, and one thousand two hundred and fifteen, of compiled laws of eighteen hundred and seventy-one, relative to officers having the care and superintendence of highways and bridges, and their general powers and duties, and sections two, four, five, six, seven, eight, and nine of chapter twenty-four, being sections one thousand two hundred and seventeen, one thousand two hundred and nineteen, one thousand two hundred and twenty, one thousand two hundred and twenty-one, one thousand two hundred and twenty-two, one thousand two hundred and twenty-three, and one thousand two hundred and twenty-four of compiled laws of eighteen hundred and seventy-one, relative to persons liable to work on highways and making assessment therefor, and sections three, fifteen, sixteen, seventeen, eighteen, twenty, twenty-one, twenty-two, twenty-three, and one of chapter twenty-five, being sections one thousand two hundred and twenty-eight, one thousand two hundred and forty, one thousand two hundred and forty-one, one thousand two hundred and forty-two, one thousand two hundred and forty-three, one thousand two hundred and forty-five, one thousand two hundred and forty-six, one thousand two hundred and forty-seven, one thousand two hundred and forty-eight, and one thousand two hundred and fifty-one of compiled laws of eighteen hundred and seventy-one, relative to the duties of overseers in regard to the performance of labor on highways, the performance of such labor or the commutation therefor and application of moneys by the commissioners, and sections two, three, four, seven, eight, eleven, fourteen, fifteen, sixteen, and one of chapter twenty-six, being sections one thousand two hundred and fifty-three, one thousand two hundred and fifty-four, one thousand two hundred and fifty-five, one thousand two hundred and fifty-eight, one thousand two hundred and fifty-nine, one thousand two hundred and sixty-two, one thousand two hundred and sixty-five, one thousand two hundred and sixty-six, one thousand two hundred and sixty-seven, and one thousand two hundred and seventy-eight of compiled laws of eighteen hundred and seventy-one, relative to laying out, altering, and discontinuing public roads, and sections two, four, five, and six of chapter twenty-seven, being sections one thousand two hundred and ninety, one thousand two hundred and ninety-two, one thousand two hundred and ninety-three, and one thousand two hundred and ninety-four of compiled laws of eighteen hundred and seventy-one, relative to the obstruction of highways, encroachments thereon, and penalties, and sections one, three, four, six, seven, eight, two, and three of chapter twenty-eight, being sections one thousand three hundred and one, one thousand three hundred and three, one thousand three hundred and four, one thousand three hundred and six, one thousand three hundred and seven, one thousand three hundred and eight, one thousand three hundred and

B

C

D

LIST OF JOINT RESOLUTIONS.

———————

LIST OF CONCURRENT RESOLUTIONS.

———◆———

LAWS OF MICHIGAN

[No. 1.]

AN ACT to amend section twelve of an act entitled "An act to provide for determining and regulating the tolls, and for the care, charge, and operating of Portage Lake and Lake Superior Ship Canal," approved April twenty-fifth, eighteen hundred and seventy-three.

SECTION 1. *The People of the State of Michigan enact,* That section twelve of an act entitled "An act to provide for determining and regulating the tolls, and for the care, charge, and operating of Portage Lake and Lake Superior Ship Canal," approved April twenty-fifth, eighteen hundred and seventy-three, be amended so as to read as follows: *Section amended*

SEC. 12. That the said board of control shall, upon the request of the Governor, proceed to establish rates of toll, and appoint a superintendent as provided in section two of this act; and the said board shall direct and fix the time when such superintendent shall take possession and charge of said canal: *Provided,* That nothing herein contained shall be construed as entitling any person, company, or corporation to the certificate of the Governor that said canal has been completed, until the title to said canal, as between the United States, the State of Michigan, and any person, company, or corporation claiming the same or any interest therein has been fully and definitely settled by the final order, judgment, or decree of some court of competent jurisdiction, unless otherwise settled to the satisfaction of the Governor. And it shall be the duty of the Attorney General to commence such proceedings as he may deem advisable, or intervene on behalf of the State in any suit or proceeding now pending, or which may hereafter be commenced, for the purpose of settling such question and protecting the rights of the State in said canal. *Board of control, under direction of the Governor, to establish rates of toll, appoint superintendent, etc.* *Proviso—title to canal to be settled before certificate of completion is given.* *Duty of the Attorney General in relation thereto.*

SEC. 2. This act shall take immediate effect.

Approved January 14, 1875.

[No. 2.]

AN ACT to provide for the purchase of books for the State Library.

SECTION 1. *The People of the State of Michigan enact,* That the sum of one thousand five hundred dollars for each of the years one thousand eight hundred and seventy-five and one thousand *Amount appropriated.*

eight hundred and seventy-six, be, and the same is hereby appropriated out of any money in the State Treasury to the credit of the general fund not otherwise appropriated, for the purchase of books for the State library.

How drawn and expended.

SEC. 2. The money so appropriated shall be drawn from the State Treasury, upon the warrant of the Auditor General, and shall be expended by the State Librarian, with the advice and consent of the Governor, for the purpose aforesaid.

SEC. 3. This act shall take immediate effect.

Approved February 2, 1875.

[No. 3.]

AN ACT to amend act number one hundred and twenty (120) of the session laws of eighteen hundred and seventy-three, the same being an act providing for the location, establishment, and organization of an additional asylum for the insane.

Section amended

SECTION 1. *The People of the State of Michigan enact*, That section eight of act number one hundred and twenty (120) of the session laws of eighteen hundred and seventy-three (1873), being an act entitled "An act providing for the location, establishment, and organization of an additional asylum for the insane," be amended so as to read as follows:

Compensation of board.

SEC. 8. Each of the members of said board shall be entitled to receive his actual traveling expenses and the sum of three dollars per day for the time actually spent in discharge of his duties under this act, to be audited by the board of State Auditors.

SEC. 2. This act shall take immediate effect.

Approved February 2, 1875.

[No. 4.]

AN ACT to amend "An act to provide for the incorporation of associations, conventions, conferences, or religious bodies, for literary, religious, or other benevolent purposes," approved March twenty-seven, eighteen hundred and sixty-seven, being sections three thousand one hundred and thirty-one, three thousand one hundred and thirty-two, and three thousand one hundred and thirty-three of chapter one hundred and eight of the compiled laws of eighteen hundred and seventy-one, by adding thereto two new sections, to be numbered sections four and five.

Sections added.

SECTION 1. *The People of the State of Michigan enact*, That an act entitled "An act to provide for the incorporation of associations, conventions, conferences, or religious bodies, for literary, religious, or other benevolent purposes," approved March twenty-seven, eighteen hundred and sixty-seven, being sections three thousand one hundred and thirty-one, three thousand one hundred and thirty-two, and three thousand one hundred and thirty-three of chapter one hundred and eight of the compiled laws of eighteen hundred and seventy-one, be and the same is hereby amended by adding thereto two new sections to be numbered sections four and five, as follows:

SEC. 4. Such articles of association may be executed singly or in duplicate, and shall be acknowledged before some officer authorized to take the acknowledgment of deeds, and the original articles so acknowledged, or one of such duplicate originals, shall be filed in the office of the Secretary of State; and either of such original articles, or a copy of the same certified by the Secretary or Deputy Secretary of State, shall be receivable in all courts as evidence of such incorporation. *Articles of association, how executed and where filed.*

SEC. 5. The articles of association shall set forth the purposes of the incorporation, and the mode of selection and term of office of the trustees, and may provide for the first board by name instead of by future election, if desired. They may also provide for acting as auxiliary to any religious conference, synod, or convention within the State of Michigan, incorporated or unincorporated, and for the choice of trustees, in whole or in part, by such religious conference, synod, or convention, and for receiving and executing trusts for their benefit, as well as for other purposes within the meaning of this act. But all such trusts in their hands shall be for purposes to be executed and expended within the State of Michigan. *What to set forth.*

SEC. 2. This act shall take immediate effect.

Approved February 2, 1875.

[No. 5.]

AN ACT to amend section one (1) of "An act relative to levies of executions on real estate," being section four thousand six hundred and eighty-five (4685), in chapter one hundred and sixty-five (165) of the compiled laws of eighteen hundred and seventy-one.

SECTION 1. *The People of the State of Michigan enact,* That section one in chapter one hundred and sixty-five (165), being section four thousand six hundred and eighty-five (4685) of the compiled laws of eighteen hundred and seventy-one, entitled "An act relative to levies of executions on real estate," be so amended as to read as follows: *Section amended*

(4685.) SECTION 1. *The People of the State of Michigan enact,* That no levy by execution on real estate, made after this act shall take effect as a law, shall be valid against *bona fide* conveyances made subsequent to such levy, until a notice thereof containing the name of the parties to the execution, a description of the premises levied upon, and the date of such levy, shall be filed by the officer making the same, in the office of the register of deeds of the county where the premises are situated; and such levy shall be a lien thereon only from the time when such notice shall be so deposited. And such register shall thereupon enter on such notice a minute of the time of receiving the same, and shall record the same in a book *Notice of levy to be filed with register of deeds.* *Duty of register.*

to be kept for that purpose; and shall make an index to such record in such manner as shall be convenient for public reference, of the names of parties to the execution, as stated in said notice; *Fees.* and such officer shall receive, for making and filing the notice as aforesaid, the sum of fifty cents; and such register of deeds shall receive for recording the same, the same fees as are allowed by law for recording notices of the pendency of suits in chancery, which fees the said officer shall add to the cost to be collected by such execution; and shall in like manner collect the same; and when-*Certificate of* ever such execution shall be fully paid, satisfied, or discharged, it *satisfaction.* shall be the duty of the clerk of the court that issued such execution, to give to the defendant a certificate, under the seal of the court, that the same is satisfied or discharged; and such certificate may be recorded in the same manner as is provided for the recording of such notice.

Approved February 4, 1875.

[No. 6.]

AN ACT to amend section thirteen of an act entitled " An act to provide for the organization of the supreme court, pursuant to section two of article six of the constitution," approved February sixteenth, eighteen hundred and fifty-seven, being section four thousand eight hundred and ninety-six of the compiled laws of eighteen hundred and seventy-one, as amended by act number one hundred and twenty-six of the session laws of eighteen hundred and seventy-three.

Section amended   SECTION 1. *The People of the State of Michigan enact,* That section thirteen of an act entitled " An act to provide for the organization of the supreme court, pursuant to section two of article six of the constitution," approved February sixteenth, eighteen hundred and fifty-seven, being section four thousand eight hundred and ninety-six of the compiled laws of eighteen hundred and seventy-one, as amended by act number one hundred and twenty-six of the session laws of eighteen hundred and seventy-three, be and the same is hereby amended so as to read as follows:

Quorum.   (4896.) SEC. 13. Three judges shall be sufficient to form a quorum for the transaction of business by the supreme court, organized under the provisions of this act, and the court shall have the *Jurisdiction and* same jurisdiction and powers which have been conferred by the *powers.* constitution and laws now in force upon the present supreme court. *Terms of court.* Four terms of the supreme court shall be held annually, commencing Tuesday after the first Monday of January, April, June, and October; which shall be called respectively the January, April, June, and October terms of said court. All the terms of said court shall be held at the supreme court room in the city of Lan-*Special terms.* sing, in the county of Ingham. The court may hold special or adjourned terms, and shall continue its session a sufficient number of days at each term to hear all the causes ready for hearing, and all causes and questions not decided at the term when the same are submitted, shall be determined early in the next succeeding term.

Sec. 2. This act shall take immediate effect.

Approved February 4, 1875.

[No. 7.]

AN ACT to amend sections seven, eleven, fifteen, sixteen, nineteen, twenty, twenty-two, and twenty-three of an act entitled "An act to provide a municipal court of the city of Detroit to be called 'The Superior Court of Detroit,'" approved March twenty-eight, eighteen hundred and seventy-three, and to add six new sections thereto, to stand as sections twenty-four, twenty-five, twenty-six, twenty-seven, twenty-eight, and twenty-nine.

SECTION 1. *The People of the State of Michigan enact,* That Sections sections seven, eleven, fifteen, sixteen, nineteen, twenty, twenty- amended. two, and twenty-three of an act entitled "An act to provide for a municipal court in the city of Detroit, to be called 'The Superior Court of Detroit,'" approved March twenty-eight, eighteen hundred and seventy-three, be and the same are hereby amended so as to read as follows:

SEC. 7. The clerk of said court shall be appointed by the judge Clerk, how apthereof, and a memorandum of such appointment shall be entered pointed. upon the record of said court. Such clerk shall hold his office for Term of office. the term of two years from and after the first day of June, and until his successor is duly appointed and qualified. But the first appointment under this section shall not take effect until the first day of January, one thousand eight hundred and seventy-six. The Removal. judge shall have the power at any time to remove such clerk for incompetency, or serious neglect in the performance of his duties; and in case of such removal, or of a vacancy in said office by the death of said clerk, or otherwise, the judge shall fill the unexpired term by a new appointment.

SEC. 11. Before any suit at law shall be commenced in said court, Court fees. there shall be paid to the clerk of said court, by the party com- [See Sec. 25.] mencing such suit. the sum of four dollars; and before any judgment shall be entered in any such suit, there shall be paid by the prevailing party to said clerk the sum of five dollars. And before any suit or proceeding in chancery shall be commenced there shall be paid to said clerk by the complainant, or party instituting such proceeding, the sum of five dollars; and before any decree shall be entered on any bill taken as confessed by all the defendants, the further sum of five dollars. And a like sum shall be paid upon the granting of any order to sell the real estate of infants, where the same is not resisted, and also before the entry of any decree upon bill and demurrer or plea to be paid by the party in whose favor such decree shall be granted, and in all other cases, the further sum of ten dollars. The moneys so paid shall be for the To be for the use use of said city, and shall be paid daily by the clerk to the city of the city, and paid over by treasurer and placed to the credit of the general fund, and the clerk.

same shall be held to be in full of all entry fees, jury fees, and all fees of the clerk of said court in any such suit from the commencement thereof to and including the issuing of execution or other

To be taxed as costs.

final process. The sum or sums so paid shall be taxed as costs of suit in favor of the party paying the same, if he be the prevailing party in such suit, in addition to any other costs to which he may

Proviso.

be entitled by law: *Provided*, That if a jury shall not be demanded, the sum so to be paid before entry of judgment shall be two dollars.

Practice and rules of Superior Court.

SEC. 15. The practice and proceedings in said superior court shall be the same as those prescribed by law for circuit courts in this State, unless otherwise limited by this act; and the rules prescribed by the supreme court for the guidance and practice of circuit courts shall be the rules of said superior court, so far as

Proviso.

the same may be applicable: *Provided*, That the judge of said court shall have full power and authority to establish from time to time such rules of practice in said court as shall have been first approved by the supreme court. The supreme court shall also direct the time when such rules shall go into effect, and the mode in which they shall be published.

Terms.

SEC. 16. There shall be at least six regular terms of said superior court held in each year, and the time of commencement of terms for each year shall be fixed by the judge of said court in the month of May in each year, and notices of the times of holding such terms shall be published for two weeks in one of the daily papers published in the city of Detroit.

Selection of jurors.

SEC. 19. On the tenth days of May and November in each year, between the hours of ten and twelve in the forenoon, the judge and clerk of said court and the sheriff of the county of Wayne shall meet together in the office of the clerk of said court, and shall proceed in public to select from the last annual assessment roll of said city (which roll the proper custodian shall produce before them), a list of two hundred persons to serve as jurors in

Qualifications.

said superior court; the persons so selected to be qualified electors of said city, of fair character, of sound mind, and capable of understanding and speaking intelligibly the English language.

List, by whom signed and where filed.

Said list shall be signed by said judge, clerk, and sheriff, and shall be filed in the office of the clerk of said court. If either of said

In case of absence of either officer.

officials shall not attend at the time and place aforesaid, the meeting shall stand adjourned from day to day for five days, and if on either of said days they shall meet together, between said hours, at such place, they shall then make such list; and if on the last adjourned day any two of them shall so meet, one being absent, they shall proceed to make, sign, and file such list of jurors. The

Time for which persons selected are liable to serve.

persons whose names are set forth in said list shall be liable to serve as jurors for six months, or until a new list shall be made as

Practice of court in drawing, summoning, etc., of jurors, imposing of penalties, etc.

aforesaid. The practice and proceedings in said court, excepting as provided in this section relative to drawing, summoning, exempting, and excusing jurors and talesmen, and imposing penalties upon them for non-attendance, shall be the same as the practice and proceedings in the recorder's court of said city as prescribed by sections thirty-five, thirty-six, thirty-seven, thirty-eight, thirty-nine, forty, forty-one, forty-two, forty-three, forty-four, forty-five, forty-six, and forty-seven of chapter six of an act entitled " An act to revise the charter of the city of Detroit," approved February fifth, eighteen hundred and fifty-seven ; but all talesmen who may be directed by said court to be summoned for the term, shall be drawn from the jury box in like manner, as near as may be, as are the jurors of the original panel, and the persons whose names shall be so drawn shall be entered on the minute of the drawing mentioned in said section forty, together with the fact that they have been drawn as talesmen, and a *venire facias* shall be made out by the clerk and delivered to the sheriff for service, which shall command him to summon the persons therein named to appear forthwith and serve as jurors in said court. Every person who shall directly or indirectly ask to be placed upon said list shall thereby render himself ineligible to serve as a juror in said court for one year thereafter, and his name shall in no case be placed upon such list during that period. It shall be a good cause of challenge, in addition to all other challenges allowed by law, that any person summoned as juror or as talesman, shall have acted as a juror in a court of record in said city, or have asked to be placed upon said list as above mentioned, during a year preceding such challenge. Cause for ineligibility of juror.
Cause of challenge.

SEC. 20. The common council of the said city shall provide a proper court-room for the accommodation of said superior court, together with an office for the clerk as near to said court-room as can conveniently be procured, and all necessary furniture, fuel, books, and stationery, for the use of the court, and in the office of the clerk. Court room, office for clerk, stationery, etc.

SEC. 22. That a stenographer for said superior court shall be appointed by the Governor on the recommendation of the judge of said court. The person so appointed shall take and subscribe the official oath prescribed by the constitution, which oath shall be administered by the presiding judge. He shall be deemed an officer of the court, and shall hold the position during the pleasure of the Governor ; provided the court shall have power to suspend him for incompetency or misconduct, and in such case of suspension he shall thereafter cease to hold the office of stenographer, unless by order of the court his suspension be rescinded. Stenographer.
Oath, term of office, etc.

SEC. 23. In case of the death or resignation of the stenographer, the Governor shall, on receiving notice from the presiding judge of such fact, appoint a successor to the office ; but in case of sickness or temporary absence of the stenographer, or his suspension as above provided, the judge may appoint some competent person to act in his absence. Vacancy, how filled.

SEC. 2. That said act be further amended by adding thereto six new sections, to be numbered sections twenty-four, twenty-five, twenty-six, twenty-seven, twenty-eight, and twenty-nine, to read as follows : Section added.

SEC. 24. It shall be the duty of said stenographer to attend upon the court during each term thereof, and to take full stenographic Duty of stenographer.

notes of all testimony given upon the trial of each issue of fact
before the court or jury, and in trials by jury also to take full stenographic notes of the instructions given by the court to the jury.
Salary.   Said stenographer shall receive a salary of two thousand dollars
per annum, to be paid in monthly installments out of the city
treasury.

Court fees. (See   SEC. 25. Each and every issue of fact at law or in chancery, tried
Sec. 11.   before the court or jury, shall be taxed three dollars, to be paid by
the plaintiff, at the commencement of the trial, into the hands of
the clerk, and by him paid into the city treasury as other fees mentioned in this act. In case the plaintiff in any suit shall refuse to
pay such fee, the defendant in the cause shall, on payment to the
clerk of said fee, be entitled to judgment as of nonsuit. The prevailing party shall have the amount so paid by him taxed in his
costs as proper disbursement.

Testimony, how   SEC. 26. The court may in its discretion order the testimony in
taken.   any and all suits in chancery to be taken orally in open court, in
whole or in part, in which case a fee of three dollars shall be first
paid to the clerk by the complainant, and such testimony shall be
taken by the stenographer of said court in like manner and with
the same effect as in suits at law; said court shall have the same
power to appoint special commissioners and make references to
them or to the circuit court commissioners of Wayne county as is
given to the circuit court of said county.

When finding is   SEC. 27. If, before judgment in any cause, tried by the court
demanded, the   without a jury, either party shall demand a finding upon the facts,
judge may
require copy of   or of law, such party shall furnish to the judge, within a reason-
testimony.   able time, to be specified by him, a copy of so much and such part
of the testimony, taken from the reporter's minutes, as the judge
shall require, and if such party shall neglect or refuse to furnish
such copy within the time specified, the party making such demand shall be deemed to have waived the same, and judgment may
be entered without such finding.

Judgment in   SEC. 28. Whenever any cause shall have been properly placed
case of neglect   upon the docket of said court for four times, whether successive or
to try cause.
otherwise, and the same shall not have been tried, the court may
at the close of any future term, if said cause shall have been again
duly placed upon the docket of said term, direct a judgment as of
nonsuit to be entered therein against the plaintiff for want of
prosecution.

Trials in pro-   SEC. 29. Whenever at the close of any term of said court the
gress at close of   trial of a cause shall be in progress, such trial shall continue until
term to be con-
tinued until   the same is determined, and the continuance of such trial shall not
determined.   be construed as prolonging said term, nor to prevent the commencement of the succeeding term, previously designated as herein required.

SEC. 30. This act shall take immediate effect.

Approved February 4, 1875.

[No. 8.]

AN ACT to amend section one of an act entitled "An act to provide for the transfer of the insane inmates of the Soldiers' Home at Detroit, or of any county jail in this State, who have been soldiers or marines of the United States, to the credit of the State of Michigan, and who are not criminals, to the Insane Asylum at Kalamazoo, the same being act number ninety-one of the session laws of eighteen hundred and seventy-three," approved April fifteen, eighteen hundred and seventy-three.

SECTION 1. *The People of the State of Michigan enact*, That section one of an act entitled "An act to provide for the transfer of the insane inmates of the Soldiers' Home at Detroit, or of any county jail in this State, who have been soldiers or marines of the United States, to the credit of the State of Michigan, and who are not criminals, to the Insane Asylum at Kalamazoo," be amended so as to read as follows : *Section amended.*

SECTION 1. All persons who have been soldiers or marines of the United States from the State of Michigan, and who are, or may become insane, and who are not criminals, may, by order of the State Military Board, be transferred, under the same rules and regulations as govern the admission of county patients, to the Insane Asylum at Kalamazoo, and there be provided for at the expense of the State. *Transfer of certain insane persons to the asylum at Kalamazoo.*

SEC. 2. This act shall take immediate effect.

Approved February 18, 1875.

———

[No. 9.]

AN ACT making appropriations for the heating and ventilating apparatus for the new Capitol, and for improvements in said building.

SECTION 1. *The People of the State of Michigan enact*, That the sum of seventy thousand dollars is hereby appropriated out of the State building fund in the State Treasury for the purpose of purchasing and putting in the new capitol building the necessary boilers and other apparatus for warming and ventilating the said building. *Amount appropriated for heating apparatus, ventilation, etc.*

SEC. 2. The further sum of thirty thousand dollars is hereby appropriated out of the State building fund in the State Treasury, to be expended by the board of State Building Commissioners, in their discretion, for proposed changes in the roof, the steps to the east, north, and south porticoes, and the interior finish of said buiding. *Amount appropriated for proposed changes.*

SEC. 3. The amounts appropriated by sections one and two of this act shall be apportioned by the Auditor General and incorporated in the State tax, one-half of the same in the tax for the year eighteen hundred and seventy-six and one-half in the tax for the year eighteen hundred and seventy-seven, and the amounts, when collected, shall be placed by him to the credit of the State building fund. *Provision to meet appropriations.*

2

Idem.

SEC. 4. Should any portion of the amount to be apportioned and collected in the State tax for the year eighteen hundred and seventy-six, as provided in section three of this act, be required by the board of State Building Commissioners before the same shall be collected and placed to the credit of the State building fund, the Auditor General is hereby authorized to advance the amount so required from the general fund, the amount so advanced to be returned to the general fund when the same shall have been collected.

SEC. 5. This act shall take immediate effect.

Approved February 18, 1875.

[No. 10.]

AN ACT to amend an act entitled " An act for the incorporation of hospitals or asylums in cases where valuable grants or emoluments have been made to trustees for such purposes," being chapter one hundred and four, section three thousand and thirty-two of the compiled laws of eighteen hundred and seventy-one, to provide for apprenticing destitute children.

Section amended

SECTION 1. *The People of the State of Michigan enact,* That section five of an act entitled " An act for the incorporation of hospitals or asylums, in cases where valuable grants or emoluments have been made to trustees for such purposes," approved March twenty, eighteen hundred and sixty-three, being chapter one hundred and four, section three thousand and thirty-two, of the compiled laws of eighteen hundred and seventy-one, be amended so as to read as follows:

Trustees may apprentice destitute children.

SEC. 5. The trustees of said corporation, or a majority of them, are hereby authorized and empowered to indenture or apprentice to responsible persons, any destitute or foundling children now, or which may be hereafter, in charge or care of said corporation, until such children shall respectively become of lawful age, and to make such indenture in each case as binding and effective in all respects as if said trustees were the lawful parents or guardians of said children:

Proviso.

Provided, Said trustees shall have power to withdraw such child from any person to whom he or she may be indentured, when in their opinion the interests of the child may require it. No

Trustees not entitled to compensation.

trustees of said corporation shall be entitled to any compensation except under some special employment by the board or authority expressed in the original deed or instrument of trust.

SEC. 2. This act shall take immediate effect.

Approved February 18, 1875.

[No. 11.]

AN ACT making appropriations for the State Normal School.

Amount appropriated.

SECTION 1. *The People of the State of Michigan enact,* That the State Treasurer shall transfer from the general fund the sum of seventeen thousand and three hundred dollars for the year eighteen hundred and seventy-five, and seventeen thousand and three hundred dollars for the year eighteen hundred and seventy-six, which sums are hereby appropriated to the Normal School interest fund and shall be drawn from the treasury in the manner now provided by law in relation to that fund.

SEC. 2. This act shall take immediate effect.

Approved February 18, 1875.

[No. 12.]

AN ACT to amend sections three hundred and thirty-eight, three hundred and thirty-nine, three hundred and forty, and three hundred and forty-one of the compiled laws of eigh'een hundred and seventy-one, being sections one, two, three, and four of an act entitled " An act to create a board of fund commissioners, and to define their powers and duties," approved April two, eighteen hundred and forty-eight.

SECTION 1. *The People of the State of Michigan enact*, That sections three hundred and thirty-eight, three hundred and thirty-nine, three hundred and forty, and three hundred and forty-one of the compiled laws of eighteen hundred and seventy-one, being sections one, two, three, and four of an act entitled " An act to create a board of fund commissioners, and to define their powers and duties," be amended so as to read as follows : *Sections amended.*

(338.) SECTION 1. The Governor, State Treasurer, and Auditor General are hereby constituted a board of fund commissioners. *Board of fund commissioners.*

(339.) SEC. 2. Whenever after paying or reserving a sum sufficient to meet all liabilities payable from the general fund, for the current expenses of the State government and for the payment of interest on State indebtedness, provided for by law, there shall be in the State Treasury a surplus over and above such liabilities, or any moneys applicable to the payment of State indebtedness, the board aforesaid shall have power and it shall be their duty to invest the same as they may find for the best interest of the State in the purchase of bonds and other liabilities of the State. *Board shall invest surplus in Treasury, in State liabilities.*

(340.) SEC. 3. Said board may, at any time in their discretion, cause a notice to be published by not less than three insertions in two or more daily papers, in each of the cities of Detroit and New York, that proposals for the sale of bonds or other evidences of debt of this State, not then due, will be received by the fund commissioners at the seat of government, at any time prior to a day specified in said notice, and which shall be at least two weeks subsequent to the first publication of said notice in either of the cities aforesaid. The commissioners shall have discretionary power to accept or reject any or all of said proposals, but in case of acceptance preference shall in all cases be given to the lowest bids, and to those bonds or other evidences of debt first to become due. If the said board are unable to purchase such unmatured bonds at rates, in their judgment, for the interest of the State, they may invest such sums, or portion thereof applicable to the payment of *Shall advertise before purchasing.* *May purchase U. S. bonds in certain cases.*

said bonds, in United States bonds, and re-convert them when, in their judgment, the bonds of this State can be substituted for the United States bonds so purchased.

Account of treasurer with respect to such purchases. (341.) SEC. 4. The State Treasurer shall be charged on the books of the Auditor General with the amount of discount allowed on the purchase of the bonds or other liabilities above mentioned, and upon cancelment of the same, shall be credited with the payment thereof at their par value, and in case any premium is paid on the purchase of said bonds or other liabilities, he shall be credited with the amount of premium paid. In case of the purchase of bonds, as herein provided, the discount, if there be any, shall be credited to, or the premium paid shall be charged to, the fund from which the money used in such purchase is disbursed.

SEC. 2. This act shall take immediate effect.

Approved February 18, 1875.

[No. 13.]

AN ACT to amend sections eighteen and twenty of chapter one hundred and seventy-eight of the compiled laws of eighteen hundred and seventy-one, relative to attachments.

Sections amended. SECTION 1. *The People of the State of Michigan enact,* That sections eighteen and twenty of chapter one hundred and seventy-eight be amended so as to read as follows:

When suit may be commenced by attachment. (5266.) SEC. 18. Any plaintiff shall be entitled to an attachment against a defendant in any action founded on a judgment or on a contract, express or implied, if such plaintiff, or some person in his behalf, shall make and file with the justice an affidavit, specifying as near as may be the amount due to the plaintiff, and containing a further statement, either that the deponent knows or has good reason to believe: either

First, That the defendant has assigned, disposed of, or concealed, or is about to assign, dispose of, or conceal, any of his property, with the intent to defraud his creditors; or

Second, That he is about to remove any of his property from the county in which such application is made, or from the county where the defendant resides, with the like intent; or

Third, That he fraudulently contracted the debt, or incurred the obligation, respecting which the suit was brought; or

Fourth, That the defendant has absconded to the injury of his creditors, or does not reside in this State, and has not resided therein for one month immediately preceding the time of making the application.

When plaintiff entitled to warrant. (5268.) SEC. 20. In actions other than those founded on judgment or contract, the plaintiff shall be entitled to a warrant, if he or some person in his behalf shall make and file with the justice an affidavit specifying the nature of the demand, and containing a statement that the deponent has good reason to believe: either

First, That the defendant has committed a trespass, or other wrong, to the damage of the plaintiff; or

Second, That the defendant has incurred a penalty or forfeiture by the violation of some law of this State, which the person filing such affidavit has a right to prosecute in the name of the people of this State, or otherwise.

SEC. 2. This act shall take immediate effect.

Approved February 18, 1875.

[No. 14.]

AN ACT to organize the county of Baraga, and to locate the county seat thereof.

SECTION 1. *The People of the State of Michigan enact,* That townships fifty, fifty-one, fifty-two, and fifty-three north, of range thirty west; townships forty-seven, forty-eight, forty-nine, fifty, fifty-one, fifty-two, and fifty three north, of range thirty-one west; townships forty-seven, forty-eight, forty-nine, fifty, fifty-one, and fifty-two north, of range thirty-two west; townships forty-seven, forty-eight, forty-nine, fifty, fifty-one, and that part of town fifty-two north lying east of Sturgeon River, of range thirty-three west; that part of town forty-seven north, lying east of the south branch of Sturgeon river, townships forty-eight, forty-nine, fifty, and that part of townships fifty-one and fifty-two north lying east of Sturgeon River, of range thirty-four west; that part of townships forty-seven, forty-eight, forty-nine and fifty north, lying east of the Sturgeon River, or the south branch thereof, of range thirty-five west, is hereby detached from the county of Houghton, and is hereby organized into a county to be known and designated as the county of Baraga. *County of Baraga organized.*

SEC. 2. The county seat of said county is hereby established at the village of L'Anse. *County seat.*

SEC. 3. Nothing herein contained shall be construed as conferring upon the county of Baraga the lands belonging to the county of Houghton, but lying within said county of Baraga. But the vacant lands belonging to the county of Houghton, whether lying within the county of Baraga or elsewhere, shall be apportioned between the counties of Houghton and Baraga, in the same manner as the other property of Houghton county is to be apportioned under existing laws. *Apportionment of vacant lands.*

SEC. 4. There shall be elected in the said county of Baraga, at the next annual meeting in the several townships in said county, to be held on the first Monday of April, in the year eighteen hundred and seventy-five, all the several county officers to which by law the said county is entitled, and said election shall in all respects be conducted and held in the manner prescribed by law for holding elections for county and state officers, and said officers so elected shall, after having duly qualified according to law, enter upon the duties of their respective offices on the first Monday of May following, and hold the same until the first day of January, in the year eighteen hundred and seventy-seven. The county officers of Houghton shall exercise all the powers and perform all *Election of county officers.*

the duties now devolving on them in the territory taken from said county until the county officers of Baraga shall be elected and qualified.

Board of canvassers.

SEC. 5. And the board of canvassers of said county under this act shall consist of the presiding inspectors of elections from each township therein, and said inspectors shall meet at the village of L'Anse, in said county, on the second Tuesday after the election, and organize by appointing one of their number chairman and another secretary of said board, and shall thereupon discharge all duties of a board of county canvassers for county and state officers.

Judicial relation.

SEC. 6. The said county of Baraga shall have concurrent jurisdiction on Lake Superior with the counties contiguous thereto, and shall form a part of the twelfth judicial circuit.

SEC. 7. This act shall take immediate effect.

Approved February 19, 1875.

[No. 15.]
AN ACT for the protection of inn and hotel keepers.

Landlord who keeps safe for custody of money, etc., and posts notices of same, not liable for losses.

SECTION 1. *The People of the State of Michigan enact,* That hereafter every landlord or keeper of a public inn or hotel in this State, who shall constantly have in his inn or hotel an iron safe, in good order, and suitable for the safe custody of money, jewelry, or other valuable articles belonging to his guests or customers, and shall keep posted conspicuously at the office, and on the inside of every entrance door of every public, sleeping, bar, reading, sitting, and parlor room of his inn or hotel, notices to his guests and customers that they must leave money, jewelry, and other valuables with the landlord, his agent, or clerk, for safe keeping, that he may make safe deposits of the same in the place required for that purpose, shall not be liable for any money, jewelry, or other valuables of gold or silver, or rare and precious stones, that may be lost, if the same is not delivered to said landlord, hotel, or innkeeper, his agent, or clerk, for deposit, unless such loss shall occur by the hand, or through the negligence of the landlord, or by a clerk, or a servant employed by him in such hotel or inn: *Pro-*

Proviso.

vided, That nothing herein contained shall apply to such amount of money and valuables as is usual, common, and prudent for any such guest to retain in his room or about his person.

Punishment for obtaining food, credit, etc., with intent to defraud.

SEC. 2. Every person who shall at any hotel or inn order, or cause to be furnished any food or accommodation, with intent to defraud the owner or proprietor of such hotel or inn out of the value of such food or accommodation, and every person who shall obtain credit at any hotel or inn, by the use of any false pretense or device, or by depositing at such hotel or inn any baggage of value less than the amount of such credit, or of the bill of such person incurred ; and any person who, after obtaining credit or accommodation at any hotel or inn, shall abscond from such hotel or inn, and shall surreptitiously remove his baggage or property therefrom, with intent to defraud the owner or keeper thereof,

shall, upon conviction, be adjudged guilty of a misdemeanor; and
on conviction thereof shall be punished by imprisonment in the
county jail not exceeding sixty days, or by fine not exceeding one
hundred dollars, or by both such fine and imprisonment, in the
discretion of the court.

Approved February 25, 1875.

[No. 16.]

AN ACT to provide for the incorporation of Tribes and Councils
of The Improved Order of Red Men, and to repeal chapter one
hundred and twenty-two of the compiled laws, being an act to
provide for the incorporation of societies of Pocahontas Tribes
of Improved Order of Red Men.

SECTION 1. *The People of the State of Michigan enact,* That the Who may incorporate under this act. Great Council and subordinate Tribes of the Improved Order of Red Men of the State of Michigan may be incorporated in pursuance of the provisions of this act.

SEC. 2. Any ten or more persons, residents of this State, being members of any Great Council of the Improved Order of Red Men of the State of Michigan, desirous to become incorporated, may make and execute articles of association, under their hands and seals, which articles of association shall be acknowledged before some officer authorized by law to take acknowledgment of deeds, and shall set forth: *(Incorporation by members of any Great Council of The Improved Order of Red Men. Articles of association.)*

First, The names of the persons associating in the first instance, and their places of residence; *(What to set forth.)*

Second, The corporate name by which such association shall be known in the law, and the place of its business office;

Third, The object and purpose of such association, which shall be to promote the general welfare of the fraternity known as the "Improved Order of Red Men," and the period for which it is incorporated, not exceeding thirty years.

SEC. 3. A copy of said articles of association, together with a copy of the charter and constitution of said Great Council, shall be filed with the Secretary of State, and thereupon the persons who shall have signed such articles of association, their associates and successors, shall be a body politic and corporate, by the name expressed in such articles of association, and by that name they and their successors shall have succession, and shall be persons in the law, capable to purchase, take, receive, hold, and enjoy, to them and their successors, estates real and personal, of suing and being sued, and to have a common seal, which may be altered or changed at their pleasure: *Provided,* That the value of such real and personal estate shall not exceed the sum of ten thousand dollars, and that they and their successors shall have power to give, grant, sell, lease, demise, and dispose of said real and personal estate, or part thereof, at their will and pleasure, and the proceeds, rents, and incomes shall be devoted exclusively to the charitable and benevolent purposes of the Improved Order of Red Men. *(Copy of articles, etc., to be filed with Secretary of State. Powers of corporation. Proviso—real and personal estate of corporation limited.)*

Powers to establish rules, regulations, and elect officers, etc.

Said corporation shall have full power to make and establish rules, regulations, and by-laws for regulating and governing all the affairs and business of said corporation not repugnant to the constitution and laws of this State, or of the United States, and to designate, elect, or appoint from its members such officers, under such name and style as shall be in accordance with the constitution of the Great Council of the United States.

Evidence of corporation.

SEC. 4. A copy of the record of such articles of association, under the seal of the State, duly certified according to law, shall be received as *prima facie* evidence in all courts of this State of the existence and due incorporation of such corporation.

Power to charter subordinate Tribes and make rules, etc., for their government.

SEC. 5. Such corporation, when duly formed, shall have power to institute and charter subordinate tribes of said order within this State, and from time to time to make, ordain, constitute, and establish such general laws and by-laws, ordinances and regulations for the government of such subordinate tribes not repugnant to law or to the constitution or regulations of the Great Council of the Improved Order of Red Men of the United States, as to them shall seem proper and necessary, and in case of violation or noncompliance with such ordinances, by-laws, and regulations, to revoke and annul the charter granted to such subordinate tribes:

Proviso—existing tribes subject to control of Great Council as heretofore.

Provided, That the existing subordinate tribes heretofore duly chartered by the Great Council of Michigan, or of the United States, shall be subject to the control of the said Great Council under this act as heretofore, and in the same manner, and to the same extent as those that may hereafter be instituted and chartered under this act.

Incorporation by members of Tribes of Improved Order of Red Men.

SEC. 6. Any seven or more persons, residents of this State, being members of a tribe of Improved Order of Red Men, having been duly chartered by the Great Council of the Improved Order of Red Men of this State, desirous to become incorporated, may make

Articles of association.

and execute articles of association under their hands and seals, specifying, as provided in article two of this act, and file a copy of such articles with the clerk of the county in which such corporation shall be formed, which shall be recorded by such clerk in a

Powers of corporation.

book to be kept in his office for that purpose; and thereupon the persons who shall have signed said articles of association, their associates and successors, shall be a body politic and corporate, by the name expressed in such articles of association; and by that name they and their successors shall have succession, and shall be persons in the law, capable to purchase, hold, enjoy, grant, sell, give, lease, and demise real and personal estate, of suing and being sued, and may have a common seal, and change and alter the same at pleasure; and a certified copy of the record of such articles of association, under the seal of the county where the said record is kept, shall be received as *prima facie* evidence in all courts of this State of the existence and due incorporation of such corporation:

Proviso—real and personal estate of corporation limited.

Provided, That the value of such real and personal estate shall not exceed the sum of ten thousand dollars, and that they and their successors shall have authority and power to give, grant, sell, lease, demise, and dispose of said real and personal estate, or part thereof, at their will and pleasure, and the proceeds, rents, and income shall be devoted exclusively to the charitable and benevolent purposes of the Improved Order of Red Men.

SEC. 7. Any corporation formed in pursuance of this act may erect and own such suitable edifice, building, or hall as to such corporation shall seem proper, with convenient rooms for the meetings of the tribes or councils of the Improved Order of Red Men; and for that purpose may create a capital stock of not more than ten thousand dollars, to be divided into shares of not more than ten dollars each; and any such corporation may take, purchase, hold, and own such suitable lot or parcel of ground as may be convenient for the purpose of a cemetery, and may make all lawful rules and regulations for the disposition of lots and the burial of the dead therein as to such corporation may seem proper. May erect edifices, etc., and create a capital stock therefor. May own ground for cemetery.

SEC. 8. All corporations formed under this act shall be subject to the provisions of chapter one hundred and thirty of the compiled laws of this State, so far as the same may be applicable to corporations formed under this act, and the Legislature may alter or amend this act at any time. Subject to chap. 180, C. L., so far as applicable.

SEC. 9. Chapter one hundred and twenty-two of the compiled laws, being an act to provide for the incorporation of societies of Pocahontas Tribes of Improved Order of Red Men, is hereby repealed. Act repealed.

Approved February 25, 1875.

[No. 17.]

AN ACT to amend sections seventy and ninety-three of an act entitled "An act to provide for a uniform assessment of property, and for the collection and return of taxes thereon," being sections one thousand and thirty-six and one thousand and fifty-nine of the compiled laws of eighteen hundred and seventy-one.

SECTION 1. *The People of the State of Michigan enact,* That sections seventy and ninety-three of an act entitled "An act to provide for a uniform assessment of property, and for the collection and return of taxes thereon," being sections one thousand and thirty-six and one thousand and fifty-nine of the compiled laws of eighteen hundred and seventy-one, be amended so as to read as follows: Sections amended

(1036.) SEC. 70. Any person may pay the taxes, or any one of the several taxes, on any parcel of lands returned as aforesaid, or on any undivided share thereof, with interest calculated thereon from the first day of February next after the same were assessed, at the rate of ten per cent per annum, and the office charges, and four per cent as a collection fee, to the treasurer of the county in which the lands are situated, at any time before they are sold for taxes, or to the State Treasurer on the certificate of the Auditor General, at any time before the twentieth day of September next preceding the time appointed for such sales: *Provided,* That on all taxes Payment of taxes after return. Proviso.

remaining unpaid on the first day of June next after the same were assessed, interest shall be computed at the rate of twenty per cent per annum from the said first day of June.

Redemption of lands.
(1059.) SEC. 93. Any person owning any of the lands sold as aforesaid, or any interest therein, may on or at any time previous to the thirtieth day of September next succeeding such sale redeem any parcel of said lands, or any part or interest in said lands, by showing to the satisfaction of the Auditor General or county treasurer that he owns only that part or interest in the same which he proposes to redeem, and by paying, at his option, into the State Treasury, or to the treasurer of the county where such land is situated, the amount for which such parcel was sold, or such portion th reof as the part or interest redeemed shall amount to, with in rest thereon at the rate of twenty-five per cent per annum; which interest shall be paid by the State Treasurer to the purchaser.

SEC. 2. This act shall take immediate effect.
Approved February 25, 1875.

[No. 18.]
AN ACT to organize the county of Isle Royal.

County of Isle Royal organized.
SECTION 1. *The People of the State of Michigan enact,* That the several islands in Lake Superior, known as Isle Royal, and the islands adjacent thereto, shall be organized into a separate county, by the name of Isle Royal, and the inhabitants thereof, entitled to all the rights, privileges, and immunities to which by law the inhabitants of other organized counties of this State are entitled.

Election of county officers.
SEC. 2. There shall be elected in the said county of Isle Royal on the first Tuesday in July next, all the several county officers to which by law the said county is entitled, and the said election and the canvass thereof shall in all respects be conducted and held in the manner prescribed by law for holding elections and canvasses for county and State offices: *Provided,* That the canvass of such election shall be held at the place of holding the election in the township of Isle Royal, on the Monday next following said election, and said county officers shall immediately be qualified and enter upon the duties of their respective offices, and their several terms of office shall expire at the same time that they would have expired had they been elected at the last general election; *And provided further,* That until such county officers are duly elected and qualified, the duties of such county officer shall be discharged by the several persons elected to fill the same for the county of Keweenaw at the last general election.

Time and place of holding canvass, etc.

Board of canvassers.
SEC. 3. The board of canvassers of said county, under this act, shall consist of the inspectors of elections from each township therein; and said inspectors shall meet at the time and place designated in this act; and shall organize by appointing one of their number chairman, and another secretary of said board; and shall thereupon proceed to discharge all the duties of a board of

county canvassers, as in ordinary cases of elections for county and state officers.

SEC. 4. The sheriff, county clerk, and county treasurer of said county, to be elected as provided for in this act, shall designate a suitable place in the township of Isle Royal for holding the circuit court in said county; they shall also designate suitable places in the same township (as near as practicable to the place designated by them for holding the circuit court in said county), for holding the offices of the sheriff, county clerk, county treasurer, register of deeds, and judge of probate of said county, until the county seat for said county shall be established, and shall make and subscribe a certificate in writing, describing the place thus designated, which certificate shall be filed and safely preserved by the county clerk; and after such certificate shall be thus filed, the places thus designated shall be the places of holding the circuit court and county officers, [offices] until the board of supervisors shall establish the county seat of said county, and until suitable accommodations shall be provided for said court and county offices at the county seat; and it is hereby made the duty of the board of supervisors of said county, on or after the year one thousand eight hundred and eighty, to designate and establish the county seat of said county. *Place of holding circuit court and county offices.*

Board of supervisors to establish the county seat.

SEC. 5. The said county of Isle Royal shall have concurrent jurisdiction on Lake Superior with the other counties contiguous thereto. *Jurisdiction.*

SEC. 6. The said county of Isle Royal shall constitute a part of the twelfth judicial circuit of Michigan. *Judicial circuit.*

SEC. 7. This act shall take immediate effect.

Approved March 4, 1875.

[No. 19.]

AN ACT to repeal section four hundred and thirteen of the compiled laws of eighteen hundred and seventy-one, being section six of act number one hundred and twenty-two of the session laws of eighteen hundred and sixty-one, being an act entitled "An act to provide means for the redemption of the bonds of the State maturing January first, eighteen hundred and sixty-three," approved March eleven, eighteen hundred and sixty-one.

SECTION 1. *The People of the State of Michigan enact,* That section four hundred and thirteen of the compiled laws of eighteen hundred and seventy-one, being section six of act number one hundred and twenty-two of the session laws of eighteen hundred and sixty-one, being an act entitled "An act to provide means for the redemption of the bonds of the State maturing January first, eighteen hundred and sixty-three," approved March eleven, eighteen hundred and sixty-one, be and the same is hereby repealed. *Section repealed.*

SEC. 2. This act shall take immediate effect.

Approved March 10, 1875.

[No. 20.]

AN ACT authorizing and instructing the Governor of the State of Michigan to convey private land claims numbers sixty-eight and seventy-six to the United States, to be appropriated for the improvement of the Saint Mary's Falls Canal.

Governor authorized to convey certain lands to U. S.

SECTION 1. *The People of the State of Michigan enact*, That the Governor of the State of Michigan is hereby authorized and instructed to convey to the United States private land claims numbers sixty-eight and seventy-six, in the county of Chippewa, and State of Michigan, to be appropriated for the improvement of the Saint Mary's Falls Canal, and for no other purpose, and reserving to the State of Michigan civil and criminal jurisdiction over said lands and premises.

Lands so conveyed, how appropriated.

Jurisdiction.

SEC. 2. This act shall take immediate effect.

Approved March 10, 1875.

[No. 21.]

AN ACT for the relief of certain societies.

Society may change name at regular meeting.

SECTION 1. *The People of the State of Michigan enact*, That whenever any church or religious society shall desire to change its corporate name, the same may be done by a vote of two-thirds of the society, conference, vestry, session, synod, or official board, so desiring to change its name as aforesaid, present and voting at a regular meeting of the same; previous notice having been given of such proposed change at least twenty [20] days before such meeting.

Notice of such meeting.

Certificate of vote.

SEC. 2. Whenever such vote shall be taken, the clerk or secretary of the meeting shall make a certificate of the fact, which certificate shall be countersigned by the presiding officer of the meeting, rector, presiding elder, or minister, and this certificate shall be acknowledged before some officer authorized to take acknowledgment of deeds.

Where recorded.

SEC. 3. Such certificate shall be recorded in the office of the county clerk for the county in which such society is located, and when so recorded the said society shall be known in law by the new name, and shall be entitled to all the rights and privileges of the original society as it regards property, real and personal, deeds and franchises, and shall be subject to and liable for all debts and obligations of the corporation by the former name, the same as if the name had not been so changed.

Rights and privileges.

SEC. 4. This act shall take immediate effect.

Approved March 10, 1875.

[No. 22.]

AN ACT to provide for the use of the proceeds of the sale of educational lands in defraying the expenses of the State government.

SECTION 1. *The People of the State of Michigan enact,* That all money received into the State Treasury from the sale of lands, and placed to the credit of the University fund, the Agricultural College fund, the Normal School fund, the Primary School fund, or the five per cent Primary School fund, on and after the first day of March, eighteen hundred and seventy-five, shall be used in defraying the expenses of the State government. Proceeds of educational lands used in defraying expenses of State government.

SEC. 2. This act shall take immediate effect.

Approved March 10, 1875.

[No. 23.]

AN ACT to amend section twenty of chapter one hundred and forty-four, relating to university and school lands, being section three thousand eight hundred and thirty-six of the compiled laws of eighteen hundred and seventy-one.

SECTION 1. *The People of the State of Michigan enact,* That section twenty of chapter one hundred and forty-four, relating to university and school lands, being section three thousand eight hundred and thirty-six of the compiled laws of eighteen hundred and seventy-one, be amended so as to read as follows: Section amended.

(3836.) SEC. 20. In all cases where rights of a purchaser shall have become forfeited under the provisions of this chapter, by his failure to pay the amount due upon his certificate of purchase, if such purchaser, his heirs or assigns shall, before the time appointed for the sale of the lands described in such certificate, at public auction, pay to the commissioner of the land office, the full amount then due and payable upon such certificate, and twenty-five cents on each dollar of such amount in addition thereto, together with all taxes remaining due and unpaid upon said lands, such payment shall operate as a redemption of the rights of such purchaser, his heirs and assigns; and said certificate from the time of such payment, shall be in full force and effect, as if no such forfeiture had occurred: *Provided, however,* That in case the lands described in any certificate of purchase shall not be redeemed after the forfeiture before the day of sale, and the same shall be purchased at such public sale, or from the State at private sale, after such public offering in the manner now provided by law, by any person, then, and in that case, such purchaser shall pay at the date of such purchase, into the State treasury, the amount required by law for the purchase of lands at such forfeited sales, together with all taxes and charges due and unpaid thereon; and the treasurer shall be required to give his receipt therefor, which shall state in full the amount paid, together with the description of the lands on which the same is paid, and the name of such purchaser; and no certificate shall be Redemption of forfeited lands prior to date of sale. Proviso—purchase at, or subsequent to time appointed for the sale. Receipt of treasurer.

Certificate of purchase.

issued to such subsequent purchaser until after the expiration of one year from and after the date of such public offering, during which time said certificate-holder, his heirs or assigns, shall have

Redemption after sale.

a right to redeem said lands from the effects of such forfeiture by paying into the State treasury all interest, penalty, and charges due upon such certificate, as is now provided by law, and all taxes and other charges due and unpaid thereon, together with interest at the rate of twenty-five per cent per annum, on all sums paid by such subsequent purchaser, from the date of such sale up to the date of such redemption; and in case of such redemption, the State Treasurer shall refund to the party whose purchase has been canceled by such redemption, the full amount so paid by such subsequent purchaser, together with interest on the same from the date of such payment into the treasury up to the date of such redemption, at the rate of twenty-five per cent per annum.

SEC. 2. This act shall take immediate effect.

Approved March 10, 1875.

[No. 24.]

AN ACT to amend section ten (10) of chapter six (6), being section forty-one (41) of the compiled laws of eighteen hundred and seventy-one, relative to notice of election to fill vacancy.

Section amended

SECTION 1. *The People of the State of Michigan enact*, That section ten of chapter six of the compiled laws of eighteen hundred and seventy-one (being compiler's section forty-one), be and the same is amended so as to read as follows:

Secretary of State to give notice of election to fill vacancy.

(41.) SEC. 10. When a vacancy shall occur in the office of judge of the supreme court, of judge of the circuit court, regent of the University, or member of the State Board of Education, thirty days or more before a general election, the Secretary of State shall, at least twenty days before such election, cause a written notice to be sent to the sheriff of each of the counties within the election district in which such vacancy may occur, which notice shall state in which office the vacancy occurred, and that such vacancy will be supplied at the next general election.

SEC. 2. This act shall take immediate effect.

Approved March 10, 1875.

[No. 25.]

AN ACT to provide for the distribution of the statutes of the United States furnished to this State by act of Congress, approved June twenty, eighteen hundred and seventy-four.

Distribution of U. S. statutes by State Librarian.

SECTION 1. *The People of the State of Michigan enact*, That the State Librarian, upon the receipt of the statutes of the United States, furnished to the State as provided by act of Congress, approved June twenty, eighteen hundred and seventy-four, shall distribute one copy each to the offices of the Governor, the Secretary of State, the Auditor General, the State Treasurer, the Commissioner of the State Land Office, the Attorney General, the Commissioner of Railroads, the Insurance Commissioner, and the Superintendent of Public Instruction; one copy to each of the justices of the supreme court, to each of the circuit judges and judges of the superior courts of this State, and one copy to be kept in the office of the county clerk of each county in this State; ten copies to the State University, five for the general and five for the law library; one copy to the library of the Agricultural College; twelve copies to the State library; in all cases the officers receiving the said statutes shall deliver them to their successors in office; and after retaining fifty volumes for future use, the balance, if any, may be distributed to the incorporated libraries and colleges of this State, upon application and payment of charges for the delivery of the same.

SEC. 2. This act shall take immediate effect.

Approved March 10, 1875.

[No. 26.]

AN ACT to provide for the incorporation of the Independent Order of Philanthropists, of the State of Michigan.

SECTION 1. *The People of the State of Michigan enact,* That grand and subordinate lodges of the Independent Order of Philanthropists, of the State of Michigan, may be incorporated in pursuance of the provisions of this act. Grand and subordinate lodges may incorporate under this act.

SEC. 2. That any ten or more persons, with their associates and successors, shall constitute the grand lodge of the Independent Order of Philanthropists, of the State of Michigan; and they are hereby authorized to make and execute, under their hands and seals, articles of association, which said articles of association shall be acknowledged before some officer of this State having authority to make [take] acknowledgments of deeds, and shall set forth: Incorporation of grand lodges.
Articles of association.

First, The names of persons so associating in the first instance, and their places of residence; What to set forth

Second, The corporate name by which such association shall be known in the law, and the place of its business office;

Third, The object and purpose of such association, which shall be to promote the general welfare of the fraternity known as the Independent Order of Philanthropists, of the State of Michigan, and the period for which it is incorporated, not exceeding thirty years.

SEC. 3. A copy of said articles of association, together with a copy of the constitution of said grand lodge, shall be filed with the Secretary of State, and thereupon the persons who shall have signed such articles of association, and their associates and successors, shall be a body politic and corporate, under the name of the grand lodge of the Independent Order of Philanthropists, of the State of Michigan, and by that name they and their associates shall have succession, and shall be persons in the law, capable to purchase, take, receive, hold, and enjoy, to them and their succes- Copy of articles and constitution to be filed with Secretary of State.

Power to hold real and personal estate, etc.

sors, estates real and personal, of suing and being sued, and they and their successors may have a common seal, which may be changed and altered at their pleasure: *Provided*, That the value **Such real and personal estate limited.** of such real and personal estate shall not exceed the sum of fifty thousand dollars, and that they, and their successors, shall have authority and power to give, grant, sell, lease, demise, and dispose of said real estate, or part thereof, at their will and pleasure, and the proceeds, rents, and incomes shall be devoted exclusively to the charitable and benevolent purposes of the Independent Order of Philanthropists, of the State of Michigan. Said corporation **Rules, regulations, etc.** shall have full power and authority to make and establish rules, regulations, and by-laws for regulating and governing all the affairs and business of said corporation, according to the laws of this State and the United States, and to designate, elect, or appoint, from its members, such officers, under such name and style as shall be in accordance with the customs of their order.

Copy of articles as evidence of incorporation. SEC. 4. A copy of the record of said articles of association, under the seal of the State, duly certified according to law, shall be received as *prima facie* evidence in all courts of this State of the existence and due incorporation of such corporation.

Chartering of subordinate lodges. SEC. 5. Such corporation, when duly formed, shall have power to institute and charter subordinate lodges within this State, and from time to time to make, ordain, constitute, and establish such constitution, general laws and by-laws, ordinances, and regulations, as it shall judge proper for the regulation and government of such subordinate lodges, not repugnant to the laws of this State.

Corporations formed under this act subject to Chap. 130, C. L. SEC. 6. All corporations formed under this act shall be subject to the provisions of chapter one hundred and thirty of the compiled laws of eighteen hundred and seventy-one, so far as the same may be applicable to corporations formed under this act; and the legislature may alter and amend this act at any time.

Approved March 10, 1875.

[No. 27.]

AN ACT to authorize railroad companies to cut decayed or dangerous trees standing within a certain distance of either side of their track.

Railroad companies required to cut dangerous trees. SECTION 1. *The People of the State of Michigan enact,* That any railroad company owning, controlling, or operating any line or lines of railroad in this State, be and is hereby authorized and required to cut any tree or trees that are dangerous and liable to fall or blow over and obstruct such track.

Approved March 10, 1875.

[No. 28.]

AN ACT to amend section forty-eight of chapter eighteen of the compiled laws of eighteen hundred and seventy-one, being consecutive section eight hundred and seventy-five, relative to the militia.

SECTION 1. *The People of the State of Michigan enact*, That section forty-eight of chapter eighteen of the compiled laws of eighteen hundred and seventy-one, being consecutive section eight hundred and seventy-five, be and the same hereby is amended so as to read as follows: *Section amended.*

(875.) SEC. 48. All officers, non-commissioned officers, and privates, shall receive for their services for each day actually spent by them on duty, in case of riot, tumult, breach of the peace, resistance of process, or whenever called upon in aid of the civil authorities, and for the time necessarily spent by them in traveling from their homes to the place of rendezvous, and in returning to their homes, the following compensation, together with necessary rations and forage, to wit: To each private one dollar per day; to each non-commissioned officer and musician one dollar and twenty-five cents per day; to all commissioned officers of the line, and to the field, staff, and other commissioned officers, the pay proper of officers of the army of the same rank in the service of the United States, together with all necessary rations and forage; and for each horse of all mounted officers and men one dollar per day. Such compensation, and such rations and forage, and the cost of all ammunition used, or purchased for use by any officer [in command] of any State troops so called out, and the cost of all necessary transportation of such troops from their place of rendezvous to the place or places where they are ordered and sent under such call, and in returning to their homes, shall be audited and allowed by the Auditor General, upon the certificate of the commanding officer of such troops, approved by the Quartermaster General. The Auditor General shall, upon auditing and allowing such accounts, draw his warrant upon the State Treasurer therefor, who is hereby authorized and directed to pay the same. And any such sums are hereby appropriated out of any moneys in the general fund not otherwise appropriated; and the Auditor General shall charge all such moneys as drawn to the county where such service is rendered, to be collected and returned to the general fund, in the same manner as any State taxes are required to be by law. *Compensation of troops for services in quieting riots, etc., and provision for payment of same*

Approved March 12, 1875.

4

[No. 29.]

AN ACT to amend section six thousand nine hundred and eighteen, being section seven of chapter two hundred and eighteen of the compiled laws of eighteen hundred and seventy-one, relative to the foreclosure of mortgages by advertisement.

Section amended

SECTION 1. *The People of the State of Michigan enact,* That section six thousand nine hundred and eighteen, being section seven of chapter two hundred and eighteen of the compiled laws of eighteen hundred and seventy-one, relative to the foreclosure of mortgages by advertisement, be and it is hereby amended so as to read as follows :

Distinct farms, lots, etc., when not occupied as one parcel, to be sold separately.

SEC. 7. If the mortgaged premises consist of distinct farms, tracts, or lots not occupied as one parcel, they shall be sold separately, and no more farms, tracts, or lots shall be sold than shall be necessary to satisfy the amount due on such mortgage at the date of the notice of sale, with interest and the costs and expenses allowed by law ; but if distinct lots be occupied as one parcel, they may in such case be sold together.

Approved March 12, 1875.

[No. 30.]

AN ACT to provide for the exercise by religious societies of corporate powers for certain purposes.

Election of trustees and designation of corporate name.

SECTION 1. *The People of the State of Michigan enact,* That when there is organized within this State any diocese, synod, conference, district, or other organization, being an association of congregations or societies of a religious denomination, which shall desire to possess corporate powers in order to effectuate the purposes of such organization, such diocese, synod, conference, or board of district stewards, at a meeting thereof, held and conducted according to the rules and regulations of such organization or association, there being present at such meeting a majority of the members constituting such organization, may elect trustees in number not more than nine nor less than three, and also designate the corporate name by which such trustees and their successors in office shall be known.

Certificate of election.

SEC. 2. It shall be the duty of the officer presiding over such election to give to such trustees a certificate of their election under his hand and seal, specifying the name by which such trustees and their successors shall thereafter be known. Such certificate shall

To be acknowledged and recorded by county clerk.

be acknowledged by the person making the same before some officer authorized to take acknowledgment of deeds, which certificate and the acknowledgment thereof shall be recorded by the county clerk of the county in which such meeting was held, in a book provided for such or similar purposes ; such clerk shall be entitled to receive ten cents for each folio for recording the same ; and thereafter such trustees and their successors shall be a body corporate by the name expressed in such certificate ; they and their

successors shall hold their office for the term of one year, or until Term of office.
the organization or association first making such election elect
others to succeed them.

Sec. 3. Such trustees may have a common seal, and may alter Powers of corporation relative
the same at pleasure, and by their corporate name may take into to the enjoyment
their possession, hold, and enjoy all the property, real or personal, of real and personal property,
purchased for, devised, granted, or conveyed to them for the use etc.
and benefit of such religious organization; they may also in such
corporate name sue and be sued in all courts, recover and hold all
debts, demands, rights, and privileges, and when such organization
shall so order by vote, at a meeting thereof, a majority of all
the members composing such organization being present and
voting therefor, such trustees may sell and convey, mortgage, or
lease any real estate belonging to such organization or held by
them as such trustees: *Provided,* Such trustees shall, before sell- Proviso relative
ing any part thereof, apply to the circuit court of the county in to the sale of real estate and the
which such organization is situated, and if said court shall deem application of the
it proper to make an order for the sale of any real estate belong- moneys arising therefrom.
ing to such organization, it may also direct the application of
any money arising therefrom to such uses as the same organization, with the consent and approbation of such circuit court, shall
conceive to be most for the interest of the corporation to which
the real estate so sold did belong.

Approved March 12, 1875.

[No. 31.]

AN ACT for the relief and regulation of the educational, charitable,
reformatory, and penal institutions of the State.

Section 1. *The People of the State of Michigan enact,* That Funds may be drawn from
the trustees of the Michigan Institution for Educating the Deaf State Treasury
and the Dumb, and the Blind, the board of control of the Reform during certain months for cur-
School, the board of control of the State Public School, are hereby rent expenses.
severally authorized to draw from the general fund of the State
Treasury, in the months of January, February, and March, in the
years in which the regular sessions of the Legislature are held, such
amount of money as shall be made to appear to the Auditor General
to be necessary to meet the current expenses of the institution for
which the money is asked during said months, which amount drawn
shall not exceed one-fourth the amount appropriated for current Amount limited.
expenses for such institution for the year preceding said regular
sessions of the legislature.

Sec. 2. That all amounts so drawn shall be considered as an Funds so drawn considered an
advance to the institution drawing the money on any appropriation advance.
made by the legislature at its regular session for the year in which
the appropriation is made, and shall be deducted therefrom.

Sec. 3. It shall be the duty of said boards, and the boards of all Certain informa-
other educational, charitable, reformatory, and penal institutions tion to be includ-ed in annual
of the State, at the time of making their annual reports, to report reports.
in detail the number and names of the various professors, superin-

tendents, officials, and all other employes, and the wages or salary
paid to each, and what, if any, other emoluments are allowed, and
to whom.

SEC. 4. This act shall take immediate effect.

Approved March 12, 1875.

———

[No. 32.]

AN ACT to organize the county of Otsego.

Otsego county organized. SECTION 1. *The People of the State of Michigan enact*, That the
county of Otsego, consisting of the territory embraced by the present county of Otsego, being townships twenty-nine, thirty, and
thirty-one north, of ranges one, two, three, and four west, and
township thirty-two north, of ranges one, two, and three west, be
and the same is hereby organized into a separate county by the
name of Otsego, and the inhabitants thereof shall be entitled to
all the privileges, powers, and immunities to which, by law, the inhabitants of other organized counties in this State are entitled.

Election of county officers. SEC. 2. At the township meeting of the several townships in said
county, to be held on the first Monday of April next, there shall
be an election of all the county officers to which, by law, the said
county is entitled, who shall hold their several offices until the first
day of January, in the year of our Lord eighteen hundred and
seventy-seven, and until their successors shall have been elected
and qualified; said election shall be conducted in the same way, by
the same officers, and the returns thereof made in the same manner, as near as may be, as is now required by law in the election of
county officers in this State.

Canvass of votes. SEC. 3. The county canvass of the votes cast for county officers
shall be held on the second Tuesday succeeding the election, at the
village of Otsego Lake, in the county aforesaid; and said canvass
shall be conducted in the same way, and by the same officers as the
requirements of law now provide in organized counties, as nearly
as may be, by the appointment by the board of canvassers of one
of their own number to act as secretary to said board of county
canvassers.

Location of county seat determined by vote of electors. SEC. 4. The location of the county seat of said county shall be
determined by the vote of the electors of said county at a special
election, which is hereby appointed to be held by the several townships of said county, on the first Monday in October, eighteen hundred and seventy six. There shall be written or printed on the
ballots there polled, by the qualified electors of said county, the
name of one place, and the place which shall receive the highest
number of votes cast at such election shall be the county seat of
the county of Otsego.

Duty of inspectors of election. SEC. 5. It shall be the duty of the several boards of township
inspectors in each of the townships of the said county to conduct the
elections authorized by the provisions of this act, and to make returns thereof in accordance with the general provisions of law for
conducting general elections in this State, so far as the same may
be applicable thereto.

SEC. 6. The board of county canvassers for the special election for locating the county seat shall consist of the persons appointed on the day of such special election by the several boards of township inspectors, and said board of county canvassers shall meet on the second Tuesday succeeding the day of said special election, at the village of Otsego Lake, in the county aforesaid, and having appointed one of their number chairman, and the county clerk of said county acting as secretary, shall proceed to canvass the votes, and determine the location of the county seat in accordance therewith, and it shall be duty of the clerk of said board to file a copy of the determination of said board as to the location of the county seat, signed and certified by him, and countersigned by the chairman, with the Secretary of State, and with the township clerks of the several townships in said county. *County canvassers to determine result of election for location of county seat.*

SEC. 7. The county seat for said county of Otsego shall be temporarily located at the village of Otsego Lake, in said county, until the county seat has been located as provided for in section four of this act. *Temporary county seat.*

SEC. 8. The said county of Otsego, when so organized, shall be in the eighteenth judicial circuit. *Judicial circuit.*

SEC. 9. The register of deeds of said county shall make, or cause to be made, a transcript of all records made in other counties which are necessary to be and appear upon the records of said county of Otsego; and the board of supervisors of said county shall, within one year after the first meeting of the board, make provision for defraying the expense of the same. *Register of deeds to make transcript of records, etc. Payment of expense.*

SEC. 10. The Secretary of State is hereby directed to furnish the township clerk of the township of Otsego Lake with a certified copy of this act; and it shall be the duty of said clerk to give the same notice of the elections to be held under the provisions of this act that is required by law to be given by the sheriff of organized counties. *Secretary of State to furnish clerk with certified copy of this act. Clerk to give notice of elections.*

SEC. 11. This act shall take immediate effect.

Approved March 12, 1875.

[No. 33.]

AN ACT to prohibit the use of naphtha, or any product of coal oil or petroleum for lighting passenger cars.

SECTION 1. *The People of the State of Michigan enact,* That every railroad corporation operating or doing business in this State is hereby prohibited from running any passenger cars of its own, or those of any other corporation doing business in this or any other State, which are lighted by naphtha, or by any illuminating oil or fluid, made in part from naphtha, or wholly or in part from coal oil or petroleum. Any railroad corporation which violates the provisions of this act shall forfeit a sum not exceeding five hundred dollars. *Railroad corporations prohibited from running passenger cars lighted by naphtha, etc. Penalty.*

Approved March 17, 1875.

[No. 34.]

AN ACT to authorize the board of supervisors of the counties of
Houghton and Baraga to cause the boundary line between said
counties to be surveyed.

Survey authorized.

SECTION 1. *The People of the State of Michigan enact*, That
the board of supervisors of the counties of Houghton and Baraga
are hereby authorized to proceed jointly and cause to be surveyed
the boundary line between said counties, along the Sturgeon River,
so as to determine the sections and fractional sections of land situated in either county along the western boundary line of said
By whom made. Baraga county. Said survey shall be made by one or more competent persons, and shall be verified by the oath of such person or
Duplicates to be persons, and duplicates thereof shall be filed with the county clerk of
filed with county each county, who shall keep the same safely filed, and shall record
clerks.
A copy duly them in the book of miscellaneous records of said county. A copy
verified to be of said survey, duly verified and certified by both boards of super-
filed with Au-
ditor General. visors, shall also be filed in the office of the Auditor General. The
Expense, how expense of making the survey shall be borne by both of said coun-
borne. ties equally.

SEC. 2. This act shall take immediate effect.
Approved March 17, 1875.

[No. 35.]

AN ACT to amend section fourteen [14] of an act entitled " An
act to amend sections two and fourteen of chapter eighty-eight
of the compiled laws of eighteen hundred and seventy-one,
entitled ' An act to authorize the formation of corporations for
the running, booming, and rafting of logs,' " approved March
seventh, eighteen hundred and seventy-three.

Section amended

SECTION 1. *The People of the State of Michigan enact*, That
section fourteen of an act entitled " An act to amend sections two
and fourteen of chapter eighty-eight of the compiled laws of
eighteen hundred and seventy-one, entitled ' An act to authorize
the formation of corporations for the running, booming, and rafting of logs,' " approved March seven, eighteen hundred and
seventy-three, be, and the same is hereby amended so as to read as
follows :

Corporation may
hold real estate,
etc.

SEC. 14. Every such corporation shall, by their corporate name,
have power to acquire, use, and hold all such real and personal
estate, by lease or purchase, as shall be necessary for the purpose
of carrying on the business of such corporation, with the full right
of selling and disposing thereof, when not further needed for the
Proviso. use of such corporation : *Provided*, That their real estate shall not
May construct exceed eight thousand acres. They shall have power and the right
booms.
in any of the navigable waters of this State, named in their articles of association, to construct, use, and maintain all necessary
booms for the business of such corporation : *Provided always*,
Proviso. That they shall first have obtained from the owner or owners of

the shores along which, or in front of which, they desire to construct such boom or booms, either by lease or purchase, their permission to erect and maintain such boom or booms in front of his or their lands: *And provided further*, That such boom or booms shall be so constructed, and so far as practicable used, as to allow the free passage of boats, vessels, crafts, logs, timber, lumber, or other floatables, along such waters. They shall have power to make all necessary contracts for the driving, booming, rafting, and running logs, lumber, timber, and other floatables. They shall have power to carry on the business of driving, booming, rafting, and running logs, timber, lumber, or other floatables, or either of them, as they may from time to time determine: and for the use of said boom or booms in the care and custody of logs, timber, lumber, and other floatables, in all cases where no rate is fixed by contract, to charge and collect a uniform and reasonable sum for boomage, and for such boomage, and for driving, rafting, or running of logs, timber, lumber, and other floatables, such corporation shall have a lien on the logs, timber, or other floatables, driven, boomed, rafted, or run; and such corporation shall be entitled to retain the possession of such logs, timber, lumber, or other floatables, or so much thereof as may be necessary to satisfy the amount of such boomage, and reasonable charges for driving, rafting, or running of logs, timber, lumber, and other floatables, and all expenses for taking care of the same, until the same shall be determined, satisfied, and paid in the manner hereinafter prescribed; and whenever any such logs, timber, lumber, or other floatables shall be delivered by any duly authorized corporation to any other duly authorized corporation, for transportation or delivery at its proper destination, such lien shall remain a lien upon such logs, timber, lumber, or other floatables, for the benefit of said first corporation, until the same shall have reached its proper destination; and said first corporation shall be deemed not to have lost its lien on the said logs, timber, lumber, and other floatables, and shall have the power to take and retain possession of the same, in common with any other party having a subsequently acquired lien thereon, or so much of the same as may be necessary to satisfy the amount of such boomage, and reasonable charges for driving, rafting, or running of logs, timber, lumber, or other floatables, until the same shall be determined, satisfied, and paid in the manner hereinafter prescribed; and all charges for running, driving, booming, towing, or rafting of saw logs and lumber by such corporation shall be by the thousand feet, board measure.

Approved March 17, 1875.

(margin notes: Boom not to obstruct navigation. Powers of corporation. Compensation for use of booms. s, etc. Charges for booming, etc., of logs and lumber.)

[No. 36.]

AN ACT to amend section three thousand five hundred and eighty-two of the compiled laws of eighteen hundred and seventy-one, relative to the duties of school inspectors.

Section amended. SECTION 1. *The People of the State of Michigan enact,* That section three thousand five hundred and eighty-two of the compiled laws of eighteen hundred and seventy-one be and is hereby amended so as to read as follows:

Notice in case new district is formed. (3582.) SECTION 1. Whenever the board of school inspectors of any township shall form a school district therein, it shall be the duty of the clerk of such board to deliver to a taxable inhabitant of such district a notice in writing of the formation of such district, describing its boundaries, and specifying the time and place of the first meeting, which notice, with the fact of such delivery, shall be Notice, etc., in entered upon record by the clerk. And whenever said board shall case boundary or number of dis- alter the boundaries or change the number of said school district, trict is changed. it shall be the duty of the clerk of said board to deliver to the director of every district affected by the alteration, a notice in writing, stating what alterations have been made, and a diagram showing the boundary lines of the district as thus changed.

Approved March 17, 1875.

[No. 37.]

AN ACT to amend section one of "An act establishing a State agency for the care of juvenile offenders," approved April twenty-nine, eighteen hundred and seventy-three.

Section amended SECTION 1. *The People of the State of Michigan enact,* That section one of an act entitled "An act establishing a State agency for the care of juvenile offenders," approved April twenty-nine, eighteen hundred and seventy-three, be and the same is so amended as to read as follows:

Appointment of agents in the several counties. SECTION 1. *The People of the State of Michigan enact,* That the Governor may appoint in each county of this State, an agent of the board of State commissioners for the general supervision of charitable, penal, pauper, and reformatory institutions, who shall hold his office at the pleasure of the Governor. Before entering Oath of office. upon the duties of his office, and within thirty days after receiving notice of his appointment, said agent shall take and file with the county clerk of the county for which he was appointed, the oath of office prescribed by the constitution of this State, and upon such Notice of qual- qualification it shall be the duty of the county clerk to immediately ification to mag- transmit notice thereof to the circuit judge, the probate judge, istrates. each justice of the peace, and all other magistrates of the county having competent jurisdiction for the trial of juvenile offenders. Compensation. Said agent shall receive as compensation for his time and services, his actual expenses necessarily incurred while engaged in the performance of his duties under this act, on being fully stated in account and verified by the affidavit of the agent, together with the sum of three dollars in full for his services in each case investigated and reported upon as hereinafter prescribed, when approved by the Governor, shall be paid by the State Treasurer on the warrant of the Auditor General, out of any money in the treasury not otherwise appropriated : *Provided*, That the sum so allowed for the services of such agent in any county except the county of Wayne, shall not in any one year exceed the sum of one hundred dollars, and that in the county of Wayne the sum so allowed for such services shall not in any one year exceed the sum of two hundred dollars. *Proviso—limit of compensation.*

Approved March 19, 1875.

[No. 38.]

AN ACT relative to the use of sleeping, parlor, and chair cars upon the railroads of this State.

SECTION 1. *The People of the State of Michigan enact*, It shall be lawful for any railroad company operating any railroad within this State, to construct or use for the transportation of passengers, sleeping cars, parlor cars, or chair cars, for the use of such passengers as may desire to use the same, and such company may make such reasonable rules and regulations concerning the use of these, as such company may think proper, and may charge a reasonable compensation for such use in addition to the regular passenger fares allowed by law. *Lawful for companies to use sleeping cars, etc., and make rules concerning their use, etc.*

SEC. 2. Nothing herein contained shall release any such railroad company from its obligations to furnish first class passenger cars for the use of the public for the regular passenger fares now fixed by law. *Not released from furnishing first class passenger cars.*

SEC. 3. This act shall take immediate effect.

Approved March 19, 1875.

[No. 39.]

AN ACT to legalize the election of the officers of certain school districts.

SECTION 1. *The People of the State of Michigan enact*, That the action heretofore had of the electors in each and every school district in this State in electing the officers of such districts in any manner other than by ballot is hereby declared legal and valid. *Election of school district officers legalized.*

Approved March 20, 1875.

[No. 40.]

AN ACT to repeal an act entitled "An act to provide for the uniform inspection of lumber," approved March twenty-five, eighteen hundred and seventy-one, and the act amendatory thereof, approved April ten, eighteen hundred and seventy-three.

SECTION 1. *The People of the State of Michigan enact*, That the act entitled "An act to provide for the uniform inspection of lum- *Act repealed.*

5

ber," approved March twenty-five, eighteen hundred and seventy-one, and the act amendatory thereof, approved April ten, eighteen hundred and seventy-three, be and the same is hereby repealed, **Saving certain rights.** saving all rights which may have accrued or which may exist under said act at the time this repeal shall take effect.

SEC. 2. This act shall take immediate effect.

Approved March 20, 1875.

[No. 41.]
AN ACT to organize the county of Roscommon.

Roscommon county organized. SECTION 1. *The People of the State of Michigan enact,* That the county of Roscommon, consisting of the territory embraced by the present unorganized county of Roscommon, be and the same is hereby organized into a separate county by the name of Roscommon, and the inhabitants thereof shall be entitled to all the privileges, powers, and immunities to which by the law the inhabitants of other organized counties in this State are entitled.

Election of county officers. SEC. 2. At the township meeting of the several townships in said county, to be held on the first Monday of April next, there shall be an election of all the county officers to which by law the said county is entitled, who shall hold their several offices until the first day of January, in the year of our Lord one thousand eight hundred and seventy-seven, and until their successors shall have been elected and qualified; said election shall be conducted in the same way, by the same officers, and the returns thereof made in the same manner, as near as may be, as is now required by law in the election of county officers in this State.

Location of county seat determined by vote of electors. SEC. 3. The location of the county seat of said county shall be determined by the vote of the electors of said county by ballot, at a special election to be held for that purpose on the first Monday of July, eighteen hundred and seventy-seven. The ballots may be written or printed, or part written and part printed, and shall each designate one place for the location of the county seat, and the vote shall be canvassed and returns thereof made in the same manner as near as may be as provided in section two of this act, and the place which shall receive the highest number of votes cast at such election shall be the county seat of Roscommon county; **Canvass of votes for county seat.** and the county canvass shall be had within the same time, and in the same manner, as near as may be, as is now required by law in general elections in this State.

Canvass of votes for county officers. SEC. 4. The county canvass of the votes cast for county officers shall be held on the second Tuesday succeeding the election, at Roscommon station, in the county aforesaid; and said canvass shall be conducted in the same way as the requirements of law now provide in organized counties, as nearly as may be. The board of county canvassers shall have power to appoint one of their own number secretary of said board, and it shall be the duty of the secretary of said board to file a copy of the determination of said

board as to the location of the county seat, signed and certified by
him, and countersigned by the chairman, with the clerk of said
county within ten days after he shall have qualified.

SEC. 5. The county treasurer, sheriff, and county clerk of said *Location of temporary county seat.*
county, are hereby authorized and required to locate the county
seat temporarily, until located as provided by section three of this
act, and shall file with the Secretary of State, and the county clerk,
each a certificate, signed by a majority of them, describing the
place where they have located the same.

SEC. 6. All suits, proceedings, and other matters now pending, *Suits, etc., now pending.*
or that may be pending on the second Tuesday succeeding the first
Monday of April next, before any court or justice of the peace of
the county of Midland shall be prosecuted to final judgment and
execution, and all taxes heretofore levied shall be collected in the *Taxes heretofore levied.*
same manner as though this act had not passed.

SEC. 7. The register of deeds of said county shall make or cause *Register of deeds to make transcript of records, etc.*
to be made, a transcript of all records made in other counties,
which are necessary to appear upon the records of said county of
Roscommon; and the board of supervisors of said county shall, *Payment of expense.*
within one year after the first Monday of April next, make provision for defraying the expense of the same.

SEC. 8. The said county of Roscommon shall be a part of the *Judicial circuit.*
twenty-first judicial circuit.

SEC. 9. The Secretary of State is hereby directed to furnish the *Secretary of State to furnish copy of this act.*
clerk of the township of Higgins a certified copy of this act; and
it shall be the duty of said clerk to give the same notice of the *Clerk to give notice of election.*
election to be held under the provisions of this act that is required
by law to be given by the sheriff of organized counties.

SEC. 10. This act shall take immediate effect.

Approved March 20, 1875.

[No. 42.]

AN ACT to amend sections eight and fourteen, and to repeal section
thirteen of chapter twelve of the compiled laws of eighteen hundred and seventy-one, being consecutive sections six hundred and
forty-three, six hundred and forty-eight and six hundred and
forty-nine, relating to the powers and duties of townships, and
election and duties of township officers, and to add eight new
sections thereto, to stand as sections one hundred and four, one
hundred and five, one hundred and six, one hundred and seven,
one hundred and eight, one hundred and nine, one hundred and
ten and one hundred and eleven, repealing chapter one hundred
thirty-nine of the compiled laws of eighteen hundred and seventy-one, relating to county superintendents of schools.

SECTION 1. *The People of the State of Michigan enact,* That *Section amended*
sections eight and fourteen of chapter twelve of the compiled laws
of eighteen hundred and seventy-one, being consecutive sections
six hundred and forty-three and six hundred and forty-nine, relating to the powers and duties of townships, and election and duties

of township officers, be and the same are hereby amended so as to read respectively as follows, and that section thirteen of said chapter twelve, being compiler's section number six hundred and forty-eight be hereby repealed, and that eight new sections be added thereto to stand as sections one hundred and four, one hundred and five, one hundred and six, one hundred and seven, one hundred and eight, one hundred and nine, one hundred and ten, and one hundred and eleven, and to read respectively as follows:

Section repealed.

Sections added.

Annual township meetings, when held.

SEC. 8. The annual meeting of each township shall be held on the first Monday of April in each year, and at such meeting there shall be an election for the following officers: one supervisor, one township clerk, one treasurer, one school inspector, one superintendent of schools, one commissioner of highways, so many justices of the peace as there are by law to be elected in the township, and so many constables as shall be ordered by the meeting, not exceeding four in number.

Officers to be elected.

Terms of office.

SEC. 14. Each of the officers elected at such meetings, except justices of the peace, shall hold his office for the term of one year, and until his successor shall be elected and duly qualified.

Township superintendents of schools to examine teachers.

SEC. 104. The township superintendent of schools elected in each of the townships of this State shall have power, and it is hereby made his duty, to examine all persons offering themselves as teachers for the primary schools in his township, and shall hold meetings for that purpose at least twice in each year, and it shall be his duty to give two weeks' public notice of the time and place of said meetings by posting written or printed notices thereof in four of the principal places in his township. Such examination may be conducted by either oral or written questions or by both, at the option of said superintendent, and all examinations shall be in public.

Shall hold meetings for that purpose at least twice in each year.

Examinations, how conducted.

Certificates, to whom granted.

SEC. 105. He shall grant certificates in such form as shall be prescribed by the superintendent of public instruction, licensing as teachers all persons whom, on a thorough and full examination, he shall deem qualified in respect to moral character, learning, and ability to instruct and govern a school. No person shall be accounted a qualified teacher within the meaning of the primary school law, nor shall any school officer employ or contract with any person to teach in any of the primary schools in this State, who has not a certificate in force from such township superintendent, or from other lawful authority: *Provided, however,* That the certificates heretofore granted by the county superintendent of schools shall be valid for the time for which they were given, unless sooner revoked by the township superintendent of schools. *Provided further,* That should any superintendent of schools engage in teaching any primary school in his township his election or appointment to such office shall be deemed as qualifying him under the law.

Qualified teachers; no others to be employed.

Proviso—certificates of county superintendents to hold good.

Township superintendents qualified teachers.

Three grades of certificates.

SEC. 106. There shall be three grades of certificates granted by the township superintendent of schools, in his discretion, as follows: the certificate of the first grade shall be granted only to those who shall have taught at least one year with ability and success, and

First.

it shall be valid throughout the township in and for which it was granted for two years. The certificate of the second grade shall be granted to those who pass a good examination, and shall be valid throughout the township for one year. The certificate of the third grade shall license the holder thereof to teach in a specified district six months; but no certificate shall be granted to any person who shall not pass a satisfactory examination in orthography, reading, writing, geography, grammar, and arithmetic. The township superintendent may revoke any teacher's certificate for any reason which would have justified him in withholding the same when given, for neglect of duty, for incompetency to instruct and govern a school, or for immorality, or they may suspend within their jurisdiction the effect of any teacher's certificate for immorality or incompetency to instruct and govern a school; but no certificate shall be revoked or suspended without a personal visit or hearing, unless the holder thereof shall, after reasonable notice, neglect or refuse to appear before the superintendent for such purpose. The superintendent shall keep a record of all certificates granted or annulled by him. showing to whom issued, together with the date, grade, and duration of each certificate, and the reason for annulling, when requested by the teacher, and shall deliver such record with all other books and papers belonging to his office to his successor. *(margin: Second. Third. Revocation of certificates, etc. Record of certificates.)*

SEC. 107. It shall be the duty of the township superintendent to visit each of the schools in his township at least twice in each year, to examine carefully the discipline, the mode of instruction, and into the progress and proficiency of the pupils, and to make a record of the same; to counsel with the teachers and district boards as to the courses of study to be pursued, and as to any improvement in discipline and instruction in the schools; to note the condition of the school-houses, and the appurtenances thereto, and to suggest plans for new school-houses to be erected, and for warming and ventilating the same, and for the general improvement of school-houses and grounds; to inquire into the condition of district and township libraries, and to advise, if necessary, for the better management thereof; to promote by such means as he may devise the improvement of the schools in his township, and the elevation of the character and qualifications of the teachers thereof; to consult with the teachers and school boards as to the best method to secure the more general and regular attendance of the children at school. It shall be the duty of the township superintendent to receive all blanks and communications that may be directed to him by the Superintendent of Public Instruction, and to dispose of the same in the manner directed by the said superintendent. He shall be subject to such rules and instructions as the Superintendent of Public Instruction may from time to time prescribe, and he shall make reports to the Superintendent of Public Instruction, at such times, in such manner, and upon such subjects as he may direct. *(margin: Superintendent to visit and examine schools. To note condition of school houses, etc. To inquire into condition of libraries. To receive and dispose of blanks sent him by superintendent of public instruction. To be subject to rules, etc., of said superintendent and report to him.)*

SEC. 108. No superintendent or teacher of schools shall act as agent for any author, publisher, or bookseller, or shall directly or *(margin: Superintendents or teachers not to act as agents) for booksellers, etc.* indirectly receive any gift or reward for his influence in recommending the purchase or use of any library or school book or school apparatus, or furniture whatever. Any act herein prohibited done by said superintendent shall be deemed a violation of his oath of office, and any employment of said superintendent by any author, publisher, or bookseller for that purpose shall be deemed a misdemeanor. *Township clerk to notify county clerk of election of superintendent.* It shall be the duty of the township clerk annually, immediately after the election and qualification of the township superintendent of schools, to transmit a written statement of the name and postoffice address of the person so elected and qualified, to *County clerk to send list of superintendents to superintendents of public instruction.* the county clerk, whose duty it shall be to make up a list of the names and postoffice address of the persons so reported to him by the township clerks of such county, to file such list in his office, and forward a copy thereof to the Superintendent of Public Instruction.

Compensation of superintendent. SEC. 109. The compensation for the services required of the township superintendent of schools, shall be two dollars a day for each day necessarily devoted to the discharge of the duties of his office, together with such stationery, postage, and printing as may be necessary for the discharge of his duties, the same to be audited by the township board, and paid as other expenses of the township.

Schools exempt from provisions of this act. SEC. 110. All schools which by a special enactment may have a board authorized to inspect and grant certificates to the teachers employed by the same, shall be exempt from the provisions of this *School officers in certain districts may examine teachers.* act as to inspection of teachers. The officers of every school district which is or shall hereafter be organized in whole or part in any city in this State, where no special enactments shall exist in regard to the inspection of teachers therein, shall have power to inspect and license, or cause to be inspected, teachers for such district; and such license shall be valid not to exceed two years.

Chapter repealed SEC. 111. That chapter one hundred and thirty-nine of the compiled laws of eighteen hundred and seventy-one, entitled "An act to provide for county superintendents of schools, and to amend section ninety-one, and to repeal sections seventy-four, eighty-five, eighty-six, eighty-seven, eighty-eight, eighty-nine, and ninety of chapter seventy-eight of the compiled laws," approved March thirteenth, eighteen hundred and sixty-seven, is hereby repealed. And the sections named in the title recited in this section, are hereby fully repealed.

SEC. 2. This act shall take immediate effect.

Approved March 20, 1875.

[No. 43.]

AN ACT to repeal chapter eighty-four of the compiled laws of eighteen hundred and seventy-one, being "An act to provide for the formation of companies to construct canals or harbors and improve the same."

Chapter repealed. SECTION 1. *The People of the State of Michigan enact,* That chapter eighty-four of the compiled laws of eighteen hundred and seventy-one, being "An act to provide for the formation of companies to construct canals or harbors and improve the same," approved March thirteen, eighteen hundred and sixty-one, and amendments thereto, be and the same is hereby repealed. But all corporations legally formed and existing under such chapter shall nevertheless continue to have legal existence for the purpose of closing up their business only in accordance with the provisions of chapter one hundred and thirty of the compiled laws of eighteen hundred and seventy-one. *Corporations already formed.*

SEC. 2. This act shall take immediate effect.

Approved March 20, 1875.

[No. 44.]

AN ACT to amend section four of an act entitled "An act to amend chapter one hundred and fourteen of the revised statutes, entitled 'Of proceedings against debtors by attachment,'" being consecutive section six thousand four hundred and thirty-one of the compiled laws of eighteen hundred and seventy-one.

SECTION 1. *The People of the State of Michigan enact,* That section four of an act entitled "An act to amend chapter one hundred and fourteen of the revised statutes, entitled 'Of proceedings against debtors by attachment,'" being consecutive section six thousand four hundred and thirty-one of the compiled laws of eighteen hundred and seventy-one, be and the same hereby is amended so as to read as follows: *Section amended*

(6431.) SEC. 4. The judge or commissioner shall have full power to issue subpœnas, and if necessary, attachments to compel the attendance of witnesses to testify in such cases, and may, in his discretion, require the party moving for such dissolution to give security for the costs of such proceedings; and may order the costs of such proceedings to be paid by the party against whom the decision shall be in the premises, and may issue execution therefor, returnable in sixty days from its date. *Attendance of witnesses in application for dissolution of attachment.*

Approved March 20, 1875.

[No. 45.]

AN ACT to authorize the trustees of the Michigan Asylum for the Insane to convey certain State land in the village of Kalamazoo, for the purpose of extending Howard street.

SECTION 1. *The People of the State of Michigan enact,* That the board of trustees of the Michigan Asylum for the Insane are hereby authorized to convey, by quit-claim deed, to the village of Kalamazoo, in the county of Kalamazoo, all the interest of the State of Michigan in and to a strip of land two rods in width, north and south, commencing at the present western terminus of Howard street, in said village, and extending west to Asylum *Land that may be conveyed.*

avenue, for the purpose of extending said Howard street to said Asylum avenue, to be used for a public street or highway.

SEC. 2. This act shall take immediate effect.

Approved March 20, 1875.

[No. 46.]

AN ACT to amend section four thousand two hundred and fifty-seven of the compiled laws of eighteen hundred and seventy-one, the same being an act entitled " An act to provide for recording patents for lands, and for other purposes."

Section amended SECTION 1. *The People of the State of Michigan enact,* That section four thousand two hundred and fifty-seven of the compiled laws of eighteen hundred and seventy-one, being an act entitled " An act to provide for recording patents for lands and for other purposes," be so amended as to read as follows:

Register to record patents or certified copies thereof. It shall be the duty of the register of deeds in the several counties of this State to receive for record and record all patents for lands from the United States or this State, or any copy thereof, duly certified by the Commissioner of the United States General Land Office, or by the Commissioner of the State Land Office of this State, in the same manner and with like effect as by existing law he is required to receive and record deeds and conveyances.

Approved March 20, 1875.

[No. 47.]

AN ACT to amend section forty-two of chapter one hundred and fifty, being section four thousand two hundred and forty-four of the compiled laws of eighteen hundred and seventy-one, relative to alienation by deed, and the proof and recording of conveyances, and the canceling of mortgages.

Section amended SECTION 1. *The People of the State of Michigan enact,* That section forty-two of chapter one hundred and fifty, being section four thousand two hundred and forty-four of the compiled laws of eighteen hundred and seventy-one, be and the same is hereby amended so as to read as follows:

Discharge of mortgage by certificate of mortgagee, circuit court or register in chancery. (4244.) SEC. 42. Any mortgage shall also be discharged upon the record thereof by the register of deeds in whose custody it shall be, whenever there shall be presented to him a certificate executed by the mortgagee, his personal representative or assigns, acknowledged, approved and certified as in this chapter provided, to entitle conveyances or instruments in writing in any wise affecting the title to lands to be recorded, specifying that such mortgage has been paid, or otherwise satisfied or discharged ; or upon the presentation to such register of deeds of the certificate of the circuit court, signed by the judge of said court, and under the seal thereof, certifying that it has been made to appear to said court that said mortgage has been duly paid, or upon the presentation to such register of deeds of a certificate of the register in chancery of the county, and under the seal thereof, certifying that a decree of foreclosure of any such mortgage has been duly entered in his office, and that the records in his office shows that such decree has been fully paid and satisfied.

Approved March 20, 1875.

[No. 48.]

AN ACT to re-organize the tenth judicial circuit and create the twenty-first judicial circuit.

SECTION 1. *The People of the State of Michigan enact,* That the county of Saginaw shall be formed into and constitute a judicial circuit, to be known and designated as the tenth judicial circuit. *Tenth circuit.*

SEC. 2. That the counties of Gratiot, Isabella, Clare, Midland, Roscommon, and Gladwin shall be formed into and be one judicial circuit, to be known as the twenty-first judicial circuit. *Twenty-first circuit.*

SEC. 3. The qualified voters of the counties mentioned in section two of this act shall, on the first Monday in April, in the year of our Lord one thousand eight hundred and seventy-five, elect a circuit judge, who shall hold his office, commencing on the first day of May, eighteen hundred and seventy-five, for the term of six years, or until his successor is elected and qualified. *Election of judge. Term of office.*

SEC. 4. The judge of the tenth judicial circuit shall continue to hold his office as judge of said circuit, as herein re-organized, for the remainder of his unexpired term, and until his successor is elected and qualified. *Time judge of present tenth circuit to retain office.*

SEC. 5. It shall be the duty of the sheriff of the several counties mentioned in section two of this act, at least ten days previous to the first Monday in April, in the year one thousand eight hundred and seventy-five, to notify the township clerk of each township, and ward inspectors of election in each ward of any city in their respective counties, of said election of circuit judge, and the township clerks and ward inspectors shall post notices in the usual manner for such election in townships and wards at least three days previous to the day of election. *Election, sheriff to notify. Township clerks, etc., to post notices.*

SEC. 6. The said election for circuit judge shall be conducted and returns made as provided by law for the election of circuit judges for the several judicial circuits of this State, and the State board of canvassers shall, without delay, on the receipt of the certified statement of the votes given in said counties named in the second section of this act, proceed to canvass the said votes, and to deliver to the person elected a copy of their determination as required by law. *Manner of conducting. Canvassers of votes.*

SEC. 7. All acts or parts of acts contravening the provisions of this act are repealed. *Acts repealed.*

SEC. 8. This act shall take immediate effect.

Approved March 20, 1875.

[No. 49.]

AN ACT to provide for a municipal court in the city of Grand Rapids, to be called " The Superior Court of Grand Rapids."

Superior court
of Grand Rapids
SECTION 1. *The People of the State of Michigan enact,* That there shall be a municipal court in and for the city of Grand Rapids, which shall be called " The Superior Court of Grand Rapids," which shall be a court of record and have a seal to be provided by said city, and whose first term shall commence on the first Tuesday of June, in the year of our Lord one thousand eight hundred and seventy-five.

Judge, first
election and
term of office.
SEC. 2. On the first Monday of April, in the year eighteen hundred and seventy-five, the qualified voters of the city of Grand Rapids shall elect a judge of said court, whose title and office shall be " Judge of the Superior Court of Grand Rapids," and who shall hold his office for six years, and until his successor shall be elected and qualified. Notice of election. Notice of such election shall be given by the clerk of the city of Grand Rapids in the manner prescribed by law in case of the election of city officers for said city: Proviso. *Provided,* That five days' notice of the first election shall be deemed sufficient, and at such election the person receiving the highest number of votes for said office shall be declared duly elected thereto. Laws applicable
to election. The provisions of law relative to holding elections of city officers in said city, canvassing the votes and making returns thereof so far as applicable, shall regulate and apply to elections of the judge of said court.

Oath of office.
SEC. 3. Any judge of said court before entering upon the duties of his office, shall take and subscribe the oath of office prescribed by article eighteen of the constitution of this State. Such oath may be taken before any officer authorized to administer oaths, and shall be filed in the office of the clerk of the city of Grand Rapids.

Elections after
the first.
SEC. 4. On the first Monday of April next preceding the expiration of the term of any judge of said court, his successor in said office shall be elected in the same manner and upon the same notice as that herein prescribed for the election of the judge of said court.

Vacancy in office
of judge, how
filled.
SEC. 5. If in case of absence from the city of the judge of said superior court, illness, or any legal disqualification, or if a vacancy occur in his office, the judge of the circuit of which Kent county shall form a part shall act as the judge of said superior court, and as such judge shall have and exercise all the powers and duties of the judge of said court until he shall resume his office or such vacancy be filled. It shall be the duty of the common council of said city to cause an election to be held in said city to fill any vacancy in the office of the judge of said superior court, the same as is provided by the charter of said city in case of vacancies in the office of mayor thereof.

Salary of judge.
SEC. 6. The judge of said superior court shall receive from the treasury of the State of Michigan the same annual salary as may be payable to circuit judges, and payable quarterly; he shall also

receive from the treasury of the city of Grand Rapids such additional salary as shall be sufficient with the sum so received from the State, to make the salary of said judge two thousand five hundred dollars, to be paid quarterly on the order of the common council.

SEC. 7. The clerk of the county of Kent shall be *ex officio* clerk Clerk. of said court.

SEC. 8. The clerk of said court, before entering upon the duties To take oath and of his office, shall take the constitutional oath to be administered give bond. by said judge, and shall give a bond to the people of the State of Michigan, in the penal sum of ten thousand dollars, to be approved by the judge of said court, for the faithful discharge of the duties of said office. The condition of such bond shall be in sub- Condition of stance as follows: WHEREAS, the above bounden ———, is the bond. clerk of the superior court of Grand Rapids, now, therefore, the conditions of the above obligations is such, that if the said ———, shall faithfully, truly, and impartially, enter and record all orders, decrees, judgments, and proceeding of the said court, and faithfully and impartially perform all other duties of his said office, and shall pay over all moneys that may come into his hands as such clerk, and shall deliver to his successor in office all the books, records, papers, seals, and other things belonging to his said office, then the above obligation to be void, otherwise in full force.

SEC. 9. It shall be the duty of said clerk to keep a true record Duty of clerk in of the proceedings, in proper books, to be provided for that purpose keeping records, by the common council of the city of Grand Rapids, at the expense etc. of said city; to file and safely keep all papers and books belonging or pertaining to said court, and to enter and record all orders, decrees, judgments, and proceedings of said court. He shall sign Shall sign and and seal all writs and process issuing from said court, and shall seal writs, administer oaths, have power generally to administer oaths and affidavits, and to do etc. all acts authorized by law to be done by clerks of circuit courts of this State. Said clerk, with the approval of the judge of said court, Deputies. may appoint one or more deputy clerks, as may be authorized by the common council of said city, and may remove the same. The Compensation, compensation of such deputies shall be fixed by the common etc. council of said city, and shall be payable from the city treasury. Such deputies shall give such security as shall be required by ordinance of the common council for the performance of the duties of their office, and they shall have the same powers as are given to said clerk.

SEC. 10. The clerk of said court shall receive an annual salary Salary of clerk. of one thousand dollars, to be paid by the city of Grand Rapids upon the order of the common council, in quarterly installments, and said sum shall be in full of all clerks' fees or perquisities of every kind and nature, and of services rendered in any cause pending or determined in said court.

SEC. 11. Before any suit at law shall be commenced in said court, Court fees. there shall be paid to the clerk of said court by the party commencing such suit the sum of four dollars, and before any judgment or final decree shall be entered in any such suit, there shall be paid by the prevailing party to said clerk the sum of three

To be for the use of the city and paid over by the clerk. dollars. The moneys so paid shall be for the use of said city, and shall be paid weekly by the clerk to the city treasurer and placed to the credit of the general fund; but upon a re-trial of any cause

Additional fees upon re-trial. by a jury an additional fee of three dollars shall be paid by the party moving for such re-trial; and the sums so as aforesaid paid shall be held to be in full of all clerks, entry and jury fees in any such suit from the commencement thereof to and including the issuing of execution or other final process. The sum or sums

Fees to be taxed as costs. so paid shall be taxed as costs of suit in favor of the party paying the same, if he be the prevailing party in such suit, in addition to any other costs to which he may be entitled by law: *Provided,* That

Proviso. if a jury shall not be demanded, the sum so to be paid before entry of judgment shall be two dollars.

Sheriff or deputy to attend court, serve writs, etc. SEC. 12. The sheriff of the county, or such deputy or deputies as the judge of said court may direct, shall attend the sittings of said court, and he and they shall have the power, and it shall be their duty, under the direction of said sheriff, to execute all lawful precepts and commands of said court, and serve all lawful writs

Fees. and process issuing therefrom. The fees of said sheriff and his deputies for services rendered in said court, and in all actions pending therein, shall be the same as those prescribed by law for similar services; but any portion of such fees, which, if the services had been rendered in a circuit court, would be chargeable to the county, shall be allowed by the common council of the city of Grand Rapids, and paid from the treasury of said city.

Jurisdiction of superior court. SEC. 13. The said superior court shall have original jurisdiction and concurrent jurisdiction with the circuit court for the county of Kent, in all civil actions of a transitory nature, where the debt or damages are one hundred dollars or over, and in which the defendants, or one of them, if there be more than one defendant, shall have been served with a copy of the declaration, or with process within the city of Grand Rapids, or in which the plaintiff shall reside in the city of Grand Rapids, and the defendants, or one of them, if there be more than one defendant, shall be served with a copy of the declaration, or with process in Kent county. Said court shall also have jurisdiction of all actions of trespass *quare clausum,* for injuries committed upon any land situated in the city of Grand Rapids; all actions of ejectment for the possession of land situated in said city; all actions commenced by attachment against nonresidents, where the property attached is at the time of service of the writ of attachment within said city; and the same jurisdiction as the circuit court for the county of Kent, in all cases in equity in which any complainant or defendant shall be a resident of the city of Grand Rapids, or in which the subject matter of such suit shall be situated or located in said city, and in all cases of foreclosure of mortgages upon land situated in the city of Grand Rap-

Exclusive jurisdiction in certain cases. ids; and said court shall also have exclusive jurisdiction of all actions at law of a civil nature, which may be brought by or against the city of Grand Rapids, or which may be brought by or against the board of education of the city of Grand Rapids, and said court shall also have exclusive appellate jurisdiction of all actions brought before the police court of the city of Grand Rapids, or any justice of the peace for the said city, for a violation of the charter of said city, or any of the by-laws and ordinances of said city, where the sentence of imprisonment shall be thirty days or more, or where the fine, penalty, or forfeiture imposed shall amount to twenty-five dollars or over, exclusive of costs. Said court shall have and exercise all of and the same jurisdiction that is vested in the recorder's court of the city of Grand Rapids, in and by Titles VI. and VII. of the revised charter of said city, and acts amendatory thereto.

SEC. 14. Said court shall have power to issue all lawful writs and process, and to do all lawful acts which may be necessary and proper to carry into complete effect the powers and jurisdiction given by this act, and especially to issue all writs and process, and to do all acts which the circuit courts of this State within their respective jurisdictions may in like cases issue and do, by the laws of the State of Michigan. All copies of declarations filed for commencement of suit, writs of subpœna, all writs of execution, and other writs of process, may be served beyond the limits of said city, which may in like cases be filed in the circuit court of said county, or issued by said circuit court, and authorized by law to be served outside the limits of the county. *Powers of court.* *Service of writs, etc., outside city limits.*

SEC. 15. The practice and proceedings in said superior court shall be the same as those prescribed by law for circuit courts in this state, unless otherwise limited by this act; and the rules prescribed by the supreme court for the guidance and practice of circuit courts, shall be the rules of said superior court, so far as the same may be applicable; but the said court may have the same power of making rules for said court as is given to circuit courts or the judges thereof. *Practice and rules of superior courts.*

SEC. 16. There shall be four regular terms of said superior court held [in] each year, and the time of commencement of terms for each year shall be fixed by the judge of said court in the month of May of each year, and notices of the times of holding such terms shall be published for two weeks in one of the daily papers published in the city of Grand Rapids. *Terms.*

SEC. 17. Any complainant or defendant in any cause in equity, who may think himself aggrieved by any decision, decree, or order made therein by said superior court, may appeal therefrom to the supreme court; such appeal may be taken in such like cases, and the proceedings on appeal shall be similar in all respects to those prescribed by statute in cases of appeals from circuit courts; and the supreme court may issue all writs of error, *certiorari*, prohibition, *mandamus*, and other writs directed to the said superior court or the judge thereof, as it may issue directed to the circuit courts or the judge thereof; and shall have like superintending control over the said superior court as is given by the constitution or by law to the supreme court over said circuit courts. *Appeal.*

SEC. 18. Said court may make and adopt rules of practice for such court, in respect to time for pleading and serving notices of *Court may adopt certain rules of practice.*

trial and other notices, and filing notes of issue. The same costs

Taxing of costs. may be taxed in favor of the prevailing party as are authorized to be taxed in circuit courts, except as heretofore provided in this act.

Selection of jurors. SEC. 19. On the tenth day of May next after the passage of this act, and annually thereafter on the tenth days of November and May in each year, between the hours of ten and twelve in the forenoon, the judge and clerk of said court and the sheriff of the county of Kent, shall meet together in the office of the clerk of said court, and shall proceed in public to select from the last annual assessment roll of said city (which roll the proper custodian shall produce before them), a list of one hundred persons to serve as jurors in said superior court; the persons so selected to be qual-

Qualifications. ified electors of said city, of fair character, of sound mind, and capable of understanding and speaking intelligibly the English language.

List, by whom signed and where filed. Said list shall be signed by said judge, clerk, and sheriff, and shall be filed in the office of the clerk of said court. If either of said offi-

In cases of absence of either official. cials shall not attend at the place and time aforesaid, the meeting shall stand adjourned from day to day for five days, and if on either of said days they shall meet together between said hours at such place, they shall then make such list; and if, on the last adjourned day any two of them shall so meet, one being absent, they shall

Time for which persons selected are liable to serve. proceed to make, sign, and file such list of jurors. The persons whose names are set forth in said list shall be liable to serve as jurors for six months, or until a new list shall be made as aforesaid.

Council shall provide court room, etc. SEC. 20. The common council of the said city shall provide a proper court room for the accommodation of said superior court, and all necessary furniture, fuel, books, and stationery for the use of the court and in the office of the clerk thereof.

Removal of causes from circuit to superior court. SEC. 21. If either party to any cause now pending in the circuit court for the county of Kent, and within the jurisdiction of said superior court, shall, after the taking effect of this act, or if the defendant in the case of a suit within such jurisdiction, hereafter commenced, at the time of entering his appearance in said circuit court, shall file a petition for the removal of the cause into the said superior court for the city of Grand Rapids, and shall offer good and sufficient security for entering in said last mentioned court, on the first day of its next term, copies of all papers filed, and proceedings had in said cause in the said circuit court, and also for his there appearing and entering special bail in the cause, if special bail was originally requisite therein, it shall then be the duty of the said circuit court for the county of Kent to accept the surety and proceed no further in the cause; and any bail that shall originally have been taken shall be discharged; and the copies of said papers and proceedings being so entered and filed as aforesaid in such superior court for the city of Grand Rapids, the cause shall then proceed in the same manner as if it had been originally brought in said court; and any attachment of the goods or estate of the defendants, by the original process, shall hold the goods or estate so attached to answer the final judgment in the same manner as they would have been held to answer final judgment had it been rendered by the court in which the suit was commenced:

Provided, however, That no cause pending in said circuit court, **Proviso.** when this act takes effect, shall be thereafter removed, under the provisions of this section, during a trial or hearing thereof.

SEC. 22. The causes pending and undisposed of in the recorder's **Causes pending** court for the city of Grand Rapids on the first Tuesday of June, **court to be** in the year of our Lord one thousand eight hundred and seventy- **determined by** five, shall be heard and determined by the judge of the superior **superior court.** court of said city, and for that purpose the clerk of the said re- corder's court, or other proper custodian thereof, shall, on or before the said first Tuesday of June, in the year of our Lord one thou- sand eight hundred and seventy-five, deliver all records, files, books, papers, and every thing appertaining to said recorder's court, to the clerk of the said superior court.

SEC. 23. This act shall take immediate effect.

Approved March 24, 1875.

[No. 50.]

AN ACT to authorize judges of probate to require new bonds from executors, guardians, administrators, special administrators and trustees.

SECTION 1. *The People of the State of Michigan enact,* That **Judge of probate** the judge of probate of any county in this State may require a new **may require new** bond to be given by any executor, guardian, administrator, special **tions, etc. and** administrator or trustee, whenever he shall deem it necessary or **existing sureties.** proper, after due notice given as he may direct, and on filing such new bond, may discharge the existing sureties from future respon- sibility, when it satisfactorily appears that no injury can result therefrom to any person interested in the estate: *Provided, how-* **Proviso.** *ever,* That such existing sureties shall not be discharged from liability upon such bond until a new bond shall have been filed, with sureties approved by the judge of probate: *Provided further,* **Proviso.** That such existing sureties shall not be discharged from any liability incurred prior to the filing of such new bond, and the old bond shall be retained by the judge of probate for the benefit of all persons who may be interested therein.

SEC. 2. This act shall take immediate effect.

Approved March 24, 1875.

[No. 51.]

AN ACT to amend sections sixty-eight and eighty of chapter one hundred and thirty-six of the compiled laws of eighteen hun- dred and seventy-one, being compiler's sections three thousand six hundred and thirty-eight and three thousand six hundred and forty-nine, relating to primary schools.

SECTION 1. *The People of the State of Michigan enact,* That **Sections** sections sixty-eight and eighty of chapter one hundred and thirty- **amended.**

six of the compiled laws of eighteen hundred and seventy-one, being compiler's sections three thousand six hundred and thirty-eight and three thousand six hundred and forty-nine, relating to primary schools, be and hereby are amended so as to read as follows:

Board of school inspectors. SEC. 68. The school inspector and the township superintendent of schools elected at the annual township meeting, together with the township clerk, shall constitute the township board of school inspectors, and the superintendent of schools shall be the chairman thereof, and the township clerk the clerk thereof.

Superintendent to furnish township clerk list, etc., of qualified teachers. SEC. 80. It shall be the duty of the superintendent of schools to furnish the township clerk a list of the names of all persons to whom he has given certificates to teach in such township, with the date and term of each, and if any are revoked, the name and date of such revocation, and the board of school inspectors, before making their annual report to the county clerk, shall examine said **Certain districts shall not receive public money.** list, and if in any school district a school shall not have been taught for the time required by law during the preceding school year by a qualified teacher, no part of the public money shall be distributed to such district; although the report from such district shall set forth that a school has been so taught, and it shall be the duty of the board to certify to the facts in relation to any such districts [district] in their reports to the county clerks **Proviso—certificates granted by State Normal School, etc., valid.** [clerk]: *Provided, however,* That a certificate in force provided by law to be given to graduates of the State Normal School, or a certificate from other lawful authority, shall be recognized as valid as to the district employing a teacher holding such certificate.

SEC. 2. This act shall take effect March thirty-one, eighteen hundred and seventy-five.

Approved March 24, 1875.

[No. 52.]

AN ACT to amend section one of act number one hundred and nine of the session laws of eighteen hundred and seventy-three, entitled " An act to provide for the collection of statistical information of the insane, deaf, dumb, and blind in this State, and to repeal a joint resolution relative to statistical information of the insane, deaf, dumb, and blind, approved April three, eighteen hundred and forty-eight, being section one thousand eight hundred and eighty-three, chapter fifty-two, of the compiled laws of eighteen hundred and seventy-one," approved April seventeen, eighteen hundred and seventy-three.

Section amended SECTION 1. *The People of the State of Michigan enact,* That section one of an act entitled " An act to provide for the collection of statistical information of the insane, deaf, dumb, and blind in this State, and to repeal a joint resolution relative to statistical information of the insane, deaf, dumb, and blind, approved April three, eighteen hundred and forty-eight, being section one thousand eight hundred and eighty-three, chapter fifty-two, of the compiled laws of eighteen hundred and seventy-one," approved April seventeen, eighteen hundred and seventy-three, be amended so as to read as follows:

SECTION 1. It shall be the duty of the supervisor or assessor of each township and ward in this State at the time of making his general assessment and assessment roll for his township or ward in each year, to ascertain and set down in a blank prepared for that purpose, the names of all insane, deaf, dumb, and blind persons in his township or ward, showing the person's age, general health, habits, and occupation ; the kind, degree, and duration of such affliction ; the sex ; whether married or single or widowed; whether under medical treatment; the pecuniary ability of the person thus afflicted, and of the relatives of such person liable for his or her support, and such further information relative to these classes of persons as may be thought useful. Such supervisor or assessor shall deliver said blank to the county clerk of his county on or before the fifteenth [day] of June, and the county clerk shall forthwith transmit said blank to the Secretary of State, who shall present an abstract of the information thus obtained to the Governor on the thirtieth day of September, or as soon as practicable thereafter. *Supervisors or assessors to collect statistics relative to the insane, deaf, dumb, and blind.* *Blanks containing statistics to be delivered to county clerk.* *Clerk to forward forthwith to Secretary of State.*

SEC. 2. This act shall take immediate effect.

Approved March 25, 1875.

[No. 53.]

AN ACT.to provide for the incorporation of Societies of St. Patrick.

SECTION 1. *The People of the State of Michigan enact,* That any number of persons of Irish birth or extraction, who may now or hereafter be residents of this State, or the descendents of such persons, may be incorporated in pursuance of the provisions of this act. *Who may incorporate.*

SEC. 2. Any ten or more persons, residents of this State, being of Irish birth, or their descendants as aforesaid, desiring to become incorporated, may make and execute articles of association, under their hands and seals, which said articles of association shall be acknowledged before some officer of this State having authority to take acknowledgments of deeds, and shall set forth, *Articles of association.*

First, The names of the persons associating, and their place of residence; *What to set forth.*

Second, The location of the association of which they are members;

Third, The corporate name by which such association shall be known in the law: *Provided,* That each association incorporated under this act shall be known as "The Society of Saint Patrick" of (the name of the city, village, or township where such association is located, and if more than one such association is located in the same city, village, or township, the same shall be designated by number);

Fourth, The object and purpose of such association, which shall

7

be to provide for the relief of distressed members and their families, the visitation of the sick, the burial of the dead, and to aid and assist the widows and orphans of deceased members. The

Limit of period of incorporation. period for which such association shall be incorporated shall not exceed thirty years.

Copy of articles to be filed and recorded in office of county clerk. SEC. 3. A copy of said articles of association shall be filed with the county clerk of the county in which such corporation shall be formed, and upon payment of a fee of seventy-five cents shall be recorded by such clerk in a book to be kept in his office for that purpose, and thereupon the persons who shall have signed said articles of association, their associates and successors, shall be a

Body politic and corporate. body politic and corporate by the name expressed in such articles of association, and by that name they and their successors shall have succession, and shall be persons in the law, capable of suing and being sued, and they and their successors may have a common seal, and the same may change and alter at pleasure, and a certified

Copy of record evidence in court. copy of the record of such articles of association, under the seal of the county where said record is kept, shall be received as *prima facie* evidence in all courts in this State of the existence and due incorporation of such corporation.

May hold estates SEC. 4. Every corporation formed in pursuance of this act shall be capable in its corporate name of purchasing, taking, receiving, holding to itself, and enjoying estates both real and personal: *Pro-*

Proviso. *vided,* That the value of such real and personal estate shall not exceed the sum of one hundred thousand dollars, and that they and their successors shall have full authority and power to give, grant, sell, mortgage, lease, devise, and dispose of said real and personal estate, or part thereof, and other estate, real and personal, may acquire instead thereof, at their will and pleasure; and the proceeds shall be devoted exclusively to the charitable and benevolent purposes set forth in section two,

May make by-laws, elect or appoint officers, etc. SEC. 5. Said corporations shall have full force and authority to make and establish rules, regulations, and by-laws for regulating and governing all the affairs and business of said corporation, not contrary to the laws of this State or of the United States, and to designate, elect, or appoint, from among their number such officers, under such names and style as shall be in accordance with the constitution or charter of said society, who shall have the supervision or control and management of the affairs of said corporations.

May erect halls, create a capital stock, etc. SEC. 6. Any corporations formed in pursuance of this act may erect and own such suitable edifices, buildings, or halls as such corporations shall deem necessary, with convenient rooms for the meeting of said society, and for that purpose may create a capital stock of not more than sixty thousand dollars, to be divided into shares of not more than twenty-five dollars each.

Subject to provisions of chapter 73, Compiled Laws. SEC. 7. All corporations formed under the provisions of this act shall be subject to the provisions of chapter seventy-three (73) of the compiled laws of this State, so far as the same may be applicable to corporations formed under this act, and the legislature may alter or amend this act at any time.

Approved March 26, 1875.

[No. 54.]

AN ACT to facilitate the inspection of the records and files in the offices of the registers of deeds.

SECTION 1. *The People of the State of Michigan enact*, That the registers of deeds in this State shall furnish proper and reasonable facilities for the inspection and examination of the records and files in their respective offices, and for making memorandums or transcripts therefrom during the usual business hours, to all persons having occasion to make examination of them for any lawful purpose: *Provided*, That the custodian of said records and files may make such reasonable rules and regulations with reference to the inspection and examination of them as shall be necessary for the protection of said records and files, and to prevent the interference with the regular discharge of the duties of said register: *And provided further*, That said register of deeds may prohibit the use of pen and ink in making copies or notes of records and files. Registers shall furnish proper facilities for inspection of records and files.
Proviso—rules for the protection of records, etc.
Proviso—use of pen and ink prohibited.

SEC. 2. This act shall take immediate effect.

Approved March 26, 1875.

[No. 55.]

AN ACT to amend an act entitled "An act to provide for the payment of the salaries of the military officers of the State," approved April fifteenth, eighteen hundred and seventy-one, being section nine hundred and twenty-four, in chapter eighteen of the compiled laws of eighteen hundred and seventy-one.

SECTION 1. *The People of the State of Michigan enact*, That section one of an act entitled "An act to provide for the payment of the salaries of the military officers of the State," approved April fifteenth, eighteen hundred and seventy-one, being section nine hundred and twenty-four, in chapter eighteen of the compiled laws of eighteen hundred and seventy-one, be and the same is hereby amended so as to read as follows: Section amended

SECTION 1. *The People of the State of Michigan enact*, That there be and the same is hereby appropriated, out of any money in the treasury to the credit of the military fund not otherwise appropriated, the following sums for the salaries of the military officers herein named, for the year eighteen hundred and seventy-five, and annually thereafter: for the salary of the Adjutant General, the sum of ten hundred dollars; for the salary of the Quartermaster General, the sum of six hundred dollars; for the salary of the Inspector General, the sum of six hundred dollars, and such further sum as may be necessary to pay his actual necessary traveling expenses, not exceeding one hundred and fifty dollars. Appropriation.
Salaries.

Approved March 26, 1875.

[No. 56.]

AN ACT to amend section two of act number three hundred and
sixty-three of the session laws of eighteen hundred and seventy-
three, entitled "An act to provide for the appointment of a stenographer for the recorder's court of the city of Detroit."

Section amended. SECTION 1. *The People of the State of Michigan enact*, That
section two of act number three hundred and sixty-three of the
session laws of eighteen hundred and seventy-three, entitled "An
act to provide for the appointment of a stenographer for the recorder's court of the city of Detroit," be and the same is hereby
amended so as to read as follows:

Stenographer
deemed officer of
court, his duty
and salary.
SEC. 2. The person so appointed shall be deemed an officer of
the court, and it shall be his duty to attend at each session thereof,
and to take full stenographic notes of the testimony and of the
charge of the court in all cases brought in the name of the people
of the State of Michigan ; and in case the judge shall desire it, he
shall make a legible transcript of his notes, which shall be filed by
the clerk and preserved as part of the files in the cause, subject to
the inspection and use of both parties. And for the performance
of this duty he shall receive as a compensation a salary not to exceed twelve hundred dollars per annum, which shall be paid in
monthly installments out of the county treasury.

Approved March 26, 1875.

[No. 57.]

AN ACT to repeal an act to provide for licensing the keeping of
dogs.

Act repealed. SECTION 1. *The People of the State of Michigan enact*, That
" An act to provide for licensing the keeping of dogs," approved
April thirtieth, eighteen hundred and seventy-three, be and the
same is hereby repealed.

SEC. 2. This act shall take effect March thirty-one, eighteen hundred and seventy-five.

Approved March 26, 1875.

[No. 58.]

AN ACT to amend section ten of an act entitled " An act to establish a State Public School for dependent and neglected children,"
approved April seventeen, eighteen hundred and seventy-one,
and to add three new sections to said act (as amended by act
number one hundred and forty-four of session laws of eighteen
hundred and seventy-three, approved April twenty-four, eighteen hundred and seventy-three), to be known as sections twenty,
twenty-one, and twenty-two.

Section amended. SECTION 1. *The People of the State of Michigan enact*, That
section ten of an act entitled " An act to establish a State Public

School for dependent and neglected children," approved April seventeen, eighteen hundred and seventy-one, as amended by act number one hundred and forty-four, session laws of eighteen hundred and seventy-three, approved April twenty-four eighteen hundred and seventy-three, be amended so as to read as follows:

SEC. 10. It shall be the duty of said board of control to meet once in three months on its own adjournments, and oftener if necessary; that the said board shall elect from its own number, a president, secretary, and treasurer, each of whom shall hold his office during the pleasure of said board; that the said treasurer shall give his bond to the people of this State, with two or more sufficient sureties to be approved by said board and the Governor, in the penal sum of at least ten thousand dollars, or in such additional penal sum as said board may require, conditioned for the faithful performance of the duties required of him by law, and to account for and pay over as required by law, all moneys received by him as such treasurer. The said board of control shall establish a system of government for the institution, and shall make all necessary rules and regulations for enforcing discipline, imparting instruction, preserving health, and for the [proper] physical, intellectual, and moral training of the children. The said board shall appoint a superintendent, a matron, and such other officers, teachers, and employes as shall be necessary, who shall severally hold their offices or places during the pleasure of said board, and that said board shall prescribe their duties, and fix their salaries, subject to the approval of the Governor.

Board of control to meet quarterly.

Bond of treasurer.

Government of school.

Officers for school.

SEC. 2. That there shall be added to said act three new sections, to stand as sections twenty, twenty-one, and twenty-two of said act, to read as follows:

Sections added.

SEC. 20. The said board of control shall make out biennially, and report to the legislature at its regular session, a detailed statement of the operations of said institution, for the two years closing with the fiscal year preceding said session, which shall include a report of the treasurer of the board of all receipts and disbursements for the same period. It shall also be the duty of said board to cause to be made out by the superintendent or other proper officer, and forwarded to the office of the Superintendent of Public Instruction, on or before the first day of November in each year, a report for the fiscal year, setting forth the condition of the institution, the amount of receipts and expenditures, the number of teachers and other officers and compensation of each, the number of inmates that have received instruction, the studies pursued, and the books used; also the mode of instruction and discipline prescribed, and such other information and suggestions as may be deemed important, or the Superintendent of Public Instruction may require, to embody in the report of his department. The members of said board shall be allowed the expenses necessarily incurred by them in the discharge of their official duties, and three dollars per day for their official services actually and necessarily performed, which shall be audited by the board of State Auditors.

Board of control to report biennially to Legislature.

Report to superintendent of public instruction.

What to set forth.

Compensation of members of board.

SEC. 21. That whenever the superintendents of the poor of any

Examination of
children before
sending to
school—duty of
superintendents
of the poor. county shall bring any child before the judge of probate for examination as to his alleged dependence, as provided in section sixteen
of this act, they shall present to said judge an application in writing, which shall be filed in his office, for such examination, which
shall be signed by at least two of said superintendents, in which
they shall certify that in their opinion the child named is dependent on the public for support, and that he has no parents against
whom his support can be enforced, as provided in chapter forty-
nine of the compiled laws of eighteen hundred and seventy-one.

Board may con-
sent to adoption
of children. SEC. 22. The [that] said board of control is hereby authorized to
consent to the adoption of any child who has or shall become an in-
mate of said institution, by any person, pursuant to the provisions
of an act entitled "An act to provide for changing the names of
minor adopted children and other persons," approved February
two, eighteen hundred and sixty-one, and that on such adoption
and proceedings had under such act, whereby the child takes the
name and becomes the heir of the person so adopting him or her,
then said board of control shall cease to be the guardian of said
child.

SEC. 3. This act shall take immediate effect.

Approved March 26, 1875.

[No. 59.]

AN ACT to provide for recording certified copies of lost deeds, and
other instruments affecting the title to real estate.

Manner of per-
fecting the rec-
ords when deeds,
etc., affecting
lands in two or
more counties
shall have been
destroyed before
being recorded in
all the counties,
when the same
shall have been
recorded in any
one of them. SECTION 1. *The People of the State of Michigan enact*, In all
cases where a deed, mortgage, or other instrument affecting the
title to real estate, shall have been, or shall be executed, affecting
land in two or more counties, and when the same shall have been
duly recorded in the office of the register of deeds in any county in
which any part of the lands to be affected thereby is situate, and
such instrument shall have been lost or destroyed before being recorded in other counties in which land affected thereby shall be
situate, it shall be lawful for any party or parties, interested in such
lost deed or other writing, or in the real estate the title to which
shall be affected thereby, to apply to the judge of the probate
court of the county where such real estate may be situate in which
the record shall not have been made, for an order to record a duly
certified transcript of such deed, mortgage, or other instrument, in
such county, and thereupon such judge of probate shall give notice
by publication, in accordance with the practice of such court, for
three successive weeks, of such application, and of the time and
place when and where a hearing will be had thereon, and on such
hearing, if it shall appear to such probate judge that such deed,
mortgage, or other instrument was duly executed and has been
legally recorded in any county in this State, and that the same was
lost or destroyed before being recorded in other counties in which
real estate to be affected thereby was situate, such probate judge
shall make an order authorizing a certified transcript of such deed,

mortgage, or other writing, to be recorded in said county, and shall annex a duly certified copy of such order to such copy of such deed, mortgage, or other instrument, and thereupon such certified copy of deed, mortgage, or other instrument, and such order authorizing a record thereof, may be recorded in the office of the register of deeds of the county in which such order shall be made, and such record shall have the same force and effect as the record of the original would have had, had the same been recorded before being lost or destroyed.

Approved March 26, 1875.

[No. 60.]

AN ACT to amend section three thousand nine hundred and thirty-four of the compiled laws of eighteen hundred and seventy-one, being section eight of an act entitled " An act to provide for the selection, care, and disposition of the lands donated to the State of Michigan by act of Congress, approved July second, eighteen hundred and sixty-two, for the endowment of colleges for the benefit of agriculture and the mechanic arts," approved March eighteen, eighteen hundred and sixty-three.

SECTION 1. *The People of the State of Michigan enact,* That section three thousand nine hundred and thirty-four of the compiled laws of eighteen hundred and seventy-one, being section eight of an act entitled " An act to provide for the selection, care, and disposition of the lands donated to the State of Michigan by act of Congress approved July second, eighteen hundred and sixty-two, for the endowment of colleges for the benefit of agriculture and the mechanic arts," approved March eighteen, eighteen hundred and sixty-three, be amended to read as follows: Section amended

(3934.) SEC. 8. The money received from the sale of said lands shall be paid into the State Treasury, and shall be placed in the general fund, but the amount thereof shall be placed to the credit of the Agricultural College fund upon the books of the Auditor General, and the annual interest thereon computed at seven per cent, shall be regularly applied under the direction of the State Board of Agriculture to the support and maintenance of the State Agricultural College, where the leading object shall be,— without excluding other scientific and classical studies, and including military tactics,—to teach such branches of learning as are related to agriculture and mechanic arts, in order to promote the liberal and practical education of industrial classes in the several pursuits and professions of life. How money received from sale of lands to be disposed of. How interest shall be disposed of. Leading object of college.

SEC. 2. This act shall take immediate effect.

Approved March 26, 1875.

[No. 61.]

AN ACT to amend section three of article two of act number one hundred and ninety-eight of the session laws of eighteen hundred and seventy-three, entitled " An act to revise the laws providing for the incorporation of railroad companies, and to regulate the running and management, and to fix the duties and liabilities of all railroad and other corporations owning or operating any railroad in this State," approved May one, eighteen hundred and seventy-three.

Section amended   SECTION 1. *The People of the State of Michigan enact,* That section three of article two of act number one hundred and ninety-eight of the session laws of eighteen hundred and seventy-three, entitled " An act to revise the laws providing for the incorporation of railroad companies, and to regulate the running and management, and to fix the duties and liabilities of all railroad and other corporations owning or operating any railroad in this State," approved May one, eighteen hundred and seventy-three, be amended so as to read as follows:

Classification of directors, their election and term of office.   SEC. 3. At any meeting of stockholders for the election of directors, it shall be lawful for the stockholders to classify the directors in three equal classes, as ·near as may be, one of which classes shall hold their office for one year, one for two years, and one for three years, and until their successors are respectively elected ; and at all subsequent elections directors shall be elected for three years to fill the places made vacant by the class whose term of office shall expire at that time. In case no such classification shall at any time be made, the persons elected at any such meeting shall hold their office for one year, and until their successors shall be elected ; and it shall be the duty of the directors to provide for by by-law and to call ; and in case of their neglect so to do, a majority of the stockholders may call an annual election of directors, at such time and place as may be appointed, in some county in which the road is to, or shall run, and at which time and place there shall be a general meeting of the stockholders in

Special meetings of stockholders. person or by proxy. And a special meeting of the stockholders may be called at any time by the directors, or by the stockholders owning not less than one-fourth of the stock in value, by giving notice of such meeting as hereinafter provided. At least thirty

Notice thereof. days' notice of the time and place of every general or special meeting of the stockholders shall be given in one or more daily newspapers printed in the city of Detroit, and also in one or more newspapers printed in the county where the principal office of the

Proviso. company is situated, if it be not in said city: *Provided,* That such notice, when given by the stockholders, shall state the object of

Evidence of notice perpetuated by affidavit. such meeting. Evidence of such notice may be perpetuated by the affidavit of any person having knowledge thereof, and at any meeting of the stockholders held pursuant to this act. The stock-

Removals from office. holders representing a majority in value of the stock may remove from office any of the directors, or other officer of the company, and elect others in their stead. And the president, and directors, and officers, and agents of the company, in the exercise of their respective powers and duties, shall at all times be governed by, and be subject to, such rules, regulations, and directions, as the stockholders holding a majority in value of the stock may adopt at such meeting (and at every such meeting it shall be competent for any stockholder to appear and vote by proxy as well as in person). If at any meeting of the stockholders, a majority in value of the stock which, by the provisions of section one of article two of this act, is entitled to vote, is not represented in person or by proxy, the same shall be adjourned by such as are present from day to day, not exceeding three days, without doing any business. when, if such majority do not appear and attend, the meeting shall be dissolved. *(margin: Majority of stock controls. Proxy. Adjournments, etc.)*

Approved March 26, 1875.

[No. 62.]

AN ACT granting and defining the powers and duties of incorporated villages.

CHAPTER I.

SECTION 1. *The People of the State of Michigan enact,* That all villages hereafter incorporated shall be subject to the provisions of this act.

SEC. 2. The boundaries of the village, the time and place for the first election therein, the time and manner of registering voters, and the manner of giving notice of such election, shall be provided for by the special act incorporating such village. *(margin: Act incorporating must fix boundaries, provide for first election, etc.)*

SEC. 3. On the day of election, and at the hour for the opening of the polls, the qualified electors present shall choose from among their number present three inspectors of election, who shall be qualified electors under the constitution, and who shall take the oath prescribed by law to be taken by inspectors of election. All persons residing within said village, and having the qualification of electors under the constitution, shall be permitted to vote at such election. *(margin: Inspectors of first election. Voters at first election.)*

SEC. 4. The inspectors of such election, after the close of the polls, shall canvass the ballots, and declare and determine the result. *(margin: Inspectors to canvass ballots and declare result.)*

SEC. 5. All villages hereafter incorporated shall be bodies politic and corporate under and by the corporate name assumed by or designated for them as hereinbefore provided, and by such name may sue and be sued, contract and be contracted with, acquire and hold real and personal property for the purposes for which they were incorporated, have a common seal, and change the same at pleasure, and exercise all the powers in this act conferred. *(margin: Corporation shall be body politic and corporate.)*

SEC. 6. Service of process in suits against corporations organized under this act may be made on the president or clerk of the village, or, in their absence, upon any of the trustees thereof, by leaving *(margin: Service of process in suits against corporation.)*

8

certified copies of such process with the officer served, at least eight days before the return day of such process.

Board of registration. SEC. 7. The village clerk and two of the trustees to be appointed each year by the the the council shall be the village board of registration.

Completion of registration of electors. On the Saturday previous to the day of holding any annual or special election, and on any other days that the village council may appoint, the board shall be in session for the purpose of completing the registration of the electors of the village. Notice of the time and place of such meeting shall be given with the notice of said election.

Rules for making and completing registration. SEC. 8. In making and completing any such registration, the board shall proceed in the same manner and conform to the same rules, as near as may be, as are provided by law for registering electors in townships.

CHAPTER II.

OFFICERS.

Officers elected. SECTION 1. In villages incorporated subject to the provisions of this act the following officers shall be elected, viz: a president, six trustees, one clerk, one treasurer, one street commissioner, one assessor, and one constable, and the president and trustees shall **Village council.** constitute the village council.

Officers appointed. SEC. 2. The council shall appoint a village marshal, an engineer of the fire department, and may appoint a village attorney, a village surveyor, one or more fire wardens, a pound-master, and such number of policemen and night watchmen as they shall deem expedient. The council may also, from time to time, provide by ordinance for the appointment of, and appoint for such term as may be provided by the ordinance, such other officers whose election or appointment is not herein specially provided for, as they shall deem necessary for the execution of the powers granted by this act, and may remove the same at pleasure. The powers and duties of all such officers shall be prescribed by ordinance.

Time of appointment. SEC. 3. Appointments to office by the council, excepting appointments to fill vacancies, shall be made on the second Monday in April in each year; but appointments which for any cause shall not be made on that day may be made at any subsequent regular meeting of the council.

Term of office of certain officers. SEC. 4. The president, clerk, treasurer, street commissioner, assessor, and constable shall hold their respective offices for the term of one year from the second Monday of March of the year when elected, and until their successors are elected and qualified and enter upon the duties of their offices.

Term of office of trustees. SEC. 5. The trustees shall hold their offices for the term of two years from the second Monday in March of the year when elected, and until their successors are qualified and enter upon the duties of their offices; except that at the first election held in any village incorporated, subject to the provisions of this act, six trustees shall be elected, three for the term of one year, and three for the term of two years, from the second Monday of March in the year when

elected, and annually thereafter three trustees shall be elected for
the term of two years.

SEC. 6. All officers appointed by the president or council, ex- *Term of office of appointed officers.*
cept officers appointed to fill vacancies in elective offices, shall
hold their respective offices until the second Monday of April
next after such appointment, and until their successors are qualified and enter upon the duties of their offices, unless a different
term of office shall be prescribed in this act, or in the ordinance
creating the office. Officers appointed to fill vacancies shall hold *Term when appointed to fill vacancy.*
the office for the residue of the term in which the vacancy oc-
curred. All persons elected or appointed to office shall enter upon *When officers to enter upon their duties.*
the duties thereof upon taking the oath of office, and filing the
requisite security, if any is required of them.

SEC. 7. No person shall be elected or appointed to any office un- *Who eligible to office.*
less he shall be an elector of the village. All officers of the vil-
lage, elected or appointed, shall take and subscribe the oath of *Oath of office.*
office prescribed by the constitution of the State, and file the
same with the clerk, and in case of failure to do so, within ten days
after receiving notice of their election or appointment, shall be
deemed to have declined the office.

SEC. 8. Every officer elected or appointed in the village, before *Official bond.*
entering upon the duties of his office, and within the time prescribed for filing his official oath, shall file with the village clerk
such bond or security as may be required by law, or by any ordinance or requirement of the council, and with such sureties as
shall be approved by the council, conditioned for the due performance of the duties of his office, except that the bond or security
given by the clerk shall be deposited with the treasurer.

SEC. 9. The council, or president, or other officer whose duty *Examination as to sufficiency of sureties.*
it shall be to judge of the sufficiency of the proposed sureties of
any officer or person of whom a bond or any security may be required by this act, or by any ordinance or direction of the council,
shall inquire into the sufficiency of such sureties, and examine
them on oath as to their property. Such oath may be administered by the president, or any trustee, or other person authorized
to administer oaths. Such examination shall be reduced to writing *To be in writing and filed with bond.*
and signed by the surety, and annexed to and filed with the instru-
ment to which it relates, and no member of the common council
shall sign any official bond relating to the village corporation, un- *Signing of bond by member of council.*
der penalty of vacating his office; but such bond, if so signed and
filed, shall be legal and valid.

SEC. 10. The council may also at any time, require any officer *Council may require new bond.*
to execute and file with the clerk of the village additional or new
official bonds, with such new or further sureties as said council
shall deem requisite for the interest of the corporation. Any failure to comply with such requirement within a reasonable time,
shall subject the officer to immediate removal from office by the
council.

VACANCIES IN OFFICE.

Resignations.

SEC. 11. Resignations of officers shall be made to the council, subject to their approval and acceptance.

Acts by which officers are vacated.

SEC. 12. If any officer shall cease to be a resident of the village during his term of office, the office shall be thereby vacated. If any officer shall be a defaulter, the office shall thereby be vacated.

Idem.

SEC. 13. If any person elected or appointed to office shall fail to take and file the oath of office, or shall fail to give the bond or security required for the due performance of the duties of his office, within the time herein limited therefor, the council may declare the office vacant, unless previously thereto he shall file the oath and give the requisite bond or security.

Vacancies, how filled.

SEC. 14. A vacancy in the office of president, or of any trustee, occurring more than six months before an annual election, shall be filled by a special election. A vacancy in the office of any trustee occurring within six months before an annual election, shall be filled by appointment of the council. Vacancies in any other office shall be filled by appointment by the council, within twenty days after the vacancy occurs, or if the vacancy be an elective office it may be filled by an election or by appointment, in the discretion of the council.

Liabilities of officers and sureties.

SEC. 15. The resignation or removal of any officer shall not, nor shall the appointment or election of another to the office, exonerate such officer or his sureties from any liability incurred by him or them.

Delivery of books, moneys, etc., to successors.

SEC. 16. Whenever any officer shall resign or be removed from office, or the term for which he shall have been elected or appointed shall expire, he shall, on demand, deliver over to his successor in office, all the books, papers, moneys, and effects in his custody as such officer, and in any way appertaining to his office; and every

Violation a misdemeanor.

person violating this provision shall be deemed guilty of a misdemeanor, and may be proceeded against in the same manner as public officers generally for the like offense under the general laws of this State, now or hereafter in force and applicable thereto; and every officer appointed or elected shall be deemed an officer within the meaning and provisions of such general laws of the State.

CHAPTER III.

ELECTIONS.

Annual elections.

SECTION 1. After the first election an annual election of officers shall be held on the second Monday in March in each year, at such place in the village as the council shall designate.

Special elections.

SEC. 2. Special elections may be appointed by resolution of the council, and held at such times as they shall determine, the purpose and object of which shall be fully set forth in the resolution appointing such election.

Inspectors of election.

SEC. 3. The president and clerk of the village and one of the trustees, or any three of the trustees, to be appointed by the council, shall be the inspectors of election. The president, when pres-

ent, shall be chairman, and the others shall be clerks of the board
of inspectors.

SEC. 4. Notice of the time and place of holding any election, Election notice.
and of the officers to be elected, and the questions to be voted upon
shall, except as herein otherwise provided, be given by the clerk, at
least eight days before such election, by posting such notices in
three public places in the village, and by publishing a copy thereof
in a newspaper in the village, if any is published therein, the same
length of time before the election; and in case of a special election, the notice shall set forth the purpose and object of the election as fully as the same are required to be set forth in the resolution appointing such election.

SEC. 5. The council shall provide and cause to be kept by the Ballot boxes.
clerk, for use at all elections, suitable ballot-boxes of the kind
required by law to be kept and used in townships.

SEC. 6. On the day of elections, in accordance with law, the polls Opening and
shall be opened at eight o'clock in the morning, and shall be kept closing of the
open until five o'clock in the afternoon, at which hour they shall polls.
be finally closed. The inspectors shall cause proclamation to be
made of the opening and closing of the polls.

SEC. 7. All elections in said village shall be conducted, as nearly Manner of con-
as may be, in the manner provided by law for holding general elec- ducting elections
tions in the State, except as herein otherwise provided; and the Powers of
inspectors of such elections shall have the same powers and author- inspectors.
ity for the preservation of order, and for forcing obedience to their
lawful commands during the time of holding the election and the
canvass of the votes, as are conferred by law upon inspectors of
general elections held in this State.

SEC. 8. Immediately after closing the polls, the inspectors of Canvass by
election shall, without adjourning, publicly canvass the votes re- inspectors.
ceived by them, and declare the result; and shall, on the same day, Statement of
or on the next day, make a statement in writing, setting forth in result, and cer-
words at full length the whole number of votes given for each tificate.
office, the names of the persons for whom such votes for each office
were given, and the number of votes so given for each person;
and the whole number of votes given upon each question voted
upon, and the number of votes given for and against the same,
which statement shall be certified under the hands of the inspectors to be correct; and they shall deposit such statement and cer- To be deposited
tificate on the day of election, or on the next day, together with with village
said poll lists and the register of electors, and the boxes contain- clerk.
ing said ballots, in the office of the village clerk.

SEC. 9. The council shall convene on Thursday next succeeding Council to deter-
each election, at their usual place of meeting, and determine the mine result of
result of the election upon each question and proposition voted election.
upon, and what persons were duly elected at the said election to
the several offices respectively; and thereupon the clerk shall make
duplicate certificates of such determination, showing the result of
the election upon any question or proposition voted upon, and
what persons are declared elected to the several offices respectively;
one of which certificates he shall file in the office of the county

clerk of the county in which the village is located, and the other shall be filed in the office of the village clerk.

Tie to be determined by lot. SEC. 10. If there shall be no choice for any office by reason of two or more candidates having received an equal number of votes, the council shall, at the meeting mentioned in the preceding section, determine by lot between such persons which shall be considered elected to such office.

Notice to persons elected, etc. SEC. 11. It shall be the duty of the village clerk, within five days after the meeting and determination of the council, as provided in this chapter, to notify each person elected, in writing, of his election; and he shall also, within five days after the council shall appoint any person to any office, in like manner notify such person of the appointment.

Clerk to report neglect to file oath and bond. SEC. 12. Within one week after the expiration of the time in which any official bond or oath of office is required to be filed, the clerk shall report in writing to the council the names of all persons elected or appointed to any office, who shall have neglected to file such oath or bond.

CHAPTER IV.

DUTIES OF OFFICERS.

Duties of president. SECTION 1. The president shall be the chief executive officer of the village. He shall preside at the meetings of the council, and shall from time to time give the council information concerning the affairs of the corporation, and recommend such measures as he may deem expedient. It shall be his duty to exercise supervision over the affairs of the village, and over the public property belonging thereto, see that the laws relating to the village, and the ordinances and regulations of the council are enforced.

Conservator of the peace. SEC. 2. The president shall be a conservator of the peace, and may exercise within the village the powers conferred upon sheriffs to suppress disorder; and shall have authority to command the assistance of all able-bodied citizens to aid in the enforcement of the ordinances of the council, and to suppress riot and disorderly conduct.

May remove or suspend. SEC. 3. The president may remove any officer appointed by him at any time, and may suspend any policeman for neglect of duty. **May examine books, etc.** He shall have authority at all times to examine and inspect the books, records, and papers of any agent, employe, or officer of the corporation, and shall perform generally all such duties as are or may be prescribed by the ordinances of the village.

President pro tempore. SEC. 4. In the absence or disability of the president, or of any vacancy in his office, the president *pro tempore* of the council shall perform the duties of the president.

Duties of village clerk. SEC. 5. The village clerk shall keep the corporate seal, and all the documents, official bonds, papers, files, and records of the village, not by this act or the ordinances of the village entrusted to some other officer: he shall be clerk of the council, shall attend its meetings, record all its proceedings, ordinances, and resolutions, and shall countersign and register all licenses granted; he shall, when required, make and certify under the seal of the village, copies of the papers and records filed and kept in his office; and such copies shall be evidence in all places of the matters therein contained, to the same extent as the originals would be; he shall possess and exercise the powers of township clerk so far as the same are required to be performed within the village, except as to filing chattel mortgages; and he shall have authority to administer oaths and affirmations.

SEC. 6. The village clerk shall be the general accountant of the village; and all claims against the corporation shall be filed with him for adjustment; after examination thereof, he shall report the same, with all accompanying vouchers and counter-claims of the village and the true balance as found by him, to the council for allowance, and when allowed shall draw his warrant upon the treasurer for the payment thereof, designating thereon the fund from which payment is to be made, and take proper receipts therefor; but no warrant shall be drawn upon any fund after the same has been exhausted. When any tax or money shall be levied, raised, or appropriated, the clerk shall report the amount thereof to the village treasurer, stating the objects and funds for which it is levied, raised, or appropriated, and the amounts thereof to be credited to each fund. *Further duties of clerk.*

SEC. 7. The village clerk shall have charge of all the books, vouchers, and documents relating to the accounts, contracts, debts, and revenues of the corporation; he shall countersign and register all bonds issued, and keep a list of all property and effects belonging to the village, and of all its debts and liabilities; he shall keep a complete set of books, exhibiting the financial condition of the corporation in all its departments, funds, resources, and liabilities, with a proper classification thereof, and showing the purpose for which each fund was raised; he shall record all official bonds of the village, in a book prepared for the purpose; he shall also keep an account with the treasurer, in which he shall charge him with all the moneys received for each of the several funds of the village, and credit him with all warrants drawn thereon, keeping an account with each fund. *Idem.*

SEC. 8. The clerk shall report to the council, whenever required, a detailed statement of the receipts, expenditures, and financial condition of the village, of the debts to be paid, and moneys necessary to meet the estimated expenses of the corporation, and shall perform such other duties pertaining to his office as the council may require. *Financial report, etc.*

SEC. 9. The village treasurer shall have the custody of all moneys, bonds other than official, mortgages, notes, leases, and evidences of value, belonging to the village. He shall receive all moneys belonging to and receivable by the corporation, and keep an account of all receipts and expenditures thereof. He shall pay no money out of the treasury, except in pursuance of and [by] authority of law, and upon warrants signed by the clerk and president, which shall specify the purpose for which the amounts thereof are to be paid. He shall keep an account of, and be charged *Duties of treasurer.*

with, all taxes and moneys appropriated, raised or received for each fund of the corporation, and shall keep a separate account of each fund, and shall credit thereto all moneys raised, paid in, or appropriated therefor, and shall pay every warrant out of the particular fund raised for the purpose for which the warrant was issued.

Monthly report. SEC. 10. The treasurer shall render to the clerk on the first Monday of every month, if required, a report of the amounts received and credited by him to each fund, and on what account received, and the amounts paid out by him from each fund during the preceding month, and the amount of money remaining in **Annual report.** each fund on the day of his report. He shall also exhibit to the council annually on the first Monday in March, and as often and for such period as the council shall require, a full and detailed account of the receipts and disbursements of the treasury since the date of his last annual report, classifying them therein by the funds to which such receipts are credited and out of which such disbursements are made, and the balances remaining in each fund; **Filing and publication of the same.** which account shall be filed in the office of the clerk, and shall be published in one of the newspapers of the village if any be published therein.

Treasurer's vouchers. SEC. 11. Said treasurer shall take vouchers for all money paid from the treasury, showing the amount and fund from which payment was made, which vouchers upon settlement with the proper officers of the village shall be surrendered and filed with the village clerk.

Not to use public moneys for private purposes SEC. 12. The treasurer shall keep all moneys in his hands belonging to the village separate and distinct from his own moneys, and he is hereby prohibited from using, either directly or indirectly, the corporation moneys, warrants, or evidences of debt in his custody or keeping, for his own use or benefit, or that of any **Penalty.** other person; any violation of the provisions of this section shall work a forfeiture of his office, and the council, on proof of the fact, are authorized to declare the office vacant and appoint his successor for the remainder of his term.

Powers and duties of marshal. SEC. 13. The village marshal shall be the chief of the police of the village. As police officer he shall be subject to the direction of the president and council. It shall be his duty to see that all the ordinances and regulations of the council, made for the preservation of quiet, good order, and for the safety and protection of the inhabitants of the village, are promptly enforced. As peace officer he shall within said village be vested with all the powers conferred upon sheriffs for the preservation of quiet and good order. He shall serve and execute all process directed or delivered to him, in all proceedings for violations of the ordinances of the village. Such process may be served any where within the county in which said village is located.

Shall keep record of arrests, etc. SEC. 14. The marshal shall keep a record of all arrests and the cause thereof, and shall enter therein, within twenty-four hours after any person shall be arrested, the name of the person so arrested, the cause of the arrest, the age and nationality of the person arrested, and if discharged without being taken before a court, the reason for such discharge, which record shall be the property of the village.

SEC. 15. The marshal shall report in writing and on oath to the council at their first meeting in each month, all arrests made by him and the cause thereof, and all persons discharged from arrest during the month ; also the number remaining in confinement for breaches of the ordinances of the village ; the amount of all fines and fees collected by him. All moneys collected or received by the marshal, unless otherwise directed by this act, shall be paid into the village treasury during the same week when received, and the treasurer's receipt therefor shall be filed with the clerk. *Monthly report.* *Weekly payment of moneys received.*

SEC. 16. The marshal may collect and receive the same fees for services performed by him as are allowed to constables for like services. *Fees.*

SEC. 17. The village surveyor shall have and exercise within the village, the like powers and duties as are conferred by law upon county surveyors; and the like effect and validity shall be given to his official acts, surveys, and plats as are given by law to the acts and surveys of county surveyors. He shall make all necessary plats, maps, surveys, diagrams, and estimates required by the council or officers of the village, relating to the public improvements, buildings, grounds, and streets of the village ; and all plats, maps, surveys, and diagrams made by him as such surveyor shall be the property of the village, and shall be delivered by him to his successor in office. *Powers and duties of surveyor.*

SEC. 18. It shall be the duty of the street commissioner to perform, or cause to be performed, all such labor, repairs, and improvements upon the highways, streets, sidewalks, alleys, bridges, reservoirs, drains, culverts, sewers, public grounds, and parks, within the village, as the council shall direct to be done by or under his supervision; and to oversee and do whatever may be required of him in relation thereto by the council. *Powers and duties of street commissioner.*

SEC. 19. He shall make a report to the council, in writing and on oath, once in each month, giving an exact statement of all labor performed by him, or under his supervision, and the charges therefor ; the amount of material used, and the expense thereof, and the street or place where such material was used, or labor performed ; and further showing the items and purpose of all expenses incurred since his last preceding report. *Monthly report.*

SEC. 20. The constable of the village shall have the like powers and authority in matters of civil and criminal nature, and in relation to the service of all manner of process, as are conferred by law upon constables in townships, and shall receive the like fees for his services. He shall have the power also to serve all process issued for breaches of the ordinances of the village; and shall be subject to the same liabilities and duties as constables elected in townships. *Powers and authority of constable,*

SEC. 21. The assessor shall perform such duties in relation to assessing property and levying taxes in the village as are prescribed by this act. *Duties of assessor.*

SEC. 22. The president and trustees shall serve without compensation. All other officers, except where other provision is made *Compensation of officers.*

9

herein or by law regulating fees for services, shall receive such compensation as the council shall prescribe.

CHAPTER V.

VILLAGE COUNCIL.

Authority, and of whom composed.	SECTION 1. The legislative authority of villages subject to the provisions of this act shall be vested in a council consisting of the president and trustees.

President.	SEC. 2. The president of the village shall be president of the council, and preside at the meetings thereof.

President pro tempore.	SEC. 3. On the second Monday in April in each year, or as soon thereafter as may be, the council shall appoint one of their number president *pro tempore* of the council, who in the absence of the president shall preside at the meetings thereof, and exercise the powers and duties of president. In the absence of the president and president *pro tem.*, the council shall appoint one of their number to preside.

Stated meetings.	SEC. 4. The council shall hold regular stated meetings for the transaction of business, at such times as it shall prescribe, not less than one of which shall be held in each month. The president or Special meetings. any three members of the council may appoint special meetings thereof, notice of which, in writing, shall be given to each trustee, or be left at his place of residence, at least twenty-four hours before the meeting.

SEC. 5. All meetings and sessions of the council shall be public. Quorum. A majority of the council shall make a quorum for the transaction of business; a less number may adjourn from time to time, and compel the attendance of absent members in such manner as shall Acts requiring a two-thirds vote of trustees elect. be prescribed by ordinance. But no office shall be created or abolished, nor any tax or assessment be imposed; street, alley, or public ground be vacated, real estate or any interest therein sold or disposed of, unless by a concurring vote of two-thirds of all the Vote on appropriations. trustees elect. No money shall be appropriated except by ordinance or resolution of the council; nor shall any ordinance be passed, nor any resolution appropriating money be adopted, except by a concurring vote of all the trustees elect.

Manner of conducting business of council.	SEC. 6. The council shall prescribe the rules of its own proceedings, and keep a record thereof. All votes for special improvements, or appropriating money, shall be taken by yeas and nays, and shall be so entered upon the journal.

Officers prohibited from being interested in any contract.	SEC. 7. No member of the council, nor any officer of the corporation, shall be directly or indirectly interested in any contract or service made by, or to be performed for the corporation: *Pro-* Proviso. *vided,* That this shall not prevent officers receiving compensation Penalty. authorized by this act. Any violation of the provisions of this section shall work forfeiture of the office, and on proof thereof, the council may declare the office vacant.

CHAPTER VI.

ORDINANCES.

Style, vote on passage, etc,	SECTION 1. The style of all ordinances shall be: "The village of ———— ordains." All ordinances shall require, for their passage, the concurrence of a majority of the council. No ordinance imposing a penalty shall take effect in less than twenty days after its passage.

SEC. 2. The council may impose penalties for violating the ordinances of the village, but no fine shall exceed one hundred dollars, nor imprisonment exceeding ninety days; and if imprisonment be adjudged in any case, it may be in the village prison, or in the county jail of the county in which the village is located, in the discretion of the court. *Penalties for violation.*

SEC. 3. All ordinances, when regularly enacted, shall be recorded by the clerk of the council, in a book to be called " the record of ordinances," and it shall be the duty of the president and clerk to authenticate the same by their official signatures upon such record. *Record of ordinances, etc.*

SEC. 4. Within one week after the passage of any ordinance, the same shall be published in a newspaper printed in the village, if any is published therein, otherwise copies of the ordinance shall, within the same time, be posted in three of the most public places in the village; and the clerk shall, immediately after such publication or posting, enter in the record of ordinances, in a blank space to be left for such purpose under the record of the ordinance, a certificate under his hand, stating the time and place or places of such publication or posting. Such certificates [certificate] shall be *prima facie* evidence of the due publication and posting of the ordinance. *Publication.* *Certificate of publication.* *Legal value of same.*

SEC. 5. Whenever it shall be necessary to prove any of the laws, regulations, or ordinances of any village, or any resolution adopted by the council thereof, the same may be read in all courts of justice and in all proceedings: *Proof of ordinances, etc., in court.*

First, From a record thereof kept by the village clerk ;

Second, From a copy of the ordinance, or of the record thereof, certified by the clerk under the corporate seal of the village ;

Third, From any volume of ordinances purporting to have been written or printed by authority of the council.

SEC. 6. Any justice of the peace of the village, or of the township in which the village or some part of it is situated, shall have authority to hear, try, and determine all causes and suits arising under the ordinances of the village, and to inflict punishments for violations thereof, as provided in the ordinances. *Who may try suits for violation of ordinances.*

SEC. 7. Whenever a penalty shall be incurred for the violation of any ordinance, and no provision shall be made for the imprisonment of the offender upon conviction therefor, such penalty may be recovered in an action of debt, or in assumpsit. And when a corporation shall incur a penalty for the violation of any such ordinance, the same shall be sued for in one of the actions aforesaid. *Recovery of penalties.*

SEC. 8. Every village shall be allowed the use of the jail of the county in which it is located, for the confinement of all persons liable to imprisonment under the ordinance thereof, or under any of the provisions of this act; and the sheriff, or other keeper of such jail, or other place of confinement or imprisonment, shall receive and safely keep any person committed thereto as aforesaid, until lawfully discharged.   In all cases of imprisonment for *Village prisoners may be confined in county jail.*

Expenses of same.

breaches of the penal laws of this State, such receiving and keeping in such jail shall be at the expense of the county in which the village is located; in all other cases it shall be at the expense of the village.

Setting forth of ordinance in complaint, pleadings, etc.

Sec. 9. It shall not be necessary in any suit, proceeding, or prosecution for the violation of any ordinance to state or set forth such ordinance or any of the provisions thereof, in any complaint, warrant, process, or pleading therein; but the same shall be deemed sufficiently set forth or stated by receiving [reciting] its title and the date of its passage or approval. And it shall be a sufficient statement of the cause of action in any such complaint or warrant, to set forth substantially, and with reasonable certainty as to time and place, the act or offense complained of, and to allege the same to be in violation of an ordinance of the village, referring thereto by its title and the date of its passage or approval.

Statement of cause of action in complaint, etc.

Appeal to circuit court.

Sec. 10. Any person convicted of a violation of any ordinance of the village may appeal to the circuit court for the county in which the village is located, which appeal shall be taken within the same time and in the same manner as is provided by law for appeals from judgments rendered by justices of the peace.

Village prison, etc.

Sec. 11. The council shall have power to provide and maintain a village prison, and such watch or station houses as may be necessary.

Security for costs in certain cases.

Sec. 12. In all prosecutions for violations of the ordinance of the village, commenced by any person other than the [an] officer of the village, the court may require the prosecutor to file security for the payment of the costs of the proceedings, in case the defendant is acquitted.

CHAPTER VII.

POWERS OF COUNCIL.

Powers and authority, and exercise thereof.

Section 1. Every village subject to the provisions of this act shall, in addition to such other powers as are conferred, have the general power and authority granted in this chapter, and the council may pass such ordinances in relation thereto as they may deem proper, namely:

First, To restrain and prevent vice and immorality;

Second, To punish vagrants, disorderly persons, and common prostitutes;

Third, To abate nuisances, and preserve the public health;

Fourth, To prohibit and suppress disorderly and gaming houses;

Fifth, To regulate, license, or suppress billiard tables and ball alleys;

Sixth, To suppress gaming;

Seventh, To license saloons, taverns, and eating-houses;

Eighth, To regulate and license public shows and exhibitions;

Ninth, To license auctioneers, and to regulate or prohibit sales of property at auction, except sales made pursuant to some of order of court or public law;

Tenth, To license and regulate hacks and other public vehicles;

Eleventh, To provide for and regulate the inspection of provision, firewood, and hay, on the public markets;

Twelfth, To provide for the inspection of weights and measures;

Thirteenth, To prohibit bathing in [the] public waters of the village;

Fourteenth, To regulate or prohibit the selling or storing of combustible or explosive materials within the village, and to regulate and restrain the making of fires in the streets or other open spaces in the village;

Fifteenth, To purchase and regulate cemeteries;

Sixteenth, To make ordinances for the organization and regulation of the fire department, and for the prevention and extinguishment of fires;

Seventeenth, To enact all ordinances and make all such regulations, not in violation of the constitution and general laws of the State, as may be necessary for the safety and good government of the village and the general welfare of its inhabitants. General authority to enact ordinances.

SEC. 2. The council of any village may make such provisions as they shall deem expedient, for the support and relief of poor persons residing in the village. Support of poor.

SEC. 3. The council may provide and maintain one or more pounds within the village, and may appoint poundmasters, prescribe their powers and duties, and fix their compensation, and shall have the same authority concerning pounds, as township boards have by the general law, except as herein otherwise provided. Pounds, poundmasters, etc.

SEC. 4. Any village may acquire, purchase, and erect such public buildings as may be required for the use of the corporation, and may purchase, appropriate, and own such real estate as may be necessary for public grounds, parks, markets, public buildings, and other purposes necessary or convenient for the public good, and for the execution of the powers conferred in this act; and such buildings and grounds, or any part thereof, may be sold at public sale, or leased, as occasion may require. Public buildings, real estate, etc.

SEC. 5. When the council shall deem it for the public interest, grounds and buildings for the village prison, hospital, pest-house, cemetery, and water-works may be purchased, erected, and maintained beyond the corporate limits of the village; and in such cases the council shall have authority to enforce beyond the corporate limits of the village, and over such lands, buildings, and property, in the same manner and to the same extent as if they were within the village, all such ordinances and police regulations as may be necessary for the care and protection thereof, and for the management and control of the persons kept or confined in such prison, pest-house, or hospital. Prison, pest-house, etc., beyond corporate limits.

SEC. 6. The council shall have authority to lay out, establish, or vacate and discontinue public parks and grounds within the village, and to improve, light, and ornament the same, and to regulate the use thereof, and to protect the same and the appurtenances thereof from obstruction, encroachment, and injury. Council may lay out and control public parks, etc.

SEC. 7. The council shall have supervision and control of all public highways, bridges, streets, avenues, alleys, sidewalks, and Supervision of public highways, bridges, etc.

public grounds within the village, and shall have the like authority over the same as is given by the general laws of this State.

Construction of sidewalks and cross-walks. SEC. 8. The council shall have control of all sidewalks in the public streets and alleys of the village, and may prescribe the grade thereof, and change the same when deemed necessary. They shall have the power to construct and maintain sidewalks and cross-walks in the public streets and alleys, and charge the expense of the sidewalks upon the lots and premises adjacent to and abutting upon such walks.

Council may require owners of lots to construct sidewalks adjacent thereto. SEC. 9. The council shall also have authority to require the owners and occupants of lots and premises to construct and maintain sidewalks in the public streets adjacent to and abutting upon such lots and premises, and to keep them in repair at all times, and to construct and lay the same upon such lines and grades, and of such width, materials, and manner of construction, and within such time, as the council shall by ordinance or resolution prescribe, and to keep the same free from obstructions, snow, ice, filth, or any nuisance.

In case of failure council may construct. SEC. 10. If the owner or occupant of any lot or premises shall fail to construct or maintain any particular sidewalk as mentioned and prescribed in the last section, the council may cause such side-**Expense of same.** walk to be constructed or repaired at the expense of such owner or occupant, and the amount of all expenses incurred by the council thereby shall be levied as a special assessment upon the lot or premises adjacent to and abutting upon such sidewalk.

Signs, awnings, etc. SEC. 11. The council shall have power to regulate and prohibit the placing of signs, awnings, awning-posts, and of other things upon or over sidewalks, and to regulate or prohibit the construction and use of openings in the sidewalks, and of all vaults, structures, and excavations under the same.

Council may establish streets, sidewalks, water-courses, etc. SEC. 12. The council shall have power to lay out and establish, open, make, and alter such streets, lanes, and alleys, sidewalks, highways, water-courses, and bridges as they may deem necessary for the public convenience; and if they shall require the lands of **Manner of acquiring private property for such purpose.** any person for such purpose, the said president and trustees shall give notice to the owner or party interested, his, her, or their agent or attorney, either by personal service or by written notice posted in at least three public places in said village, three weeks next preceding the meeting of the said president and trustees for **Council may purchase.** the purpose aforesaid, and the said council are hereby authorized to contract for and purchase such lands of such owners for the **Proceedings when purchase cannot be made.** purpose aforesaid; and in case such owner or owners refuse to sell or convey such lands or premises for the purpose aforesaid, or the parties fail to agree, it shall and may be lawful for the council to order and direct the clerk to issue a *venire facias*, directed to the marshal, or to any constable of the county in which said village or any part thereof may be situate, commanding him to summon and **Jury.** return a jury of twelve disinterested freeholders, residing without the limits of said village, to appear before any justice of the peace of said village at a time to be therein stated, to inquire into the necessity of using such grounds or premises, and the just compensation to be made therefor to the owner or owners of or to the person or persons interested in such lands or premises; which jury *Jury to view premises, assess damages, etc.* being first duly sworn by said justice faithfully and impartially to inquire into the necessity of using such lands or premises, and the just compensation to be made therefor, and after having viewed the premises, if they shall deem it necessary for the village to use said lands, shall inquire and assess such damages and recompense as they may think proper to award to the owner or owners of such lands and premises according to their respective estates and interests therein; and the said justice shall, upon the return of such *Judgment.* assessment or verdict, render judgment therefor, confirming the same; and such sum or sums so assessed, together with the costs, *Payment of damages.* shall be paid or tendered, or, in case the party entitled to such damages and compensation is not a resident of such village, then upon deposit of the amount for his benefit with the treasurer of said village, before such street, lane, alley, or highway shall be opened, established, or altered, to the claimant or claimants thereof. It shall thereupon be lawful for the president and trustees to cause the said lands and premises to be occupied and used for the purposes aforesaid: *Provided*, That any party claiming *Proviso—appeal to circuit court.* damages as aforesaid may have the right to remove such proceedings by appeal to the circuit court for the county in which such proceedings were had, upon giving notice of his, her, or their intention so to do, to said justice, in writing, within ten days, or in case such party does not reside in said village, then within thirty days after the rendition of such verdict and the judgment thereon as aforesaid; and, upon filing a transcript of the proceedings aforesaid, duly certified by said justice, within forty days after the verdict and judgment as aforesaid in the said circuit court, the same proceedings shall thereafter be had thereon as is prescribed by law in other cases of appeal: *Provided*, That if the final judg- *Proviso relative to costs.* ment of said court shall not exceed the damages assessed before the said justice at least five dollars the party appealing shall pay the costs occasioned by such appeal.

CHAPTER VIII.

IMPROVEMENTS AND ASSESSMENTS.

SECTION 1. The cost and expense of the following improvements, *Certain improvements to be paid for from general fund.* including the necessary lands therefor, viz: for public buildings and offices for the use of the village officers, engine-houses, and structures for the fire department, for water-works, cemeteries, and parks, watch-houses, village prisons, and lands appropriated for streets, shall be paid from the proper general funds of the village. When, by the provisions of this law, the cost and expenses of any *Making of special assessments.* local or public improvement may be defrayed in whole or in part by special assessment upon lands abutting upon and adjacent to, or otherwise benefited by the improvement, such assessment may be made as in this chapter provided.

SEC. 2. There shall be a board of assessors in every village, con- *Board of assessors, their compensation and duties.* sisting of three members, who shall be freeholders and electors in the village, to be appointed by the council. They shall take the

constitutional oath of office. The compensation shall be prescribed by the council. Special assessments, authorized by this act,
shall be made by such board. If a member of the board shall be
interested in any special assessment directed by the council, they
shall appoint some other person to act in his stead in making the
assessment, who, for the purposes of that assessment, shall be a
member of the board.

Amount of
special assess-
ment to be
declared by reso-
lution of coun-
cil.SEC. 3. When the council shall determine to make any public
improvement and defray the whole or any part of the cost and ex-
penses thereof by special assessment, they shall so declare by resolution stating the improvement, and what part or proportion of the
expenses thereof shall be paid by special assessment, and what
part, if any, from the general funds of the village, and shall designate the district or lands and premises upon which the special
assessments shall be levied.

Estimates, plats,
etc., deposited
with village
clerk.SEC. 4. Before ordering any public improvement, any part of the
expense of which is to be defrayed by special assessment, the
council shall cause estimates of the expense thereof to be made, and
also plats and diagrams, when practicable, of the work and of the
locality to be improved, and deposit the same with the village
Notice thereof.clerk for public examination; and they shall give notice thereof
and of the proposed improvement or work, and of the district to
be assessed, by publication for two weeks at least in one of the
newspapers of the village, if any be published therein, or if not, by
posting notices in three public places in the village.

What cost and
expense shall
include, and per
cent of special
assessments.SEC. 5. The costs and expenses of any improvement which may
be defrayed by special assessment shall include the costs of surveys,
plans, assessments, and costs of construction. In no case shall the
whole amount to be levied by special assessment upon any lot or
premises for any one improvement exceed twenty-five per cent of
the value of such lot or land, as valued and assessed for State and
county taxation in the last preceding tax roll. Any cost exceeding that per cent, which would otherwise be chargeable on such lot
or premises, shall be paid from the general funds of the village.

Special assess-
ments, when
levied.SEC. 6. Special assessments, to defray the estimated cost of any
improvement, shall be levied or collected before the making of the
improvement.

Assessment roll.SEC. 7. When any special assessment is ordered, the board of
assessors shall make out an assessment roll, entering and describing therein all lots, premises, and parcels of land to be assessed,
with the names of the persons (if known) chargeable with the
assessments thereon, and shall levy thereon and against such persons the amount to be assessed in proportion to the benefits such
property shall receive from the making such local improvement,
Report of com-
pletion.and when such assessment is completed the board shall report the
same to the council.

Special assess-
ment filed with
village clerk.SEC. 8. When any special assessment shall be reported by the
board of assessors to the council, as in this chapter directed, the
same shall be filed in the office of the village clerk, and numbered.
Notice of meet-
ing to review.Before adopting the assessment, the council shall cause notice to
be published for two weeks at least in some newspaper of the vil-

lage, if any be published therein, or if not, to be posted in three public places for the same length of time, of the filing of the same with the clerk, and appointing a time when the council and board of assessors will meet to review the assessment. Any person objecting to the assessment may file his objections thereto with the clerk. Objections filed with clerk.

SEC. 9. At the time appointed for that purpose as aforesaid, the council and board of assessors shall meet, and there, or at some adjourned meeting, review the assessment; and the council shall correct the same if necessary, and confirm it as reported or as corrected; or they may refer the assessment back to the board for revision, or annul it and direct a new assessment, in which case the same proceedings shall be had as in respect to the previous assessment. When a special assessment shall be confirmed, the village clerk shall indorse a certificate thereof upon the roll, showing the date of confirmation. Review, correction, and disposition of roll. Certificate of date of confirmation.

SEC. 10. When any special assessment shall be confirmed by the council, it shall be final and conclusive; but no such assessment shall be confirmed, except by the concurrence of two-thirds of the council. Confirmation final. Vote thereon.

SEC. 11. All special assessments shall, from the date of the confirmation thereof, constitute a lien upon the respective lots or parcels of land assessed, and shall be a charge against the persons to whom assessed until paid. Assessments a lien on land and charge against persons.

SEC. 12. Should any special assessment prove insufficient to pay for the improvement or work for which it was levied, and the expenses incident thereto, the council may, within the limitations prescribed for such assessments, make an additional *pro rata* assessment to supply the deficiency; and in case a larger amount shall have been collected than was necessary, the excess shall be refunded ratably to those by whom it was paid. Additional assessments to supply deficiency Surplus refunded

SEC. 13. Whenever any special assessment shall, in the opinion of the council, be invalid by reason of irregularity or informality in the proceedings, or if any court of competent jurisdiction shall adjudge such assessment to be illegal, the council shall, whether any part of the assessments have been paid or not, have power to cause a new assessment to be made for the same purpose for which the former assessment was made. All the proceedings on such reassessment and for the collection thereof shall be conducted in the same manner as provided for the original assessment, and whenever any sum or any part thereof levied upon any premises in the assessment so set aside has been paid and not refunded, the payment so made shall be applied upon the re-assessment on said premises, and the re-assessment shall to that extent be deemed satisfied. New assessments to be made in case of irregularity. Proceedings.

SEC. 14. When any special assessment shall be confirmed, and be payable as hereinbefore provided, the council may direct the assessment so made in the special assessment roll to be collected; and thereupon, the village clerk shall attach his warrant to a certified copy of said special assessment roll, therein commanding the village marshal to collect from each of the persons assessed in said roll the amount of money assessed to and set opposite his name Council may direct collection of such assessment.

10

therein ; and in case any person named in said roll shall neglect
or refuse to pay his assessment upon demand, then to levy and collect the same by distress and sale of the goods and chattels of such
person ; and that he pay the money so collected into the treasury,
and return said roll and warrant, together with his doings thereon,
in sixty days from the date of such warrant.

Seizure and sale of goods. SEC. 15. Upon receiving said assessment roll and warrant, the
marshal shall proceed to collect the amounts assessed therein. If
any person shall neglect or refuse to pay his assessment upon demand, the marshal shall seize and levy upon any personal property
found within the village, or elsewhere within the county, belonging
to such person, and sell the same at public auction, first giving six
days' notice of the time and place of such sale, by posting such
notices in three of the most public places in the village or town-
ship where such property may be found. **Disposition of proceeds.** The proceeds of such
sale, or so much thereof as may be necessary for that purpose, shall
be applied to the payment of the assessment, and a percentage of
Costs of sale. five per centum upon the amount of the assessment for the costs
and expenses of said seizure and sale, and the surplus, if any, shall
be paid to the person entitled thereto.

Disposition of money by marshal, and return of roll and warrant. SEC. 16. The marshal shall pay the moneys, and all percentage
collected by him, into the village treasury, and take the treasurer's
receipt therefor and file the same with the clerk. He shall also
make return of said assessment roll and warrant to the village
clerk according to the requirement of the warrant, and if any of
the assessments in said roll shall be returned unpaid, the marshal
shall attach to his return a statement, verified by affidavit, containing a list of the persons delinquent, and a description of the
lots and premises upon which the assessments remain unpaid, and
the amount unpaid on each.

Renewal of warrant. SEC. 17. Said warrant may be renewed from time to time by the
clerk, if the council shall so direct, and for such time as they shall
determine, and during the time of such renewal the warrant shall
have the same force, and the marshal shall perform the same duties
and make the like returns as above provided. In case any assess-
Assessments finally returned unpaid re-assessed with interest. ment shall be finally returned by the marshal unpaid, as aforesaid,
the same may be transferred to and re-assessed in the next annual
village tax roll, in a column headed " special assessments," with interest included at the rate of ten per cent from the date of the
confirmation of the assessment, and be collected and paid in all
respects as provided for collecting the village taxes.

Manner of collecting special assessments by suit. SEC. 18. At any time after a special assessment has become payable, the same may be collected by suit, in the name of the village,
against the person assessed, in an action of assumpsit, in any court
having jurisdiction of the amount. In every such action a declaration upon the common count for money paid shall be sufficient.
The special assessment roll and a certified copy of the order or resolution confirming the same shall be *prima facie* evidence of the
regularity of all the proceedings in making the assessment, and of
the right of the village to recover judgment therefor.

CHAPTER IX.

FINANCE AND TAXATION.

SECTION 1. The council of any village, subject to the provisions of this act, shall have authority to raise, by general tax upon all the real and personal property liable to taxation in said village (exclusive of taxes for highway and street purposes), such sum not exceeding in any one year one and one-fourth of one per cent of the assessed value of such property, as they shall deem necessary for the purpose of defraying the general expenses and liabilities of the corporation, and to carry into effect the powers in this act granted. The moneys so raised shall constitute a "general fund." *Authority of council to raise money by taxation.*

SEC. 2. The council shall also have power to raise, by general tax upon all the real and personal property aforesaid, such sum not exceeding one-half of one per cent of the assessed value of said property, as they shall deem necessary for highway and street purposes. Such moneys shall constitute a "general highway fund," and shall be expended exclusively for working and improving the highways, streets, lanes, and alleys of the village. *Highway taxes, how raised, etc.* *General highway fund.*

SEC. 3. The council shall have power to levy and cause to be collected, in each year, a poll tax of one dollar upon every male inhabitant of the village between the ages of twenty-one and fifty years, excepting active members of the fire department, and such other persons as are exempted by general law from the payment of such tax. All moneys collected by virtue of this section shall be paid into the general highway fund. *Poll-tax.*

SEC. 4. The council may, for the purpose of purchasing grounds for a cemetery, raise by general tax a sum not exceeding in any one year one-fourth of one per cent of the assessed value of the property in the village: *Provided*, That the whole amount which may be so raised for the purchase of grounds for such purpose, shall not at any time exceed five thousand dollars. *Cemetery grounds.* *Proviso.*

SEC. 5. Within two weeks next preceding any annual village election, the council shall audit and settle the accounts of the treasurer and other officers of the village, and so far as practicable, of all persons having claims against the village, and shall make out a statement in detail of the receipts and expenditures of the corporation during the preceding year, which statement shall distinctly show the amount of all taxes raised during the year for all purposes, and the amount raised for each fund; the amount levied by special assessment, and the amount collected on each; also the items and amounts received from all other sources during the year; also the several items of all expenditures made during the year, and the objects thereof, classifying the same for each purpose separately, and containing such other information as shall be necessary to a full understanding of the financial concerns of the village. *Auditing of accounts of officers, etc.* *Annual financial statement.*

SEC. 6. Said statement, signed by the president and clerk, shall be filed in the office of the village clerk, and a copy thereof published in a newspaper of the village at least five days previous to the next annual village election, if one is published therein. *Statement filed with clerk and published.*

76 LAWS OF MICHIGAN. [1875.

Assessment roll.

SEC. 7. The assessor of any village subject to the provisions of this act shall, on or before the second Monday in May, in each year, make an assessment roll, containing the names of the resident persons liable to be taxed, a full description of all the real estate, the estimated value of each tract or parcel, and the aggregate valuation of the personal estate of each person liable to be taxed, and the names of all persons liable to pay a poll tax in the village; and shall set down in such roll the valuation of such property, at its fair cash value, placing the value of the real and personal property in separate columns.

Notice of completion and review of roll.

SEC. 8. Immediately after the completion of such assessment roll, the assessor shall give notice thereof, and of the time and place in said village, when and where the assessment will be reviewed, and that any persons deeming themselves aggrieved by the assessment may then be heard. Such notice shall be given by posting copies thereof in six public places in the village, not less than five days before the day of review.

Board of review of assessments, and its powers and duties.

SEC. 9. The assessor and village clerk shall constitute a board of review of the assessments. At the time appointed for the review, the board shall meet at the place designated in the notice and continue in session two days, for the purpose of reviewing and correcting such assessments; and for such purpose the board of review shall have the same powers, and perform the like duties in all respects, as are conferred upon and required of supervisors in townships, in reviewing assessments made by them. They shall hear the complaints of all persons considering themselves aggrieved by such assessment, and if it shall appear that any person has been wrongfully assessed, or omitted from the roll, the board shall correct the roll in such manner as they shall deem just.

Board shall make record of changes.

SEC. 10. Said board of reviewers shall make a record of all changes made in the roll, which record shall be signed by them, and deposited with the village clerk.

Board to certify roll to council.

SEC. 11. Immediately after the review of the assessment roll as aforesaid, the board of review shall certify the roll under their hands to the village council.

Council to certify roll back to assessor.

SEC. 12. The council, after an examination of the assessment roll, shall certify the same back to the assessor, together with the amount which they require to be raised by general tax, for highway and other general purposes; and all amounts of special assessments which they require to be re-assessed upon any lands, premises, or against any person, with a particular description of the lands and property to be re-assessed, and the amounts to be re-assessed upon each parcel of land, and the name or names, so far as known, of the persons chargeable with such tax, which certificate, endorsed upon or annexed to the roll, shall be signed by the president and village clerk.

Completing of roll by assessor.

SEC. 13. Upon receiving the assessment roll, with the certificate of the several amounts to be raised thereon, as provided in the preceding section, the assessor shall proceed to estimate, apportion, and set down in columns opposite to the several valuations of real and personal property on the roll, in proportion to the individual and particular estimates and valuations, the respective sums in dollars and cents, apportionable to each; placing the general fund taxes and all general taxes, except those for highway purposes, in one column; the general highway taxes in another column; all special assessment taxes in another column; and shall also set down in another column on the roll, one dollar opposite the name of every person liable to pay a poll tax in the village, and the total of all taxes assessed to each valuation shall be carried into the last column of the roll. The assessor shall also foot up the amounts carried to the last column as aforesaid, and certify upon the roll the aggregate amounts of the taxes levied therein.

SEC. 14. After extending the taxes as aforesaid, the assessor shall cause said assessment roll, certified under his hand, to be delivered to the village marshal, with the warrant of the president of the village annexed thereto, directing and requiring him to collect from the several persons named in said roll, the several sums mentioned therein opposite to their respective names, as a tax or assessment, and authorizing him, in case any person named therein shall neglect or refuse to pay such sums, to levy the same by distress and sale of his, her, or their goods and chattels, together with the costs and charges of such distress and sale, and directing him to pay all taxes collected to the treasurer of the village by a certain day therein to be named—not less than thirty nor more than fifty days from the date of said warrant. *Delivery of roll to marshal with warrant of president annexed.*

SEC. 15. The president may renew said warrant from time to time, by order of the council, and for such time as the council shall direct. *President may renew warrant.*

SEC. 16. Immediately upon receiving the tax roll, with the warrant thereto annexed, as provided in section fourteen, the marshal shall proceed to collect the taxes levied therein according to the direction of said warrant, together with such percentage thereon for collection fees as shall be authorized by the village council. *Marshal to collect taxes in accordance with warrant.*

SEC. 17. In case any person shall neglect or refuse to pay any tax imposed upon any real or personal property belonging to him, as aforesaid, the marshal shall levy the same by distress and sale of the goods and chattels of the said person liable to pay the same, wherever such goods and chattels may be found, either in said village or elsewhere in the county where such village is located, first giving public notice of such sale in the manner and for the time required by law in case of such sales made by township treasurers, and for such purpose and for the collection of the taxes aforesaid, the marshal may bring suit therefor, and shall have all the powers and perform the like duties, so far as applicable, as are conferred upon or required of township treasurers, in the collection of taxes levied in townships. *Distress and sale.* *Notice of sale.* *Suit for collection of taxes.*

SEC. 18. Within one week after collecting or receiving any taxes assessed in said roll, the marshal shall pay the same into the village treasury, whether the time for the return of his roll and warrant shall have arrived or not. *When money to be paid into treasury.*

SEC. 19. Within one week after the expiration of the time limited in the warrant for the collection of the taxes levied in said roll, *Return of warrant and tax roll.*

or within one week after the time to which said warrant may have been renewed or extended, the marshal shall make return of said warrant and tax roll, and a statement on oath, showing the amount of all taxes remaining unpaid, and a description of all lands upon which the taxes remain unpaid, and the amount delinquent upon each parcel. All taxes levied upon lands so returned as delinquent, shall be and remain a lien thereon until paid.

SEC. 20. The treasurer of the village shall preserve, in books to be kept by him for that purpose, a list of all lands returned by the marshal to him as delinquent for taxes assessed thereon as aforesaid; and upon taxes so returned interest shall be charged at the rate of fifteen per cent per annum from the date of the return of the warrant until paid. If such taxes and interest shall remain unpaid for the period of one year from the date of said return of warrant, the treasurer shall cause the land charged with the tax and interest aforesaid, or so much thereof as may be necessary to pay the tax and interest, to be sold at public auction for that purpose.

SEC. 21. Before any lands shall be sold for delinquent taxes as provided in the preceding section the treasurer shall give notice for not less than six weeks, by publication, once in each week, in a newspaper published in the village, if any shall be printed therein; and if not, then by posting notices, for the same length of time before the sale, in three of the most public places in said village, of the time and place of said sale, with a description of the lands to be sold, and the amount of taxes, charges, and interest remaining unpaid thereon.

SEC. 22. On the day mentioned in the notice, the treasurer shall commence the sale of the lands upon which any taxes or assessments and interest remain unpaid, and continue the same from day to day until all are sold; and shall sell so much of each description of said lands as will pay the taxes, assessments, interest, and costs of sale, as aforesaid.

SEC. 23. If less than the whole of any description or parcel of land shall be sold for the taxes, the portion sold shall be taken from the north end or side of such description. If any parcel or description of such lands shall not be sold for want of bidders, the treasurer shall bid off the same to and for the village, and shall give a certificate of such sale, which shall have the like effect in all respects as if the same had been given to any other purchaser, except that lands so bid off to the village shall continue liable to be taxed in the same manner as if they were not the property of the village, and such taxes shall be a lien upon such lands.

SEC. 24. At such sale the treasurer shall give the purchaser of any such lands a certificate in writing, describing the land purchased, and the amount paid therefor, and stating the time when he will be entitled to a deed of the lands.

SEC. 25. At any time within one year after such sale, any person owning any parcel of land so sold, or any interest therein, may redeem such land, or such interest therein, by paying to the village treasurer the amount for which the land was sold, or such portion

thereof as his part interest amounts to, with interest thereon at the
rate of fifteen per cent per annum.

SEC. 26. If any lot or description of land sold as aforesaid, or any Conveyance of
part thereof, shall not be redeemed as aforesaid within one year land to pur-
from the date of said sale, the treasurer shall, at the expiration of chaser.
said year, execute to the purchaser, or to his or her heirs or assigns,
a conveyance of the land sold, or of that part thereof not redeemed,
which said conveyance shall, in case all the proceedings previous
to the execution of the deed have been regular and according to
law, vest in the purchaser, or to whomsoever it shall be given, an
estate in fee simple; and said conveyance shall be *prima facie* evi- Evidence of
dence of the regularity of all the proceedings connected therewith, regularity of
from the valuation of the land by the assessors to the date of the proceedings, etc.
deed inclusive, and of the title in fee of the grantee therein named.
And every such conveyance, duly executed and acknowledged by
said treasurer, may be given in evidence in the same manner as
other deeds of conveyance.

CHAPTER X.

SECTION 1. Previous notice of any application for the charter of Notice of appli-
any village incorporated under this act or any special act of incor- cation for
poration, shall be given by the publication of the proposed amend- charter, etc.
ments in some newspaper published in the village incorporated
under said charter, and if there be no newspaper published in such
village the same shall be published in any newspaper published in the
county in which such village is located. Such proposed amendment shall be published at least three successive weeks before the
bill proposing such amendments shall be introduced into the Legislature, and some evidence of such publication shall accompany the
bill proposing the same.

SEC. 2. This act shall take immediate effect.

Approved April 1, 1875.

[No. 63.]

AN ACT to amend section nine of act number one hundred and
one of the session laws of eighteen hundred and seventy-three,
entitled "An act to amend sections seven hundred and ninety-
three, seven hundred and ninety-nine, and eight hundred of the
compiled laws of eighteen hundred and seventy-one, being sections two, eight, and nine of an act entitled 'An act to provide
for taking the census and statistics of this State,' approved February nine, eighteen hundred and fifty-three," approved April
seventeen, eighteen hundred and seventy-three.

SECTION 1. *The People of the State of Michigan enact,* That sec- Section amended
tion nine of an act entitled "An act to amend sections seven hundred and ninety-three, seven hundred and ninety-nine, and eight
hundred of the compiled laws of eighteen hundred and seventy-
one, being sections two, eight, and nine, of an act entitled 'An act
to provide for taking the census and statistics of this State,' ap-

proved February nine, eighteen hundred and fifty-three," approved
April seventeen, eighteen hundred and seventy-three, be amended
so as to read as follows:

Report by Secretary of State. (800.) SEC. 9. The Secretary of State shall condense, in a tabular form, the census and statistical returns made to him, and, as soon as may be, cause six thousand copies to be published and Distribution thereof. bound, and transmit four copies to each organized township in the State, one for the use of the supervisor, one for the use of the township clerk, and two to be deposited in the township clerk's office; and twenty-five copies to the mayor of the city of Detroit, and ten copies to the mayor of every other city in the State, and two copies to the president of each incorporated village, for the use of the several city and village libraries. He shall also cause one hundred copies to be deposited in the State library of this State, and also transmit one copy to each of the members of this legisla- Proviso. ture, and its officers: *Provided*, That in counties having less than five thousand inhabitants, the supervisor in each town shall be entitled to three dollars for taking the census and statistics in his town, extra.

SEC. 2. This act shall take immediate effect.

Approved April 1, 1875.

[No. 64.]

AN ACT to require railroad companies to notify the Commissioner of Railroads and coroners of accidents occurring on their roads, and the investigations of the same.

Notice of accidents. SECTION 1. *The People of the State of Michigan enact,* That every railroad corporation doing business in this State shall cause immediate notice of any accident which may occur on its road, attended with loss of life to any person, to be given to a coroner of the county residing nearest to the place of accident, and shall also give notice within twenty-four hours to the Commissioner of Railroads of any such accident, or of any accident falling within a description of accidents of which said commissioner may, by general regulation, require notice to be given. For each omission to give such notice the corporation shall forfeit a sum not exceeding one hundred dollars.

Commissioner to investigate causes of accidents. SEC. 2. The Commissioner of Railroads shall investigate the causes of any accident on a railroad resulting in loss of life, and of any accident not so resulting, which, in his judgment, shall require investigation.

Approved April 1, 1875.

[No. 65.]

AN ACT to amend sections twelve, fourteen, one, eighty-six, eighty-seven, eighty-nine, and three, of chapter twelve, being sections six hundred and forty-seven, six hundred and forty-

nine, six hundred and ninety-five, seven hundred and twenty-
nine, seven hundred and thirty, seven hundred and thirty-two,
seven hundred and thirty-five, of compiled laws of eighteen
hundred and seventy-one, relative to the powers and duties
of townships, and election and duties of township officers, and
sections one, two, three, five, eight, eleven, twelve, thirteen,
fourteen, two, three, four, five, one, one, and one, of chapter
twenty-three, being sections one thousand one hundred and
ninety-two, one thousand one hundred and ninety-three, one
thousand one hundred and ninety-four, one thousand one hundred and ninety-six, one thousand one hundred and ninety-
nine, one thousand two hundred and two, one thousand two
hundred and three, one thousand two hundred and four, one
thousand two hundred and five, one thousand two hundred and
seven, one thousand two hundred and eight, one thousand two
hundred and nine, one thousand two hundred and ten, one
thousand two hundred and twelve, one thousand two hundred
and fourteen, and one thousand two hundred and fifteen, of
compiled laws of eighteen hundred and seventy-one, relative to
officers, having the care and superintendence of highways and
bridges, and their general powers and duties, and sections two,
four, five, six, seven, eight, and nine, of chapter twenty-four,
being sections one thousand two hundred and seventeen, one
thousand two hundred and nineteen, one thousand two hundred and twenty, one thousand two hundred and twenty-one,
one thousand two hundred and twenty-two, one thousand two
hundred and twenty-three, and one thousand two hundred and
twenty-four, of compiled laws of eighteen hundred and seventy-one, relative to persons liable to work on highways and
making assessment therefor, and sections three, fifteen, sixteen,
seventeen, eighteen, twenty, twenty-one, twenty-two, twenty-
three, and one, of chapter twenty-five, being sections one thousand
two hundred and twenty-eight, one thousand two hundred and
forty, one thousand two hundred and forty-one, one thousand two hundred and forty-two, one thousand two hundred and forty-three, one thousand two hundred and forty-
five, one thousand two hundred and forty-six, one thousand
two hundred and forty-seven, one thousand two hundred and
forty-eight, and one thousand two hundred and fifty-one, of
compiled laws of eighteen hundred and seventy-one, relative
to the duties of overseers in regard to the performance of
labor on highways, the performance of such labor or the commutation therefor and application of moneys by the commissioners, and sections two, three, four, seven, eight, eleven, fourteen, fifteen, sixteen, and one, of chapter twenty-six, being sections one thousand two hundred and fifty-three, one thousand
two hundred and fifty-four, one thousand two hundred and fifty-
five, one thousand two hundred and fifty-eight, one thousand
two hundred and fifty-nine, one thousand two hundred and
sixty-two, one thousand two hundred and sixty-five, one thousand two hundred and sixty-six, one thousand two hundred and

11

sixty-seven, and one thousand two hundred and seventy-eight of compiled laws of eighteen hundred and seventy-one, relative to laying out, altering, and discontinuing public roads, and sections two, four, five, and six, of chapter twenty-seven, being sections one thousand two hundred and ninety, one thousand two hundred and ninety-two, one thousand two hundred and ninety-three, and one thousand two hundred and ninety-four, of compiled laws of eighteen hundred and seventy-one, relative to the obstruction of highways, encroachments thereon and penalties, and sections one, three, four, six, seven, eight, two, and three, of chapter twenty-eight, being sections one thousand three hundred and one, one thousand three hundred and three, one thousand three hundred and four, one thousand three hundred and six, one thousand three hundred and seven, one thousand three hundred and eight, one thousand three hundred and ten, and one thousand three hundred and eleven, of compiled laws of eighteen hundred and seventy-one, relative to the erection, repairing, and preservation of bridges, and sections two and five, of chapter twenty-nine, being sections one thousand three hundred and seventeen, one thousand three hundred and twenty-one, of compiled laws of eighteen hundred and seventy-one, relative to miscellaneous provisions of a general nature, and sections one, three, four, one, two, and four, of chapter thirty-one, being sections one thousand three hundred and thirty-five, one thousand three hundred and thirty-seven, one thousand three hundred and thirty-eight, one thousand three hundred and forty, one thousand three hundred and forty-one, and one thousand three hundred and forty-three, of compiled laws of 1871, relative to private roads, and sections nine and fourteen, of chapter forty-seven, being sections one thousand seven hundred and fifty-three, one thousand seven hundred and fifty-eight, of compiled laws of eigthteen hundred and seventy-one, relative to the draining of swamps, marshes, and low lands, and sections two, three, and four, of chapter sixty-eight, being sections two thousand one hundred and thirty, two thousand one hundred and thirty-one, two thousand one hundred and thirty-two, of compiled laws of eighteen hundred and seventy-one relative to the spread of Canada thistles, and sections twenty-seven and forty-five, of chapter seventy-eight, being sections two thousand five hundred and eighty-seven and two thousand six hundred and five, of compiled laws of eighteen hundred and seventy-one, relative to plank road companies, being the various sections defining the powers and duties of the commissioners of highways, and adding a new section thereto.

Sections amended

SECTION 1. *The People of the State of Michigan enact,* That sections twelve, fourteen, one, eighty-six, eighty-seven, eighty-nine, and three, of chapter twelve, being sections six hundred and forty-seven, six hundred and forty-nine, six hundred and ninety-five, seven hundred and twenty-nine, seven hundred and thirty, seven hundred and thirty-two, seven hundred and thirty-five, of com-

piled laws of eighteen hundred and seventy-one, relative to the
powers and duties of townships, and election and duties of township officers, and sections one, two, three, five, eight, eleven, twelve,
thirteen, fourteen, two, three, four, five, one, one, and one, of chapter twenty-three, being sections one thousand one hundred and
ninety-two, one thousand one hundred and ninety-three, one thousand one hundred and ninety-four, one thousand one hundred and
ninety-six, one thousand one hundred and nine-nine, one thousand
two hundred and two, one thousand two hundred and three, one
thousand two hundred and four, one thousand two hundred and
five, one thousand two hundred and seven, one thousand two hundred and eight, one thousand two hundred and nine, one thousand
two hundred and ten, one thousand two hundred and twelve, one
thousand two hundred and fourteen, and one thousand two hundred and fifteen, of compiled laws of eighteen hundred and seventy-one, relative to officers having the care and superintendence
of highways and bridges, and their general powers and duties, and
sections two, four, five, six, seven, eight, and nine, of chapter
twenty-four, being sections one thousand two hundred and seventeen, one thousand two hundred and nineteen, one thousand two
hundred and twenty, one thousand two hundred and twenty-one,
one thousand two hundred and twenty-two, one thousand two
hundred and twenty-three, and one thousand two hundred and
twenty-four, of compiled laws of eighteen hundred and seventy-
one, relative to persons liable to work on highways and making
assessment therefor, and sections three, fifteen, sixteen, seventeen,
eighteen, twenty, twenty-one, twenty-two, twenty-three, and one,
of chapter twenty-five, being sections one thousand two hundred
and twenty-eight, one thousand two hundred and forty, one thousand two hundred and forty-one, one thousand two hundred and
forty-two, one thousand two hundred and forty-three, one thousand
two hundred and forty-five, one thousand two hundred and forty-
six, one thousand two hundred and forty-seven, one thousand two
hundred and forty eight, and one thousand two hundred and fifty-
one, of compiled laws of eighteen hundred and seventy-one, relative to the duties of overseers, in regard to the performance of labor on highways, the performance of such labor or the commutation therefor and application of moneys by the commissioners,
and sections two, three, four, seven, eight, eleven, fourteen, fifteen,
sixteen and one, of chapter twenty-six, being sections one thousand two hundred and fifty-three, one thousand two hundred and
fifty-four, one thousand two hundred and fifty-five, one thousand
two hundred and fifty-eight, one thousand two hundred and fifty-
nine, one thousand two hundred and sixty-two, one thousand two
hundred and sixty-five, one thousand two hundred and sixty-six,
one thousand two hundred and sixty-seven, and one thousand two
hundred and seventy-eight, of compiled laws of eighteen hundred
and seventy-one, relative to laying out, altering, and discontinuing
public roads, and sections two, four, five, and six, of chapter
twenty-seven, being sections one thousand two hundred and ninety,
one thousand two hundred and ninety-two, one thousand two

hundred and ninety-three, and one thousand two hundred and
ninety-four, of compiled laws of eighteen hundred and seventy-
one, relative to the obstruction of highways, encroachments
thereon, and penalties, and sections one, three, four, six, seven,
eight, two, and three, of chapter twenty-eight, being sections one
thousand three hundred and one, one thousand three hundred and
three, one thousand three hundred and four, one thousand three
hundred and six, one thousand three hundred and seven, one
thousand three hundred and eight, one thousand three hundred
and ten, and one thousand three hundred and eleven, of compiled
laws of eighteen hundred and seventy-one, relative to the erection,
repairing, and preservation of bridges, and sections two and five,
of chapter twenty-nine, being sections one thousand three hundred
and seventeen, one thousand three hundred and twenty-one, of
compiled laws of eighteen hundred and seventy-one, relative to
miscellaneous provisions of a general nature, and sections one,
three, four, one, two, and four, of chapter thirty-one, being sections one thousand three hundred and thirty-five, one thousand
three hundred and thirty-seven, one thousand three hundred and
thirty-eight, one thousand three hundred and forty, one thousand
three hundred and forty-one, and one thousand three hundred
and forty-three, of compiled laws of 1871, relative to private roads,
and sections nine and fourteen, of chapter forty-seven, being sections one thousand seven hundred and fifty-three, one thousand
seven hundred and fifty-eight, of compiled laws of eighteen hundred and seventy-one, relative to the drainage of swamps, marshes,
and low lands, and sections two, three, and four, of chapter sixty-
eight, being sections two thousand one hundred and thirty, two
thousand one hundred and thirty-one, two thousand one hundred
and thirty-two, of compiled laws of eighteen hundred and seventy-
one, relative to the spread of Canada thistles, and sections twenty-
seven and forty-five, of chapter seventy-eight, being sections two
thousand five hundred and eighty-seven and two thousand six
hundred and five, of compiled laws of eighteen hundred and seventy-one, relative to plank road companies, being the various sections defining the powers and duties of the commissioners of highways, and adding a new section thereto, be amended so as to read
as follows:

Commissioner of highways. SEC. 2. All the powers heretofore exercised, and duties performed, by the board of highway commissioners of the several
townships, shall hereafter be exercised and performed by the commissioner of highways in said townships, and the term of office of
the commissioners of highways, elected in the years of eighteen hundred and seventy-three and eighteen hundred and seventy-four,
shall expire when this act takes effect.

Term of office. (647.) SEC. 12. The commissioner of highways shall hold his
office for one year, and until his successor shall be elected and
qualified.

What officers elected at town-ship meetings to hold for one year. (649.) SEC. 14. Each of the officers elected at such meetings,
except justices of the peace and school inspectors, shall hold his
office for one year and until his successor shall be elected and duly
qualified.

(695.) SEC. 1. *The People of the State of Michigan enact,* That Vacancy in office of overseer of highways, how filled in certain cases. whenever any vacancy shall occur in the office of overseer of highways, which the commissioner of highways shall be unable to fill under existing provisions of law, it shall be his duty and he is hereby authorized to designate some other overseer of highways of the same township, to perform the duties of such vacated office; and the person so designated shall have the same powers, be subject to the same orders, and liable to the same penalties as overseers chosen in township meetings.

(729.) SEC. 86. Any commissioner or overseer of highways may Commissioner and overseer may be indicted for deficiency in highways. be prosecuted, by indictment, for any deficiency in the highways within his limits, occasioned or continued by his fault or neglect, and on conviction thereof may be fined in any sum not exceeding fifty dollars.

(730.) SEC. 87. Each commissioner of highways, before entering Bonds of commissioner. upon the duties of his office, and within the time limited by law for filing his official oath, shall give bonds, with one or more sufficient sureties, to the township, in the penal sum of five hundred dollars, to be approved by the supervisor or township clerk, conditioned for the faithful performance of the duties of his office, and the faithful disbursement of all moneys that may come into his hands by virtue of his office. Said commissioner may require any Bonds of overseers. one or all of said overseers of highways, before entering upon the duties of their office, to give bond with one or more sufficient sureties, in such sum as may be required by said commissioner, and to be approved by him, conditioned for the faithful performance of the duties of their office, and the faithful disbursement of all moneys that may come into their hands by virtue of their office.

(732.) SEC. 89. The township clerk of each township shall be the Clerk of commissioner, and his duties. clerk of the commissioner of highways, and shall, under his direction, record his proceedings in a suitable book, to be provided by said clerk for that purpose, at the expense of the township, and shall keep an accurate account of all orders drawn by said commissioner on the township treasurer, stating the amount of each, and in whose favor the same was drawn; and all books and papers relating to the business of said commissioner shall be preserved and kept by said clerk in his office.

(735.) SEC. 3. Should any of said townships neglect to elect over- Commissioner to fill vacancies in office of overseer. seers of highways, as provided in this act, or should the office for any cause become vacant, or should a new road district or districts be formed in any of the townships, it shall be the duty of the commissioner of highways of the township to fill such vacancies, and appoint an overseer of highways for any new road district, who shall hold his office until the next annual township meeting, and until his successor is elected and qualified according to law.

(1192.) SEC. 1. The commissioner of highways in each township Duties of commissioner. in this State shall have the care and superintendence of highways and bridges therein, and it shall be his duty:

First, To give directions for the repairing of roads and bridges within his township;

Second, To regulate the roads already laid out, and to alter such of them as he shall deem inconvenient;

Third, To cause such of the roads used as highways as have been laid out, but not sufficiently described, and such as shall have been used for twenty years, but not recorded, to be ascertained, described, and entered of record in the township clerk's office;

Fourth, To cause the highways and the bridges over streams intersecting highways to be kept in repair;

Fifth, To divide his township into so many road districts as he shall judge convenient, by writing under his hand, to be entered of record in the township clerk's office; but no such division shall be made within five days next preceding an annual township meeting;

Sixth, To assign to each of the said districts such of the inhabitants liable to work on highways as shall reside in such districts, or own lands therein ; and

Seventh, To require the overseer [overseers] of highways, from time to time, and as often as he shall deem it necessary, to have all persons assessed to work on the highways perform their labor thereon with such teams, carriages, sleds, or implements as said commissioner shall direct.

To lay out and discontinue roads.

(1193.) SEC. 2. The commissioner of highways shall have power, in the manner and under the restrictions hereinafter provided, to lay out and establish, upon actual survey, such new roads in his township as he may deem necessary, and to discontinue such old roads and highways as shall appear to him to have become unnecessary.

To render account to township board.

(1194.) SEC. 3. The commissioner of highways of each township shall render to the township board at the annual meeting of such board in each year, an account in writing, stating:

First, The labor assessed and performed in his township;

Second, The sums paid for delinquencies and commutations, and other moneys received by him, and the application thereof;

Third, The improvements which have been made on the roads and bridges in his township during the year preceding such report, and the condition of such roads and bridges; and,

Fourth, The improvements necessary to be made on the same, and an estimate of the probable expense thereof beyond what the labor to be assessed in that year will accomplish.

Duties of overseers of highways.

(1196.) SEC. 5. It shall be the duty of the overseers of highways:

First, To repair and keep in order the highways, within the several districts for which they shall have been elected or appointed, respectively;

Second, To warn all persons assessed to work on the highways in their respective districts, to come and work on such highways, according to law;

Third, To cause the noxious weeds within the limits of the highways in their respective districts to be cut down and destroyed twice in each year, once before the first day of July, and again before the first day of September, and the requisite labor shall be considered highway work; and,

Fourth, To collect all sums due for delinquencies and commutation money, and to execute all lawful orders of the commissioner of highways.

(1199.) SEC. 8. The commissioner of highways of each township *Guide posts.* shall cause guide posts, with proper inscriptions and devices thereon, to be erected and kept in repair at the intersection of all post-roads in his township, and at the intersection of such other roads therein as he may deem necessary.

(1202.) SEC. 11. If any person chosen to the office of overseer *When commissioner to appoint overseers, etc.* of highways shall refuse to serve, or if his office shall become vacant, the commissioner of highways shall, by warrant under his hand, appoint some other person in his stead; and the overseers so appointed shall have the same powers, be subject to the same orders, and liable to the same penalties as overseers chosen in township meetings.

(1203.) SEC. 12. The commissioner of highways making such *Warrant of appointment to be filed, notice to be given, etc.* appointment shall cause such warrant to be filed in the office of the township clerk, who shall forthwith give notice thereof to the person appointed, which person shall give written notice of his acceptance to such clerk within ten days after receiving notice of his appointment.

(1204.) SEC. 13. Every overseer of highways who shall refuse or *Penalty for neglect, etc., by overseer.* neglect to perform any of the duties required of him by law, or which may be lawfully enjoined on him by the commissioner of highways of his township, and for the omission of which a penalty is not hereinafter provided, shall for any such neglect or refusal, forfeit the sum of ten dollars.

(1205.) SEC. 14. It shall be the duty of the commissioner of high- *When commissioner to prosecute for penalty.* ways of each township, whenever any person resident of his <u>town</u>-ship shall make complaint that any overseer of highways in such township has refused or neglected to perform any of the duties required of him by law, or shall give or offer to such commissioner sufficient security to indemnify him against the costs which may be incurred in prosecuting for the penalty annexed to such refusal or neglect, forthwith to prosecute such overseer in the name of the people of this State, for the recovery of such penalty. If any over- *When overseer liable.* seer of highways shall neglect or refuse to warn the residents of his district liable to do work on the highways, to do such work as the law requires and his warrant directs, such overseer shall be liable to pay for all the work not so done or commuted for, at the rate of sixty-two and a half cents per day; and it shall be the duty of the commissioner of highways in each township to prosecute any overseer who may so neglect or refuse to do his duty, before any justice of the peace, or any other court of competent jurisdiction, and collect of him what he may be liable to pay under the provisions of this act, unless such overseer shall show satisfactory cause to such justice of the peace, or such court, why he should not pay the same: *Provided*, That in all cases where judgment shall be *Proviso—on recovery of judgment not further liable.* recovered against any such overseer under the provisions of this section, such overseer shall not be further liable to an action for the penalty incurred by such neglect or refusal.

(1207.) SEC. 2. The clerk, in transcribing. where characters, ini- *How clerk to transcribe defective highway records.* tials, signs, and figures are used in the survey bills herein required to be transcribed, shall write the same in words at full length, but the name of the highway commissioner, where there is no order establishing the survey as a public highway, shall be omitted.

When transcribed commissioner to meet at the office of township clerk.

(1208.) SEC. 3. Where the clerk of any township shall have transcribed the survey bills of his township according to the provisions of the preceding sections of this act, it shall be his duty to give notice thereof to the commissioner of highways of his township, and it shall be the duty of said commissioner, within ten days after the receipt of such notice, to meet at the office of such township clerk.

Commissioner to establish as highways. such of the roads as public interest may require.

Proviso.

(1209.) SEC. 4. When so met, it shall be the duty of said commissioner, and he is hereby authorized, to affix his order and determination, establishing as public highways so many roads as there are survey bills transcribed according to the provisions of this act, or so many thereof as in his opinion the public interest may require: *Provided,* That nothing herein shall be construed as authorizing the commissioner of highways to establish by his order, or in any manner to affect the record of any road, except such as was surveyed, opened, and traveled as late as January first, eighteen hundred and forty-nine.

Determination of commissioner to be recorded.

(1210.) SEC. 5. The said commissioner, after having made his order upon the corrected copies of the survey bills, as prescribed in the last preceding section of this act, shall deliver the same to the township clerk, whose duty it shall be to cause the same to be filed and recorded as provided in chapter twenty-five, section one, of the revised statutes of eighteen hundred and forty-six.

Care of streets of unincorporated villages.

(1212.) SEC. 1. *Be it enacted by the Senate and House of Representatives of the State of Michigan,* That such streets of recorded, but unincorporated, village plats, as the commissioner of highways shall deem to be required for public highways, shall be included in the several road districts of the respective townships in which they are situated, and shall be subject to the care and superintendence of the commissioner and overseers of highways relative to repairs, and in like manner as other highways are now by law provided for.

Proceedings on the opening of roads between adjoining townships.

(1214.) SEC. 1. *The People of the State of Michigan enact,* That whenever a road shall have been laid out and established on the line between adjoining townships, upon the petition of twelve freeholders of either township, the commissioners of highways of the respective townships shall meet upon the line of such road and make an examination into the condition of the same, and if in their opinion the public good require the opening of such road, or the improvement of the same, and that the highway labor assessed thereon is insufficient to open such road or make such improvement,

Contracts to be let.

How paid.

Amount to be assessed.

they shall proceed to let contracts for the opening and improvement of such road, and when such contracts are completed and accepted, give orders upon the treasurer of the township to which such road or part of road belonged, payable out of any money raised or to be raised for that purpose, and notify the supervisors of said township or townships of the amount of such order, and it shall be the the duty of the supervisor to assess the same upon the taxable property of the township in the same manner as other township taxes are assessed and collected: *Provided,* Such contract _{Proviso.} shall not exceed fifty dollars in any one year on any one road in such township.

(1215.) SEC. 1. *The People of the State of Michigan enact,* That _{Commissioner not to have power over State roads.} no commissioner of highways of any township of this State shall hereafter attempt to discontinue any State road, or presume to exercise any such powers over any such road.

(1217.) SEC. 2. The commissioner of highways of each town- _{Assessment of highway tax.} ship shall be in attendance at the office of the supervisor, on the first Thursday after the third Monday of May in each year, for the purpose of assessing a highway tax, and he shall have free access to the assessment roll until he shall have completed his assessment.

(1219.) SEC. 4. The commissioner of highways in each township _{Statement and description of property.} shall make out from the assessment roll a separate list and statement of the valuation of all taxable personal property, and a description of all lots or parcels of land, within each road district in such town- ship, inserting in a separate part of such list, descriptions of lands owned by non-residents of the township, with the value of each lot or parcel set down opposite to such description, as the same shall appear on the assessment roll; and if such lot or tract was not separately described in such roll, then in proportion to the valua- tion which shall have been affixed to the whole tract of which such lot or parcel forms a part.

(1220.) SEC. 5. In making the estimate and assessment of high- _{Highway labor, how and by whom estimated.} way labor, the commissioner shall proceed as follows :

First, Every male inhabitant in each road district being above _{Who to be assessed.} the age of twenty-one and under the age of fifty, except pensioners of the United States, and other soldiers and sailors honorably dis- charged, who are disabled from performing manual labor by reason of wounds received or disease contracted while in the service of the United States, paupers, idiots, and lunatics, shall be assessed one day ;

Second, The residue of the highway labor to be assessed, not _{Residue of high- way labor, how apportioned.} exceeding one day's work upon one hundred dollars of the valua- tion, shall be apportioned upon the estate, real and personal, of every inhabitant in each of the road districts in such township, and upon each tract or parcel of land in the respective road dis- tricts of which the owners are non-residents, as the same shall appear by the assessment roll ;

Third, The commissioner shall affix to the name of each person _{Commissioner to give number of days persons and property to be assessed.} named in the lists furnished by the overseers, and not assessed upon the assessment roll, and also to each valuation of property within the several road districts, the number of days which such person or property shall be assessed for highway labor, adding one day to the assessment of each person liable to a poll-tax and assessed upon the township assessment roll.

(1221.) SEC. 6. The township clerk shall, under the direction of _{Township clerk to make dupli- cate lists, etc.} the commissioner, make duplicates of the several lists, which shall be subscribed by the commissioner; one of which lists for each road district, shall be filed by such clerk in his office, and the other shall be forthwith delivered to the overseer of highways of the district in which the highway labor therein specified is assessed.

Persons omitted from list rated by overseers. (1222.) SEC. 7. The names of persons left out of any such list, and who ought to have been included therein, and of new inhabitants who have not in the same year been assessed in some other place for highway labor, shall be from time to time added to the several lists, and rated by the overseers in proportion to their taxable real and personal property, as others are rated on such lists by the commissioner, to work on the highways, subject to an appeal to the commissioner.

Credit to persons working private roads. (1223.) SEC. 8. It shall be the duty of the commissioner of highways of each township to credit such persons as live on private roads, and work the same, so much upon their assessment on account of such work as such commissioner may deem necessary to improve and keep such private roads in repair, or he may annex any such private road to some highway district.

Assessment of land occupied by tenant. (1224.) SEC. 9. Whenever the occupant of any land not owned by him shall be assessed therefor by the commissioner, he shall distinguish in his assessment list the amount charged upon such land from the personal tax, if any, of such occupant; but when any such land shall be assessed in the name of the occupant, the owner thereof shall not be assessed during the same year to work on the highways on account of such land.

Commutation for work, etc. (1228.) SEC. 3. Every person liable to work on the highways, shall work the whole number of days for which he shall have been assessed; but every such person other than an overseer, whether resident or non-resident, may elect to commute for the same, or any part thereof, at the rate of one dollar for each day; in which case such commutation money shall be paid to the overseer of highway of the district in which the labor is required to be performed, and shall be applied and expended by such overseer in the purchase of implements, or construction and repair of the roads and bridges in the same district, except when said taxes are otherwise appropriated or disposed of by law.

Overseer to make list of non-resident lands when assessed labor is unpaid. (1240.) SEC. 15. Every overseer of highways shall, between the first and fifteenth days of November, in each year, when required by the commissioner of highways, make out and deliver to such commissioner a list of all the lands of non-residents and of persons unknown, which are taxed upon his list, on which the labor assessed has not been paid, and the amount of labor unpaid; also, a list of **Also, list of resident lands and property.** all lands and personal property assessed as resident, upon which the owner or occupant shall have refused or neglected to work on the highway, after being duly notified by the overseer; and said **Affidavit of overseer.** overseer shall make and subscribe to an affidavit thereon, before some person competent to administer oaths, or before the commissioner of highways, that he has given such notice as is required by law, and that the labor assessed upon the lands and personal property so returned has not been performed, and remains unpaid.

Supervisor to cause delinquent highway taxes to be collected, etc. (1241.) SEC. 16. The supervisor of each township shall cause the amount of such arrearages of labor, estimating the same at one dollar for each day, to be levied on the lands so returned, and to be collected in the same manner that the contingent charges of the township are collected; and the same when collected shall be paid into the township treasury, to be applied by the commissioner of highways in the construction and improvement of roads and bridges in the road district for the benefit of which the labor was originally assessed, except when said taxes are otherwise appropriated or disposed of by law.

(1242.) SEC. 17. Every overseer of highways shall, between the first and fifteenth days of November, render to the commissioner of highways an account, in writing, verified by his oath, to be administered by the commissioner of highways, or some other person competent to administer oaths, and containing: *Overseer's account to commissioner.*

First, The names of all persons assessed to work on the highway in his district; *Contents.*

Second, The names of all those who have actually worked on the highway, with the number of days they have so worked;

Third, The names of all those against whom judgments have been recovered by virtue of this chapter, and the sums so recovered;

Fourth, The names of all those who have commuted, and the amounts paid by them, and the manner in which the moneys arising from judgments and commutations have been expended by him;

Fifth, A list of all the non-resident lands in his district upon which labor has been performed or commuted for.

(1243.) SEC. 18. Every such overseer shall, immediately upon the rendering of such account, pay over to the township treasurer all moneys collected by him for judgments and commutations, and remaining unexpended, to be applied by the commissioner in the construction and improvement of roads and bridges in the road district of the overseer who paid over the same. *Overseers to pay over moneys in their hands, etc.*

(1245.) SEC. 20. No money shall be drawn by the commissioner of highways from the township treasury in payment of any labor, contract, or materials furnished, except by an order signed by him, and accompanied by his certificate that the labor has been actually performed, or the contract fulfilled, or materials furnished, for which the amount of such warrant is to apply in payment. *Highway moneys, how drawn.*

(1246.) SEC. 21. Whenever the commissioner of highways shall determine to appropriate any portion over ten dollars of the moneys accruing to his township, on account of non-resident highway taxes, in the repairing or construction of roads or bridges therein, he shall contract at public auction with the lowest bidder giving good and sufficient security for the performance thereof; and not less than ten days' notice shall be given by said commissioner of the time and place of letting such contracts, by posting up such notice in at least three of the most public places in his township. *Letting of contracts for repairs, etc.*

(1247.) SEC. 22. The commissioner of highways shall, between the first and fifteenth of November in each year, call upon each overseer of highways of his township for the purpose of procuring the returns mentioned in sections fifteen and seventeen of this chapter, and shall deposit the returns mentioned in section fifteen *Commissioner to procure returns of overseers, and deposit same with supervisor.*

of this chapter with the supervisor of his township, whose duty it shall be to enter the value of such delinquent highway tax so returned on the assessment roll of his township, under its appropriate heading, and against the description of property so delinquent.

(1248.) SEC. 23. It shall be the duty of the Auditor General, at the time of transmitting blanks for the use of supervisors in making out their assessments, to transmit blanks with proper headings, for the use of [the] commissioner of highways, in making lists of highway taxes; also, blanks for the proper return of overseers, mentioned in sections fifteen and seventeen of this chapter.

(1251.) SECTION 1. *The People of the State of Michigan enact,* That the supervisor and highway commissioner of each organized township be and they are hereby authorized, in their discretion, to purchase at the expense and for the use of their township, one of Nathaniel Potter's rut-scrapers, or machine for improving roads, together with the right to make and use the same in said township.

(1253.) SEC. 2. Whenever the commissioner of highways shall be applied to, as mentioned in the preceding section, to lay out, alter, or discontinue any highway, he shall, within five days thereafter, issue a written notice, stating the object of such application, and appointing a time and place of meeting the commissioner of highways, which shall be served by said commissioner on the owners or occupants of lands through which it is proposed to lay out, alter, or discontinue such road, either personally or by a copy left at the residence of said owner or occupant, at least ten days before the time of said meeting; and if no person shall reside upon such lands, and the owner thereof shall not reside in the township, no other service of said notice shall be required than by posting up the same in three public places in the township ten days before the time of meeting.

(1254.) SEC. 3. The commissioner shall, at the time appointed, as provided in the last preceding section, proceed to view the premises described in said application and notice, and ascertain and determine the necessity of laying out and altering or discontinuing such highway, and justly and impartially appraise the damage thereon, if any is claimed, and shall, within five days thereafter, make a return of his doings, in writing, signed by him, which return shall state his action in regard to such application, and his award of damages, if any, and to whom payable, if known; and such return shall be filed in the office of the township clerk, with the application for such highway, and copy of notice attached thereto: *Provided,* That he may adjourn from time to time, in his discretion, not to exceed twenty days from the time of first meeting, and shall make his returns to the township clerk within five days from the time of last meeting.

(1255.) SEC. 4. Upon laying out, altering, or discontinuing a highway on the line between adjoining township [townships], or upon determining what part of such highway shall be made and repaired by each township, the commissioners of such adjoining townships shall act jointly, and application may be made to the commissioner of either township, who shall notify the commissioner of the adjoining township of the time and place of meeting; and said commissioners of adjoining townships shall proceed as before provided, and their return shall be filed in the office of the township clerk of each township, and each township shall have all the rights and be subject to all the liabilities in relation to the part of such highway to be made and repaired by such township, as if the same was located wholly in such township.

(1258.) SEC. 7. All highways heretofore regularly laid out and established, in pursuance of existing laws, are hereby declared to be legal highways, subject to alteration or discontinuance the same as other highways; and the commissioner shall have power to lay out and establish highways on section lines, through unenclosed lands, according to the provisions of this act, without the application therefor provided in section one of this act. *Existing highways legalized.*

(1259.) SEC. 8. Whenever a highway shall be laid out or altered, the commissioner shall, if he shall deem the same necessary, cause an accurate survey to be made of the line of said road, and shall file the minutes of such survey in the office of the township clerk of the township in which such road is situated; and the premises belonging to any highway shall be a parcel of land not less than two rods wide on each side of the line of said survey, or each side of any section line on which any highway shall be established. *Commissioner may cause survey on laying out, etc., of highway. Line of survey to be the center of the road.*

(1262.) SEC. 11. Any person who shall conceive himself aggrieved by any determination of the commissioner as to the necessity of laying out, altering, or discontinuing such highways, or in their award of damages, may, within ten days after such determination, appeal therefrom to the township board of said township, or in case of a road on the line of townships, where the determination shall have been made by the commissioners of adjoining townships, to the township boards of such adjoining townships: *Provided,* That any commissioner who may be a member of the township board shall not act on such appeal. *Person aggrieved in the laying out, etc., of highway may appeal to township board. Proviso.*

(1265.) SEC. 14. In cities and villages application can be made by ten freeholders, as provided in section one of this act, to the corporate authorities of such city or village; and such corporate authorities shall have power, upon such application, to lay out and establish, open, alter, or discontinue such streets, commons, lanes, alleys, sidewalks, highways, water-courses, and bridges, as may be necessary for the public convenience; and such corporate authorities shall be governed by the regulations that are required in this act to be observed by the commissioner of highways and township clerk, except as to appeal; and the city or village clerk, or recorder, shall discharge the like duties as are imposed upon the township clerk by the provisions of this act: *Provided,* That this act shall not be construed to change the manner of opening such roads, streets, alleys, lanes, commons, highways, bridges, or water-courses as now provided for in the charter of an incorporated city or village. *Proceedings as to laying out, etc., streets in cities and villages. Proviso.*

(1266.) SEC. 15. The damage or compensation awarded by the commissioner of highways, township board, or city or village authorities, shall be assessed, levied, and collected upon the taxable *Damages, how assessed and collected.*

property of such township, city, or village, in the same manner as other taxes are levied and collected.

Removal of fences, how, effected. (1267.) SEC. 16. When the damage or compensation aforesaid shall have been paid or tendered to the persons entitled thereto, or an order on the treasurer of the proper township, city, or village for the amount of such damages shall have been executed and delivered, or tendered to such person or persons, said commissioner of highways of any township, village, or city authorities of any city or village, shall then give notice to the owner or occupant of the land through which any such highway, street, lane, alley, or common shall have been laid out, altered, or established, and require him, within such time as they shall deem reasonable, not less than sixty days after giving such notice, to remove his fence or fences; and in case such owner or occupant shall neglect or refuse to remove his fence or fences within the time specified in such notice, the said commissioner, or city or village authorities, shall have full power, and it shall be their duty, to enter with such aid and assistance as shall be necessary upon the premises, and remove such fence or fences, and open such highway, street, lane, alley, or common without delay, after the time specified in such notice shall

Proviso. have expired: *Provided*, That in townships no person shall be required to move his fence or fences between the first day of April and the first day of November.

Relative to laying out, etc., of roads on State line. (1278.) SEC. 1. *The People of the State of Michigan enact,* That the commissioner of highways of any township of this State lying along the line of any other State shall, upon a petition of twelve or more freeholders, as is provided for in other cases for laying out highways in this State, has power, and it shall be his duty, to meet with any officer or officers of such adjoining States, entrusted with the power of laying out or discontinuing highways, as may be required on said State line, and shall have power to lay a highway of any width, which, added to the width on the other side of such State line, shall make a highway which shall not exceed four rods nor be less than three rods in width, to be surveyed, examined, and recorded as other highways on lines between townships of this State.

Removal of encroachments on highways. (1290.) SEC. 2. In every case where a highway shall have been laid out and opened, and the same has been or shall be encroached upon by any fence, building, or other encroachments, the commissioner of highways may make an order under his hand, requiring the occupant of the land through or by which such highway runs, and of which such fence, buildings, or other encroachments form a part of the enclosure, to remove such encroachments beyond the limits of such highway within thirty days; and he shall cause a

Commissioner to cause copy of order of removal to be served on occupant. copy of such order to be served upon such occupant, and every such order shall specify the width of the road, the extent of the encroachment, and the place or places in which the same shall be, with reasonable certainty.

Proceedings in case encroachment be denied. (1292.) SEC. 4. If the occupant upon whom a copy of such order shall be served shall deny such encroachment, the commissioner shall apply to some justice of the peace of the county for a precept,

which shall be issued by said justice, directed to any constable of
the county, commanding him to summon six disinterested freeholders thereof, to meet at a certain day and place, and not less
than four days after the issuing thereof, to inquire into the premises; and the constable to whom such precept shall be directed
shall give at least three days' notice to the commissioner of highways of the township, and to the occupant of the land, of the time
and place at which such freeholders are to meet.

(1293.) SEC. 5. On the day specified in the precept, the jury so summoned shall be sworn by such justice, well and truly to inquire whether any such encroachment has been made as described in the order of the commissioner, and by whom; and the witnesses produced by either party shall be sworn by the justice, and the jury shall hear the proofs and allegations which may be produced and sub-mitted to them; and in case any person so summoned as a juror shall not appear, or shall be incompetent, his place may be sup-plied by a talesman, as in other cases. *Idem.*

(1294.) SEC. 6. If the jury find that any such encroachment has been made by the occupant of the land, or any former occupant thereof, they shall make and subscribe a certificate in writing, of the particulars of such encroachment, and by whom made, which shall be filed in the office of the township clerk; and the occupant of the land, whether such encroachment shall have been made by him, or by any former occupant, shall remove the same within thirty days after the filing of such certificate, under the penalty of one dollar for each day after the expiration of that time during which such encroachments remain unremoved, and if not removed within the thirty days as herein provided, the commissioner may remove the same at the expense of the occupant of the land, to be collected in the same manner as is provided in section seven of this chapter for the collection of costs: *Provided*, The said en-croachments shall not be required to be removed, nor penalty col-lected for said encroachments, if the same be by fence or fences for the protection of hedge or hedges, unless the road be so fenced up as to render it less than two rods wide. *Proceedings for the removal of obstructions.* *Penalty.* *Proviso.*

(1301.) SEC. 1. Whenever it shall appear to the board of super-visors of any county that any one of the townships in such county would be unreasonably burdened by erecting or repairing any necessary bridge or bridges in such township, such board of super-visors may cause such sum of money to be raised and levied upon the county as will be sufficient to defray the expenses of erecting or repairing such bridge or bridges, or such part of such expenses as they may deem proper; and such moneys when collected, shall be paid to the township treasurer of the township in which the same are to be expended, and to be applied by the commissioner of highways of such township to the purpose for which the same was raised. *When moneys may be raised by county for build-ing bridges.*

(1303.) SEC. 3. The commissioner of highways of any township, or common council of any city, or organized company, or the vil-lage council of any village, may put up and maintain, at the ex-pense of their township, city, or company, or village, as the case *Notice on certain bridges relative to riding or driving.*

may be, in conspicuous places at each end of any bridge in such township, city, or village, maintain at the public or company charge, and the length of whose chord is not less than twenty-five feet, a notice with the following words in large characters: "One dollar fine for riding or driving on this bridge faster than a walk;" and in case such bridge shall be over one hundred feet in length, or shall have a draw or turn table therein for the purpose of opening the same, such notice may be: "Ten dollars fine for riding or driving on this bridge faster than a walk, or driving on more than ten head of cattle at a time;" or such other sum, not to exceed twenty-five dollars, may be mentioned in such notice, as the said commissioner of highways of any township, common council of any city, or organized company, or the village council of any village under whose control or management any such bridge may be, shall deem proper.

Penalty for violation. (1304.) SEC. 4. Whoever shall ride or drive faster than a walk, or shall drive more than ten head of cattle at a time, upon any bridge upon which such notice shall have been placed, and shall there be, shall forfeit for every such offense the sum mentioned in such notice, and the same may be collected in the name of such highway commissioner, city, company, or village authorities, as the case may be, or by criminal prosecution.

Injury or destruction of certain bridges. (1306.) SEC. 6. If any bridge over any stream intersected by a highway in any township in this State, or in any village incorporated under the general law for the incorporation of villages, or in any city or village not having, by the terms of its charter, the exclusive control of the construction and repair of any such bridges, and not being within the corporate limits of any city or village above excepted, has been within the last year, or shall hereafter be injured or destroyed by the occurrence of a freshet, or **Commissioner to repair, etc.** from any other cause, it shall be the duty of the highway commissioner of such township, on application in writing, signed by at least six freeholders thereof, to proceed with all convenient dispatch to repair or reconstruct such bridge, as the case may require, under his personal supervision, or by letting a contract therefor, under existing provisions of law: *Provided,* That the **Proviso.** highway commissioner of such township shall, upon a personal examination of the situation, determine that the public interest and convenience require such repairs to be made, or that such bridge **Further proviso.** ought to be rebuilt: *And provided,* That the sum to be expended for such repairs or re-construction shall not, in any one year, exceed one thousand dollars in any one organized township.

Payment for labor etc., for the same. (1307.) SEC. 7. In payment for the labor performed, materials furnished, and necessary expenses incurred for the purpose in the last preceding section specified, the said highway commissioner is hereby authorized to draw and issue his orders upon the township treasurer, redeemable out of the proceeds of the tax to be levied and collected therefor in the manner provided by the following section.

Moneys therefor, how raised (1308.) SEC. 8. For the purpose of levying and collecting such tax, the said highway commissioner shall furnish the township clerk with the amount of all the orders drawn by him for the objects aforesaid, on or before the first Monday of October thereafter; and the said township clerk shall thereupon include such amount in the statement of moneys to be raised for township purposes, to be by him delivered to the supervisor, under the provisions of existing law.

(1310.) SEC. 2. In all cases where the owner or owners, occupiers, or possessors of any such mill or mills, or other water-works, shall refuse or neglect to make such bridge or bridges, or shall refuse or neglect to keep the same in good repair, it shall be the duty of the commissioner of highways of the township in which such highway may be, to proceed forthwith to erect or repair such bridge or bridges, at the expense of the person or persons whose duty it was to have erected or repaired such bridges. *Duty of commissioner in case of neglect of owners of mills, etc., to maintain bridges over races.*

(1311.) SEC. 3. The expenses so made or incurred by said commissioner of highways, in erecting or repairing such bridge or bridges, shall be a legal charge against the owner or owners, occupiers, possessors of such mill or mills, or other water-works; and it shall be the duty of the said commissioner of highways to prosecute the person or persons so chargeable, on an action of assumpsit, for the expenses so made or incurred, and to cause the damages recovered in such prosecution to be applied toward the payment of said expenses. *Expense of repairs, etc., a legal charge against owners, etc.*

(1317.) SEC. 2. Any person who shall (except as hereinafter provided) willfully injure, deface, tear, or destroy any tree or shrub thus planted along the margin of the highway, or purposely left there for shade or ornament, shall forfeit a sum not less than five, nor more than one hundred dollars for each offense, which sum may be recovered in any court of competent jurisdiction: *Provided*, That whenever it shall appear to the commissioner of highways in any town in this State, that any shade or ornamental trees or shrubs are an obstruction or an injury to any highway, said trees or shrubs may be cut down and removed by order of the commissioner of highways. *Penalty for injuring trees planted along highway. Proviso—when trees, etc., may be cut down.*

(1321.) SEC. 5. But if any such injury shall be done within any road district by the overseer of highways of such district, or with his assent, or if any overseer of highways of any road district shall refuse or neglect to prosecute for any such injury done within his district, it shall be the duty of the commissioner of highways of the town within which such district is situated to prosecute for such injury in an action of trespass on the case, and cause the damages to be recovered in such prosecution to be expended in the repair of roads in the district within which such injury shall have been done. *When commissioner to prosecute for injuring highway.*

(1335.) SECTION 1. *The People of the State of Michigan enact,* That whenever application shall be made to the commissioner of highways of any township for a private road, he shall give notice to the owner or occupant of the land over which the road is proposed to be laid out, to meet on a day and at a place certain, for the purpose of aiding in the striking of a jury to determine as to the necessity or propriety of such road; at which time and place *Private road, application for.*

13

Jury, how selected.

the jury shall be selected in the following manner, to wit: said commissioner of highways shall direct some disinterested person to write down the names of eighteen disinterested freeholders, from which list the owner or occupant of said land, and the applicant for said road, shall strike out three names each, and the balance remaining on such list shall form said jury. In case either said owner or occupier, or said applicant, shall refuse to strike, said commissioner shall strike for the party so neglecting or refusing. Said commissioner shall issue a citation to said freeholders to appear before them forthwith, to determine as to the necessity or propriety of such road, and the damages resulting therefrom in case such road shall be deemed necessary by them.

Duty of jury.

(1337.) SEC. 3. If they shall determine that the road so applied for is necessary, they shall make and subscribe a certificate of such determination, and also their appraisal of the damages, and shall deposit the same with the commissioner of highway of the township; and the said commissioner of highways shall thereupon lay out the road, describing the same particularly by its bounds, courses, and distances, and cause a record thereof to be made in the clerk's office of the proper townships.

How road shall be laid out.

Applicant to pay damages and expenses.

(1338.) SEC. 4. The damages of the owner or owners, or occupant of the land through which such road shall be laid, when ascertained as hereinbefore provided, together with expenses of proceedings, shall be paid by the person applying for the road, and when such damages and expenses are paid, the commissioner of highways of the township shall proceed to open the road.

When paid road to be opened.

Temporary highways, when and how to be laid out.

(1340.) SECTION 1. *The People of the State of Michigan enact*, That whenever any two or more owners of any pine or other timbered lands in any township, shall wish to have a temporary highway laid out, they may, by writing, under their hands, make application to the commissioner of highways of the township for that purpose, who shall proceed to lay out such temporary highway in all respects as provided by the law in force at the time of said application in relation to laying out other highways, except as hereinafter provided.

Duty of commissioner or jury, and when road shall cease.

(1341.) SEC. 2. When any such application shall be made, the commissioner or jury shall proceed to view the premises described in such application, and any such tracts of pine or other timbered land in the vicinity as they may deem necessity, and ascertain and determine the necessity of laying out such highway for the purpose of removing the saw-logs, timber, or lumber, from any pine or other timbered lands, and the length of time that such highway will be necessary, and they shall state such time in their proceedings, and at the expiration of said time such highway shall cease; but no

Exception.

such highway shall be laid out along and upon, and so as to occupy any road made or caused to be made by the owner of said land, or by any person with the consent of said owner, and used by the person or persons who made the same, unless such owner shall consent thereto in writing. If the owner of the land across which

Owner may designate route.

such highway is desired, shall appear before the commissioner or jury at the time and place fixed by them to determine such necessity, and shall designate a route for such highway, which shall be,

in the opinion of such commissioner or jury, reasonably direct
and practicable for the purpose desired by such applicants, it shall
be the duty of the commissioner or jury, in case they determine
such highway to be necessary, to lay the same upon the route designated by such owner.

(1343.) SEC. 4. In case any tract of land across which such road *Notice of meeting of commissioner when land is unoccupied.*
shall be laid out shall be unoccupied, it shall not be necessary to
serve the notice of the meeting of the commissioner personally or
by leaving the same at the residence of the owner, but it shall be
sufficient to post the same in three public places in the township
ten days before the time of meeting.

(1753.) SEC. 9. Said commissioner shall give at least fifteen days' *Drain commissioner to give notice for meeting to let contracts for construction of drains.*
public notice in some newspaper published and circulating near
such drain or drains, of the time or times when, and the place or
places where he will meet parties to contract for the excavation
and construction of such drain or drains, such place or places to be
convenient of access by the people resident near and interested in
the proposed drain or drains; and at least three such notices shall
also be posted in the most public places of travel and resort in each
township, and as near as may be along the line of such proposed
drain, at least ten days next preceding such meeting. Said com- *Notice of day and place for exhibiting surveys and apportionment of cost of construction, and review and correction thereof.*
missioner shall also name, in or in connection with such published
and posted notices, a convenient place near such drain or drains,
and a time not less than three days nor more than five days prior
to the day fixed in said notices for letting the construction of such
drain or drains, at which time and place he will exhibit surveys of
the proposed drain or drains, and descriptions of the several parcels
of land by him deemed to be benefited thereby, and the amount and
description, by divisions and subdivisions, of the proposed drain or
drains by him apportioned to the owner of each description of land
to construct, and to each township to construct, on account of *Hearing of reasons for reviewing and correcting apportionment.*
drains benefiting highways, if any such benefit there be, and hear
reasons, if any are offered, why such apportionments should be
reviewed and corrected. And said commissioner shall also give at *Notice to resident owner, etc., of lands assessed, of meeting for review, etc.*
least six days' notice, in writing to each and every resident owner
or occupant of any of the lands assessed for the incidental expenses,
damages and expense of construction of drains as mentioned in
section eight of this act, of such meeting for review and correction
of apportionments. And if at this time two-thirds of the persons *Protest of two-thirds shall suspend construction.*
whose lands are to be taxed for such drain or drains enter a protest
against said drain, and pay the costs and expenses up to this time,
all proceedings for the construction of said drain or drains shall be
suspended for one year. Between such day of hearing and review *Apportionment revised.*
and the appointed day of letting, the commissioner shall, if need
be, revise his apportionments of such drain or drains. At the time *Each land owner may contract for making his portion of the ditch.*
and place for letting named in said notices, the owner of each such
parcel of land, or his or her agent or attorney, may appear and make
and execute to said commissioner a contract or contracts, with good
and sufficient surety for the faithful performance of the excavation
and construction, within the time limited by said commissioner
in such contract or contracts, of so much of such drain or drains as

said commissioner has adjudged to be set off to such land. When

When contract let to the lowest bidder. any part of such drain or drains is offered to be let, and the owner of the land to which it is assigned, or his or her agent or attorney, shall not at once and without unnecessary delay enter into contract as aforesaid to excavate and construct the same as provided in this section, it shall be the duty of said commissioner to let the same to the lowest responsible bidder or bidders therefor, who shall execute **Contractor to fill contract with surety.** and file a contract or contracts, with good and sufficient surety, as aforesaid, with said commissioner, for the faithful performance of the excavation and construction of the same, according to said **Where expense of the same shall be levied.** contract or contracts; and the cost of such excavation and construction, and its portion of the incidental expense and damages, shall be levied and assessed upon the land to which such part or parts of said drain or drains have been assigned as aforesaid. If, at **Letting of contracts may be postponed.** the time of letting said drain or drains according to said notice, no suitable land owners or bidders for the construction of the same, or any part thereof, appear to take or bid and contract with good and sufficient security, for the construction and completion of the whole of the same, or for any other cause by said drain commissioner deemed important and sufficient, he may postpone and adjourn such letting, in whole or in part, and from time to time to such other time or times, to be by him at the time of such adjournment publicly announced, as shall to him seem meet and proper, but not in all more than thirty days from and after the time of the letting at first advertised and noticed as aforesaid. At the hearing and the **Commissioner of highways may act for township at meeting for hearing and letting.** letting provided for in this section, the commissioner of highways of any township named in said notice, and to which has been assigned any construction of drain or tax for incidental expenses or damages on account of benefit by such drain or drains to highways, may appear and act in behalf of such township. Any taxes so **Taxes on State lands reported to Commissioner of State Land Office.** assessed on State lands shall be at once reported by said commissioner to the Commissioner of the State Land Office, who shall enter on the books of his office against each description of such State land the amount of drain taxes assessed thereon, and no patent shall issue for such lands until said drain taxes are paid or **When persons held to have waived right of appeal.** otherwise provided for. Any person resident in said county failing or neglecting to file, in writing, with said commissioner, on or before such appointed day of hearing and review, his claim for damages or objections to such assessments, shall be held to have waived his claim for damages and his right to appeal.

Drains in highways, overseers to keep open. (1758.) SEC. 14. Drains may be laid along, within the limits of, or across any public road; and when any shall be so laid out and constructed, or where any road shall hereafter be constructed along or across any such drain, it shall be the duty of the overseers of highways, in their respective districts, to keep the same open and **Bridge for same.** free from all obstructions; and when any such drain shall cross a public highway, the commissioner of highways of the proper township shall build and keep in repair a suitable bridge over the same; **Township to pay apportionment of commissioner.** and the township to which any road along or across which any drain has been made belongs, shall pay towards the construction of such drain such sum, including the cost of building such bridge, as the drainage commissioner shall estimate, as aforesaid, as the benefit accruing to such road from such drain. A drain may be laid along any railroad when necessary, but not to the injury of such road; and when it shall be necessary to run a drain across a railroad, it shall be the duty of such railroad company, when notified by said drain commissioner to do so, to make the necessary opening through said road, and to build and keep in repair a suitable culvert. Drain along or across railroads.

(22:0¼) SEC. 2. It shall be the duty of the overseer or commissioner of highways in any township to see that the provisions of this act shall be carried out within their respective highway districts, and they shall give notice to the owner, possessor, or occupier of any land within said district, whereon Canada thistles shall be growing and in danger of going to seed. requiring him to cause the same to be cut down within five days from the service of such notice ; and in case such owner, possessor, or occupier shall refuse or neglect to cut down the said Canada thistles, the overseer or commissioner of highways shall enter upon the land, and cause all such Canada thistles to be cut down, with as little damage to growing crops as may be, and he shall not be liable to be sued in an action of trespass therefor: *Provided*, That where such Canada thistles are growing upon non-resident lands, it shall not be necessary to give notice before proceeding to cut down the same. Duty of overseer or commissioner relative to destruction of of Canada thistles Proviso.

(2131.) SEC. 3. Each overseer or commissioner of highways shall keep an accurate account of the expense incurred by him in carrying out the provisions of the preceding section of this act, with respect to each parcel of land entered upon therefor, and shall offer a statement of such expense, describing by its legal description the land entered upon and verified by oath, to the owner, possessor or occupier of such resident lands, requiring him to pay the amount. In case such owner, possessor, or occupier shall refuse or neglect to pay the same within thirty days after such application, said claim shall be presented to the township board of the township in which such expense was incurred, and said township board is hereby authorized and required to audit and allow such claim, and order the same to be paid from the fund for general township purposes of said township, out of any moneys in the township treasury not otherwise appropriated. The said overseer or commissioner of highways shall also present to the said township board a similar statement of the expense incurred by him in carrying out the provisions of said section, upon any non-resident land, and the said township board is hereby authorized and required to audit and allow the same in like manner. Expenses incurred, account of to be kept. Allowance of. Expenses incurred on non-resident lands.

(2132.) SEC. 4. The supervisor of the township shall cause all such expenditures as have been so paid from the township treasury, under the provisions of this act, to be severally levied on the lands so described in the statements of the overseers or commissioner of highways, and to be collected in the same manner as delinquent highway taxes are collected ; and the same, when col- Expenses paid to be levied on lands.

lected, shall be paid into the township treasury, to reimburse the
outlay therefrom aforesaid.

Plank road company may use highway.

(2587.) SEC. 27. Any plank road company which shall be organized under this act is hereby authorized to enter upon, take, and
use any public highway on the route of said plank road, and to
construct thereon, or any part thereof, their plank road, with all
necessary fixtures and appurtenances: *Provided,* The consent of

Proviso—consent of certain township officers, or majority of freeholders required.

the supervisor, highway commissioner, and township clerk, or a
majority of them, in each town through which such road passes,
or, instead thereof, the consent of a majority of the freeholders residing on that part of the highway so to be taken, shall be first obtained ; and such company, during the construction of such plank
road, shall in no wise unnecessarily obstruct or prevent travel on
such highway.

Liable for damages sustained by road being out of repair.

(2605.) SEC. 45. Any such corporation shall be liable for all
damages that may be sustained by any person or persons, to themselves or property, in consequence of neglect or omission to keep
such road in good condition or repair ; and if such company shall

Penalty for taking toll when road is out of repair, and how collected.

continue to take toll for passing over that portion of their road
which may be out of repair, so as to make the passage of teams or
vehicles inconvenient or dangerous, for six days at any one time,
they shall pay therefor a penalty of fifty dollars, which may be
sued for and recovered by the prosecuting attorney of the county
in which such portion of their road may be situated, on complaint
on oath of any person, to be paid, when collected, to the treasurer
of such county for the benefit of township libraries in such
county, or such prosecution may be instituted by the highway
commissioner of any township in which the portion of the road so
out of repair lies, upon the application of ten freeholders residing
in such township.

SEC. 3. This act shall take effect from and after the first Monday
of April, 1875.

Approved April 1, 1875.

[No. 66.]

AN ACT to amend an act entitled "An act to prevent animals
from running at large in the public highways," being section
four of chapter fifty-nine, being section (2030) of the compiled
laws of eighteen hundred and seventy-one.

Section amended

SECTION 1. *The People of the State of Michigan enact,* That
section four of chapter fifty-nine, being section two thousand and
thirty of the compiled laws of eighteen hundred and seventy-one,
being an act entitled "An act to prevent animals from running at
large in the public highways," be amended so as to read as follows :

Duty of person after making seizure of animals.

(2030.) SEC. 4. Whenever any such person shall seize and take
into custody or possession any animal under the authority of the
next preceding section, it shall be the duty of such person to
forthwith cause a description of said animal or animals to be entered upon a book to be kept by the clerk of the town, city or vil-

lage in which such animals were taken up, and shall thereupon Notice of sale. give immediate notice to a justice of the peace, or a commissioner of highways of the town, city, or village in which such seizure and possession shall have been taken, and such justice or commissioner shall thereupon give notice by affixing the same in three public and conspicuous places in said town, city, or village, one of which shall be the district school-house nearest the residence of such justice or commissioner, that such animal or animals will be sold at public auction, at some convenient place (to be specified in such notice) in said town, city, or village, not less than fifteen nor more than thirty days from the time of the affixing of such notice. The same justice or commissioner shall proceed to sell the said animals for cash, and out of the proceeds thereof shall, in the first place, retain the following fees and charges for his services in giving said notice and making such sale, viz.: for the first horse Fees. sold three dollars, and for every additional horse one-half dollar; for each cow, calf, or other cattle, not exceeding five in number, one dollar; and for every additional cow, calf, or other cattle, twenty-five cents; and for every sheep or swine, not exceeding five in number, one-half dollar; and for every additional sheep or swine, ten cents; together with a reasonable compensation, to be estimated by such justice or commissioner, to be paid the person making the seizure for the care and keeping of said animal or animals, from the time of the seizure to the sale thereof. If there Disposal of surplus money. shall be any surplus money arising from said sale, the said justice or commissioner shall retain the same in his hands, and pay the same to the owner or owners of said animal or animals, after a reasonable demand therefor, and satisfactory proof of such ownership: *Provided*, Such owner or owners shall appear and claim Proviso—surplus to be claimed within one year. such surplus moneys within one year after sale. And if the owner or owners of such animal or animals shall not appear and demand such surplus moneys within one year after such sale has been made, he shall be forever precluded from recovering any part of such moneys; and the same shall be paid to the treasurer of the town for the use of the town, and his receipt therefor shall be a legal discharge of said justice or commissioner: *Provided*, That Proviso—redemption of animal. any animal sold in pursuance of this act may be redeemed any time within six months following such sale, by paying the expenses of such custody and sale, and a reasonable compensation for keeping the same.

SEC. 2. This act shall take immediate effect.

Approved April 2, 1875.

[No. 67.]

AN ACT making appropriations for the institution for educating the deaf and dumb, and the blind, for the years eighteen hundred and seventy-five and eighteen hundred and seventy-six.

SECTION 1. *The People of the State of Michigan enact,* That Appropriation to defray current expenses for 1875–6. the sum of forty-five thousand dollars for the year eighteen hundred and seventy-five and the sum of forty thousand dollars for the year eighteen hundred and seventy-six, or such portions of said sums as may be necessary, are hereby appropriated to defray the current expenses of the institution for educating the deaf and dumb, and the blind.

Further sum for improvement, etc.

SEC. 2. The sum of ten thousand five hundred dollars, or so much thereof as may be necessary, is hereby appropriated for grading and ornamenting the grounds, for building sidewalks, for building one ice-house, for building one barn, for building partitions in and ventilating dormitories, for building water-closets for dormitories, for buying and furnishing fifty additional beds, for building two hundred rods of board fence, and for digging one well. The above sum to be used in amounts for the various items as estimated by the trustees of said institution as found in their biennial report for the year eighteen hundred and seventy-four.

Further sum for foremen, assistants, etc.

SEC. 3. To pay foremen and assistants in the cabinet, shoe and basket shops and the printing office, the sum of four thousand dollars for the year eighteen hundred and seventy-five, and the sum of four thousand dollars for the year eighteen hundred and seventy-six, or so much of said sums as may be necessary, is hereby appropriated.

Provision to meet appropriations.

SEC. 4. The several sums mentioned in this act are hereby appropriated out of the general fund, and passed to the credit of the asylum fund for the benefit of the institution for educating the deaf and dumb and the blind; and shall be paid to the board of trustees at such time and in such manner and amounts only as are or may be provided by law, and may be made to appear to the Auditor General to be necessary for the immediate wants of said institution; and in no case shall a greater sum be drawn at one time from the State treasury than five thousand dollars.

Mem.

SEC. 5. Of the above mentioned sums, the Auditor General shall add to and incorporate with the State tax for the year eighteen hundred and seventy-five, the sum of fifty-four thousand two hundred and fifty dollars, and for the year eighteen hundred and seventy-six the sum of forty-nine thousand two hundred and fifty dollars, which sums when collected shall be passed to the credit of the general fund.

SEC. 6. This act shall take immediate effect.

Approved April 8, 1875.

[No. 68.]

AN ACT to incorporate State and subordinate granges.

What granges may be incorporated under this act.

SECTION 1. *The People of the State of Michigan enact,* That State, county, or district and subordinate granges of the order of the Patrons of Husbandry in the State of Michigan may be incorporated under the provisions of this act.

Articles of association for incorporating a State grange.

SEC. 2. Any thirteen or more persons, residents of this State, and of lawful age, and members of a State grange of the Patrons of Husbandry of the State of Michigan, and appointed for that pur-

pose by the executive committee of said State grange, may, under
the direction of said executive committee, for the purpose of incorporating a State grange of the order of the Patrons of Husbandry,
make and execute articles of association under their hands and
seals, which articles shall be acknowledged before some officer having authority to take the acknowledgment of deeds, and shall set
forth :

First, The names of the persons so associating in the first in- *What to set forth.*
stance, and their places of residence ;

Second, The corporate name by which such association shall be
known in the law, and the place or places which shall be deemed
to be the place of its business office ;

Third, The object and purpose of such corporation, which shall
be to advance the social, moral, intellectual, and material interests
of the members of the corporation ;

Fourth, The period of the existence of the corporation, which
shall not exceed thirty years.

SEC. 3. Such articles of association shall have endorsed thereon, *Proof of the due*
or annexed thereto, an affidavit made by not less than three of the *execution there-of, etc.*
signers thereof, sworn to before some officer in this State author-
ized to administer oaths, showing that the persons whose names
are signed to said articles of association are members of the State
grange of the Patrons of Husbandry, and that they have been appointed by the executive committee of said State grange to make
and execute said articles for the purpose of incorporating a State
grange, as aforesaid, and that such articles of association are made
and executed in accordance with the direction of said executive
committee.

SEC. 4. A copy of said articles of association, and of the certifi- *Copy of articles,*
cate of acknowledgment thereof, and of said affidavit, with an affi- *etc., to be filed and recorded in*
davit thereto attached, showing the same to be true copies of said *office of Secre-tary of State.*
original articles, certificate, and affidavit, which affidavit so at-
tached shall be made by one or more of the signers of said articles,
shall be filed and recorded in the office of the Secretary of State ;
and thereupon the persons who shall have signed said articles of
association, their associates and successors, being masters of the
subordinate granges of the order of the Patrons of Husbandry in
this State, together with such other persons (if any) as shall be
designated for that purpose in the articles of association aforesaid,
shall be a body politic and corporate, under and by the name ex- *Body politic and*
pressed in such articles of association ; it being hereby intended *corporate.*
and provided that the persons who shall be the members and compose the corporation created as aforesaid, shall be composed of the
persons signing such articles of association as aforesaid, and all the
other masters of the subordinate granges of the Patrons of Husbandry in this State, during their continuance in office as such
masters, and until their successors in office shall be chosen and
enter upon the duties of their offices, together with such other
persons as may be designated for that purpose in such articles of
association as aforesaid ; and the corporation formed under such *Powers of cor-*
articles of association as aforesaid, shall by the name designated in *poration.*

such articles, have succession, and be capable of suing and being sued, of contracting and being contracted with, and of purchasing, receiving, and holding real and personal estate, by deed, gift, grant, or devise, and may have a common seal and may alter the same at pleasure, and shall have full power to give, grant, convey, lease, mortgage, sell, and dispose of any and all of such real and personal estate; but the rents, income, and proceeds of all such property and estate shall be devoted exclusively to the objects for which the corporation is formed; and the amount of the real and personal estate owned by such corporation at any one time, shall not exceed the sum of one hundred thousand dollars in value.

Amount of property limited.

SEC. 5. Such corporation shall have power and authority to designate, elect, and appoint from its members such officers and agents, under such name and style, as shall be in accordance with the constitution of the national grange of the order of the Patrons of Husbandry, and as shall be provided for by the articles of association or by-laws (or both) of the corporation, and such corporation shall have authority to make all such rules, regulations, and by-laws, not repugnant to law, or to the constitution and regulations of the national grange of the order of the Patrons of Husbandry, as may be necessary and convenient for the regulation, management, and government of the affairs, business, property, and interests of the corporation; and such corporation may change the location of its business office whenever desirable.

Officers and agents.

Rules, by-laws, etc.

SEC. 6. A copy of the record of the articles of association of every such corporation formed as aforesaid, filed in the office of the Secretary of State, and certified by him under the seal of State, shall be received in all courts and places as *prima facie* evidence of the existence and due incorporation of such corporation.

Copy of record evidence in court.

SEC. 7. Any thirteen or more persons, of lawful age, residents of this State, and being members of any county, district, or subordinate grange of the Patrons of Husbandry, duly chartered by the national grange, by charter approved by the State grange, desirous to become incorporated, may make and execute articles of association, specifying therein, as provided in section two of this act, and acknowledge the same as specified in said section two, and file a copy of such articles, together with a copy of the charter granted as aforesaid by said national grange, in the office of the county clerk of the county where the business office of the grange is located, and the same shall be recorded by such county clerk, in a book to be kept in his office for that purpose; and thereupon, the persons who shall have signed such articles of association, together with their associates and successors who shall sign such articles, shall be a body politic and corporate, by the name expressed in such articles of association, and by that name they and their successors shall have succession, and by that name may sue and be sued, contract and be contracted with, and may have a common seal, which they may alter at pleasure, and may purchase, take, receive, own, and hold real and personal estate, and the same or any part thereof grant, sell, mortgage, lease, and convey at pleasure. But every such corporation shall be limited as to the amount of estate which

Incorporation of county, district, and subordinate granges.

Articles of association.

Filed and recorded in office of county clerk.

Body politic and corporate.

Powers.

Amount of estate limited.

it may hold, and the disposition to be made thereof, and of the income and proceeds therefrom, by the provisions of section four of this act, and a copy of the record of the articles of association, and of the charter thereto attached, certified by the county clerk, under the seal of the county where such record is kept, shall be received in all courts and places in this State as *prima facie* evidence of the existence and due incorporation of every grange incorporated under this section. *Copy of record evidence in court.*

SEC. 8. Every county, district, and subordinate grange incorporated under this act, shall have power and authority to designate, elect, and appoint from its members such officers, under such name and style as shall be in accordance with the constitution of the national grange, and the regulations of the State grange, and as may be provided for in the articles of association or by-laws of the corporation; and shall also have authority to make all such by-laws, rules and regulations, not repugnant to the laws of the United States or of this State, nor repugnant to the constitution and regulations of the national grange or State grange, as may be necessary and convenient for the regulation, management, and government of the affairs, business, property, and interests of the corporation; and may change the location of its business office whenever expedient, but notice of such change shall be filed and recorded in the office of the county clerk, where the record of its articles of association are kept. And every corporation organized under this act may, for the purpose of effecting the objects and purposes of the corporation, create a capital stock, and divide the same into convenient shares, and make all such rules and regulations in respect to the same, and the management thereof, and for the collection of assessments and calls upon such shares, as may be expedient. *Appointment of officers.* *By-laws rules, etc.* *Change of location of business office.* *May create a capital stock, etc.*

SEC. 9. All corporations formed under this act shall, in all things not herein otherwise provided, be subject to the provisions of chapter one hundred and thirty of the compiled laws of eighteen hundred and seventy-one, so far as the same may be applicable to corporations formed under this act, and the legislature may alter or amend this act at any time. *Subject to provisions of chapter 130, C. L. 1871.*

SEC. 10. This act shall take immediate effect.

Approved April 8, 1875.

[No. 69.]

AN ACT to organize the county of Gladwin.

SECTION 1. *The People of the State of Michigan enact*, That the present unorganized county of Gladwin, be and the same is hereby organized into a separate county by the name of Gladwin, and the inhabitants thereof shall be entitled to all the privileges, powers, and immunities to which, by law, the inhabitants of other organized counties in this State are entitled. *Gladwin county organized.*

SEC. 2. At the township meeting of the several townships in said county to be held on the first Monday of April next, there shall be an election of all the county officers to which other *First election of county officers.*

counties in this State are entitled, who shall hold their several offices until the first day of January, in the year of our Lord eighteen hundred and seventy-seven, and until their successors shall have been elected and qualified. Said election shall be conducted in the same way, by the same officers, and the returns thereof made in the same manner as near as may be, as is now required by law in the election of county officers in this State.

Canvass of votes.   SEC. 3. The county canvass of the votes cast for county officers, shall be held on the second Tuesday succeeding the election at the village of Gladwin in the county aforesaid, and said canvass shall be conducted in the same way and by the same officers as the requirements of law now provide in organized counties as nearly as may be, and the board of canvassers shall have power to appoint one of their number secretary of said board.

Location of county seat determined by commissioners.   SEC. 4. The location of the county seat of said county shall be determined by three commissioners, and W. Grout, O. O. Chappell, and James Dow, are hereby appointed such commissioners, who shall on or before the first day of June, eighteen hundred and seventy-five, determine the location of the county seat of said county, and make a certificate describing the location thereof, which certificate shall be signed by a majority of said commissioners and filed with the clerk of the county of Gladwin, and a certified copy of said certificate shall by the county clerk be filed with the Secretary of State.

Suits, etc., now pending.   SEC. 5. All suits, proceedings, and other matters now pending, or that shall be pending on the second Tuesday after the first Monday in April next, before any court, or before any justice of the peace of the county of Midland, shall be prosecuted to final judgment and execution. And all taxes which have been heretofore levied shall be collected in the same manner as though this act had not passed.

Taxes heretofore levied.

Judicial circuit.   SEC. 6. The said county of Gladwin shall be in and a part of the twenty-first judicial circuit.

Register of deeds to make transcript of records, etc.   SEC. 7. The register of deeds of said county shall make, or cause to be made, a transcript of all records made in other counties which are necessary to be and appear upon the records of said county; and the board of supervisors of said county shall within one year, make provision for defraying the expense of the same.

Payment of expense.

Secretary of State to furnish certified copy of this act.   SEC. 8. The Secretary of State is hereby directed to furnish the township clerk of the township of Gladwin with a certified copy of this act; and it shall be the duty of said clerk to give the same notice of the elections to be held under the provisions of this act that is required by law to be given by the sheriff of organized counties.

Clerk to give notice of election.

SEC. 9. This act shall take immediate effect.

Approved April 8, 1875.

[No. 70.]

AN ACT supplemental to an act entitled "An act to provide for the collection of statistical information of the insane, deaf, dumb, and blind in this State," etc.; being act one hundred and nine of the laws of eighteen hundred and seventy-three, approved April seventeenth, eighteen hundred and seventy-three.

SECTION 1. *The People of the State of Michigan enact,* That it shall be the duty of the county clerk of each county, to make and forward to the trustees of the institution for the deaf and dumb, and the blind, on or before the first day of December of each year, on blanks to be furnished by the Secretary of State for that purpose, a copy, in detail, of so much of the statistical report of each supervisor or assessor, as is required by an act to provide for the collection of statistical information of the insane, deaf, dumb, and blind in this State, etc., being act one hundred and nine of the laws of eighteen hundred and seventy-three, approved April seventeen, eighteen hundred and seventy-three, as relates to the deaf, dumb, and blind, in each county respectively. *(County clerk to furnish certain information to trustees of Deaf, Dumb, and Blind Institute.)*

Approved April 8, 1875.

[No. 71.]

AN ACT to amend section one (1) of act number one hundred and twenty-four (124) of the session laws of eighteen hundred and seventy-three, entitled "An act to establish a board of commissioners to increase the product of the fisheries, and to make an appropriation therefor," approved April nineteen, eighteen hundred and seventy-three.

SECTION 1. *The People of the State of Michigan enact,* That section one (1) of act number one hundred and twenty-four (124) of the session laws of eighteen hundred and seventy-three, entitled "An act to establish a board of commissioners to increase the product of the fisheries and to make an appropriation therefor," approved April nineteen, eighteen hundred and seventy-three, be amended so as to read as follows: *(Section amended)*

SECTION 1. *The People of the State of Michigan enact,* That it shall be the duty of the Governor, by and with the advice and consent of the senate, to appoint three persons, residents of this State, who shall constitute a board of fish commissioners. The persons so appointed shall hold their office, one for two years, one for four years, and one for six years; and their successors to be appointed at the expiration of the several terms of office, shall each hold their terms of office for six years. It shall be the duty of the persons so appointed to select a suitable location for a State fish-breeding establishment, for the artificial propagation and cultivation of whitefish and such other kinds of the better class of food fishes as they may direct, upon the best terms possible. Said *(Board of fish commissioners. Terms of office. Their duties.)*

State Treasurer to pay actual expenses.

board may receive from the State Treasurer all the expenses actually disbursed by them while in discharge of their respective duties.

SEC. 2. This act shall take immediate effect.

Approved April 8, 1875.

[No. 72.]

AN ACT to confirm and legalize all acts changing representative districts passed prior to the enumeration of eighteen hundred and seventy-four, and to confirm records, taxes, and official acts in territory affected by such changes.

Preamble; decision of the Supreme Court.

Whereas, The supreme court of this State has decided that an act of the legislature passed in eighteen hundred and seventy-three for the purpose of enlarging the boundaries of the city of Detroit, and which did, in fact, annex to said city of Detroit, territory which before then was in a representative district other than the one to which said territory was annexed, was void, as being in conflict with section four of article four of the constitution of this State ; and

Effect of such decision.

Whereas, Said decision, if applied to all existing acts on that subject of like character which have been passed since the enumeration of eighteen hundred and seventy and prior, would unsettle and throw into confusion a large portion of the territory in this State, affect the legality of the records of deeds, mortgages, and other instruments, the validity of taxes assessed, and the election of officers in many cases ;

Now, therefore, For the purpose of settling all questions which might be raised by reason of legislation of the character indicated, and to ratify and confirm all such acts and proceedings thereunder,

Acts legalized.

SECTION 1. *The People of the State of Michigan enact,* All acts and parts of acts heretofore passed by the legislature and approved by the governor changing the boundaries of cities, townships, or counties, by taking territory from one representative district and placing the same in another, or transferring territory from one representative district to another, shall be and the same are hereby ratified and confirmed.

Records, taxes levied, etc., held to be legal.

SEC. 2. All records made in the office of any register of deeds, all suits commenced and pending, or determined, all taxes levied, and all other official acts in or concerning territory so transferred, which would have been legal and valid had the division of territory taken place next subsequent to an enumeration of the inhabitants, shall be held to be as legal and valid as if the territory transferred from one representative district to another had been so transferred at a session next subsequent to such general enumer-

Proviso.

ation: *Provided,* That nothing in this act contained shall be held as affecting or intending to affect the particular case which was decided by the supreme court in the recital above alluded to.

SEC. 3. This act shall take immediate effect.

Approved April 8, 1875.

[No. 73.]

AN ACT making appropriations for the maintenance of patients at the Michigan Asylum for the Insane, and for certain repairs, renewals, and additions.

SECTION 1. *The People of the State of Michigan enact,* That the sum of seventeen thousand and five hundred dollars be and is hereby appropriated out of the State treasury to the Michigan Asylum for the Insane, for the maintenance of patients for the fiscal year eighteen hundred and seventy-five; also, for the same fiscal year the further sum of twenty-one thousand and two hundred and fifty dollars for the following purposes, viz.: For repairs and renewals of building and furniture one thousand dollars; for new steam-boilers and the reconstruction of the boiler-house, ten thousand dollars; for constructing a covered way between the kitchen and center building, one thousand one hundred dollars; for additional laundry apparatus, one thousand dollars; for an additional stairway, one hundred dollars; for woven wire mattresses (three hundred), two thousand five hundred and fifty dollars; for a laundry wagon, two hundred dollars; for fencing, four hundred dollars; for reconstructing coils and coil chambers, one thousand one hundred dollars; for dispensary fixtures, nine hundred dollars and a steam engine, nine hundred dollars; for the male department and for the reimbursement of sums paid for litigation and for sinking a well, two thousand dollars; also, for the same fiscal year the further sum of six thousand and seven hundred dollars for completing and furnishing the male department. *(margin: Appropriations for 1875.)*

SEC. 2. That there be and hereby is appropriated out of the State treasury to the Michigan Asylum for the Insane the sum of seventeen thousand and five hundred dollars for the maintenance of patients for the fiscal year eighteen hundred and seventy-six; also, for the same fiscal year the further sum of six thousand dollars for the following purposes, viz.: For repairs and renewals of building and furniture, one thousand dollars; for the erection of a porter's lodge and gateway, one thousand two hundred dollars; for stone flags, five hundred dollars; for arching and tiling the kitchen floors, nine hundred and fifty dollars; for a microscope and medical apparatus, five hundred and fifty dollars; for excavation at the ice-pond, iron lamp-posts, and covered seats for female patients, seven hundred dollars; and for a new steam pump and attachments, one thousand one hundred dollars. *(margin: Appropriations for 1876.)*

SEC. 3. That there be and hereby is appropriated out of the State treasury to the Michigan Asylum for the Insane the sum of seventeen thousand and five hundred dollars for the maintenance of patients for the fiscal year eighteen hundred and seventy-seven; and also for the same fiscal year the further sum of two thousand dollars for the repairs and renewals of buildings and furniture. *(margin: Appropriations for 1877.)*

SEC. 4. That the moneys appropriated hereby may be drawn from the State treasury upon the warrant of the Auditor General, in such sums and at such times as shall be made to appear to him *(margin: Moneys, how drawn, expended, etc.)*

necessary; they shall be expended only for the purposes specified, and their receipt and disbursement shall be accounted for by duplicate vouchers and monthly accounts current, as provided for by act number one hundred and forty-eight of the laws of eighteen hundred and seventy-three.

Deficiency in certain items, how supplied. SEC. 5. Should the sums appropriated in sections one and two of this bill, for repairs and renewals of buildings and furniture, be insufficient to meet the necessary expenditures for that purpose, the Superintendent and Trustees of said Asylum may draw an amount not to exceed one thousand dollars for the year eighteen hundred and seventy-five, and one thousand dollars for the year eighteen hundred and seventy-six, from any fund heretofore appropriated to said Asylum, said amount thus drawn to be used for renewal and repairs of buildings and furniture.

SEC. 6. This act shall take immediate effect.

Approved April 8, 1875.

[No. 74.]

AN ACT to provide for a supply of water for the University of Michigan.

Appropriation. SECTION 1. *The People of the State of Michigan enact*, That for the purpose of supplying the University of Michigan with water, there shall be and is hereby appropriated out of any funds in the treasury of the State of Michigan not otherwise appropriated, the How drawn and expended. sum of five thousand dollars. Said moneys shall be expended under the direction of the board of regents of the said University, and shall be drawn from the treasury on the presentation of the proper voucher of the treasurer of the said board to the Auditor General, and on his warrant to the State Treasurer; and no money shall be drawn by virtue of this act by such regents, unless they shall have first filed with the Auditor General an estimate and statement showing the purpose for which such moneys is required, and none shall be drawn further than is required to pay for labor done, and materials furnished.

Approved April 8, 1875.

[No. 75.]

AN ACT to amend sections one and eight of chapter ninety of the compiled laws of eighteen hundred and seventy-one (compiler's sections two thousand eight hundred and six and two thousand eight hundred and thirteen), relating to co-operative associations.

Sections amended. SECTION 1. *The People of the State of Michigan enact*, That section one of chapter ninety (compiler's section two thousand eight hundred and six), of the compiled laws of eighteen hundred and seventy-one, entitled "An act to authorize the formation of co-operative associations, by mechanics, laboring men, or others," be amended to read as follows:

SECTION 1. Any five or more persons who shall be desirous of uniting as mechanics, laboring men, or in any other capacity, in any co-operative association for the purpose of purchasing all manner of groceries, provisions, and any other articles of merchandise, and selling the same for cash, or otherwise, to all the stockholders and others, at such reasonable prices over the cost thereof, as will enable the members of such association to obtain such commodities at the smallest practicable rate of cost; and also, if necessary, to manufacture any such articles of trade or merchandise, such as flour, meal, boots, shoes, clothing, and to vend the same as aforesaid; or for the purpose of cultivating or raising vegetables, fruits, or other produce, or animals, for food for said members, or to vend the same as aforesaid; or who may be desirous of engaging as stockholders in any association for the conducting of a general agricultural or horticultural business, or any combination of the two, for the purpose of growing or producing general or special agricultural, horticultural, orchard, garden, or nursery products, whether for the use of such stockholders, or for sale to oth r persons,—may become incorporated for that purpose, by executing one or more duplicate articles of agreement, as hereinafter specified, by signing and acknowledging the same before some officer authorized to take such acknowledgments; and upon the execution and acknowledgment of such articles, the signers thereof, and those who may thereafter become associated with them, shall become a body politic, for the purposes set forth in said articles. *Who may incorporate.*

SEC. 2. Section eight (compiler's section two thousand eight hundred and thirteen) of said chapter, shall be amended to read as follows: *Section amended*

SEC. 8. Any and all associations heretofore organized under the provisions of the statute to which this act is amendatory, and which shall have filed articles of association, in accordance with the provisions of said statute, shall be held to have a valid corporate existence thereunder, notwithstanding any alleged want of conformity with the objects of said statute, if the same shall be in conformity with said statute as now amended; and such corporations shall be held to have such valid existence without farther action on their part for such purpose; and any co-operative association, now in existence in this State, and not incorporated, shall be entitled to all the benefits of this statute, by complying with the provisions thereof, and may, by a vote of a majority of such co-operative association or company, to be taken according to its existing by-laws, determine to avail itself of the provisions of this statute, and to take and assume corporate powers thereunder; and may, by a like vote, transfer to such corporation, so formed under this statute, all its property, real, personal, and mixed; and thereupon such corporation to which said property is so transferred, shall take the same in the same manner, to the same extent, and with the like effect, as the same was previously owned and held by the association so transferring the same; and may, in its corporate name, sue for and collect all dues and demands, subscriptions and other benefits belonging to such original and unincorporated association: *Associations now in existence entitled to benefits of this act.* *May transfer property to corporation formed under this act.*

Proviso. *Provided, however,* That the said corporation, so taking such property as aforesaid, shall take the same subject to all liens and trusts, both legal and equitable, to which the same was subject before said transfer, and shall also be liable for all debts and obligations of such previous association, and shall pay the same to the full extent of the value of such property at the time of so taking the same.

Approved April 9, 1875.

[No. 76.]

AN ACT making an appropriation for the support of the State Public School, and providing for the construction of additional buildings, for the purchase of land, and for making other improvements to that institution.

Appropriation for current expenses.

SECTION 1. *The People of the State of Michigan enact,* That the sum of twenty-five thousand dollars be and the same is hereby appropriated out of the general fund, to meet the current expenses of the State Public School for the year eighteen hundred and seventy-five, and the further sum of thirty thousand dollars be and the same is hereby appropriated out of the general fund, to meet the current expenses of the State Public School for the year eighteen hundred and seventy-six. That the further sum of twelve thousand five hundred and sixty-five dollars be and the same is hereby appropriated out of the general fund for the following named purposes for the State Public School: for cows, three hundred dollars; for library for the children, five hundred dollars; for trees, fencing, and grading, one thousand dollars; for furniture, one thousand five hundred dollars; for a team, harness, and sleigh, five hundred dollars; for deficit in the construction account, six thousand five hundred dollars; for the Coldwater Gas Light Company, for extending gas pipe to the premises of said institution, eighteen hundred and forty dollars; for the same company, for laying gas pipe from the street to the building, four hundred and twenty-five dollars. That the further sum of twenty-three thousand nine hundred dollars be and the same is hereby appropriated out of the general fund, for the following named purposes, for the State Public School: for building, heating, lighting, and furnishing three cottages for children, thirteen thousand five hundred dollars; for raising the wings of the main building another story, one for school rooms and the other for dormitories for employes, eight thousand dollars; for heating, lighting, and furnishing the second stories of the wings, one thousand four hundred dollars; and for establishing mechanical industries for the children, five hundred dollars. That the further sum of two thousand dollars be and the same is hereby appropriated out of the general fund, with which sum the board of control of the State Public School is hereby authorized to purchase for the State such land as said board of control shall select and determine, for the use of said institution.

Margin notes: For sundries. / For buildings, etc. / For purchase of land.

That the further sum of two thousand dollars be and the same is hereby appropriated out of the general fund for the use of the State Public School, for the following named purposes: for general necessary repairs on the main building and cottages, and for the more effectually perfecting the means for heating and ventilating the water-closets, and sewerages of the institution. And the further sum of five thousand dollars be and the same is hereby appropriated out of the general fund for the use of the State Public School for the purpose of constructing and furnishing a hospital for the use of said institution.

For repairs to buildings, etc.

SEC. 2. That the several sums appropriated by the provisions of this act, shall be passed to the credit of the State Public School, and paid to the board of control of that institution, or its treasurer, at such times, and in such amounts and manner as is now provided by law, and by this act, and as may be made to appear to the Auditor General to be necessary.

To whom paid and the time and manner of payment.

SEC. 3. That one-half of the aggregate sum of the appropriations made by this act, the Auditor General shall add to and incorporate with the tax for the year eighteen hundred and seventy-five, and the other half of the aggregate sum of the appropriations made by this act, the Auditor General shall add to and incorporate with the tax for the year eighteen hundred and seventy-six, which sums when collected, shall be passed to the credit of the general fund.

How raised.

SEC. 4. The expense of transportation of children who may be sent to said school pursuant to law shall be audited by the board of State Auditors, and paid out of the general fund.

Expense of transporting children to school, how paid.

SEC. 5. This act shall take immediate effect.

Approved April 9, 1875.

[No. 77.]

AN ACT to amend section one thousand eight hundred and twenty of the compiled laws of eighteen hundred and seventy-one, being section five of "An act to revise and consolidate the several acts relating to the support and maintenance of poor persons," approved April fifth, eighteen hundred and sixty-nine

SECTION 1. *The People of the State of Michigan enact,* That section one thousand eight hundred and twenty of the compiled laws of eighteen hundred and seventy-one, being section five of "An act to revise and consolidate the several acts relating to the support and maintenance of poor persons," approved April fifth, eighteen hundred and sixty-nine, be and is hereby amended to read as follows:

Section amended

(1820.) SEC. 5. They shall have the general superintendence of all the poor who may be in their respective counties, and shall have power, and it shall be their duty:

Powers and duties of the superintendents of the poor.

First, To have charge of the county poor-house that has been or shall be erected, and to provide suitable places for the keeping of such poor, when so directed by the board of supervisors, when

To have charge of county poor-houses, etc.

houses for that purpose shall not have been erected by the county; and for that purpose to rent a tenement or tenements, and land not exceeding eighty acres, and to cause the poor of the county to be maintained at such places;

To ordain rules, etc. *Second,* To ordain and establish prudential rules, regulations, and by-laws, and for the government and good order of such places so provided, and of the county poorhouses, and for the employment, relief, management, and government of the persons therein placed;

To employ keepers, etc. *Third,* To employ one or more suitable persons to be keepers of such houses or places, and all necessary officers and servants; and to vest in them such powers for the government of such houses as shall be necessary, reserving to the paupers, who may be placed under the care of such keepers, the right to appeal to the superintendents;

To purchase materials, etc. *Fourth,* To purchase the furniture, implements, provisions, and materials, that shall be necessary for the maintenance of the poor and their employment and labor, and to sell and dispose of the proceeds of such labor as they shall deem expedient: *Provided,*

Proviso prohibiting the purchase of materials, etc., of superintendent. That no furniture, implements, provisions, or materials, shall be purchased of a superintendent of the poor; and any superintendent being the owner of any such furniture, implements, provisions, or materials, sold to or purchased by such superintendents, or interested directly or indirectly in the profits on any such furniture, implements, provisions, or materials, by commission or otherwise, shall forfeit his interest in the same; and in addition to such forfeiture, a penalty of fifty dollars for each and every violation of the prohibitions and terms of this proviso is hereby imposed, to be collected by and in the name of the county treasurer, in the same manner as the forfeiture provided for, and by section twenty-five of the act to which this act is amendatory;

To prescribe rate of allowance for bringing paupers to poorhouse. *Fifth,* To prescribe the rate of allowance to be made to any person for bringing paupers to the county poor-house, or place provided for the poor, which amount shall be paid by the county treasurer, on the production of a certificate signed by the chairman and countersigned by the secretary of the board of superintendents;

To prosecute suits, etc. *Sixth,* To commence any suit wherein they may be entitled to prosecute upon any recognizance, bond, or security taken for the indemnity, of any township or of the county, and prosecute the same to effect;

To draw on county treasurer for expenses. *Seventh,* To draw, from time to time, on the county treasurer, for all necessary expenses incurred in the discharge of their duties, which draft shall be paid by him out of the moneys placed in his hands for the support of the poor;

To render annual accounts. *Eighth,* To render to the board of supervisors of their county at their annual meeting, a detailed account of all moneys received and expended by them, or under their directions, and of all their proceedings;

To pay over moneys. *Ninth,* To pay over all moneys belonging to the county, remaining in their hands, to the county treasurer, within fifteen days after receiving the same.

Approved April 9, 1875.

[No. 78.]

AN ACT to amend section eight of chapter twenty-six, being section one thousand two hundred and fifty-nine of the compiled
laws of eighteen hundred and seventy-one, relative to laying out,
altering, and discontinuing public roads.

SECTION 1. *The People of the State of Michigan enact,* That section eight of chapter twenty-six, being section one thousand two hundred and fifty-nine of the compiled laws of eighteen hundred and seventy-one, be so amended as to read as follows:

(1259.) SEC. 8. Whenever a highway shall be laid out or altered by the commissioners of highways, they shall cause an accurate survey to be made of the line of said road; and the minutes of such survey shall give the distance and bearings of such road, and also of such roads as are not on section or quarter-lines, the distance and bearing of the commencement and ending of such road, from the nearest section corner or quarter-post; and also the distance from the intersection of such road with each and every section line, to the nearest [section] corner or quarter-post; and shall file a plat or map with the minutes of such survey, certified by the surveyor, in the office of the township clerk of the township in which such road is situated; and the premises belonging to any highways shall be a parcel of land not less than two rods wide on each side of the line of said survey, or each side of any section line on which any highway shall be established.

Approved April 9, 1875.

[No. 79.]

AN ACT to amend section three thousand and thirty-eight (3038) of the compiled laws of eighteen hundred and seventy-one, being section three of an act entitled "An act for the incorporation of charitable societies," approved February sixth, in the year of our Lord one thousand eight hundred and fifty-five.

SECTION 1. *The People of the State of Michigan enact,* That section three thousand and thirty-eight (3038) of the compiled laws of eighteen hundred and seventy one, be and the same is hereby amended so as to read as follows, to-wit:

(3038.) SEC. 3. The affairs of each corporation shall be under the general management of not less than five nor more than forty trustees to be chosen by the members thereof, and to hold office for such time, not exceeding four years, as shall be provided by the articles of association; and the articles of association may provide for a classification of the trustees so that the terms of office of the several classes shall expire at different times. The regular officers of such corporation, except the secretary and treasurer, shall form a part of said trustees. The officers may be chosen by the trustees or by the members of the corporation, as the articles shall prescribe. The by-laws of such corporation shall be adopted by the trustees, who may change them at pleasure. A majority of the

Quorum.

Delegation of powers of trustees to committees.

Amendment of articles of association.

trustees shall be a quorum to transact business. The articles of association may provide for the delegation, by the trustees, of their powers, by the by-laws, to a committee or committees of their own body. The articles of association of any such corporation may be amended at any time, by resolution passed by vote of two-thirds of the trustees. Before any such amendment shall take effect a copy of the resolution, certified by the secretary, shall be filed in the office of the Secretary of State and in the clerk's office of the county or counties in which the original articles are filed.

SEC. 2. This act shall take immediate effect.

Approved April 9, 1875.

————

[No. 80.]

AN ACT to organize the county of Presque Isle, and the townships of Presque Isle, Posen, Belknap, Rogers, and Moltke, in the county of Presque Isle.

County of Presque Isle organized.

SECTION 1. *The People of the State of Michigan enact,* That the county of Presque Isle, consisting of the territory embraced in the present county of Presque Isle, shall be, and the same is hereby organized into a separate county by the name of Presque Isle, and the inhabitants thereof shall be entitled to all the privileges, powers, and immunities to which by law the inhabitants of other organized counties in this State are entitled.

Township of Presque Isle organized.

SEC. 2. All that part of the said county of Presque Isle which lies east of the township line running between townships six and seven east, shall be organized into a township by the name of Presque Isle; and the first township meeting thereof shall be held at the house of George Johnson, on the third Monday of April next, and Frederick Burnham, George Johnson, and John Kaufman shall be the inspectors of the election.

Township of Posen organized.

SEC. 3. All that part of the said county of Presque Isle embraced in townships thirty-three, thirty-four, and thirty-five north, of range six east, shall be organized into a township by the name of Posen; and the first township meeting thereof shall be held at the house of August Paul on the third Monday of April next, and Lawrence Kowalsky, Andrew Miminger, and Charles Ehmke shall be the inspectors of the election.

Township of Belknap organized.

SEC. 4. All that part of the said county of Presque Isle which is embraced in township thirty-three north, ranges two, three, four, and five east, and township thirty-four north, range five east, shall be organized into a township by the name of Belknap; and the first township meeting thereof shall be held at the school-house on section seventeen, township thirty-four north, of range five east, on the third Monday of April next, and John D. McKenzie, Frederick Nagle, and William Meridith, shall be the inspectors of the election.

Township of Moltke organized.

SEC. 5. All that part of said county of Presque Isle, which is embraced in township thirty-four north, ranges two, three, and four east, and township thirty-five north, ranges two, three, and four east, shall be organized into a township by the name of Moltke; and the first township meeting thereof shall be held at the house of Stephen Reiger, on the third Monday of April next, and Andrew E. Banks, Stephen Reiger, and Frederick Sorgenfrei shall be the inspectors of the election.

SEC. 6. All the remainder of said county of Presque Isle not em- *Township of Rogers organized.* braced in the township named in the foregoing sections of this act, are hereby organized into a township by the name of Rogers; and the first township meeting thereof shall be held at the union school house in the village of Rogers City on the third Monday of April next, and Leonard C. Crawford, Hermon Hoift, and Frederick D. Larke shall be the inspectors of election.

SEC. 7. The county seat of said county shall be and remain at *County seat.* Rogers City, in said county of Presque Isle, until such time as the same shall be changed in accordance with law.

SEC. 8. At the township meeting of the several townships of said *First election of county officers.* county, to be held on the third Monday of April next, there shall be an election of all the county officers to which the said county is entitled, whose term of office shall expire on the first day of January, eighteen hundred and seventy-seven, and when their successors shall have been elected and qualified. Said election shall be conducted in the same way, by the same officers, and the returns thereof made in the same manner, as near as may be, as the same now required by law in the election of county officers in this State.

SEC. 9. The county canvass of votes cast for county officers *Canvass of votes.* shall be held on the second Tuesday succeeding the election at the court house in Rogers City aforesaid, and said canvass shall be conducted in the same way and by the same officers, as the requirements of law now provide for organizing counties, as nearly as may be, by the appointment by the board of canvassers of one of their own number to act as secretary for the board of county canvassers.

SEC. 10. Said county shall be in the eighteenth judicial circuit. *Judicial circuit.*
SEC. 11. This act shall take immediate effect.
Approved April 9, 1875.

[No. 81.]

AN ACT to amend sections one, two, and three of an act entitled "An act to authorize and empower the board of control of State swamp lands to make an appropriation of State swamp lands to aid in the construction of a railroad from the straits of Mackinaw to Marquette harbor on Lake Superior," approved March twenty-one, eighteen hundred and seventy-three, and an act amendatory thereof, approved March twenty-four, eighteen hundred and seventy-four.

SECTION 1. *The People of the State of Michigan enact,* That *Sections amended.* sections one, two, and three of an act entitled "An act to authorize and empower the board of control of State swamp lands to make an appropriation of State swamp lands to aid in the construction of a railroad from the straits of Mackinaw to Marquette harbor on Lake Superior," being act number thirty-six of the session laws of eighteen hundred and seventy-three, approved March twenty-one, eighteen hundred and seventy-three, and the act amendatory thereof, approved March twenty-four, eighteen hundred and seventy-four, be amended as follows, viz:

Board of control may make appropriation of swamp lands.

SECTION 1. *The People of the State of Michigan enact,* That to secure the early construction of a railroad from the straits of Mackinaw to Marquette harbor on Lake Superior, and for the purposes of drainage and reclamation, the board of control of State swamp lands are hereby authorized and empowered, if by them deemed expedient, and to the best interest of the State and to the section of country to be penetrated by said railroad, to appropriate not to exceed sixteen sections of State swamp lands per mile to any railroad company that shall construct and complete such railroad in running order on or before December thirty-one, eighteen hundred and seventy-seven : *Provided, however,* That if from the financial condition of the country and the present discredit of all railway investments, difficulties shall occur in raising the money for the construction of said railroad, which may delay its inception and progress, the rights of the company to the grant and privileges hereby authorized shall not be forfeited by reason of the non-completion of the road at the time specified : *Provided,* The progress of the work be such at said time as to render the completion thereof assured to the satisfaction of the said board of control, within a reasonable time thereafter, not exceeding one additional year, and the same shall be actually completed within that time.　Said board of control of State swamp lands in their discretion may award and convey to the company constructing said railroad, the number of acres earned, upon the completion of any twenty mile sections of said railroad : *Provided further,* That said sections are completed ready for the rolling stock, and the said Board of Control shall deem the same necessary to facilitate the completion of said railroad.

Proviso.

Conveyance upon completion of twenty mile sections of road.

Further proviso.

Power and authority of board.

SEC. 2. To promote and further the construction of said railroad, and for the better protection of the interests of the State, the board of control as aforesaid shall have full power and authority over said lands, the reservation necessary, and the privileges requisite in the application of such lands to such a purpose : *Provided,* That such lands shall be selected from the vacant and unreserved State swamp lands in the counties of Mackinaw, Chippewa, Schoolcraft, and Marquette : *And provided further,* That the said board of control shall make no contract exempting said lands from taxation for any period longer than the time during which they shall remain unsold by the railroad company which shall become entitled to the privileges of this grant : *Provided,* No such exemption shall in any event be for a longer term than sixteen years from the time such lands are patented : *And provided further,* That in no event shall any claim exist against the State for any deficiency in the number

Where lands to be selected.

Time lands may be exempt from taxation limited.

Proviso—no claim to exist against State for deficiency in quantity of land.

of acres that may be donated under the provisions of this act, it being the intention to provide for the donation of all the unappropriated State swamp lands in the counties hereinbefore named, not exceeding the sixteen sections to the mile.

SEC. 3. The said board of control shall have power to modify or amend any contract already made for the construction of said railroad, or negotiate any new contract with any new or other company, and to secure the construction of the said railroad, may use the increased power and authority given them by this act; and any contract made within the authority conferred upon them by this act shall be valid and binding upon all the authorities of this State. *Power of board to modify or amend contracts, etc.*

SEC. 2. This act shall take immediate effect.

Approved April 15, 1875.

[No. 82.]

AN ACT to amend an act entitled "An act to provide for the return and settlement of tax sales of county treasurers," being section one thousand one hundred and thirty-six of the compiled laws of eighteen hundred and seventy-one.

SECTION 1. *The People of the State of Michigan enact,* That section one thousand one hundred and thirty-six of the compiled laws of eighteen hundred and seventy-one be amended so as to read as follows: *Section amended*

(1136.) SECTION 1. *The People of the State of Michigan enact,* That it shall be the duty of the county treasurers of the several counties in said State to return to the Auditor General of the State one of the books, and duplicate certificates connected with the sale of lands for taxes in their respective counties, and make a settlement of said sales with said Auditor General annually, on or before the first day of December following said sales; and if any county treasurer shall refuse or willfully neglect to return to the Auditor General of the State the books, and duplicate certificates as aforesaid, he shall be liable to a penalty of one hundred dollars for each and every offense. *County treasurer to settle with Auditor General annually. Penalty for neglect.*

Approved April 16, 1875.

[No. 83.]

AN ACT making appropriations for the State Reform School for the years eighteen hundred and seventy-five and eighteen hundred and seventy-six.

SECTION 1. *The People of the State of Michigan enact,* That there be and hereby is appropriated the sum of twenty-five thousand dollars for each of the years eighteen hundred and seventy-five and eighteen hundred and seventy-six for the current expenses of the State Reform School for each of those years, and the *Appropriations for current expenses, etc., for 1875 and 1876.*

further sum of five hundred dollars for each of said years for the purchase of books and current literature for said school, and the further sum of two thousand five hundred dollars for the year eighteen hundred and seventy-five, for the purpose of lighting the buildings of said school with gas, and the further sum of one thousand dollars for the year eighteen hundred and seventy-five, to meet the expenses already incurred for a new boiler.

Further sum for repairs, etc. SEC. 2. The further sum of five thousand dollars is hereby appropriated for the following purposes: Repairs on buildings, two thousand dollars; for furniture, five hundred dollars: for kitchen furniture, two hundred dollars; for oven, three hundred and fifty dollars; for repairs on laundry and engine, five hundred dollars; for new fence, five hundred dollars; for out-houses and wash room, five hundred dollars; for improvements on farm, four hundred and fifty dollars.

Provision for payment. SEC. 3. The several sums appropriated by sections one and two of this act shall be passed to the credit of the State Reform School, from the funds already in, or from regular sources to come into, the State Treasury, and paid on the order of the Board of Control, according to law.

SEC. 4. This act shall take immediate effect.

Approved April 16, 1875.

[No. 84.]

AN ACT to amend section three thousand five hundred and ninety-three of chapter one hundred and thirty-six of the compiled laws, relative to meetings of school districts.

Section amended SECTION 1. *The People of the State of Michigan enact.* That section three thousand five hundred and ninety-three, of chapter one hundred and thirty-six, of the compiled laws, being section twelve of the primary school law, is hereby amended to read as follows:

Special meetings SEC. 12. Special meetings may be called by the district board; and it shall be the duty of said board, or any one of them, to call such meetings on the written request of not less than five legal voters of the district, by giving the notice required in the next **Time of holding annual meeting in certain districts.** succeeding section; and any district organized under the law for graded and high schools, and any district organized by a special act of the legislature that shall so determine at a regular annual meeting, or at a special meeting called for that purpose, shall thereafter hold its annual meeting on the second Monday in July; and the officers of the district shall date their terms of office from that **Proviso.** day: *Provided,* That such action shall not change the time of the commencement of the school-year or the taking of the school census. No business shall be transacted at a special meeting unless the subject is indicated in the notice of said meeting.

Approved April 16, 1875.

[No. 85.]

AN ACT to amend section twenty of chapter twenty-one of the compiled laws of eighteen hundred and seventy-one, being an act to provide for a uniform assessment of property, and for the collection and return of taxes thereon.

SECTION 1. *The People of the State of Michigan enact,* That section twenty of chapter twenty-one, being section nine hundred and eighty-six of the compiled laws of eighteen hundred and seventy-one, be amended so as to read as follows: *Section amended*

SEC. 20. On the third Monday of May, it shall be the duty of the supervisor of each of the several townships, to be present at his office from eight o'clock in the forenoon until twelve noon, and from one o'clock in the afternoon until five o'clock in the afternoon, for the purpose of reviewing his assessment, and so on the two next following days; and on the request of any person, his agent, or attorney, considering himself aggrieved, on sufficient cause being shown, to the satisfaction of the supervisor, he shall alter the assessment in such manner as shall to him appear just and equal; and to this end he may in either case examine, on oath, the person making the application, or any other person present, touching the matter, which oath the supervisor is hereby authorized to administer. And it shall also be the duty of such supervisor to be and remain at his office during the time the commissioner of highways shall be employed in assessing the highway tax or taxes of his township, and render such assistance as may be required of him by such commissioner in assessing such highway tax. *Review of assessments, when to be made by supervisor.* *Power to alter assessments.* *Supervisor to assist commissioner of highways in assessing highway tax.*

SEC. 2. This act shall take immediate effect.

Approved April 16, 1875.

[No. 86.]

AN ACT to amend sections one thousand four hundred and sixty-one, one thousand four hundred and sixty-two, one thousand four hundred and sixty-five, one thousand four hundred and seventy-six, one thousand four hundred and eighty, one thousand four hundred and ninety-six, and one thousand five hundred of the compiled laws of eighteen hundred and seventy-one, being sections of the act entitled " An act to regulate the manufacture and provide for the inspection of salt."

SECTION 1. *The People of the State of Michigan enact,* That sections one thousand four hundred and sixty-one, one thousand four hundred and sixty-two, one thousand four hundred and sixty-five, one thousand four hundred seventy-six, one thousand four hundred and eighty, one thousand four hundred and ninety-six, and one thousand five hundred of the compiled laws of eighteen hundred and seventy-one, being sections of an act entitled " An act to regulate the manufacture and provide for the inspection of salt," shall be and the same are hereby amended so as to read as follows: *Sections amended.*

Salary and expenses of inspector of salt.

(1461.) SEC. 4. The inspector shall be entitled to receive an annual salary of two thousand dollars. He shall also be allowed the further sum of five hundred dollars annually for the expense of providing and furnishing his office, and for clerk hire, stationery, books, printing and traveling expenses. His deputies shall be en-

Salaries of deputies.

titled to such sums as he may approve, not exceeding in any case the sum of one hundred dollars per month for the time actually

How paid.

employed. All salaries and expenses provided for by this act shall be retained by the inspector out of the money received under section five of this act, and accounted for and paid out by him as provided in this act; salaries to be paid monthly: *Provided*, That in

Proviso.

case the amount of money received for the inspection of salt, according to the provisions of section five, shall not be sufficient to pay the salaries and expenses of the inspector and his deputies, as provided herein, that the amount of such deficiency shall be deducted from said salaries *pro rata* to each.

Two mills paid for each bushel inspected.

(1462.) SEC. 5. Each person, firm, company, and corporation engaged in the manufacture of salt, or for whom any salt shall be inspected, shall from time to time, as salt is inspected, or offered for inspection, pay on demand to the inspector, or the deputy of the district where the salt is inspected, two mills for each bushel of

Proviso.

salt inspected or offered for inspection: *Provided*, That the same may be required to be paid in advance: *And provided further*,

Proviso.

That but one inspection fee shall be paid upon the same salt. In

Neglect or refusal to pay.

case any person, firm, company or corporation shall neglect or refuse to pay such inspection fees, on demand, at his, their or its office or manufactory, the party so refusing shall be liable to an action therefor, in the name of the inspector; and the certificate of inspection, with proof of the signature of the inspector or deputy giving the same, shall be *prima facie* proof of the liability, and the extent of liability of the party so in default; and it shall be lawful for the inspector and his deputies to refuse to inspect salt manufactured at the works so in default, until the amount due is

Moneys received to be paid to inspector.

paid; all money received by or paid to any deputy inspector under this section shall be forthwith paid to the inspector. The inspector

Inspector shall keep accounts.

shall keep just and true accounts of all money received under this section, and an account of the amounts received from or paid by each person, firm, company and corporation engaged in the manufacture of salt, and all other things appertaining to the duties

Books and accounts shall be open for inspection, etc.

of the office, and the said books and accounts shall always during office hours be subject to the inspection and examination of any person who may wish to examine them, shall be deemed the books of the office, and shall be handed· over to his successor in office, together with all the money and effects appertaining to the office.

Location of office.

(1465.) SEC. 8. The inspector shall keep his principal office in either Saginaw or Bay county, and the deputy for the district in which such office is located may occupy the same office. This

Office hours.

office shall be open at all times during business hours. All the

Reports of deputies.

books, records and accounts shall be kept at this office, and each deputy shall, at least once in each month make a written report, by mail or otherwise, to the inspector, of the salt inspected by him during the month, stating for whom, and the quantity and quality thereof. Abstracts of these reports shall be entered in books provided for that purpose. Said inspector shall, in proper books, keep a full record and account of all his transactions; and such books shall also be open for the examination of all persons wishing to examine the same during office hours. `Record of same.`

(1476.) SEC. 19. Each inspector or deputy shall deliver to the party for whom he shall inspect salt, a certificate of the quantity and quality inspected, and shall thereupon direct the employes of the manufacturer to brand and mark, under his personal supervision, with durable paint, the package containing the salt so inspected, with the surname of the inspector at length, and the initials of his christian name, with the addition of the word "Inspector," in letters at least one inch in length, and shall also cause to be marked or branded by the employes of the manufacturer upon the head of the barrel, cask, or package, the weight prescribed for such barrel, cask, or package by the inspector, when such weights are in conformity to the rules and regulations prescribed by the inspector in that regard; and if such weights do not correspond to the rules and regulations, he shall cause the same to be repacked so as to conform thereto. `Certificate of inspection.` `Brand.` `Weights to conform to rules prescribed by inspector.`

(1480.) SEC. 23. The inspector and his deputies, in their daily examination of the several salt manufactories, shall examine all bins of salt for the purpose of ascertaining whether any salt is packed contrary to the provisions of the foregoing section. `Inspector shall examine all bins of salt.`

(1496.) SEC. 39. In case of any vacancy from any cause, in the office of the inspector, the deputy who has been longest continuously in office shall possess the powers and perform the duties of inspector until such vacancy shall be filled; and the bond of the inspector and his sureties shall continue to be liable for the acts of all the deputies until such vacancy shall be filled. `Who to act in case of vacancy.`

(1500.) SEC. 43. In case the inspector shall, at the time of making any annual report, have a surplus of money arising from the inspection fees in this act provided for, in his hands, he shall apportion back and pay such surplus to the persons, firms or corporations for whom salt has been inspected during the last preceding year in proportion to the amounts paid by them respectively for inspection fees: *Provided,* That in no case shall the State be held liable for any obligation or expenditure in consequence of any of the provisions of this act. `How inspector to dispose of surplus money.` `Proviso.`

SEC. 2. This act shall take immediate effect.

Approved April 16, 1875.

[No. 87.]

AN ACT to amend section nineteen of an act entitled " An act to
provide for the organization of the supreme court, pursuant to
section two of article six of the constitution," approved February sixteen, eighteen hundred and fifty-seven, being section four
thousand nine hundred and one of the compiled laws of eighteen
hundred and seventy-one.

Section amended. SECTION 1. *The People of the State of Michigan enact*, That
section nineteen of an act entitled " An act to provide for the organization of the supreme court, pursuant to section two of article
six of the constitution," approved February sixteen, eighteen hundred and fifty-seven, being section four thousand nine hundred
and one of the compiled laws of eighteen hundred and seventy-one,
be and the same is hereby amended so as to read as follows :

Appointment of (4901.) SEC. 19. The clerk of the county of Ingham may, in ad-
deputy county dition to the general deputy which he may now appoint by law,
clerk to act as appoint a deputy who shall act as clerk of the supreme court. And
clerk of supreme such appointee shall be authorized to perform all the duties as
court. clerk of the said court. And he shall receive, in addition to the
Compensation. compensation now allowed by law, annually the sum of three hundred dollars, which sum shall be paid quarterly, out of any moneys
in the treasury belonging to the general fund not otherwise appropriated.

Approved April 16, 1875.

[No. 88.]

AN ACT to exempt private burial grounds and places of interment for the dead from taxation and levy on execution or attachment.

Authority to lay SECTION 1. *The People of the State of Michigan enact*, That
out and make it shall be lawful for any person or persons in this State to lay out
deed of land as and survey any tract of land, not included within the corporate
private burial limits of any city or village, which may be owned by such person
ground. or persons, as a private burial ground for the use of their families
or descendants for purposes of interment of members of such families and descendants, and for no other purpose, not exceeding in
quantity one acre of land, and may make a deed of the same to
some person or persons to be named therein as trustees, with such
provisions for continuing such trusteeship as they shall deem
necessary, which said deed shall be acknowledged by such persons
making the same, in the same manner as other deeds of land, and
shall be recorded in the county where such land shall lie.

Such land a SEC. 2. Such land so laid out and described in said deed, when
grant forever for recorded in the register's office of the county where such land lies,
such purposes. shall operate as a grant forever of the land described in such deed
to said trustees and their successors forever, for the purposes described in said deed ; and no sale, judgment, or decree shall be made
Effect of such which shall have the effect to divert the same from the objects of
grant.

said grant, set forth in such deed; and the same shall not be **taxed** for any purpose, or be subject to any sale for taxes, or any execution, attachment, or other order of sale made by any court; and any deed made by said trustees or their successors, or upon any sale made for taxes, or upon any execution, or decree, or order of sale made by any court of said lands, or any part thereof, or any tenements, tombs or other structures thereon and appurtenant thereto, shall be void and shall convey no interest or title to the grantee named in such deed.

Approved April 16, 1875.

[No. 89.]

AN ACT to amend sections six, fifteen, and twenty-three of an act entitled " An act to authorize the formation of corporations for mining, smelting, or manufacturing iron, copper, mineral coal, silver, or other ores or minerals, and for other manufacturing purposes," approved February five, eighteen hundred and fifty-three, being sections two thousand eight hundred and forty-one, two thousand eight hundred and fifty, and two thousand eight hundred and fifty-eight of the compiled laws of eighteen hundred and seventy-one.

SECTION 1. *The People of the State of Michigan enact,* That sections six, fifteen, and twenty-three of an act entitled " An act to authorize the formation of corporations for mining, smelting, or manufacturing iron, copper, mineral coal, silver, or other ores or minerals, and for other manufacturing purposes," approved February five, eighteen hundred and fifty-three, being sections two thousand eight hundred and forty-one, two thousand eight hundred and fifty, and two thousand eight hundred and fifty-eight of the compiled laws of eighteen hundred and seventy-one, be and the same are hereby amended so as to read as follows : *[margin: Sections amended.]*

(2841.) SEC. 6. The amount of the capital stock in every such corporation shall be fixed and limited by the stockholders in their articles of association, subject to the following limitations and requirements : *[margin: Capital stock.]*

First, The capital stock shall not be less than ten thousand dollars in any case ; *[margin: Minimum.]*

Second, The capital stock of any one corporation engaged in mining or manufacturing iron, steel, silver, lumber, or copper, shall not exceed two million five hundred thousand dollars ; *[margin: Maximum.]*

Third, The capital stock of any other corporation organized or existing under the provisions of this act, shall not exceed five hundred thousand dollars; *[margin: Idem.]*

Fourth, The capital stock of each corporation shall be divided into shares of twenty-five dollars each ; *[margin: Shares.]*

Fifth, Subject to the foregoing limitations the capital stock and number of shares may be increased at any meeting called for that purpose, by a vote of two-thirds in interest of the entire capital *[margin: How increased.]*

stock of the corporation, and at such meeting the stockholders shall have power to make all necessary provisions for calling in and cancelling the old, and issuing new certificates of stock.

Corporation may hold real estate. (2850.) SEC. 15. Any corporation organized or existing under the provisions of this act, shall have power to acquire and hold real estate in fee, by lease, or otherwise, to the following extent for the purpose of carrying on its business, to wit: Any corporation **Limit.** organized or existing under this act shall be allowed to hold three thousand acres of land; any corporation engaged in lumbering or in mining, smelting or manufacturing iron, steel, copper, or the ores thereof, shall be allowed to so acquire and hold fifty thousand acres of land; no corporation shall hold more lands than is permitted by this section, unless authorized by some other act of the legislature, and all conveyances of land heretofore made by or to any corporation organized or existing under this act, are hereby confirmed and declared as valid and effectual, to all intents and purposes, as if made under the present provisions of this section. **Sales of property heretofore made, valid.** When any corporation has heretofore disposed of its property, by sale or lease, in the usual manner in which corporations perform such acts, and has done the same in good faith and for a fair and valuable consideration, then such sale or lease is hereby declared legal and valid, although not done in the manner provided in section two thousand eight hundred and eighty-eight of the compiled laws of eighteen hundred and seventy-one.

Liability of directors for neglecting to comply with certain provisions. (2858.) SEC. 23. If the directors of any such corporation willfully neglect or refuse to comply with the provisions, and to perform the duties required of them by sections three, five, eighteen, and nineteen of this act, they shall be deemed guilty of a misdemeanor, and shall, upon conviction, be punished by a fine not exceeding one thousand dollars each, or by imprisonment in the **Liability for neglecting to make report.** county jail not exceeding one year; and such directors shall also be subject to a penalty of twenty-five dollars per day for each day after the first of August, in each year, that they willfully neglect or refuse to make the reports required by law.

SEC. 2. This act shall take immediate effect.

Approved April 16, 1875.

[No. 90.]

AN ACT to provide for the election of trustees of graded school districts by ballot, in the Upper Peninsula.

What districts may elect board of trustees. SECTION 1. *The People of the State of Michigan enact,* That any school district in the Upper Peninsula, containing more than one hundred children between the age of five and twenty years, may elect a district board consisting of six trustees: *Provided,* **Proviso.** The district shall so determine at an annual meeting, by a vote of two-thirds of the legal voters attending such meeting: *Provided* **Further proviso.** *also,* That the intention to take such vote shall be expressed in the notice of such annual meeting. When such change in the district board shall have been voted, the voters at such annual meeting shall proceed immediately to elect by ballot, from the qualified voters of the district, two trustees for a term of one year, two for a term of two years, and two for a term of three years; and annually thereafter two trustees shall be elected in the manner aforesaid, whose terms of office shall be three years, and until their successors shall have been elected and filed their acceptances.

Approved April 22, 1875.

[No. 91.]

AN ACT to amend sections fifteen and seventeen of act number seventy-nine of the session laws of eighteen hundred and seventy-three entitled "An act to provide for the appointment of a commissioner of railroads, and to define his powers, duties, and fix his compensation," approved April tenth, eighteen hundred and seventy-three.

SECTION 1. *The People of the State of Michigan enact,* That section fifteen and seventeen of act number seventy-nine of the session laws of eighteen hundred and seventy-three, entitled "An act to provide for the appointment of a commissioner of railroads, and to define his powers, duties, and fix his compensation," approved April ten, eighteen hundred and seventy-three, be amended so as to read as follows:

SEC. 15. Every corporation owning a road in use shall, at rea- sonable times and for a reasonable compensation, draw over the same the merchandise and cars of any other corporation or individual having connecting tracks: *Provided,* Such cars are of the proper gauge, are in good running order, and properly loaded: *Provided further,* That nothing herein contained shall apply to the drawing of the cars of stock car-loaning companies. If the corporations cannot agree upon the stated periods at which the cars shall be so drawn, or the compensation to be paid, the said commissioner shall, upon petition of either party and notice to the other, and after hearing the parties interested, determine the rate of compensation and fix such periods, having reference to the convenience and interest of the corporation or corporations, and the public to be accommodated thereby, and the award of the commissioner shall be binding upon the respective corporations interested therein until the same shall have been revised, or alterations shall be made within one year after the award. Any rail- road corporation refusing to comply with the provisions of this section shall be liable to a penalty not exceeding five hundred dollars.

SEC. 17. Whenever, in the opinion of the commissioner of rail- roads, the safety of the public would be more efficiently secured by stationing a flagman to signal trains where a highway or street is crossed by any railroad, or when one railroad crosses or intersects another railroad, or by the building of a gate or bridge at such highway, street or railroad crossing or intersection, or street railway crossing, he shall direct the corporation or corporations owning or operating any such railroad or railroads to station a flagman, or to erect and maintain a bridge or gate at such crossing as the public safety may demand; and in case such flagman is directed to be stationed, or gate or bridge directed to be erected and maintained where one railroad crosses or intersects another, the expense thereof shall be borne jointly in equal proportions by the companies owning or controlling each of said railroads. Any corporation or corporations neglecting or refusing to construct and maintain such gate or bridge, or to maintain such flagman so directed as aforesaid, shall each forfeit for every such neglect or refusal the sum of one hundred dollars, and the further sum of ten dollars for every day which such neglect or refusal shall continue; and if said flagman shall neglect to display his flag, or perform such other duties as may be required of him by said commissioner, he shall for every such neglect be liable to a fine of ($25) twenty-five dollars, and shall also be liable for all damages sustained by any person by reason of such neglect, to be recovered in an action of tort: *Provided*, The corporation owning or operating any such railroad shall not be released from liability therefor, but shall be subject to the same liability at the option of the aggrieved party.

Forfeiture.

Proviso.

SEC. 2. This act shall take immediate effect.

Approved April 22, 1875.

[No. 92.]

AN ACT to prohibit any person entering into any contract with any city or village while a member of the common council of such city, or of the common council or board of trustees of such village.

Member of council not to enter into contract with city or village.

SECTION 1. *The People of the State of Michigan enact,* That it shall be unlawful for any person to enter into any contract with any city or village while he is a member of the common council of such city, or of the common council or board of trustees of such village, for which contract he is to receive from such city or village a valuable consideration, except as may be expressly authorized by the charter of such city or village, or by any other law of this State.

Penalty.

SEC. 2. In case any person violates any of the provisions of this act, he shall be deemed guilty of a misdemeanor, and shall, upon conviction, be punished accordingly.

Approved April 22, 1875.

[No. 93.]

AN ACT to amend sections seven thousand five hundred and sixty-three, seven thousand five hundred and sixty-four, seven thousand five hundred and sixty-five, seven thousand five hundred and sixty-six, and seven thousand six hundred and twenty-three, of the compiled laws of eighteen hundred and seventy-one, relative to offenses against property.

SECTION 1. *The People of the State of Michigan enact,* That sections seven thousand five hundred and sixty-three, seven thousand five hundred and sixty-four, seven thousand five hundred and sixty-five, seven thousand five hundred and sixty-six, and seven thousand six hundred and twenty-three, of the compiled laws of eighteen hundred and seventy-one, relative to offenses against property, shall be and the same are amended so as to read as follows: *Sections amended.*

(7563.) SEC. 12. Every person who shall break and enter, in the night-time, any office, shop, store, railroad depot, warehouse, mill, school-house, or factory, not adjoining to or occupied with a dwelling-house, or any railroad car, shop, boat, or vessel, within the body of any county, with intent to commit the crime of murder, rape, robbery, or any other felony or larceny, shall be punished by imprisonment in the State prison not more than fifteen years. *Penalty for breaking and entering an office, etc., in night time.*

(7564.) SEC. 13. Every person who shall enter in the night-time, without breaking, or shall break and enter in the day-time, any dwelling-house, or any out-house thereto adjoining, kept therewith, or any office, shop, store, railroad car, railroad depot, warehouse, mill, or factory, or any ship, boat, or vessel, within the body of any county, with intent to commit the crime of murder, rape, robbery, or any other felony or larceny, the owner or any other person lawfully therein being put in fear, shall be punished by imprisonment in the State prison not more than ten years. *Penalty for entering dwelling, etc., in night, without breaking, or breaking in in day time, etc.*

(7565.) SEC. 14. Every person who shall enter any dwelling-house in the night-time, without breaking, or shall break or enter in the day-time, any dwelling-house, or any out-house thereto adjoining and occupied therewith, or any church, office, shop, store, railroad car, railroad depot, warehouse, mill, school-house, or factory, or any ship, boat, or vessel lying within the body of any county, with intent to commit the crime of murder, rape, robbery, or any other felony or larceny, no person lawfully therein being put in fear, shall be punished by imprisonment in the State prison not more than five years, or by a fine not exceeding five hundred dollars, and by imprisonment in the county jail not more than one year: *Provided,* That every person who shall unlawfully break into any railroad freight car, or unlawfully enter the same without breaking, with intent to obtain carriage in such car, the same being a part of a freight train, shall be punished by a fine not exceeding two hundred dollars, or imprisonment in the house of correction or county jail not more than six months, or both such fine and imprisonment. *Penalty for entering dwelling, etc., without putting in fear lawful occupant.* *Proviso, penalty for unlawfully entering freight car to obtain carriage.*

Embezzlement, etc., of railroad tickets by officer of road.

(7623.) SEC. 5. If any officer, agent, or employe, of any incorporated railroad company shall fraudulently embezzle, dispose of, or convert to his own use any passenger railroad tickets which have come to his hands or charge by virtue of his office or employment, he shall be punished by imprisonment in the State prison, not exceeding ten years, or by fine not exceeding three thousand dollars, or both, at the discretion of the court.

What may be included in a charge in any prosecution under this section.

In any prosecution under this section, it shall be lawful to include in a charge, as one offense, all acts constituting such offense committed between certain days set forth; and it shall be sufficient to set forth by their value a general description of the tickets alleged to have been unlawfully taken; and it shall be sufficient to maintain the charge if it shall be proved upon the trial that any such tickets were, within the period set forth, embezzled, disposed of, or converted as alleged.

Approved April 22, 1875.

[No. 94.]

AN ACT to repeal section two of an act entitled "An act to compel children to attend school," approved April fifteen, eighteen hundred and seventy-one, being section three thousand seven hundred and thirty-eight of the compiled laws of eighteen hundred and seventy-one.

Section repealed.

SECTION 1. *The People of the State of Michigan enact,* That section two of an act entitled "An act to compel children to attend school," approved April fifteen, eighteen hundred and seventy-one, being section three thousand seven hundred and thirty-eight of the compiled laws of eighteen hundred and seventy-one, shall be and the same is hereby repealed.

Approved April 22, 1875.

[No. 95.]

AN ACT to provide for the examination of certain forfeited and part-paid agricultural college, salt spring, and other lands.

Commissioner of State Land Office authorized to examine certain lands, etc.

SECTION 1. *The People of the State of Michigan enact,* That the Commissioner of the State Land Office in his discretion be, and he is hereby authorized and empowered, to cause the lands hereinafter designated in this act to be examined, and their value and condition ascertained.

Kinds of lands to be examined.

SEC. 2. The lands to be examined under this act are known as the forfeited and part-paid agricultural college, salt spring, asylum, primary school, and swamp lands of the State.

Commissioner to appoint supervisors as agents and define their duties.

SEC. 3. Said Commissioner is hereby authorized to appoint and designate the supervisors of each of the organized townships within which any of the lands to be examined may be located, as examining agents, whose duties in the premises shall be fully defined in a letter of instructions, which it will be the duty of said commissioner to furnish to each person who shall be appointed under this act : *Provided,* That if said Commissioner shall deem it for the best interests of the State, he may, by and with the advice and consent of the Governor, appoint one or more persons as such examining agents, to act in the place of any supervisors, to make examinations in unsettled and unimproved localities. Proviso— other persons may be appointed.

SEC. 4. It shall be the duty of the Commissioner of the State Land Office to furnish each of said agents with plats and descriptions of all of the lands that it will be the duty of such agents to examine, together with all such other information and instruction relating to said lands, or to their duties as such agents, as may be sufficient to enable said agents, after careful personal examination of said lands, to report fully as to their character, value, and condition, at the time of examination ; and in case any of said lands have been trespassed upon and their value deteriorated thereby, said agent shall carefully estimate and report the amount and character of timber probably cut and removed, the date of the cutting, and by whom. To furnish plats, descriptions, etc., to agents. Reports of agents when lands have been trespassed upon.

SEC. 5. The Governor, the State Treasurer, and the Commissioner of the State Land Office, be and are hereby empowered and constituted a board of control, to carry out the provisions of this act, to examine and act upon the reports made by the said agent or agents ; and if in the opinion of the board the best interest of the State would be promoted by changing the price, or terms, of these lands, the said board may alter, by reducing or advancing the price per acre, or conditions of payment : *Provided,* That not less than twenty-five per cent. of the purchase money is paid at the time of purchase. And when the price and terms are so fixed, the said board shall fix the time when the change, if any, is made, will take effect, and cause the same to be published. Board of control to carry out provisions of this act, and its powers and duties. Proviso.

SEC. 6. Said agents shall receive as compensation for their services such sum or sums as the board of State auditors shall determine and allow, including necessary expenses, which bills for services and expenses shall be itemized and sworn to, and made upon forms furnished by the Commissioner of the Land Office, the same to be paid out of the general fund, and apportioned to the several funds, according to the expenses attending the examination of lands belonging to the different classes herein mentioned. Compensation of agents.

SEC. 7. This act shall take immediate effect.

Approved April 22, 1875.

[No. 96.]

AN ACT providing for the location, establishment, and organization of a State house of correction, and making appropriation therefor.

SECTION 1. *The People of the State of Michigan enact,* That the sum of one hundred and fifty thousand dollars be and is hereby appropriated for the purpose of the erection and construc- State house of correction, appropriation therefor.

tion of a State house of correction according to the plans, specifications, and estimates of the commissioners appointed under act number one hundred and seventy of the session laws of eighteen hundred and seventy-three, subject to such alterations and modifications as may be made by the governor and the commissioners hereafter to be appointed under the provisions of section three of this act; which said sum of money shall be incorporated in the State tax as follows: seventy-five thousand dollars for each of the years one thousand eight hundred and seventy-five and one thousand eight hundred and seventy-six.

Appropriation, how raised.

Location.

SEC. 2. The said State house of correction shall be located at Ionia, upon the site selected by the commissioners appointed under said act number one hundred and seventy of the session laws of eighteen hundred and seventy-three, and donated to the State under the provisions of said act.

Board of commissioners and their duties.

SEC. 3. The governor shall appoint three persons, who shall constitute a board of commissioners, whose duty it shall be to erect and construct said house of correction according to the plans, specifications, and estimates mentioned in section one of this act:

Proviso, entire cost limited.

Provided, however, That the entire cost of said State house of correction shall not exceed, when completed, the sum of two hundred and seventy thousand dollars.

Board shall advertise for proposals for constructing.

SEC. 4. Said board of commissioners shall, as soon as practicable after their appointment, advertise for a time not less than six weeks in such papers as they may select in this State for proposals for constructing said State house of correction or any portion thereof in accordance with the plans and specifications heretofore mentioned. All contracts for labor or materials to be used in the erection and construction of said State house of correction, requiring an expenditure of more than five hundred dollars, shall be let to the lowest responsible bidder or bidders; and advertisement of such shall be published in the Detroit daily papers not less than thirty days before the time appointed for opening bids, the advertisement thus provided for to specify the time and place when the bids or proposals made in pursuance thereof shall be opened. All bids or proposals thus made shall be sealed, and shall not be opened at any time or place other than that designated in the advertisement. All or any bids or proposals received by said commissioners may be by them rejected, and whether accepted or rejected shall, after decision thereon by said commissioners, be deposited in the office of the Secretary of State. No contract made by the commissioners shall be binding until approval of the Governor in writing shall be endorsed thereon. When so approved said contract shall be filed with the Auditor General, who shall file the same in his office, and shall make and certify a copy thereof and deliver such copy to the said commissioners: *Provided,* That, after the building of said State house of correction has so far advanced as to receive and keep prisoners, the said board of commissioners shall have power and authority, with the approval of the Governor, to buy materials for, and employ such prisoners upon the completion of said work.

Certain contracts to be let to the lowest responsible bidder.

Bids to be sealed, etc.

Commissioners may reject.

Where deposited.

Contracts to be approved by Governor.

To be filed with Auditor General, who shall furnish certified copies to commissioners.

Proviso—prisoners may be employed.

SEC. 5. In letting contracts said commissioners shall not obli- *Limit of amount that may be paid to contractor.* gate the State to pay to any contractor any money other than that to which said contractor may be justly entitled by reason of labor or materials already furnished and supplied, and in no event shall more than eighty-five per cent of the amount called for in any contract to be paid to the contractor named therein before the completion of his contract and its acceptance by the commissioners: *Provided*, That every contractor performing service or work or *Proviso—contractor to give bonds.* furnishing materials under this act, shall enter into such bonds with sureties, for the proper performance of his contract, as shall be required by said board of commissioners, and approved by the Governor.

SEC. 6. The said board of commissioners shall appoint some *Superintendent and secretary.* proper person, not of their number, to superintend under their direction the erection and construction of the State house of correction provided for in this act, and they shall also appoint a secretary, not of their number, whose duties shall by them be prescribed. Such superintendent and secretary thus appointed shall *Compensation.* each receive for his services a reasonable compensation, to be established by the board and approved by the Governor; and before *To take oath and give bond.* entering upon the discharge of his duties shall each take the oath prescribed by the constitution and laws of this State, and give bond for the faithful performance of the duties of his office in the penal sum of ten thousand dollars.

SEC. 7. Each of the members of said board of commissioners *Compensation of members of board.* shall be entitled to receive his actual traveling expenses and the sum of three dollars per day for the time actually spent in the discharge of his duties under this act, which compensation and expenses shall be audited by the board of State auditors.

SEC. 8. Payments for work or materials for said house of cor- *Payments for. work, etc., how made.* rection shall be made as follows: vouchers for the amount to be paid shall be certified by the said commissioners and presented to the Auditor General, who shall draw his warrant upon the State Treasurer for the amount to be paid.

SEC. 9. It shall be the duty of the said secretary of the said *Secretary to render accounts current to Auditor General, etc.* board of commissioners to render quarter-yearly to the Auditor General accounts current of all transactions, with an estimate and statement showing the purpose for which payments have been paid, and an estimate showing the amount which has accrued to the contractors, and the amount of percentage retained.

SEC. 10. Said commissioners, before they enter upon the dis- *Oath of commissioners, where filed.* charge of the duties of their office, shall each take and subscribe the constitutional oath of office, and file the same in the office of the Secretary of the State, and the treasurer of said board of com- *Treasurer to give bond.* missioners shall give his bond to the people of the State of Michigan in the penal sum of twenty thousand dollars, with two or more sufficient sureties, approved by the Governor, for the faithful performance of the duties required of him, and to properly account for all moneys received by him under this act.

SEC. 11. No commissioner appointed under this act shall be di- *Commissioners not to be interested in contracts.* rectly or indirectly interested in any contract or contracts for the erection or construction of said State house of correction or the furnishing of labor or materials for the same.

Commissioners may draw from general fund for immediate use.

SEC. 12. Said board of commissioners are hereby authorized at any time to draw from the general fund of the State Treasury such amounts of money within the appropriation made by this act, as they shall deem necessary for the immediate commencement and carrying on of the erection of said State house of correction. The amounts so drawn shall be considered as an advance to the said State house of correction upon the appropriation made by

Reimbursement. this act, and such amounts shall be deducted from said State house of correction fund and returned to the general fund when such appropriation shall have been collected and paid into the State Treasury.

SEC. 13. This act shall take immediate effect.

Approved April 22, 1875.

[No. 97.]

AN ACT to prevent the setting of guns and other dangerous devices.

Setting of a spring gun, etc., deemed a mis-demeanor.

SECTION 1. *The People of the State of Michigan enact,* That if any person shall set any spring or other gun, or any trap or device operating by the firing or explosion of gunpowder or any other explosive, and shall leave or permit the same to be left, except in the immediate presence of some competent person, he shall be

Killing of person by gun so set deemed man-slaughter.

deemed to have committed a misdemeanor; and the killing of any person by the firing of a gun or device so set shall be deemed to be manslaughter.

SEC. 2. This act shall take immediate effect.

Approved April 22, 1875.

[No. 98.]

AN ACT to amend section twelve of article two, and sections one, two, four, seven, thirteen, and fifteen of article four of act num-ber one hundred and ninety-eight, of the session laws of eight-een hundred and seventy-three, entitled "An act to revise the laws providing for the incorporation of railroad companies, and to regulate the running and management, and to fix the duties and liabilities of all railroad and other corporations owning or operating any railroad in this State," approved May one, eighteen hundred and seventy-three.

Sections amended.

SECTION 1. *The People of the State of Michigan enact,* That section twelve of article two, and sections one, two, four, seven, thirteen, and fifteen, of article four of act number one hundred and ninety-eight of the session laws of eighteen hundred and seventy-three, entitled "An act to revise the laws providing for the incorporation of railroad companies, and to regulate the running and management, and to fix the duties and liabilities of all railroad and other corporations owning or operating any railroad in this State," approved May one, eighteen hundred and seventy-three, be amended so as to read as follows:

ARTICLE II.

SEC. 12. All railroad companies shall keep their ticket offices open for the sale of tickets at least twenty minutes immediately preceding the departure of all passenger trains from every regular passenger station from which any such passenger trains are to start from or stop at, between the hours of seven o'clock in the morning and eleven o'clock in the evening; and the conductors of all such passenger trains shall announce, or cause to be announced, the name of the station in each passenger car of every such train, twice inside each passenger car of every such train, the door of said car being closed at the time of such announcement, within a reasonable time before the arrival of any passenger train at every station at which said train from notice given is to stop. At junctions, crossings, and points where trains leave in different directions, at or near the same time, the conductor of each train shall announce, or cause to be announced, distinctly, in each passenger car of his train, before starting, the direction in which his train is to go. For each violation of the provisions of this section, the railroad company whose employes do not comply with the provisions of this section in every respect, shall forfeit the sum of one hundred dollars for each violation of the same. *Ticket offices must be kept open twenty minutes. Stations announced twice in cars. Direction train is to go announced. Penalty for violation of provisions of section.*

ARTICLE IV.

SEC. 1. On and after the thirty-first day of October, eighteen hundred and seventy-three, no regular passenger trains shall be run in this State without an air brake or some equally effective device for checking the speed of the train, to be approved by the commissioner of railroads, which may be applied by the engineer to each passenger car composing the train; and every railroad company, person or corporation owning or operating a railroad in this State, which shall permit any such trains to be run on such road without such brake shall forfeit for every train so run, the sum of fifty dollars, to recover which, such company, person or corporation shall be liable in an action on the case, to be brought in behalf of the people of this State, and the money so realized shall be paid into the State treasury. *Air-brake upon passenger trains. Forfeiture for running trains without air-brake.*

SEC. 2. On and after July thirty-first, eighteen hundred and seventy-three, every company, person, or corporation owning or operating a railroad within this State, shall construct and maintain a gate or gates, or bridge, or maintain a flagman to signal trains at every highway or street crossing on the line of such road, where the same shall be required by the commissioner of railroads, as hereinafter provided. Any company, person, or corporation neglecting or refusing to construct or maintain such gate or gates, or bridge, or to maintain such flagman where so required as *Flagman, gate, or bridge at street crossings. Forfeiture for not maintaining.*

aforesaid, shall forfeit for every such neglect or refusal the sum of one hundred dollars, and the further sum of ten dollars for every day while such neglect or refusal shall continue.

Gates, location and construction of. SEC. 4. All gates which, by the provisions of this act, are under the direction of the commissioner of railroads, may be required to be constructed at street or highway crossings, shall be built in such manner, and within such time, and of such material as shall be approved by the commissioner of railroads, and shall be located on the highway or street on one or both sides of the railroad track or tracks, as the commissioner may deem the public safety to require, and shall be so constructed as when closed to obstruct and prevent any passage across such railroad or railroads from the side on which such gate may be located. There shall be **Person to be always in charge of.** a person in charge of every such gate at all hours of the day and night, and it shall be his duty to close the same at the approach of a train of cars, or of a locomotive, and to keep it open at all other **His duties.** times; and it shall be the duty of the gate-keeper on either side of one or more tracks, to close the gate of which he is in charge on the approach of a train of cars or locomotive, on either track. **Penalty for neglect.** For every neglect of such duty, such person, upon conviction thereof, shall pay the sum of twenty-five dollars, or be imprisoned in the county jail for the period of ninety days, or both, in the **Expense for erection, etc., of gates, shared equally by companies.** discretion of the court. The expense incurred in the erection and maintenance of the gates provided for in this section, and of the necessary gate-keepers, shall be shared equally by the railroad companies alongside whose tracks the gates shall be located.

Corporation to furnish employes copies of rules. SEC. 7. It shall be the duty of every railroad corporation in this State to furnish to each of its employes of every grade a printed or written copy of its rules and regulations relative to their **Penalty for violating rule of company.** respective duties, and any conductor, engineer, servant, or other employe of any such railroad corporation, who shall knowingly violate any of the printed or written rules or regulations of such company, shall be subject to a fine of not less than twenty-five dollars nor more than one hundred dollars, or to an imprisonment in the county jail not more than three months, or both such fine and imprisonment, in the discretion of the court.

Bell and whistle on locomotive, where used and penalty for neglect to use. SEC. 13. A bell of at least thirty pounds weight and a steam whistle shall be placed on each locomotive engine, and said whistle shall be twice sharply sounded at least forty rods before the crossing is reached; and after the sounding of the whistle the bell shall be rung continuously until the crossing is passed, under a penalty of one hundred dollars for every neglect: *Pro-* **Proviso.** *vided,* That at street crossings within the limits of incorporated cities or villages, the sounding of the whistle may be omitted unless required by the common council or board of trustees of any such city or village; and the company shall also be liable for all damages which shall be sustained by any person by reason of such **Sign-boards at street crossings.** neglect. Every railroad corporation shall, and they are hereby required to cause boards to be placed, well supported by posts or otherwise, and maintained at each public road or street, where the same is crossed by the railroad and on the same level. The boards

shall be elevated so as not to obstruct the travel and to be easily
seen by travelers; and on each side of said board shall be painted,
in letters of not less than twelve inches in height, the words " railroad crossing;" but such boards need not be put up in cities or
villages unless required by the proper officers thereof. This provision shall not apply to boards already erected.

SEC. 15. Every railroad company formed under this act, or *Fences, cattle-guards, etc.*
any former act, and every corporation owning or operating any such
railroad shall erect and maintain fences on the sides of their respective roads of the height and strength of a division fence required by
law, with fences and cattle-guards at all highway and street crossings, sufficient to prevent cattle or other animals from getting on
such railroad; also gates or bars convenient for farm crossings.
Until such fences and cattle-guards, or ditches, shall be duly made, *Liability previous to fencing, etc.*
such company or corporation owning or operating such road shall
be liable for all damages done to cattle or other animals thereon,
which may result from the neglect of such company or corporation maintaining or operating such road to construct and maintain such fences, cattle-guards, or ditches, as aforesaid; and after
such fences, cattle-guards, or ditches shall be duly made and maintained, such company or corporation shall not be liable for any
such damages, unless negligently or willfully done. And every
corporation owning or operating any such railroad shall, within six
months from the time any section or portion of such road is fin-
ished and put in general use by running regular trains thereon,
and in case of roads now in use within six months from the time
this act shall take effect, shall erect and maintain such fences or
obstructions as aforesaid. Any violation of the provisions of this *Penalty for violation of provisions of section.*
section by any railroad company or corporation owning or operat-
ing such railway, shall be punished by a penalty of two hundred
dollars per week for each and every week that they shall fail to
comply with the provisions of this section: *Provided,* That if *Proviso excepting roads north of the mouth of Saginaw river.*
such fences or obstructions are not built as aforesaid, along such
portions of any such line of road as is or may be situate north of
a line extending due west from the mouth of the Saginaw river,
the corporation owning or operating such line of road shall not be
liable to said penalty of two hundred dollars per week, but shall be
liable to all the other provisions of this section; and if any person *Penalty for having animals within fences and cattle-guards, or making openings in fences, etc.*
shall ride, lead, or drive, or intentionally permit any horse or other
animal upon such road and within such fences and cattle-guards
or ditches, other than farm crossings, or shall injure or destroy, or
make openings or passages through or over such fences, cattle-
guards, or ditches, or neglect to close any gates or bars immediately after passing through the same, without the consent of such
company or corporation, he shall, for every such offense, be liable
to a fine not exceeding one hundred dollars, and shall also pay all
damages which shall be sustained thereby to the party aggrieved.

Approved April 22, 1875.

[No. 99.]

AN ACT relative to proceedings in criminal cases in circuit courts.

Duty of judge when person shall plead guilty

SECTION 1. *The People of the State of Michigan enact,* That whenever any person shall plead guilty to an information filed against him in any circuit court, it shall be the duty of the judge of such court, before pronouncing judgment or sentence upon such plea, to become satisfied, after such investigation as he may deem necessary for that purpose, respecting the nature of the case, and the circumstances of such plea, that said plea was made freely, with full knowledge of the nature of the accusation, and without undue influence. And whenever said judge shall have reason to doubt the truth of such plea of guilty, it shall be his duty to vacate the same, direct a plea of not guilty to be entered, and order a trial of the issue thus formed.

Approved April 22, 1875.

[No. 100.]

AN ACT to amend section seven thousand five hundred and eighty of chapter two hundred and forty-five of the compiled laws of eighteen hundred and seventy-one, relative to embezzlement by officers of corporations, and others.

Section amended

SECTION 1. *The People of the State of Michigan enact,* That section seven thousand five hundred and eighty of chapter two hundred and forty-five of the compiled laws of eighteen hundred and seventy-one, relative to embezzlement by officers of corporations, and others, be and the same is hereby amended so as to read as follows:

Embezzlement deemed a larceny.

(7580.) SEC. 29. If any officer, agent, clerk, or servant of any incorporated company, or of any city, township, incorporated town, or village, school district, or other public or municipal corporation, or if any clerk, agent, or servant of any private persons, or of a copartnership, except apprentices and other persons under the age of sixteen years, shall embezzle or fraudulently dispose of or convert to his own use, or shall take or secrete with intent to embezzle and convert to his own use, without consent of his employer or master, any money or other property of another, which shall have come to his possession, or shall be under his charge by virtue of such office or employment, he shall be deemed by so doing, to have committed the crime of larceny.

Approved April 22, 1875.

[No. 101.]

AN ACT relating to the formation of co-operative associations by mechanics, laboring men, and others, being a bill to amend section six (6), of chapter ninety (90), of the compiled laws.

Section amended

SECTION 1. *The People of the State of Michigan enact,* That section six (6), of chapter ninety (90), of the compiled laws of

eighteen hundred and seventy-one, be amended so as to read as
follows:

SEC. 6. Stockholders and directors shall be severally and jointly liable for all debts for labor performed for said corporation; and for all goods, wares, and merchandise sold and delivered to any such association, each of the stockholders or directors thereof shall be held liable to the amount of his capital stock therein, and no more; but no execution shall issue against such director or stockholder individually, until a judgment be first obtained for such goods, wares, and merchandise against said association, and execution thereon be returned unsatisfied, in whole or in part. *Individual liability.*

Approved April 22, 1875.

[No. 102.]

AN ACT making an appropriation for a copper roof for the new
State Capitol.

SECTION 1. *The People of the State of Michigan enact,* That the sum of ten thousand dollars, or so much thereof as may be necessary in the judgment of the board of the State building commissioners, is hereby appropriated out of the State building fund in the State treasury, to be used by the said board for the purpose of defraying the expense of putting upon the roof of the new State capitol a covering of copper: *Provided,* That the copper to be used for the purpose aforesaid, shall be produced within the State of Michigan: *Provided further,* That pure sheet copper be furnished to the State at a cost not exceeding twenty-five and one-half cents per pound. *Appropriation. Proviso. Further proviso.*

SEC. 2. The Auditor General and State Treasurer are hereby directed to transfer on the first day of January, eighteen hundred and seventy-seven, the above mentioned sum of ten thousand dollars from the general fund to the credit of the State building fund. *Transfer of sum from General to State building fund.*

Approved April 22, 1875.

[No. 103.]

AN ACT to amend section twenty-eight of an act entitled "An act
to revise and consolidate the several acts relative to the support
and maintenance of poor persons," approved April five, eighteen
hundred and sixty-nine, being section one thousand eight hundred and forty-three of the compiled laws of eighteen hundred
and seventy-one.

SECTION 1. *The People of the State of Michigan enact,* That section twenty-eight of "An act to revise and consolidate the several acts relating to the support and maintenance of poor persons," approved April five, eighteen hundred and sixty-nine, being section one thousand eight hundred and forty-three of the compiled laws of eighteen hundred and seventy-one, be and the same is hereby amended so as to read as follows: *Section amended.*

Superintendents of poor shall make annual report to Secretary of State.

(1843.) SEC. 28. It shall be the duty of the superintendents of the poor of each county, on the fifteenth day of October in each year, to report to the Secretary of State, in such form as such Secretary shall direct, the condition of such poor-house during the preceding year; which report shall contain a statement of the number

What report shall contain.

of paupers, insane, idiots, blind, mutes, and the average number of each class maintained during the preceding year; also, the cost of supporting such persons in the poor-house, the salary of the keeper thereof, the amount paid for medical attendance, the estimated amount earned by paupers, and their nationality, the amount paid for the transportation of paupers, the amount paid to supervisors for services, the amount paid to superintendents of the poor, the number of persons who have received temporary relief outside of the poor-house during the year, and the amount paid for such relief, the value of county farms, including buildings, the value of all personal property belonging or attached to such poor-house and farm, and the income received from the county farm. Such report shall also contain a statement of the general condition of the farm-house and other buildings, the manner in which paupers are treated, how they are fed, clothed, and in what manner such persons are cared for; how the insane and idiots are kept, and what are their accommodation and treatment; how the pauper children are educated; what the facilities are for bathing, heating, and ventilation, and to include all other information necessary to give a complete account of the condition of such poor-house.

Approved April 22, 1875.

[No. 104.]

AN ACT to repeal section four thousand two hundred and fourteen of the compiled laws of eighteen hundred and seventy-one, relative to alienation by deed.

Section repealed.

SECTION 1. The People of the State of Michigan enact, That section four thousand two hundred and fourteen of the compiled laws of eighteen hundred and seventy-one, relative to alienation by deed, be and the same is hereby repealed.

Acknowledgment of married women to deed, how taken.

SEC. 2. Hereafter the acknowledgment of any married woman to a deed of conveyance or other instrument affecting real property, may be taken in the same manner as if she were sole.

Approved April 22, 1875.

[No. 105.]

AN ACT to amend section five thousand two hundred and twenty-five of the compiled laws of eighteen hundred and seventy-one, relative to appeals from probate courts.

Section amended.

SECTION 1. The People of the State of Michigan enact, That section five thousand two hundred and twenty-five of the com-

piled laws of eighteen hundred and seventy-one, be and the same
is hereby amended so as to read as follows:

(5225.) SEC. 34. After an appeal is claimed and notice thereof *Proceedings stayed by appeal.*
given at the probate office, all further proceedings in pursuance of
the sentence, order, decree, or denial appealed from shall cease
until the appeal shall be determined: *Provided*, That when an *Proviso—appointment of special administrators, etc.*
appeal is taken from a decree, admitting or denying probate of a
will, the probate court may appoint one or more special administrators to take charge of and protect the estate, with such powers,
not exceeding those of a general administrator, as the said probate
court may deem necessary, and by order may confer in the particular case; and no appeal shall be allowed from the appointment
of such special administrator or administrators.

SEC. 2. This act shall take immediate effect.

Approved April 23, 1875.

[No. 106.]

AN ACT to amend section one of an act entitled "An act to extend
certain rights and privileges to persons who are tax-payers, but
not qualified voters in school districts," approved February eight,
eighteen hundred and fifty-five, being compiler's section three
thousand seven hundred and five of the compiled laws of eighteen
hundred and seventy-one.

SECTION 1. *The People of the State of Michigan enact*, That *Section amended.*
section one of an act entitled "An act to extend certain rights and
privileges to persons who are tax-payers, but not qualified voters in
school districts," approved February eight, eighteen hundred and
fifty-five, being compiler's section three thousand seven hundred
and five of the compiled laws of eighteen hundred and seventy-one,
be amended so as to read as follows:

SECTION 1. Every person of the age of twenty-one years, who *Certain persons entitled to vote and hold office.*
has property liable to assessment for school taxes in any school
district, and has been a resident therein three months preceding
any district meeting, shall be a qualified voter in said meeting.
And all persons who are entitled by the laws of this State to vote
at township and county elections, and who have resided in said
district three months as aforesaid, shall be entitled to vote on all
questions arising in said district when the raising of money by tax
is not in question, and all such persons shall be eligible to office in
such school district.

Approved April 23, 1875.

[No. 107.]

AN ACT to require supervisors, directors and overseers to make certain annual reports to the county superintendents of the poor.

Annual reports to superintendents of poor.

SECTION 1. *The People of the State of Michigan enact,* That it shall be the duty of any director or overseer of the poor authorized by law to furnish relief to poor persons, and of the supervisors of each township and ward in this State, annually hereafter, on or before the first day of October, to make and transmit to the county superintendent of the poor of the county in which such

What to contain.

township or ward is situated, a full statement or report of the number of poor persons who have been relieved by them during the year, with the amount paid for their relief, the amount paid for transportation and for medical attendance for such persons, and such other facts as shall show fully the whole sum expended by said supervisors, directors, or overseers of the poor for such purpose,

Secretary of State to furnish blanks.

including his charges for services; and such report shall be made in such form as the Secretary of State may prescribe, and said Secretary of State shall prepare, and annually transmit blanks for that purpose; and such report shall be made by the supervisors of townships that make their poor a township charge, as well as from all other supervisors authorized by law to furnish relief to poor persons.

Penalty for refusal to make report.

SEC. 2. Any supervisor, director, or overseer of the poor who shall refuse to make such report shall be guilty of a misdemeanor, and on conviction thereof may be punished as prescribed by law for the commission of such offense.

Approved April 23, 1875.

[No. 108.]

AN ACT to provide for the compilation and distribution of the election laws to certain county, township, and city officers.

Compilation and publication of election laws with decisions of of Supreme Court thereon.

SECTION 1. *The People of the State of Michigan enact,* That the Secretary of State and Attorney General are hereby directed, previous to the first day of January, eighteen hundred and seventy-six, to compile and procure to be printed in pamphlet form, all the laws of this State now in force relative to elections, together with a brief digest of the decisions and rulings of the supreme court

Distribution.

thereon, and that the Secretary of State forward to each of the county clerks in this State a sufficient number of copies to furnish one to each election board of every city, ward, and organized township in this State, and it shall be the duty of each county clerk in the several counties to make the distribution at least one month previous to the next general election.

Approved April 23, 1875.

[No. 109.]

AN ACT to amend section five hundred and forty of the compiled laws of eighteen hundred and seventy-one, relative to county clerks.

SECTION 1. *The People of the State of Michigan enact,* That section five hundred and forty of the compiled laws of eighteen hundred and seventy-one, relative to county clerks, shall be and the same is hereby amended so as to read as follows:

(540.) SEC. 63. Each county clerk shall appoint one or more deputies, to be approved by the circuit judge, one of whom shall be designated in the appointment as the successor of such clerk in case of vacancy from any cause, and may revoke such appointment at his pleasure, which appointment and revocation shall be in writing, under his hand, and filed in the office of the county treasurer, and the deputy, or deputies, may perform the duties of such clerks.

Approved April 23, 1875.

Section amended

County clerk to appoint deputies.

May revoke appointment.

[No. 110.]

AN ACT to repeal section four thousand three hundred and eighty-nine, chapter one hundred and fifty-six, of the compiled laws of eighteen hundred and seventy-one, the same being " An act to provide for the administration and distribution of. estates of intestates."

SECTION 1. *The People of the State of Michigan enact,* That section four thousand three hundred and eighty-nine (4389), chapter one hundred and fifty-six (156) of the compiled laws of eighteen hundred and seventy-one (1871), the same being an act entitled " An act to provide for the administration and distribution of estates of intestates," be and the same is hereby repealed.

SEC. 2. This act shall take immediate effect.

Approved April 23, 1875.

Section repealed.

[No. 111.]

AN ACT to legalize the record of the Coit and Curtis partition plat of lands in the city of Grand Rapids, in the county of Kent.

Whereas, The record of the original plat of township (7) seven north, part of range (11) eleven and (12) twelve west and marked A ; and of the original plat of part of sections (19) nineteen and (30) thirty in township (7) seven north, of range (11) eleven west, and marked B, as surveyed by E. C. Martin in January, eighteen hundred and fifty-four, for the division of property between Daniel W. Coit and Benjamin Curtis, of the city, county, and State of New York, as the same were recorded in the office of the register of deeds of Kent county, Michigan, was destroyed by the fire which destroyed a

Preamble.

19

large portion of the records of the county of Kent in said register's office, in January, eighteen hundred and sixty;

And whereas, The said original plats were again recorded in
liber number two of plats of Kent county, on pages twenty-two
and twenty-three, in said register's office, April fourteenth, eighteen
hundred and seventy;

And whereas, The record of said plats so made is the only record
of the same now in existence;

And whereas, The premises and all portions thereof contained
in said plat are necessarily described in all conveyances and papers
pertaining thereto, by the descriptions thereof laid down in said
record, and according to the same; therefore be it enacted as
follows:

Record of original plats declared public. SECTION 1. *The People of the State of Michigan enact,* That
said record of said original plats, known as "Coit and Curtis parti-
tion plat," as the same appears on said pages twenty-two and
twenty-three of liber two of plats of said Kent county in said
register's office, is hereby declared to be and established as a public record, and in all the courts in this State, and in all suits and
proceedings therein, and before all officers of this State having
jurisdiction in such suits and proceedings, and shall be and are
prima facie evidence of the matters thereof, and of all things
therein stated, and shall have the same virtue and effect as, by
present provisions of law, the records of the office of register of
deeds do possess.

SEC. 2. This act shall take immediate effect.

Approved April 23, 1875.

[No. 112.]

AN ACT to amend act number forty-three of the laws of eighteen
hundred and sixty-nine, being an act entitled " An act to provide for the draining of swamps, marshes, and other low lands,"
approved March twenty-two, eighteen hundred and sixty-nine,
the same being section one thousand seven hundred and fifty-
three of the compiled laws of eighteen hundred and seventy-one.

Section amended SECTION 1. *The People of the State of Michigan enact,* That
section nine of act number forty-three of the session laws of
eighteen hundred and sixty-nine, being an act entitled " An act to
provide for the draining of swamps, marshes, and other low lands,"
approved March twenty-two, eighteen hundred and sixty-nine, the
same being section one thousand seven hundred and fifty-three of
the compiled laws of eighteen hundred and seventy-one, be amended
so as to read as follows:

Notice for meeting to let contracts for construction of drain. (1753.) SEC. 9. Said commissioner shall give at least fifteen
days' public notice in some newspaper published and circulating
near such drain or drains of the time or times when, and the
place or places where he will meet parties to contract for the excavation and construction of such drain or drains; such place or

places to be convenient of access by the people resident near, and interested in the proposed drain or drains; and at least three such notices shall also be posted in the most public places of travel and resort in each township, and as near as may be along the line of such proposed drain, at least ten days next preceding such meeting. Said commissioner shall also name in, or in connection with such published and posted notices, a convenient place near such drain or drains, and at a time not less than three days nor more than five days prior to the day fixed in said notices, for letting the construction of such drain or drains; at which time and place he will exhibit surveys of the proposed drain or drains, and descriptions of the several parcels of land by him deemed to be benefited thereby; and the amount and description, by divisions and subdivisions, of the proposed drain or drains by him apportioned to the owner of each description of land to construct, and to each township to construct, on account of drains benefiting highways, if [any] such benefit there be, and hear reasons, if any are offered, why such apportionments should be reviewed and corrected. And said commissioner shall also give at least six days' notice in writing, to each and every resident owner or occupant of any of the lands assessed for the incidental expenses, damages, and expense of construction of drains, as mentioned in section eight of this act of such meeting for review and correction of apportionment. And if at this time two-thirds of the persons whose lands are to be taxed for such drain or drains enter a protest against said drain, and pay the costs and expenses up to this time, all proceedings for the construction of said drain or drains shall be suspended for one year. Between such day of hearing and review and the appointed day of letting, the commissioner shall, if need be, revise his apportionment of such drain or drains. At the time and place for letting named in said notices, the owner of each such parcel of land, or his or her agent or attorney, may appear and make and execute to said commissioner a contract or contracts, with good and sufficient surety for the faithful performance of the excavation and construction within the time limited by said commissioner, in such contract or contracts, of so much of such drain or drains as said commissioner has adjudged or set off to such land. When any part of such drain or drains is offered to be let, and the owner of the land to which it is assigned, or his or her agent or attorney, shall not at once, and without unnecessary delay, enter into contract as aforesaid, to excavate and construct the same, as provided in this section, it shall be the duty of said commissioner to let the same to the lowest responsible bidder or bidders therefor, who shall execute and file a contract or contracts, with good and sufficient surety as aforesaid, with said commissioner, for the faithful performance of the excavation and construction of the same, according to said contract or contracts; and the cost of such excavation and construction and its portion of the incidental expenses and damages shall be levied and assessed upon the land to which such part or parts of said drain or drains have been assigned as aforesaid. If at the time of the letting of said drain or drains, accord-

Letting of contracts may be postponed. ing to said notice, no suitable land owners or bidders for the construction of the same or any part thereof, appear to take or bid and contract, with good and sufficient surety, for the construction and completion of the whole of the same, or for any other cause by said drain commissioner deemed important and sufficient, he may postpone and adjourn such letting, in whole or in part, and from time to time, to such other time or times, to be by him at the time of such adjournment publicly announced, as shall to him seem meet and proper, but not in all more than sixty days from and after the time of the letting at first advertised and noticed as aforesaid. At the hearing and the letting provided for in this section, the commissioner of highways of any township named in said notice, and to which has been assigned any construction of drain or tax for incidental expenses or damages on account of benefit by such drain or drains to highways, may appear and act in behalf of such township. Any taxes so assessed on State lands shall be at once reported by said commissioner to the Commissioner of the State Land Office, who shall enter on the books of his office, against each description of such State land, the amount of drain taxes assessed thereon, and no patent shall issue for such lands until said drain taxes are paid or otherwise provided for. Any person resident in said county failing or neglecting to file in writing, with said commissioner, on or before such appointed day of hearing and review, his claim for damages, or objections to such assessments, shall be held to have waived his claim for damages and his right to appeal: *Provided*, That in case, from sickness or other good and sufficient cause, the commissioner is not able to be present in person on the day of exhibiting surveys and apportionment, and reviewing and correcting the same, or on the day of letting the contracts, it shall be competent for him to cause an adjournment of the same through his duly authorized agent or attorney.

Commissioner of highways may act for township at meeting for hearing and letting.

Taxes on State lands reported to Commissioner of State Land Office.

When persons held to have waived right of appeal, etc.

Proviso—in case of sickness, etc., commissioner may postpone the letting of contracts, etc.

SEC. 2. This act shall take immediate effect.

Approved April 23, 1875.

[No. 113.]

AN ACT to provide for paying the outstanding interest-bearing warrants of the University of Michigan.

Appropriation. SECTION 1. *The People of the State of Michigan enact*, That there shall be and is hereby appropriated out of any funds in the treasury of the State of Michigan not otherwise appropriated, the sum of thirteen thousand dollars, or so much thereof as may be necessary, for the purpose of paying the outstanding interest-bearing warrants on the treasury of the University of Michigan. Said money shall be drawn from the treasury on the presentation of said warrants accompanied by the proper voucher of the treasurer of the board of regents of the University of Michigan to the Auditor General, and on his warrant to the State Treasurer.

How drawn.

SEC. 2. This act shall take immediate effect.

Approved April 23, 1875.

[No. 114.]

AN ACT making an appropriation for a stone cornice and balustrade for the new State capitol.

SECTION 1. *The People of the State of Michigan enact,* That Appropriation. the sum of sixty-five thousand dollars, or so much thereof as may be necessary in the judgment of the board of State building commissioners, is hereby appropriated out of the State building fund in the State treasury, to be applied under the direction of said board, for the purpose of putting a stone cornice and balustrade upon the new State capitol, instead of the galvanized iron cornice and balustrade provided for by the plans and specifications for said building.

SEC. 2. The amount appropriated by section one of this act shall Apportionment be apportioned by the Auditor General and incorporated in the State of same. tax, one-half of the same in the tax for the year eighteen hundred and seventy-six, and one-half in the tax for the year eighteen hundred seventy-seven, and when collected shall be placed by him to the credit of the State building fund : *Provided,* That should any Proviso. portion of the amount hereby appropriated be required by the board of State building commissioners for the purpose hereinbefore mentioned. [before] the same shall be collected and placed to the credit of the State building fund, the Auditor General is hereby authorized to advance the amount so required from the general fund, the amount so advanced to be returned to the general fund when the same shall have been collected.

SEC. 3. This act shall take immediate effect.

Approved April 23, 1875.

[No. 115.]

AN ACT to amend section nine of chapter sixty-four, being section two thousand one hundred and one, of the compiled laws of eighteen hundred and seventy-one, relative to the penalty for maiming pigeons near nestings.

SECTION 1. *The People of the State of Michigan enact,* That Section amended section nine of chapter sixty-four, being section two thousand one hundred * and one, of the compiled laws of eighteen hundred and seventy-one, relative to the penalty for maiming pigeons near nestings, be amended so as to read as follows:

(2101.) SEC. 9. No person or persons shall use any gun or guns, or Penalty for fire-arms, to maim, kill. or destroy any wild pigeon or pigeons, at maiming pigeons or within five miles of the place or places where they are gathered etc. near nestings, in bodies for the purpose of brooding their young, known as pigeon nestings; and no person or persons shall use any gun or guns, or fire-arms, to maim, kill, or destroy any wild pigeon or pigeons within their roostings anywhere within the limits of this State;

---

* The words "one hundred" are in the law as approved by the Governor, but not in the bill as passed by the Legislature.

and no person or persons shall, with trap, snare, or net, or in any other manner, take or attempt to take, or kill or destroy, or attempt to kill or destroy, any wild pigeon [or pigeons], at or within two miles of such nesting place at any time from the beginning of the nesting until after the last hatching of such nesting, anywhere within the limits of this State; and every person offending against the provisions of this section, or any part thereof, shall be subject to a penalty of fifty dollars, with costs of suit.

Approved April 23, 1875.

[No. 116.]

AN ACT making an appropriation for the support of the State Agricultural College, to pay the expenses of the State Board of Agriculture, and for repairs and other improvements at the State Agricultural College.

Appropriations for support of college and expenses of board.

SECTION 1. *The People of the State of Michigan enact,* That there shall be and is hereby appropriated out of the State treasury the sum of eight thousand six hundred and thirty-eight dollars, for the year one thousand eight hundred and seventy-five, and the sum of seven thousand six hundred and thirty-eight dollars, for the year one thousand eight hundred and seventy-six, for the use and support of the State Agricultural College, and to pay the expenses of the State Board of Agriculture. Of the above appropriation, one thousand dollars shall be invested in books for the library.

Appropriations for buildings, improvements, museum, etc.

SEC. 2. There shall be and is hereby appropriated out of the State treasury, the sum of five thousand five hundred and fifty dollars for buildings and repairs; one thousand six hundred and seventy dollars for stock, experiments, and farm improvements; seven hundred and seventy dollars for horticultural department; one thousand and seventy-five dollars for chemical department; six hundred and forty-six dollars for museum; two thousand seven hundred dollars for steam works, repairs, and furniture at boarding hall; three hundred dollars for safe in secretary's office; and eight hundred dollars for Cedar River bridge; said amounts embraced in this section, aggregating thirteen thousand five hundred and eleven dollars, to be paid, one-half of the same in the year one thousand eight hundred and seventy-five, and one-half in the year one thousand eight hundred and seventy-six; which said moneys

How drawn and expended.

provided for in this act, or so much thereof as may be necessary, shall be expended under the direction and control of the State board of agriculture for the purposes aforesaid, and shall be drawn from the treasury on the presentation of the proper certificates of said board to the Auditor General, and on his warrant to the State Treasurer.

SEC. 3. This act shall take immediate effect.

Approved April 23, 1875.

[No. 117.]

AN ACT making appropriation for the board of fish commissioners for the year eighteen hundred and seventy-five and the year eighteen hundred and seventy-six.

SECTION 1. *The People of the State of Michigan enact,* That the sum of seven thousand dollars is hereby appropriated for the year eighteen hundred and seventy-five, commencing July first, eighteen hundred and seventy-five and ending June thirty, eighteen hundred and seventy-six, and a like sum for the year eighteen hundred and seventy-six, commencing July first, eighteen hundred and seventy-six and ending June thirty, eighteen hundred and seventy-seven, for the necessary expense incurred by the board of fish commissioners, which the State Treasurer shall pay to said board on the warrant of the Auditor General, from time to time, as their vouchers for such expenses shall be exhibited and approved.

Sec. 2. This act shall take immediate effect.

Approved April 23, 1875.

Appropriation.
How paid.

[No. 118.]

AN ACT to authorize the judge of probate of Washtenaw county to appoint a probate register, and prescribing his duties and compensation.

SECTION 1. *The People of the State of Michigan enact,* That the judge of probate of the county of Washtenaw shall have power to appoint a probate register for said county, who shall receive such annual salary as the board of supervisors shall prescribe, not exceeding six hundred dollars, payable monthly from the county treasury. Such probate register shall have power to receive petitions, fix the time of hearing, administer oaths, and do all other acts required by the judge of probate, except judicial acts.

Sec. 2. This act shall take immediate effect.

Approved April 23, 1875.

Probate register, his salary and powers.

[No. 119.]

AN ACT to amend sections three and five, of chapter one hundred and twenty-five, of the compiled laws of eighteen hundred and seventy-one, being compiler's sections three thousand two hundred and seventy-three and three thousand two hundred and seventy-five, relative to skating rinks and parks.

SECTION 1. *The People of the State of Michigan enact,* That sections three and five of chapter one hundred and twenty-five of the compiled laws of eighteen hundred and seventy-one, being compiler's numbers three thousand two hundred and seventy-three and three thousand two hundred and seventy-five, be amended so as to read as follows:

Sections amended.

Articles of
association,
where filed, etc.

(3273.) SEC. 3. The articles of such association shall be filed in the office of the Secretary of State, and a duplicate of said articles shall be filed and recorded at length, in the office of the county clerk in the county where such association is located; and

Body politic and corporate.

thereupon all persons who shall have subscribed to the same, and all persons who shall from time to time become stockholders in such company, shall be a body politic and corporate, by the name specified in such articles, and by such name they and their successors shall have succession, and in their corporate name be capable in law of owning, holding, or purchasing and disposing of, in any manner, any real or personal property or estate whatsoever, not exceeding in value fifty thousand dollars, and they shall be capable and liable of suing and being sued in all courts of law and equity in this State, and may have a common seal, and may alter and change the same at pleasure.

Amount of capital shall be fixed by stockholders, etc.

(3275.) SEC. 5. The amount of the capital stock of every such corporation shall be fixed and limited by the stockholders in their articles of association, and shall in no case be more than fifty thousand dollars, and shall be divided into shares of twenty-five dollars each; and such certificates of stock shall be signed by the president and secretary of the company, and sealed with its corporate seal.

Approved April 23, 1875.

[No. 120.]

AN ACT to amend sections nine and ten of chapter two hundred and forty-seven, being sections seven thousand six hundred and sixty-one, and seven thousand six hundred and sixty-two of the compiled laws of eighteen hundred and seventy-one, relative to offenses against public justice.

Sections amended.

SECTION 1. *The People of the State of Michigan enact.* That sections nine and ten of chapter two hundred and forty-seven, being sections seven thousand six hundred and sixty-one, and seven thousand six hundred and sixty-two of the compiled laws of eighteen hundred and seventy-one, relative to offenses against public justice, be so amended as to read as follows:

Penalty for corrupting or attempting to corrupt jurors and others.

(7661.) SEC. 9. Every person who shall corrupt or attempt to corrupt any circuit court commissioner, auditor, juror, arbitrator, or referee, by giving, offering, or promising any gift or gratuity whatever, with intent to bias the opinion or influence the decision of such circuit court commissioner, auditor, juror, arbitrator, or referee in relation to any matter which may be pending in the court, or before an inquest, or for the decision of which such arbitrator or referee shall have been appointed or chosen, shall be punished by imprisonment in the State prison for not more than five years, or by fine not exceeding one thousand dollars, and imprisonment in the county jail not more than one year.

Accepting bribes by jurors and others.

(7662.) SEC. 10. If any person summoned as a juror or chosen or appointed as an arbitrator, or if any circuit court commissioner or auditor shall corruptly take anything to give his verdict, award, or report, or shall corruptly receive any gift or gratuity whatever, from a party to any suit, cause, or proceeding, for the trial or decision of which such juror shall have been summoned, or for the hearing or determination of which such circuit court commissioner, auditor, arbitrator, or referee shall have been chosen or appointed, he shall be punished by imprisonment in the State prison not more than five years, or by fine not exceeding one thousand dollars, and imprisonment in the county jail not more than one year.

Approved April 24, 1875.

[No. 121.]

AN ACT to amend section forty-one (41) of chapter two hundred and sixteen (216) of the compiled laws of eighteen hundred and seventy-one, being compiler's section six thousand eight hundred and eighty-one, for the collection of penalties, forfeitures, and fines of forfeited recognizances.

SECTION 1. *The People of the State of Michigan enact,* That Section amended section forty-one of chapter two hundred and sixteen of the compiled laws of eighteen hundred and seventy-one, being compiler's section six thousand eight hundred and eighty-one, be so amended as to read as follows:

SEC. 41. Every county treasurer shall keep an accurate account of Disposition of moneys collected for fines, etc. all moneys paid to him on account of fines, penalties, and forfeitures, separate and distinct from all other accounts, and shall credit the same to the library fund, and he shall account therefor to the board of supervisors at each annual meeting of such board. And When county treasurer to bid off real estate. in case of the sale of any real estate upon an execution upon judgment rendered for the breach of any recognizance in any criminal case, it shall be the duty of the county treasurer, in case there are no bidders to the full amount of any such judgment or the value of the property advertised, to bid off the same ; and in case the same How to dispose of same. shall not be redeemed within the time allowed by law for the redemption thereof, to sell the same for the best price he can obtain therefor, and place the money received in the general fund.

SEC. 2. This act shall take immediate effect.

Approved April 24, 1875.

[No. 122.]

AN ACT to amend section seventeen of chapter fifty-five, being section two thousand of the compiled laws of eighteen hundred and seventy-one, relative to gaming or betting at cards or dice.

SECTION 1. *The People of the State of Michigan enact,* That Section amended section seventeen of chapter fifty-five, being section two thousand of the compiled laws of eighteen hundred and seventy-one, rela-

tive to gaming or betting at cards or dice, be and is amended so as
to read as follows:

Penalty for playing at billiards, cards, etc., for purpose of gaming.

(2000.) SEC. 17. If any person shall play at billiards, cards, dice,
nine-pins, or any other unlawful game, at any such table or alley
kept or used as mentioned in the two last preceding sections, or
shall play at cards or dice, for the purpose of gaming or betting
upon such cards or dice, at any place within this State, he shall
forfeit a sum not less than two dollars nor more than one hundred
dollars for each offense.

Approved April 24, 1875.

[No. 123.]

AN ACT to amend section twelve of chapter seventy-nine of the
revised satutes of eighteen hundred and forty-six, being section
four thousand six hundred and thirty-nine of the compiled laws of eighteen hundred and seventy-one, relative to sales
on execution.

Section amended

SECTION 1. *The People of the State of Michigan enact*, That
section twelve of chapter seventy-nine of the revised statutes of
eighteen hundred and forty-six, being section four thousand six
hundred and thirty-nine of the compiled laws of eighteen hundred and seventy-one, be amended so as to read as follows:

Certificate of sale or record thereof evidence of regularity of sale, etc.

SEC. 12. Such certificate shall be recorded in a book to be kept
for that purpose by the register of deeds, in whose office the same
are filed, and the original certificate, or the record thereof, or a
transcript of such record, duly certified by the register of deeds,
shall be *prima facie* evidence of the facts therein set forth, and of
the regularity of the sale and all proceedings in the cause anterior
thereto.

Approved April 24, 1875.

[No. 124.]

AN ACT to amend section four (compiler's section three thousand
eight hundred and twenty) of chapter one hundred and forty-
four of the compiled laws of eighteen hundred and seventy-one,
relative to university and primary school lands.

Section amended

SECTION 1. *The People of the State of Michigan enact*, That
section four (compiler's section three thousand eight hundred and
twenty) of the compiled laws of eighteen hundred and seventy-one
be amended so as to read as follows:

Certificate of purchase, what further to set forth.

(3820.) SEC. 4. The said certificate shall further set forth that in
case of the non-payment of the interest due by the first day of
March, or within sixty days thereafter, in each and every year, or
of the taxes for the preceding year, within the time aforesaid, by
the purchaser or purchasers, or by any person claiming under him
or them, then the said certificate shall, from the time of such fail-

ure, be utterly void and of no effect, and the said commissioner may take possession thereof and re-sell the same as hereinafter provided.

Approved April 24, 1875.

[No. 125.]

AN ACT to amend section one of chapter two hundred and sixty-six, being section eight thousand and eighteen of the compiled laws of eighteen hundred and seventy-one, relative to county jails, and the regulation thereof.

SECTION 1. *The People of the State of Michigan enact,* That section one of chapter two hundred and sixty-six, being section eight thousand and eighteen of the compiled laws of eighteen hundred and seventy-one, relative to county jails and the regulation thereof, be so amended as to read as follows: *(Section amended)*

(8018.) SECTION 1. The common jails in the several counties in the charge of the respective sheriffs shall be used as prisons: *(Jails to be used as prisons.)*

First, For the detention of persons charged with offenses and duly committed for trial;

Second, For the confinement of persons committed pursuant to a sentence upon conviction of an offense, and of all other persons duly committed for any cause authorized by law; and the provisions of this section shall extend to persons detained or committed by the authority of the courts of the United States, as well as the courts and magistrates of this State.

Approved April 24, 1875.

[No. 126.]

AN ACT to amend chapter forty of the compiled laws of eighteen hundred and seventy-one, entitled "Brokers and exchange dealers," being "An act relative to brokers and exchange dealers," approved February eleven, eighteen hundred and fifty-nine, by adding two new sections thereto, to stand as sections six and seven of said act.

SECTION 1. *The People of the State of Michigan enact,* That chapter forty of the compiled laws of eighteen hundred and seventy-one be and the same is hereby amended by the addition of the following sections, to stand as sections six and seven of said act: *(Chapter amended.)*

SEC. 6. No person or firm doing business under this act shall advertise or put up signs, or use any device or contrivance whatever, tending to convey the impression that the place of business of such person or firm is an organized bank; but in all such cases such person or firm, if they advertise at all, must use their individual or firm name, and state in such advertisement the names of every member of such co-partnership or firm; in case any person or persons shall violate any of the provisions of this section, they shall be deemed guilty of a misdemeanor, and shall each, upon conviction, be punished by a fine of not more than two hundred *(Advertisements, signs, etc.)* *(Penalty for violating provisions of this section.)*

Proviso.
dollars and costs, or by imprisonment of not more than six months in the county jail: *Provided*, The words " bank," " banking office," or "exchange office," as a sign over the door or on the building, or used on notes, checks, or drafts, in connection with the individual or firm name, shall not be deemed a violation of the foregoing.

Penalties, how collected.
SEC. 7. The State Treasurer shall, when his attention is called to violations of any of the provisions of this act, refer the same to the Attorney General, who shall proceed, when warranted by the evidence, to collect the penalties as herein set forth; and all suits or proceedings for the violation of any of the provisions of this act shall be first commenced in the circuit court of the county in which the business office of said person or firm is located.

Approved April 24, 1875.

[No. 127.]

AN ACT to provide for the payment to railroad companies of certain moneys collected by the agent of the State from trespassers upon the lands of said companies.

State Auditors to audit and allow moneys upon proof of collection from trespasses, etc.
SECTION 1. *The People of the State of Michigan enact*, That the Board of State Auditors be and are hereby directed to audit and allow to the several railroad companies of this State the amount of moneys collected, or which may hereafter be collected and paid into the State treasury (less the expenses incident to such collection) from trespassers upon lands which were granted by the United States to this State for railroad purposes, by act of June three, eighteen hundred and fifty-six, the title to which has become vested in such companies, upon proof satisfactory to said board, that such moneys were collected from trespasses actually committed upon the lands of such railroad companies, and that the title to such lands has actually become vested in the companies making application for such moneys.

How moneys to be drawn.
SEC. 2. When such amount shall have been ascertained and audited, said board shall certify to the Auditor General the amount thereof, who shall draw his warrant upon the State Treasurer, payable to the order of the proper officer of such railroad companies, and the State Treasurer shall pay the same out of the fund to which said moneys may have been credited: *Provided*, That such companies shall not be indebted to the State for specific State tax or otherwise.

Approved April 27, 1875.

[No. 128.]

AN ACT for the establishment of a homœopathic medical department of the University of Michigan.

Board of regents authorized to establish.
SECTION 1. *The People of the State of Michigan enact*, The Board of Regents of the University of Michigan are hereby au-

thorized to establish a homœopathic medical college, as a branch
or department of said university, which shall be located at the city
of Ann Arbor.

SEC. 2. The Treasurer of the State of Michigan shall, on the Appropriation.
first day of January, eighteen hundred and seventy-six, pay out of
the general fund, to the order of the treasurer of the Board of Regents, the sum of six thousand dollars, and the same amount on
the first day of January of each year thereafter, which moneys
shall be used by said Regents exclusively for the benefit of said
department.

Approved April 27, 1875.

[No. 129.]

AN ACT to amend section five of chapter eighty, being section
two thousand six hundred and twenty-nine of the compiled
laws of eighteen hundred and seventy-one, relative to the formation of telegraph companies.

SECTION 1. *The People of the State of Michigan enact,* That Section amended
section five of chapter eighty, being section two thousand six hundred and twenty-nine of the compiled laws of eighteen hundred
and seventy-one, relative to the formation of telegraph companies,
be and the same is hereby amended so as to read as follows:

(2629.) SEC. 5. Such association is authorized to enter upon, Where author-
and construct, and maintain lines of telegraph through, along, and ized to construct
upon any of the public roads and highways, or across or under any
of the waters within the limits of this State, by the erection of
the necessary fixtures, including posts, piers, or abutments for sus-
taining the cords or wires of such lines: *Provided,* That the same Proviso.
shall not be so constructed as to incommode the public use of said
roads or highways, or injuriously interrupt the navigation of said
waters; nor shall this act be so construed as to authorize the construction of any bridge across any of the waters of this State:
And provided further, That this act shall not be construed to au- Further proviso
thorize any such association to injure, deface, tear, cut down, or etc., planted
destroy any tree or shrub planted along the margin of any high- along highways
way in this State, or purposely left there for shade or ornament. or destroyed.
Said association, instead of running or placing their wires on posts, Wires may be
may, if they choose, run or place the same under ground, with a ground.
suitable or proper covering for the protection of the same; and
any part of this act, or any law made or to be made, providing for
the appraisement of damages to any person injured by the construction or maintenance of such line or lines, shall be construed
to include damages occasioned by the construction of said lines
under ground, as provided by this act.

SEC. 2. This act shall take immediate effect.

Approved April 27, 1875.

[No. 130.]

AN ACT to provide for the payment of the State militia for services rendered, under a call of the Governor, in Marquette and
Montcalm counties, in eighteen hundred and seventy-four.

Appropriaticn.   SECTION 1. *The People of the State of Michigan enact*, That
there be and hereby is appropriated out of any money in the treasury to the credit of the military fund, a sum sufficient for the payment of the officers, non-commissioned officers, musicians, and
privates of the State militia for services rendered under the orders
of the Governor, in the year eighteen hundred and seventy-four,
in the counties of Marquette and Montcalm.

Amount of com-   SEC. 2. Such officers, non-commissioned officers, musicians, and
pensation, and
payment of the   privates, shall receive such compensation as they would be entitled
same.   to under section forty-eight of chapter eighteen of the compiled
laws of eighteen hundred and seventy-one. Such compensation
shall be audited and allowed by the Auditor General upon the
certificate of the commanding officer of the militia rendering such
. service, approved by the Quartermaster-General. The Auditor
General upon auditing and allowing the accounts for such service
shall draw his warrant upon the State Treasurer therefor, who is
hereby authorized and directed to pay the same.

By payment   SEC. 3. Upon the payment of such sum or sums of money the
State acquires
certain rights   State of Michigan shall thereby acquire and hold all the rights
which it may
enforce against   (if any), which the parties to whom such payment is made, had
counties.   or might have had against the counties of Marquette or Montcalm, and shall have the right to take any and all lawful means to
enforce said claim against said counties for the services of said
officers, non-commissioned officers, musicians, and privates, for the
service mentioned in sections one and two of this act.

SEC. 4. This act shall take immediate effect.

Approved April 27, 1875.

———

[No. 131.]

AN ACT to provide for the safe keeping of public moneys.

"Public mon-   SECTION 1. *The People of the State of Michigan enact*, That
eys" defined.   all moneys which shall come into the hands of any officer of the
State, or of any officer of any county, or of any township, school
district, highway district, city or village, or of any other municipal
or public corporation within this State, pursuant to any provision
of law authorizing such officer to receive the same, shall be denominated public moneys within the meaning of this act.

Public moneys to   SEC. 2. It shall be the duty of every officer charged with the
be kept separate
from all other   receiving, keeping, or disbursing of public moneys to keep the
funds.   same separate and apart from his own money, and he shall not com-
mingle the same with his own money, nor with the money of any
other person, firm, or corporation.

How used.   SEC. 3. No such officer shall, under any pretext, use, nor allow
to be used, any such moneys for any purpose other than in accord-

ance with the provisions of law; nor shall he use the same for his
own private use, nor loan the same to any person, firm, or corporation without legal authority so to do.

SEC. 4. In all cases where public moneys are authorized to be deposited in any bank, or to be loaned to any individual, firm, or corporation, for interest, the interest accruing upon such public moneys shall belong to and constitute a general fund of the State, county, or other public or municipal corporation, as the case may be. *Interest on public moneys to constitute a general fund.*

SEC. 5. In no case shall any such officer, directly or indirectly, receive any pecuniary or valuable consideration as an inducement for the deposit of any public moneys with any particular bank, person, firm, or corporation. *Officers not to receive consideration for deposit of money with particular bank, etc.*

SEC. 6. The provisions of this act shall apply to all deputies of such officer or officers, and to all clerks, agents, and servants of such officer or officers. *Provisions of this act to apply to deputies, etc.*

SEC. 7. Any person guilty of a violation of any of the provisions of this act shall, on conviction thereof, be punished by a fine not exceeding one thousand dollars, or imprisonment in the county jail not exceeding six months, or both such fine and imprisonment in the discretion of the court: *Provided,* That nothing in this act contained shall prevent a prosecution under the general statute for embezzlement in cases where the facts warrant a prosecution under such general statute. *Penalty for violating provisions of this act. Proviso.*

SEC. 8. Any officer who shall willfully or corruptly draw or issue any warrant, order, or certificate for the payment of money in ex-cess of the amount authorized by law, or for a purpose not author-ized by law, shall be deemed guilty of a misdemeanor, and may be punished as provided in the preceding section. *Penalty for illegal payment of money.*

Approved April 27, 1875.

[No. 132.]

AN ACT to organize the county of Ogemaw, and to locate the county seat thereof.

SECTION 1. *The People of the State of Michigan enact,* That the county of Ogemaw, consisting of the territory embraced in the present county of Ogemaw as attached to Iosco for judicial pur-poses, be and the same hereby is organized into a separate county by the name of Ogemaw, and the inhabitants thereof shall be en-titled to all the privileges, powers, and immunities to which by law the inhabitants of other organized counties in this State are entitled. *Ogemaw county organized.*

SEC. 2. The county seat of said county of Ogemaw shall be es-tablished at West Branch Station, on the Jackson, Lansing and Saginaw Railroad: *Provided,* That a block of land shall be do-nated by owners of land at said place for permanent use of the county for county buildings: *And provided further,* That a building suitable for county purposes shall be erected at said point, *County seat. Proviso. Proviso.*

by said owners of land, to be used gratuitously for three years by said county of Ogemaw.

First election of county officers. Sec. 3. At the township meetings of the several townships in said county, on the first Monday of April next, there shall be an election of all the county officers to which said county is entitled, whose terms of office shall expire on the thirty-first day of December, eighteen hundred and seventy-six, and when their successors shall have been elected and qualified. Said election shall be conducted in the same way, by the same officers, and the returns thereof be made in the same manner, as near as may be, as is now required by law in the elections of county officers of this State.

Canvass of votes. Sec. 4. The county canvass of the votes cast for county officers shall be held on the second Tuesday succeeding the election, at the hotel of Weideman and Wright, at West Branch; and said canvass shall be conducted in the same manner, and by the same officers, as the requirements of law now provide in organized counties, as nearly as may be, by the appointment, by the board of canvassers, of one of their own number to act as secretary to said board of canvassers.

Judicial circuit. Sec. 5. Said county shall be in the eighteenth judicial circuit, and shall be entitled to at least one court in each year.

Board of canvassers at first election. Sec. 6. The following named persons, viz.: C. L. Nauman, Z. H. Wright, and M. P. Moor, are hereby authorized to and shall act as the board of county canvassers at said election to be held as herein authorized.

Sec. 7. This act shall take immediate effect.

Approved April 27, 1875.

––––

[No. 133.]

AN ACT to amend sections six and eighteen of act number eighty-three of the session laws of eighteen hundred and fifty-one, the same being sections two thousand six hundred and fifty and two thousand six hundred and sixty-one of the compiled laws of eighteen hundred and seventy-one, being "An act to authorize the incorporation of bridge companies."

Sections amended. Section 1. *The People of the State of Michigan enact,* That sections six and eighteen of act number eighty-three of the session laws of eighteen hundred and fifty-one, the same being sections two thousand six hundred and fifty, and two thousand six hundred and sixty-one of the compiled laws of eighteen hundred and seventy-one, being "An act to authorize the incorporation of bridge companies," be and the same is hereby amended [so] as to read as follows:

Supervisors to fix rates of toll for passing bridge. (2650.) Sec. 6. The board of supervisors of the county in which any such bridge is to be constructed shall, at the time of granting such assent to the construction of such bridge, or previous to any toll being taken for passing the same, fix and establish the rates of toll to be paid for passing such bridge, and if such bridge shall be situated in more than one county, the board of supervisors of each county shall, at the request of the directors of such company, and at the expense of the company, meet on some day to be agreed upon, at the site of such bridge, and shall act as one board, and may appoint their own clerk and chairman, in determining such rates of toll; and in either case such rates of toll shall be certified by such board, and a printed copy of such certificate shall be at all times kept up in some conspicuous place on such bridge; and if such company or any gate-keeper in their employ, shall at any time take or receive any greater sum for toll than shall have been so fixed, such company shall be liable to a penalty of ten dollars for every such offense, with costs of suit, to be recovered by the person aggrieved; and after said tolls shall have been so fixed, they shall remain without any change for the term of ten years, when they may be again fixed by the supervisors as aforesaid for a further term of not less than five years, with the same effect; but such toll shall not at any time be reduced so that the sum shall amount to less than fifteen per cent a year upon the cost of the bridge after deducting expenses of maintaining and operating the same. If any such bridge should at any time be out of repair, so as to render the passage of teams and vehicles dangerous or inconvenient, no tolls shall be taken or received for passing over the same, till the same shall be repaired and put in good order. For every violation of this provision, the company shall forfeit and pay to the party aggrieved a penalty of ten dollars for such violation, together with all damages that may be sustained by reason of such bridge not being kept in repair.

[margin: Certified copy of rates to be posted on bridges, and penalty for taking illegal toll.]

[margin: Tolls to remain fixed ten years.]

[margin: Minimum of toll.]

[margin: Not to be taken if bridge is out of repair.]

[margin: Penalty for so doing.]

(2661.) SEC. 18. Any person who shall forcibly or fraudulently pass the toll-gate or toll-house of any bridge erected pursuant to the provisions of this act, not having paid the legal toll, or any person who shall aid another, or shall permit anything under his or her control, to be used by any person to aid such person in forcibly or fraudulently passing such toll-gate or toll-house, not having paid the legal toll, shall for each offense be liable to a fine not exceeding ten dollars to be sued for and recovered by such company in an action of debt or assumpsit: *Provided*, Nothing in this section shall be so construed as to authorize the taking of tolls on any such bridge contrary to the provisions of section six of this [the] act to which this is an amendment.

[margin: Penalty for not paying toll.]

[margin: Proviso.]

Approved April 27, 1875.

[No. 134.]

AN ACT to amend section thirty-two of chapter one hundred and eighty-eight of the compiled laws of eighteen hundred and seventy-one, relative to the taking of depositions.

SECTION 1. *The People of the State of Michigan enact*, That section thirty-two of chapter one hundred and eighty-eight, being section five thousand eight hundred and seventy-eight of the com-

[margin: Section amended]

piled laws of eighteen hundred and seventy-one, be and the same
is hereby amended so as to read as follows:

Commission may be awarded after interlocutory judgment, etc. (5878.) SEC. 32. On application of the plaintiff in any action,
after entry of defendant's default in such action for want of plea,
or after obtaining interlocutory judgment in such action, a commission may be awarded in the like cases and in the same manner
as if an issue of fact had been joined; and the depositions thereon
may be used in evidence in any proceedings to assess the plaintiff's
damages, with the like effect as herein provided in case of a trial;
and in case such default or such interlocutory judgment shall be
set aside and a trial be had, then such deposition may be read in
evidence upon such trial.

Approved April 27, 1875.

AN ACT to amend section seventy-eight of chapter twenty-one of
the compiled laws of eighteen hundred and seventy-one, being
compiler's section one thousand and forty-four, relative to the
sale of lands for delinquent taxes and the conveyance and redemption thereof.

Section amended SECTION 1. *The People of the State of Michigan enact,* That
section seventy-eight of chapter twenty-one of the compiled laws
of eighteen hundred and seventy-one, being compiler's section ten
hundred and forty-four, relative to the sale of lands for delinquent
taxes, and the conveyance and redemption thereof, be amended so
as to read as follows:

Auditor General shall make statement of land specifying amount of taxes due, etc. SEC. 78. On the first day of July of each year, the Auditor General shall make out a separate statement of all such lands as the
taxes shall remain due upon in each of the respective counties,
specifying the amount of taxes due on each parcel, the interest
thereon computed, as is provided in section seventy of this act, to
the first day of October thereafter, together with the cost of advertising, postage, expense of sale, and returns thereon, and conveyances, which shall be charged at one dollar upon each parcel of
land contained in such list; and accompanying or preceding such
statements the Auditor General shall cause to be published as hereinafter shall be provided, a list of all lands not sold by the several
county treasurers at the time prescribed by law, on account of
error in advertising or other cause, not affecting the legality of the
assessment or requiring a rejection of the taxes thereon, and on
which the taxes, interest and charges still remain unpaid, or not
otherwise discharged, for the taxes of any year prior to that for
which the statements above mentioned are made up; also, a notice
of sale by the county treasurer of state tax lands, and deeds given
by the Auditor General to purchasers at such sales, or their assigns,
shall take effect according to the year's tax for which the deed
may be given, the deed for the latest year's tax taking precedence,
and the interest on such re-advertised lists shall be computed

at the same rate as in other cases, up to the time of the ensuing annual tax sales.

Sec. 2. This act shall take immediate effect.

Approved April 27, 1875.

———

[No. 136.]

AN ACT to amend sections four thousand four hundred and one and four thousand four hundred and six, being sections one and .six of chapter one hundred and fifty-seven of the compiled laws of eighteen hundred and seventy-one, relative to the inventory and collection of the effects of deceased persons.

SECTION 1. *The People of the State of Michigan enact,* That ·sections four thousand four hundred and one and four thousand four hundred and six, being sections one and six of chapter one hundred and fifty-seven of the compiled laws of eighteen hundred and seventy-one, relative to the inventory and collection of the effects of deceased persons, be amended so as to read as follows: *Section amended*

(4401.) SECTION 1. Every executor or administrator shall, within thirty days after his appointment, make and return into the probate court a true inventory of the real estate, and of all the goods, chattels, rights and credits of the deceased which shall have come to his possession or knowledge, excepting only that an executor who shall be a residuary legatee, and shall have given bond to pay all the debts and legacies, as provided by law, shall not be required to return an inventory. *Making and return of inventory.*

(4406.) SEC. 6. The personal estate of the deceased, including all growing crops of grain, grass, and fruit not disposed of by special mention in the will of the deceased, and by said will plainly directed to pass with the real estate, which shall come into the hands of the executor or administrator, shall be first chargeable with the payment of the debts and expenses; and if the goods, chattels, rights, and credits in the hands of the executor or administrator shall not be sufficient to pay the debts of the deceased and the expenses of administration, the whole of his real estate, except the widow's dower, or so much thereof as may be necessary, may be sold for that purpose by the executor or administrator, after obtaining license therefor in the manner provided by law. *Personal estate first chargeable with payment of debts, and if not sufficient real estate to be sold.*

Approved April 27, 1875.

———

[No. 137.]

AN ACT to authorize the supervisor and commissioner of highways to purchase the interest of any plank road or toll road company for that portion of such road situated in their respective townships.

SECTION 1. *The People of the State of Michigan enact,* That the supervisor and commissioner of highways of the several townships in this State may negotiate with, and purchase the interest *Authority to purchase plank or toll roads.*

of any plank road or toll road company for that portion of their road situated in their respective townships, and draw their orders on the township treasurer for the same, in the same manner as orders are drawn for the support of roads and bridges: *Provided,*

Proviso. That no contract shall be binding, and no orders shall be drawn or money paid until the qualified voters of the township in which such road is located shall at some township meeting, or at some special meeting called for that purpose, so order. In case the qual-

Money raised by tax. ified voters shall order the money paid or orders issued, it shall be lawful for the supervisor of such township to levy the amount upon the taxable property of the township in the same manner as township taxes are levied.

On purchase road to become public highway. SEC. 2. When such purchase is made and completed said road shall become a public highway and be subject to all the provisions of law the same as other township roads.

Approved April 27, 1875.

[No. 138.]

AN ACT to amend sections one, two, and three, of chapter sixty-five, of an act entitled " An act to authorize dissection in certain cases, for the advancement of science," being sections twenty-one hundred and ten, twenty-one hundred and eleven, and twenty-one hundred and twelve, of the compiled laws of eighteen hundred and seventy-one.

Sections amended. SECTION 1. *The People of the State of Michigan enact,* That sections one, two, and three, of chapter sixty-five, of an act entitled " An act to authorize dissection in certain cases, for the advancement of science," the same being sections twenty-one hundred and ten, twenty-one hundred and eleven, and twenty-one hundred and twelve, of the compiled laws of eighteen hundred and seventy-one, be amended so as to read as follows:

Provision for furnishing University and Detroit Medical College with certain subjects for dissection. (2110.) SECTION 1. *The People of the State of Michigan enact,* That any member of either of the following boards of officers, to wit: the board of health of any city, village, or township in the State, the mayor or common council of any city, and any officer or board having direction, management, charge, or control in whole or in part of any prison, house of correction, or jail in the State, shall deliver the dead bodies of such persons as may be required to be buried at the public expense, when so requested by letter or otherwise, to any member of the medical faculty of the University of Michigan, or Detroit Medical College, when there shall be deposited with such board or officer sufficient money to defray the expense and trouble of packing and preparing the same for shipment, which shall not exceed the sum of fifteen dollars for each subject, shall deliver, within forty-eight hours after the death of such person, to the express company or freight company at the nearest railroad station, properly placed in a plain coffin as for burial, and inclosed in a strong box, plainly directed to the person and place as directed by the consignee making such deposit, to be shipped to such consignee to be used by him for the advancement of anatomical science, preference being always given to the faculty *Preference to medical faculty of University.* of the medical department of the University of Michigan for their use in the instruction of medical students, and after they have made their orders and deposit of money as aforesaid; and such *Officer making shipment to take receipt, etc.* board or officers shall take the usual shipping receipt for such packages, and shall notify the consignee of such shipment by letter, mailed on the day the packages are delivered to the express company or freight company at the railroad depot. In no case shall the *Cost of bodies to students.* faculty or the regents be entitled to require or receive from any medical student or students for any such body furnished therein, any sum of money in excess of the actual cost of procuring the same. Any of said officers who shall neglect to comply with any *Penalty for neglect to furnish body.* such request after being tendered or receiving the money so required to be deposited, shall be subject to a penalty of one hundred dollars for each body that he neglects to ship as aforesaid, one-half of which shall go to the party making the demand and deposit as aforesaid: *Provided,* That the University and each and every med- *Proviso.* ical institution shall not receive into their possession such bodies as are procured in this State other than those provided for by the provisions of this act, and every individual or party violating this provision shall be deemed guilty of a misdemeanor.

(2111.) SEC. 2. No such dead body shall be shipped as aforesaid. *When bodies not to be surrendered.* if within twenty-four hours after death or before such body shall be shipped any relatives or friends of the deceased who will bury the body at his own expense, or shall require to have the body buried; or if such deceased person was a stranger or traveler, the dead body shall in all such cases be buried.

(2112.) SEC. 3. No such dead body shall be sold or delivered to *Bodies must not be sold to be taken out of State, etc.* any person to be taken out of the State, nor shall any such dead body be shipped to any person or place out of the State, or be used within the State for any purpose except for the prosecution of anatomical science. Any person violating any of the provisions *Penalty for violating provisions of act.* of this act shall be punished by a fine of not less than fifty, or more than one hundred dollars, or by imprisonment in the county jail not less than one or more than three months, or by both such fine and imprisonment, at the discretion of the court.

SEC. 2. This act shall take immediate effect.

Approved April 27, 1875.

[No. 139.]

AN ACT to provide for paying the expenses of the supervision of such products of soil and mine, works of art, and manufactured articles as the citizens of Michigan may send to the Centennial Exhibition to be held in Philadelphia, State of Pennsylvania, during the year eighteen hundred and seventy-six.

SECTION 1. *The People of the State of Michigan enact,* That *Board of managers and their duties.* the Governor is hereby authorized to appoint a board of managers,

consisting of four persons, representing the agricultural, pomological, mining, and manufacturing interests of this State, whose
duty it shall be to supervise the forwarding to the place of the
Centennial Exhibition in Philadelphia, to be held between the
months of April and October, in the year eighteen hundred and
seventy-six, all such articles, whether of art, or the products of
soil and mine, or of manufacturers, that any of the citizens of
Michigan may desire to send to such exhibition, and shall provide
storage for them at the place of shipment, and make such arrange-
ments for freight and conveyance as shall best serve the interest

Proviso.

of the owners of said articles: *Provided,* That the cost of transportation shall be paid by the owners of said articles.

Expense.

SEC. 2. The members of said board of managers shall be entitled,
for their services, to a sum sufficient to defray their actual and
necessary disbursements in the discharge of their duties, and for
personal expenses while actually engaged in the performance of
the duties of said board.

Appropriation.

SEC. 3. That the sum of seven thousand five hundred dollars, or
so much thereof as may be necessary, be and the same is hereby
appropriated from the general fund for the purpose of paying the
expenses of said board, as above described.

How drawn
from treasury.

SEC. 4. Upon satisfactory vouchers of expenses incurred, exhibited by the managers to the Governor, it shall be the duty of
the Auditor General, upon the requisition of the Governor, to draw
his warrant on the State Treasurer for such sum or sums not exceeding the amount hereby appropriated, as may be necessary, to
be used for the purpose hereinbefore prescribed.

Governor to be
chairman of
board, etc.

SEC. 5. The Governor shall be chairman of the board of managers, and shall have power to remove any of said managers, for
good and sufficient cause, and to appoint others in their place.

SEC. 6. This act shall take immediate effect.

Approved April 28, 1875.

[No. 140.]

AN ACT to amend sections one thousand seven hundred and seventy-eight, one thousand seven hundred and seventy-nine, one
thousand seven hundred and eighty, one thousand seven hundred
and eighty-one, one thousand seven hundred and eighty-two,
one thousand seven hundred and eighty-three, one thousand
seven hundred and eighty-five, one thousand seven hundred and
eighty-six, one thousand seven hundred and eighty-seven, one
thousand seven hundred and eighty-eight, one thousand seven
hundred and eighty-nine, one thousand seven hundred and ninety, one thousand seven hundred and ninety-four, one thousand
seven hundred and ninety-five, and one thousand eight hundred
of the compiled laws of eighteen hundred and seventy-one, being
sections one, two, three, four, five, six, eight, nine, ten, eleven,
twelve, thirteen, seventeen, eighteen, and twenty-three of chap-

ter forty-eight, relative to establishing water-courses, and locating ditches or drains.

SECTION 1. *The People of the State of Michigan enact,* That sections one thousand seven hundred and seventy eight, one thousand seven hundred and seventy-nine, one thousand seven hundred and eighty, one thousand seven hundred and eighty-one, one thousand seven hundred and eighty-two, one thousand seven hundred and eighty-three, one thousand seven hundred and eighty-five, one thousand seven hundred and eighty-six, one thousand seven hundred and eighty-seven, one thousand seven hundred and eighty-eight, one thousand seven hundred and eighty-nine, one thousand seven hundred and ninety, one thousand seven hundred and ninety-four, one thousand seven hundred and ninety-five, and one thousand eight hundred of the compiled laws of eighteen hundred and seventy-one, being sections one, two, three, four, five, six, eight, nine, ten, eleven, twelve, thirteen, seventeen, eighteen, and twenty-three of chapter forty-eight, relative to establishing water-courses, and locating ditches or drains, be amended so as to read as follows: *(Sections amended.)*

(1778.) SECTION 1. There shall be elected at the annual township meeting in the year eighteen hundred and seventy-six, and biennially thereafter, in each of the organized townships of the State, one township drain commissioner, who shall hold his office for the term of two years, or until his successor is elected and qualified. *(Election of township drain commissioner.)* Before entering upon the duties of his office, and within ten days after his election or appointment, each drain commissioner shall subscribe and take the oath required by the constitution of this State, before the township clerk of his township, or some other officer authorized to administer oaths, and file the same with the township clerk. *(Oath of office.)* The drain commissioner of each township shall have power under this act to establish and open water-courses, to locate and construct ditches or drains in his township, and to alter, enlarge, extend, and clear those already located, laid out, and established under any law of this State: *(Powers.)* *Provided,* That whenever a vacancy shall occur in the office provided for in this act, the same shall be filled by the township board of such township; and it shall be their duty to fill such vacancy within thirty days after such vacancy shall occur: *(Proviso—vacancy in office.)* *Provided further,* That the drain commissioner [commissioners] elected in the several townships at the last annual township meeting held therein, shall continue to hold his office until his successor is elected and qualified. *(Further proviso—time present commissioners to continue in office.)*

(1779.) SEC. 2. When any person or persons shall make application to the drain commissioner of any township to establish and open a water-course, or to locate and construct a ditch or drain, and shall give such commissioner good and sufficient security, in writing, to pay all costs and expense of whatever kind pertaining to the action of said commissioner about such application in case such application shall not be granted, the drain commissioner shall immediately proceed to examine, personally, the line of the proposed water-course, ditch, or drain, and if in his opinion it is proper *(Action of commissioner on application to open a water-course, construct ditch or drain.)*

or necessary, and for the good of the public health that the application should be granted, he shall try to obtain a conveyance to the county of the lands necessary therefor, and a release of the damages from every person through whose land such water-course, ditch, drain, or drains are to pass; if he obtains such conveyance and release, he shall proceed to make such examination, by surveys or otherwise, as may be necessary to determine the route, width, length, and dimensions thereof, and the lands to be benefited thereby; he shall establish such water-course, or locate such ditch or drain. He shall proceed to apportion the opening or construction of the same, and the apportioning of the cost and expenses in the same manner as provided in sections six and nine of this act; but

If not sufficient cause for application, commissioner to so determine. if on such examination it shall appear that there was not sufficient cause for making such. application, the commissioner shall so determine. **Applicants liable for costs and expenses.** Said applicants shall be liable to said commissioner for the amount of all costs and expenses incurred by him in making such determination; and if the said applicants shall neglect to pay the same on demand thereof being made, said commissioner may recover the same in an action of assumpsit, or on the case, before any justice of said county. **Appointment of time and place for examination upon application and notice thereof.** If the drain commissioner does not decide adversely to the application, or cannot obtain a conveyance and a release of the damages, as aforesaid, from every person through whose land such ditch, drain, or water-course is to pass, he shall at once appoint a time and place for an examination upon such application, and shall give notice thereof, in writing, to all persons interested in such ditch, drain, or water-course who reside in such township, which notice shall be served upon each of such persons at least five days before the day appointed as aforesaid, by delivering a copy to such persons, or by leaving a copy at the residence of such persons, with some person of suitable age; and when **When notice to be published, etc.** any person or persons interested in such water-course, ditch, or drain, reside out of such township, or any minor, minors, insane, or incompetent person or persons are interested in such water-course, ditch, or drain, the drain commissioner shall publish such notice once a week for three successive weeks, next before such day appointed, in a newspaper of general circulation in the county in which such township lies, or when there is no newspaper in said county, in a newspaper of general circulation in an adjoining county, unless he shall serve written notice as above provided, on all such persons living out of such townships, and on the guardian or guardians whose wards are interested in such water-course, ditch, or drain; in which case the person upon whom such notice is made shall have one day's notice for every twenty miles travel (excluding Sundays) from their residence to such place appointed, in addition to the five days' notice provided above; and a copy of such notice, with an affidavit of service, or publication, or both, shall be taken as evidence that the same has been regularly served **Commissioner may administer oath.** or published. Said drain commissioner may administer any oath provided for in this chapter.

(1780.) SEC. 3. Said drain commissioner, at the time and place appointed, as provided in the preceding section, shall hear all persons asking to be heard, and he may re-examine such water course Powers and duties of commissioner relative to application. or line of proposed ditch, or drain, and for that purpose shall have power to enter upon any lands in his township, and may also adjourn such examination and hearing from time to time as to him shall seem proper, by publicly announcing the time and place to which such adjournment is made.

(1781.) Sec. 4. If said drain commissioner, after hearing, or if the Applicants liable for costs, etc., when drain decided not necessary. jury or commissioners hereinafter provided for, shall decide that it is not necessary to establish and open such water course, or to locate and construct such ditch or drain through the lands mentioned in the application, then said applicant or applicants shall be liable to said drain commissioner for all just and legal costs, charges, and expenses, and if not paid on demand, may be collected in the same manner as provided in section two of this act: *Provided*, That the Proviso—hearing of application before examination of line. said drain commissioner may, after receiving the application and bond, or security mentioned in section two of this act, proceed to appoint a time and place for the hearing of such application, and to give the required notice before making a personal examination of the line mentioned therein.

(1782.) Sec. 5. After such examination and hearing, if said Proceedings in case drain is found necessary. drain commissioner does not decide adversely to the application, he shall cause a survey and measurement of the line of the proposed water-course, ditch, or drain, to be made, if he deems it necessary ; he shall establish the commencement and terminus of said water-course, ditch or drain ; he shall determine the route, width, length, and average depth thereof; and if all the owners of the Proceedings when owners of land do not release claim for compensation. land through which said water-course, ditch, or drain is to run shall not convey the necessary land to the county and release all claim for damages or compensation, the drain commissioners shall immediately make a list of twenty-four disinterested freeholders residing in the vicinity of such land, and in the same county, from which said commissioner shall strike off the names of six, and the owners of such land six ; but if such owners do not appear at such examination and hearing, or appearing, refuse or neglect to act, then said drain commissioner shall strike off other six, and the remaining twelve shall be deemed elected ; and said commissioner Sheriff or constable to summon jurors. shall at once issue a *venire* signed by him, directed to the sheriff, or any constable of said county, commanding him to summon said jurors, naming them, to be and appear before him forthwith, or at such other time as he shall direct, not more than three days from the date of said *venire*, to serve as jurors to decide as to the necessity of establishing and opening the proposed water-course and taking the land therefor ; or as to the necessity of locating and constructing such ditch or drain and taking the land therefor (as the case may be), and to determine the amount of damage sustained by any person or persons owning or interested in any of the lands through which such water-course, ditch, or drain is to pass. If all the jurors shall not appear within one hour of the time of appearance named in said *venire*, said drain commissioner shall direct the sheriff or constable in attendance, if any, otherwise some other officer or disinterested person, to summon talesmen to

22

complete the panel. It is hereby made the duty of such sheriff, constable, or other officer or person to perform the duties required
Oath of jurors of him by this act. When the panel shall be full said drain commissioner shall administer unto the jury an oath well and truly to examine and determine the necessity of establishing and opening such water-course and the necessity of taking the land therefor, or the necessity of locating and constructing such ditch or drain, and the necessity of taking the land therefor, as the case may be, said
Jury to examine line of ditch, etc. jury shall thereupon proceed to examine the line of the proposed water-course, ditch, or drain described in the application. If the
Determination of jury when found necessary. jurors be of the opinion that it is necessary for the good of the public health, as well as a benefit to the land in the vicinity thereof, to take such land and to establish and open such water-course, or to locate and construct such ditch or drain, they shall so deter-
Evidence of location of water-course, etc. mine; such determination, when reduced to writing and signed by the jurors, shall be *prima facie* evidence of the establishment or location of such water-course, ditch, or drain, and shall be deemed a sufficient conveyance to vest the fee of the lands necessary for such water-course, ditch, or drain in the county in which it is situated, in trust to, and for the uses and purposes of drainage, and for no other use or purpose whatever, and such determination may be acknowledged before some officer authorized to take acknowledgments of deeds, and recorded in the office of the register of deeds in the
Assessment of damages. county where such lands lie; they shall proceed to assess the damages which any person or persons may sustain by reason thereof, and shall certify in writing their doings, and the amount of damages so assessed and payable to each individual, and deliver the certificate
Proceedings when jury cannot agree. to the drain commissioner. If said jury cannot agree, another jury may be chosen and sworn in like manner as the first, on the same or some other day, to be appointed by said commissioner, who shall act and make return as aforesaid, and successive jurors may be chosen, sworn, and act as aforesaid, until they shall agree, if the parties
Application to judge of probate for appointment of commissioners. interested desire it; or the said drain commissioner may then, or in the first instance, apply to the probate court of his county for the appointment of three commissioners to act in place of said jury, who shall take the same oath and perform the same duties
Proviso. prescribed above for said jury: *Provided*, That if said jury or commissioners shall certify in their return that it is not necessary to establish such water-course, or to locate and construct such ditch, or drain, on or near the line mentioned in the application, no successive jury or commissioners shall be chosen within one year thereafter; but if said jury or commissioners shall certify that a water-course, ditch, or drain is necessary under the application, on some other line, then the drain commissioner, upon renewing the bond or security as provided in the second section of this act, may proceed to establish the water-course, or locate the ditch or drain on the line proposed by the jury or commissioners; and another jury or commissioners may be called or appointed as hereinbefore provided.

(1783.) SEC. 6. If the jury or commissioners shall return that it is necessary to establish such water-course or locate such ditch or drain, and necessary to take the land therefor, and shall award the just damag s or compensation therefor. to be paid to the owners of said land, said drain commissioner shall, as soon thereafter as may be, proceed to apportion the opening of such water-course, or the construction of such ditch or drain, to each and every parcel of land to be drained or benefited thereby, in such proportion as he shall deem just and right; describing such parts so assigned to each parcel of land by division stakes, to be placed at the commencement of each part or portion, with the number of the same marked thereon on the side designated by the number; when such water-course, ditch or drain, will benefit the highway as well as the public health, said .drain commissioner shall assign the opening or construction thereof, of such part or parts as seem to him just, to the township to which such highway belongs or in which it is situated. If such highway is on the line between townships. then such part or parts, with the consent of the drain commissioner of the other township, or townships, may be assigned in equitable proportion between the townships. He shall make an official certificate of his doings showing the establishment of such water-course or location of such ditch or drain ; also the courses, distances, depth, width, and termination of the same, and further showing what portions of such water-course, ditch. or drain he has apportioned to be opened and maintained by each piece or tract of land to be drained or benefited thereby. as well as the portion assigned to the township, and the length and number of such portion, which certificate, together with all other papers in the case, shall be attached together and filed in the office of the clerk of the township in which such water-course ditch, or drain is to be opened, to be preserved as the records of such township for the benefit of those interested ; and such clerk shall make an entry, in a book kept for that purpose, of papers so filed, showing the kind of paper and date of entry, and showing in what part of such township such water-course is established, or ditch or drain located, and name thereof, which entry shall be *prima facie* evidence of the existence of such papers at the date of such entry. and of their having been duly filed at such date; and such award and apportionment of labor as aforesaid when duly filed as aforesaid, shall thenceforth be a lien upon each piece or tract of land so drained and benefited, and an obligation against the owners thereof: *Provided,* That in case of application for clearing, or straightening any natural water-course, it shall not be necessary to level and survey the same, but simply to divide the water-course into sections.

(1785.) SEC. 8. When such water-course is established, ditch or drain located. and apportionment for the opening or construction thereof made, and papers fi ed as provided in the foregoing section, by agreement of parties or by act of the commissioner, it shall be the duty of each owner of the land upon which such apportionment is made, to fully open such portion of such water-course, ditch or drain, as has been apportioned to his land on or before the twentieth day of October next after such papers are filed ; and in all cases parties shall have at least three months to complete such

Marginal notes:

When ditch. etc., found necessary, commissioner to apportion the same.

Official certificate of commissioner and where filed.

Entry to be made of same in a book for that purpose.

Award, etc., lien upon land.

Proviso.

When ditch, etc., shall be opened.

When commissioner to contract for construction. work. If any portion of such water-course, ditch or drain is not opened by the time provided, said drain commissioner shall, as soon as practicable, cause the same to be done, either by public letting to the lowest responsible bidder or private contract: *Provided,* That Proviso. the aggregate amount of said private contract shall not exceed the sum of twenty-five dollars, on such reasonable terms as he may be able to procure; and he shall give to the persons who shall have performed their contracts thereon, certificates showing the amount and value of the labor performed by such persons, on each contract respectively, with a description of the land against which such labor was performed.

Apportionment of costs, etc. (1786.) SEC. 9. Said drain commissioner shall apportion all the just fees, costs, and expenses (which may include prospective costs and expenses) of all the officers and persons engaged in any manner in establishing such water-course, or locating such ditch or drain, upon the lands drained or benefited thereby, as well as upon the township, in such proportion as shall to him seem just; he Apportionment of damage. shall also, in the same manner, apportion the damage or compensation awarded by the jury or commissioners of appraisal, to certain of the owners of the lands through which such water-course, ditch, or drain runs, except that the lands to the owner of which such damage or compensation is to be paid, shall not be liable to the apportionment of any part of such damage or compensation: Proviso. *Provided,* If such owner or owners are benefited by such water-course, ditch, or drain, then such benefits shall be taken into consideration by the jury or commissioners of appraisal, and by them deducted from the damage or compensation; and he shall apportion all the fees, costs, and the value of the labor of opening any portion of such water-course, ditch, or drain caused to be opened by him under the provisions of the foregoing section, to the land, as well as upon the township, to which the opening of such portion Statement showing apportionment and where filed. was apportioned; and he shall make a statement in writing, signed by him, showing his apportionment to each tract of land, of the fees, costs, and expenses of officers and other persons in establishing such water-course or locating such ditch or drain; also of the damage or compensation to be paid to owners of land as aforesaid, and of fees, costs, and value of labor of opening each and every portion of such water-course, ditch, or drain, caused to be opened by said drain commissioner as aforesaid, showing further the amount out of such apportionments to be paid to each and every person entitled thereto; and where compensation is to be paid to the owner of land through which such water-course, ditch, or drain is to run, and the name of such [owner] is known, then name him as the owner of such land, which statement shall be subscribed and sworn to by said drain commissioner, before the township clerk or some other officer authorized to administer oaths, and shall be filed in the office of the township clerk on or before the tenth day of November next, after such water-course is established, or ditch or Proviso. drain is located: *Provided,* That if three months shall not have elapsed from the time of the apportionment of the labor for opening such water-course, or for the construction of such ditch or drain, to the twentieth day of October next following, or the contract for performing the same is not let by the said tenth day of November, then such statement or any part thereof may be filed on or before the tenth day of November next thereafter.

(1787.) SEC. 10. If the owners of land upon which such apportionment is made, or agreed to be made, do not pay to the township treasurer the apportionment upon their lands respectively, and file a receipt therefor with the township clerk, on or before the fifteenth day of November next after the filing of such statement, the township clerk shall certify to the supervisor, on or before the twentieth day of November, all such apportionments which remain unpaid. The supervisor shall levy such apportionments upon the said lands upon which the apportionments are made, placing the tax in a column entitled "ditch tax." in the same manner that delinquent highway taxes are required by law to be levied; he shall at the same time, in the same manner as township taxes are required by law to be levied, levy all sums apportioned to the township, upon the entire taxable property of the township, placing the tax in the column entitled "ditch tax." The several amounts so levied shall be collected by the township treasurer, in the same manner as other taxes, and when collected shall be received into the township treasury, together with the money paid by the owners of the land as aforesaid; and shall be credited to the particular ditch fund to which it belongs, and shall be paid out only to the person or persons entitled to receive the same, on order of the township board. In case of failure to levy such taxes, or any part thereof, within the time and in the manner herein provided. it shall be lawful to levy each sum remaining unpaid, and collect the same next year, with the same force and effect as the same might or could have been the first year. *Apportionment not paid, to be assessed and collected same as certain other taxes.*

Disposition of same.

May be levied and collected second year.

(1788.) SEC. 11. The township treasurer shall retain in his hands the amount of the several ditch taxes as specified in his warrant. If any of the taxes authorized to be levied under the provisions of this act shall remain unpaid, and the township treasurer shall be unable to collect the same from the owner or occupant of the premises assessed, he shall make return at the same time and manner as lands are returned for State and county taxes. The land so returned shall be subject to sale and redemption the same as lands returned for other taxes. *Township treasurer to retain ditch taxes. Unpaid taxes returned same as State and county taxes.*

(1789.) SEC. 12. The drain commissioner shall have power, upon application therefor, to clear, open, or to straighten any natural water-course in his township; to locate a tile, or other underground drain, and construct the same; or partly tile, or underground, and partly open, as he may deem proper. He shall proceed in the same manner as required by this act to establish water-courses and locate ditches or drains: *Provided*, That the notice required by the second section of this act, shall state distinctly the kind of drain proposed to be located and constructed. *Commissioner may clear, etc., natural water-course.*

May locate tile drain, etc.

Proviso.

(1790.) SEC. 13. Water-courses may be established, or ditches or drains located along, within the l.mits of, or across any public road; and when any shall be so established, located, and opened *Ditches, etc., may be established across public roads.*

or constructed, it shall be the duty of the overseers of highways,
in their respective districts, to keep the same open and free from
Bridges over the same. all obstructions. When any such water-course, ditch, or drain
shall cross a public highway, the commissioner or commissioners
of highways of the proper townships, shall build and keep in repair a suitable bridge over the same, except in cases where a plank
road crosses such ditch or water-course, then it shall be the duty
of such plank road company to erect and maintain such bridge.
Farm crossings. It shall be lawful for the township board of any township in which
such water-course is established, ditch or drain located, to provide
for and maintain suitable farm crossings over such water-course,
Proviso. ditch or drain ; *Provided,* The owners of the land on either side
consent thereto.

Proceedings by justice under appeal. (1794.) SEC. 17. The said justice of the peace shall, on receiving such notice of, and reasons for, appeal, and the said agree-
ment and security duly approved, immediately appoint a time
and place for hearing such appeal, in the town or towns where the
act complained of occurred, and give notice thereof in writing to
the party appealing, and the drain commissioner or commissioners
appealed from; and on the day appointed, or on some day to
which the hearing shall be adjourned, he shall proceed to hear
and determine the appeal, and may reverse, in whole or in part
the doings of said drain commissioner or commissioners, or make
such order in the premises as may be right and lawful under this
act, and send a copy thereof to such township drain commissioner
or commissioners, and to the party appealing ; and said township
drain commissioner or commissioners shall execute the same, or
said justice of the peace may proceed to execute the same, and in the
same manner and with like effect as the township drain commissioner or commissioners might, or could do under this act, if no
appeal was made ; and in all cases wherein the township drain
commissioners are interested, the justice shall act : *Provided,* That
Proviso. whenever a township drain commissioner shall be elected and
qualified, who is not interested in such appeal, the said justice
may, in his discretion, certify the proceedings had by him on
such appeal to such disinterested township drain commissioner,
who shall proceed in the matter in all respects as if the same
had been originally commenced before him.
Compensation for services under this act. (1795.) SEC. 18. The said drain commissioners and justices of the
peace shall receive two dollars, and the same rate for parts of days,
for each day actually employed. Township clerks shall receive ten
cents for each paper filed in his office, and one dollar for making
the certificate mentioned in section ten of this act. Publishers of
newspapers shall receive for publishing legal notices and furnishing evidence of such publication not more than seventy cents per
folio for the first insertion, and thirty-five cents per folio for each
subsequent insertion. Judges of probate shall receive fifty cents
for the appointment of commissioners and certificate thereof.
Commissioners of appraisal shall receive one dollar and fifty cents
for each day, and seventy-five cents per each half day, and six
cents per mile for travel (in going only); jurors one dollar each

per day, and fifty cents per each half day, and six cents per mile
for travel (in going only); sheriffs and constables for serving *venire*
seventy-five cents, and ten cents per mile actually traveled in making service; laborers, such fees as shall seem to such commissioner
just, not to exceed one dollar and fifty cents per day. The township board of the township in which such water-course is established, ditch or drain located, shall draw orders in favor of each of
such officers and laborers for the amount to which they are entitled, as shown by the statement of the drain commissioner filed
with the township clerk. They shall likewise draw orders in favor
of each person entitled to damage or compensation on account of
such water-course, ditch, or drain running across his land; also,
in favor of each person who has performed labor under contract
from said drain commissioner, in opening a portion of such
water-course, or constructing such ditch or drain, as shown by said
statement, which order shall be drawn on the township treasurer
of the township in [which] such water-course, ditch. or drain lies,
and made payable by the first day of February next after the date
thereof; and if such water-course, ditch, or drain lies in more
than one township, then the township board of the township in
which the most of such water-course. ditch, or drain lies, shall
draw all the orders on the township treasurer of that township,
and the township treasurers of the other townships shall pay over
all the money in their hands on account of such water-course,
ditch, or drain, by the first day of February aforesaid, to the township treasurer on which such orders are drawn; and the township
treasurer or the township treasurers on which such orders are
drawn, shall in all cases pay such orders from the particular fund
upon which they are drawn. When such orders are presented to
such treasurers after such first day of February, and they have not
funds in their hands to pay them, they shall endorse the date of
such presentation, after which such orders shall draw interest till
paid. A separate fund shall be kept for the moneys collected for
each water-course, ditch, or drain, which fund shall be applied exclusively for the construction of such water-course, ditch, or drain.

(1800.) SEC. 23. The Secretary of State shall, on or before the
first day of June next, cause to be prepared suitable forms to be
used in the execution of this act, and shall publish a sufficient
number of copies of the act of which this is amendatory, with the
forms annexed, to furnish at least one copy to each township clerk,
and one copy to each drain commissioner in the State.

SEC. 2. This act shall take immediate effect.

Approved April 28, 1875.

Marginal notes: Township board to draw orders on treasurer for services and damage. — Relative to orders and collection of taxes when ditch is in more than one township. — Separate fund for ditches. — Secretary of State to prepare forms to be used in execution of this act, etc.

[No. 141.]

AN ACT to regulate the sale of wheat, and to prevent the sale or offering for sale of wheat not grown in Michigan as Michigan wheat, and to prevent the mixing of foreign wheat with the Michigan product.

Penalty for selling, etc., as Michigan wheat, wheat not raised in Michigan.

SECTION 1. *The People of the State of Michigan enact*, That if any person or persons shall knowingly sell or offer for sale, or cause to be sold or offered for sale, any wheat not raised in Michigan, falsely pretending or representing to the public or any purchaser, or in the market, by any brand, device, or representation, or by word or writing, that the same is a Michigan product, such person or persons shall be deemed guilty of a misdemeanor, and on conviction thereof shall be punished by a fine not exceeding one thousand dollars and not less than two hundred dollars, or by imprisonment in the county jail for a period not exceeding six months, or both fine and imprisonment, in the discretion of the court.

Penalty for selling, etc., mixed wheat as wholly Michigan wheat.

SEC. 2. If any person or persons shall knowingly mix or cause to be mixed any wheat not raised in Michigan with Michigan wheat with intent to sell or offer the mixture for sale under the representation that the same is wholly Michigan wheat, such person or persons shall be deemed guilty of a misdemeanor, and on conviction thereof shall be punished by fine not exceeding one thousand dollars and not less than two hundred dollars, or by imprisonment in the county jail for a period not exceeding six months, or both by fine and imprisonment, in the discretion of the court.

Person selling liable for damages.

SEC. 3. Any person or persons who shall sell to another any wheat as Michigan wheat or the product of this State, knowing the same to be in whole or in part the product of any other State or country, shall be liable to the person or persons to whom the same is so sold in an action on this statute for double the amount of damages which he shall have sustained by reason of any breach in the contract of sale.

Exception to foregoing provisions.

SEC. 4. The provisions of the foregoing section [sections] of this act shall not apply in cases where wheat is brought to market in this State by teams from adjoining localities in other States.

Approved April 28, 1875.

[No. 142.]

AN ACT to regulate the sale of tickets by railroad companies at special rates and on special conditions.

Authority to issue tickets at special rates, etc.

SECTION 1. *The People of the State of Michigan enact*, That any railroad corporation doing business in this State may make contracts for the conveyance of passengers upon designated trains, for a specific distance, at fixed times, at such reduced rates of fare as the parties may agree upon. Tickets may be issued for such passengers, upon which shall be plainly printed the terms upon which they may be used. Such tickets shall not entitle the holder to ride upon any train not therein designated, or at any time beyond that stipulated therein.

Approved April 28, 1875.

[No. 143.]

AN ACT to repeal an act entitled "An act to regulate the transportation of freight and passengers, and the management of railroads of this State not incorporated under an act entitled 'An act to provide for the incorporation of railroad companies,' as approved February twelve, eighteen hundred and fifty-five," approved April seventeen, eighteen hundred and seventy-one, being sections two thousand three hundred and ninety-nine, two thousand four hundred, two thousand four hundred and one, two thousand four hundred and two, and two thousand four hundred and three of the compiled laws of eighteen hundred and seventy-one.

SECTION 1. *The People of the State of Michigan enact*, That Act repealed. an act entitled "An act to regulate the transportation of freight and passengers, and the management of railroads of this State not incorporated under an act entitled 'An act to provide for the incorporation of railroad companies,' as approved February twelfth, eighteen hundred and fifty-five;" approved April seventeen, eighteen hundred and seventy-one, being sections two thousand three hundred and ninety-nine, two thousand four hundred, two thousand four hundred and one, two thousand four hundred and two, and two thousand four hundred and three of the compiled laws of eighteen hundred and seventy-one, be and the same is hereby repealed.

SEC. 2. This act shall take immediate effect.

Approved April 28, 1875.

[No. 144.]

AN ACT to provide for the payment of the transportation of the State militia called out by the Governor to prevent breaches of the peace in Marquette and Montcalm counties in the year eighteen hundred and seventy-four.

SECTION 1. *The People of the State of Michigan enact*, That a Appropriation. sum not to exceed two thousand dollars be and hereby is appropriated out of any money in the treasury to the credit of the military fund for the payment of the cost of transportation of the State militia called out by the Governor to prevent breaches of the peace in Marquette and Montcalm counties in the spring and summer of eighteen hundred and seventy-four.

SEC. 2. The Auditor General is hereby authorized to audit and Auditor General to allow claims allow all just claims for transportation of such State militia so and draw war- called out from their place of rendezvous to the place or places rant on treas-urer.

23

where ordered and sent and their return from such place or places to their place of rendezvous, and shall draw his warrant upon the State Treasurer therefor, who is hereby authorized and directed to pay the same.

By payment, State acquires certain rights which it may enforce against counties.

SEC. 3. Upon the payment of such sum or sums of money the State of Michigan shall thereby acquire and hold all the rights (if any), which the parties to whom such payment is made had or might have had against the counties of Marquette or Montcalm, and shall have the right to take any and all lawful means to enforce said claim against said counties for the services of said officers, non-commissioned officers, musicians, and privates, for the transportation mentioned in sections one and two of this act.

SEC. 4. This act shall take immediate effect.

Approved April 28, 1875.

[No. 145.]

AN ACT to authorize the printing and distribution of the laws relative to drainage and highways.

Secretary of State to publish and distribute.

SECTION 1. *The People of the State of Michigan enact,* That the Secretary of State is hereby authorized and directed as soon as practicable after the adjournment of this legislature, to compile and publish in pamphlet form all the laws of this State relating to drainage and highways, and forward to the county clerk of each county a number sufficient; and it shall be his duty to supply one copy of said laws to each county drain commissioner, and one to each township drain commissioner and highway commissioner in this State.

SEC. 2. This act shall take immediate effect.

Approved April 28, 1875.

[No. 146.]

AN ACT to amend sections sixteen, twenty-two, twenty-three' twenty-eight, twenty-nine, and thirty of chapter one hundred and seventy-one of revised statutes of eighteen hundred and forty-six, being sections eight thousand and thirty-three, eight thousand and thirty-nine, eight thousand and forty, eight thousand and forty-five, eight thousand and forty-six, and eight thousand and forty-seven of the compiled laws of eighteen hundred and seventy-one, relative to county jails.

Sections amended.

SECTION 1. *The People of the State of Michigan enact,* That sections sixteen, twenty-two, twenty-three, twenty-eight, twenty-nine, and thirty of chapter one hundred and seventy-one of revised statutes of eighteen hundred and forty-six, being sections eight thousand and thirty-three, eight thousand and thirty-nine, eight thousand and forty, eight thousand and forty-five, eight thousand and forty-six, and eight thousand and forty-seven of the compiled laws of eighteen hundred and seventy-one, be and the same are hereby amended so as to read as follows:

(8033.) SEC. 16. In each county of this State the judge of the circuit court together with the county superintendents of the poor, shall be inspectors of the jails respectively. Inspectors of jails.

(8039.) SEC. 22. It shall be the duty of the keeper of every county prison to present to every circuit court to be held in his county, at the opening of such court, a calendar stating— Keeper of county prison to present calendar to court

First, The name of every prisoner then detained in such prison;

Second, The time when such prisoner was committed, and by virtue of what process or precept; and

Third, The cause of the detention of every such person.

(8040.) SEC. 23. It shall be the duty of such court during the term thereof to inquire into the cause of the commitment of every person confined in such prison upon any criminal charge who shall not have been indicted, or against whom no information shall have been filed, and unless satisfactory cause shall be shown to such court for detaining such person in custody or upon bail, as the case may require, to cause such person to be discharged. When persons not indicted to be discharged by court.

(8045.) SEC. 28. If any person lawfully imprisoned in any jail, workhouse, or house of correction, under sentence of confinement at hard labor, shall break such prison and escape, he shall be punished by imprisonment in the State prison or county jail not more than three years, in addition to the unexpired portion of the time for which he was originally imprisoned. Penalty for breaking jail, etc. when under sentence of confinement at hard labor.

(8046.) SEC. 29. If any person lawfully imprisoned in any jail, workhouse, or house of correction for any cause not mentioned in the preceding section shall break such prison and escape, he shall be punished by imprisonment either in the State prison or county jail not more than one year, in addition to the unexpired portion of the term for which he was originally sentenced. Penalty for breaking prison in other cases.

(8047.) SEC. 30. If any person lawfully imprisoned for any cause in any prison or place of confinement, established by law, other than the State prison, shall forcibly break the same with intent to escape, or shall by any force or violence attempt to escape therefrom, although no escape be effected, he shall be punished by imprisonment in the county jail not more than one year, in addition to any term for which he was held in prison at the time of such breaking or attempting to escape. And if any person lawfully imprisoned in any prison or place of confinement established by law, awaiting examination, trial, or sentence for any crime or offense, or charged with any crime or offense, shall forcibly break such prison with intent to escape, or shall by any force or violence attempt to escape therefrom, although no escape be effected, he shall be deemed guilty of a misdemeanor, and upon conviction thereof shall be punished accordingly. Punishment for attempting to escape.

Approved April 28, 1875.

[No. 147.]

AN ACT to amend section thirteen of chapter two hundred and forty-four, being section seven thousand five hundred and twenty-two of the compiled laws of eighteen hundred and seventy-one, relative to an attempt to commit the crime of murder by poisoning, drowning, or strangling.

Section amended

SECTION 1. *The People of the State of Michigan enact*, That section thirteen of chapter two hundred and forty-four of the compiled laws of eighteen hundred and seventy-one, be amended so as to read as follows:

Penalty for attempting to murder by poisoning, etc.

(7522.) SEC. 13. If any person shall attempt to commit the crime of murder by poisoning, drowning, or strangling another person, or by any means not constituting the crime of assault with intent to murder, every such offender shall be punished by imprisonment in the State prison for life, or any number of years.

Approved April 28, 1875.

[No. 148.]

AN ACT to allow the members of the Legislature from the Upper Peninsula of Michigan the sum of five dollars per day during the present session of the Legislature.

Preamble.

Whereas, By the Constitution of this State, section fifteen, article four, the Legislature may allow five dollars per day to the members of the Legislature from the Upper Peninsula of Michigan; therefore,

Allowance.

SECTION 1. *The People of the State of Michigan enact*, That the members of the Legislature from the Upper Peninsula of Michigan shall receive five dollars per day during the present session of said Legislature.

SEC. 2. This act shall take immediate effect.

Approved April 28, 1875.

[No. 149.]

AN ACT to amend section eight of an act entitled "An act to authorize the formation of telegraph companies," approved March twenty-six, eighteen hundred and fifty-one, being section two thousand six hundred and thirty-two of the compiled laws of eighteen hundred and seventy-one.

Section amended

SECTION 1. *The People of the State of Michigan enact*, That section eight of an act entitled "An act to authorize the formation of telegraph companies," approved March twenty-six, eighteen hundred and fifty-one, being section two thousand six hundred and thirty-two of the compiled laws, shall be amended so as to read as follows:

Liability of stockholders.

(2632.) SEC. 8. The stockholders of every association organized in pursuance of this act shall be, jointly and severally, individually liable for the payment of all debts and demands for labor performed and materials furnished for such association, which shall be contracted, or which shall be or shall become due during the time of their holding such stock; but no stockholder shall be proceeded against for the collection of any such debt or demand against such association, until judgment thereon shall have been obtained against the association, and an execution returned unsatisfied in whole or in part, or unless such association shall be dissolved; and every stockholder against whom any such recovery shall have been had for labor and materials furnished, shall have the right to recover the same of the other stockholders in said corporation, in ratable proportion to the amount of stock they shall respectively hold.

SEC. 2. This act shall take immediate effect.

Approved April 28, 1875.

[No. 150.]

AN ACT to amend sections two and five of chapter eighty-seven of revised statutes of eighteen hundred and forty-six, being sections four thousand eight hundred and fifty-eight and four thousand eight hundred and sixty-one of the compiled laws of eighteen hundred and seventy-one, relative to masters, apprentices, and servants.

SECTION 1. *The People of the State of Michigan enact,* That sections two and five of chapter eighty-seven of revised statutes of eighteen hundred and forty-six, being sections four thousand eight hundred and fifty-eight and four thousand eight hundred and sixty-one, of the compiled laws of eighteen hundred and seventy-one, be and the same are hereby amended so as to read as follows: *(Sections amended.)*

(4858.) SEC. 2. Such consent shall be given—

First, By the father of the infant. If he be dead or be not in a legal capacity to give his consent, or if he shall have abandoned and neglected to provide for his family, and such fact be certified by a justice of the peace of the township and endorsed on the indenture; then, *(Consent, by whom given.)*

Second, By the mother. If the mother be dead, or be not in a legal capacity to give such consent or refuse; then,

Third, By the guardian of such infant duly appointed. If such infant have no parent living, or none in a legal capacity to give consent, and there be no guardian; then,

Fourth, By any two justices of the peace of the township where such infant may reside;

Fifth, By the recorder of any city in the county, or by the probate judge of such county.

(4861.) SEC. 5. The county superintendents of the poor in the several counties, or the recorder of any city of the county, or the probate judge of such county, and upon the relation of any person they or either of them, are hereby authorized and required to institute inquiry, and to examine witnesses on oath as to the merits of the *(When superintendents of the poor, etc., may bind out minors.)*

case, and shall keep a record of proceedings, and file the same in
the county clerk's office, and may bind out any child under the
ages above specified who shall be sent to any county poor-house, or
who is or shall become chargeable, or whose parent or parents
shall become chargeable to such county, to be clerks, apprentices,
or servants, until such child, if a male, shall be twenty-one years
old, and if a female shall be eighteen years old, or until her mar-
riage within that age, which binding shall be as effectual as if such
child had bound himself or herself with the consent of his or her
father.

Approved April 29, 1875.

[No. 151.]

AN ACT to amend section eighteen, being section four thousand
five hundred and twelve, chapter one hundred and sixty of the
compiled laws of eighteen hundred and seventy-one, relative to
the partition and distribution of estates.

Section amended SECTION 1. *The People of the State of Michigan enact,* That
section eighteen, being section four thousand five hundred and
twelve, chapter one hundred and sixty of the compiled laws of
eighteen hundred and seventy-one, relative to the partition and
distribution of estates, be amended so as to read as follows:

Partition, when conclusive. (4512.) SEC. 18. The partition, when finally confirmed and established, shall be conclusive on all the heirs and devisees, and all
persons claiming under them, and upon all persons interested;

Certified copy of report, where recorded, etc. "and the judge of probate shall cause a duly certified copy of the
report to be recorded in the office of the register of deeds for the
county, and the expense thereof shall be a charge against the estate, to be paid out of the funds thereof in the same manner as
other costs of administration; and such record shall be notice of
all matters therein contained, and shall be evidence thereof."

Approved April 29, 1875.

[No. 152.]

AN ACT to amend section nine of chapter one hundred and thirty
of the revised statutes of eighteen hundred and forty-six, being
section six thousand nine hundred and twenty of the compiled
laws of eighteen hundred and seventy-one, relative to foreclosure by advertisement.

Section amended SECTION 1. *The People of the State of Michigan enact,* That
section nine of chapter one hundred and thirty of the revised statutes of eighteen hundred and forty-six, being section six thousand
nine hundred and twenty of the compiled laws of eighteen hundred and seventy-one, be amended so as to read as follows:

Deed on sale. SEC. 9. The officer or person making the sale shall forthwith
execute, acknowledge, and deliver to each purchaser, a deed of the
premises bid off to him; and if the lands are situated in several

counties he shall make separate deeds of the lands in each county, and [shall] specify therein the precise amounts for which each parcel of land therein described was sold. And he shall endorse upon each deed the time when the same will become operative in case the premises are not redeemed according to law. Such deed or deeds shall, as soon as practicable, and within twenty days after such sale, be deposited with the register of deeds of the county in which the land therein described is situated, and the register shall endorse thereon the time the same was received, and for the better preservation thereof, shall record the same at length in a book to be provided in his office for that purpose. In case such premises shall be redeemed, the register of deeds shall, at the time of destroying such deed, as provided in section twelve of this chapter, write on the face of such record the word "Redeemed," with a reference to the record, showing such fact and stating at what date such entry is made, and signing such entry with his official signature.

Endorsement of time when deed will become operative.

Deed to be deposited with register of deeds, etc.

Duty of register in case premises are redeemed.

Approved April 29, 1875.

[No. 153.]

AN ACT to amend section thirty-eight, being section four thousand three hundred and fifty-nine, chapter one hundred and fifty-four of the compiled laws of eighteen hundred and seventy-one, relative to wills of real and personal estate.

SECTION 1. *The People of the State of Michigan enact,* That section thirty-eight, being section four thousand three hundred and fifty-nine, chapter one hundred and fifty-four of the compiled laws, relative to wills of real and personal estate, be amended so as read as follows :

Section amended

(4359.) SEC. 38. An attested copy of every will devising lands, or any interest in lands, and of the probate thereof, shall be recorded in the office of the register of deeds of the county in which the lands thereby devised are situated ; "and it shall be the duty of the judge of probate to cause such registration to be made, and the expense thereof shall be a charge against the estate, and shall be paid in the same manner as other expenses of administration are."

Attested copy of will shall be recorded in office of register of deeds.

Approved April 29, 1875.

[No. 154.]

AN ACT to amend section ten of chapter two hundred and one, being section six thousand four hundred and six of the compiled laws of eighteen hundred and seventy one, relative to proceedings against debtors by attachment.

SECTION 1. *The People of the State of Michigan enact,* That section ten of chapter two hundred and one, being section six thousand four hundred and six of the compiled laws of eighteen

Section amended

hundred and seventy-one, relative to proceedings against debtors by attachment, be amended so that the same shall read as follows:

When real estate bound by attachment. SEC. 10. Real estate attached shall be bound, and the attachment shall be a lien thereon from the time when a certified copy of the attachment, with a description of the real estate attached, shall be deposited in the office of the register of deeds in the county where the real estate attached is situated.

Approved April 29, 1875.

[No. 155.]

AN ACT to amend section five thousand nine hundred and sixty-eight of the compiled laws of eighteen hundred and seventy-one, relating to evidence.

Section amended SECTION 1. *The People of the State of Michigan enact,* That section five thousand nine hundred and sixty-eight of the compiled laws of eighteen hundred and seventy-one be and the same is hereby amended so as to read as follows:

Parties not to testify in relation to certain matters. (5968.) SEC. 101. That when a suit or proceeding is prosecuted or defended by the heirs, assigns, devisees, legatees, or personal representatives of a deceased person, the opposite party, if examined as a witness on his own behalf, shall not be admitted to testify at all in relation to matters which, if true, must have been equally within the knowledge of such deceased person; and when any suit or proceeding is prosecuted or defended by any surviving partner or partners, the opposite party, if examined as a witness in his own behalf, shall not be admitted to testify at all in relation to matters which, if true, must have been equally within the knowledge of the deceased partner, and not within the knowledge of any one of the surviving partners.

Approved April 29, 1875.

[No. 156.]

AN ACT to amend sections eight, fourteen, and thirty-eight of chapter twenty-one, being sections nine hundred and seventy-four, nine hundred and eighty, and ten hundred and four, of the compiled laws of eighteen hundred and seventy-one, relative to taxation of shares in national or State bank stock.

Section amended SECTION 1. *The People of the State of Michigan enact,* That sections eight, fourteen, and thirty-eight of chapter twenty-one, being sections nine hundred and seventy-four, nine hundred and eighty, and ten hundred and four of the compiled laws of eighteen hundred and seventy-one, relative to taxation of shares in national or State bank stock, be and is hereby amended so as to read as follows:

Excepted cases. (974.) SEC. 8. The excepted cases referred to in the preceding section, and not included in said section three, are the following:

First, All goods, wares, and merchandise, or stock in trade, including stock employed in the business of the mechanics' arts, in any township other than where the owner resides, shall be taxed in the township where the same may be, if the owner hire or occupy a store, mill, shop or warehouse therein, and shall not be taxable where the owner resides ; and all shares in national or State banks, shall be taxed in the township or city where the bank is located, and not elsewhere ; *Provided,* That shares owned by persons residing within the county where such bank is located shall be assessed in the township, city, or village where the owner thereof resides. Proviso.

Second, All horses, mules, and neat cattle, sheep and swine, kept throughout the year, other than where the owner resides, shall be assessed to such owner in the township where they are kept ;

Third, All personal property of non-residents of this State shall be assessed to the owner or to the person having the possession or control thereof, in the township or city where the same may be, or in case the same is in transit, at the place of destination within the State ;

Fourth, All personal property belonging to minors under guardianship shall be assessed to the guardian in the township where he is an inhabitant, and the personal property of every other person under guardianship shall be assessed to the guardian in the township of which the ward is an inhabitant ;

Fifth, All personal property held in trust by an executor, administrator, or trustee, the income of which is to be paid to any married woman or other person, shall be assessed to the person having possession or charge of such property, in the township of which he is an inhabitant, whether such married woman or other person reside within or without this State ;

Sixth, Personal property placed in the hands of any corporation, as an accumulating fund for the future benefit of heirs or other persons, shall be assessed to the persons for whose benefit the same is accumulating, if within this State ; otherwise to the person so placing it, or his executors or administrators, until the trustees shall be appointed to take charge of such property, or of the income thereof ;

Seventh, The personal estate of persons deceased, which shall be in the hands of executors or administrators, shall be assessed to the executors or administrators in the township where the deceased last dwelt, until they shall give notice to the supervisors that the estate has been distributed and paid over to the parties interested ;

Eighth, All property held by any religious society as a ministerial fund shall be assessed to the treasurer of such society ; and if such property consists of real estate, it shall be taxed in the township where such property lies ; if it consists of personal property, it shall be taxed in the township where such society usually holds its meetings.

(980.) SEC. 14. Every person of full age and sound mind, and every firm, body politic or corporate, shall when called upon as hereinafter provided forthwith make a full and true statement in writing Statement to supervisors, who to make and what to contain.

to the supervisor of the township or ward in which he resides, in which shall be distinctly and truly set forth a correct description of all the real estate and personal property not by this act exempt from taxation, and not by the laws of this State subject to a specific tax, of which he or she is the owner or the holder, as guardian, parent, husband, or trustee, executor, administrator, receiver, accounting officer, partner, agent, or factor; and also all moneys and credits owned or held as aforesaid, and the cashier of any State or national bank in said township or ward, when called upon as aforesaid, shall also truly and fully set forth the names and residence of all the parties owning shares or stock in such bank, the number and amount of such shares owned by said parties respectively, as the same shall appear upon the books of said bank, and in case of neglect or refusal so to do, said cashier shall be deemed guilty of a misdemeanor.

Power of board of supervisors to make new tax roll and extend time.

(1004.) SEC. 38. The board of supervisors of any county shall have power to authorize the making out a new tax roll; to extend and determine, by resolution, the time when each collector or township treasurer in their county shall make his return to the county treasurer, but such time shall in no case exceed two months from the time fixed by the last previous section; and when an extension is had each township treasurer, or other collecting officer, shall be authorized to levy and collect all taxes as if such extension had

When collector not to receive benefit of extension.

not been granted; but no collector or township treasurer shall receive the benefit of such extension until he shall have paid over to the county treasurer, or other officer authorized to receive the same, all moneys collected by him up to the first day of February

Interest on taxes extended.

which may be due; and in all cases interest shall be charged on all taxes extended from the first day of February at the rate and in the manner provided in section seventy of this act; and for the

Collector to call for taxes remaining unpaid.

purpose of collecting the taxes remaining unpaid he shall call at least once upon the person taxed, if a resident, or at the place of his usual residence in the township, and shall demand payment of the taxes charged to him on such list; and in case of any tax assessed upon the shares of capital stock of any bank in such township he shall call upon the cashier of such bank and demand payment thereof, and thereupon it shall be the duty of such cashier to pay the same, and charge the amount so paid against

Proviso.

the shares of stock so taxed: Provided, That the township boards of any township, or the common council of any city, shall have the power to extend the time for the collection one month whenever the boards of supervisors have neglected to so extend the time, and when the township board of a township, or the common council of a city, shall have extended the time as aforesaid, such extension shall be duly certified by the township clerk of the township, or the proper certifying officer of the city, to the county clerk of the county.

SEC. 2. This act shall take immediate effect.
Approved April 29, 1875.

[No. 157.]

AN ACT to amend section three of an act entitled " An act relative to the imprisonment of parties in civil suits in certain cases," approved March twenty-seven, eighteen hundred and sixty-seven, being compiler's section seven thousand three hundred and eighty-four of the compiled laws of eighteen hundred and seventy-one.

SECTION 1. *The People of the State of Michigan enact,* That §ection amended section seven thousand three hundred and eighty-four, chapter two hundred and thirty-eight of the compiled laws of eighteen hundred and seventy-one, being section three of an act entitled " An act relative to the imprisonment of parties in civil suits in certain cases,"approved March twenty-seven, eighteen hundred and sixty-seven, be amended so as to read as follows:

(7384.) SEC. 3. That whenever, in any civil cause or action, any When county defendant shall have been committed to jail in default of bail, and free from by reason thereof shall be detained in any county jail, the expenses of board and detention of such defendant shall in no case be, or constitute a charge against the county. In such case the Plaintiff to pay sheriff or keeper of such jail shall give to the plaintiff or his attorney in such suit or action, notice that the expenses of keeping and detention of such defendant must be paid in advance; and no Sheriff not sheriff or keeper of such jail shall be required to retain such defendant in jail any longer than such expenses of board and keeping are paid in advance.

SEC. 2. This act shall take immediate effect.
Approved April 29, 1875.

[No. 158.]

AN ACT to amend an act entitled "An act to provide for the opening and improvement of roads on the line of adjoining townships," being compiler's section one thousand two hundred and fourteen, chapter twenty-three of the compiled laws of eighteen hundred and seventy-one, approved March nineteen, eighteen hundred and sixty-three, and to add three new sections thereto.

SECTION 1. *The People of the State of Michigan enact,* That Act amended. " An act to provide for the opening and improvement of roads on the line of adjoining townships," being compiler's section one thousand two hundred and fourteen, chapter twenty-three of the compiled laws of eighteen hundred and seventy-one, approved March nineteen, eighteen hundred and sixty-three, be amended so as to read as follows, and that there be added to the same three new sections to stand as sections two, three, and four respectively, following said recited section one thousand two hundred and fourteen, and to read as follows:

(1214.) SECTION 1. That whenever a road shall have been laid Proceedings on out and established on the line between adjoining townships, upon the petition of twelve freeholders of either township, the commis-

sioner of highways of the respective townships shall meet upon
the line of such road and make an examination into the condition
of the same, and if in their opinion the public good requires the
opening or improvement of such highway, they shall proceed to
open and improve the same as hereinafter provided.

When commissioner shall proceed to open road. SEC. 2. If a road shall have been laid out and established on the
line between adjoining townships, as aforesaid, and either town-
ship shall have opened and improved the road or part of road belonging to such township, the commissioner of highways of the
township neglecting or refusing to open and improve the road or
part of road belonging to the same, shall, upon the petition of
twelve freeholders of either township, proceed to open and improve
the road or part of road belonging thereto.

When commissioner to let contracts, etc. SEC. 3. Whenever the highway labor assessed thereon in any one
year shall be insufficient to open and improve such highway, the
said commissioner shall proceed to let contracts for such opening
and improvement, and when said contracts are completed and accepted, give orders upon the treasurer of the township to which
such road or part of road belongs, payable out of any money raised
or to be raised for that purpose, and notify the supervisor of said
township or townships of the amount of such order or orders, and
it shall be the duty of the supervisor so notified to assess the same
upon the taxable property of the township in the same manner as
other township taxes are assessed and collected: *Provided,* Such
Proviso. contracts shall not exceed fifty dollars in any one year on any one
road.

Liability of supervisor or commissioner who fails to discharge duty. SEC. 4. Every supervisor or commissioner of highways who shall
neglect or refuse to discharge the duties imposed upon him by the
provisions of this act, shall be liable to a fine of twenty-five dollars.

Approved April 29,

[No. 159.]

AN ACT to amend sections five, thirteen, and twenty-nine of "An
act to provide for the draining of swamps, marshes, and other
low lands," approved March twenty-two, eighteen hundred and
sixty-nine, being compiler's sections one thousand seven hundred
and forty-nine, one thousand seven hundred and fifty-seven, and
one thousand seven hundred and seventy-three of the compiled
laws of eighteen hundred and seventy-one.

Sections amended. SECTION 1. *The People of the State of Michigan enact,* That
sections five, thirteen, and twenty-nine, of "An act to provide for the
draining of swamps, marshes, and other low lands," approved March
twenty-two, eighteen hundred and sixty-nine, being compiler's sections one thousand seven hundred and forty-nine, one thousand
seven hundred and fifty-seven, and one thousand seven hundred
and seventy-three of the compiled laws of eighteen hundred and
seventy-one, be and are hereby amended so as to read as follows:

(1749.) Sec. 5. If such release cannot be obtained in a reasonable time, said commissioner shall issue an order, under his hand, directed to the sheriff, or any constable of said county, to write down the names of twenty-four freeholders, residents of said county, and not interested in the drain or drains in reference to which they are to act, and qualified to be jurors in the circuit court in said county. Such officer shall thereupon write down the names of twenty-four such persons, and give notice to said commissioner, and to such of the persons through whose lands such drain or drains will run, who reside in the township or townships through or into which such drain or drains will pass, and can be found therein, that he will leave such names at the house of some justice of the peace, in one of said townships, naming such justice, the place and time to be named in such notice, and the time not less than four days from the time of giving such notice, and that at said place and time, a jury will be struck from such list of names. At the time and place appointed, said commissioner shall strike off six names, and the person or persons interested in said drain or drains shall strike off a like number; and if either or both parties fail to strike off, such sheriff or constable shall do so for him or them, and the names remaining on such list shall form the jury; and thereupon said commissioner shall issue a *venire*, under his hand, directed to any constable or to the sheriff of said county, commanding him to summon said jury, to be and appear before said commissioner, at a time and place to be named in said *venire*, to determine the necessity for the construction of any such drain or drains, and the amount of damage sustained by any person or persons owning or interested in any of the lands through which such drain or drains may be constructed. If the jury shall not all appear within one hour after the time of appearance named in said *venire*, said commissioner shall direct the officer to summon a sufficient number of competent jurors, as aforesaid, as talesmen, to complete the panel; and when the panel shall be full, said commissioner shall administer unto each juror an oath, well and truly to examine and determine the necessity for constructing said drain or drains, and to assess the damages sustained by any person or persons, owning or interested in the lands through which the same shall pass. Said jury shall thereupon proceed to examine such swamp, marsh, or other low land, to determine the necessity for constructing such drain or drains, and if they shall, on a careful examination of the whole matter, be of the opinion that it is necessary for the good of the public health, as well as a benefit to the land in the vicinity thereof, to construct said drain or drains, they shall so determine. Such determination, when reduced to writing and signed by the jurors, shall be *prima facie* evidence of the location of such drain or drains, and shall be deemed a sufficient conveyance to vest the fee of the lands necessary for such drain or drains in the county in which it is situated, in trust to and for the uses and purposes of drainage, and for no other use or purpose whatever; and such determination may be acknowledged before some officer authorized to take acknowledgments of deeds, and recorded in the office of the register

of deeds in the county where such lands lie. The jury shall proceed to assess the damages which any person or persons shall sustain
by reason of the construction of the same, and shall certify, in
writing their doings and the amount of damages so assessed, to
said commissioner; and said jurors shall each be entitled to receive
one dollar per day, and six cents per mile for traveling, in going to
the place or places where such drain or drains shall be located, to
be paid according to the provisions of this act.

Assessment of damages and certificate to commissioner.

Per diem and mileage.

(1757.) SEC. 13. Said commissioner shall have power to re-locate
any drain or drains, and to alter or vary the size, or extend the line
thereof, with the consent of the contractor or contractors, if such
extension be necessary to provide a suitable outlet; and the power
herein conferred on said commissioner for digging and draining
shall also extend to and include deepening and widening, and
clearing out any ditches or drains which have heretofore been, or
may hereafter be constructed; also, straightening, cleaning out,
and deepening the channels of creeks and streams; but no expense,
exceeding one hundred dollars, on any one drain or creek, shall
be charged and assessed as aforesaid, unless upon such application
as provided for in section four of this act.

Power of commissioner to re-locate, alter, and extend drains, etc.

Limit of expense.

(1773.) SEC. 29. It shall be the duty of every person owning land,
across which a drain has been, or may be lawfully constructed by
the county drain commissioner, to keep so much of such drain as
lies upon his lands, which are in any manner benefited by such
drain or ditch, open and in good repair. If such owner shall refuse or neglect to keep such drain open and in good repair, it shall
be lawful, and the duty of said commissioner, on application to
him in writing of five freeholders, residents near the obstructed
parts of such drain, to open and repair the same; and the costs
and expenses of such repairs shall be collected by said commissioner of such delinquent owner; or such costs and expenses, with
one year's interest on the same, may be reported to the board of
supervisors, who shall order the same to be assessed by the supervisor of the proper township, on the real and personal estate of
such delinquent owner, and the same shall be collected and paid
over to the county treasurer, and passed to the fund for such drain;
Provided, That if such expenses shall exceed twenty-five dollars,
the same application shall be had as in section four of this act,
and the expense of such repairs shall be assessed on the several
parcels of land previously assessed for the construction of such
drain; and such assessment shall be reported, collected, paid over,
and passed to the fund of such drain as in this act provided.

How drain to be kept in repair.

Proviso.

Approved April 29, 1875.

[No. 160.]

AN ACT to legalize the election of directors of consolidated railroad companies in certain cases.

SECTION 1. *The People of the State of Michigan enact,* That
all elections of directors for consolidated railroad companies held

Election legalized.

before the consolidation agreement shall have been filed with the Secretary of State, shall in all suits and proceedings be of the same force and effect as if the said election had been held after the filing of said agreement: *Provided*, Said election was held after the consolidation agreement was sanctioned by the stockholders. *Proviso.*

Sec. 2. This act shall take immediate effect.

Approved April 29, 1875.

[No. 161.]

AN ACT to amend section two of an act entitled " An act to organize the county of Gladwin," approved April eight, eighteen hundred and seventy-five.

Section 1. *The People of the State of Michigan enact*, That *Section amended* section two of an act entitled " An act to organize the county of Gladwin," approved April eight, in the year of our Lord one thousand eight hundred and seventy-five, be and the same is hereby amended so as to read as follows:

Sec. 2. There shall be held in the several townships of Glad- *Election of officers and their* win county, on Tuesday, the first day of June next, a special elec- *term of office.* tion, for county officers of said county, at which election there shall be elected all the county officers to which the said county is entitled, who shall hold their several offices until the first day of January, in the year of our Lord eighteen hundred and seventy-seven, and until their successors shall have been elected and qualified. Said election shall be conducted in the same way, by the same officers, and the returns thereof made in the same manner as near as may be, as is now required by law in the election of county officers in this State.

Sec. 2. This act shall take immediate effect.

Approved April 29, 1875.

[No. 162.]

AN ACT relative to changing the sureties on bonds by judges of probate.

Section 1. *The People of the State of Michigan enact*, That *When probate* when the sureties or the penal sum in any bond given to the pro- *court may require new* bate court are insufficient, the probate court, on the petition of *bond.* any person interested, and after notice to the principal in the bond, may require a new bond with such surety or sureties, and in such penal sum as the court shall direct.

Sec. 2. Any surety may, upon his petition to the probate court, *Discharge of* be discharged from all further responsibility, if the court, after due *surety on his petition, etc.* notice to all persons interested, deems it reasonable and proper, and the principal may thereupon be required to give a new bond.

Sec. 3. If the principal fails to give a new bond within such *Removal in case* time as is ordered by the court, he may be removed and some other *of failure to give* person appointed in his stead. *new bond.*

Liability of sureties when new bond is required.

SEC. 4. When a new bond is so required, the sureties in the prior bond are liable for all breaches of the condition committed before the new bond is approved by the judge.

SEC. 5. This act shall take immediate effect.

Approved April 29, 1875.

[No. 163.]

AN ACT to amend an act entitled "An act to designate the holidays to be observed in the acceptance and payment of bills of exchange and promissory notes, in the holding of courts, and relative to the continuance of suits," approved March eight, eighteen hundred and sixty-five, being compiler's section one thousand five hundred and fifty-nine of the compiled laws of eighteen hundred and seventy-one.

Act amended.

SECTION 1. *The People of the State of Michigan enact,* That an act entitled "An act to designate the holidays to be observed in the acceptance and payment of bills of exchange and promissory notes, in the holding of courts, and relative to the continuance of suits," approved March eight, eighteen hundred and sixty-five, being compiler's section one thousand five hundred and fifty-nine of the compiled laws of eighteen hundred and seventy-one, be and the same is hereby amended so as to read as follows:

Certain days considered as is Sunday, for certain purposes.

(1559.) SECTION 1. That the following days, viz: the first day of January, commonly called New Year's day, the twenty-second day of February, commonly called Washington's birth-day, the fourth [day] of July, the twenty-fifth day of December, commonly called Christmas day, the thirtieth day of May, commonly called Decoration day, and any day appointed or recommended by the Governor of this State, or the President of the United States, as a day of fasting and prayer or thanksgiving, shall, for the purposes of presenting for payment or acceptance, and of protesting notice of the dishonor of bills of exchange, bank checks, and promissory notes, made after this act shall take effect, also for the holding of courts, be treated and considered as the first day of the week, commonly called Sunday:

Proviso.

Provided, That in case any of the holidays shall fall upon a Sunday, then the Monday following shall be considered as the said holiday:

Further proviso —return or adjourn day of any suit.

Provided also, That in case the return or adjourn day in any suit, matter, or hearing before any court shall come on any day so appointed or recommended by the Governor of this State, or the President of the United States, as a day of thanksgiving, or fasting and prayer, such suit, matter, or proceeding, commenced or adjourned as aforesaid, shall not, by reason of coming on any day recommended by the Governor of this State, or the President of the United States, as a day of thanksgiving, or fasting and prayer, abate, but the same shall stand continued on the next succeeding day, at the same time and place, unless the next day shall be the first day of the week, or a holiday, in which case the same shall stand continued to the day next succeeding said first day of the week or holiday, at the same time and place: *Pro- Further proviso* *vided further,* That whenever the first day of the general term of —first day of term of circuit any circuit court, as fixed by the order of a circuit judge, shall fall court. upon either of the days first above named, such court may be adjourned to the next succeeding secular day: *Provided further,* Further proviso That nothing in this section shall make invalid a presentation, —presentation of commercial demand, or notice of dishonor of commercial paper on any such paper on such days. holiday other than Sunday, in cases where the same shall not have been presented on the secular day next preceding such holiday.

SEC. 2. This act shall take immediate effect.

Approved April 29, 1875.

[No. 164.]

AN ACT to repeal section four thousand two hundred and four of the compiled laws of eighteen hundred and seventy-one, relative to alienation by deed.

SECTION 1. *The People of the State of Michigan enact,* That Section repealed. section four thousand two hundred and four of the compiled laws of eighteen hundred and seventy-one, relative to alienation by deed, shall be and the same is hereby repealed.

Approved April 29, 1875.

[No. 165.]

AN ACT to facilitate the collection of damages for trespass on lands.

SECTION 1. *The People of the State of Michigan enact,* In all Party may cases where a party has a right of action for the taking of tim- waive tort and bring assumpsit. ber or other trespass on lands, it shall be lawful for the party having such right of action to waive the tort and bring assumpsit.

SEC. 2. When tort is waived, as provided in the preceding sec- Plaintiff may tion, the plaintiff may commence his suit by attachment against commence suit by attachment, the property of the defendant, as in other cases, and his affidavit etc. for such attachment shall state the amount due him as near as may be, and the fact that the damages are unliquidated shall not prevent the bringing and maintaining of such writ.

Approved April 29, 1875.

[No. 166.]

AN ACT to authorize counties, townships, cities, and villages to raise money by taxation for the payment of their bonds, issued to aid in the construction of railroads.

SECTION 1. *The People of the State of Michigan enact,* That Authority to the board of supervisors of any county, the township board levy tax for payment of bonds. of any township, the common council of any city, or the common

25

council or board of trustees of any village which issued its bonds to aid in the construction of any railroad in this State prior to the twenty-sixth day of May, in the year of our Lord one thousand eight hundred and seventy, are hereby authorized and empowered to provide, by a tax to be collected from the taxable property in any such county, township, city, or village, such sum or sums of money as may be necessary to pay the principal and interest due or to become due upon any such bonds issued by such county, township, city, or village, and which has been negotiated prior to the twenty-sixth day of May, eighteen hundred and seventy, or upon any judgment obtained upon any such bond against any county, township, city, or village.

Levy and collection of tax.

SEC. 2. The board of supervisors of any county, the township board of any such township, the common council of any such city, or the common council or board of trustees of any such village, at the time of raising the tax for general county, town, city, or village purposes, may cause the amount necessary to be raised by tax for the payment of the principal and interest due upon such bonds, or which shall become due upon them within one year next after the time of raising said general tax according to the conditions of such bonds, to be placed in the general assessment roll of said county, township, city, or village, in a separate column, which said tax shall be levied, assessed, and collected in the same manner and subject to the same provisions as other general taxes for county, town, city, or village purposes.

Corporations may issue new bonds.

Interest.

SEC. 3. Any county, township, city, or village may provide for the payment of the principal and interest due and unpaid at the time this act shall go into effect, upon such bonds, by the issue of new bonds, at a rate of interest not exceeding ten per cent per annum, and for such sums each, and for such a length of time as the board of supervisors, the township board, the common council of the city, or the common council or board of trustees of the village, shall direct. Such bonds shall have attached thereto the necessary and usual interest coupons, corresponding in dates and numbers with the bonds to which they are attached. Such bonds shall, if issued by a county, be executed by the chairman of the board of supervisors and the clerk of such board; if by a city, they shall be executed by the mayor and clerk, or recorder thereof, as the case may be, under the seal of said city; and if issued by a township, they shall be executed by the supervisor and clerk thereof; and if issued by a village, they shall be executed by the president and clerk, or recorder thereof, as the case may be.

Coupons.

Who to execute bonds.

Levy of tax, annually, for payment of new bonds and interest.

SEC. 4. In case any county, township, city, or village shall issue any bonds in accordance with the provisions of section three of this act, such county, township, city, or village shall, each year, by its proper authorities, so long as such bonds remain unpaid, levy, assess, and collect, upon the taxable property of such county, township, city, or village, a sufficient sum of money to pay all bonds, or the interest upon the same as the same shall become due; and the full faith and credit of any county, township, city, or village, so issuing any such bonds, is hereby pledged for the full pay-

ment of both principal and interest thereon; and the same are
hereby made a valid and legal charge upon the taxable property of
the county, township city, or village issuing the same.

Sec. 5. In case the boundaries of any county, township, city, *Where tax shall be levied when boundaries of corporation have been changed.*
or village shall have been enlarged, or diminished, since the time
of issuing any of the bonds mentioned in section one of this
act, the taxes hereinbefore provided for, shall be collected only
from the taxable property within the boundaries of such county,
township, city, or village as they existed at the time of [the] issuing
of such bonds.

Sec. 6. This act shall take immediate effect.

Approved April 30, 1875.

[No. 167.]

AN ACT to amend section one hundred and thirty-seven of chapter one hundred and thirty-six, compiler's section three thousand six hundred and ninety-six of the compiled laws of eighteen hundred and seventy-one, an act entitled "An act relative
to primary schools."

Section 1. *The People of the State of Michigan enact,* That *Section amended*
section one hundred and thirty-seven of chapter one hundred and
thirty-six, compiler's section three thousand six hundred and
ninety-six of the compiled laws of eighteen hundred and seventy-
one, be so amended as to read as follows:

(3696.) Sec. 137. Any person may send scholars to a district *Non-residents may send to school.*
school who are members of his own family, in a district in which
he does not reside: *Provided,* He pays taxes in the district to an *Proviso.*
amount equal to the amount per scholar of the cost of supporting
the said district school.

Approved April 30, 1875.

[No. 168.]

AN ACT to amend section seven thousand five hundred and
eighty-five of the compiled laws of eighteen hundred and
seventy-one, relative to offenses against property.

Section 1. *The People of the State of Michigan enact,* That *Section amended*
section seven thousand five hundred and eighty-five of the compiled laws of eighteen hundred and seventy-one, relative to offenses
against property, shall be and the same is hereby amended so as to
read as follows:

(7585.) Sec. 34. If any person to whom any money, goods, or *Embezzlement of goods, etc., which may be the subject of larceny, deemed larceny.*
other property which may be the subject of larceny, shall have
been delivered, shall embezzle or fraudulently convert to his own
use, or shall secrete with the intent to embezzle, or fraudulently
use such goods, money, or other property, or any part thereof, he

shall be deemed by so doing to have committed the crime of larceny.

Approved April 30, 1875.

[No. 169.]

AN ACT to provide for the punishment of collecting agents and other persons who refuse to pay over moneys collected by them.

Liability of agent who fails to pay over moneys collected.

SECTION 1. *The People of the State of Michigan enact,* That if any banker, broker, collecting agent, or any person who holds himself out to the public as a collecting agent, converts to his own use, or neglects or refuses to pay over any money collected by him for another, within a reasonable time after demand, he shall be deemed guilty of a misdemeanor, and shall, upon conviction thereof, be punished by imprisonment in the county jail not more than one year, or by fine not exceeding four times the amount so received,

Proviso.

or both, in the discretion of the court: *Provided,* That the provisions of this act shall only apply to collections of drafts, notes, accounts, or bills of lading, where the written instructions were to remit or pay over such collection when so collected, or any part thereof, and that the party to whom such instructions were given has neglected to comply therewith.

Approved April 30, 1875.

[No. 170.]

AN ACT to repeal an act entitled " An act to authorize the cities, townships, and incorporated villages of the State of Michigan to aid in the construction and maintenance of wagon, gravel, cobble-stone, pounded stone, and plank roads," passed in eighteen hundred and sixty-seven, being sections one thousand two hundred and seventy-nine, one thousand two hundred and eighty, one thousand two hundred and eighty-one, one thousand two hundred and eighty-two, one thousand two hundred and eighty-three, and one thousand two hundred and eighty-four of the compiled laws of eighteen hundred and seventy-one.

Act repealed.

SECTION 1. *The People of the State of Michigan enact,* That the act passed in eighteen hundred and sixty-seven, entitled " An act to authorize the cities, townships, and incorporated villages of the State of Michigan to aid in the construction and maintenance of wagon, gravel, cobble-stone, pounded stone, and plank roads," shall be, and the same is hereby repealed.

SEC. 2. This act shall take immediate effect.

Approved April 30, 1875.

[No. 171.]

AN ACT to amend section one of an act entitled "An act to provide for the payment of the salaries of the State officers," approved April seventeen, eighteen hundred and seventy-one, being section four hundred 'and twenty of the compiled laws of eighteen hundred and seventy-one.

SECTION 1. *The People of the State of Michigan enact,* That *Section amended* section one of an act entitled "An act to provide for the payment of the salaries of the State officers," approved April seventeen, eighteen hundred and seventy-one, being section four hundred and twenty of the compiled laws of eighteen hundred and seventy-one, be and is hereby amended to read as follows:

SECTION 1. That there be and the same is hereby appropri- *Appropriation.* ated out of any moneys in the treasury, to the credit of the general fund, not otherwise appropriated, the following sums, for *Salaries.* the salaries of the State officers for the year eighteen hundred and seventy-five, and each year thereafter: For the Governor, one thou- *Governor.* sand dollars; for the salaries of the Justices of the Supreme Court, *Justices of Supreme Court.* four thousand dollars each; for the salaries of the judges of the circuit courts, and the judge of the recorder's court of the city of *Judges, etc.* Detroit, fifteen hundred dollars each; for the salaries of the Audi- *State officers.* tor General, State Treasurer, Secretary of the Board of Agriculture, and Superintendent of Public Instruction, one thousand dollars each; for the salaries of the Commissioner of the State Land Office, the Secretary of State, and the Attorney General, eight hundred dollars each; for the salary of the State Librarian, one thousand dollars; for the salaries of the Deputy State Treasurer, *Deputies.* and the Deputy Auditor General, fifteen hundred dollars each; for the salaries of the Deputy Secretary of State, and the Deputy Commissioner of the State Land Office, fourteen hundred dollars each; for the salary of the Deputy Superintendent of Public Instruction, thirteen hundred dollars; for the salary of the private *Governor's private secretary.* secretary of the Governor, eight hundred dollars; for the salary of the book-keeper and draughtsman of the land office, one thousand *Book-keepers.* dollars; for the salaries of the book-keeper of the land office, the book-keeper of the State Treasurer's office, and the book-keeper of the Auditors General's office, one thousand dollars each; for the *Clerks.* salary of the clerk of the Attorney General, one thousand dollars; for the salaries of the four regular clerks of the Auditor General, and one regular clerk of the Secretary of State, and one regular clerk of the Commissioner of the State Land Office, one thousand dollars each; for the salaries of all other clerks of the Auditor General, a sum not exceeding one thousand dollars each; for the salaries of such additional clerks in the State Land office, State Treasurer's office, office of the Secretary of State, of the State Board of Health, and office of the Superintendent of Public Instruction, as may be necessary, not exceeding at the rate of one thousand dollars each per annum for the time employed.

SEC. 2. This act shall take immediate effect.

Approved April 30, 1875.

[No. 172.]

AN ACT to author'ze the judge of probate of the county of St.
Joseph to appoint a clerk, and to authorize the board of Supervisors of said county to fix the compensation for such clerk.

Clerk to judge of
probate, his du-
ties and powers.

SECTION 1. *The People of the State of Michigan enact.* That
the judge of probate of the county of St. Joseph may appoint a
clerk, whose duty it shall be to keep the record of the proceedings
in the probate court of said county, as required by the judge of
probate; and such clerk may hear petitions for hearings. make certificates and orders, sign and seal process issued out of the probate court, and attest the same in the name of the judge of probate, and do all other acts required of said judge, except making
judicial decisions.

Order of appoint-
ment.

SEC. 2. Whenever such clerk shall be appointed by such judge
of probate, pursuant to the provisions of this act, such judge of
probate shall make an order of appointment, and the same shall
be entered at large on the record of the proceedings of such probate court.

Oath of office.

SEC. 3. Any person appointed clerk of the probate court by virtue of the provisions of this act shall, before entering upon the
duties of the office, take and subscribe the oath prescribed by the
constitution of this State.

Compensation.

SEC. 4. It shall be the duty of the board of supervisors of the
county of St. Joseph to fix the compensation of such clerk, which
shall not be less than three, nor more than six hundred dollars per
annum, to be paid in the same manner as provided by law for the
payment of compensation for county clerks.

Consent of
board of super-
visors required.

SEC. 5. No proceedings shall be taken under this act except with
the consent of the board of supervisors of said county of St. Joseph.

SEC. 6. This act shall take immediate effect.
Approved April 30, 1875.

[No. 173.]

AN ACT to reduce the penalty for non-payment of taxes on lands
known as railroad lands.

One-half of cer-
tain interest
penalty remitted.

SECTION 1. *The People of the State of Michigan enact,* That
one-half the interest penalty required to be paid by section
ninety-three of "An [act] to provide for a uniform assessment of
property, and for the collection and return of taxes thereon," approved April six, eighteen hundred and sixty-nine, which penalty
was incurred by several of the land grant railroads, so called, while
said section was in force, by the failure of the roads or companies
to pay the taxes of eighteen hundred and seventy-three on what
are known as railroad lands assessed to them, be and the same is
hereby remitted to said roads or companies: *Provided,* The taxes

Proviso.

are paid in the counties where the lands lie, within ninety days
from and after the approval of this act.

SEC. 2. In the payment of said taxes the treasurers of the several counties wherein said lands lie, are hereby directed to collect only one-half of the interest penalty on such railroad lands, of such penalty. *Directions to treasurers.*

SEC. 3. If it shall appear that any of said railroad lands shall have been struck off at the sale thereof, in October, in the year of our Lord one thousand eight hundred and seventy-four, to individuals, such lands shall be subject, upon redemption, to the penalty of twenty-five per cent. to be paid to said purchaser, and the remainder of the penalty shall be and is hereby remitted to said roads. *Relative to penalty on lands sold in 1874.*

SEC. 4. This act shall take immediate effect.

Approved May 1, 1875.

[No. 174.]

AN ACT to amend sections three and sixteen of chapter twenty-five, being sections one thousand two hundred and twenty-eight and one thousand two hundred and forty-one of compiled laws of eighteen hundred and seventy-one, relative to the duties of overseers in regard to the performance of labor on highways, the performance of such labor or the commutation therefor, and application of moneys by the commissioners.

SECTION 1. *The People of the State of Michigan enact,* That sections three and sixteen of chapter twenty-five, being sections one thousand two hundred and twenty-eight and one thousand two hundred and forty-one of compiled laws of eighteen hundred and seventy-one, relative to the duties of overseers in regard to the performance of labor on highways, the performance of such labor or the commutation therefor, and application of moneys by the commissioners, be amended so as to read as follows: *Sections amended.*

(1228.) SEC. 3. Every person liable to work on the highways, shall work the whole number of days for which he shall have been assessed; but every such person other than an overseer, whether resident or non-resident, may elect to commute for the same, or any part thereof, at the rate of one dollar for each day; in which case such commutation money shall be paid to the overseer of highways of the district in which the labor is required to be performed, and shall be applied and expended by such overseer in the purchase of implements, or construction and repair of the roads and bridges in the same district. *Commutation for work on highways, etc.*

(1241.) SEC. 16. The supervisor of each township shall cause the amount of such arrearages of labor, estimating the same at one dollar for each day, to be levied on the lands so returned, and to be collected in the same manner that the contingent charges of the township are collected; and the same when collected shall be paid into the township treasury. to be applied by the commissioner of highways in the construction and improvement of roads and bridges in the road district for the benefit of which the labor was originally assessed. *Supervisor to cause delinquent taxes to be collected, etc.*

Approved May 1, 1875.

[No. 175.]

AN ACT for the apportionment of Senators in the State Legislature.

Senate districts. SECTION 1. *The People of the State of Michigan enact,* That this State shall be and is hereby divided into thirty-two Senate districts, and each district be entitled to one Senator, which shall be constituted as follows, viz :

First District.—The first district shall consist of the second, third, fourth, seventh, and the tenth wards of the city of Detroit, and the townships of Greenfield, Hamtramck, and Grosse Point, in the county of Wayne, and the election returns shall be made to the clerk's office in the county of Wayne.

Second District.—The second district shall consist of the first, fifth, sixth, eighth, and ninth wards of the city of Detroit, and the election returns shall be made to the clerk's office, in the county of Wayne.

Third District.—The third district shall consist of the twelfth ward of the city of Detroit, and the townships of Brownstown, Canton, Dearborn, Ecorse, Huron, Livonia, Monguagon, Nankin, Plymouth, Redford, Romulus, Springwells, Sumpter, Taylor, Van Buren, and the city of Wyandotte, in the county of Wayne, and the election returns shall be made to the clerk's office in the county of Wayne.

Fourth District.—The fourth district shall consist of the county of Washtenaw.

Fifth District.—The fifth district shall consist of the county of Monroe.

Sixth District.—The sixth district shall consist of the county of Lenawee.

Seventh District.—The seventh district shall consist of the county of Jackson.

Eighth District.—The eighth district shall consist of the county of Calhoun.

Ninth District.—The ninth district shall consist of the county of Hillsdale.

Tenth District.—The tenth district shall consist of the counties of Branch and St. Joseph, and the election returns shall be made to the clerk's office of the county of St. Joseph.

Eleventh District.—The eleventh district shall consist of the county of Kalamazoo.

Twelfth District.—The twelfth district shall consist of the counties of Van Buren and Cass, and the election returns shall be made to the clerk's office of the county of Van Buren.

Thirteenth District—The thirteenth district shall consist of the county of Berrien.

Fourteenth District.—The fourteenth district shall consist of the county of Allegan.

Fifteenth District.—The fifteenth district shall consist of the counties of Barry and Eaton, and the election returns shall be made to the clerk's office of the county of Eaton.

Sixteenth District.—The sixteenth district shall consist of the counties of Ingham and Clinton, and the election returns shall be made to the clerk's office of the county of Ingham.

Seventeenth District.—The seventeenth district shall consist of the counties of Livingston and Shiawassee, and the election returns shall be made to the clerk's office of the county of Shiawassee.

Eighteenth District.—The eighteenth district shall consist of the county of Oakland.

Nineteenth District.—The nineteenth district shall consist of the county of Genesee.

Twentieth District.—The twentieth district shall consist of the counties of Macomb and Lapeer, and the election returns shall be made to the clerk's office of the county of Macomb.

Twenty-first District.—The twenty-first district shall consist of the county of St. Clair.

Twenty-second District.—the twenty-second district shall consist of the counties of Sanilac, Tuscola, and Huron, and the election returns shall be made to the clerk's office in [the] county of Tuscola.

Twenty-third District.—The twenty-third district shall consist of the county of Saginaw.

Twenty-fourth District.—The twenty-fourth district shall consist of the counties of Ionia and Montcalm, and the election returns shall be made to the clerk's office in the county of Ionia.

Twenty-fifth District.—The twenty-fifth district shall consist of the county of Kent.

Twenty-sixth District.—The twenty-sixth district shall consist of the counties of Ottawa and Muskegon, and the election returns shall be made to the clerk's office in the county of Ottawa.

Twenty-seventh District.—The twenty-seventh district shall consist of the counties of Newaygo, Oceana, Mecosta, Osceola, Lake, Mason, and Manistee, and the election returns shall be made to the clerk's office in the county of Mecosta.

Twenty-eighth District.—The twenty-eighth district shall consist of the counties of Midland, Gladwin, Roscommon, Gratiot, Isabella, Clare, and the election returns shall be made to the clerk's office in the county of Midland.

Twenty-ninth District.—The twenty-ninth district shall consist of the counties of Bay, Iosco, Ogemaw, Alcona, Oscoda, Alpena, Montmorency, and Presque Isle, and the election returns shall be made to the clerk's office in the county of Bay.

Thirtieth District.—The thirtieth district shall consist of the counties of Wexford, Missaukee, Kalkaska, Grand Traverse, Benzie, Leelanaw, Crawford, Otsego, Antrim, Charlevoix, Emmet, Manitou, and Cheboygan, and the election returns shall be made to the clerk's office in the county of Grand Traverse.

Thirty-first District.—The thirty-first district shall consist of the counties of Mackinac, Chippewa, Schoolcraft, Delta, Menominee, Marquette, and Baraga, and the election returns shall be made to the clerk's office in the county of Marquette.

26

Thirty-second District.—The thirty-second district shall consist of the counties of Houghton, Ontonagon, Keweenaw, and Isle Royal, and the election returns shall be made to the clerk's office in the county of Houghton.

Returns of counties forming one district.

The election returns of each county forming one district shall be made to the county clerk's office in such county.

Approved May 1, 1875.

[No. 176.]

AN ACT to amend sections one, two, three, twelve, thirteen, fourteen, and twenty-four of chapter seventy-three of the compiled laws of eighteen hundred and seventy-one, being compiler's section two thousand two hundred and fifty-seven, two thousand two hundred and fifty-eight, two thousand two hundred and fifty-nine, two thousand two hundred and sixty-eight, two thousand two hundred and sixty-nine, two thousand two hundred and seventy, and two thousand two hundred and seventy-nine, relating to savings associations.

Sections amended.

SECTION 1. *The People of the State of Michigan enact*, That sections one, two, three, twelve, thirteen, fourteen, and twenty-four of chapter seventy-three of the compiled laws of eighteen hundred and seventy-one, being compiler's sections two thousand two hundred and fifty-seven, two thousand two hundred and fifty-eight, two thousand two hundred and fifty-nine, two thousand two hundred and sixty-eight, two thousand two hundred and sixty-nine, two thousand two hundred and seventy, and two thousand two hundred and seventy-nine, relating to savings associations, be amended so as to read as follows:

Authorizing offices of deposit and loan.

SECTION 1. Any five persons or more desirous of organizing an association under the provisions of this act, may associate themselves together and establish offices of deposit and loan of money, upon the terms and conditions and subject to the liabilities and restrictions prescribed in this act, but the aggregate amount of the capital stock of any such association shall not be less than twenty thousand dollars nor more than one hundred thousand dollars.

Aggregate amount of capital stock.

One-half at least of said capital stock shall be paid in in cash before any such association shall commence business or receive any deposits or make any loans, and the balance shall be paid in in cash within one year thereafter; *Provided*, That when the capital stock exceeds fifty thousand dollars the said balance above fifty thousand dollars may be paid in when the trustees shall so order.

One-half paid in before business is commenced.

Proviso.

Certificate of association, what to specify.

SEC. 2. Such persons, under their hands and seals, shall make a certificate in writing, which shall specify—

First, The name assumed to distinguish such association, and to be used in all its dealings;

Second, The place where the operations of deposit and loan of such association are to be carried on, designating the particular county, city, town, or village, at which place such association shall keep an office for the transaction of its business;

Third, The amount of the capital stock of such association, and the number of shares into which the same is divided;

Fourth, The name and place of residence of the shareholders, and the number of shares held and owned by each of them respectively;

Fifth, The period at which such association shall commence and terminate, and which period shall not exceed thirty years;

Sixth, The names and place of residence of the several trustees and officers, and the number of shares of the capital stock of such association owned and held by each of said trustees and officers, which certificate shall be proved or acknowledged and recorded in the office of register of deeds of the county where any office of such association shall be established, and a copy thereof shall be filed in the office of the State Treasurer. *Acknowledgment and record.*

SEC. 3. The certificate required by the last preceding section to be recorded in the office of [the] register of deeds of the county, and filed in the office of the State Treasurer as aforesaid, or copies thereof duly certified by either of said officers, may be used as evidence in all courts and places for and against such association. *Effect of certified copy of certificate of association.*

SEC. 12. Every association so organized shall have power to sue and be sued, plead and be impleaded, answer and be answered, in all suits arising from or growing out of its business, under and by virtue of this act, in all courts of competent jurisdiction. They shall at all times be subject to examination and inspection by the authorized bank inspector of this State, as is or may be provided for by law for the inspection of banks, or savings banks. *Power to sue, etc. Subject to inspection by State bank inspector.*

SEC. 13. The board of trustees of every such association shall report to the State Treasurer on the first Monday of January and July in each year the condition of such association at the time such report is made. Such report shall state the amount of paid up capital then in said association; the number of savings depositors; the amount of savings deposits, which shall mean deposits upon which interest is paid, according to the advertised terms as set forth in their books of deposit as furnished depositors; the amount of all other deposits; the amount of surplus fund; the amount of moneys on hand; the real and personal estate owned by such association, and the value thereof; the amount loaned on securities, as provided in sections four and five of this act, and the amount upon each class; the amount and kind of all other loans; the names and residence of the trustees and officers for the time being, and any other matters affecting the safety of their deposits and interests of their creditors, as the State Treasurer may require; and also at such other times and in such form and manner of their condition on any day past, which the said State Treasurer may require, and shall publish said statements as required in this act. If such association shall neglect to make out and transmit the statement required in this section, for one month beyond the period when the same is required to be made, or shall willfully violate any of the provisions of this act, such association may be deemed insolvent, and may be proceeded against and dissolved in the same *Semi-annual report to State Treasurer. Contents of report. Association failing to make report, et., deemed insolvent.*

manner as any other corporation may be proceeded against and dissolved.

Publication of reports. SEC. 14. The State Treasurer shall embody all such reports received by him in his annual report; and whenever, upon knowl-

Power of Attorney General on notification by treasurer to close up affairs of association. edge, information, or belief, derived from said reports, or from any other source, he shall deem it necessary for the interests of the creditors of any such association, or that its business is being conducted in a manner inconsistent with the provisions of this act, or any of the laws of this State, he shall notify the Attorney General of the State of such fact, who shall have full power, and it is hereby made his duty to proceed to close up the affairs of such association, in any court of competent jurisdiction, and according to the laws in such case made and provided.

Increase of capital stock. SEC. 24. Whenever any such increase shall be made, the board of trustees shall certify thereto, under their hands, and acknowledge the same before some officer authorized to take the acknowledgment of deeds, and shall cause a copy thereof to be filed with the State Treasurer, and with the clerk of the county in which the association is located, who shall attach the same to the articles of incorporation now on file in their respective offices; the pay-

Payment of increase to be in cash, etc. ment of such increase shall be in cash, one-half of which shall be within thirty days, and before the board of trustees shall certify to the said increase as hereinbefore provided, and the balance within

Proviso. one year thereafter: *Provided,* That nothing herein shall apply to or in any manner affect existing banks organized under the laws as they now exist.

Approved May 1, 1875.

* * *

[No. 177.]

AN ACT to release witnesses in criminal cases from giving bail.

Need not give bail except required by judge. SECTION 1. *The People of the State of Michigan enact,* It shall not be necessary in any criminal case for any witness to give bail for his appearance as a witness in such cause, unless required to do so by the order of a judge of a court of record. All laws contraven-

Laws repealed. ing this act are hereby repealed.

SEC. 2. This act shall take immediate effect.

Approved May 1, 1875.

* * *

[No. 178.]

AN ACT to amend sections sixty-two, sixty-five, sixty-nine, and seventy-three, of chapter twelve, relating to the protection and preservation of township records, books and papers, being sections six hundred and ninety-eight, seven hundred and one, seven hundred and five, and seven hundred and nine, of the compiled laws of eighteen hundred and seventy-one.

Sections amended. SECTION 1. *The People of the State of Michigan enact,* That sections sixty-two, sixty-five, sixty-nine, and seventy-three of chapter twelve, relating to the powers and duties of townships, and election and duties of township officers, be and the same are amended so as to read as follows:

(698.) SEC. 62. The supervisor shall preserve and keep all books, assessment rolls, and other papers belonging to his office, in a safe and suitable place, but not in any saloon, restaurant, public inn, hotel, place of public amusement, nor in any place where intoxicating drinks of any kind are kept or sold, or where gaming or plays of chance of any kind are carried on, or where they will be exposed to unusual hazard from fire or theft, and he shall deliver the same on demand to his successor in office, and on application of any person he shall give certified copies of any such papers, or abstracts from any assessment roll, or books in his office; and for making any such copies or abstracts he shall be entitled to receive from the person applying therefor six cents for each folio; but no such copy or abstract and certificate shall be required for less than twelve and a half cents; and such certified copies or abstracts shall be presumptive evidence of the facts therein contained. *Supervisor to preserve books, etc., and furnish certified copies. Fees for copies.*

(701.) SEC. 65. The township clerk of each township shall have the custody of all the records, books, and papers of the township, when no other provision is made by law; and he shall duly file and safely keep all certificates of oaths and other papers required by law to be filed in his office, and record such as are required by law to be recorded therein; such records, books, and papers shall not be kept in any saloon, restaurant, public inn, hotel, place of public amusement, nor in any place where intoxicating drinks of any kind are kept or sold, or where gaming or plays of chance of any kind are carried on, nor where they will be exposed to unusual hazard of fire or theft, and he shall deliver the same on demand to his successor in office; he shall also open and keep an account with the treasurer of his township, and shall charge such treasurer with all funds which shall come into his hands by virtue of his office, and shall credit him with all moneys paid out by him on the order of the proper authorities of the township, and shall enter the date and amount of all vouchers in a book kept by said clerk in said office; he shall also open and keep a separate account with each of the several funds belonging to his township, and shall credit each of said funds with such amounts as properly belong to them, and shall charge them severally with all warrants drawn on the township treasurer and payable from said funds respectively. *Township clerk to keep records, etc., of township.*

(705.) SEC. 69. Each township clerk shall, within the time limited for filing his oath of office and before entering upon the duties of his office, give a bond to the township in such sum and with such sureties as the township board shall require and approve, conditioned for the faithful discharge of the duties of his office according to law, and especially for the safe keeping of the records, books, and papers of said township in the manner required by law, and for their delivery on demand to his successor in office, which bond shall be filed in the office of the supervisor; he shall also appoint a deputy, who shall take an oath of office and file the same with the clerk, and in case of the absence, sickness, death, or other *Township clerk to give bond. To appoint deputy; duties of deputy.*

disability of the clerk, such deputy shall perform the duties of such clerk, and receive the same compensation as the clerk would have been entitled to receive therefor.

Township board to settle with treasurer and other officers. (709.) SEC. 73. The said board shall, at their annual meeting in each year, examine and audit the accounts of the township treasurer for all moneys received and disbursed by him as such treasurer; and they shall also audit and settle the accounts of all other township officers who are authorized by law to receive or disburse any public moneys by virtue of their offices; they shall also have **To enforce statute for protection of records, etc.** power and it shall be their duty to cause the provisions of the statute for the protection and preservation of township records, books, and papers to be enforced; and they shall determine the amount of the bond and the number of sureties to be required from the township clerk, as provided by law, in each year, within the thirty days next preceding the annual township election.

SEC. 2. This act shall take immediate effect.

Approved May 1, 1875.

[No. 179.]

AN ACT to amend section five of chapter twenty-four of the compiled laws of eighteen hundred and seventy-one, being an act relative to persons liable to work on highways, and making assessments therefor.

Section amended SECTION 1. *The People of the State of Michigan enact,* That section five of chapter twenty-four of the compiled laws of eighteen hundred and seventy-one, being compiler's section one thousand two hundred and twenty, being an act relative to persons liable to work on highways, and making assessments therefor, be and the same is hereby amended so as to read as follows:

Highway labor, how and by whom established. SEC. 5. In making the estimate and assessment of highway labor, the commissioner shall proceed as follows:

How to be assessed. *First.* Every male inhabitant in each road district, being above the age of twenty-one, and under the age of fifty, except pensioners of the United States, and other soldiers and sailors honorably discharged, who are disabled from performing manual labor by reason of wounds received, or diseases contracted while in the service of the United States, paupers, idiots, and lunatics, shall be assessed one day;

Residue of highway labor, how apportioned. *Second,* The residue of the highway labor to be assessed not exceeding one-half day's work upon one hundred dollars valuation shall be apportioned upon the estate, real and personal, of every inhabitant in each of the road districts in such township, and upon each tract or parcel of land in the respective road districts of which the owners are non-residents as the same shall appear by the assessment roll;

Commissioner to fix number of days persons and property shall be assessed. *Third.* The commissioner shall affix to the name of each person named in the lists furnished by the overseers and not assessed upon the assessment roll, and also to each valuation of property within the several road districts, the number of days which such person

or property shall be assessed for highway labor, adding one day to
the assessment of each person liable to a poll tax and assessed upon
the township assessment roll.

SEC. 2. This act shall take immediate effect.

Approved May 1, 1875.

[No. 180.]

AN ACT to amend sections fifty and fifty-one, being compiler's
sections six thousand two hundred and fifty-two and six thousand two hundred and fifty-three, chapter one hundred and
ninety-five of the compiled laws of eighteen hundred and seventy-one, and the act amendatory thereto, approved April twenty-nine, eighteen hundred and seventy-three, relative to the
action of ejectment.

SECTION 1. *The People of the State of Michigan enact,* That Sections
sections fifty and fifty-one, being compiler's sections six thousand amended.
two hundred and fifty-two and six thousand two hundred and fifty-
three of chapter one hundred and ninety-five of the compiled laws
of eighteen hundred and seventy-one, as amended by an act approved April twenty-nine, eighteen hundred and seventy-three, relative to the action of ejectment, be amended so as to read as
follows:

(6252) SEC. 50. Whenever in any action of ejectment the plain- When defendant
tiff, or any one or more of the plaintiffs, if there be more than allowed value of
one, shall recover, the defendant or defendants shall be allowed improvements.
compensation for buildings and improvements on the premises recovered, erected, or made by him or them, by any person through
whom he or they claim title, to the extent that such buildings and
improvements shall increase the present value of said premises:
Provided, The defendant or defendants, or the person through Proviso.
whom he or they claim title, shall have been in the actual, peaceable occupation of the premises recovered, for six years before
the commencement of the action : *Or provided,* The same shall Proviso.
have been so occupied for a less time than six years under a color
of title and in good faith.

(6253.) SEC. 51. In all actions of ejectment, if any defendant Estimating value
wish to avail himself of the provisions for compensation contained and value of
in the last preceding section, he may file a claim in writing, to premises with-
compensation for buildings and improvements on the premises in ments.
controversy, setting forth therein the character of the occupation,
and the time thereof, and a request that the jury find whether the
premises have been actually and peaceably occupied by the defendant, or the person through whom he claims title, and the time of
such occupation, and determine the increased value of the premises
by reason thereof, a copy of which, with notice of the filing thereof,
shall be served on the plaintiff or his attorney, at least ten days before the first day of the term at which such cause may be tried.
The plaintiff may then file a request in writing, that the jury also
find and determine what would have been the value of the prem-

ises at the time of the trial, if no buildings had been erected or improvements made or waste committed, a true copy of which, with notice of filing shall be served on the defendant or his attorney, at least five days before the first day of the term at which such cause may be tried. The jury, in all cases in which the above matters shall be submitted to them, shall, by their verdict, if they find for the plaintiff, also find and determine upon said matters.
Approved May 1, 1875.

[No. 181.]
AN ACT to provide for the inspection of illuminating oils manufactured from petroleum, or coal oils.

State inspector of oils, appointment of. SECTION 1. *The People of the State of Michigan enact,* That the Governor shall appoint a suitable person, resident of the State, who is not interested in manufacturing, dealing, or vending any illuminating oils manufactured from petroleum, as State Inspector of Oils, whose *Term of office.* term of office shall be two years from the date of appointment, or until his successor shall be appointed and shall *To test oils offered for sale.* qualify. It shall be the duty of said State Inspector to examine and test the quality of all such oils offered for sale by any manufacturer, vender, or dealer, and if upon such testing, or examination, the oils shall meet the requirements hereinafter specified, he shall *Brand.* fix his brand or device, viz.: "Approved," with the date, over his official signature, upon the package, barrel, or cask containing the same, and it shall be lawful for any manufacturer, vender, or dealer to sell the same as an illuminator; but if the oil so tested shall not meet said requirements, he shall mark in plain letters on said package, cask, or barrel, over his official signature, the words "Rejected *Unlawful to sell rejected oils.* for illuminating purposes," and it shall be unlawful for the owner thereof to sell such oil for illuminating purposes; and if any person shall sell, or offer for sale such rejected oil, he shall be deemed guilty of a misdemeanor, and shall be punished as provided in section four of this act.

Deputy inspectors. SEC. 2. The State Inspector provided for in this act, is hereby empowered to appoint a suitable number of deputies, which deputies are hereby empowered to perform the duties of inspection, and shall be liable to the same penalties as the State Inspector: *Pro- Proviso.* *vided,* That the State Inspector may remove any of said deputies *Inspectors to provide themselves with instruments and inspect oils when called upon.* for reasonable cause. It shall be the duty of the inspector and his deputies, to provide themselves at their own expense, with the necessary instruments and apparatus for testing the quality of said illuminating oils, and when called upon for that purpose, to promptly inspect all oils hereinbefore mentioned, and to report as *Test.* dangerous all oils which, by reason of being adulterated, or for any other reason, will, at the temperature of one hundred and fifty degrees of Fahrenheit's thermometer, take fire when a well-lighted match is applied thereto or plunged therein, or which will emit a combustible vapor at the temperature of one hundred and forty degrees of Fahrenheit's thermometer: *Provided,* The quantity of oil used in this test shall not be less than half a pint; and it shall be the duty of said inspector to designate, by his brand, the temperature at which said oil will ignite. The oil tester adopted Oil tester. and recommended by the Michigan State Board of Health shall be used by the inspector and his deputies.

SEC. 3. Every person appointed State Inspector or deputy in- Oath of inspect-spector shall, before he enters upon the discharge of the duties of or and deputies. his office, take an oath or affirmation, prescribed by the constitution and laws of this State, and the State inspector shall also execute a Bond of inspect-bond to the State of Michigan, in such sum and with such surety or. as shall be approved by the Secretary of State, conditioned for the faithful performance of the duties imposed upon him by this act, which bond shall be for the use of all persons aggrieved by the acts or neglect of said inspector; and the same shall be filed with the clerk of the county where the inspector resides. The deputy Bond of deputy. inspector shall execute a bond to the State of Michigan in such sum and with such surety as shall be approved by the judge of probate, and file the same with the county clerk in the county where the deputy inspector resides. Said inspector or deputy in- Fees for inspec-spector shall be entitled to demand and receive from the owner or tion. party calling on him, or for whom he shall inspect, the sum of forty cents for a single barrel, package, or cask, [and] thirty cents each when not exceeding five in number; twenty-five cents each when not exceeding ten in number, and ten cents for each addi-tional barrel, package, or cask so inspected and branded by him; and it shall be the duty of every inspector or deputy inspector to keep Record of oils a true and accurate record of all oils so inspected and branded by inspected. him, which record shall state the date of inspection, and number of gallons or barrels, and the name of the person for whom in-spected; and the record shall be open to the inspection of any and all persons interested. And it shall be the duty of every deputy Deputies to inspector, within one month after the inspection by him of any report monthly to principal. oils hereinbefore mentioned, to make a true and accurate return thereof to his principal. All illuminating oils manufactured or Inspection of refined in this State shall be inspected before removed from the tured in this manufactory or refinery. And if any person or persons, whether, State. manufacturer, vender, or dealer, shall sell or attempt to sell to any Penalty for sell-person in this State, any illuminating oils, whether manufactured ing, etc., before inspection. in this State or not, before having the same inspected as provided in this act, he shall be deemed guilty of a misdemeanor, and he shall be subject to a penalty in any sum not exceeding five hun-dred dollars; and if any manufacturer, vender, or dealer of either Penalty for or any of said illuminating oils shall falsely brand the package, branding falsely, etc. cask or barrel containing the same, as provided in the sections one and two of this act, or shall use packages, casks, or barrels having the inspector's brand thereon, without having the oil inspected, he shall be deemed guilty of a misdemeanor, and he shall be subject to a penalty in any sum not exceeding five hundred dollars, nor less than one hundred dollars, or be imprisoned in the county jail not exceeding six months, or both, at the discretion of the court.

SEC. 4. It shall be the duty of the inspector, or any deputy in-

27

Inspector or
deputy to enter
complaint.

spector who shall know of the violation of any of the provisions of sections one and three of this act, to enter complaint before any court of competent jurisdiction against any persons so offending.

Inspectors not to
traffic in oils.

SEC. 5. No inspector or deputy inspector shall, while in office, traffic directly or indirectly in any article which he is appointed to inspect. For the violation of this section he shall be liable to the penalty not exceeding ten hundred dollars.

No person to
adulterate, or
sell or use certain oils or their
products.

SEC. 6. No person shall fraudulently adulterate, for the purpose of sale or for use, any coal or kerosene oils to be used for lights, in such a manner as to render them dangerous to use; nor shall any person knowingly sell or offer to sell, or knowingly use such adulterated oil, nor shall any person knowingly sell or offer for sale or knowingly use any coal or kerosene oil, or any of the products thereof, which, by reason of being adulterated, or for any other reason will, at the temperature of one hundred and fifty degrees of Fahrenheit's thermometer, take fire when a well-lighted match is applied thereto or plunged therein, or which will emit a combustible vapor at the temperature of one hundred and forty degrees

Proviso.

of Fahrenheit's thermometer: *Provided,* That the quantity used in the test shall not be less than one-half pint: *And further pro-*

Further proviso.

vided, That the gas or vapor from said oils may be used for illuminating purposes when the oils from which said gas or vapor is generated are contained in reservoirs under ground outside the building illuminated or lighted by said gas. Any person violating

Penalty for violating provisions
of this act.

the provisions of this act shall be deemed guilty of a misdemeanor, and shall upon conviction thereof be punished by imprisonment in the county jail not more than one year, or by fine not exceeding four hundred dollars, or by both fine and imprisonment, in the discretion of the court.

Acts repealed.

SEC. 7. All acts or parts of acts contravening the provisions of this act are hereby repealed.

SEC. 8. This act shall take immediate effect.

Approved May 1, 1875.

[No. 182.]

AN ACT to amend sections one and seventeen of " An act to create a Board of State Swamp Land Commissioners, and to repeal act number seventy-six of the session laws of eighteen hundred and sixty-seven," being sections four thousand and three and four thousand and nineteen of the compiled laws of eighteen hundred and seventy-one.

Sections
amended.

SECTION 1. *The People of the State of Michigan enact,* That sections one and seventeen of " An act to create a Board of State Swamp Land Commissioners, and to repeal act number seventy-six of the session laws of eighteen hundred and sixty-seven," being sections four thousand and three and four thousand and nineteen of the compiled laws of eighteen hundred and seventy-one, be and the same is hereby amended so as to read as follows:

(4003.) SEC. 1. The Governor may appoint a commissioner, who Appointment of shall be denominated "The State Swamp Land Commissioner." State Swamp He shall hold his office for two years, unless removed by the Governor, and he shall receive a salary at the rate of twelve hundred Term of office, dollars per annum, which shall be in full for all services, except necessary and reasonable expenses, and one clerk, stationery for the office, and necessary printing: *Provided*, That in case the business of the office should increase to such an extent at any time that to an assistant. said commissioner should be unable to make all the necessary examinations of work and attend to the other duties of his office, then said commissioner, with the consent of the board of control, may appoint an assistant to perform for the time being such work, and make such examinations as said commissioner may instruct and direct, and said assistant shall make his reports of such work and examinations to said commissioner, who shall be responsible therefor; and for such services said assistant shall receive the sum of three dollars per day, together with his necessary expense, said bill for services and expenses to be itemized and sworn to and approved by both the Governor and said Commissioner, and shall be allowed the same as other bills by the Board of State Auditors. And said Commissioner shall have the same powers, and perform Powers of commissioner. all the duties in relation to State roads and swamp lands in the upper peninsula of Michigan, as are prescribed in the act to which this is amendatory, for the "Board of State Swamp Land Road Commissioners," in relation to State roads and swamp lands in the lower peninsula of Michigan.

(4019.) SEC. 17. Nothing contained in this act shall be construed Construction of as authorizing the appropriation of any lands in the upper peninsula to aid in constructing roads or ditches in the lower peninsula.

SEC. 2. This act shall take immediate effect.

Approved May 1, 1875.

[No. 183.]

AN ACT to amend sections one and fourteen of an act entitled "An act for the relief of school districts," being sections three thousand seven hundred and thirteen and three thousand seven hundred and twenty-six of the compiled laws of eighteen hundred and seventy-one, as amended by act forty-two of the laws of eighteen hundred and seventy-two, approved March twenty-ninth, eighteen hundred and seventy-two.

SECTION 1. *The People of the State of Michigan enact,* That Sections sections one and fourteen of an act entitled "An act for the relief amended. of school districts," being sections three thousand seven hundred and thirteen and three thousand seven hundred and twenty-six of the compiled laws of eighteen hundred and seventy one, as amended by act number forty-two of the laws of eighteen hundred and seventy-two, approved March twenty-ninth, eighteen hundred and seventy-two, [are hereby amended so as to read as follows:]

Voters may designate school-house site by two-thirds vote.

SEC. 1. The qualified voters of any school district, when lawfully assembled, may designate by a vote of two-thirds of those present, such number of sites as may be desired for school-houses, and may change the same by a similar vote at any regular meeting.

School districts may borrow money for erection of school-houses, etc.

SEC. 14. School districts may by a two-thirds vote of the qualified electors of said district present at any annual meeting, or special meeting called for that purpose, borrow money, and may issue bonds of the district therefor, to pay for a school-house site, or sites, and to erect and furnish school buildings, as follows:

Amount limited. Districts having less than thirty children between five and twenty years of age, may have an indebtedness not to exceed three hundred dollars; districts having thirty children of like age, may have an indebtedness not to exceed five hundred dollars; districts having fifty children of like age, may have an indebtedness not to exceed one thousand dollars; districts having one hundred children of like age, may have an indebtedness not to exceed three thousand dollars; districts having two hundred children of like age, may have an indebtedness not to exceed eight thousand dollars; districts having three hundred children of like age, may have an indebtedness not to exceed fifteen thousand dollars; districts having four hundred children of like age, may have an indebtedness not to exceed twenty thousand dollars; districts having five hundred children of like age, may have an indebtedness not to exceed twenty-five thousand dollars; and districts having eight hundred children or more, of like age, may have an indebtedness

Proviso. not to exceed thirty thousand dollars: *Provided*, That in districts having less than thirty children between five and twenty years of age, the amount voted to be raised by tax for the purposes herein mentioned shall not exceed five hundred dollars in the same year that any bonded indebtedness is incurred as authorized by this

Further proviso. section: *Provided further*, That in all proceedings under this act, the acting director, assessor, and one person appointed by the district board shall constitute a board of inspection, who shall cause a poll list to be kept, and a suitable ballot box to be used, which shall be kept open two hours, and said ballotings shall be conducted in the same manner as at township elections.

Approved May 1, 1875.

[No. 184.]

AN ACT to amend section two of chapter one hundred and sixty-two, being compiler's section four thousand five hundred and thirty-one of the compiled laws of eighteen hundred and seventy-one, relative to the specific performance by executors and administrators of the contracts of deceased persons for the conveyance of real estate.

Section amended SECTION 1. *The People of the State of Michigan enact*, That section two of chapter one hundred and sixty-two, being compiler's section four thousand five hundred and thirty-one of the com-

piled laws of eighteen hundred and seventy-one, be and the same
is hereby amended so as to read as follows:

(4531.) SEC. 2. On the presentation of a petition by any person Notice of hearclaiming to be entitled to such conveyance from any executor or ing of petition administrator, setting forth the facts upon which such claim is of real estate of predicated, the judge of probate shall make an order appointing a deceased person.
time and place for hearing such petition, a copy of which order
shall be published at least once in each week for four successive
weeks, before the time fixed for such hearing, in such newspaper
or newspapers in this State as the court shall direct, or cause a
copy of such order to be personally served upon the heirs at law
or other parties interested in said estate, at least twenty days before the day of said hearing.

Approved May 1, 1875.

[No. 185.]

AN ACT to define and establish the boundary line between the
counties of Mackinac and Chippewa.

SECTION 1. *The People of the State of Michigan enact,* That Boundary.
the boundary line between the counties of Mackinac and Chippewa be and the same is hereby established as follows, to-wit:
Commencing at a point in Lake Huron south of the line between
ranges two and three (2 and 3) east, thence north to the north
boundary of township forty-one (41) north, thence west to the line
between ranges one and two (1 and 2) east, thence north to the
north boundary of township forty-two (42) north, thence west to
the meridian, thence north on said meridian to the north boundary
of township forty-three (43) north, thence west on said township
line to the line between ranges six and seven (6 and 7) west, thence
north on said township line to the north boundary of township
forty-four (44) north, thence west to the line between ranges seven
and eight (7 and 8) west, thence north to the north boundary of
township forty-five (45), thence west on the north boundary of
township forty-five (45), to the line between ranges twelve and
thirteen (12 and 13) west.

Approved May 1, 1875.

[No. 186.]

AN ACT to provide for an appropriation to enable the board of
regents to establish and maintain a dental school in connection
with the medical department of the State university.

SECTION 1. *The People of the State of Michigan enact,* That Appropriation.
there shall be, and is hereby appropriated out of any funds in the
treasury of the State of Michigan, not otherwise appropriated, the
sum of three thousand dollars for each of the years eighteen hundred and seventy-five and eighteen hundred and seventy-six, for
the purpose of enabling the board of regents to establish and main-

tain a dental school in connection with the medical department of the State university. The above mentioned sum shall be drawn from the treasury, on the presentation of the proper voucher of the treasurer of said board to the Auditor General, and on his warrant to the State Treasurer.

Approved May 1, 1875.

[No. 187.]

AN ACT for the incorporation of manufacturing companies.

HOW FORMED.

Persons associated for manufacturing purposes a body politic and corporate.

SECTION 1. *The People of the State of Michigan enact,* That any number of persons, not less than three, who, by articles of agreement in writing, have associated, or shall associate according to the provisions of this act, under any name assumed by them, for the purpose of engaging in, and carrying on any kind of manufacturing business, and who shall comply with all the provisions of this act, shall, with their successors and assigns, constitute a body politic and corporate, under the name assumed by them in their articles of association: *Provided,* No two companies shall assume the same name.

Proviso.

Articles of association.

SEC. 2. The articles of agreement of every such association shall be signed by the persons associating in the first instance, and acknowledged before some person authorized by the laws of this State to take the acknowledgment of deeds.

Capital stock.

SEC. 3. The amount of capital stock in every joint stock corporation formed under this act, shall not be less than ten thousand dollars, and shall be fixed and limited by the stockholders in their article of association, and shall be divided into shares of twenty-five dollars each ; but every such corporation may increase its capital stock, and the number of shares therein, at any meeting of the stockholders called for that purpose, or at any annual meeting, by a vote of two-thirds in interest of its stockholders. The amount of capital stock shall not exceed twenty-five hundred thousand dollars.

What articles of association to contain.

SEC. 4. The stockholders of every corporation formed under this act shall, in their articles of association, distinctly and definitely state the term of the existence of such corporations, which term shall not exceed thirty years; and said stockholders shall also distinctly and definitely state, in said articles, the purpose for which every such corporation shall be established, and it shall not be lawful for said corporation to divert its operations or appropriate its funds to any other purpose, except as hereinafter stated.

First meeting of stockholders.

Notice.

SEC. 5. When any number of persons shall have associated according to the provisions of this act, any two of them may call the first meeting of the stockholders, at such time and place as they may appoint, by giving notice thereof by publishing the same in some newspaper published in the county where its operations are to be carried on, and if there is no newspaper published in such county, then by publishing the said notice in some newspaper published in an adjoining county, at least two weeks before the time appointed for such meeting. But said notice may be waived by a writing, signed by all the subscribers to the capital stock of said corporation, specifying the time and place for said first meeting, which writing shall be entered at full length upon the records of the corporation; and the first meeting of any such corporation, which has been held pursuant to such written waiver of notice, shall be valid. *How notice of, may be waived.*

SEC. 6. The stock, property, affairs, and business of every such corporation shall be managed by not less than three nor more than nine directors, who shall be chosen annually by the stockholders, at such time and place as shall be provided by the by-laws of said corporation, and who shall be stockholders, and shall hold their offices for one year, and until others shall be chosen in their stead. *Directors, the number, how chosen, etc.*

SEC. 7. If an election of directors in any such corporation shall not take place at the annual meeting thereof, in any year, such corporation shall not thereby be dissolved, but an election may be had at any time thereafter to be fixed upon, and notice thereof to be given by the directors: *Provided*, That in case the directors shall refuse or neglect so to do, any three of the stockholders may call a meeting of the stockholders for the election of directors, by giving the notice as prescribed in section five of this act. *In case not elected at annual meeting.* *Proviso.*

SEC. 8. The directors of every such corporation shall choose one of their number to be president, and one of their number to be vice president, and shall also choose a secretary and treasurer, which two last mentioned officers shall reside, and have their place of business, and keep the books of said corporation within this State; and shall choose such other officers as the by-laws of the corporation shall prescribe, all of which said officers shall hold their offices until others shall be chosen in their stead: *Provided*, That if the stockholders shall so elect, the same person may hold the office of secretary and treasurer. *Directors to choose officers.* *Proviso.*

SEC. 9. The directors of such corporation, for the time being, shall have power to fill any vacancy which may happen in their board by death, resignation, or otherwise, for the current year. *Directors may fill vacancy in their board.*

DUTIES OF OFFICERS.

SEC. 10. Before any corporation formed under this act shall commence business, the president shall cause the articles of association to be recorded, at the expense of said corporation, in the office of the Secretary of State of this State, and in the office of the county clerk of the county in which said corporation is to transact its business. The Secretary of State and the county clerk in whose office such articles of association shall be recorded, shall each certify upon every such articles of association recorded by him, the time when it was received, with a reference to the book and page where the same is recorded; and the record, or transcript of the record, certified by the Secretary of this State under the seal thereof, shall be received in all the courts of this State as *prima facie* evidence of the due formation, existence, and capacity of such corporation in any suit or proceedings brought by or against the same. *Articles to be recorded by Secretary of State and county clerk.* *Legal value of record or transcript certified by Secretary of State.*

Quorum at
meetings of
directors and of
stockholders. SEC. 11. A majority of the directors of every such corporation, convened according to the by-laws, shall constitute a quorum for the transaction of business; and the stockholders holding a majority of the stock, at any meeting of the stockholders, shall be capable of transacting the business of that meeting, except as herein otherwise provided; and at all meetings of such stockholders each share shall be entitled to one vote. Stockholders may appear and vote in person or by proxy duly filed.

Stockholders may vote by proxy.

Subscription to stock may be called in by directors.

SEC. 12. The directors may call in the subscription to the capital stock of such corporation by installments, in such proportion, and at such times and places as they shall think proper, by giving notice thereof, as the by-laws shall prescribe; and in case any stockholder shall neglect or refuse payment of any such installment for the space of thirty days after the same shall have become due and payable, and after he shall have been notified thereof, said corporation may recover the amount of said installment from such negligent stockholder in any proper action for that purpose, or so much of the stock of said delinquent stockholder as may be necessary to pay such installment so due, may be sold by the directors at public auction at the office of the secretary of the corporation, giving at least thirty days' notice of such sale in some newspaper published in the county where said office is located, if there is a newspaper published in such county, if not, then in some newspaper published in some adjoining county; and in case of a sale of said stock, the proceeds thereof shall be first applied in payment of the installment called for, and the expenses of the sale, and the residue, if any, shall be refunded to the delinquent stockholder. In case the proceeds of such sale shall be insufficient to pay said installment, said corporation may recover the balance from such negligent stockholder. Such sale shall entitle the purchaser to all the rights of a stockholder to the extent of the shares so purchased.

Recovery of subscription when stockholder refuses payment.

Rights of the purchaser of stock.

Annual report.

Publication of.

What to contain.

By whom signed.

Where filed.

Penalty for neglect to make, by directors.

SEC. 13. Every such company shall annually, within the month of January, make a report, which shall be published in some newspaper published in the town, city, or village, or if there be no newspaper published in said town, city, or village, then in some newspaper published nearest the place where the business of said company is carried on, which shall state the amount of capital and of the proportion actually paid in, and the amount of its existing debts, which report shall be signed by the president and a majority of the trustees, and shall be verified by the oath of the president or secretary of said company, and filed in the office of the clerk of the county where the business of the company shall be carried on; and if any of said directors of any such company shall willfully neglect or refuse to make the report required by this section, they shall each be liable and subject to a penalty of twenty-five dollars, and in addition thereto, the sum of five dollars for each and every secular day after the first day of March in each year, during the pendency of such neglect or refusal, which penalty shall be for the use and benefit of the general fund of the county in which such corporation is required to file its report, and the amount so forfeited may be recovered in an action of debt brought in the name of the board of

Penalty shall be for use of county.

Recovery of penalty.

supervisors of the county entitled to the same, and it shall be the
duty of the county clerk at each annual meeting of the board of
supervisors of any such county, to lay before such board a statement
of the names of all corporations in said county who have failed to
make the report required by this act, and such board shall thereupon proceed to collect such forfeiture or forfeitures, according to
law.

THEIR POWERS.

SEC. 14. All corporations organized and established under the
provisions of this act shall be capable to sue and be sued, plead and
be impleaded, answer and be answered unto, appear and prosecute to final judgment in any court or elsewhere; to have a common seal, and to alter the same at pleasure; to elect, in such manner as they shall determine, all necessary officers; to fix their compensation, and define their duties; to ordain and establish by-laws
for the government and regulation of their affairs, and to alter and
repeal the same; and to employ all such agents, mechanics, and
other laborers as they shall think proper. *Corporation may sue and be sued, etc. May have seal. May elect officers, etc. May establish by-laws, employ agents, etc.*

SEC. 15. Every such corporation shall, by its corporate name, have
power to acquire and hold such lands, tenements and hereditaments,
and such other property of every kind as shall be necessary for
the purposes of said corporation, and such other lands, tenements,
and hereditaments as shall be taken in payment of, or as security
for debts due to such corporation, and to manage and dispose of the
same at pleasure. *Authority to acquire and hold property.*

SEC. 16. The books of every such corporation containing their
accounts, shall be kept, and shall at all reasonable times be open in
the city, village, or town where such corporation is located, or at the
office of the treasurer of such corporation, within this State, for
inspection of any of the stockholders of said corporation; and
said stockholders shall have access to the books and statements of
said corporation, and shall have the right to examine the same in
said city, village, or town, or at said office; and as often as once in
each year, a true statement of the accounts of said corporation
shall be made and exhibited to the stockholders by order of the di-
rectors. *Books to be open for inspection of stockholders. Annual statement to stockholders.*

SEC. 17. The stock of every such corporation shall be deemed
personal property, and be transferred only on the books of such
corporation, in such form and manner as their by-laws shall prescribe; and such corporation shall at all times have a lien upon
all the stock or property of its members, invested therein, for all
debts due from them to such corporation. *Stock deemed personal property.*

SEC. 18. Every such corporation may amend its articles of association by the specification of any other lawful business in which
two-thirds of its stockholders in interest may desire to engage; but
before it shall commence any business under its amended articles,
other than such as was distinctly and definitely specified in its
original articles, the president and directors shall cause such of
the amended articles as specify the purpose for which such corpo-
ration is formed, subscribed by two-thirds of its stockholders in in- *Amendment of articles of association.*

terest, to be recorded in the same manner, and with the like effect, as the original articles of association.

Removal of place of business

SEC. 19. Any corporation organized under the provisions of this act may remove its place of business from any city, village, or town in this State, where it is or may be located, to any other city, village, or town in this State, by a vote of two-thirds of its stockholders in interest. But in case of a removal from one county to another, the president and secretary of such corporation shall attach to their articles of association a certificate that such corporation has thus removed, and said articles of association, together with said certificate, shall be left for record immediately on such removal, in the office of the county clerk of the county to which such corporation shall remove, and they shall be recorded by such clerk, at full length, in the book kept by him for such purpose.

Certificate of removal deposited with Secretary of State.

And the president and secretary of such corporation shall, immediately on such removal, cause a certificate thereof to be deposited with the Secretary of State, which certificate shall be recorded by him in the book kept for the record of articles of corporation.

President and directors to make certificate of increase of capital stock.

SEC. 20. When any such corporation shall increase its capital stock as provided in section three of this act, the president and a majority of the directors shall, within thirty days thereafter, make a certificate thereof, which shall be signed by them, and re-

Record of same.

corded as is provided in the tenth section of this act.

Return of articles and certificate after recording.

SEC. 21. The Secretary of State, and any county clerk, after recording the articles of association and certificates specified by this act to be recorded by them, shall return the same, each with his endorsement of record thereon, to said corporation; and for re-

Fees for recording.

cording the articles of association and certificates required in this act, the Secretary of State and county clerk shall each be entitled to receive at the rate of twenty cents for each folio.

LIABILITIES FOR NEGLECT OF DUTIES.

Liability of stockholders when capital stock has been refunded.

SEC. 22. If the capital stock of any such corporation shall be withdrawn, and refunded to the stockholders before the payment of all the debts of the corporation for which such stock would have been liable, the stockholders of such corporation shall be jointly and severally liable to any creditor of such corporation, in an action founded on this statute, to the amount of the sum refunded to him or them respectively.

Liability of assenting directors for paying dividends when corporation is insolvent.

SEC. 23. If the directors of any such corporation shall declare and pay a dividend when the corporation is insolvent, or any dividend the payment of which would render it insolvent, knowing such corporation to be insolvent, or that the payment of such dividend would render it so, the directors assenting thereto shall be jointly and severally liable in an action founded on this statute for all debts due from such corporation at the time of paying or declaring such dividend.

Liability for violating provisions of this act.

SEC. 24. If any corporation organized under this act shall violate any of its provisions, the directors ordering or assenting to such violation, shall be jointly and severally liable, in an action founded on this statute, for all debts contracted after such violation as aforesaid, to the extent of three times the amount paid in on the stock standing in the name of such director in any such company.

LIENS ON STOCK, HOW ENFORCED.

SEC. 25. Any corporation organized under this act, which has a lien upon the stock of any stockholder therein as provided by the seventeenth section, may give notice to such stockholder that unless he shall pay his indebtedness to said corporation within three months from the time of giving such notice, then such corporation will proceed to sell and transfer the stock of such stockholder in said corporation; and upon default of payment said corporation may sell the stock of such indebted stockholder as hereafter provided, and any such corporation may prescribe by its by-laws the manner of giving the notice required by this section. *Notice to delinquent stockholder of sale of stock.*

SEC. 26. Such corporation may at any time within six months after it shall have given the notice required by the preceding section to such indebted stockholder of its intention to sell such stock, and the three months' notice shall have expired, advertise in one or more newspapers published in the county where such corporation is located, and if there is no newspaper published in said county, then in a newspaper published in an adjoining county, giving at least three weeks' notice of the time and place when and where such stock will be sold; and at the time and place of sale, shall state the amount due from such stockholder to such corporation, and may then proceed to sell for cash, at public auction, to the highest bidder therefor, so much of the stock of such indebted stockholder as shall pay in full the indebtedness of such stockholder to such corporation, together with the necessary costs of sale; and if the sale of the entire stock of such indebted stockholder shall not be sufficient to pay in full the claim of said corporation on said stock, such corporation shall credit the amount received for such stock, less the costs of sale, to said indebted stockholder, and may proceed to collect the remainder of their debt by any proper action for that purpose. *Publication of notice of sale.* *Sale.* *Proceedings when entire stock not sufficient to pay indebtedness.*

SEC. 27. Whenever the purchasers of said stock shall have complied with the conditions of said sale, the corporation shall issue new certificates of stock to such purchasers, or to their order, and shall cancel upon the books of the corporation the certificates of such indebted stockholders, and the new certificates so issued shall entitle the holders thereof to all the privileges, rights, and interests of a stockholder in such corporation. *New certificates issued to purchasers of stock.*

SEC. 28. Whenever any stockholder in any such corporation shall have made a transfer or assignment of his stock as security for his indebtedness to a third party, and afterwards shall become a debtor to such corporation, such corporation may sell the equity of redemption of such stock, in the same manner as is provided for the sale of stock on which it has a lien, and shall credit the amount received from such sale to such indebted stockholder. Such corporation may require the party holding a transfer or assignment of such stock, to give a statement to the treasurer of such corpo- *Sale of stock assigned as security to third party.* *Statement to treasurer of amount for which stock is pledged.*

ration under oath, of the amount for which said stock was pledged;
Forfeiture for not making. and if said party shall not give such a statement at or before the
time such sale is to take place, he shall forfeit all claim and lien
on such stock or any part thereof, and such corporation may sell
the same as herein provided.

Certain rights not affected by provisions of preceding sections. SEC. 29. Nothing contained in the four preceding sections shall
affect any lien or right acquired by any other party by virtue of
any attachment or levy of execution upon the stock of any stockholder in any such corporation.

GENERAL PROVISIONS.

Liability of stockholders for labor performed, and the enforcement of the same. SEC. 30. The stockholders of all corporations organized under
this act shall be individually liable for all labor performed for such
corporations, which said liability may be enforced against any
stockholder by action founded on this statute, at any time after an
execution shall be returned unsatisfied, in whole or in part, against
the corporation, or at any time after an adjudication in bankruptcy
against said corporation, and the amount due on such execution
shall be *prima facie* evidence of the amount recoverable, with
costs, against any such stockholder; and if any stockholder shall
be compelled by any such action to pay the debts of any creditor,
or any part thereof, he shall have the right to call upon all the responsible stockholders to contribute their equal part of the sum so
paid by him as aforesaid, and may sue them, jointly or severally, or
any number of them, and recover in such action the amount due
from the stockholder or stockholders so sued.

Service of legal process, on whom made. SEC. 31. Service of any legal process against any corporation
formed under this act may be made on the president, secretary, or
treasurer, or if neither of them can be found in the county in
which, by their articles of association, they are to do business,
then such service may be made by posting a true copy thereof on
some conspicuous place at the business office of the company in
said county.

Taxation. SEC. 32. All corporations formed under this act shall be liable to
be assessed for all real and personal estate held by them in this
State, at its true value, and shall pay thereon a tax for township,
village, city, county, and State purposes, the same as other real
and personal estate; and such tax shall be assessed, collected, and
paid in the same manner as other taxes on real and personal estate
are required to be assessed, collected, and paid: *Provided*, Nothing
Proviso. herein contained shall authorize the taxing of the capital stock of
such corporation as such capital stock.

Certain articles exempt from seizure by execution. SEC. 33. That all articles of machinery, materials for manufacturing, or manufactured articles belonging to any such company,
shall be free from seizure by execution or distress, for any debts or
claims for rents or services, in whose hands soever they may be,
except such execution or claim be against such company.

Act subject to Chap. 130, C. L. SEC. 34. Companies formed under this act shall be subject to the
provisions of chapter one hundred and thirty of the compiled laws
of eighteen hundred and seventy-one, so far as applicable.

SEC. 35. Every manufacturing corporation organized under the provisions of chapter ninety-five of the compiled laws of eighteen hundred and seventy-one, may at any time, by a vote of a majority in interest of its stockholders, or by an agreement in writing signed by a majority in interest of its stockholders, dissolve its organization, and organize under this act, by filing with the Secretary of State and county clerk of the county where the business of said corporation is transacted, a certified copy of the record of the vote of said stockholders, or of the agreement of said stockholders; which said copies shall be recorded as provided in the tenth section of this act; and after perfecting its organization according to the provisions of this section, it shall be entitled to all the rights, and privileges, and immunities contained in this act, and the property, effects, and rights of action of the former corporation shall pass to, and be vested in, the corporation so organized under this act; and the debts, liabilities, and demands existing against the former corporation so dissolved, shall be and remain debts, liabilities, and demands against the newly organized corporation, and may be prosecuted against it in like manner, and to the like effect, as they might have been against the corporation so dissolved; and all conveyances and grants of real or personal property heretofore made to any corporation so dissolved, are hereby confirmed and declared as effectual and valid to all intents and purposes to the corporation so organized under this act, as if made under the [present] provisions of this act.

Certain corporations may dissolve and organize under this act.

Approved May 1, 1875.

[No. 188.]

AN ACT to regulate the catching of fish in certain waters of this State.

SECTION 1. *The People of the State of Michigan enact,* That no person shall extend any pound, trap, stake, or set-net of any kind, or any other device for the purpose of taking fish in Lake Erie (within the jurisdiction of this State), further than one mile in a easterly direction measured from a line running from Point Mouille, in township of Berlin, in Monroe county, in this State, to Stony Point, in said county, nor further than one mile out from a line running from Stony Point to Raisin Point, in said county, nor further than one mile out from a line running from Raisin Point to Bay Point, or North Cape, of Maumee Bay, at the State line between the States of Michigan and Ohio. Nets, or other devices for taking fish, extending from the shores of islands in Lake Erie within this State, shall not be extended further than one mile from shore of said islands.

Limit for fishing with net, etc., in Lake Erie.

SEC. 2. No person shall use any pound, trap, stake, or set-net, or device of any kind for taking fish, in the Detroit river, or the head of Lake Erie to Point Morrille, one mile in a easterly direction from said point, nor in Lake St. Clair within a radius of two miles from the different mouths or outlets of St. Clair river, or

In Detroit river, head of Lake Erie and Lake St. Clair.

within a radius of the same distance from the present light-house near the outlet of Lake St. Clair within the waters of this State.

Relative to the use of nets, etc., in Lakes Erie and St. Clair, and St. Clair river. Sec. 3. No person shall use any net whatever, or device of any kind for the purpose of catching fish, in the waters of Lakes Erie or St. Clair, within this State, beyond such limits as may be designated in this act. No person shall use any pound, trap, stake, fike, set-net, or device of any kind for taking fish, in the St. Clair river within the jurisdiction of this State, excepting as provided for in section four of this act.

Sweep nets not to exceed a certain length. Sec. 4. No sweep net exceeding one hundred and fifty fathoms in length shall be used in any waters in this State for the purpose of taking fish. No sweep net exceeding sixty fathoms in length shall be used in the waters of Detroit river or St. Clair river within the boundaries of this State.

Attaching of nets, etc., to bridges across Detroit and St. Clair rivers, prohibited. Sec. 5. No person shall attach, either directly or indirectly, to any bridge across either of said Detroit river or St. Clair river, or to any pier, part, or appurtenance of said bridge, any net or device by which the passage of fish shall be prevented or impeded. No bridge company, or other company, or person having the control of such bridge, shall license or permit, either for hire or gratuitously, any such net or device to be in any way attached thereto, or to any part thereof.

Catching white fish in certain waters, between certain dates, prohibited. Sec. 6. It shall not be lawful for any person to catch or take whitefish, between the twentieth day of November and the first day of March succeeding in each year, in any of said waters of Lake Erie or Detroit and St. Clair rivers ; and immediately after said twentieth day of November, all nets, piles, stakes, and all other appliances of every kind which have been used in the business of fishing, shall be carried or caused to be carried to the shore, or inside the channel bank, by the person or persons who have used them ; and they shall also cause the ground beneath the waters where such fishing has been carried on, to be cleared, so far as may be reasonable to be done, from all debris and material found thereon, which has resulted from said business.

Penalty for attempting to divert the natural running of white fish. Sec. 7. Any person who shall attempt to divert the natural progress or running of whitefish within any of the waters mentioned in the different sections of this act, by shingling, or any other device calculated to frighten or divert such fish from their natural course, shall forfeit the sum of one hundred dollars, and imprisonment not exceeding sixty days, at the discretion of the court. Pound nets or seines shall not be construed to come within the provisions of this section, when used in compliance with this act.

Trial and penalty for offending against provisions of this act. Sec. 8. Any person charged with offending against the provisions of this act, may be tried before a justice of the peace of the county in which the offense is charged to have been committed, in the same manner as other offenders are tried where the justice has jurisdiction, and upon conviction such person shall be subject to a fine not exceeding fifty dollars, for each and every offense, and to imprisonment in the county jail until such fine is paid ; but not for a period exceeding sixty days.

SEC. 9. It shall be the duty of said commissioners of State fisheries, or of the sheriffs of the different counties in their respective jurisdictions, to enforce the provisions of this act, and when upon information or otherwise, said commissioners or sheriffs shall discover any violations thereof, to institute the necessary proceedings to punish such violation. Who to enforce provisions of this act.

SEC. 10. No part of this act shall be construed as a prohibition upon fishing with hooks, or with spears, or any instrument or device similar in principle of its operation to such hooks or spears, at any time, and in any waters, nor upon fishing with sweep nets of any length not exceeding one hundred and fifty fathoms, in the waters where pound, stake, trap, or set-nets, or set devices of any kind for taking fish, may be used under the provisions of this act. Relative to fishing with hooks, spears, etc.

SEC. 11. It shall not be lawful to use sweep nets within two miles of the mouths of St. Clair river during the months of December, January, and February, in each year, nor to use seines in the above named locality during the spawning season of black bass. Sweep nets, etc., use of, in St. Clair river.

SEC. 12. Nothing in this act contained shall prohibit the catching of soft fish, sturgeon, pike, or carnivorous fish at any time. Relative to catching of soft fish, etc.

Approved May 1, 1875.

[No. 189.]

AN ACT to repeal act number fifty-one of the session laws of eighteen hundred and seventy-two, entitled "An act to amend sections fifteen and eighteen of act number one hundred and fifty-five of the session laws of eighteen hundred and sixty-nine, entitled 'An act to amend act number seventy-six of the session laws of eighteen hundred and sixty-seven, entitled An act for the appointment of a commissioner to be known as the Swamp Land State Road Commissioner,' approved March twenty-first, eighteen hundred and sixty-seven, by adding six new sections thereto, to stand as sections fourteen, fifteen, sixteen, seventeen, eighteen, and nineteen," approved April fifth, eighteen hundred and sixty-nine.

SECTION 1. *The People of the State of Michigan enact,* That act number fifty-one of the session laws of eighteen hundred and seventy-two, entitled "An act to amend sections fifteen and eighteen of act number one hundred and fifty-five of the session laws of eighteen hundred and sixty-nine, entitled 'An act to amend act number seventy-six of the session laws of eighteen hundred and sixty-seven, entitled An act for the appointment of a commissioner to be known as the Swamp Land State Road Commissioner,' approved March twenty-first, eighteen hundred and sixty-seven by adding six new sections thereto, to stand as sections fourteen, fifteen, sixteen, seventeen, eighteen, and nineteen," approved April fifth, eighteen hundred and sixty-nine, be and the same is hereby repealed. Act repealed.

SEC. 2. This act shall take immediate effect.

Approved May 1, 1875.

[No. 190.]

AN ACT to repeal section thirteen of an act to amend chapter ninety-four of the revised statutes in relation to criminal proceedings, being section five thousand five hundred and sixty-five of the compiled laws of eighteen hundred and seventy-one, relating to appeals in criminal cases from justice's courts.

Section repealed. SECTION 1. *The People of the State of Michigan enact,* That section five thousand five hundred and sixty-five of the compiled laws of eighteen hundred and seventy-one, be and the same is hereby repealed,—relating to appeals in criminal cases from justice's courts.

Approved May 1, 1875.

[No. 191.]

AN ACT to amend sections twenty-five and twenty-six of chapter two hundred and forty-four, being sections seven thousand five hundred and thirty-four and seven thousand five hundred and thirty-five of the compiled laws of eighteen hundred and seventy-one, relative to offenses against the lives and persons of individuals.

Sections amended. SECTION 1. *The People of the State of Michigan enact,* That sections twenty-five and twenty-six of chapter two hundred and forty-four, being sections seven thousand five hundred and thirty-four and seven thousand five hundred and thirty-five of the compiled laws of eighteen hundred and seventy-one, relative to offenses against the lives and persons of individuals, be so amended as to read as follows:

Unlawfully confining any person, how punished. (7534.) SEC. 25. Every person who willfully and without lawful authority shall forcibly or secretly confine or imprison any other person within this State against his will, or shall forcibly carry or send such person out of this State, or shall forcibly seize and confine, or shall inveigle or kidnap any other person with intent either to cause such person to be secretly confined or imprisoned in this State against his will, or in any way held to service against his will, shall be punished by imprisonment in the State prison not more than ten years, or by fine not exceeding one thousand dollars.

Where offense may be tried. (7535.) SEC. 26. Every offense mentioned in the preceding section may be tried either in the county in which the same may have been committed or in any county in or through which the person so seized, taken, inveigled, kidnapped, or whose services shall be so sold or transferred, shall have been taken, confined, held, carried, or brought; and upon the trial of any such offense, the consent thereto of the person so taken, inveigled, kidnapped, or confined, shall not be a defense, unless it shall be made satisfactorily to appear to the jury that such consent was not obtained by fraud nor extorted by duress or by threats.

Approved May 1, 1875.

[No. 192.]

AN ACT to amend section two of an act entitled "An act relative
to the costs of proceedings in criminal cases," approved March
thirteen, eighteen hundred and forty-nine, being section seven
thousand four hundred and eighty-nine of the compiled laws of
eighteen hundred and seventy-one.

SECTION 1. *The People of the State of Michigan enact,* That
section two of an act entitled "An act relative to the costs of proceedings in criminal cases," approved March thirteen, eighteen
hundred and forty-nine, being sections seven thousand four hundred
and eighty-nine of the compiled laws of eighteen hundred and
seventy-one, be and the same is so amended as to read as follows :
(7489.) SEC. 2. That whenever any person shall attend any
court as a witness, in behalf of the people of this State, upon request of the public prosecutor, or upon a subpœna, or by virtue of
any recognizance for that purpose, he shall be entitled to the following fees : For attending in a court of record, one dollar for each
day, and fifty cents for each half day; for attending in a justice'
court or upon an examination, seventy-five cents for each day, and
thirty-seven and a half cents for each half day, and for traveling,
at the rate of ten cents per mile in going to the place of attendance, to be estimated from the residence of such witness, if within
the State; if without this State, from the boundary line which
witness passed in going to attend the court.
Approved May 1, 1875.

(margin notes: Section amended / Fees of witnesses in criminal cases.)

[No. 193.]

AN ACT to amend sections one, three, five, six, eight, and nine of
an act entitled "An act to prohibit the maintaining of suits in
equity by judgment creditor's bill, to provide a remedy at law
in lieu thereof, and to repeal sections twenty-four and twenty-
five of chapter ninety of the revised statutes of eighteen hundred and forty-six;" the same being sections six thousand five
hundred and thirteen, six thousand five hundred and fourteen,
six thousand five hundred and fifteen, six thousand five hundred
and seventeen, six thousand five hundred and eighteen, six thousand five hundred and twenty, and six thousand five hundred
and twenty-one of the compiled laws of eighteen hundred and
seventy-one.

SECTION 1. *The People of the State of Michigan enact,* That
sections one, three, five, six, eight, and nine of an act entitled "An
act to prohibit the maintaining of suits in equity by judgment
creditor's bill, to provide a remedy at law in lieu thereof, and to
repeal sections twenty-four and twenty-five of chapter ninety of
the revised statutes of eighteen hundred and forty-six," approved
June twenty-eight, eighteen hundred and fifty-one, be and the same
are hereby amended so as to read as follows:

(margin note: Sections amended.)

29

Judgment debtor, in certain cases, to make discovery of property on oath. SEC. 1. That when an execution against the property of a judgment debtor, issued to the sheriff of the county in which he resides, or, if he reside out of the State, to the sheriff of the county in which the judgment was recorded, or a transcript thereof filed, shall be returned unsatisfied in whole or in part, the judgment creditor may obtain an order from the judge of the court in which the judgment was obtained, or from the judge of the circuit court for the county in which the defendant resides, or from the circuit court commissioner of any such county, or of the county in which a transcript may have been filed as aforesaid, requiring the judgment debtor to appear and make discovery on oath, concerning his property or any debts due or to become due to him, before such judge or commissioner, at a time and place specified in the order.

Where party and witnesses to be examined. SEC. 3. If the party or witness reside in the county where the order is made, he shall be required to attend before the judge of the circuit court, or before the commissioner for such county; if in any other county, before a referee, as provided in section seven of this act. In the latter case the examination shall be taken in writing and certified to the court or judge.

May appoint receivers, and forbid transfers, etc., of property. SEC. 5. The judge may also by an order appoint a receiver of the property of the judgment debtor, with the like powers and authority as receivers heretofore appointed by courts of equity in this State. The judge or commissioner may also by an order forbid a transfer of the property of the judgment debtor and any interference therewith, and such order shall have the like effect as an injunction from a court of equity.

Actions by receiver against person claiming interest in property of debtor. SEC. 6. If it appear that the person or persons so brought before the judge or commissioner by the aforesaid judgment creditor, claims an interest in the property of the judgment debtor, adverse to him, such interest shall be recovered only in an action by the receiver; but the judge or commissioner may, by an order, forbid a transfer or other disposition of such interest till a sufficient opportunity be given to the receiver to commence the action; but such receiver shall bring no action unless at the request of the judgment creditor, and at his expense in case of failure, and he may require such reasonable security against all costs as he may think proper, before commencing such action.

Fees allowed to creditor, etc. SEC. 8. The judge may allow to the judgment creditor, or to any party examined, whether a party to the action or not, witness fees and disbursements, and a fixed sum in addition, not exceeding thirty dollars, as costs.

Liability of party or witness for disobeying order of judge. SEC. 9. If any party or witness shall disobey any order of the judge or commissioner, made in pursuance of this act, and duly served, such party or witness may be punished by the judge, as for a contempt, in the same manner as the circuit court may punish for contempt.

Approved May 1, 1875.

[No. 194.]

AN ACT to repeal act number one hundred and fifty-five of the session laws of eighteen hundred and sixty-nine, entitled "An act to amend act number seventy-six of the session laws of eighteen hundred and sixty-seven, entitled 'An act for the appointment of a commissioner, to be known as the Swamp Land State Road Commissioner,' approved March twenty-first, eighteen hundred and sixty-seven, by adding six new sections thereto, to stand as sections fourteen, fifteen, sixteen, seventeen, eighteen, and nineteen."

SECTION 1. *The People of the State of Michigan enact,* That act number one hundred and fifty-five of the session laws of one thousand eight hundred and sixty-nine, entitled "An act to amend act number seventy-six of the session laws of one thousand eight hundred and sixty-seven, entitled 'An act for the appointment of a commissioner to be known as the Swamp Land State Road Commissioner,' approved March twenty-first, one thousand eight hundred and sixty-seven, by adding six new sections thereto, to stand as sections fourteen, fifteen, sixteen, seventeen, eighteen, and nineteen," approved April fifth, one thousand eight hundred and sixty-nine, be and the same is hereby repealed. *Act repealed.*

SEC. 2. This act shall take immediate effect.

Approved May 1, 1875.

———

[No. 195.]

AN ACT to amend section two of chapter sixty-three, being section two thousand and ninety of the compiled laws of eighteen hundred and seventy-one, relative to the protection of fish and the preservation of fisheries.

SECTION 1. *The People of the State of Michigan enact,* That section two of chapter sixty-three, being compiler's section two thousand and ninety of the compiled laws of eighteen hundred and seventy-one, be and the same are amended soas to read as follows: *Section amended*

SEC. 2. There shall be erected and maintained in each dam across any stream which by law is a public highway, by the owner or occupant thereof, or by any person or persons, or the officers of any corporation using the waters thereof, through the medium of any canal or race, sufficient and permanent shutes or fish ladders, to admit the passage of fish in such stream during the months of April, May, and June, in each year ; and if the owner or occupant of any such dam, or person or persons, or the officers of any corporation using the waters thereof through the medium of any canal or race, shall neglect or refuse for the period of sixty days, to construct and maintain such shutes or fish ladders as aforesaid, whenever requested in writing so to do by the Fish Commissioner of this State, such person or persons, or officers of any corporation, shall be deemed guilty of a misdemeanor, and for each and every *Erection of shutes.* *Neglect to erect.*

Penalty.   sixty days that such person or persons, or officers of such corporation, shall so neglect or refuse, he or they shall be punished by a fine not exceeding five hundred dollars, or by imprisonment in the county jail not exceeding ninety days, or by both such fine and imprisonment, in the discretion of the court.

Section added.   SEC. 2. There shall be added to said act one section to stand as section four, to read as follows:

Erection of shutes by corporations owning dams.   SEC. 4. In respect to the construction and maintenance of fish shutes or fish ladders at dams owned by corporations, the duties and liabilities imposed by this act shall devolve and be imposed upon the president and secretary of such corporation.

Approved May 1, 1875.

[No. 196.]

AN ACT to amend sections thirty-two and sixty-eight of chapter twenty-one, being sections nine hundred and ninety-eight and one thousand and thirty-four of the compiled laws of eighteen hundred and seventy-one, relative to the duties of the county clerk and Auditor General.

Sections amended.   SECTION 1. *The People of the State of Michigan enact,* That sections thirty-two and sixty-eight of chapter twenty-one, being sections nine hundred and ninety-eight and ten hundred and thirty-four of the compiled laws of eighteen hundred and seventy-one, relative to the duties of the county clerk and Auditor General, be amended so as to read as follows:

Certificates of apportionment of taxes.   (998.) SEC. 32. The clerk of the board of supervisors shall, immediately after such apportionment, make out two certificates of the amount apportioned to be assessed upon the property of each township, for State, county, township, fractional school districts, and other purposes, one of which he shall deliver to the county treasurer, and the other to the supervisor of the proper township or ward; and the county treasurer shall charge the amount of the State and county taxes specified in such certificate to the proper

County clerk to keep account with treasurer.   township, ward, or city. The county clerk shall also open and keep an account with the treasurer of his county, and shall charge such treasurer with all funds which shall come into his hands by virtue of his office, and shall credit him with all moneys paid out by him on the order of the proper authorities of his county. He shall also open and keep a separate account with each of the several funds belonging to his county, and shall credit each of said funds with such amounts as properly belong to them, and shall charge them severally with all warrants drawn on the county treasurer, and payable from said funds respectively.

Transcript of lands delinquent for taxes to be forwarded to Auditor General.   (1034.) SEC. 68. Such transcript, so made, compared, and certified, shall be forwarded by the county treasurer to the Auditor General, by the first day of March next after the return of such statement; but such transcript shall be receivable at any time during said month of March; and when received by the Auditor General the amount thereof shall be placed to the credit of the proper

When receivable, etc.

county on the books in his office, and a receipt of the same given to the county treasurer.

Approved May 1, 1875.

[No. 197.]

AN ACT to appropriate lands to aid in the construction of a railroad from the village of L'Anse, in the county of Baraga, to the village of Houghton, in the county of Houghton.

SECTION 1. *The People of the State of Michigan enact,* That to secure the early construction of a railroad from the village of L'Anse, in the county of Baraga, to the village of Houghton, in the county of Houghton, and for the purposes of drainage and reclamation, there are hereby appropriated five (5) sections of State swamp lands per mile. *Appropriation.*

SEC. 2. The State swamp lands hereby appropriated and reserved to further the construction of said railroad, are those lying in the counties of Baraga, Houghton, and Keweenaw, and thirty sections in the eastern and southern portions of the county of Ontonagon. *Location of lands.*

SEC. 3. To further the construction of said railroad and for the better protection of the interests of the State, the Board of Control of State Swamp Lands shall have full power and authority over said lands, the reservations necessary, and the limitations and privileges requisite in the application of such lands to such purpose. *Authority over lands vested in Board of Control of State Swamp Lands.*

SEC. 4. Said board may confer such lands upon any corporation that shall enter into bonds to the State of Michigan, satisfactory to said board, to complete said road within five years from the time the said lands are conferred upon such corporation ; said road to be of the standard gauge of four feet eight and one-half inches. *Board may confer lands upon corporation.*

SEC. 5. And if said lands shall be conferred by said board upon any corporation under the provisions of this act, such corporation shall be entitled to receive patents for fifty (50) sections of lands upon the completion and acceptance by said board of any section of ten continuous miles. *When corporation to receive patents.*

SEC. 6. Said lands shall become taxable as fast as they are conveyed to said railroad company. *When lands to become taxable.*

SEC. 7. This act shall take immediate effect.

Approved May 1, 1875.

[No. 198.]

AN ACT to authorize the board of trustees of the Michigan institution for educating the deaf, the dumb, and the blind to convey certain State land in the city of Flint for street purposes.

SECTION 1. *The People of the State of Michigan enact,* That the board of trustees of the Michigan institution for educating the *Authority to convey.*

deaf and dumb, and the blind, are hereby authorized to convey by
quit-claim deed to the city of Flint, in the county of Genesee, all
the interest of the State of Michigan in and to a strip of land not
exceeding two rods in width across the west end of the triangular
piece of land owned by the State of Michigan, and lying north of
the grounds of the institution for the deaf, dumb, and blind, in
the fourth ward of the city of Flint, beginning at a point on the
Lands described. north side of the Miller road, so called, where the east line of land
owned by Ira Wright intersects said road, and running in a north-
erly direction across said State land, on a line parallel with the
east line of said land owned by Ira Wright, to the northern wagon
road, so called, for the purpose of laying out and establishing a
Proviso. street: *Provided*, That no expense for laying out, establishing,
or in any way improving such street shall ever be chargeable to
Further proviso. the State: *And provided further*, That a strip of land of the
same width and length, is conveyed to said city, for the same purpose, by the owner of the property adjoining on the west.

SEC. 2. This act shall take immediate effect.

Approved May 1, 1875.

[No. 199.]

AN ACT to amend an act entitled "An act to authorize the supreme court to appoint a crier," approved February twenty-fifth,
eighteen hundred and sixty-one, by adding a new section thereto.

Act amended. SECTION 1. *The People of the State of Michigan enact*, That
an act entitled "An act to authorize the supreme court to appoint
a crier," be and the same is hereby amended by adding thereto a
new section, to read as follows:

On filing of bond SEC. 2. Upon filing with the clerk of said court the bond required
crier empowered by law to be given by sheriffs with sureties to be approved by the
to serve order, chief justice of said court, said crier shall have power to serve all
etc. orders, processes, or writs issued from said court, and shall receive
for such service the fees allowed by law to sheriffs.

SEC. 3. This act shall take immediate effect.

Approved May 1, 1875.

[No. 200.]

AN ACT to amend section thirty-one of chapter one hundred
and fifty-three of the revised statutes of eighteen hundred and
forty-six, being section seven thousand five hundred and forty
of the compiled laws of eighteen hundred and seventy-one,
relative to exposing children with intent to abandon them.

Section amended SECTION 1. *The People of the State of Michigan enact*, That
section thirty-one of chapter one hundred and fifty-three of the
revised statutes of eighteen hundred and forty-six, being section
seven thousand five hundred and forty of the compiled laws of

eighteen hundred and seventy-one, be and the same is hereby amended so as to read as follows:

(7540.) Sec. 31. If the father or mother of any child under the age of six years, or any other person, shall expose such child in any street, field, house, or other place, with intent to injure or wholly to abandon it, he or she shall be punished by imprisonment in the State prison not more than ten years.

Approved May 1, 1875.

Punishment for exposing child with intent to injure or abandon.

[No. 201.]

AN ACT to amend sections one and eight of an act entitled " An act to revise and consolidate the several acts relating to the protection of game, and for the better preservation of elk, deer, birds, and wild fowl," approved April third, eighteen hundred and sixty-nine, being sections two thousand and ninety-three and two thousand one hundred of the compiled laws of eighteen hundred and seventy-one, as amended by act number forty-six of the session laws of eighteen hundred and seventy-three.

SECTION 1. *The People of the State of Michigan enact,* That sections one and eight of an act entitled " An act to revise and consolidate the several acts relating to the protection of game, and for the better preservation of elk, deer, birds, and wild fowl," approved April third, eighteen hundred and sixty-nine, being sections two thousand and ninety-three and two thousand one hundred of the compiled laws of eighteen hundred and seventy-one, as amended by act number forty-six of the session laws of eighteen hundred and seventy-three, be and is hereby amended so as to read as follows:

Sections amended.

(2093.) Sec. 1. That no person or persons shall pursue, or hunt, or kill any wild elk, wild buck, doe, or fawn, save only in the Upper Peninsula from the first day of August, and in the Lower Peninsula from the fifteenth day of September, to the fifteenth day of December in each year, or kill or destroy by any means whatever, or attempt to take or destroy any wild turkey, at any time during the year, except in the months of October, November, and December in each year, or kill or destroy by any means whatever, any woodcock until after the fifth day of July, or any prairie chicken, or pinnated grouse, ruffled grouse, commonly called partridge or pheasant, or any wood duck, teal duck, or mallard duck, or any water fowl, save only from the first day of September in each year to the first day of January next following.

When game may be hunted.

(2100.) Sec. 8. That any railroad, express company, or other common carriers, or any of their agents or servants, or other persons having any of the above named birds or animals in their possession for transportation, or shall transport the same, after the expiration of ten days next succeeding the time limited and prescribed for the killing of such birds or animals, shall be punished by fine not less than ten dollars, nor more than one hundred dol-

Penalty for transporting at certain times.

Proviso. lars: *Provided*, That such penalty shall not apply to the transportation of live quail which are to be kept alive throughout the winter, or to the transportation of such birds or animals in transitu through this State, from other States where it is lawful to kill such birds or animals at the time of such transportation.

Approved May 3, 1875.

[No. 202.]

AN ACT to amend section one of act number one hundred and seventy-four of the session laws of eighteen hundred and fifty-five, being section seven thousand six hundred and ten of the compiled laws of eighteen hundred and seventy-one, entitled "An act to prevent the wrongful taking, detaching from the ground, or injuring any fruit trees, shade trees, ornamental shrub, plant, vine, or vegetable."

Section amended SECTION 1. *The People of the State of Michigan enact,* That section one of act number one hundred and seventy-four of the session laws of eighteen hundred and fifty-five, being compiler's section seven thousand six hundred and ten of the compiled laws of eighteen hundred and seventy-one, be amended so as to read as follows:

Wrongful taking of fruit trees, etc., how punished. (7610.) SEC. 1. That any person who shall wrongfully take and carry away from any place, any fruit tree, ornamental tree, shade tree, ornamental shrub, or any plant, vine, bush, or vegetable there growing, standing, or being, with intent to deprive the owner thereof, or who shall without right and with wrongful intent, detach from the ground, or injure any fruit tree, ornamental tree, shade tree, ornamental shrub, or any plant, vine, bush, or vegetable, shall be guilty of a misdemeanor, and on conviction thereof be punished by imprisonment in the county jail not more than six months, or by fine not exceeding two hundred and fifty dollars, or by both such fine and imprisonment, in the discretion of the court:

Proviso. *Provided,* That when the damage to the owner does not exceed the sum of twenty-five dollars, the punishment shall be a fine not exceeding one hundred dollars, or imprisonment in the said jail not exceeding three months, or by both such fine and imprisonment, in the discretion of the court.

Approved May 3, 1875.

[No. 203.]

AN ACT to amend section four thousand four hundred and seven of the compiled laws of eighteen hundred and seventy-one, relative to the inventory and collection of the effects of deceased persons, as amended by act number one hundred and forty-seven of the session laws of eighteen hundred and seventy-three.

Section amended SECTION 1. *The People of the State of Michigan enact,* That section four thousand four hundred and seven of the compiled laws of eighteen hundred and seventy-one, relative to the inventory and collection of the effects of deceased persons, as amended by act number one hundred and forty-seven of the session laws of eight-reu hundred and seventy-three, be and the same is hereby amended so as to read as follows:

(4407.) SEC. 7. The executor or administrator shall be entitled to the possession of the personal estate of the deceased until assignment or distribution of the same to heirs, legatees, or other persons entitled thereto, by order of the probate court, or until the estate is finally settled. *Time executor or administrator shall be entitled to possession of personal estate.*

Approved May 3, 1875.

[No. 204.]

AN ACT to amend an act entitled "An act to amend section five of an act entitled 'An act to protect fish and preserve the fisheries of this State,' approved March twenty-first, eighteen hundred and sixty-five, being section two thousand and seventy-six of the compiled laws of eighteen hundred and seventy-one," approved April fifteen, eighteen hundred and seventy-three.

SECTION 1. *The People of the State of Michigan enact*, That an act entitled "An act to amend section five of an act entitled 'An act to protect fish and preserve the fisheries of this State,' approved March twenty-first, eighteen hundred and sixty-five, being section two thousand and seventy-six of the compiled laws of eighteen hundred and seventy-one," approved April fifteen, eighteen hundred and seventy-three, be and the same is hereby amended so as to read as follows: *Section amended*

(2076.) SEC. 5. No person shall catch or take from any lake, river, or stream of this State, by any means whatsoever, any speckled trout from the first [day] of September in any year until the first day of May following thereafter; nor shall any person catch or take any grayling, by any means whatsoever, from any such lake, river, or stream, from the first day of November, in any year, until the first day of June following thereafter; nor shall any person purchase, buy, or sell any such fish during said prohibited time; nor shall any person take or catch any speckled trout or grayling, in any such lake, river, or stream, by means of a spear, net, or seine, or in any other manner whatever, except by hook and line, at any time during the year. In all prosecutions under this act it shall be *prima facie* sufficient on the part of the people to show that the defendant was found in possession of any such fish at any time within the period when the catching or taking of such fish is prohibited as aforesaid. It is hereby made the duty of the prosecuting attorney, the sheriff and his deputies, and every constable of any county, and the supervisor of any township, to prosecute any person for a violation of any of the provisions of this section when complaint is made before a justice of the peace. It shall be lawful, however, for the Superintendent of Fisheries to give permits in writing to any person to catch or take any such fish in such manner *When speckled trout or grayling must not be caught. Prosecutions, evidence in, etc. Permit for catching for propa-gation.*

as such superintendent shall direct, at any season of the year, for the purposes of propagation ; but in any prosecution for a violation of any of the provisions of this section, such permission must be shown affirmatively by the defendant.

SEC. 2. This act shall take immediate effect.

Approved May 3, 1875.

[No. 205.]

AN ACT to organize a school of mines in the University of Michigan, the establishment of additional professorships, and making appropriations for maintenance of the same.

School of mines authorized.

SECTION 1. *The People of the State of Michigan enact,* That the board of regents of the University of Michigan, are hereby authorized to establish a school of mines in connection with the polytechnic department of that institution, to be called the school of mines of the University of Michigan.

Professorships authorized.

SEC. 2. The board of regents are hereby authorized to establish and maintain in the University of Michigan at least three professorships : one of mining engineering, one of metallurgy, and one of architecture and design, with the necessary assistant instructors.

Appropriation for professorships, general expenses of school of mines, etc.

SEC. 3. That for the professorships and assistant instructors mentioned in section two, and also for the general expenses of said school of mines, and of the professorship of architecture and design, there shall be assessed upon the taxable property of the State for the year eighteen hundred and seventy-five, and also for the year eighteen hundred and seventy-six, the sum of eight thousand dollars for each of said years, which sum shall be paid to the treasurer of the board of regents of the University of Michigan, in two equal sums, on the first days of May and November of the year eighteen hundred and seventy-six, and of the year eighteen hundred and seventy-seven, upon a requisition of the treasurer of said board of regents, the requisition being accompanied by a certificate of the president and secretary of said board, stating that the amount so drawn, is to be applied to the purpose specified in this section.

Regents to commence equipment of school.

SEC. 4. The board of regents shall commence the equipment of said school with the necessary engines, boilers, and machinery, serviceable models or furnaces, pumps, hoisting apparatus, and other mechanical mining appliances; serviceable models of shaftwork, mining structures, bridges, transportation cars, roads, appliances for crushing, stamping, washing, and reduction of rock and ores, the display of tools, implements, apparatus, drawings, maps, photographs, and specimens of minerals and metals and all else needful and necessary for imparting to students the highest theoretical and best practical instruction, according to the constant improvements from time to time made in the methods of mining and quarrying, and in architecture and design.

Appropriation for purposes mentioned in section four.

SEC. 5. That there be appropriated hereby from any money in the treasury of the State of Michigan not otherwise appropriated, the sum of two thousand five hundred dollars for the year eighteen hundred and seventy-five (1875), and two thousand five hundred dollars for the year eighteen hundred and seventy-six (1876), to be expended under the direction of the board of regents of the University of Michigan, for the purposes mentioned in section four of this act; that this sum so appropriated shall be placed by the Auditor General to the credit of the University of Michigan, designated as "special fund for the establishment of the school of mines," and shall not be diverted to any other purpose.

SEC. 6. There is hereby appropriated for the specified purpose *Idem.* of carrying out the provisions of section four of this act, the sum of five thousand dollars; and the same shall be incorporated in the State tax as follows, to wit: for the year eighteen hundred and seventy-five (1875), two thousand five hundred dollars ; for the year eighteen hundred and seventy-six (1876), two thousand five hundred dollars; which taxes, when and as collected, shall be credited up to the general fund of the State to reimburse the same for the amount drawn from it as provided for in section five.

SEC. 7. That the sum appropriated, as provided for in section *Payment of moneys to treasurer of board of regents.* five of this act, shall be paid to the treasurer of the board of regents of the University in any sum or sums he may require, upon his filing with the Treasurer of the State of Michigan his voucher, accompanied by the certificate of the president and secretary of the board of regents of the University of Michigan, certifying that the sum so asked for is needed to liquidate obligations of the University then already incurred and due for the purposes specified in section five of this act.

SEC. 8. The board of regents shall yearly hereafter, in the annual *Certain statements to be included in annual report of regents.* report of the University, include a detailed statement of the expenditures out of the above appropriations for their respective objects.

SEC. 9. The president of the University shall be provided at all *Certain statistical tables to be furnished president.* reasonable times, upon application, for the purposes of the school of mines, with abstracts of all statistical tables and other information resulting from mining and quarrying, that shall come into the possession of the various State offices.

Approved May 3, 1875.

[No. 206.]

AN ACT to apportion anew the representatives among the several counties and districts of this State.

SECTION 1. *The People of the State of Michigan enact,* That *Ratio of representation.* the House of Representatives shall hereafter be composed of members elected agreeably to a ratio of a representative for every fourteen thousand persons, including civilized persons of Indian descent, not members of any tribe, in each organized county, and one representative for a fraction equal to a moiety of said ratio, and not included therein; that is to say, within the county of Wayne, ten; within the county of Kent, four; within the counties of Washtenaw, Lenawee, Jackson, Calhoun, Berrien, Oakland, St.

Clair, and Saginaw, three each; within the counties of Monroe, Hillsdale, Branch, St. Joseph, Van Buren, Allegan, Kalamazoo, Barry, Eaton, Ingham, Clinton, Shiawassee, Genesee, Macomb, Lapeer, Bay, Ottawa, Ionia, and Marquette, two each; within the counties of Cass, Livingston, Sanilac, Huron, Tuscola, Gratiot, Manistee, Mecosta, Oceana, Newaygo, Muskegon, Montcalm, and Houghton, one each.

The counties of Isabella and Clare shall compose a representative district, and be entitled to one representative, and the election returns of said district shall be made to the county of Isabella.

The counties of Midland, Iosco, Gladwin, Roscommon, and Ogemaw shall compose a representative district, and be entitled to one representative, and the election returns of said district shall be made to the county of Midland.

Alpena, Alcona, Presque Isle, Oscoda, and Montmorency shall constitute a representative district, and shall be entitled to one representative, the election returns to be made to the county of Alpena.

The counties of Lake and Mason shall constitute a representative district, and be entitled to one representative, the election returns to be made to the county of Mason.

The counties of Osceola, Missaukee, Kalkaska, and Crawford shall constitute a representative district, and be entitled to one representative, the election returns to be made to the county of Osceola.

The counties of Leelanaw and Benzie shall constitute a representative district, and be entitled to one representative, the election returns to be made to the county of Leelanaw.

The counties of Grand Traverse and Wexford shall constitute one representative district, and be entitled to one representative, the election returns to be made to the county of Grand Traverse.

The counties of Antrim, Charlevoix, Emmet, Manitou, and Otsego shall constitute a representative district, and be entitled to one representative, the election returns to be made to the county of Charlevoix.

The counties of Cheboygan, Mackinac, Chippewa, and Schoolcraft shall constitute a representative district, and be entitled to one representative, the election returns to be made to the county of Cheboygan.

The counties of Delta and Menominee shall constitute a representative district, and be entitled to one representative, the election returns to be made to the county of Delta.

The counties of Ontonagon, Isle Royal, Baraga, and Keweenaw shall constitute a representative district, and be entitled to one representative, the election returns to be made to the county of Keweenaw.

Approved May 3, 1875.

[No. 207.]

AN ACT making appropriations for the building of a hospital in connection with the University of Michigan, and for the equipment of the same with hospital stores and furniture.

SECTION 1. *The People of the State of Michigan enact*, That there shall be and is hereby appropriated out of any moneys in the treasury of the State of Michigan not otherwise appropriated, the sum of five thousand five hundred dollars, for the purpose of building a hospital in connection with the University of Michigan, which said money shall be expended under the direction of the board of regents of [the] said University, and shall be drawn from the treasury on the presentation of the proper voucher of the treasurer of the said board to the Auditor General; and on his warrant to the State Treasurer; and no money shall be drawn by virtue of this act by such regents unless they shall have first filed with the Auditor General an estimate and statement showing the purpose for which said money is required; and none shall be drawn further than is required to build such hospital in payment for labor and material furnished. *(Appropriation.)* *(How drawn, etc.)*

SEC. 2. There shall be and is hereby appropriated out of any moneys in the treasury of Michigan not otherwise appropriated, the further sum of two thousand five hundred dollars, to be expended under the direction of the board of regents of said University for equipments, supplies, and such hospital stores as they shall deem necessary for the maintenance of such hospital, which said moneys shall be drawn from the treasury on the presentation of the proper voucher of the treasurer of the said board to the Auditor General and on his warrant to the State Treasurer: *Provided*, That no money shall be drawn from the State treasury under this act until the citizens of Ann Arbor shall have first contributed and deposited the sum of four thousand dollars with the treasurer of the said board of regents, which said moneys shall be disposed of as the other moneys appropriated in this act. *(Further appropriation for equipments, etc.)* *(Proviso.)*

SEC. 3. This act shall take immediate effect.

Approved May 3, 1875.

[No. 208.]

AN ACT to amend section one of an act to provide for the better security of public records, being section seven thousand seven hundred and fifty-one of the compiled laws of eighteen hundred and seventy-one.

SECTION 1. *The People of the State of Michigan enact*, That section one of an act to provide for the better security of public records, being section seven thousand seven hundred and fifty-one of the compiled laws of eighteen hundred and seventy-one, be amended so as to read as follows: *(Section amended)*

SEC. 1. That all books, papers, or records, belonging or in anywise appertaining to the offices of clerk, treasurer, register of *(What to be deemed public records.)*

deeds, or judge of probate, of the several counties, and also all books, papers, and records belonging or in any wise appertaining to the offices of the several townships and school district officers of this State, are hereby declared to be public property, belonging to the people of the State of Michigan, to be used and preserved by and under the direction of said officers, and be by them preserved during their continuance in office; and any person or persons who shall willfully carry away, mutilate, or destroy any of such books, papers, records, or any part of the same, and any person or persons who shall retain and continue to hold the possession of any books, papers, records, or parts thereof, belonging to the aforesaid offices of clerk, treasurer, register of deeds, or judge of probate of the several counties, or to the offices of the several township and school district officers of this State, and shall refuse to deliver up said books, papers, records, or parts thereof to the proper officer having charge of the office to which the said books, papers, or records belong, upon demand being made by such officer, shall, on conviction thereof, be deemed guilty of a misdemeanor, and shall be punished by fine not exceeding one thousand dollars, or imprisonment in the State prison not exceeding three years.

Penalty for mutilating or wrongfully retaining.

Approved May 3, 1875.

[No. 209.]

AN ACT to provide for an appropriation for the benefit of the Pioneer Society of the State of Michigan for the years eighteen hundred and seventy-five and eighteen hundred and seventy-six.

Appropriation, and how expended.

SECTION 1. *The People of the State of Michigan enact,* That there is hereby appropriated from the general fund, until the Legislature shall by law otherwise direct, to the Pioneer Society of the State of Michigan, the sum of five hundred dollars for each of the years eighteen hundred and seventy-five and eighteen hundred and seventy-six, to be expended by said society in collecting, embodying, arranging, and preserving in authentic form, a library of books, pamphlets, maps, charts, manuscripts, papers [paintings], printing, statuary, and other materials illustrative of the history of Michigan, to rescue from oblivion the memory of its early pioneers, to obtain and preserve narratives of their exploits, perils, and hardy adventures; to secure facts and statements relative to the history, genius, progress, or decay of our Indian tribes; to exhibit faithfully the antiquities, and the past and present resources of Michigan, and in paying other necessary incidental expenses of the society; but no part of such appropriation shall ever be paid for services rendered by its officers to the society.

Account of expenditures to be kept and transmitted to Governor

SEC. 2. It shall be the duty of the executive committee of the said Pioneer Society of the State of Michigan, to keep an accurate account of the manner of expenditure of the said sum of money hereby appropriated, and transmit the same with the vouchers

.therefor to the Governor of this State biennially, to be by him laid before the Legislature.

SEC. 3. This act shall take immediate effect.

Approved May 3, 1875.

[No. 210.]

AN ACT to repeal chapter two hundred and forty-one of the compiled laws of eighteen hundred and seventy-one, relative to the protection of the rights and liberties of persons claimed as fugitive slaves.

SECTION 1. *The People of the State of Michigan enact,* That chapter two hundred and forty-one of the compiled laws of eighteen hundred and seventy-one, relative to the protection of the rights and liberties of persons claimed as fugitive slaves, be and the same is hereby repealed.   *Chapter repealed*

Approved May 3, 1875.

[No. 211.]

AN ACT to amend section forty-six of chapter one hundred and fifty-four, of revised statutes of eighteen hundred and forty-six, being section seven thousand five hundred and ninety-seven of the compiled laws of eighteen hundred and seventy-one, relative to malicious injury to dams, reservoirs, and canals.

SECTION 1. *The People of the State of Michigan enact,* That section forty-six of chapter one hundred and fifty-four of revised statutes of eighteen hundred and forty-six, being section seven thousand five hundred and ninety-seven of the compiled laws of eighteen hundred and seventy-one, be and the same is hereby amended so as to read as follows :   *Section amended*

(7597.) SEC. 46. Every person who shall willfully and maliciously break down, injure, remove, or destroy any dam, reservoir, canal, or trench, or any gate, flume, flash-boards, or other appurtenances thereof, or any levee or structure for the purpose of conveying water to any such dam or reservoir, or any of the wheels, mill-gear, or machinery of any mill, or shall willfully or wantonly, without color of right, draw off the water contained in any millpond, reservoir, canal, or trench, shall be punished by imprisonment in the State prison not more than five years, or by fine not exceeding five hundred dollars and imprisonment in the county jail not more than one year.   *Penalty for malicious injury to dams, reservoirs, etc.*

Approved May 3, 1875.

[No. 212.]

AN ACT to amend section three of the revised statutes of eighteen hundred and forty-six, being section six hundred and thirty-eight of the compiled laws of eighteen hundred and seventy-one.

Section amended

SECTION 1. *The People of the State of Michigan enact.* That section three of the revised statutes of eighteen hundred and forty-six, being section six hundred and thirty-eight of the compiled laws of eighteen hundred and seventy-one, be and the same is hereby amended so as to read as follows:

Inhabitants of townships may raise money to defray expenses.

(638.) SEC. 3. The inhabitants of each township shall have power at any legal meeting, by a vote of the qualified electors thereof, to grant and vote sums of money, not exceeding such amounts as are or may be limited by law, as they shall deem necessary for defraying all proper charges and expenses arising in the

Officers prohibited from creating debt, etc.

township; nor shall any board, officer, or officers, create any debt or liability against the township, or issue any warrant, certificate, or order, for the payment of money, except when the creation of such debt or liability, or the payment of such money, has been authorized by such vote or by the provisions of law.

Approved May 3, 1875.

[No. 213.]

AN ACT to revise and consolidate the laws relative to the State Prison and the government and discipline thereof, and to repeal all acts inconsistent therewith.

State Prison, location and use of.

SECTION 1. *The People of the State of Michigan enact.* There shall continue to be maintained in this State, a State Prison at Jackson, in the county of Jackson, in which convicts sentenced for life or otherwise, shall be securely confined, employed at hard labor, and governed for the purpose of punishment and reformation in the manner hereinafter provided.

OFFICERS.

General supervision vested in Governor.

SEC. 2. The general supervision of the State Prison shall be vested in the Governor, and he shall visit it semi-annually, and oftener if he shall deem necessary. He shall investigate its management, examine its condition, inquire into any alleged abuses or neglect of duty, and may, in connection with the inspectors, make such changes in the general discipline of the prison as he may deem proper and best.

Officers.

SEC. 3. The officers of the prison shall consist of three inspectors, one warden, who shall be the principal keeper, one deputy warden, one clerk, one agent, one chaplain, one physician and surgeon, and as many keepers and guards as the warden and inspectors may deem necessary. Each of said officers, before entering upon the duties of his office, shall take and subscribe the official

oath prescribed in the constitution, and file the same with the Oath of office.
Auditor General.

SEC. 4. The said inspectors shall be appointed by the Governor, Appointment of inspectors and their term of office.
by and with the advice and consent of the Senate, and may be re-
moved by him at his discretion, which removal, with the cause
thereof, shall be reported to the Legislature at its next session.
The inspectors now in office shall continue to hold such offices for
the terms for which they were respectively appointed, unless sooner
removed by the Governor. At the expiration of the terms of office
for which the present inspectors have been appointed, and biennially thereafter, there shall be appointed by the Governor, as
aforesaid, one inspector, who shall hold his office for the term of
six years, unless sooner removed therefrom. Appointments to fill Vacancies.
vacancies occurring during the recess of the Legislature, shall be
made only until the close of the next session, or until a successor
is appointed, with the concurrence of the Senate, and qualified.

SEC. 5. The warden shall be appointed by the Governor, by and Warden, how appointed and term of office.
with the advice and consent of the Senate, and shall hold his office
for the term of two years, and until his successor shall be appointed and qualified, unless sooner removed by the Governor.

SEC. 6. The deputy warden, clerk, agent, physician, and chap- Other officers, how appointed.
lain, shall be appointed by the board of inspectors, and shall hold
their respective offices during the pleasure of the board; and the
keepers, and all other officers shall be appointed by the warden,
with the assent of the inspectors, and hold their offices during the
pleasure of the board of inspectors.

SEC. 7. No inspector of the State Prison shall be warden thereof, No officer to hold any other appointment in prison, or be interested in any contract, etc.
or be concerned in the business of such agency, or hold any other
appointment or place connected with the prison; and no person
shall be appointed an inspector, warden, deputy, agent, or clerk, or
to any other employment in the prison, who is a contractor in the
prison, or the agent or employé of such contractor, or who is interested, directly or indirectly, in any kind of business carried on
in such prison. And no inspector, warden, or any other officer of
the prison shall be directly or indirectly interested in any contract,
purchase, or sale, for or on account of such prison.

SEC. 8. No officer of the prison shall employ the labor of any Officers not to employ labor of convicts.
convict upon any work in which he or any other officer shall be in-
terested.

SEC. 9. Neither the warden nor any officer appointed by the Officers not to engage in private business.
warden and inspectors shall be employed in any business for pri-
vate emolument, or which does not pertain to the duties of his
office.

SEC. 10. The warden, clerk, deputy, keepers, guards, and other Certain officers exempt from military and jury duties.
necessary attendants shall, while in the actual employ of the State,
as such officers, guards, and attendants respectively, be exempt
from military and jury duties.

SEC. 11. It shall be the duty of the warden and other officers, Inspectors to be admitted into prison, and books, etc., to be exhibited to them.
whenever requested, to admit the inspectors, or either of them,
into every part of said prison; to exhibit to them, or either of
them, on demand, all the books, papers, accounts, and writings

31

pertaining to the prison, or to the business, government, discipline, or management thereof, and to render them every other facility in their power, to discharge their duties under this act.

INSPECTORS.

Monthly meetings. SEC. 12. The inspectors shall meet at the prison at least as often as once in each month, and as much oftener as the proper control and management thereof shall require. A majority of the mem- **Quorum.** bers shall constitute a quorum for the transaction of business. All **Record of orders, etc.** orders and resolutions of the board shall be entered on its journal. At the first meeting after the appointment of an inspector for the **To choose president.** full term, the members shall choose one of their number president of the board. The clerk of the prison shall attend their meetings **Clerk of prison to attend meetings, keep minutes, etc.** and shall keep regular minutes of their proceedings, and of all rules and regulations adopted by them, which shall be recorded in a book provided for that purpose, signed by the inspectors present at each meeting, and kept in the prison office.

Inspectors to establish rules, etc. SEC. 13. It shall be the duty of the inspectors to make and adopt all such general rules and regulations for the government and discipline of the prison as they may deem expedient, and from time to time to change and amend the same as circumstances may require. In making such rules and regulations, they shalt as far as practicable, consistent with the discipline of the prison, adopt such as shall in their judgment best conduce to the reformation of **Copy of rules to be furnished officers, guards, and convicts.** convicts. A printed copy of the rules and regulations shall be furnished to every officer and guard at the time he is appointed and sworn, and so much thereof as relates to the duties and obli- gations of the convicts shall be hung up in a conspicuous place in each cell and shop, and such rules shall be written or printed in a language known to the convict occupying the cell. The inspectors **Inspectors to examine departments, etc.** shall at their regular meeting examine all the different depart- ments of the prison, and inquire into all matters connected with the government, discipline, and police thereof; the punishment and employment of the convicts therein confined; the books, ac- counts, and vouchers of the warden, clerk, and agent; the money concerns and contracts for work; the purchases and sales of the articles provided for such prison or sold on account thereof; and whether the convicts are properly fed, clothed, and governed. **To inquire into improper conduct of officers.** They shall also inquire into any improper conduct which may be alleged to have been committed by the warden or any other officer or employe of the prison, and for that purpose may issue subpœnas to compel the attendance of witnesses, and the production of books, papers, and writings before them with like effect, and subject to the same penalties for disobedience as in cases of trial before justices of the peace, and may examine any witness produced be- fore them on oath to be administered by the president of the board, or in his absence by some other member thereof.

Inspectors may unite offices of agent and clerk. SEC. 14. The board of inspectors,in their discretion, may unite the offices of agent and clerk, and impose the duties thereof upon the clerk, who shall discharge the same in the manner prescribed by law, and the rules and regulations of the board. But for the performance of such duties the clerk shall in no case receive compensation as agent and clerk, but only such sum as may be allowed him for his services as clerk.

SEC. 15. The inspectors may make such regulations in regard to the food, rations, clothing, and bedding of the convicts, as the health, well-being, and circumstances of each may require; but all diet, rations, clothing, beds, and bedding, shall be plain, of good quality, and in sufficient quantity for the sustenance and comfort of the convicts. Regulations relative to food, clothing, etc.

SEC. 16. The inspectors shall annually, and as much oftener as they may deem necessary, require reports from the warden and other officers of the prison, in relation to any and all matters connected with the management, business, discipline, moneys, and property of the prison, and with the condition, conduct and employment of the convicts confined therein; and they shall, on or before the thirtieth day of November in each and every year, make out and transmit to the Governor, a report made up to the thirtieth of September of the current year, showing the condition of the prison, together with a detailed statement of its receipts and expenditures; the estimates of expenses for buildings, repairs, and all other purposes for the next succeeding year; the number of the officers, with their several salaries; the contracts entered into during the year for the employment of convicts; the name of each contractor in the prison, with the number of convicts employed by him, and the price paid for their labor; the whole number of convicts in the prison, and the whole number received during the year, with the names of the counties from whence they were received, and the crimes of which they were convicted; the number discharged, died, escaped, or pardoned; the changes or additions, if any, to the prison buildings, and the cost thereof; together with such other facts and suggestions as may fully exhibit the entire workings of the prison during the year. Reports of warden and other officers.
Annual report of inspectors.

SEC. 17. The inspectors shall cause a full and accurate inventory of all and singular the machinery, fixtures, goods, chattels, and property of every nature and description belonging to the State in and about the prison, to be made in each year at the time of making their annual report; and said property shall be appraised on oath by two disinterested and competent appraisers to be appointed for that purpose by said inspectors, and a copy of such inventory and appraisal shall be appended to the annual report of the inspectors. Inventory of property of State in and about prison.

SEC. 18. The inspectors shall be allowed for their services respectively four dollars for each and every day actually and necessarily occupied in inspecting the prison and inquiring into the management thereof, and their actual traveling expenses in going to and from the prison, to be verified on oath, and paid by the State Treasurer on the warrant of the Auditor General. Compensation of inspectors.

WARDEN.

SEC. 19. The warden shall reside in the State Prison, in apartments to be assigned him by the inspectors, and he shall be in Residence.

constant attendance at the prison, except when absent on some necessary duty, in which case his duties during his absence shall be performed by the deputy; and in no case shall the warden and **Bond.** deputy warden be absent from the prison at the same time. Before entering upon the duties of his office, the warden shall execute to the people of this State a bond with two or more sufficient sureties, in the penal sum of twenty thousand dollars, conditioned that he shall faithfully account for all money and property that may come into his hands by virtue of his office, and perform all the duties incumbent upon him as such warden, according to law; which bond shall be approved by the inspectors, and filed in the office of the Auditor General.

Daily journal of proceedings in prison. SEC. 20. The warden shall also keep a daily journal of the proceedings of the prison, in which he shall note every infraction of the rules and regulations of the prison by any officer or guard thereof, which shall come to his knowledge, and make a memorandum of every complaint made by any convict, of cruel or unjust treatment from his overseer or other officer of the prison, or a want of good and sufficient food or clothing; and also of every infraction of the rules and regulations of the prison by any prisoner, naming him and specifying the offense, and also what punishment, and the extent thereof, if any was awarded; which journal shall be laid before the inspectors at every stated meeting, and at every special meeting when demanded.

Duties of warden. SEC. 21. It shall be the duty of the warden, under the rules and regulations adopted by the board of inspectors for the government of the prison:

First, To exercise a general superintendence over the government, discipline, and police of the prison, and to superintend all the business concerns thereof;

Second, To give necessary directions to all the inferior officers, keepers, and guards, and to examine whether they have been careful and vigilant in their respective duties;

Third, To examine daily into the state of the prison, and the health, conduct, and safe keeping of the prisoners;

Fourth, To use every proper means to furnish employment to the prisoners, most beneficial to the State and best suited to their several capacities;

Fifth, To superintend any manufacturing and mechanical business that may be carried on by the State, pursuant to law, within the prison; to receive the articles manufactured, and to sell and dispose of the same for the benefit of the State;

Sixth, To take charge of the real and personal estate attached to the prison;

Seventh, To inquire into the justice of any complaints made by any of the convicts relative to their provisions, clothing, or treatment;

Eighth, To read to the convicts at least once in each month, the rules and regulations of the prison so far as the same relate to such convicts, and to make such explanations of the same as he shall deem proper;

Ninth, And generally to have charge of all the departments of the prison and its officers as its executive head.

SEC. 22. The said warden, under the direction of the inspectors, shall be the custodian of all funds belonging to the said prison, whether arising from the avails of the labor of convicts, the sales of manufactured articles, or appropriations made by the legislature and drawn from the State treasury. Custodian of funds of prison.

SEC. 23. The warden shall make a monthly report to the inspectors, stating the names of all convicts received into the prison during the preceding month, the counties in which they were tried, the crimes of which they were convicted, the nature and duration of their sentence, their former trade, employment, or occupation, their habits, color, age, place of nativity, degree of instruction, and a description of their persons; and also stating in such report the names of all convicts pardoned, discharged, escaped, or died during said month; and he shall also make out and render, for the same time, a full and accurate statement and account of all moneys received by him from every source by virtue of his office, including all moneys taken from convicts, or received as the proceeds of property taken from them, and of all sums paid and expended by him, with the vouchers therefor, and stating also the balance in his hands at the time of rendering such account. Monthly report to inspectors.

SEC. 24. The warden shall on the thirtieth day of September or within twenty days thereafter in every year, make and deliver to the inspectors of the prison a report, exhibiting a complete and comprehensive view of the transactions of the prison during the preceding year, stating the number of convicts confined therein, the various kinds of business in which they are employed, the number employed in each branch, and the profit or loss, if any, arising to the State therefrom; also a full and true account of all moneys received on account of the prison under his charge, and all the moneys expended for the use thereof, together with an inventory of the goods, raw materials, and other property of the State then on hand, and with such other particulars in relation to the prison as the inspectors shall require. Annual report to inspectors.

CLERK.

SEC. 25. The clerk of the prison, before entering on the duties of his office, shall execute a bond to the people of this State, with sufficient sureties, to be approved by the inspectors, in the penal sum of ten thousand dollars, conditioned that he will keep a true, honest, and faithful record of the accounts of the prison, and pay over all moneys belonging to the prison that may come into his hands as such clerk; and will faithfully discharge all the duties of such office as prescribed by law and the rules and regulations of the prison, which bond shall be filed in the office of the Auditor General. Bond.

SEC. 26. It shall be the duty of the clerk of the prison:

First, To attend at the prison daily during the proper business hours, unless by the direction of an inspector or of the warden he is otherwise engaged in transacting business on account of the prison; Duties.

Second, To keep the books and accounts of the prison in such a manner as to exhibit clearly all the financial transactions relating to it; to also keep a register of convicts, in which shall be entered in alphabetical order the name of each convict, the crime of which he is convicted, the date of his conviction, term of sentence, from what county, and by what court sentenced, his place of nativity, age, occupation, complexion, stature, number of previous convictions, and whether previously confined in a prison in this or any other State, together with when and how he was discharged. The inspectors may require such additional facts to be stated on the register as they may deem proper;

Third, To do all such writing as may be required of him by the inspectors and warden relating to the affairs of the prison.

AGENT.

Bond.

SEC. 27. The agent before entering upon the duties of his office shall execute a bond to the people of this State, with sufficient sureties to be approved by the inspectors, in the penal sum of ten thousand dollars, conditioned that he will discharge all the duties devolved upon him by virtue of said office faithfully, and with direct reference to the best interests of the State, said bond to be deposited with the Auditor General.

Duties.

SEC. 28. The agent shall purchase all the forage, fuel, and lights, and all supplies for the kitchen and hospital, and all articles for manufacturing and repairs in the State shops, and make all sales for the prison under the direction of the warden, and subject to such rules and regulations as the inspectors may prescribe. He shall take bills for all supplies and materials purchased by him, at the time of such purchase; and the persons to whom any bill shall be paid shall in all cases make an affidavit, stating that the articles specified in the account were actually furnished, and that the same was paid in cash by the warden. The agent shall keep a regular and correct account of all purchases and sales made by him in books to be furnished for that purpose, and which shall be open at all times to the inspection of the warden or any member of the board of inspectors. All other articles and supplies shall be purchased as directed by the inspectors.

CHAPLAIN.

Duties.

SEC. 29. It shall be the duty of the chaplain of said prison:

First, To perform religious services in the prison, under such regulations as the inspectors may prescribe, and to attend to the spiritual wants of the convicts;

Second, To visit the convicts in their cells, for the purpose of giving them moral and religious instruction;

Third, To furnish at the expense of the State a bible of such version as the convict may choose, and also a prayer book of such kind as the convict may choose, to each convict, and such other reading matter as the inspectors may consider for the best interests of such convicts;

Fourth, To take charge of the library;

Fifth, To visit daily the sick in the hospital;

Sixth, To make an annual report to the inspectors for each year ending the thirtieth day of September, relative to the religious and moral conduct of the convicts during such year, stating therein what services he has performed, and the results of his instruction, together with any other facts relative to said convicts he may deem proper to report;

Seventh, When required by the inspectors, to give instruction in the common branches of an English education, and at such time and in such manner as the board of inspectors shall prescribe;

Eighth, To conduct funeral services at the burial of each convict who shall die in the prison; and the warden shall, as soon as practicable after the death of a convict, fix a time for such services, and immediately notify the chaplain thereof, that he may be prepared to officiate thereat.

PHYSICIAN.

SEC. 30. It shall be the duty of the physician of the prison; Duties.

First, To attend at all times to the wants of the sick convicts, whether in the hospital or in their cells, and to bestow upon them all necessary medical service;

Second, In company with the hall master, to examine weekly the cells of the convicts, for the purpose of ascertaining whether they are kept in a proper state of cleanliness and ventilation, and if they are not so kept to point out to said hall master the deficiencies, and report the same monthly to the inspectors;

Third, To prescribe the diet of sick convicts, and his directions in relation thereto shall be strictly followed; and to be present at and superintend all corporeal punishments which may be inflicted in the prison;

Fourth, To keep a daily record of all admissions to the hospital, and of cases treated in the cells or elsewhere, indicating the sex, color, nativity, age, occupation, habits of life, crime, period of entrance and discharge from the hospital, and disease;

Fifth, To make a yearly report to the inspectors of the sanitary condition of the prison during the year, which report shall also contain a condensed statement of the information contained in his daily record;

Sixth, To make all such other reports as the inspectors may from time to time require.

SEC. 31. It shall be the duty of such physician, in case of any convict claiming to be unable to labor by means of sickness, to examine such convict; and if it is his opinion upon such examination that such convict is unable to labor, he shall immediately certify the same to the warden, and such convict shall thereupon be relieved from labor and admitted to the hospital, or placed in his cell or elsewhere for medical treatment, as said physician shall direct, having a due regard for the safe keeping of such convict; and such convict shall not be required to labor so long as in the opinion of said physician such disability shall continue; and whenever said physician shall certify to the warden that such convict is sufficiently recovered to be able to labor, said convict shall be required to labor, but not before.

Purchase of medicines and hospital stores. SEC. 32. The necessary medicines and other hospital stores for the use of the prison shall be purchased from time to time by the agent of the prison, with the advice of the physician, and under the direction of the inspectors.

SALARIES.

Annual salaries. SEC. 33. There shall be paid monthly at the office of the State Prison to the officers thereof the following annual salaries, to wit: To the warden, fifteen hundred dollars, but the board of inspectors may increase the same to a sum not exceeding two thousand dollars, if in their judgment they shall deem it for the best interests of the prison to do so; to the deputy warden, one thousand dollars, with discretion in the board of inspectors to increase the same to a sum not exceeding twelve hundred dollars; to the clerk, twelve hundred dollars, with power in the board of inspectors to increase the same to a sum not exceeding fifteen hundred dollars; to each of the keepers, seven hundred dollars, with authority in the board of inspectors to increase the same to a sum not exceeding eight hundred dollars; to the physician, a sum not exceeding one thousand dollars; and to the chaplain, a sum not exceeding one thousand dollars, as the inspectors in their discretion may deem for the best interests of the prison; and the agent, keepers, guards, and all other employes of the prison shall be paid such compensation as the inspectors shall deem just and reasonable, and shall direct. **Not to be increased without concurrence of Governor.** None of the salaries fixed at the sums aforesaid shall be increased within the limit above authorized without the knowledge and concurrence of the Governor. **Warden allowed use of house, etc.** The warden shall, in addition to his salary, be allowed the use of house, fire-wood and lights, and provisions for his family, and for guests who visit him on business connected with the prison, from the stock provided for the use of the prison; and the deputy warden shall be allowed the use of the house known as the deputy's house, free of rent. **Officers not allowed perquisites.** And no officer or other person employed in or about the prison shall be permitted to receive in any way perquisites, emoluments, or supplies for themselves or their families from the prison, other than the compensation allowed by law. **Inspectors may require certain employes boarded in prison.** The inspectors may, if they shall deem it for the interest of the prison, require the keepers, guards, and such of the employes as they may designate, to be lodged and messed or boarded in the prison, and for that purpose may furnish lodging rooms in a plain and substantial manner, and supply provisions from the prison stock, which shall be cooked and prepared by the labor of convicts, and served at such times and in such place as the inspectors may direct.

DISCIPLINE—GOOD TIME.

Convicts to be kept at hard labor. SEC. 34. All convicts in the State Prison other than such as are confined in solitude for misconduct in the prison, shall be kept constantly employed at hard labor at an average of not less than ten hours a day (Sundays excepted), unless incapable of laboring by reason of sickness or other infirmity.

SEC. 35. Whenever there shall be a sufficient number of cells in Convicts to be kept singly in cells. the prison, it shall be the duty of the warden to keep each prisoner singly in a cell at night, and also during the day time when unemployed.

SEC. 36. The keepers shall preserve proper discipline among the Punishment. convicts under their charge, and the warden or deputy warden may punish them for misconduct in such manner and under such regulations as shall be adopted by the board of inspectors: *Provided,* Proviso. That punishment by showering with cold water, or whipping with the lash on the bare body, shall in no case be allowed; and the Record of. warden or deputy shall, as soon as the next day after inflicting punishment on any convict, enter, in a book to be kept for that purpose, a written memorandum thereof, signed by him, stating the offense committed, and the kind and extent of the punishment inflicted, but in no case shall brutal or inhuman punishment be inflicted on a convict.

SEC. 37. When several convicts combined, or any convict alone, Duty of officers in case of violence or attempt to escape. shall offer violence to any officer or guard of the prison, or to any other convict or person, or do, or attempt to do any injury to the building, or any workshop, or to any appurtenances thereof, or attempt to escape, or resist, or disobey any reasonable command, the officers of the prison shall use all suitable means to defend themselves, to enforce the observance of discipline, to secure the persons of the offenders, and to prevent any such attempt to escape. But the provisions of this section shall not be published in the rules and regulations of the prison, and shall not be posted up in the cells therein, or read to the convicts by the warden at the time of reading the other rules as prescribed in the eighth subdivision of section twenty-one of this act.

SEC. 38. No spirituous or fermented liquor shall, on any pretense whatever, be sold in the State Prison, or in any building appurtenant thereto, or on the land granted to the State for the use and benefit of the prison; and no such liquors shall be given to or suffered to be used by any convict or any employe in the prison, unless he is sick, and then only under the special direction of the physician. Liquor not to be sold or used in prison.

SEC. 39. The board of inspectors shall prescribe a cap, or uniform, to be worn while on duty by the several officers of the prison, except the inspectors, physician, and chaplain, which shall be made with marks or indications plainly designating the rank of each officer wearing the same. Uniform of officers.

SEC. 40. The board of inspectors may establish a proper scale or rate of debits and credits for good conduct or misconduct, which shall be a part of the rules of discipline of the prison, and in a book to be kept for that purpose may cause to be entered up at the end of each month, the total of credits to which each prisoner may be entitled; and they shall require the warden, on the first day of each month, by means of cards or otherwise, to announce such result to each prisoner. Debits and credits for conduct to be kept, and the results announced to prisoners monthly.

SEC. 41. The warden of the prison shall keep a record of each and all infractions of the rules of discipline by convicts, with the Record of infractions of rules.

32

names of the convict or convicts offending, and the date and character of each offense, which record shall be placed before the inspectors at each regular meeting of the board; and every convict **Deductions from term of sentence for good conduct.** sentenced for any term less than life, who shall have no infraction of the rules and regulations of the prison, or laws of the State recorded against him, shall be entitled to a deduction from his sentence for each year, and *pro rata* for any part of a year when the sentence is for more or less than one year, as follows: From and including the first year up to the third year, a deduction of two months for each year. From and including the third year up to the fifth year, a deduction of seventy-five days for each year. From and including the fifth year up to the seventh year, a deduction of three months for each year. From and including the seventh year up to the tenth year, a deduction of one hundred and five days for each year. From and including the tenth year up to the fifteenth year, a deduction af four months for each year. From and including the fifteenth year up to the twentieth year, a deduction of five months for each year. From and including the twentieth year up to the period fixed for the expiration of the sentence, six months for each year. The inspectors shall allow each convict **Allowance for a faithful performance of duties.** who has performed in a faithful, orderly, and peaceable manner, all the duties assigned to him, and who has become entitled to a deduction from his sentence, as aforesaid, from time to time, as they may judge best, five per cent of the value of each day's labor actually performed by such convict, to be computed on the average rate per day paid by contractors for convict labor in the prison, and the inspectors may cause such earnings to be paid either to the family of the convict, or applied to his benefit in such manner, in such sums, and at such times as they may think proper. The inspectors shall provide by rule how much of the good time and money thus earned a convict shall forfeit for one or more viola- **Diminution of time far those now in prison.** tions of the prison rules. The warden, in computing the diminution of time for those now in the prison, shall allow them for the good time made up to the time this act takes effect, in accordance with the provisions of law previously in force, and thereafter it shall be computed in accordance with the terms of this section. When- **Convictions under separate sentences regarded one continuous sentence.** ever a convict has been committed under several convictions, with separate sentences, they shall be construed as one continuous sentence in the granting or forfeiting of good time.

Certain privileges granted to prisoners sentenced to solitary confinement for life. SEC. 42. The convicts which have been or may be sentenced to solitary confinement in the State Prison at hard labor for life, may be released from solitary confinement and employed as other convicts are, whenever and for such times as the inspectors may by resolution direct; and the inspectors are authorized to allow such convicts, under such restrictions as they may deem necessary and proper, to correspond with near relatives and friends.

CONTRACTS.

Contracts for the labor of convicts, by whom and in what manner let. SEC. 43. Whenever the inspectors shall direct a contract to be made for letting and hiring the labor of the convicts, it shall be the duty of the warden, under the direction of the inspectors, to proceed to make such contracts in the following manner:

First, He shall cause a notice to be published in one daily paper printed in the city of Jackson, in one daily paper published in the city of Detroit, in one daily paper published in the city of Grand Rapids, and in one paper published in the city of Lansing, at least three weeks previous to the day appointed for letting the labor of the convicts, stating that sealed proposals will be received therefor, and specifying the number of convicts to be let, the length of time, which shall not exceed ten years, and the last day on which bids will be received;

Second, The inspectors may in their discretion authorize the warden to designate what articles, or class of articles, shall be manufactured;

Third, Each bid shall specify each article proposed to be manufactured, and the number of square feet of shop room which will be required;

Fourth, Each bid shall be accompanied by a bond, with good and sufficient sureties to the satisfaction of the inspectors, and in such sum as they may direct, conditioned that in case the bid is accepted by the warden, the bidder will, on entering into a contract in pursuance of the bid, execute a bond with two or more good sureties in a sum satisfactory to the inspectors, conditioned for the faithful performance of such contract on his part, and no bid or proposal shall be received unless such bond shall accompany the same;

Fifth, The bids shall be opened by the warden, in the presence of the board of inspectors, at their next meeting after the last day specified for receiving bids, and the labor shall be awarded to the highest bidder, if the price bid, in the judgment of the inspectors, be a fair and reasonable compensation for such labor. If, however, the inspectors shall deem it against the interest of the State or the welfare of the convicts, that the articles specified should be manufactured in the prison, the bid may be rejected;

Sixth, If any bid or bids shall be rejected for the reasons aforesaid, or either of them, the warden may decline to close the contract, and may thereafter, under the direction of the inspectors, proceed again to advertise the letting of contracts for such labor until the same shall be successful;

Seventh, The contracts made by the warden shall be reduced to writing and approved by the inspectors, or a majority of them, and one copy of every contract shall be filed in the prison office. But such contract shall not be executed by the warden until the bond for the performance of the conditions thereof specified in subdivision four of this section, shall be made and approved by the inspectors;

Eighth, In thus contracting the labor of the prisoners hereafter, there shall be inserted in every contract a stipulation that the State shall retain the right of full control through its proper officers over them, and that it reserves the right to govern the prisoners and to change the disciplinary rules of the prison, and to forbid any work, or mode or manner of doing the same, that is injurious to the health or dangerous to the person of the prisoner, and also such time of the convict as the inspectors may from time to time judge proper for imparting instruction; and that the warden, under the order and direction of the board of inspectors, may exclude from the prison premises any contractor or his agent or agents or employes who may be guilty of any misconduct in the prison;

Ninth, The said contracts shall also contain a stipulation that the State shall have a lien upon the machinery, tools, and stock of the contractors which are or may hereafter be within the workshop or prison yard, for all moneys due or to become due for convict labor; and authorizing the warden at any time after such moneys become due, to detain such property and to advertise and sell the same, by giving at least four weeks' notice in four daily papers published in the State prior to such sale; and the surplus money, if any, arising from such sale, after paying what is due to the State, shall be paid to the contractor or contractors to whom the property belongs.

Employment of convicts not employed on contracts. SEC. 44. All convicts not employed on contracts may be employed by the warden, with the approval of the inspectors, in the performance of work for the State, in such manner as he shall think most conducive to the interests of the State and the welfare of the convict, or they may be temporarily hired, which hiring shall terminate whenever their labor is required on any contract.

Employment of convicts in case their labor cannot be contracted. SEC. 45. If the warden shall be unable to let the labor of the convicts on contract at reasonable rates, so that any considerable number are without employment, he may, under the direction of the inspectors, with the approval of the Governor, prepare shop room, procure simple and inexpensive machinery and material, and employ such convicts in the manufacture of any articles that in the opinion of the inspectors can be made in the prison to advantage and profit for the benefit of the State.

Purchase of raw material for manufacture. SEC. 46. The agent, under the direction of the inspectors, may also purchase such raw materials as may be necessary, to be manufactured in the prison, and to be paid for by the warden out of any money in his hands belonging to the State.

Contracts for convict labor to be performed outside prison walls. SEC. 47. It shall and may be lawful for the warden of the State prison, acting by and with the advice and consent of a majority of the inspectors of the prison, and in accordance with the regulations at the time in force, to make contracts for supplying convict labor for terms not exceeding two years, to parties whose places of business may be outside the prison walls, and so located that the convicts may be conveniently taken from the prison in the morning and returned to the same at night, at not less than one dollar per day for each convict so employed: *Provided,* That before any Proviso. such contract shall be executed the warden of the prison shall transmit to the inspectors a statement and estimate, in writing, showing what precautions are proposed to prevent the escape of the convicts so contracted; the extra expense of guards and keepers, and of clothing, if any, by such plan; and showing what the profit or loss to the State would be by such contract, as compared with the average price paid for labor within the prison walls, and

with the average which he will probably be able to obtain for the
same during the time for which it is proposed to contract the labor
of said convicts: *And provided further*, That it shall be inserted Further proviso.
as a proviso in every such contract, that the same may be canceled
at any time, by the vote of a majority of the inspectors of the
prison.

SEC. 48. The said warden shall also have authority, under such Convicts may be employed in quarrying stone, etc.
regulations as the inspectors may adopt, and subject to the control
of said inspectors, to employ the said convicts in quarrying stone,
or other labor useful in the erection or repair of the building or
walls of the prison.

SEC. 49. Any person supplying any convict with weapons, money, Penalty for aiding convict to escape.
clothing, or disguises, with intent to assist him in escaping from
custody, or who shall in any way assist such convict in his endeavors to escape, shall be liable, upon conviction, to the same punishment as though such act had been done within the prison walls,
and every such convict who shall escape, and every person aiding
such escape from such custody, shall be liable to the same penalties
as though he had broken prison and escaped, or assisted in such
breaking or escape.

REMOVALS AND ESCAPES.

SEC. 50. The inspectors of the State Prison and of the State State Prison and State House of Correction, transfer of prisoners from one to the other.
House of Correction shall meet together quarter-yearly, alternately
at each prison ; and it shall be their duty, acting in conjunction,
to ascertain the number of convicts confined in each prison, their
conduct, and as far as possible their offenses and character; and
if it shall appear that either prison has, or is likely to have, more
convicts than there are cells therein, or that there is a greater number of convicts in either one than can well be accommodated therein,
or that such convicts where they are cannot be employed profita-
bly to the State, or whenever in the judgment of the said boards so
acting jointly, the interests of the State, or the health or improvement of the convicts, or any of them, demand it, or when it is
otherwise material or in furtherance of justice, the said inspectors
so acting jointly as aforesaid, shall have and hereby are invested
with the power to transfer prisoners from one prison to the other,
and may by warrant, directed to the warden or superintendent of
the prison from which it is deemed desirable to remove any convicts, direct him to forthwith transport such convicts to the other
prison, designating them by name, and the agent or superintendent to whom such warrant is directed shall at once cause the convicts so ordered to be removed to be safely and securely transported
to the prison to which they are to be sent, and shall deliver such
convicts with the certified copies of their sentences to the warden
or superintendent of the prison to which they shall be removed,
and the warden or superintendent of such prison shall receive and
keep them according to their sentences, as if they had been originally committed to such prison. All necessary expenses of such
removal of convicts shall be deemed a part of the incidental expenses of the prison from which they shall be removed.

Removal of convicts in case of pestilence.
SEC. 51. In case any pestilence or contagious disease shall break out among the convicts in prison, or in the vicinity of the prison, the inspectors may cause the convicts therein to be removed to some suitable place of security, where such of them as may be sick, shall receive all necessary care and medical attendance, and such convicts shall be returned as soon as it may be safe to do so to the prison, and there confined according to their respective sentences, if the same be unexpired.

In case of fire.
SEC. 52. Whenever by reason of the State Prison, or any building contiguous thereto, or near such prison, being on fire, there shall be reason to apprehend that the convicts therein may be injured or endangered by such fire, or may escape, the warden may remove such convicts to some safe and convenient place, and there confine them so long as may be necessary to avoid the danger.

Removal of convict to testify in criminal prosecution.
SEC. 53. If any convict confined in the State Prison shall be considered an important witness in behalf of the people of this State, upon any criminal prosecution against any other person by the prosecuting attorney conducting the same, it shall be the duty of any officer or court, authorized by law to allow writs of *habeas corpus*, upon the affidavit of such prosecuting attorney, and a showing to the satisfaction of the court that such convict is a material and important witness on the trial of the cause, to grant a *habeas corpus* for the purpose of bringing such convict before the proper court to testify upon such prosecution. And in every case where a convict shall be removed from the prison to testify on any trial as provided in this section, he shall be securely kept in the jail of the county to which he shall have been removed, subject only to be taken into court to testify on such trial, and after his testimony shall have been given he shall be by the sheriff of the county forthwith returned to the prison, there to serve out the remainder of his term.

Time from escape to return of prisoner to be served after expiration of sentence.
If any prisoner shall be retaken, the time between the escape and his recommittal shall not be computed as part of the term of imprisonment, but he shall remain in the prison a sufficient length of time after the term of his sentence would have expired if he had not escaped, to equal the period of time he may have been absent by reason of such escape.

Reward for convicts who have escaped.
SEC. 54. Whenever any convict shall escape from the prison, it shall be the duty of the warden to take all proper measures for the apprehension of such convict, and for that purpose he may offer a reward, not exceeding fifty dollars, for the apprehension and delivery of such convict; but with the consent of the board of inspectors, such reward may be increased to a sum not exceeding five hundred dollars. All suitable rewards and other sums of money, necessarily paid for advertising and apprehending any convict who may escape from the prison, shall be audited by the Auditor General and paid out of the State treasury.

PROPERTY OF CONVICT.

Warden to take charge of, etc.
SEC. 55. It shall be the duty of the warden to take charge of any property which any convict may have with him at the time of entering the prison; the warden shall sell or preserve the same,

c nd place the proceeds thereof at interest, for the benefit of such onvict or his representatives.

SEC. 56. Such warden shall keep a correct account of all such operty, and shall pay the amount, or the proceeds thereof, or re- rn the same to the convict when discharged, or to his legal representatives in case of his death, and in case of the death of such convict without being released, if no legal representative shall demand such property within five years, then the same shall be applied to the use of the State.

To keep account of and return to prisoner.

DISCHARGE.

SEC. 57. When any convict shall be discharged from prison by pardon or otherwise, the warden shall furnish such convict with clothing, if he be not already provided for, not exceeding ten dollars in value, and such sum of money not exceeding ten dollars, as the warden may deem necessary and proper; and the board of inspectors may, in their discretion, furnish such convict with a further sum of money not exceeding fifteen dollars, whenever in their opinion the necessities of the convict are such as require the same. The warden shall also allow and pay to the convict such sum as such convict may earn by doing over-work for contractors, under such regulations as the inspectors may prescribe; such over-work to be charged and collected of the contractors in the same manner as the regular labor of the convicts.

Convicts to be furnished clothing and money.

Pay for over-work.

VISITORS.—EDUCATION.

SEC. 58. The following persons shall be authorized to visit the prison at pleasure, namely: The Governor, Lieutenant Governor, members of the Legislature, State officers, the judges of the supreme and circuit courts, prosecuting attorneys, sheriffs, members and officers of any board authorized by law to visit the same, and all regular officiating ministers of the gospel; and no other person shall be permitted to go within the walls of the prison where convicts shall be confined, except by special permission of the warden, or under such regulations as the inspectors shall prescribe.

Who may visit prison at pleasure.

SEC. 59. It shall be lawful for the inspectors to establish uniform rules for the admission of visitors within the prison, and they may prescribe a reasonable sum, not exceeding twenty-five cents, to be charged each individual for one admission. The warden shall procure suitable tickets, which shall be sold by the clerk, who shall keep an account of such sales and pay over the money received to the warden daily. The keeper at the entrance to the convict department of the prison shall receive the tickets, and also keep an account of them in a book as they are received, and shall deliver them to the warden each day before the prison is closed. It shall be the duty of the inspectors to appropriate annually out of the avails of fees received from visitors the sum of five hundred dollars in the purchase of books for said prison for the use of the said convicts.

Rules for the admission of visitors, etc.

Appropriation from fees for purchase of books.

SEC. 60. No person, without the consent of the warden, shall bring into or carry out of the prison any letter or writing, or any

Letters not to be delivered to convicts, etc.

information to or from any convict; and whoever shall violate the provisions of this section shall be deemed guilty of a misdemeanor.

Instruction of prisoners. Sec. 61. The board of inspectors may expend from the earnings of the prison a sum not exceeding one thousand dollars per annum in furnishing suitable instruction in reading, writing, and such other branches of education as they may deem expedient to be taught to such of the convicts as may be benefited thereby and are desirous of receiving the same, and may also employ a teacher for said prison, who shall devote his entire time to the instruction of the convicts in the ordinary branches of a common school education.

MISCELLANEOUS PROVISIONS.

Sheriff to convey convicts to prison. Sec. 62. It shall be the duty of the sheriff of every county in which any criminal shall be sentenced to confinement in the State Prison, as soon as may be practicable after the passing of such sentence, to convey such convict to the State Prison and deliver him to the warden thereof.

Copy of sentence to be delivered with convict, etc. Sec. 63. When any convict shall be delivered to the warden of the State Prison, the officer having such convict in his charge shall deliver to such warden the certified copy of the sentence, received by such officer from the clerk of the court, and shall take from such warden a certificate of the delivery of such convict; and such certified copy of the sentence of any convict shall be evidence of the facts therein contained.

Fees and expenses of conveying convicts to prison, and payment of the same. Sec. 64. The fees and actual expenses of sheriffs in conveying convicts to the State prison shall be made out in a bill containing the items thereof, and shall be presented to the warden when the prisoner is delivered at the prison. The warden shall certify on it that the prisoner has been received, and the bill, including the sheriff's actual expenses in returning to the county from whence the prisoner was sent, shall be audited by the Auditor General and paid from the State treasury. Before drawing his warrant the Auditor General shall correct any errors in said bill, as to form, items, or amount; and the sheriff shall be paid for such services, his actual traveling expenses, and the expenses of the convict, and the sum of ($3.00) three dollars for each and every day so employed.

Convicts sentenced by courts of United States. Sec. 65. It shall be the duty of the warden of the State Prison to receive therein and safely keep, and subject to the discipline of the prison, any criminal convicted of any crime against the United States, sentenced to imprisonment therein by any court of the United States sitting within this State or elsewhere, until such sentence shall be executed, or until such convict shall be discharged by due course of law, the United States supporting such convicts and paying the expenses of executing such sentence.

Transactions to be conducted in name of warden. Sec. 66. All the fiscal transactions and dealings on account of said prison shall be conducted by and in the name of the warden, who shall be capable in law of suing and being sued in all courts and places, and in all matters concerning the said prison, by his name of office; and by that name he is hereby authorized to sue for and recover all sums of money, or any property due from any person to any former agent or warden of the said prison, or to the people of this State on account of said prison. When a controversy arises respecting any contract made by the agent on account of the prison, or a suit is pending thereon, the warden may, with the written approval of the inspectors, submit the same to the final determination of arbitrators or referees.

SEC. 67. All books of account, registers, and other documents and papers relating to the affairs of the prison, shall be considered public property, and shall remain therein; and the warden shall preserve at least one set of copies of all official reports made to the Governor respecting said prison, and a set of similar reports in relation to the prisons of other States, so far as he shall be able to obtain the same; and to accomplish this purpose there shall be printed annually, for the use of the prison, one hundred extra copies of the annual report of the inspectors, which shall be supplied to the warden for exchange with prisons of other States; and he shall annually transmit to each of the State prisons in the United States one copy of such report. *[Books of account public property. Provision for preserving prisons reports of this and other States.]*

SEC. 68. It shall be the duty of the warden and deputy warden to see that rigid economy is practiced in all matters pertaining to the prison, and in the employment of prisoners, and that duplicate receipts be taken for all expenditures made by them on account of the prison, one copy of which shall be sent to the Auditor General's office monthly. *[Economy in matters pertaining to prison required.]*

SEC. 69. The Auditor General is hereby authorized and required to draw his warrant on the treasurer for such sums as the Inspectors of the State Prison shall from time to time direct; but such sums so drawn at any one time, shall not exceed one thousand dollars; and no further sum shall be drawn until satisfactory vouchers are presented to and allowed by the Auditor General for the amount previously drawn. *[Drawing of money from treasury.]*

SEC. 70. On the removal or resignation of any warden of said prison, the Auditor General shall settle the accounts of such warden on the presentation of his books and vouchers duly authenticated for that purpose. *[Settlement with warden on removal, etc.]*

SEC. 71. The warden shall annually, on the thirtieth day of September in every year, close his account, and on or before the fifteenth day of October thereafter shall render to the Auditor General a full and true account of all moneys received by him on account of the prison, and of all moneys expended by him for the use thereof, with sufficient vouchers for the same, and also an inventory of the goods, materials, and other property of the State on hand, exhibiting a complete detail of the transactions of the prison for the year. *[Annual report of warden to Auditor General.]*

SEC. 72. To the several returns, accounts, and inventories required by the preceding section to be rendered, there shall be annexed an affidavit of the warden and clerk of the prison, stating that the same are true in every respect to the best of their knowledge and belief. *[Affidavit to be attached to returns, accounts, etc.]*

33

Accounts of warden to be audited, etc.   SEC. 73. It shall be the duty of the Auditor General to examine and audit the accounts of the warden, and to lay a statement thereof before the Legislature at each regular session thereof.

Annual report of warden to Secretary of State.   SEC. 74. It shall be the duty of the warden annually, on or before the first day of January, to report to the Secretary of State the names of the convicts pardoned or discharged during the preceding year from the prison, the counties in which they were tried, the crimes for which they were convicted, the terms for which they were severally committed, the ages and description of their persons, and, in cases of pardon, the term unexpired for which they were severally sentenced, when such pardons were granted, and the terms, if any, upon which they were granted.

Contracts, etc., heretofore made not affected by passage of this act.   SEC. 75. No lien, demand, claim, or contract heretofore established or made by the agent of the prison in behalf of the State shall be in any wise changed or affected by the passage of this act; but the rights of the State, and of all parties to contracts or obligations heretofore made, as well as the lien of the State upon property of such contractors for sums unpaid or due for the labor of convicts, shall remain as complete and as binding, and may be enforced in the same manner and as fully, as if this act had not been passed.

Acts repealed.   SEC. 76. All acts and parts of acts contravening any of the provisions of this act are hereby repealed; but all proceedings pending, and all rights and liabilities existing, acquired, or incurred at the time this act takes effect, are hereby saved, and such proceedings may be consummated under and according to the law in force at the time such proceedings were commenced.

SEC. 77. This act shall take immediate effect.

Approved May 3, 1875.

[No. 214.]

AN ACT to amend section five thousand two hundred and fifty, being section two of chapter one hundred and seventy-eight of the compiled laws of eighteen hundred and seventy-one, relative to jurisdiction of justices' courts.

Section amended   SECTION 1. *The People of the State of Michigan enact,* That section five thousand two hundred and fifty, being section two of chapter one hundred and seventy-eight of the compiled laws of eighteen hundred and seventy-one, be amended so as to read as follows:

Actions of which justice has no jurisdiction.   (5250.) SEC. 2. No justice of the peace shall have cognizance of real actions, actions for a disturbance of a right of way or other easement, actions for libel or slander, or malicious prosecutions, and actions against executors or administrators as such, except in the cases specially provided by law, nor where the title to real estate shall come in question, except as hereinafter mentioned: *Pro-*

Proviso.   *vided,* That justices of the peace may have jurisdiction in actions for damages resulting from obstructions to highways, subject to the restrictions prescribed in section one of this chapter.

Approved May 3, 1875.

[No. 215.]

AN ACT to amend section ten, being section four thousand two hundred and twelve of the compiled laws of eighteen hundred and seventy-one, chapter one hundred and fifty, relative to alienation by deed, and the proof and recording of conveyances, and the canceling of mortgages.

SECTION 1. *The People of the State of Michigan enact,* That sections ten, being section four thousand two hundred and twelve, chapter one hundred and fifty, of the compiled laws, relative to alienation by deed, and the proof and recording of conveyances, and the canceling of mortgages, be amended so as to read as follows : Section amended

(4212.) SEC. 10. In the cases provided for in the ·last preceding section, unless the acknowledgment be taken before a commissioner appointed by the Governor of this State for that purpose, such deed shall have attached thereto a certificate of the clerk or other proper certifying officer of a court of record of the county or district, or of the Secretary of State of the state or territory within which such acknowledgment was taken, under the seal of his office, that the person whose name is subscribed to the certificate of acknowledgment was at the date thereof such officer as he is thereon represented to be, and that he believes the signature of such person to such certificate of acknowledgment to be genuine, and that the deed is executed and acknowledged according to the laws of such State, territory, or district. How acknowledgment authenticated.

Approved May 3, 1875.

[No. 216.]

AN ACT to amend sections twelve and thirteen of chapter twenty-six of an act entitled " An·act relative to laying out, altering, and discontinuing highways," being sections one thousand two hundred and sixty-three and one thousand two hundred and sixty-four of the compiled laws of eighteen hundred and seventy-one.

SECTION 1. *The People of the State of Michigan enact,* That sections twelve and thirteen of chapter twenty-six, being sections one thousand two hundred and sixty-three and one thousand two hundred and sixty-four of the compiled laws of eighteen hundred and seventy-one, be amended so as to read as follows : Sections amended.

SEC. 12. Every such appeal shall be in writing, signed by the appellant, and addressed to the township board or boards, as case may be, and filed with the township clerk, who shall as soon as may be after the term limited for taking appeals shall have expired, call a meeting of the township board or boards, ten days' notice of which shall be given by said township clerk to the appellant, and one or more of said commissioners from whose determination the appeal was taken, and to each person whose lands are to be affected thereby. Such notice shall be in writing, and shall state the time and place of meeting, and a copy shall be delivered to said appel- Proceedings on appeals to township board.

lant, commissioner, and to each person to be affected thereby, or
left at their respective places of residence.

Hearing proof and allegations.
SEC. 13. The said township board or boards shall proceed at the
time and place specified in the notice to hear the proofs and allegations of the parties in respect to the necessity of laying out,
altering, or discontinuing such highway, or the award of dam-
Decision final.
ages, and their decision shall be conclusive and final. Such de-
Shall be in writing.
cision shall be reduced to writing, and signed by the board or
boards making the same, and filed in the office of the township
Proviso.
clerk: *Provided,* That if the decision, appraisal, and award of the
commissioner from which the appeal is taken be confirmed, or if
the award of damages shall be diminished, then in either case the
Costs.
appellant shall pay the whole amount of costs of such appeal,
said costs to be ascertained and determined by said board or boards,
and deducted from the amount of damages awarded, and when
there is no damages from which to pay the costs of the appeal, the
appellant shall be liable for the costs of the appeal, to be collecti-
ble in an action at law.

Approved May 3, 1875.

[No. 217.]

AN ACT to provide for the republication and sale of such of the
reports of the Supreme Court of this State as are or may become
out of print.

Republication authorized.
SECTION 1. *The People of the State of Michigan enact,* That
whenever the Chief Justice of the Supreme Court may deem it
necessary to republish any volume or volumes of the reports of the
Supreme Court of this State which are out of print, he shall request the State reporter, and it shall be his duty as soon as practicable thereafter, to cause such volume or volumes to be reprinted
and bound in a good and substantial manner, and uniform in size
with the present Michigan reports, subject to the approval of the
Proviso.
Chief Justice of the Supreme Court: *Provided,* That the edition
of any of said reports shall be deemed out of print, and the Chief
Justice shall make said request whenever such edition, as far as
held for sale by the State shall be exhausted, and the prevailing
market price of the same per volume shall be not less than double
the price at which reports of the Supreme Court are authorized to
be sold by the State.

Certain foot notes or references to be published in connection therewith.
SEC. 2. Before any volume of said reports shall be so reprinted
said reporter shall prepare or cause to be prepared and appended to
the cases contained in such volume, suitable foot notes or references to subsequent cases in the Michigan reports modifying or
affecting the decision in such cases, and cause the same to be
printed in connection therewith under his supervision; and for his
services therefor said reporter shall be allowed such reasonable
compensation by the Board of State Auditors as to them shall
Proviso.
seem just: *Provided,* If for any cause said reporter shall be unable personally to perform the duties hereby imposed, the Chief

Justice shall appoint some other person of known integrity and legal learning to perform the same, who shall be entitled to like compensation.

SEC. 3. Whenever any volume of said reports shall be repub- Number of coplished, under the provisions of this act, one thousand copies shall ies to be printed, where deposited, be printed and bound as above provided, all of which shall be de- etc. posited with the State Librarian, who shallgive his receipt to the State printer therefor, and shall hold and dispose of the same at the prices and in the manner provided in section seven of chapter one hundred and eight, being compiler's section five thousand six hundred and fifty-seven of the compiled laws of eighteen hundred and seventy-one : *Provided*, Sales therein provided for to book- Proviso. sellers, shall not be more than sufficient at any time to meet the reasonable present demands of the trade.

Approved May 3, 1875.

[No. 218.]

AN ACT to amend sections thirteen and fourteen of an act to authorize and encourage the formation of corporations to establish rural cemeteries, and to provide for the care and maintenance thereof, approved February nineteen, eighteen hundred and sixty-nine, being general sections three thousand four hundred and twenty and three thousand four hundred and twenty-one of the compiled laws of eighteen hundred and seventy-one.

SECTION 1. *The People of the State of Michigan enact*, That Sections sections thirteen and fourteen of an act to authorize and encourage amended. the formation of corporations to establish rural cemeteries, and to provide for the care and maintenance thereof, approved February nineteen, eighteen hundred and sixty-nine, being sections three thousand four hundred and twenty and three thousand four hundred and twenty-one of the compiled laws of eighteen hundred and seventy one, be and the same are hereby amended so as to read as follows :

(3420.) SEC. 13. The superintendent, landscape gardener, over- Powers of seer, and watchman in any cemetery belonging to any corporation superintendent, gardener, over- formed under this act, shall have the power to summarily arrest seer, and watch- any person or persons who shall commit any crime, misdemeanor, man to make arrests. or depredation, or be guilty of any disorderly conduct upon the grounds of such corporation. Upon any arrest being made by any Offender to be one of said officers or employes of such corporation, it shall be the conveyed before a justice for trial. duty of the one making such arrest to convey the arrested party to a justice of the peace of the proper county, and make complaint to such magistrate, under oath, as to the nature of the offense committed ; and thereupon, if the offense charged is cognizable by a Punishment. justice of the peace, under the general laws of the State, such justice shall try such person charged with committing said offense, and upon the conviction of such person, shall render judgment and inflict such punishment upon such offender, either by fine or im-

prisonment, or both, as the nature of the case may require, together
with the costs of prosecution, as the justice of the peace shall order;
but such punishment shall in no case exceed the limits fixed by
law for the offense charged. In case the offense charged shall not
be cognizable by a justice of the peace under the general laws of
this State, then such justice shall examine the accused person, and
the proceedings upon such examination shall be such as are prescribed by chapter one hundred and ninety-four of the compiled
laws of this State.

Proceedings when offense is not cognizable by such justice.

(3421.) Sec. 14. No person shall use fire-arms upon the grounds
of any cemetery owned and inclosed by any such corporation, nor
hunt game therein. No person shall enter into such inclosed cemetery by climbing or leaping over or through any fence or wall
around the same, nor direct or cause any animal to enter therein
in any such manner. Any person offending against any of the
provisions of this section shall be punished by a fine not exceeding
fifty dollars, or by imprisonment not exceeding three months, or by
both, in the discretion of the court.

Use of fire-arms prohibited.

Penalty.

Approved May 3, 1875.

[No. 219.]

AN ACT to amend sections three thousand four hundred and ten
and three thousand four hundred and fourteen of chapter one
hundred and twenty-nine of the compiled laws of eighteen hundred and seventy-one, entitled "An act to authorize and encourage the formation of corporations to establish rural cemeteries,
and provide for the care and maintenance thereof," approved
February nineteen, eighteen hundred and sixty-nine, and to add
ten new sections thereto, to stand as sections seventeen, eighteen,
nineteen, twenty, twenty-one, twenty-two, twenty-three, twenty-
four, twenty-five, and twenty-six.

SECTION 1. *The People of the State of Michigan enact,* That
sections three thousand four hundred and ten and three thousand
four hundred and fourteen of chapter one hundred and twenty-
nine of the compiled laws of eighteen hundred and seventy-one,
entitled "An act to authorize and encourage the formation of corporations to establish rural cemeteries and provide for the care and
maintenance thereof," approved February nineteen, eighteen hundred and sixty-nine, be and the same are hereby amended so as to
read as follows:

Sections amended.

(3410.) Sec. 3. The subscribers to such articles of association
shall, at the time of subscription thereto, severally pay to the treasurer named therein at least twenty per cent of the amount subscribed by each, and when the whole amount of capital mentioned
in said articles shall be subscribed and said portion thereof actually
paid in, the directors shall cause a copy of their articles of association, together with an affidavit of such treasurer that twenty per
cent of the amount of capital subscribed has actually been paid in,

Subscribers each to pay 20 per cent of amount subscribed.

to be filed in the office of the county clerk of the county in which
such association is formed.

(3414.) SEC. 7. It shall be the duty of such board of directors *Further duties of board of directors.*
to preserve good order in the grounds of such cemetery; to pro-
vide for the laying out and embellishing of the same, and to see
that they are well kept and in good condition. When the pay- *To apply two-thirds of receipts for improvements.*
ments for lands purchased shall have been fully made, to reserve
at least two-thirds of all the receipts of such corporation which
shall be derived from the sale of burial rights after the payment
of the current expenses for interest, improvements, and embellishing, until the aggregate amount thereof shall, in the opinion of
said board, be sufficient to constitute a permanent fund which,
when invested, shall produce an income large enough to meet the
expense of keeping the grounds of such cemeteries perpetually in
good condition after the same shall have once been properly laid
out, improved, and embellished according to the plan thereof; to *To invest receipts.*
invest the receipts to be reserved as aforesaid in the bonds of the
United States, or of the State of Michigan, or of municipal corporations of this State, and to use the income thereof only for the
purposes aforesaid; to cause to be issued scrip or certificates to each *To issue scrip.*
subscriber to the articles of the association, which certificates shall
specify the amount paid into the capital stock by such subscriber.
Such scrip shall be personal property and transferable by the holder
thereof, under such regulations as the board of directors may
adopt; to make a report to the annual meeting of the condition of *To make annual report.*
the association, and its receipts and disbursements for the previous
year.

SEC. 2. That the following sections be and the same are hereby *Sections added.*
added to an act entitled "An act to authorize and encourage the
formation of corporations to establish rural cemeteries and provide
for the care and maintenance thereof;" approved February nineteenth, eighteen hundred and sixty-nine, which new sections shall
stand as sections seventeen, eighteen, nineteen, twenty, twenty-one,
twenty-two, twenty-three, twenty-four, twenty-five and twenty-six
of said act.

SEC. 17. Whenever the board of directors of said corporation, *Relative to enlarging the limits of cemetery.*
the board of health of any township, or the common council,
board of health, or board of trustees of any city or village shall
deem it to be desirable and necessary to enlarge the limits of any
cemetery which has been or may be hereafter established in the
manner provided by law, and such board of directors, board of
health, board of trustees, or common council shall be unable to
agree with the owner or owners of the land which such board of
directors, board of health, board of trustees, or common council
desire to include within the limits of the cemetery to be enlarged,
as to the compensation to be paid therefor, or in case such board
of directors, board of health, board of trustees, or common council
shall, by reason of any imperfection in the title to said land, arising either from a break in the chain of title, tax-sale, mortgages,
levies, or any other cause be unable to procure a perfect, unencum-
bered title in fee simple to said land, such board of directors,

Application to
circuit judge for
jury to deter-
mine compensa-
tion, etc.

board of health, board of trustees, or common council shall authorize one or more of its members to apply to the circuit judge in
whose circuit such cemetery shall be situated, for a jury to ascertain and determine the just compensation to be made for the real
estate required by such cemetery, and the necessity for using the
same, which application shall be in writing, and shall describe the
real estate desired for enlarging such cemetery as accurately as is
required in a conveyance of real estate.

Summoning of
jury.

SEC. 18. It shall be the duty of such circuit judge, upon such
application being made to him, to issue a summons or *venire* directed to the sheriff or any constable of the county, commanding
him to summon eighteen freeholders residing in the vicinity of
such land, who are in nowise of kin to the owner of such real estate, and not interested therein, to appear before such judge, at the
time and place therein named, not less than twenty nor more than
thirty days from the time of issuing such summons or *venire*, as
a jury to ascertain and determine the just compensation to be
made for the real estate required for enlarging such cemetery, and

Notice to owner
of real estate.

the necessity for using the same, and to notify the owner or occupant of such real estate, if he can be found in the county, of the
time and place where such jury is summoned to appear, and the
object for which said jury is summoned, which notice shall be
served at least ten days before the time specified in such summons
or *venire* for the jury to appear as hereinbefore mentioned.

Notice of time
when, and place
where jury will
assemble.

SEC. 19. Thirty days' previous notice of the time when, and the
place where, such jury will assemble, shall be given by such board
of directors, board of health, board of trustees, or common council, where the owner or owners of such real estate shall be unknown, are non-residents of the county, minors, insane, *non compos mentis*, or inmates of any prison, by publishing the same in a
newspaper published in the county where such real estate is situated, or if there be no newspaper published in such county, then in
some newspaper published in the nearest county where a newspaper is published, once in each week for four successive weeks,
which notice shall be signed by the board of directors, board of
health, board of trustees, or common council, and shall describe
the real estate required for enlarging such cemetery, and state the
time when, and place where, such jury will assemble, and the object for which they will assemble, or such notice may be served on
each owner personally, or by leaving a copy thereof at his last place
of residence.

Return of sum-
mons, etc.

SEC. 20. It shall be the duty of such judge, and of the persons
summoned as jurors, as hereinbefore provided, and of the sheriff
or constable summoning them, to attend at the time and place
specified in such summons or *venire*, and the officer who summoned the jury shall return such summons or *venire* to the officer
who issued the same, with the names of the persons summoned by
him as jurors, and shall certify the manner of notifying the owner
or owners of such real estate if he was found, and if he could not

Formation of
jury.

be found in said county, he shall certify that fact. Either party
may challenge any of the said jurors for the same causes as in

civil actions. If more than twelve of said jurors in attendance
shall be found qualified to serve as jurors, the officer in attendance,
and who issued the summons or *venire* for such jury, shall strike
from the list of jurors a number sufficient to reduce the number
of jurors in attendance to twelve; and in case less than twelve of
the number so summoned as jurors shall attend, the sheriff or constable shall summon a sufficient number of freeholders to make
up the number of twelve, and the officer issuing the summons or
venire for such jury may issue an attachment for any person summoned as a juror who shall fail to attend, and may enforce obedience to such summons, *venire*, or attachment as courts of record
are authorized to do in civil cases.

SEC. 21. The twelve persons selected as the jury shall be duly *Oath of jurors.*
sworn by the judge in attendance, faithfully and impartially to inquire, ascertain, and determine the just compensation to be made
for the real estate required for enlarging such cemetery, and the
necessity for using the same in the manner proposed by such cemetery; and the persons thus sworn shall constitute the jury in such
case. Subpœnas for witness [witnesses] may be issued, and their *Witnesses.*
attendance compelled by such circuit judge in the same manner as
may be done by the circuit court in civil cases. The jury may *Jury to examine premises, etc.*
visit and examine the premises, and from such examination and
such other evidence as may be presented before them, shall ascertain and determine the necessity for using such real estate in the
manner and for the purpose proposed by such board of directors,
board of health, board of trustees, or common council, and the
just compensation to be made therefor, and if such jury shall find
that it is necessary that such real estate shall be used in the manner or for the purpose proposed by such board of directors, board
of health, board of trustees, or common council, they shall sign a *Certificate of jury.*
certificate in writing, stating that it is necessary that said real estate (describing it) should be used for enlarging such cemetery,
also stating the sum to be paid by such board of directors, board
of health, board of trustees, or common council, as the just compensation for the same. The said circuit judge shall sign and at- *Certificate of judge.*
tach to and indorse upon the certificate thus subscribed by the
said jurors a certificate stating the time when and the place where
the said jury assembled, that they were by him duly sworn, as
herein required, and that they subscribed the said certificate. He
shall also state in such certificate who appeared for the respective
parties on such hearing and inquiry, and shall deliver such certificates to said board of directors, board of health, board of trustees,
or common council.

SEC. 22. Upon filing such certificate in the circuit court of the *On filing of cer-tificate court to render judg-ment.*
county where such real estate is situated, such court shall, if it
finds all the proceedings regular, render judgment for the sum
specified in the certificate signed by such jury against such board
of directors, board of health, board of trustees, or common council, which judgment shall be collected and paid in the manner as
as other judgments are collected and paid.

SEC. 23. In case the owner of such real estate shall be un-

34

When owner is
unknown,
insane, etc.,
money to be
deposited with
county treasurer. known, insane, *non compos mentis*, or an infant, or cannot be
found within such county, it shall be lawful for said board of directors, board of health, board of trustees, or common council to
deposit the amount of such judgment with the county treasurer of
such county, for the use of the person or persons entitled thereto,
and it shall be the duty of such county treasurer to receive such
moneys, and at the time receiving it to give a receipt or certificate to the person depositing the same with him, stating the
time when such deposit was made, and for what purpose; and such
county treasurer and his sureties shall be liable on his bond for
any money which shall come into his hands under the provisions
of this act, in case he shall refuse to pay or account for the same
Proviso. as herein provided: *Provided,* That no such money shall be drawn
from such county treasurer except upon an order of the circuit
court, or judge of probate, as hereinafter provided.

Decree of court
on payment of
judgment. SEC. 24. Upon satisfactory evidence being presented to the circuit court of the county where such real estate lies, that such
judgment or the sum ascertained and determined by the jury as
the just compensation to be paid by such board of directors, board
of health, board of trustees, or common council, for such real
estate, has been paid, or that amount has been deposited according
to the provisions of the preceding section, such court shall by an
order or decree adjudge and determine that the title in fee of such
real estate shall, from the time of making such payment or deposit,
forever thereafter be vested in such board of directors, board of
health, board of trustees, or common council, or in the township,
city, or village, as the case may be, and its assigns; a copy of
Record of decree,
etc. which decree, certified by the clerk of said county, shall be recorded in the office of the register of deeds of such county, and
the title of such real estate shall thenceforth, from the time of
making such payment or deposit, be vested forever thereafter in
such board of directors, board of health, board of trustees, or common council, township, city, or village, and its assigns in fee.

When premises
may be taken
possession of. SEC. 25. Such board of directors, board of health, board of trustees, or common council may at any time after making the payment or deposit hereinbefore required enter upon and take possession of such real estate for the use of such cemetery, by such
board of directors, board of health, board of trustees, or common
council.

Proceedings in
case jury cannot
agree. SEC. 26. In case the jury hereinbefore provided for shall not
agree, another jury may be summoned in the same manner, and
the same proceedings may be had, except that no further notice of
the proceedings may be necessary, but instead of such notice the
judge may adjourn the proceedings to such time as he shall think
reasonable, not exceeding thirty days, and shall make the process
to summon a jury returnable at such time and place as the pro-
Adjournment of
proceedings. ceedings may be adjourned to. Such proceedings may be adjourned from time to time by the said judge, on the application of
either party, and for good cause to be shown by the party applying
for such adjournment, unless the other party shall consent to such

adjournment, but the adjournment [adjournments] shall not exceed three months.

SEC. 3. This act shall take immediate effect.

Approved May 3, 1875.

[No. 220.]

AN ACT to amend section (93) ninety-three of chapter (18) eighteen, being section nine hundred and twenty of the compiled laws of eighteen hundred and seventy-one, entitled "An act for the re-organization of the military forces of the State of Michigan."

SECTION 1. *The People of the State of Michigan enact,* That section ninety-three of chapter eighteen, being section nine hundred and twenty of the compiled laws of eighteen hundred and seventy-one, be amended so as to read as follows: *Section amended*

SEC. 93. For the purpose of providing the expenses necessary to carry out the provisions of this act, it shall be the duty of the Auditor General at the time of apportioning the State taxes, to apportion among the several counties of the State each year in proportion to the whole amount of real and personal property therein, as equalized by the State board of equalization, a sum equal to ten cents for each person whom it shall appear, by the return made to the proper officer, voted at the next preceding gubernatorial election for the office of Governor of this State, which sum so apportioned shall be collected in the same manner with other State taxes and shall constitute the State military fund, but no military tax shall be apportioned, levied, or collected for the year eighteen hundred and seventy-five. *Auditor General to apportion a tax to meet the expenses incurred by this act.* *No tax to be collected for 1875.*

Approved May 3, 1875.

[No. 221.]

AN ACT to amend section thirty-three of act number one hundred and forty-five of the session laws of eighteen hundred and seventy-three, approved April twenty-fourth eighteen hundred and seventy-three, being an act to amend an act to re-organize the State Agricultural College and establish a State Board of Agriculture, approved March five, eighteen hundred and sixty-one.

SECTION 1. *The People of the State of Michigan enact,* That section thirty-three of act number one hundred and forty-five of the session laws of eighteen hundred and seventy-three, approved April twenty-four, eighteen hundred and seventy-three, being an act to amend an act to re-organize the State Agricultural College and establish a State Board of Agriculture, approved March fifteen, eighteen hundred and sixty-one, be so amended as to read as follows: *Section amended*

Annual reports of the several departments to be filed with Secretary of the board.

SEC. 33. The superintendents of the farm, horticultural, and other departments, the curators of the museums, and each of the professors, shall make a written and detailed report of the workings of their several departments annually to the president of the college, which said reports shall be kept on file in the office of the secretary of the State Board of Agriculture. Agricultural opera-

Agricultural operations to be carried on experimentally.

tions on the farm shall be carried on experimentally. Careful experiments shall be made annually in field crops, in keeping, feeding, and fattening stock, and in the preparation and application of barn-yard and commercial manures, and a detailed account of them shall be published in the annual reports of the board. The college shall serve also as an experimental station, making trial from time to time of new varieties of fruits, grains, and vegetables.

What reports to contain.

The reports shall contain an account of the management of all the several fields, pastures, orchards, and gardens of the college, as designated by permanent names or numbers, and shall give an account of the preparation and enriching of the land, the planting, cultivation, harvesting, and yield of the crops and disposition of the same; the management of the stock, with a careful comparison of the cost of keeping, growth, and profit of the several breeds kept on the farm; also an account of the students' labor, specifying the amount used in each of the several departments of the college, with other details, in such a way that the reports, as issued from year to year, shall contain a continuous history of the

Proviso.

college, farm, and garden: *Provided*, That the State Board of Agriculture shall deem the same practicable or advisable.

Approved May 3, 1875.

[No. 222.]

AN ACT to amend an act entitled "An act relative to plank roads," approved March thirteenth, eighteen hundred and forty-eight, and the acts amendatory thereto, being chapter seventy-eight of the compiled laws of eighteen hundred and seventy-one, and to add one new section thereto.

Act amended.

SECTION 1. *The People of the State of Michigan enact*, That an act entitled "An act relative to plank roads," approved March thirteenth, eighteen hundred and forty-eight, and the acts amendatory thereto, be amended by adding one new section, to stand as section thirty-two.

Proceedings necessary to secure the widening of plank roads.

SEC. 32. The commissioners [commissioner] of highways of any township, the mayor of any incorporated city, or the president of any incorporated village, through any portion of which any plank road may be or shall have been constructed, whenever satisfied that the public good and safety, by reason of the amount of travel on such road, requires more than sixteen feet in width of good, smooth, and permanent road, or that that portion of any plank road which has been prepared and constructed for travel is of insufficient width, may, on at least fifteen days' written notice to the president or secretary of said company, apply to the circuit court of the county in which said township, city, or village is located for an order to widen said road-bed. The court, on such application, and on hearing the respective parties, and on reviewing the premises, if the said court shall deem such view necessary, shall make such order in the matter as to the said court may seem just and proper: *Provided*, That the court shall not have power to extend the width of said road-bed beyond two and one-half rods. Such order shall be observed by the respective parties, and may be enforced by attachment or otherwise, as said court shall direct, and the decision of said court shall be final in the matter, and said court may direct the payment of costs in the premises as shall be deemed just and equitable. Proviso.

Approved May 3, 1875.

[No. 223.]

AN ACT to amend section two thousand nine hundred and fifty-seven of the compiled laws of eighteen hundred and seventy-one, being section sixteen of chapter ninety-eight, entitled " An act in relation to life insurance companies transacting business within this State."

SECTION 1. *The People of the State of Michigan enact,* That section sixteen of chapter ninety-eight of the compiled laws of eighteen hundred and seventy-one be amended so as to read as follows: Section amended

(2957.) SEC. 16. All insurance companies insuring life within this State, and not deriving corporate existence from its laws, shall annually, at the time of filing their annual report with the Commissioner of Insurance, pay to the State Treasurer a tax of two per centum on all premiums received in cash or otherwise, by such companies or their agents within this State, or from insured parties residing therein during the preceding year; and in case of neglect or refusal of such company to pay such tax within ten days after the filing of such report, the State Treasurer may proceed to collect the same out of the interests or dividends on any securities that such company may have deposited with him, as hereinafter provided; and in case no such securities are deposited, then it shall not be lawful for the company in default to receive any application for insurance, or to issue any policy, until such tax is paid ; and any agent or officer receiving any such application, or issuing such policy, while such default continues, shall be liable to a penalty of one hundred dollars, to be collected in the same manner with the other penalties hereinbefore provided; and the specific tax herein provided for shall be in lieu of all other taxes in this State. Specific tax of two per cent to be paid by foreign companies. When State Treasurer may collect tax.

Approved May 3, 1875.

[No. 224.]

AN ACT to repeal section one hundred and twenty-four of chapter twenty-one, being section one thousand and ninety of the compiled laws of eighteen hundred and seventy-one, relative to the assessment and collection of taxes.

Section repealed. SECTION 1. *The People of the State of Michigan enact,* That section one hundred and twenty-four of chapter twenty-one, being section one thousand and ninety of the compiled laws of eighteen hundred and seventy-one, relative to the assessment and collection of taxes, shall be and the same is hereby repealed.

Approved May 3, 1875.

[No. 225.]

AN ACT to prevent the adulteration of alcoholic liquors, and to punish all persons who shall sell or offer to sell adulterated liquors and other adulterated beverages.

Penalty for adulterating liquors, or for selling or offering the same for sale. SECTION 1. *The People of the State of Michigan enact,* That if any person shall adulterate any spirituous or alcoholic liquors used or intended for drink, by mixing the same in the manufacture or preparation thereof, or by process of rectifying, or otherwise, with any deleterious drug, substance, or liquid, which is poisonous or injurious to health, except as hereinafter provided, or if any person shall sell, or offer to sell, any wine, or spirituous, or alcoholic liquors, or shall import into this State any wine or spirituous or intoxicating liquors, and sell or offer for sale such liquors, knowing the same to be adulterated, or shall sell or offer to sell any spirituous or intoxicating liquors from any barrel, cask, or other vessel containing the same, and not branded as hereinafter provided, he shall be deemed guilty of a misdemeanor, and upon conviction thereof shall be fined in any sum not exceeding five hundred dollars, nor less than fifty dollars, and shall be imprisoned in the jail of the county not more than sixty nor less than ten days.

Brand. SEC. 2. It shall be the duty of every person or persons engaged in the manufacture and sale of malt, spirituous, or alcoholic liquors, or in rectifying or preparing the same in any way, to brand on each barrel, cask, or other vessel containing the same, the name or names of the person, company, or firm manufacturing, rectifying, or preparing the same, and also these words, " Pure, and without drugs or poison."

Sale from casks etc., not branded, prohibited. SEC. 3. No person shall sell at wholesale or retail any ale, rum, wine, or other malt or spirituous liquors from any barrel, cask, or vessel, unless the same shall have been branded and marked as aforesaid.

Evidence of violation of this act SEC. 4. If any barrel, cask, or other vessel containing any drugged or poisoned liquor shall be found in the possession of any wholesale or retail dealer in liquors, or in the possession of any person holding himself out as such a dealer, it shall be deemed *prima facie* evidence of the violation of the provisions of this act.

SEC. 5. Any person who shall put into any barrel, cask, or other vessel, branded, or marked, as required by this act, any liquors drugged or adulterated as aforesaid, or who shall sell or offer for sale any such liquors, for the purpose and with the intent of deceiving any person in the sale thereof, shall be deemed guilty of an attempt to practice a fraud, and upon conviction thereof shall be imprisoned in the State prison not more than one year. *(Penalty for putting drugged liquors into branded casks, etc.)*

SEC. 6. The provisions of this act shall not be so construed as to prevent druggists, physicians, and persons engaged in the mechanical arts from adulterating liquors for medical and mechanical purposes. *(Adulteration for medical and mechanical purposes.)*

SEC. 7. Prosecutions for a violation of any of the provisions of this act may be commenced by information in the circuit court of any county, by the prosecuting attorney of the county in which the offense shall be committed, which information shall be filed with the proceedings in any previous examination before any justice of the peace, and the proceedings after the filing of the information or information and proceedings as aforesaid, shall be the same as in other criminal cases. *(Prosecutions for violation of this act.)*

Approved May 3, 1875.

[No. 226.]

AN ACT to impose a tax on the business of selling spirituous and intoxicating, malt, brewed, and fermented liquors in the State of Michigan to be shipped from without this State.

SECTION 1. *The People of the State of Michigan enact,* That every person who shall come into, or being in this State, shall engage in the business of selling spirituous and intoxicating, malt, brewed, or fermented liquors to citizens or residents of this State, at wholesale, or of soliciting or taking orders from citizens or residents of this State for any such liquors, to be shipped into this State, or furnished, or supplied at wholesale to any person within this State, by a person, copartnership, association, or corporation, not resident in this State, nor having his, their, or its principal place of business within this State, shall, on or before the fourth Friday of June in each year, pay a tax of three hundred dollars if engaged in selling, or soliciting, or taking orders for the sale of such spirituous and intoxicating liquors, and one hundred dollars for malt, brewed, or fermented liquors. Such tax shall be paid to the Auditor General, and be by him paid into the State treasury, to the credit of the general fund. *(Tax upon non-residents for selling liquor at wholesale. Payment of, to Auditor General.)*

SEC. 2. Upon the payment of such tax the Auditor General shall issue to such person a receipt therefor, and in case of loss thereof, a duplicate, when required by the person to whom the original receipt was issued. Every person making sales, or soliciting, or taking orders, as in the first section of this act provided, shall exhibit such receipt to every person to whom he makes sale, or from *(Receipt for tax. Person making sales, etc., to exhibit receipt.)*

whom he takes or solicits orders for such liquors, and shall éxhibit such receipt to any supervisor, justice of the peace, sheriff, under or deputy sheriff, city or village marshal, chief of police, policeman, or constable, when required so to do, during business hours.

Penalty for selling liquor by, and for purchasing of persons, etc., who have not paid tax. SEC. 3. Any person liable to pay a tax under this act, who shall sell any liquors, or solicit or take orders for liquors to be shipped from without this State to any person within this State, furnished or supplied by a person, copartnership, association, or corporation not resident in, or having his, their, or its principal place of business within this State, without the tax herein provided for having been paid, and having in his possession and exhibiting the receipt therefor, or a duplicate thereof; and any person residing or being in this State who shall purchase liquors from a person liable to pay a tax under this act, who has not paid such tax, or shall give an order for liquors to such person liable to pay a tax under this act, which order is to be filled, and such liquors are to be shipped from without this State to a person within this State, furnished or supplied by a person, copartnership, association, or corporation, not resident in or having his, their, or its principal place of business within this State, shall be deemed guilty of a misdemeanor, and upon conviction thereof shall be punished by a fine of not less than twenty-five nor more than one hundred dollars; and in default of payment thereof shall be imprisoned not less than ten nor more than ninety days, or both such fine and imprisonment, in the discretion of the court.

Selling at wholesale defined. SEC. 4. Selling at wholesale shall be deemed to mean and include all sales of such spirituous and intoxicating malt, brewed, or fermented liquors in quantities of five gallons or over, or one dozen quart bottles or more, or soliciting orders therefor at any one time of any person.

SEC. 5. This act shall take immediate effect.

Approved May 3, 1875.

[No. 227.]

AN ACT to promote the early construction of a railroad through the Menominee Iron Range.

Grant of land to aid in construction of railroad. SECTION 1. *The People of the State of Michigan enact,* That for the purpose of encouraging the early construction of a line of railroad from Escanaba, in the county of Delta, westerly by way of Spaulding, thence northwesterly through the Menominee Iron Range, as far west and south as section thirty-four, town forty north, of range thirty west, and from thence to the Michigamme river, and for the purposes of drainage and reclamation, the State hereby grants to the Menominee River Railroad Company, to aid in the construction of portions of such railroad on the line aforesaid, **Extent of grant and where situated.** to the extent of seven sections of the swamp lands belonging to this State per mile of said railroad to be so constructed, to be selected from the vacant and unreserved State swamp lands be-

longing to this State, in any portion or portions of the counties of
Menominee and Delta, for the construction of that portion of said
railroad from Escanaba, Delta county, to the north line of said Menominee county, and for the construction of said railroad from said
north line of Menominee county to the Michigamme river, to be selected from the vacant and unreserved State swamp lands belonging
to this State, still remaining vacant and unreserved in the counties
of Menominee and Delta aforesaid; but the title to the same shall   *When title to vest in company.*
not vest in said company except as their railroad progresses. Should
said railroad company, accepting the provisions of this act, its suc-   *When lands shall revert to people.*
cessors or assigns, fail to construct ten consecutive miles of their
line of road within one year from the passage of this act, and ten
miles of railroad each year thereafter, then all grants of land
herein made for that portion of the line of railroad not completed
shall revert to the people of this State : *Proviso, however,* That   *Proviso.*
if said railroad company shall, in any one year, construct more than
the ten miles of road hereinbefore provided for, the excess over said
ten miles shall be credited to said company on account of the
amount of road required to be built by it in the next succeeding
year or years; and said company shall be entitled to receive, of the
lands hereby granted, an amount equivalent to seven sections of
land for each mile of road so actually constructed : *Provided,*   *Proviso.*
That no lands shall be granted to said railroad company for any
railroad or portion of railroad now built.

SEC. 2. As soon as said railroad company, accepting the pro-   *Plats of route to be deposited with Secretary of State and Commissioner of Land Office, and Commissioner to withdraw lands from market.*
visions of this act, shall actually survey and adopt their line of
railroad or any part or parts thereof, on the route indicated, they
shall deposit from time to time a plat or plats thereof in the office
of the Secretary of State, and a plat or plats thereof with the Commissioner of the Land Office; and it shall be the duty of such Commissioner, upon the passage of this act and the acceptance of the
provisions thereof by said company, as in this act provided, to
withdraw from sale all the vacant and unreserved swamp lands that
belong to this State in the counties of Menominee and Delta,
until such railroad company, accepting the provisions of this act,
shall have filed with the Commissioner of the Land Office a list of
the said swamp lands so selected by it for the construction of its
line of road : *Provided,* Said list of said lands shall have been so   *Proviso.*
filed with the Commissioner of the Land Office within one year
from the date of the deposit of the plat of its said line of railroad
with said Commissioner of the Land Office.

SEC. 3. On the list of said swamp lands so selected by said   *Lands selected withdrawn from, and other lands restored to, market.*
railroad company being filed with the Commissioner of the Land
Office, as aforesaid, it shall be his duty to withdraw from sale
the swamp lands embraced in said list to the extent and amount
of seven sections per mile of the whole of said line of railroad so
proposed to be constructed by said railroad company, to be disposed of according to the provisions of this act; and to restore all
the swamp lands belonging to this State, within said limits so remaining unselected by said railroad company, to the same condi-

35

tion they were in before said withdrawal from sale, for the purpose of sale or entry.

Lands granted exempt from taxation five years. SEC. 4. All lands granted by this act to aid in the construction of said line of railroad shall be and are exempt from all taxation whatsoever, for five years from and after the date of this grant.

Governor to examine road and issue patents for lands. ·SEC. 5. Before any lands shall be conveyed, under the provisions of this act, by the Governor, he shall personally, or by some authorized agent, examine each section of ten miles or more of completed railroad, and if, after full examination, he shall approve of the construction of said ten miles or more of railroad, as·in section one of this act provided, it shall be his duty to certify the same to the Commissioner of the State Land Office, and patents shall be issued to the railroad company constructing said ten miles or more of road, by the Governor, for the lands, as provided in this act, and so on continuously for each division of ten miles or more of road actually constructed, until the completion of said line of railroad.

When this act to become obligatory. SEC. 6. Upon the filing by said company in the office of the Secretary of State of a notification of its acceptance of the provisions of this act, the same shall thereupon become obligatory upon the State as well as upon said company: *Provided,* That **Proviso.** said notification shall be given within sixty days from and after the passage of this act.

SEC. 7. This act shall take immediate effect.

Approved May 3, 1875.

[No. 228.]

AN ACT for the taxation of the business of manufacturing and selling spirituous and intoxicating malt, brewed, or fermented liquors, and to repeal act number seventeen, approved February three, eighteen hundred and fifty-five, entitled "An act to prevent the manufacture and sale of spirituous and intoxicating liquors as a beverage," and all acts amendatory thereof or in addition thereto, said acts being sections two thousand one hundred and thirty-six, two thousand one hundred and thirty-seven, two thousand one hundred and thirty-eight, two thousand one hundred and thirty-nine, two thousand one hundred and forty, two thousand one hundred and forty-one, two thousand one hundred and forty-two, two thousand one hundred and forty-three, two thousand one hundred and forty-four, two thousand one hundred and forty-five, two thousand one hundred and forty-six, two thousand one hundred and forty-seven, two thousand one hundred and forty-eight, two thousand one hundred and forty-nine, two thousand one hundred and fifty, two thousand one hundred and fifty-one, two thousand one hundred and fifty-two, two thousand one hundred and fifty-three, two thousand one hundred and fifty-four of the compiled laws of eighteen hundred and seventy-one, and also act number one hundred and fifty, of the session laws of eighteen hundred and seventy-three, entitled "An act to prevent the sale of spirituous and intoxicating drinks as a beverage, the same being a new section to chapter sixty-nine of the compiled laws of eighteen hundred and seventy-one, being an act relative to "the manufacture and sale of spirituous and intoxicating drinks as a beverage," to stand as section twenty-two.

SECTION 1. *The People of the State of Michigan enact*, That in all townships, cities, and villages of this State there shall be annually levied and collected the following tax upon the business of manufacturing, selling, or keeping for sale distilled or malt liquors, as follows: Upon the business of selling or offering for sale, spirituous or intoxicating liquors by retail, or any patent medicine, mixture, or compound, which in whole or in part consists of spirituous or intoxicating liquors, the sum of one hundred and fifty dollars; upon the business of selling or offering for sale, by retail, any fermented or brewed liquors, or any other beverage, forty dollars; upon the business of selling brewed or malt liquors at wholesale, or at wholesale and retail, one hundred dollars per annum; upon the business of selling spirituous or intoxicating liquors at wholesale, or at wholesale and retail, three hundred dollars per annum; upon the business of manufacturing brewed or malt liquors for sale, if the quantity manufactured be fifteen hundred barrels or under, fifty dollars. If over fifteen hundred barrels and not exceeding five thousand, one hundred dollars. If five thousand barrels or over, the sum of two hundred dollars per annum; upon the business of manufacturing for sale of spirituous or intoxicating liquors, three hundred dollars. No person paying a tax on spirituous or intoxicating liquors, under this act, shall be liable to pay any tax on the sale of malt, brewed, and fermented liquors. *(Tax upon manufacture and sale of liquor provided for. How levied.)*

SEC. 2. Retail dealers of spirituous and intoxicating liquors and brewed, malt, and fermented liquors, shall be held and deemed to include all persons who sell by the drink, and in quantities of five gallons or less, or one dozen quart bottles or less, at any one time to any one person. Wholesale dealers shall be held and deemed to mean and include all persons who sell or offer to sell such liquors and beverages in quantities of five gallons or over one dozen quart bottles at any one time to any one person. No tax imposed under this act shall be levied or collected from any person for selling any wine or cider made from fruits grown or gathered in this State. No druggist shall be liable to pay any tax herein imposed who sells liquors for medicinal, chemical, mechanical, and sacramental purposes only. *(Who deemed retail dealers. Who deemed wholesale dealers. Certain wine and cider exempt. Druggists who sell for medicinal purposes, etc., not liable.)*

SEC. 3. The taxes herein provided for shall be assessed, levied, and collected by the same officers, and in the same time and manner as the taxes upon personal property, except as herein otherwise provided: *Provided*, Nothing herein contained shall be construed to exempt any species of property from taxation under the general laws. All taxes shall be deemed payable and due at the time of the delivery of the assessment roll to the treasurer. *(Taxes, how assessed collected. Proviso. When due.)*

SEC. 4. The assessor of every township, ward, city, or village, shall, on or before the third Monday of May in each year, enquire and ascertain the name of every person, corporation, association, company, or *(Assessment roll.)*

copartnership engaged in carrying on any business mentioned in the first section of this act; and he shall enter in a roll, to be made by him, the name of every such person, corporation, association, company, or copartnership, and the place of doing business, the kind of business carried on, and the amount of tax to be paid, according to the provisions of this act. And he shall, before the first Wednesday after the third Monday in May, notify each person, corporation, association, company, or copartnership, whose names have been entered on said roll of said entry; such notice to be verbal, printed, or written.

Notice to persons whose names have been entered on roll.

Review and correction of roll. SEC. 5. On the first Wednesday after the third Monday in May it shall be the duty of the assessor to be present at his office from eight o'clock in the forenoon until twelve o'clock noon, and from one o'clock in the afternoon until five o'clock in the afternoon, for the purpose of reviewing such assessment roll, and so on the next two following days; and on the request of any person, corporation, company, or copartnership, his, its, or their agent or attorney considering themselves aggrieved, on sufficient cause being shown to the satisfaction of such assessor, he shall alter such assessment in such manner as may be necessary in order to conform to the provisions of this act; and he shall also upon sufficient cause being shown by any credible person, add to said roll the name of any other person, corporation, association, company, or copartnership engaged in any business liable to be taxed under the provisions of this act, the kind of business and the amount of tax to be paid according to the provisions of this act; and the said assessor shall receive two dollars per day for each day's services performed under this act, to be audited and allowed by the township board, the village trustees, or the common council, and paid out of the contingent funds of said township, village, or city.

Compensation of assessor.

Certificate upon completion of roll. SEC. 6. When said assessor has reviewed and completed his roll, it shall be his duty to attach thereto, signed by him, a certificate, which may be in the following form : " I do hereby certify that I have set down in the above assessment roll all the places where the business of manufacturing, selling, or offering for sale spirituous, intoxicating, brewed, or malt liquors is being carried on, together with the name of the corporation, person, association, company, or copartnership engaged in such business, and the particular kind of business in which each is so engaged, according to my best information and belief." And on or before the first Monday of June he shall attach to such assessment roll a warrant under his hand, commanding the county treasurer to collect such taxes in the manner prescribed by law for the collection of township, ward, city, or village taxes, assessed upon personal property, except as herein otherwise provided ; he shall deliver the said roll and warrant so completed to the treasurer of his county : *Provided, however,* That in case the above roll is not completed within the time above fixed, or is defective in any respect, the same may, by such assessor, be completed at any time thereafter and delivered to such treasurer : *Provided further,* That should any person, corporation, association, company, or copartnership be added to said roll after the time fixed

Warrant commanding county treasurer to collect taxes.

Proviso.

Proviso—notice of change in assessment roll.

for reviewing the same, as above provided, or should such roll not be completed, or such assessor not be present at his office at the time above fixed, then public notice shall be published in some newspaper printed and published in said county, setting forth the name of each person, corporation, association, company, or copartnership added to or appearing upon said roll, and fixing a time and place not less than ten days from the date of publication, at which all persons interested may appear and show cause why such assessment should not be charged as above provided, or such notice may be served personally upon each person, corporation, association, company, or copartnership, at least three days before the time fixed for such hearing.

SEC. 7. The county treasurer, upon receiving such roll, shall proceed to collect such taxes, and for that purpose shall remain in his office on the second, third, and fourth Fridays of June, and upon all taxes paid to him at any time prior to or on the fourth Friday of June, he shall add two per cent for collection fees.

Collection of taxes by county treasurer.
His fees.

SEC. 8. If any person, corporation, association, company, or copartnership shall refuse or neglect to pay the tax so assessed, within the time specified in the preceding section, such treasurer shall thereupon forthwith issue his warrant to the sheriff of said county, reciting therein the name of such person, corporation, association, company, or copartnership, the business carried on, the assessment of such tax, and date of the same, and commanding him to levy and make the amount of said assessment, with ten per cent interest from the date of such assessment, and four per cent collection fees, by distress and sale of any goods and chattels of such person or persons, corporation, association, company, or copartnership, or of any goods and chattels found in the custody or possession of such person, corporation, association, company, or copartnership, and in default thereof, then of his, her, or their lands and tenements, and to pay over the same, reserving his fees, to the county treasurer, within ten days after the same is collected.

In case of neglect to pay, treasurer to issue his warrant to sheriff.
Contents of warrant.

SEC. 9. Upon the receipt of such warrant, the sheriff shall proceed immediately to collect the same. He shall call once at the place of business of each person, corporation, association, company, or copartnership named in said warrant, and in case any person, corporation, association, company, or copartnership refuses to pay such tax, he shall levy on the goods and chattels of such persons, corporation, association, company, or copartnership, wherever found in said county, or on the bar fixtures or furniture, liquors, beverages, and other goods and chattels used in carrying on such business, which levy shall take precedence of any and all liens, mortgages, conveyances, or encumbrances on such goods and chattels so used in carrying on such business; nor shall any claim of property by any third person to such goods and chattels so used in carrying on such business avail against such levy so made by the sheriff, and no property of any person, corporation, association, company or copartnership, liable to pay a tax under the provisions of this act, shall be exempt from such levy.

Collection of taxes by sheriff.
Property of third persons used to carry on business not exempt.

Notice of time and place of sale, etc.

SEC. 10. The sheriff shall give public notice of the time and place of sale, and of the property to be sold, at least six days previous to the sale, by advertisement, to be posted up in three public places in the township, city, or village where such sale is made: *Provided*,

relative of real estate.

however, That in cases where a levy has been made upon real estate, such sheriff shall give like notice of the time and place of such sale, as in sales of real estate on execution; and all provisions of law applicable to sales of real estate upon execution shall be applicable to sales under this act, except as herein otherwise provided.

Adjournment of sale for want of bidders.

SEC. 11. In case the property so distrained or levied upon cannot be sold for want of bidders, said sheriff may adjourn such sale so often as may be necessary, not exceeding one week, however, at

Proceeding in case property sold is insufficient to satisfy writ.

any one time; and in case the property distrained or levied upon and sold is insufficient to satisfy such writ, the sheriff shall make return thereof and pay over the amount by him received, less his said fees, to said treasurer, and said treasurer shall renew said warrant, and again deliver the same to the sheriff, commanding him as before, so often as may be necessary, until the whole amount of such tax has been collected.

Assessor to add names at any time during the year and assess a pro rata tax.

SEC. 12. The assessor shall have power, and it shall be his duty, to add to said roll at any time during the year the name of any person, corporation, association, company, or copartnership engaging in any kind of business specified in the first section of this act, whose name does not appear upon such roll, and to assess against such business thereon a *pro rata* tax for the unexpired portion of such

Notice to persons whose names are thus added to roll.

year, and said assessor shall, before making such assessment, notify the person, corporation, association, company, or copartnership of a time and place at which the assessment will be made, and requiring such person to appear at the time and place mentioned and show cause, if any, why such assessment should not be made, which notice shall be personally served in the same manner as summonses issued by justices of the peace, and shall be served at least three days before the time specified therein for a hearing; and upon such assessment being made, the same proceedings shall be had in all respects as though such assessment had been made by the assessor

Proviso.

as above prescribed: *Provided, however,* That in case of neglect or refusal of said assessor to comply with the provisions of this section, then, and in that case, the said county treasurer shall have power, and it shall be his duty to make the assessment and give the notice required by this section, and the same shall be valid as though made by the assessor.

Disposition of moneys collected.

SEC. 13. All moneys collected by any treasurer under the provisions of this act, except the fees and percentage herein allowed to him as compensation, which may be retained by such treasurer as his fees, shall be by him placed to the credit of the contingent fund of the township, village, or city from which the same was collected, and the same shall be by such township, village, or city applied as other contingent funds.

County treasurer to file monthly statement with county clerk.

SEC. 14. It shall be the duty of each and every county treasurer, at least once in each and every month, to make a sworn statement containing the names of each and every person, corporation, company, or copartnership in his county, paying a tax under the provisions of this act, stating therein the residence of such person, corporation, association, company, or copartnership, the business in which such person is engaged, the place of doing business, the amount of tax paid, and date of payment of the same, and file such statement with the clerk of his county; and such county treasurer shall, on or before the twenty-fifth day of December in each year, make a full and complete report of all the facts, as shown by the reports on file in his office, and return the same to the Auditor General, and publish the same in at least two newspapers in his county, if so many there be. All blanks required to carry into effect the provisions of this act shall be prepared and furnished by the Auditor General to the county treasurers, and by them to the township, village, or city officers. *To make annual report and return same to Auditor General and publish same.* *Auditor General to furnish blanks.*

SEC. 15. Any officer willfully neglecting or refusing to perform his duty under the provisions of this act shall be liable to a penalty of one hundred dollars for each and every offense. And any person liable to pay a tax under the provisions of this act who shall neglect or refuse to pay the same, shall be deemed guilty of a misdemeanor, and upon conviction thereof shall be punished by a fine of not less than twenty-five dollars nor more than one hundred dollars, and costs of prosecution, for each and every offense, and on failure to pay such fine and costs shall be imprisoned in the county jail not less than ten nor more than ninety days, in the discretion of the court. *Penalties.*

SEC. 16. The word "assessor," as used in this act, shall be held to include supervisors, or other officers whose duty it is to make assessments in townships, wards, villages, or cities. *"Assessor," how used in this act.*

SEC. 17. In case any assessor, county treasurer, or sheriff willfully neglects or refuses to perform his duty under the provisions of this act, he shall be liable to a penalty of one hundred dollars for each and every offense; and the Governor may, in case of any such neglect or refusal, appoint some other person or persons to perform the duties prescribed by this act, who shall, upon being so appointed, have like powers and duties under this act as such assessor, treasurer, or sheriff, as the case may be. *Officers liable to penalty for neglect, and Governor may appoint others.*

SEC. 18. The act entitled "An act to prevent the manufacture and sale of spirituous or intoxicating liquors as a beverage," approved February third, eighteen hundred and fifty-five, and the several acts amendatory thereof and in addition thereto, being sections two thousand one hundred and thirty-six to section two thousand one hundred and fifty-four, inclusive, of the compiled laws of eighteen hundred and seventy-one; also act number one hundred and fifty of the session laws of eighteen hundred and seventy three, entitled "An act to prevent the sale of spirituous and intoxicating drinks as a beverage," the same being a new section to chapter sixty-nine of the compiled laws of eighteen hundred and seventy-one, being an act relative to "the manufacture and sale of spirituous and intoxicating drinks as a beverage," to stand as section twenty-two, shall be and the same are hereby repealed, saving all *Acts repealed.*

actions pending and all causes of action which have accrued at the time this act takes effect.

SEC. 19. This act shall take immediate effect.

Approved May 3, 1875.

[No. 229.]

AN ACT to amend the act entitled, "An act to provide for the draining of swamps, marshes, and other low lands," approved March twenty-two, eighteen hundred and sixty-nine, and the acts amendatory thereto.

Act amended.

SECTION 1. *The People of the State of Michigan enact,* That the act entitled "An act to provide for the draining of swamps, marshes, and other low lands," approved March twenty-two, eighteen hundred and sixty-nine, being chapter forty-seven of the compiled laws of eighteen hundred and seventy-one, be and the same is hereby amended by adding three new sections as follows:

Collection of taxes shall not be declared void because of certain errors.

SEC. 34. That the collection of the taxes levied, or ordered to be levied to pay for the location and construction of any ditch, drain, or water-course laid out and constructed under and by authority of the act entitled "An act to provide for the draining of swamps, marshes, and other low lands," approved March fifteenth, eighteen hundred and sixty-one; and the act entitled "An act to provide for the draining of swamps, marshes, and other low lands" approved March twenty-second, eighteen hundred and sixty-nine, and any acts amendatory thereto, shall not be perpetually enjoined or declared absolutely void in consequence of any error committed by the engineer or surveyor, or by the county treasurer, or by the drain commissioner in the location and establishment thereof, nor by reason of any error or informality appearing in the record of the proceedings by which any ditch, drain, or water-course shall have been located and established.

Court, in case of error, shall set proceedings aside, etc.

But the court in which any proceeding is now pending, or which may hereafter be brought to reverse or to declare void the. proceedings by which any ditch, drain, or water-course has been located or established, or to enjoin the tax levied or ordered to be levied to pay for the labor and fees aforesaid, shall, if there be manifest error, set the same aside, and allow the plaintiff in the action to come in and show wherein he has been injured thereby.

Shall appoint persons to examine premises, etc.

The court shall, on application of either party, appoint such person or persons to examine the premises or to survey the same, or both, as may be deemed necessary, and the court shall, on final hearing, make such order in the premises as shall be just and equitable, and may order such tax to remain for collection, or order the same to be levied, or may perpetually enjoin the same. or any part thereof, or if the same shall have been paid under protest, shall order the whole, or such part thereof as may be just and equitable, to be refunded, the costs of said proceedings to be apportioned amongst the parties, or to be paid out of the county treasury, as justice may require.

SEC. 35. If it shall appear in any suit or bill to restrain the collection of any assessment heretofore or hereafter made, or in any suit or proceedings, to compel the levying or making of an assessment or assessments, or taxes to pay for the location and construction of any ditch, drain, or water-course laid out and constructed under and by authority of this act, or of the acts to be which this is amendatory, that there has been no condemnation of the private property taken in the construction of said ditch, and no valid appointment of commissioners, or selection of a jury to ascertain and determine the necessity for taking and using the same, the court in which any proceedings is now pending, or may hereafter be brought to reverse or to declare void the proceedings by which any ditch, drain, or water-course shall have been located and established, or in which any suit or proceedings shall be pending, or hereafter be brought to enforce and compel the levying and collection of any assessment or tax to pay for the location and construction of any ditch, drain, or water-course laid out and constructed under and by the authority of this act, shall, at the request of either party to said suit or proceedings, and upon notice to the adverse party, appoint three disinterested and competent freeholders as commissioners to ascertain and determine the necessity for taking such lands or other property, and to appraise and to determine the damages or compensation to be allowed to the owners and persons interested in the real estate or property proposed to be taken for the purposes of constructing such ditch, or which has been taken for the purpose of constructing such ditch.

When court shall appoint commissioners to determine necessity of taking property for construction of ditch.

SEC. 36. In case the records [record] does not show that application in writing was made for the ditch, it may be proven (if such was the fact). that such application was made, and upon due proof of the loss thereof, parol or secondary evidence of the contents thereof may be given in said suit or proceedings, and the court, if satisfied that a proper application was in fact made, may make such order or decree in the premises as shall seem just and equitable.

Proceedings in case of loss of written application for ditch.

Approved May 3, 1875.

[No. 230.]

AN ACT to amend sections twenty-two, twenty-three, twenty-four, and seventy-one of chapter fifty-eight of revised statutes of eighteen hundred and forty six, as amended by act thirty-four of the laws of eighteen hundred and sixty-seven, approved February twenty-eighth, eighteen hundred and sixty-seven, as amended by act one hundred and seventy of the laws of eighteen hundred and seventy-one, approved April seventeenth, eighteen hundred and seventy-one, being sections thirty-six hundred and two, thirty-six hundred and three, thirty-six hundred and four, and thirty-six hundred and forty-one of the compiled laws of eighteen hundred and seventy-one.

SECTION 1. *The People of the State of Michigan enact,* That sections twenty-two, twenty-three, twenty-four, and seventy-one

Sections amended.

of chapter fifty-eight of revised statutes of eighteen hundred and forty-six, as amended by act thirty-four of the laws of eighteen hundred and sixty-seven, approved February twenty-eighth, eighteen hundred and sixty-seven, as amended by act one hundred and seventy of the laws of eighteen hundred and seventy-one, approved April seventeenth, eighteen hundred and seventy-one, being sections thirty-six hundred and two, thirty-six hundred and three, thirty-six hundred and four, and thirty-six hundred and forty-one of the compiled laws of eighteen hundred and seventy-one, be and the same is hereby amended so as to read as follows:

Limit of tax for school houses.   (3602.) Sec. 22. The amount of taxes to be raised in any district for the purpose of purchasing or building a school-house shall not exceed the sum of one thousand dollars in any one year, unless there shall be more than fifty children between the ages of five and twenty years residing therein; and in districts containing less than ten children, shall not exceed two hundred and fifty dollars; in districts containing over ten children and less than thirty, shall not exceed five hundred dollars.

Voters may impose tax for school-purposes.   (3603.) Sec. 23. Such qualified voters, when so assembled as aforesaid, may from time to time impose such tax as shall be necessary to keep their school-house in repair, and to provide the necessary appendages and school apparatus; and in townships having district libraries, for the support of the same, and to pay and discharge any debts or liabilities of the district lawfully incurred; and when a tax is voted or estimated by the board under the provisions of section twenty-four, and is needed for use before it can be collected, the district may borrow to an amount not exceeding the amount of the tax; and no money raised by district tax shall be used for any other purpose than that for which it was raised, without a vote of two-thirds of the tax-paying voters of the district. **Limit of tax.** The tax imposed under this section shall not exceed one-half the amount which the district is authorized to raise for building a school-house.

Relative to length of time of school, sex of teachers, amount to be raised by tax, etc.   (3604.) Sec. 24. They shall also determine at such annual meeting the length of time a school shall be taught in their district during the ensuing year, which shall not be less than nine months in districts having eight hundred children over five and under twenty years of age, and not less than five months in districts having from thirty to eight hundred children of like ages, nor less than three months in all other districts, on pain of forfeiture of their share of the two-mill tax and primary school fund; and whether by male or female teachers, or both; and it shall be the duty of the district board to estimate the amount necessary to be raised, in addition to other school funds, for the entire support of such schools, including fuel and other incidental expenses, and for deficiencies of previous year. But in districts having less than thirty scholars, such estimate, including the district's share of the primary school fund and two-mill tax, shall not exceed the sum of fifty dollars a month for the period during which school is held in such district; and previous to the second Monday in October make a written report of the amount so determined, to the supervisor of the township in which any part of said district may be situated; and the same shall be levied upon the taxable property of the district, collected and returned in the same manner as township taxes. A school month within the meaning of this act, shall consist of four weeks, of five days in each week, unless otherwise specified in the teacher's contract. *School month.*

(3641.) SEC. 71. The inspectors shall divide the township into such number of school districts as may from time to time be necessary, which districts they shall number, and they may regulate and alter the boundaries of the same as circumstances shall render proper; but no district shall contain more than nine sections of land, and each district shall be composed of contiguous territory, and be in as compact a form as may be; but no land shall be taxed for building a school-house unless some portion of every legal subdivison of said land shall be within two and one-half miles of said school-house site; and no land which has been taxed for building a school-house shall be set off into another school district, for the period of three years thereafter, except by the consent of the owner thereof. *Formation of school districts.*

SEC. 2. This act shall take immediate effect.

Approved May 3, 1875.

[No. 231.]

AN ACT to prevent the sale or delivery of intoxicating liquors, wine, and beer, to minors, and to drunken persons, and to habitual drunkards; to provide a remedy against persons selling liquor to husbands or children in certain cases.

SECTION 1. *The People of the State of Michigan enact,* That it shall not be lawful for any person to sell any spirituous or intoxicating liquor, or any wine, or beer, to any minor, or to any intoxicated person, or to any person in the habit of getting intoxicated. It shall not be lawful for any person to sell malt, spirituous, or intoxicating liquors without first having executed and delivered to the treasurer of the county in which such business is prosecuted and carried on, the bond required to be given by section five of this act. All saloons, restaurants, bars, bar rooms, in taverns or otherwise, and all places of public resort where intoxicating liquors are sold, either at wholesale or retail, shall (unless otherwise determined and directed by the board of trustees or common council of the village or city where such saloons, restaurants, bars, bar rooms are kept), be closed on the first day of the week, commonly called Sunday, and on each week-day night from and after the hour of eleven o'clock until six o'clock of the morning of the succeeding day. But this provision shall not be construed to prohibit druggists from selling such liquors at such times, upon the written request or order of some practicing physician of the town, village, or city. Any person who shall violate any of the provisions of this section shall be deemed guilty of a misdemeanor, and upon conviction thereof shall be punished by a fine of not less than twenty-five dollars nor more than one hundred dollars, and costs of prosecution, and on failure to pay such fine and costs, shall be imprisoned in the county jail not less than ten days nor more than ninety days, or both such fine and imprisonment, in the discretion of the court.

Penalty for obtaining liquors by false pretense, or for being drunk in certain places. SEC. 2. Any person who by false pretense shall obtain any spirituous or intoxicating liquors, or who shall be drunk or intoxicated in any hotel, tavern, inn, or place of public business, or in any assemblage of people collected together in any place for any purpose, or in any street, lane, alley, highway, railway or street car, by drinking intoxicating liquors, shall, on conviction thereof, be punished by a fine of five dollars, and the costs of prosecution, or be punished by imprisonment in the common jail of the county, not exceeding twenty days, or both such fine and imprisonment, in the discretion of the court.

Who may bring actions for actual and exemplary damages. SEC. 3. Every wife, child, parent, guardian, husband, or other person who shall be injured in person or property, means of support, by any intoxicated person, or by means of the intoxication of any person, shall have a right of action in his or her own name against any person or persons who shall, by selling or giving any intoxicating liquor, have caused or contributed to the intoxication of such person or persons; and shall also have a right of action against the principal and sureties to the bond hereinafter mentioned; and in any such action the plaintiff shall have a right to re-

Evidence of relationship. cover actual and exemplary damages. And in every action by any wife, husband, parent, or child, general reputation of the relation of husband and wife, parent and child, shall be *prima facie* evidence of such relation; and the amount recovered by every wife or child shall be his or her sole and separate property. Any sale or gift of

Forfeiture of lease for sale or gift of liquors. Lessee may be enjoined. intoxicating liquors by the lessee of any premises, resulting in damage, shall, at the option of the lessor, work a forfeiture of his lease; and the circuit court in chancery may enjoin the sale or giving away of intoxicating liquors by any lessee of premises which may result in loss or damage, or liability to the lessor, or any person claiming under such lessor.

Penalty for misrepresenting one's age in order to purchase liquors. SEC. 4. It any person under the age of twenty-one years shall misrepresent his age and state himself to be over twenty-one years of age in order to purchase malt, spirituous, or intoxicating liquors, he shall be deemed guilty of a misdemeanor, and upon conviction thereof shall be fined in any sum not less than five nor more than twenty-five dollars, and on failure to pay such fine shall be imprisoned in the county jail not less than five days nor more than sixty days, or both such fine and imprisonment, in the discretion of the court.

Bond. SEC. 5. Every such dealer or person shall in each and every year make, execute, and deliver to the county treasurer of the county in which he is carrying on such business, a bond to be determined by the township board of the township, or the board of trustees, or the common council of the village or city in which the parties reside, to the people of the State of Michigan, in the sum of not less than one thousand dollars nor more than three thousand dollars, with two or more sufficient sureties, who shall be freeholders, which bond shall be substantially in the following form :

Know all men by these presents that we_____ Form of bond.
as principal and_____and_____
as sureties, are held and firmly bound unto the people of the State
of Michigan in the sum of_____dollars, to the payment whereof,
well and truly to be made, we bind ourselves, our heirs, executors,
and administrators firmly by these presents. Sealed with our seals
and dated this_____day of_____A. D. 18___

Whereas, The above named principal professes to carry on the
business of_____at_____
in the county of_____and whereas, the said principal hath
covenanted and agreed and doth hereby covenant and agree as
follows, to wit: That he will not directly or indirectly by himself, his
clerk, agent, or servant, at any time, sell or deliver any spirituous or
intoxicating liquors, or any mixed liquor, a part of which is spirituous or intoxicating, to a minor, nor to any adult person whatever,
known to him to be an habitual drunkard; nor to a person in the
habit of getting intoxicated, nor to any person whose husband, wife,
parent, child, guardian, or employer, may give him notice in writing
that such person has acquired or is acquiring the habit of drinking
to excess, and is being injured thereby, except as a medicine on a
prescription of a physician; and that he will pay all damages, actual
and exemplary, that may be adjudged to any person for injuries
inflicted upon them, either in person or property, by reason of his
selling intoxicating liquors.

Now, the condition of this obligation is such that if said principal
shall well and truly keep and perform all and singular the foregoing covenants and agreements, and shall pay any judgment for
actual or exemplary damages which may be recovered against him
in any court of competent jurisdiction, then this obligation shall be
void and of no effect, otherwise the same shall be in full force and
effect.

Signed and sealed in the presence of }
_____ }
_____)
        _____ _____ L. S.
        _____ _____ L. S.
        _____ _____ L. S.

Such bond shall not be received unless the approval thereof by
the township board or the board of trustees or common council of
the village or city shall be duly certified thereon in writing, and
the principal shall not be allowed to sell spirituous or fermented
liquors in any other place than that specified in said bond without
giving notice and executing another bond in the manner above
prescribed. Whenever any condition of said bond shall be broken,
a new bond may be required by the county treasurer, and also in
case of the death, insolvency, or removal of either of the sureties,
and in any other contingency requiring it.

Approved May 3, 1875.

[No. 232.]

AN ACT to amend sections two, three, and four of "An act relative to plank road companies," approved February twelve, eighteen hundred and fifty-five, being sections two thousand six hundred and fourteen, two thousand six hundred and fifteen, and two thousand six hundred and sixteen of the compiled laws of eighteen hundred and seventy-one.

Sections amended. SECTION 1. *The People of the State of Michigan enact,* That sections two, three, and four of "An act relative to plank road companies," approved February twelve, eighteen hundred and fifty-five, being sections two thousand six hundred and fourteen, two thousand six hundred and fifteen, and two thousand six hundred and sixteen of the compiled laws of eighteen hundred and seventy-one, be so amended that said sections shall read as follows:

How plank and gravel roads to be kept. SEC. 2. Every plank road company, and the owners of any such plank road, by purchase or otherwise, shall cause to be laid down and kept closely together, and in an even manner, so that the surface shall be uniform, the plank upon its road; or if the said company or owners shall have built any portion of their road, or may hereafter build any portion of the same of gravel, or of stone so broken as to serve the purpose of gravel, they shall cause the said gravel or broken stone of proper quality and quantity to be placed upon the road and kept in a uniform manner of the width and **Default works forfeiture of toll.** depth required by law; and in case of default they shall forfeit the right to receive any toll upon such road; and the prosecuting at-**Prosecution to ascertain default.** torney of the county, on complaint of the highway commissioner of any township in which any portion of the road defectively constructed or out of repair lies, may institute a suit in the circuit court of the same county in chancery, to have such default judicially ascertained and declared; and the said circuit court in chancery for the respective counties shall have full jurisdiction of all cases arising under this act, to hear, try, and determine the same, upon bill or petition filed according to the usual course and practice of those courts.

When company may receive tolls. SEC. 3. Every plank road company shall have the right to receive tolls at any time after it shall have constructed two consecu-**Proviso.** tive miles of [the] road: *Provided,* That this section shall only apply to plank roads during the period in which they are or may have been in the course of construction, and not afterwards: *And* **Further proviso.** *provided further,* That if any plank road company, or the owner or owners of any such plank road, by purchase or otherwise, shall have heretofore, for the space of one year or more, ceased, or may hereafter cease, in like manner, to keep up the road, or any part thereof exceeding five continuous miles in length, and shall have removed its gates therefrom, and abandoned the same without the consent of the Legislature of this State, such road shall be deemed to have forfeited the right to take any toll upon said road, or any part thereof, and such forfeiture may be ascertained and enforced as provided for in section two of this act.

SEC. 4. Every plank road company shall cease to be a body cor- When company shall cease to be a body corporate
porate if within three years, or if hereafter organized, then if
within three years from the date of its organization, it shall
not have commenced the construction of its road and actually
expended thereon at least ten per cent of the capital stock; and
every plank road company which shall have so far completed
its road as to be entitled to receive tolls thereon, or upon some
portion thereof, and shall have actually commenced to receive such
tolls, shall cease to be a body corporate, if it shall hereafter neglect
for the term of five years successively to hold the annual meeting
for the election of directors, and shall hold no election of directors
during all that time.

Approved May 3, 1875.

[No. 233.]

AN ACT to re-enact and amend chapter eighty four of the compiled laws of eighteen hundred and seventy-one, relative to the
formation of corporations to construct canals or harbors and improve the same, by adding two new sections thereto, and by re-
stricting its operations to the Upper Peninsula.

SECTION 1. *The People of the State of Michigan enact,* That Chapter re-enacted and amended.
chapter eighty-four of the compiled laws of eighteen hundred and
seventy-one, being "An act to provide for the formation of companies to construct canals or harbors and improve the same," be
and the same hereby is re-enacted and amended so as to read as
follows:

SECTION 1. Any number of persons, not less than three, may be Corporations may be formed.
formed into a corporation for the purpose of constructing a canal
or harbor or improving the navigation of any river or stream in the
Upper Peninsula, by dredging out the channel, making a new entrance, and constructing canals to straighten the same, or by any
of said methods, by complying with the following requirements.
Notice shall be given in at least one newspaper printed in each Notice of construction of canal or improvement.
county where the said canal or improvement is proposed to be
constructed, at least two weeks, of the time and place or places
where books for subscribing to the stock of such company will be
opened, and of the estimated cost of said canal or improvement,
which notice may be signed by any two persons proposing to enter
upon the construction of said canal or improvement. If there be
no newspaper printed in such county, then it shall be printed in
some newspaper in an adjoining county, if any, or if none, then it
shall be printed in some newspaper in the city of Detroit, and in
the latter case notices shall also be posted in three of the most
public places in the township, city, or village where said meeting
is to be held, during the same time; and when stock to the amount Directors, when elected.
of one thousand dollars per mile of such canal or improvement so
intended to be built shall be subscribed, and five per cent paid
thereon, then the said subscribers, upon due and proper notice,
signed by any two of said subscribers, may elect directors for the

Articles of
association,
contents of.

said corporation; and thereupon they shall severally subscribe articles of association, in which shall be set forth the name of said company, the number of years the same is to be continued, the amount of capital stock, the number of shares of said stock, the number of directors, the names of those elected to hold office for the first year, the nature and extent of said canal or improvements, and the length thereof, as near as may he.

Articles to be
subscribed. ·

Filed in office of
Secretary of
State.

By-laws.

Privileges and
restrictions.

May issue bonds.

Proviso.

Sec. 2. Each subscriber to such articles of association shall subscribe thereto his name and place of residence, and the number of shares of stock taken by him. The said articles shall be filed in the office of the Secretary of State, and thereupon the persons who have so subscribed, and all persons who shall, from time to time, become stockholders in said company by assignment or otherwise, shall be a body corporate by the name specified in such articles, and as such shall be capable of suing and being sued in all courts, purchasing and acquiring all property necessary to be used in the construction and keeping in repair of said canal. or harbor, or improvement, or any works necessary for the same, and may, by such by-laws as shall be adopted by said company, prescribe the manner of calling and conducting the meetings of the stockholders, and shall possess the power and privileges, and be subject to the provisions contained in chapter fifty-five of the revised statutes of one thousand eight hundred and forty-six, so far as the same shall be applicable, and not inconsistent with the provisions of this act, and shall also have power to issue bonds to the amount of one-half the capital paid in, bearing such rates of interest as shall be directed by the board of directors: *Provided*, That no such bond shall be issued for a less sum than one hundred dollars, nor sold at less than the face thereof, without a vote of the stockholders authorizing the same.

Conditions
precedent to
filing articles.

Stockholders
not to vote
unless dues are
paid.

Sec. 3. Such articles of agreement shall not be filed in the office of the Secretary of State until five per cent of the capital subscribed shall have been paid to the directors named in the articles, nor until there is endorsed on said articles, or annexed thereto, an affidavit of two of the directors that the amount of capital stock required by the first section has been subscribed, and five per cent paid; and no stockholder shall be entitled to vote on any question which shall come before a meeting of the stockholders unless all assessments due on stock standing in his name shall have been paid.

Certified copies
of articles to be
evidence.

Sec. 4. A copy of said articles, filed in pursuance of this act, certified by the Secretary of State to be a true copy, and of the whole thereof, shall be in all courts and places presumptive evidence of the incorporation of such company and of the facts therein stated.

Board of
directors.

Notice of election

Sec. 5. The business and property of such company shall be managed by a board of not less than three nor more than seven directors, who after the first year shall be elected annually, at such time and place as the by-laws direct, and public notice shall be given of such election not less than twenty days previous thereto, in such manner as shall be prescribed by the by-laws. The election shall be made by such stockholders as shall attend for that pur- _{Each share entitled to a vote.} pose in person or by proxy. Each share shall be entitled to one vote, and the person receiving the greatest number of votes shall be declared elected. All vacancies in the board shall be filled by _{Vacancies.} the remaining directors until another election. In case the election of directors is not held on the day fixed by the by-laws, it may be held on any day thereafter fixed by the board, on giving the same notice of the time and place as in case of an annual election.

SEC. 6. A majority of the directors shall be a board for the _{Officers of board.} transaction of business. At the first meeting after their election they may elect one of their number president, and appoint such other officers as the articles of association or by-laws require.

SEC. 7. The president and directors shall have power to make _{Powers of president and directors.} and prescribe such rules and regulations respecting the transfer of the stock, either before its full payment or thereafter, and for the general management of the affairs of said association, as they may deem proper, not inconsistent with the laws of this State, and shall have power to appoint and employ officers, clerks, agents, and servants, for conducting and carrying on the business of said corporation, and fix the salaries or compensation to be paid to them. It _{Annual report to Secretary of State.} shall be the duty of the said president and directors to make, verified by the oath of some one of them, an annual report to the Secretary of State on the first day of January in each year, showing: First, the capital stock and the amount actually paid in; second, the amount expended, and for what purpose; third, the amount received from tolls, and from all other sources, distinguishing from what sources; fourth, the number and amount of dividends, and how paid; fifth, the number of men employed and their occupation.

SEC. 8. It shall be lawful for such company, their officers, engi- _{Location of route.} neers, and agents to enter upon any lands for the purpose of exploring, surveying, and locating the route of any such canal, harbor, or the improvement of any such river or stream, doing thereto no unnecessary damage, and paying any damage which may accrue; but said company shall not locate any such canal through any _{Not to be located through orchard, etc., without consent of owner} orchard over one year old, or garden, without the consent of the owner, or through any building or fixtures, or any yard or enclosure necessary for the use and enjoyment thereof, without the like consent; and when the said route or improvement shall be estab- _{When route is located company may enter upon lands.} lished by the said company, it shall be lawful for them, their officers and servants, to enter upon, take possession of, and use such lands, to the width of two hundred feet, as said company shall have purchased or obtained from the owners or occupants the right to use, and also to take and use any other lands which may be necessary for the construction of said canal, or the improvement of the navigation of such river, or the erection of any locks, gates, tollhouses, or other fixtures, or the construction of any dam that may be necessary to raise the water for the purposes of washing out any channel or harbor: *Provided,* If such dam shall obstruct any _{Proviso.} channel navigable for vessels, it shall be made during the winter months and removed before the opening of navigation, the necessity for such taking, and the damages to be paid therefor being first ascertained, and such damages paid as hereinafter provided.

Corporation not to hold lands other than those donated. SEC. 9. Said corporation shall not, in their corporate capacity, hold, purchase, or deal in any lands other than lands donated to said corporations to aid in constructing said improvements, or the lands in which their canals shall run, to the width of three hundred feet on each side of said canals, or which are donated to or purchased by said corporation for wharves or docking purposes, or which may actually be necessary for the construction and maintenance of the canals or improvements, or the fixtures connected therewith.

Proceedings to ascertain damages for entering upon lands. SEC. 10. Whenever said company shall desire to enter upon, use, or occupy any lands, or condemn any franchises or right to the use of running water, when no agreement can be made with the owners thereof, the like proceedings shall be had and taken as is provided in "An act to provide for the incorporation of railroad companies," and the acts amendatory thereto; and after the payment or tender of such damages as shall be then ascertained, may **After payment of damages may take lands.** enter upon and take the lands so appraised, for the purposes of constructing said canal, harbors, or making the improvement in such river, its fixtures and appurtenances.

Commissioner to establish rates of toll. SEC. 11. Any such company shall be authorized to charge, demand, and receive such rates of toll for the use of said canal or harbor, or for the use of any river or stream of this State, improved by said company, or for any dock, wharf, or other improvements, as may be established by three commissioners, who shall be appointed by the board of supervisors of the county where the tolls are collected, or in which the greater part of such improvements shall be constructed. Said commissioners, after making a personal examination of such canal or improvement, shall fix and establish the rate of tolls and charges for each boat, vessel, raft, or craft of any description using such canal, or passing through said improved river, or any of the works of said company, and upon the goods, merchandise, or other cargo, on said boat or vessel, which said tolls or **Tolls a lien upon boats and vessels** charges shall be a lien upon the boat or vessel using any of the improvements of said company, or having such goods or merchandise **How collected.** on board, and may be collected under the provisions of an act entitled "An act to repeal chapter one hundred and twenty-two of the revised statutes of eighteen hundred and forty-six, and the amendments thereto, and provide for the collection of demands against water-craft," approved February five, in the year of our Lord eighteen hundred and sixty-four, and shall be collected in the distribution of funds, as provided by section thirty-three of said act, under the fourth specification of said section; and it shall be **Master or clerk of boat to give statement.** the duty of the master or clerk of any such boat or vessel, on demand of the collector, or any other person authorized by said company to receive or collect such tolls or charges, to give such collector, or other person so authorized, a true and correct statement of all goods, merchandise, or other cargo, on said boat or vessel, and subject to pay any toll, or charges, which statement shall be verified by the oath of the master, or clerk of such vessel or boat. Said board of commissioners shall deliver a certified copy of such rates Copy of rates to be posted and filed. of tolls or charges to said company, a printed copy of which shall always be posted up at such place where toll is demanded, and the board shall file another copy with the Secretary of State, which shall be duly recorded in his office. A certified copy of such record Certified copy may be given in evidence. may be read in evidence in any court of this State, and shall be sufficient proof of the rates of tolls and charges due on any boat or vessel, or any goods, merchandise, or other cargo: *Provided, how-* Certain crafts not to pay toll. *ever,* That no charge whatever shall be made for the use of any river where such improvement has been made, for any boat, vessel, raft, or craft of any description which might or could have used said river before said improvements had been made: *Provided* Proviso. *further,* That the said board shall, in determining the rates of toll or charges, declare what boats, or vessels, or rafts are entitled to use said river free of charge.

SEC. 12. If any person shall willfully obstruct, or in anywise Penalty for injuring improvements, etc. injure any such canal, harbor, or improvements, or any dock, wharf, or other fixture connected therewith, or shall violate any rule or regulation established by said company, such person, or [such] boat or vessel, or other craft, as the said company may elect, shall be liable for all damages done or committed; and said damages, if Damages, how recovered. against the person, may be recovered in an action of trespass, and if proved to have been done willfully, treble damages may be re-covered. Any such claim for damages, if the company shall so elect, shall be a lien on any such boat or vessel, or other craft, and such lien may be enforced under the existing provisions of the law therefor.

SEC. 13. Whenever any canal shall cross any highway, the com- Canal across highway to be bridged. pany shall make and keep in good repair such bridges as the board of supervisors of the county in which such canal is located shall direct.

SEC. 14. The stockholders of said companies incorporated under Stockholders jointly liable for labor performed. this act shall be jointly and severally liable for all labor performed for such company; but no suit shall be brought against any indi- Suit, when brought. vidual stockholder for any debt of said company until judgment on the demand shall have been obtained against the company and execution thereon returned unsatisfied in whole or in part; and Stockholders may recover amount paid for company. any stockholder who has paid any debt of such company, either voluntarily or otherwise, shall have the right to sue and recover of such company the full amount thereof, with interest, costs, and expenses; and in case of failure to recover the amount from said company, may sue the said stockholders, or any one of them, for their due proportion thereof, which such stockholders ought to pay, and if such action for contribution shall be brought against more than one, the judgment shall specify the sum due and to be recov-ered from each of the defendants named.

SEC. 15. Any boat, vessel, raft, or craft which shall willfully Penalty for attempting to avoid toll. pass through said canal or said improvement without paying the toll required, shall be liable to pay to said company the sum of one hundred dollars, to be collected by proceeding against said boat or against the owners thereof, by attachment or otherwise.

Legislature may amend, etc.
SEC. 16. The Legislature shall, at all times hereafter, have the free right to alter, amend, or repeal this act.

Tax.
SEC. 17. Every corporation formed under the provisions of this act shall pay on the capital stock of said company all taxes assessed thereon for State, county, township, or other purposes, upon the property of said company, whether real, personal, or mixed, except penalties imposed by this act, the said tax to be estimated upon the last annual report of said corporation.

Corporations already formed may organize under this act.
SEC. 18. Any persons, or private associations, or corporations in the Upper Peninsula, who have, previous to the passage of this re-enacted and amended act, constructed any canal or harbor, or have improved the navigation of any river or stream in the Upper Peninsula within the meaning of section one of this act, when the amount of money actually expended by them in the construction of any such canal or improvement exceeds the sum of ten thousand dollars, may organize under this act, and like notice shall be given as required by section one of this act: *Pro-*
Proviso.
vided, That such persons, associations, or corporations, shall have the preference in the subscription to the stock of such company, to the amount so expended by them.

Penalty for refusing to furnish statement of cargo.
SEC. 19. In case the master or clerk of any boat or vessel shall neglect or refuse to furnish the statement as required by section eleven of this re-enacted and amended act, he shall be liable to a fine not exceeding one hundred dollars, to be sued for and be recovered by said company.

Companies may issue bonds.
SEC. 20. Any company organized under this act may borrow money, and issue bonds for the payment of the same, for the purpose of providing means for repairing, altering, or enlarging said improvements: *Provided, however,* That the amount so raised
Proviso.
shall not at any one time exceed in amount fifty per cent of the amount of the capital stock of said company.

Counties may purchase improvements.
SEC. 21. Any county through which any such improved river or stream shall pass, or in which the greater part of any such improvements have been constructed, or in which any canal shall have been constructed, within the provisions of this act, shall have the right to purchase any such canal or improvement by paying to any such company the amount of their capital stock, and the amount of all subsequent expenditure in repairing, altering, or enlarging any such canal or improvements, and interest at the rate of ten per cent per annum on said amounts, deducting from the amount of interest the net proceeds of any such company; and
Board of supervisors to assume management.
the board of supervisors of any such county to take the management of any such canal or improvement so purchased; to receive and collect tolls the same as provided for in this act; to appoint proper officers for the management of the same, with proper salaries for their services, and shall be entitled to the privileges and remedies provided in this act.

Purchase to be submitted to the electors.
SEC. 22. The board of supervisors of any such county may at any time, by a majority vote, submit the question of purchasing any such canal, harbor, or improvement, to the electors of said county; and if a majority of the electors shall decide to purchase

any such canal, harbor, or improvement, then the board of supervisors shall be authorized to purchase the same, and may for that purpose issue the bonds of said county to an amount sufficient to make such purchase.

SEC. 23. The corporations heretofore formed under said chapter eighty-four, in the Upper Peninsula, are hereby re-instated in all their rights, privileges, franchises, and property. *Reinstatement of corporations heretofore formed.*

SEC. 24. Corporations may be formed under this act, in the Upper Peninsula, for the purpose of operating and further improving any canal or improvement of any corporation formed under the act hereby re-instated, and may purchase the canal or other improvements, lands, or other property of such corporation. *Corporations may be formed for improving canal, etc., of company formed under act hereby reinstated.*

SEC. 25. This act shall take immediate effect.

Approved May 4, 1875.

[No. 234.]

AN ACT to repeal an act entitled "An act authorizing circuit courts in chancery in the county of Wayne to refer causes pending in chancery to special commissioners," being sections five thousand one hundred and ninety and five thousand one hundred and ninety-one of chapter one hundred and seventy-six of the compiled laws of eighteen hundred and seventy-one.

SECTION 1. *The People of the State of Michigan enact,* That sections one, two, and three of an act entitled "An act authorizing circuit courts in chancery, in the county of Wayne, to refer causes pending in chancery to special commissioners," approved January thirty, eighteen hundred and sixty-nine, being compiler's sections five thousand one hundred and ninety and five thousand one hundred and ninety-one of chapter one hundred and seventy-six of the compiled laws of eighteen hundred and seventy-one, be and the same are hereby repealed. *Act repealed.*

Approved May 4, 1875.

AND WHEREAS, Said harbor at Saugatuck is greatly in need of further appropriations to preserve the government work already there, and to dredge out bars that exist in said harbor, and to further improve said harbor;

AND WHEREAS, Congress has heretofore made, and continues to make, liberal appropriations of money for the improvements of harbors and rivers, in different parts of the Union, for the advancement of the general prosperity of the country;

Resolved by the Senate and House of Representatives, That our Senators and Representatives in Congress be requested to use their best endeavors to obtain an appropriation of money for the further improvement of said harbor at Saugatuck, and to improve the navigation of the Kalamazoo river to the village of Saugatuck; that said moneys be expended under the immediate direction of an officer of the United States government, detailed from the proper department for that purpose, if not contrary to the usual practice in such cases; therefore,

Resolved, That the Governor be and he is hereby requested to transmit a copy of the foregoing preamble and resolution to each of our Senators and Representatives in Congress.

Approved February 2, 1875.

[No. 3.]

JOINT RESOLUTION asking the Congress of the United States for an appropriation to repair and improve the harbor at South Haven on Lake Michigan.

WHEREAS, The rapidly increasing commerce of the port of South Haven, in the county of Van Buren, requires that the harbor should be in a condition to safely accommodate the numerous vessels frequenting said port;

AND WHEREAS, The citizens of that place have contributed largely of their private means, in addition to former appropriations from the United States government, in order to improve the harbor and protect the shipping interests of said place;

AND WHEREAS, The shore end of the north pier of the harbor has been seriously injured by the late autumnal storms, thereby causing serious obstructions to the entrance of said harbor by the formation of a bar across its channel;

AND WHEREAS, The producing and consuming interests of the country require that the means of transportation should be increased by the creation of new commercial facilities, and the preservation and improvement of present ones; therefore be it

Resolved by the Senate and House of Representatives of the State of Michigan, That the Congress of the United States be and is hereby requested to make such appropriation as will be sufficient to speedily repair and improve said harbor of South Haven; and that our Senators and Representatives in Congress be requested to use all proper efforts to secure an immediate appropriation for that purpose;

Resolved, That His Excellency the Governor be requested to transmit copies of the foregoing preamble and resolutions to each of our Senators and Representatives in Congress.

Approved February 2, 1875.

[No. 4.]

JOINT RESOLUTION for the relief of the Mining Journal Company of Marquette, Michigan.

WHEREAS, The Auditor General awarded to the Mining Journal Company, the publisher and proprietor of "The Mining Journal," a weekly newspaper published at Marquette, Marquette county, Michigan, the publication of the statements of lands to be sold for taxes in the counties of Chippewa, Schoolcraft, and Marquette at the general tax sales in October, eighteen hundred and seventy-three, which said statements were duly published by said Mining Journal Company, amounting in all, at legal rates, to the sum of thirty-one dollars and thirty cents;

AND WHEREAS, Section one thousand and forty-seven compiled laws eighteen hundred and seventy-one, provides that no printer shall be paid for publishing said statements unless he shall forward an affidavit of publication to the Auditor General within thirty days after the last publication, which affidavit was made and forwarded within the time limited by the statute, but never reached the Auditor General's office, in consequence of which the Auditor General refused to draw his warrant for the amount of said claim;

AND WHEREAS, An affidavit is now on file in said Auditor General's office, showing that the law was fully complied with by said company in publishing said statements; therefore, be it

Resolved by the Senate and House of Representatives of the State of Michigan, That the Auditor General be and he is hereby authorized to draw his warrant on the State Treasurer for said sum of thirty-one dollars and thirty cents, payable to said Mining Journal Company, to settle said claim.

Resolved, That this joint resolution take immediate effect.

Approved February 2, 1875.

[No. 5.]

JOINT RESOLUTION asking Congress for an appropriation in money for the improvement of the harbor at Saint Joseph, Benton Harbor, and New Buffalo, in the county of Berrien and State of Michigan.

WHEREAS, Congress has heretofore made appropriations for the improvement of the harbors at Saint Joseph and New Buffalo, in the county of Berrien, Michigan, which appropriations have aided materially in making said Saint Joseph an important shipping port on Lake Michigan, but have been inadequate to make said harbor at New Buffalo fully practicable;

AND WHEREAS, The proper officers of the United States government, having charge of the lake harbor improvements, have heretofore officially reported that a commodious harbor can be made at said New Buffalo, by the expenditure of a comparatively moderate sum, and that thereby important commercial interests would be developed;

AND WHEREAS, By reason of the improvement of said harbor of St. Joseph, and the commercial interests promoted thereby, a ship canal has been constructed from said harbor of Saint Joseph to the village of Benton Harbor, in said county of Berrien; and said Benton Harbor is now an important shipping port, having a custom-house, and is the outlet for the products of an enterprising and growing section of country, the prosperity of which is largely dependent upon and promoted by shipping facilities; and said harbor at St. Joseph is greatly in need of further appropriations to preserve the government work already there, and to further improve said harbor;

AND WHEREAS, Congress has heretofore made, and continues to make, liberal appropriations of money for the improvement of harbors and rivers in different parts of the Union, for the advancement of the general prosperity of the country;

Resolved by the Senate and House of Representatives of the State of Michigan, That our Senators and Representatives in Congress be requested to use their best endeavors to obtain an appropriation of money for the improvement of said harbor at New Buffalo; also an appropriation of money to improve said harbor at Saint Joseph; also an appropriation of money to construct a wing dam on the north bank of the Saint Joseph river, at said harbor of Saint Joseph, at the junction of the Saint Joseph and Paw Paw rivers, on the west or lower side of said Paw Paw, to improve the navigation of said Saint Joseph river and harbor to the village of Benton Harbor. That said moneys be expended for the specific purposes aforesaid, and under the immediate direction of an officer of the United States Government, detailed from the proper department, for that purpose, if not contrary to the usual practice in such cases.

Resolved, That the Governor be and is hereby requested to transmit a copy of the foregoing preamble and resolution to each of our Senators and Representatives in Congress.

Approved February 2, 1875.

[No. 6.]

JOINT RESOLUTION asking Congress to establish a United States judicial circuit in the Upper Peninsula of Michigan.

Resolved by the Senate and House of Representatives of the State of Michigan, That, whereas a bill has been introduced into the Congress of the United States by Hon. Jay A. Hubbell, Congressman from the ninth district, for the establishment of a United States judicial circuit in the Upper Peninsula of Michigan;

Now therefore, The Legislature of Michigan, by joint resolution, does hereby recommend the passage of said bill, and does hereby request all our Senators and Representatives in Congress to support said bill, and to do their utmost to secure its passage, believing as we do that the passage of said bill will be for the interest of the general government and the State of Michigan, and absolutely necessary that the people of the Upper Peninsula of Michigan may receive just and proper litigation.

Approved February 2, 1875.

[No. 7.]

JOINT RESOLUTION asking the Congress of the United States to aid in the improvement of the navigation of Pine River, in Charlevoix county, on Lake Michigan.

WHEREAS, The commerce of Pine River, in Charlevoix county, exceeds that of any of the harbors on the east shore of Lake Michigan (excepting those of Grand Haven, Muskegon, and Manistee), and is constantly increasing;

AND WHEREAS, The navigation of said river has been impeded and rendered difficult by the existence and formation of bars at the mouth of said Pine River;

AND WHEREAS, The people of Charlevoix county have, by voluntary labor, private subscriptions, local taxation, and issue of bonds, expended upwards of twenty thousand dollars in removing obstructions, dredging, and improving the navigation of said river;

AND WHEREAS, The State Board of Control of Michigan in eighteen hundred and seventy-two, made an appropriation of twelve thousand five hundred dollars, in State swamp lands, in aid of the improvement of said Pine River and harbor;

AND WHEREAS, By a report recently made by Colonel Mansfield of the Engineer Corps U. S. A., in charge of the harbor improvements of the eastern shore of Lake Michigan, additional aid is necessary to protect and complete the work already accomplished, and such engineer has reported in favor of the General Government aiding the said improvement; therefore,

Resolved by the Senate and House of Representatives of the State of Michigan, That the Congress of the United States be and they are hereby requested to make such appropriation as may be necessary for completing and protecting such improvement, and that our Senators in Congress be instructed, and our Representatives requested to use all proper efforts to secure an appropriation for that purpose.

Resolved, That His Excellency, the Governor, be requested to transmit copies of the foregoing preamble and resolution to each of our Senators and Representatives in Congress.

Approved February 2, 1875.

[No. 8.]

JOINT RESOLUTION asking Congress for an appropriation in money for the improvement of the harbor at Alpena, Alpena county, State of Michigan.

WHEREAS, Alpena is a city of (4000) four thousand inhabitants, with a very large shipping and commercial interest, being the outlet for the productions of Alpena and Montmorency counties, and a portion of Alcona, Oscoda, Presque Isle, and Cheboygan counties, with a daily line of mail steamers, and three weekly lines of passenger steamers, three weekly lines of steam barges, together with an average of twenty other barges and sailing vessels per week entering and clearing this port, importing supplies, provisions, merchandise, and laborers necessary for the production of one hundred million feet of lumber annually; together with a large quantity of shingles, lath, cedar posts, siding, and hemlock extract; also large exportations of fish;

WHEREAS, The United States government never has expended one dollar in the improvement of said harbor;

AND WHEREAS, Congress has made, and continues to make, liberal appropriations of money for the improvement of rivers and harbors in different parts of the Union, for the advancement of the general prosperity of the country;

WHEREAS, The condition of the harbor is such as to debar the entrance and full loading of any vessels, except those of small tonnage and light draft, therefore necessitating the extra expense of lightering a large quantity of the lumber and other products at an enormous expense, thereby greatly injuring the prosperity of the large extended territory depending on this harbor for an outlet;

WHEREAS, A commodious harbor can be made at said Alpena by the construction of piers at the mouth of Thunder Bay River, and dredging at a comparatively moderate expenditure, thereby greatly relieving and developing the commercial interests of the country;

Resolved (the Senate concurring), That our Senators and Representatives in Congress be requested to use their best endeavors to obtain an appropriation of money for the improvement of said harbor at Alpena; and to begin the work as early in the spring as the season will permit, under the immediate directions of an officer of the United States government detailed from the proper department for that purpose.

Resolved, That the Governor be and is hereby requested to transmit a copy of the foregoing preamble and resolution to each of our Senators and Representatives in Congress.

Approved February 2, 1875.

[No. 9.]

JOINT RESOLUTION asking Congress for an appropriation for the improvement of the harbor at Eagle Harbor, Keweenaw county, Michigan.

WHEREAS, An appropriation was made by Congress, six years ago, for the blasting of a channel through the reef at Eagle Harbor, and one season's work done under the supervision of the Engineering Department, and the said department have recommended a small additional appropriation to the unexpended balance, so as to enable them to put the work under contract for its completion;

AND WHEREAS, This harbor is at present the most dangerous and difficult of access of all the harbors on the shore of Lake Superior, and is relied on as the shipping point by the people of Keweenaw county, and ranks as one of the most important in the value of its imports and exports on Lake Superior;

Resolved (the Senate concurring), That our Senators and Representatives in Congress are hereby requested to use their best endeavors to obtain an appropriation of money for said harbor.

Resolved, That the Governor be and is hereby requested to transmit a copy of the foregoing preamble and resolution to each of our Senators and Representatives in Congress.

Approved February 2, 1875.

[No. 10.]

JOINT RESOLUTION relative to the Reciprocity Treaty.

WHEREAS, There is now pending in the Senate of the United States a proposed treaty with the Dominion of Canada, known as the reciprocity treaty;

AND WHEREAS, The ratification of said pending treaty by the Senate of the United States would be prejudicial to all the productive industries of this State, and especially to our agricultural, mineral, lumber, saline, and quarrying interests;

AND WHEREAS, The ratification of the proposed treaty with Canada will be a certain and grievous injury to the people and business of this State; that it is not demanded by any class of our citizens, or by any necessity of the State or the General Government, nor any claim of international sympathy or duty; that it will interfere with the revenues of the country, and by favoritism and discrimination towards a foreign people, deprive the General Government of a large revenue now collected from imports, and result in adding an equal sum to our already high domestic taxation; that the government owes its first duty and protection to our own citizens, to foster their industries and encourage the development of home manufactures and markets; therefore,

Resolved by the Senate and House of Representatives of the State of Michigan, That our Senators in Congress be and they are hereby instructed to use all honorable means to prevent the ratification of said reciprocity treaty by the Senate of the United States, and thus aid in securing the just rights of all persons who, trusting to the faith of the government, have devoted their labor and embarked their capital in developing the varied industries of our State.

Resolved, That the Governor be requested to transmit a copy of the foregoing preamble and resolution to each of our Senators in Congress.

Approved February 18, 1875.

[No. 11.]

JOINT RESOLUTION giving construction to section four (4) of act number one hundred and twenty-four (124) of the laws of eighteen hundred and seventy-three, relative to the expenses incurred by the board of commissioners on fisheries.

Resolved by the Senate and House of Representatives of the State of Michigan, That the years eighteen hundred and seventy-three and eighteen hundred and seventy-four, mentioned in section four of act number one hundred and twenty-four, laws of eighteen hundred and seventy-three, shall be construed as commencing on the first day of July, eighteen hundred and seventy-three, and the first day of July, eighteen hundred and seventy-four, and continuing for one year from said first days of July, respectively.

Approved February 20, 1875.

[No. 12.]

JOINT RESOLUTION asking Congress for an appropriation to construct a light-house and fog-bells at the West Bar of Mackinaw Island, in the county of Mackinaw, and State of Michigan.

WHEREAS, The light-house board as early as eighteen hundred and fifty-nine deemed it necessary to the interests of commerce to construct a light-house on West Bar of Mackinaw Island, and an appropriation was made therefor, but for some cause unknown said light-house was never built;

AND WHEREAS, The neglect to construct said light-house has resulted annually in great loss and damage to vessels and steamers getting aground on the shoals and bars in the Straits of Mackinaw while endeavoring to make a harbor during stormy and foggy weather;

AND WHEREAS, The great and important commerce of our lakes (exceeding our tonnage on the ocean) imperatively demands for future safety that a suitable light-house and fog-bell should be erected on the site formerly purchased by the government for said light-house on said West Bar of Mackinaw Island; therefore,

Resolved by the Senate and House of Representatives of the State of Michigan, That our Senators and Representatives in Congress be requested to use all honorable means to procure the necessary appropriation for the construction of a light-house and fog-bells on the West Bar of said island under the superintendence of the light-house board.

Resolved, That His Excellency, the Governor, be requested to transmit copies of the foregoing preamble and resolution to each of our Senators and Representatives in Congress.

Approved February 25, 1875.

———

[No. 13.]

JOINT RESOLUTION asking Congress for an appropriation in money for the improvement of the harbor at Holland, in the county of Ottawa, and State of Michigan.

WHEREAS, Congress has heretofore made appropriations for the improvement of the harbor at Holland, in the county of Ottawa, Michigan, which appropriations have aided materially in making said Holland an important shipping port on Lake Michigan;

AND WHEREAS, The proper officers of the United States government, having charge of the lake harbor improvements, have heretofore officially reported that a harbor, second to none, can be made at Holland by the expenditure of a comparatively moderate sum, and that thereby important commercial interests would be developed;

AND WHEREAS, By reason of the improvements of said harbor at Holland, and the commercial interests promoted thereby, the said Holland is now an important shipping port, having a custom-house, and is the outlet for the products of an enterprising and growing section of the country, the prosperity of which is largely dependent upon and promoted by shipping facilities;

AND WHEREAS, Said harbor at Holland is greatly in need of further appropriations to preserve the government work already there, and to dredge out bars that exist in said harbor, and to further improve said harbor;

AND WHEREAS, Congress has heretofore made, and continues to make, liberal appropriations of money for the improvement of harbors and rivers, in different parts of the Union, for the advancement of the general prosperity of the country; therefore,

Resolved by the Senate and House of Representatives, That our Senators and Representatives in Congress be requested to use their best endeavors to obtain an appropriation of money for the further improvement of said harbor at Holland; that said moneys be expended under the immediate direction of an officer of the United States government, detailed from the proper department for that purpose, if not contrary to the usual practice in such cases;

Resolved, That the Governor be and he is hereby requested to transmit a copy of the foregoing preamble and resolution to each of our Senators and Representatives in Congress.

Approved February 25, 1875.

[No. 14.]

JOINT RESOLUTION authorizing the issue of a patent to George S. Hoppin upon appraised University land certificate numbered three hundred and thirty-eight.

WHEREAS, George S. Hoppin, of Berrien county, Michigan, is the holder and rightful owner of appraised University land certificate number three hundred and thirty-eight, and has duly paid the whole amount of principal and interest therein specified, and has been in possession of the land described in said certificate, paying all taxes thereon for more than twenty-five years last past;

AND WHEREAS, The Attorney General of Michigan is of opinion that, although said George S. Hoppin is equitably entitled to have a patent issued to him on said certificate, yet that none can be so issued on account of defects in assignments appearing on said certificate;

Resolved by the Senate and House of Representatives of the State of Michigan, That the Governor of this State be and is hereby authorized to sign and cause to be issued to George S. Hoppin a patent for the lands described in said certificate whenever the same shall be presented to him with the certificate of the Commissioner of the State Land Office that the principal and interest, and all taxes and charges levied upon said lands, have been paid.

This resolution shall take immediate effect.

Approved February 26, 1875.

———

[No. 15.]

JOINT RESOLUTION asking Congress to amend the homestead law giving soldiers and sailors disabled by the loss of a limb or other equivalent disability, the amount of land to which they would be entitled without settlement upon the same as now required.

WHEREAS, Congress has provided through the homestead law for deeding to the soldiers and sailors of the war for the suppression of the rebellion, a certain amount of land on certain conditions of settlement;

AND WHEREAS, Many soldiers and sailors, through disqualifications incurred in the service, are precluded from availing themselves of its provisions; therefore

Resolved by the Senate and House of Representatives of the State of Michigan, That our Senators and Representatives in Congress be requested to use their influence in procuring such modifications of the homestead law as will enable those soldiers and sailors who, by loss of a limb, or other equivalent disability, are prevented from making the settlement required by the same, to avail themselves of the advantages of the law without actual settlement being required of them.

Resolved, That the Governor be requested to transmit a copy of the foregoing preamble and resolutions to each of our Senators and Representatives in Congress.

Approved March 10, 1875.

[No. 16.]

JOINT RESOLUTION asking Congress to so amend an act entitled " An act to enable honorably discharged soldiers and sailors, their widows and orphan children, to acquire homesteads on the public lands of the United States."

WHEREAS, The above act of Congress as it now stands gives no benefit or advantage over the general homestead law to the parties interested, except the deduction of the time served in the army or navy, or the term of enlistment (when discharged on account of wounds, etc.) from the term of settlement otherwise required to perfect title;

AND WHEREAS, Owing to the occupation and condition in life of a large majority of soldiers and sailors, whose lot as mechanics, tradesmen, etc., prevents them from entry and occupation of said lands in person, thereby making the present law as to them a dead letter, from which they derive no benefit; therefore, be it

Resolved (the Senate concurring), That our Senators and Representatives in Congress be requested to use their best endeavors to have said act amended so as to allow such soldiers, sailors, their widows and orphan children, to obtain and perfect title to homesteads on complying with the requirements of said act (as to settlement and cultivation) through agents.

Resolved, That the Governor be, and he is hereby requested to transmit a copy of the foregoing preamble and resolution to each of our Senators and Representatives in Congress.

Approved March 10, 1875.

[No. 17.]

JOINT RESOLUTION to provide for the transfer of certain moneys from the sinking fund to the general fund.

WHEREAS, It appears from the late message of the Governor to this Legislature that there has been placed to the credit of the sinking fund the sum of two hundred and sixty-six thousand eight hundred and twenty-eight dollars and forty cents, received from the general government for re-imbursements of war expenses, and the further sum of two hundred thousand dollars by authority of joint resolution of the Legislature in eighteen hundred and sixty-nine, amounting in the aggregate to four hundred and sixty-six thousand eight hundred and twenty-eight dollars and forty cents;

AND WHEREAS, Subsequent events have demonstrated that this amount of money is not needed in the sinking fund to be kept on hand in the State treasury for the purpose of meeting State indebtedness not yet due, the current and prospective receipts from specific taxes being amply sufficient for that purpose, it being evident that the unmatured bonds of the State cannot be obtained to any large extent at such rates as will justify the retaining in the sinking fund of other amounts than those expressly required by the constitution; therefore, in order to lessen the amount of taxation required for the general expenses of the State government and for special appropriations,

Resolved by the Senate and House of Representatives of the State of Michigan, That the State Treasurer and Auditor General are hereby directed to transfer the sum of four hundred and sixty-six thousand and eight hundred and twenty-eight and forty one-hundredths dollars from the sinking fund to the credit of the general fund.

Resolved, That this resolution shall take immediate effect.

Approved March 12, 1875.

[No. 18.]

JOINT RESOLUTION for publishing in pamphlet form all laws relating to the public health.

WHEREAS, It is important that health officers, and persons who give immediate attention to sanitary science in this State, should have in a form convenient for reference, all the laws in force in this State relating to the public health;

Resolved by the Senate and House of Representatives of the State of Michigan, That the Secretary of State, immediately after the final adjournment of this Legislature, be authorized and directed to compile and publish, in pamphlet form, all the laws of this State, then in force, relating to the public health; that he shall cause three thousand copies of such pamphlet to be printed; that he shall send one copy to each health officer in this State, and that he shall place one thousand copies in the hands of the Secretary of the State Board of Health, for the use of said board.

Approved March 20, 1875.

[No. 19.]

JOINT RESOLUTION for the relief of Edward A. Durant.

WHEREAS, Edward A. Durant, a resident of the city of Albany, in the State of New York, deposes and claims that on or about the first of May, in the year of our Lord one thousand eight hundred and seventy-three, he lost five coupons which he had detached from five Michigan war bounty loan bonds, numbered respectively fifty-seven, fifty-eight, fifty-nine, sixty, and sixty-one, each of said bonds bearing date May first, eighteen hundred and sixty-five, and issued pursuant to an act of the Legislature of the State of Michigan, entitled, "An act authorizing a war bounty loan," approved March two, eighteen hundred and sixty-five;

AND WHEREAS, The said Edward A. Durant claims that he has never been able to find or recover the said five lost coupons, and by reason of their loss he is justly entitled to the aggregate amount of said coupons, being the sum of one hundred and seventy-five dollars;

AND WHEREAS, Said coupons, nor any of them, have ever been paid by the State, nor presented for payment; therefore,

Be it resolved by the Senate and House of Representatives of the State of Michigan, That the board of State Auditors are hereby authorized and empowered, in their discretion, to allow to the said Edward A. Durant the value of said coupons, lost as aforesaid, not exceeding in the aggregate amount the sum of one hundred and seventy-five dollars; and on such allowance the Auditor General shall draw his warrant on the State Treasurer, in favor of the said Edward A. Durant, for the amount so audited and allowed, to be paid by him out of any moneys in the treasury belonging to the proper funds, upon which said coupons were a charge, not otherwise appropriated: *Provided*, That the said Edward A. Durant shall, before the delivery of said warrant, give to the State of Michigan a good and sufficient bond with sureties residing in Michigan, to be approved by the Auditor General and State Treasurer, indemnifying the State against the payment of said coupons, or any of them.

Approved March 20, 1875.

[No. 20.]

JOINT RESOLUTION authorizing the Board of State Auditors to examine and adjust certain specific taxes.

Resolved by the Senate and House of Representatives of the State of Michigan, That the Board of State Auditors be and they are hereby authorized and directed to examine and adjust upon the basis of an act entitled "An act to revise the laws providing for the incorporation of railroad companies, and to regulate the running and management, and to fix the duties and liabilities of all railroad and other corporations owning or operating any railroad in this State," approved May one, eighteen hundred and seventy-three, all claims of the State against the Chicago and Lake Huron Railroad Company, upon such terms as by the said board shall be deemed equitable and just in view of the law and the facts in the case.

Approved March 26, 1875.

[No. 21.]

JOINT RESOLUTION to amend the constitution of this State by striking out section forty-seven, article four, legislative department, which forbids the grant of license for the sale of intoxicating liquors.

Resolved by the Senate and House of Representatives of the State of Michigan, That the constitution of said State be amended by striking therefrom section forty-seven, article four, legislative department, which prohibits the Legislature from passing any act authorizing the grant of license for the sale of ardent spirits or other intoxicating liquors. Said amendment shall be submitted to the people of this State at the next general election, to be held on the first Tuesday succeeding the first Monday in November, in the year eighteen hundred and seventy-six; and the Secretary of State is hereby required to give notice of the same to the sheriffs of the several counties in the State, in the same manner that he is now by law required to do in case of an election of governor and lieutenant governor; and the inspectors of the election in the several townships and cities in this State shall prepare a suitable box for the reception of ballots cast for and against said amendment. Each person voting for striking out said section forty-seven, article four, legislative department, shall have written or printed on his ballot the words "Amendment relative to license for the sale of ardent spirits or other intoxicating liquors,—Yes," and each person voting against it shall have written or printed on his ballot the words "Amendment relative to license for sale of ardent spirits or other intoxicating liquors,—No." The ballots shall in all other respects be canvassed and returns made as in elections of Governor and Lieutenant Governor.

Received in the Executive office March 30, 1875.

[No. 22.]

JOINT RESOLUTION authorizing the State Treasurer to settle with all persons heretofore engaged in mining iron ore in the county of Marquette, for the specific taxes due from such persons, at the same rate required by law to be paid by corporations.

WHEREAS, Certain persons have heretofore engaged in mining iron ore in Marquette county;

AND WHEREAS, Such persons were required by law to pay a much larger specific tax on the iron ore mined by them than corporations were obliged to pay; therefore,

Resolved by the Senate and House of Representatives of the State of Michigan, That the Auditor General and State Treasurer be and are hereby authorized to collect from all such persons, specific taxes on the iron ore so mined by them, at the same rate paid by corporations on iron ore mined by such corporations; and all such persons who have heretofore paid into the State treasury specific taxes on the iron ore mined by them, the same as corporations were obliged by law to pay during the same period, shall not be required to pay any further specific tax on such iron ore heretofore mined by them.

Approved April 8, 1875.

––––––

[No. 23.]

JOINT RESOLUTION asking the Secretary of War of the United States to cause an examination of the harbor of St. Joseph, Michigan, with reference to a modification of the railroad bridge across the harbor at that place:

Resolved by the Senate and House of Representatives of the State of Michigan, That the Secretary of War of the United States be requested to cause an examination to be made of the harbor at St. Joseph, Michigan, and if it shall be found, on such examination, that the railroad bridge across said harbor is so constructed as materially to affect the commerce of said harbor and river, that he will direct such a modification to be made in said bridge as the interests of said harbor may require.

Resolved, That the Governor be and he is hereby requested to transmit a copy of the foregoing resolution to the Secretary of War.

This resolution shall take immediate effect.

Approved April 16, 1875.

––––––

[No. 24.]

JOINT RESOLUTION to authorize the Commissioner of the State Land Office, or other proper officers, to convey the southwest quarter of the southeast quarter of section number sixteen (16), in township number five south, of range number two east, to Joseph R. Smith, assignee of primary school land certificate number one thousand six hundred and sixteen.

WHEREAS, On the fourteenth day of November, in the year of our Lord one thousand eight hundred and forty-four, primary school land certificate number one thousand six hundred and sixteen, was issued by J. B. Frink, the Deputy Commissioner of the State Land Office of the State of Michigan, for the sale of the southwest quarter of the southeast quarter of section number sixteen, in township number five, south of range number two east, to Thomas B. Carpenter;

AND WHEREAS, On the first day of March, one thousand eight hundred and forty-seven, the said Thomas B. Carpenter duly assigned, in writing, said certificate to David Thomas;

AND WHEREAS, On the fifth day of March, one thousand eight hundred and fifty, the said David Thomas duly assigned, in writing, said certificate to Ezra Lewis;

AND WHEREAS, On the nineteenth day of April, in the year of our Lord one thousand eight hundred and fifty-three, the said heirs at law of said Ezra Lewis (he, the said Ezra Lewis, being dead) duly assigned, in writing, said certificate to David Thomas.;

AND WHEREAS, On the eleventh day of July, one thousand eight hundred and fifty-six, the said David Thomas duly assigned, in writing, said certificate to Joseph R. Smith, the present owner of said primary school land certificate;

AND WHEREAS, Some of said assignments have not been acknowledged by a proper officer, authorized to take acknowledgments, not deeming it necessary; and further, the said David Thomas and Ezra Lewis are and have been dead for the past ten years, and the said Thomas B. Carpenter, if not dead, his whereabouts is not known; therefore,

Resolved by the Senate and House of Representatives of the State of Michigan, That the Commissioner of the State Land Office, or other proper officer, is hereby authorized upon satisfactory proof of the matters set forth in the preamble to execute to said Joseph R. Smith, for and in behalf of the State of Michigan, a patent, or deed, in and to the land above described, on payment to the proper officers of said State, by the said Joseph R. Smith of the amount due, if any there be unpaid, to said State upon said certificate number one thousand six hundred and sixteen.

This resolution shall take immediate effect.

Approved April 16, 1875.

[No. 25.]

JOINT RESOLUTION authorizing the Governor to appoint three disinterested persons to investigate and adjust certain matters in dispute between Chancey Gates and the superintendent and trustees of the Michigan Asylum for the Insane.

WHEREAS, There is now pending in the circuit court for the county of Kalamazoo, a suit instituted by Chancey Gates, of the township of Kalamazoo, against the superintendent and trustees of the Michigan Asylum for the Insane, which suit is based upon the claim of said Gates that he has been damaged in his property in consequence of the diversion of the water from the Arcadia creek, so called, to the Michigan Asylum for the Insane; and

WHEREAS, The said Chancey Gates signifies his willingness to submit all matters in dispute between himself and the superintendent and trustees aforesaid, to three disinterested persons non-residents of said county of Kalamazoo, to be appointed by the Governor; therefore be it

Resolved by the Senate and House of Representatives of the State of Michigan, That the Governor be and he is hereby authorized and empowered to appoint three disinterested persons, non-residents of said county of Kalamazoo, who shall investigate and adjust all matters in dispute between said Chancey Gates and said superintendent and trustees, and make such award concerning such matters as in their judgment shall appear just and equitable, and such award shall be final: *Provided,* That before the Governor shall appoint the persons, as herein provided, said Gates shall sign a stipulation in writing that he will abide by the award so made.

Resolved, That in case the persons so named by the Governor, or a majority of them shall find that said Gates has been damaged in his property in consequence of the diversion of the water from said creek, as aforesaid, and that he is entitled to remuneration for damages thereby sustained, the Auditor General is hereby authorized and empowered to draw his warrant on the State Treasurer for the amount of such award, to be paid out of any funds in the treasury not otherwise appropriated, and also for such further sum as shall be authorized by the Governor for the payment of expenses incurred in obtaining such award.

Approved April 22, 1875.

[No. 26.]

JOINT RESOLUTION to provide for the exhibition of the horticultural and pomological productions of this State at the exhibition at the American Pomological Society, to be held at Chicago in 1875.

Resolved by the Senate and House of Representatives of the State of Michigan, That the Governor be and he is hereby empowered to provide for the collection and display of specimens of the horticultural and pomological productions of this State, at the exhibition of the American Pomological Society, to be held at the city of Chicago, during the autumn of the year eighteen hundred and seventy-five; and that the sum of one thousand dollars be and the same is hereby appropriated from the general fund for such purpose, to be expended under the direction of the Governor.

Approved April 23, 1875.

[No. 27.]

JOINT RESOLUTION authorizing the issue of a patent to James C. Brand upon primary school land certificate number (4,300) four thousand three hundred.

WHEREAS, James C. Brand, of Vernon, in the county of Shiawassee, State of Michigan, is now the holder of primary school land certificate number four thousand three hundred, issued by Porter Kibbee, Commissioner of the State Land Office, on the first day of October, in the year of our Lord one thousand eight hundred and fifty-three, to William Westmoreland, then of Oakland county, Michigan, for the purchase of the following described land, that is to say: the southeast quarter of the southeast quarter of section number sixteen, in township number six north, of range four east, containing forty acres, more or less;

AND WHEREAS, The said James C. Brand derives his right and title to said certificate, under, through, and by virtue of an assignment of said certificate, made and executed, signed, sealed, and acknowledged by Emma Westmoreland, administratrix of the estate of William Westmoreland, deceased, on the first day of December, eighteen hundred and fifty-four;

AND WHEREAS, Said assignment is in form such as would be required and all that would be necessary for the assignment of a mortgage of real estate by an administrator or administratrix, but is not such as to authorize the conveyance of said land by the State of Michigan ; therefore,

Resolved by the Senate and House of Representatives of the State of Michigan, That the Governor be and is hereby authorized to sign and cause to be issued to the said James C. Brand a patent for the land described in said certificate number four thousand three hundred, whenever the same shall be presented to him, with the certificate of the Commissioner of the State Land Office attached thereto certifying that the principal and interest, as well as all taxes, interest, and charges due upon said land, has been paid.

This resolution shall take immediate effect.

Approved April 29, 1875.

[No. 28.]

JOINT RESOLUTION proposing an amendment to section one, article nine of the constitution of this State, relative to the salaries of the judges of the circuit court.

Resolved by the Senate and House of Representatives of the State of Michigan, That the following amendment to the constitution of this State be and the same is hereby proposed, to stand as section one of article nine:

SECTION 1. The Governor shall receive an annual salary of one thousand dollars ; the judges of the circuit court shall each receive an annual salary of two thousand five hundred dollars; the State Treasurer shall receive an annual salary of one thousand dollars; the Auditor General shall receive an annual salary of one thousand dollars; the Superintendent of Public Instruction shall receive an annual salary of one thousand dollars; the Secretary of State shall receive an annual salary of eight hundred dollars; the Commissioner of the Land Office shall receive an annual salary of eight hundred dollars; the Attorney General shall receive an annual salary of eight hundred dollars. They shall receive no fees or perquisites whatever for the performance of any duties connected with their offices. It shall not be competent for the Legislature to increase the salaries herein provided. And be it further provided that said amendment shall be submitted to the people of this State at the next general election, to be held on the Tuesday succeeding the first Monday in November in the year eighteen hundred and seventy-six; and the Secretary of State is hereby required to give notice of the same to the sheriffs of the several counties in this State in the same manner that he is now required to do in case of an election of Governor and Lieutenant Governor; and the inspectors of elections in the several townships and cities in this State shall prepare a suitable box for the reception of ballots cast for and against said amendment. Each person voting for said amendment shall have written or printed, or partly written and partly printed, the words " Amendment relative to the salaries of circuit judges,—Yes;" and each person voting against such amendment the words " Amendment relative to the salaries of circuit judges,—No." The ballots shall in all respects be canvassed, and returns be made as in elections of Governor and Lieutenant Governor.

Received at the Executive office April 29, 1875.

[No. 29.]

JOINT RESOLUTION proposing an amendment to section one, article twenty of the constitution of this State, relative to the amendment and revision of the constitution.

Resolved by the Senate and House of Representatives of the State of Michigan, That the following amendment to the constitution of this State be and the same is hereby proposed to stand as section one of article twenty:

SECTION 1. Any amendment or amendments to this constitution may be proposed in the Senate or House of Representatives. If the same shall be agreed to by two-thirds of the members elected to each House, such amendment or amendments shall be entered on the journals respectively, with the yeas and nays taken thereon; and the same shall be submitted to the electors at the next spring or autumn election thereafter, as the Legislature shall direct, and if a majority of electors qualified to vote for members of the Legislature voting thereon shall ratify and approve such amendment or amendments, the same shall become part of the constitution.

Be it further resolved, That said constitutional amendment shall· be submitted to the people of this State at the general election, to be held on the Tuesday succeeding the first Monday in November, in the year eighteen hundred and seventy-six; and the Secretary of State is hereby required to give notice of the same to the sheriffs of the several counties of this State in the same manner that he is now required to do in case of an election of Governor or Lieutenant Governor, and the inspectors of election in the several townships and cities in this State shall prepare a suitable box for the reception of ballots cast for or against said amendment. Each person voting for said amendment shall have written or printed, or partly written and partly printed, on his ballot, the words " Amendment as to the time of submitting to the people amendments to the constitution,—Yes;" and each person voting against said amendment shall have on his ballot, in like manner, the words, "Amendment as to the time of submitting to the people amendments to the constitution,—No." The ballot shall in all respects be canvassed and returns made as in the election of Governor and Lieutenant Governor.

Received at the Executive office April 29, 1875.

[No. 30.]

JOINT RESOLUTION for the relief of Albert M. Harmon and Samuel H. Crowl.

WHEREAS, Certain pieces or parcels of lands, situated in township twenty-five north, of range six east, township twenty-five north, of range seven east, township twenty six north, of range six east, and township twenty-six north, of range seven east, were irregularly sold by the State of Michigan, to Cyrus Hewitt, and were by said Hewitt assigned to H. T. Carpenter, and by said Carpenter sold to R. McDonald, and by said McDonald sold and deeded to Albert M. Harmon and Samuel H. Crowl;

AND WHEREAS, Said McDonald, and said Albert M. Harmon, and Samuel H. Crowl were innocent purchasers, and knew nothing of any frauds in previous sales of said land;

AND WHEREAS, Said Albert M. Harmon and Samuel H. Crowl were assured when said fraud was discovered, that if they would re-convey said land to the State, that they would be refunded the amount they had in good faith paid therefor, and having so re-conveyed said lands to the State; therefore,

Resolved by the Senate and House of Representatives of the State of Michigan, That the Board of State Auditors be and they are hereby authorized and instructed to make a just and equitable settlement with said Albert M. Harmon and Samuel H. Crowl, for all lawful or equitable claims against the State, growing out of said irregular sale of said land. And upon such settlement being made, there shall be paid in cash, to said Albert M. Harmon and Samuel H. Crowl, the amount awarded by said board: *Provided,* That no interest shall be computed and allowed in such settlement: *And provided further,* That said award shall in no case be a greater sum than the State has secured therefor.

Approved April 30, 1875.

[No. 31.]

JOINT RESOLUTION requiring the Auditor General of the State to credit to the county of Isabella all moneys charged by said Auditor General to said county on account of the detaching of the unorganized county of Clare.

WHEREAS, At the session of the Legislature in the year eighteen hundred and sixty-nine, the then unorganized county of Clare was detached from the county of Isabella, and the east half thereof attached to the county of Midland, and the west half thereof attached to the county of Mecosta, for municipal and judicial purposes;

AND WHEREAS, The Auditor General did, in pursuance of said act, deduct from the credits due to the said county of Isabella the sum of ten thousand four hundred and eighty-six and thirty-six one-hundredths dollars; therefore,

Be it resolved by the Senate and House of Representatives, That the Auditor General be and he is hereby required to credit to the said county of Isabella the said amount of ten thousand four hundred and eighty-six and thirty-six one-hundredths dollars, deducted as aforesaid, and charge the same to the respective counties to which the same was credited when the change was made.

Approved April 30, 1875.

[No. 32.]

JOINT RESOLUTION asking Congress for an appropriation for the survey of a ship canal.

Resolved by the Senate and House of Representatives of the State of Michigan, That our Senators and Representatives in Congress be requested to use their influence to procure an appropriation for the survey of a ship canal across the State of Michigan from the waters of Lake Michigan to the waters of Lake Erie.

Resolved, That his Excellency the Governor be requested to transmit copies of the foregoing resolution to each of our Senators and Representatives in Congress.

Approved April 30, 1875.

[No. 33.]

JOINT RESO.'.UTION requesting the Board of State Auditors to adjust and pay certain claims of Luther Smith for State swamp land scrip, erroneously charged to him by the Commissioner of the State Land Office.

WHEREAS, The Commissioner of the State Land Office did, on the eighth day of September, eighteen hundred and seventy, erroneously allow O. K. Robinson to use one hundred and fifty dollars of " swamp land scrip," which legally belonged to Luther Smith, and at that date stood to his credit on the books of said office;

Therefore be it resolved by the Senate and House of Representatives of the State of Michigan, That the Board of State Auditors be, and they are required to adjust and allow to Luther Smith the just and equitable amount found due, with interest thereon, and that when so allowed the same be paid by the proper authority.

Approved May 1, 1875.

[No. 34.]

JOINT RESOLUTION asking Congress to admit gilling twine for fishing free of duty.

WHEREAS, The present duty on gilling twine is now forty per cent., gold; and,

WHEREAS, The fishermen as a class are unable to pay so great a tax; and,

WHEREAS, There is no gilling twine manufactured in this country that equals that imported; therefore,

Resolved by the Senate and House of Representatives of the State of Michigan, That our Senators and Representatives in Congress be requested to use their influence in procuring such change in the tariff that gilling twine may be admitted free of duty.

Approved May 1, 1875.

[No. 35.]

JOINT RESOLUTION authorizing the issue of a patent to William Lavarneway upon primary school land certificate number five thousand sixty-four (5064).

WHEREAS, It is represented that William Lavarneway, of Berrien county, Michigan, is the holder and rightful owner of primary school land certificate number five thousand sixty-four (5064), and has paid the whole amount of principal and interest specified therein;

AND WHEREAS, It is represented that the assignment conveying said school land certificate from the original purchaser, William D. Kirk, to William Lavarneway, by the administrator of the estate of William D. Kirk, deceased, was informal; therefore, be it

Resolved by the Senate and House of Representatives of the State of Michigan, That the Governor of the State be and is hereby authorized to sign and cause to be issued to said William Lavarneway, a patent for the lands described in said certificate (five thousand sixty-four), whenever the same shall be presented to him with the certificate of the Commissioner of the State Land Office endorsed thereon, certifying that the principal and interest, as well as all taxes, charges, and interest due upon said lands, have been paid: *Provided,* It be shown to the satisfaction of the Governor, that the matters recited in the preamble to this resolution are true, and that the said William Lavarneway is entitled to a patent for said land.

This resolution shall take immediate effect.

Approved May 3, 1875.

[No. 36.]

JOINT RESOLUTION asking Congress to grant relief to honorably discharged soldiers and sailors, and to the widows and orphans of deceased soldiers and sailors of the late war of the rebellion.

WHEREAS, The present Legislature has passed a resolution asking Congress to amend an act entitled " An act to enable honorably discharged soldiers and sailors, their widows and orphan children, to acquire homesteads on the public lands of the United States," so as to permit them to comply with the requirements of said act through agents;

AND WHEREAS, Numerous petitions of soldiers, sailors, and others have asked this Legislature to recommend the payment of two hundred dollars in lieu of said land; therefore

Resolved, That Congress be requested to pay to each honorably discharged soldier and sailor, their widows and orphans, two hundred dollars.

Resolved, That the Governor be and he hereby is requested to transmit a copy of the foregoing preamble and resolution to each of our Senators and Representatives in Congress.

Approved May 4, 1875.

[No. 37.]

JOINT RESOLUTION authorizing the Board of State Auditors to audit and pay the claims of the non-commissioned officers and musicians of the fifth, sixth, and seventh regiments of Michigan volunteer infantry, for services rendered in the month of August, eighteen hundred and sixty-one.

Be it resolved by the Senate and House of Representatives of the State of Michigan, That the Board of State Auditors is hereby authorized to audit the claims of the non-commissioned officers and musicians of the fifth, sixth, and seventh regiments of Michigan volunteer infantry, for services rendered the State in the month of August, eighteen hundred and sixty-one, and to draw his warrant upon the State Treasurer, payable out of the military fund, for the amounts to which he may find the said soldiers respectively are entitled under the orders and regulations in force at that time.

Be it further resolved, That the Adjutant General be required to transmit to the Auditor General copies of the records of his office bearing upon these cases, and that it shall be the duty of the Quartermaster General to present to the General Government the claim of the State for all outlays under this resolution.

This resolution shall take immediate effect.

Approved May 4, 1875.

CONCURRENT RESOLUTIONS.

[No. 1.]

CONCURRENT RESOLUTION to appoint Benjamin B. Baker of Ingham Postmaster of the Senate and House.

Resolved (the Senate concurring), That Benjamin B. Baker of Ingham be appointed postmaster of the Senate and House, to distribute all mail matter belonging to members of the Senate and House, at a compensation of three dollars per day.

Approved January 18, 1875.

[No. 2.]

CONCURRENT RESOLUTION appointing Mr. James W. King to compile and publish a manual.

Resolved (the Senate concurring), That James W. King be and he is hereby appointed to compile and publish, without delay, under the supervision of the committees on printing in the two Houses, when the same are appointed, a manual for the use of members and officers of both Houses in this and the next Legislature, and the State officers,—said manual to contain the Constitutions of the United States and of this State with all amendments thereto; the rules and joint rules of the Senate and House of Representatives of this State; a diagram of the Senate Chamber and Representative Hall; names, ages, occupation, and residence of members and officers of both Houses; a map showing the Congressional districts, the Judicial circuits of the State, the various Senatorial and Representative districts of the State, with the population thereof; a railroad map of the State; the votes for President in eighteen hundred and seventy-two and for Governor in eighteen hundred and seventy-four; the post-offices, newspapers, banking institutions, railroad routes, the latest statistics of the educational, charitable, reformatory, and penal institutions; the table of equalization for eighteen hundred and seventy-one; and such other statistical matter as is usually found in the work. The same to be printed and bound in the usual style by the State printer, and the compiler to receive for his services such sum as shall be fair and adequate; but no compensation shall be paid unless his copy shall be ready for the printer within twenty-five days from the passage of this resolution.

Approved January 18, 1875.

[No. 3.]

CONCURRENT RESOLUTION to urge the passage of bill by the Congress of the United States to equalize the bounties of soldiers and sailors.

Resolved (the Senate concurring), That our Senators and Representatives in Congress be and are hereby requested to introduce and urge the passage of a bill to equalize the bounties of the soldiers and sailors of the war for the suppression of the rebellion.

Resolved, That the Governor be requested to transmit copies of the foregoing resolution to each of our Senators and Representatives in Congress.

Approved February 2, 1875.

[No. 4.]

CONCURRENT RESOLUTION asking Congress to pass a bill granting one hundred and sixty acres of government land to soldiers and sailors, without regard to occupation.

Resolved (the Senate concurring), That our Senators and Representatives in Congress be and are hereby requested to introduce and urge the passage of a bill granting one hundred and sixty acres of government land to the surviving soldiers and sailors of the war for the suppression of the rebellion, without any restrictions connected therewith, in regard to occupation.

Resolved, That the Governor be requested to transmit copies of the foregoing resolution to each of our Senators and Representatives in Congress.

Approved February 4, 1875.

[No. 5.]

CONCURRENT RESOLUTION to arrange for the transportation of the committees to visit the State institutions.

Resolved by the House (the Senate concurring), That the chairman of the railroad committees of the Senate and House, together with Railroad Commissioner, be requested to act as a joint committee to arrange for the transportation of the committees on the asylums and other State institutions to visit and inspect the same.

Approved February 18, 1875.

[No. 6.]

CONCURRENT RESOLUTION asking Congress that pensions be granted to soldiers and widows of deceased soldiers of the war of eighteen hundred and twelve, who have been honorably discharged after five days' service.

WHEREAS, By act of Congress, approved February fourteen, eighteen hundred and seventy-one, the surviving soldiers of the war of eighteen hundred and twelve, who had served sixty days, and had been honorably discharged, and the widows of deceased soldiers who had rendered such service were granted pensions ;

AND WHEREAS, There is a class of soldiers of said war of eighteen hundred and twelve who do not come under the provisions of said act;

AND WHEREAS, Most of such soldiers, and the widows of such as are deceased, are in indigent circumstances; therefore

Resolved, (the Senate concurring), That in our opinion the provisions of said act should be so extended as to include all soldiers of the war of eighteen hundred and twelve who have been honorably discharged after five days' service, and the widows of deceased soldiers who had rendered such service, and that the rules in relation to the proof of marriages of such soldiers be modified;

Resolved, That the Governor be and he is hereby requested to cause a copy of the foregoing preamble and resolution to be forwarded to each of our Senators and Representatives now in Congress at Washington.

Approved March 10, 1875.

[No. 7.]

CONCURRENT RESOLUTION fixing the time of final adjournment.

Resolved (the Senate concurring), That from and after Thursday, the twenty-ninth day of April, the two Houses will transact no business other than for the President of the Senate and the Speaker of the House to sign enrolled bills for the approval of the Governor, and the entry of the same on the journals by the Secretary of the Senate and the Clerk of the House, and the time of final adjournment of this Legislature shall be on Tuesday, the fourth day of May, eighteen hundred and seventy-five, at twelve o'clock at noon of that day.

Filed in the office of the Secretary of State, April 27, 1875.

[No. 8.]

CONCURRENT RESOLUTION directing the Secretary of State to forward the laws, journals, and other documents to reporters of the press.

Resolved (the Senate concurring), That the Secretary of State be directed to forward the laws, journals, and all other documents of the present session of the Legislature to the reporters of the press who have been in attendance since the opening of the session.

Approved April 28, 1875.

[No. 9.]

CONCURRENT RESOLUTION instructing the Secretary of State to forward to each probate judge one copy of the general laws.

Resolved by the House of Representatives (the Senate concurring), That the Secretary of State be instructed, at the earliest practicable moment after the close of the present session of the Legislature, to forward to each probate judge one copy of all the general acts ordered to take immediate effect, said acts to be printed and bound in pamphlet form.

Approved April 28, 1875.

[No. 10.]
CONCURRENT RESOLUTION.

Resolved by the Senate (the House concurring), That the amount of postage stamps furnished by the postmaster at Lansing to the State printer, for the prepayment of postage on the daily journal, in compliance with a concurrent resolution heretofore passed at this session, be paid by the State Treasurer on the warrant of the Auditor General, to be drawn upon presentation of a bill for such postage, duly certified by said postmaster and by the foreman of the State bindery, showing that such postage stamps have been actually furnished and used for the purposes aforesaid.

Approved April 30, 1875.

[No. 11.]
CONCURRENT RESOLUTION authorizing the Secretary of the Senate and the Clerk of the House of Representatives to compile, index, and prepare for publication the journals and documents of the present Legislature.

Resolved (the Senate concurring), That the Secretary of the Senate and the Clerk of the House of Representatives be and they are hereby authorized and requested to compile and prepare for publication, and make indexes and superintend the publication of the journals and documents of the present Legislature, and when completed and certified to by the Secretary of State, they shall each be entitled to and receive for such services the sum of five hundred dollars.

Approved May 3, 1875.

NOTE.—The words and sentences enclosed in brackets in the foregoing laws and resolutions were in the engrossed copies, and passed by the Legislature, but not in the enrolled copies.

CERTIFICATE.

STATE DEPARTMENT, MICHIGAN, } ss.
      Secretary's Office,

I, E. G. D. HOLDEN, Secretary of State of the State of Michigan, do hereby certify that the date of the final adjournment of the regular session of the Legislature of this State, for the present year, was May fourth, one thousand eight hundred and seventy-five.

IN TESTIMONY WHEREOF, I have hereunto set my hand and affixed the Great
        Seal of the State of Michigan, at Lansing, this twentieth day of
[L. S.] May, in the year of our Lord one thousand eight hundred and
        seventy-five.

E. G. D. HOLDEN,
Secretary of State.

APPENDIX:

CONTAINING

CERTIFIED STATEMENTS OF BOARDS OF SUPERVISORS

RELATIVE TO THE

ERECTION OF NEW TOWNSHIPS;

ALSO,

STATE TREASURER'S ANNUAL REPORT

For the Year 1874.

APPENDIX.

———◆———

ALPENA COUNTY.

In the matter of the application of James Dempster, William Pulford, W. O. Dunn, Thomas Hunter, John Mulholland, Wm. J. Waltenbery, Louis Vansipe, James Welch, Patrick Eagan, William Boulton, Conrad Wessell, William Lewis, James Boulton, David Jones, William Lumsden, W. G. Dunham, James DeRush, Theodore Shultz, Jacob Burns, Rudolph Wintersheim, Charles Emeky, Andreas Mining, Hendrich Minning, Joseph Shant, Franz Neff, William Rezippa, Christian Yager, August Kowolsky, Charles T. Yager, Joseph Deogy, Michael Deogy, Antoine Jsdos, Michael Doias, Julius Paul, Wilhelm Fredricks, August Henry, Hoffman, Louis Preijitski, and Wm. B. Leonard, for the erection and organization of a new township.

It appearing to the board of supervisors that application has been made, and that notice thereof has been signed, posted up, and published, as in the manner required by law, and having duly considered the matter of said application, the board order and enact, that the territory described in said application, bounded as follows, to wit: towns number thirty-three north, ranges five (5), six (6), seven (7), and eight (8) east, and nine (9) east, all in the county of Presque Isle, in the State of Michigan, and towns number thirty-four north, of ranges number six (6), seven (7), and eight (8) east, in said county and State, be and the same is hereby erected into a township, to be called and known as the township of Presque Isle. The first annual township meeting thereof shall be held at the dwelling house of Lawrence Kowolsky, in said Presque Isle township, on the sixteenth day of August, in the year of our Lord, one thousand eight hundred and seventy-one, at ten o'clock in the forenoon, and at said meeting Wm. B. Leonard, Charles Ehmke and John Fisher, three electors of said township, shall be the persons whose duty it shall be to preside at such meeting, appoint a clerk, open and keep the polls, and exercise the same powers as the inspectors of election at any township meeting, as the law provides.

STATE OF MICHIGAN, } ss.
  Alpena county,

I, Cha's N. Cornell, clerk of the county aforesaid, and of the board of supervisors of said county, do hereby certify that the foregoing is a true and correct statement of the action of said board on the matters therein contained, and that the same has been compared by me with the original acts on file in my office, and that it is a true and correct transcript therefrom, and of the whole of said original act. And I further certify that the foregoing order of said board was passed by them at a meeting held at Alpena, in said county, on the twenty-ninth day of July, in the year of our Lord, one thousand eight hundred and seventy-one, as appears by their record.

In testimony whereof, I have hereunto set my hand, and affixed
[L. S.] the seal of the circuit court for said county, this six-
           teenth day of November, in the year of our Lord,
           one thousand eight hundred and seventy-four.
                    CHA'S N. CORNELL, *County Clerk.*

ANTRIM COUNTY.

In the matter of the application of E. G. Wiggins and thirty-four others, for the erection and organization of a new township.

It appearing to the board of supervisors that application has been made, and that notice thereof has been signed, posted up, and published, as in the manner provided by law, and a map having been furnished of the township affected by the proposed division, and having duly considered the matter of such application, this board do order and enact that the territory described in such application, that is to say, township twenty-nine (29) north, of range seven (7) west, be and the same is hereby detached from the township of Helena, and the same be and is hereby erected into a new township, to be called and known by the name of the "town-
Custar organ- ship of Custar." The first annual meeting therein shall be held
ized.   at the school-house of district number five, known as the "Mad-
dock's school-house," on the first Monday of April, in the year of our Lord, one thousand eight hundred and seventy-five, at nine o'clock in the forenoon, and that William B. Rush, Theodore Meade, and Darius P. McGuirk, three electors of said township, shall be the persons whose duty it shall be to preside at such meet-ing, appoint a clerk, open and keep the polls, and exercise the same powers and duties as inspectors of election at any township meet-ing, as the law provides.

STATE OF MICHIGAN, } ss.
  County of Antrim,

I, Cuthbert Parkinson, clerk of the county aforesaid, and of the board of supervisors thereof, do hereby certify the foregoing to be a true copy of the original record in my office, as enacted by the board of supervisors, at their meeting held at Elk Rapids, in said county, on the fourth day of January, one thousand eight hundred and seventy-five.

In testimony whereof I have hereunto set my hand and affixed [L. S.] the seal of the circuit court of said county, at Elk Rapids, this eighteenth day of January, in the year one thousand eight hundred and seventy-five.

CUTHBERT PARKINSON, *Clerk.*

In the matter of the application of William H. Jaquays and eighteen others, for the erection and organization of a new township.

It appearing to the board of supervisors that application has been made and that notices thereof has been signed, posted up, and published as in the manner provided by law, and a map having been furnished of the township affected by the proposed division, and having duly considered the matter of such application, this board do order and enact that the territory described in such application, that is to say: " Township thirty-one (31) north, of range six (6) west, be and the same is hereby detached from the township of Central Lake, in said county of Antrim, and that the same be and is hereby erected into a new township, to be called and known by the name Jordan organ-of the township of Jordan." The first annual meeting therein shall ized. be held at the house of William H. Jaquays on the first Monday of April, in the year of our Lord, one thousand eight hundred and seventy-five, at nine o'clock in the forenoon, and that William H. Jaquays, Gilbert H. Green, and Charles Cunningham, three electors of said township, shall be the persons whose duty it shall be to preside at such meeting, appoint a clerk, open and keep the polls, and exercise the same powers and duties as inspectors of election at any township meeting, as the law provides.

STATE OF MICHIGAN, ⎫
　County of Antrim, ⎬ ss.

I, Cuthbert Parkinson, clerk of the county aforesaid, and of the board of supervisors thereof, do hereby certify the foregoing to be a true copy of the original record in my office as enacted by the board of supervisors at their meeting held at Elk Rapids in said county on the fourth day of January, one thousand eight hundred and seventy-five.

In testimony whereof I have hereunto set my hand and affixed the seal of the circuit court of said county at [L. S.] Elk Rapids, this eighteenth day of January, in the year one thousand eight hundred and seventy-five.

CUTHBERT PARKINSON, *Clerk.*

In the matter of the application of H. W. Hitchcock and twenty others for the erection and organization of a new township.

It appearing to the board of supervisors that application has been made, and that notice thereof has been signed, posted up, and

published, as in the manner required by law, and a map having
been furnished of all the townships affected by the division, and
having duly considered the matter of said application, this board
do order and enact, that the territory described in said application,
that is to say, townships thirty (30) north, of ranges five (5) and
six (6) be and is hereby detached from the township of Forest
Home, in said county of Antrim, and be and the same is hereby
erected into a new township, to be called and known by the name
Chestonia or-ganized. of the "township of Chestonia." The first annual meeting therein shall be held at the house of William E. Stephens, on the first
Monday of April, in the year of our Lord, one thousand eight
hundred and seventy-five, at nine o'clock in the forenoon, and
that Thomas R. Van Wert, Peter T. Baldwin, and Edward Holm,
three electors of said township, shall be the persons whose duty it
shall be to preside at such meeting, appoint a clerk, open and keep
the polls, and exercise the same powers and duties as inspectors of
elections at any township meeting, as the law provides.

STATE OF MICHIGAN, } ss.
 County of Antrim, }

I, Cuthbert Parkinson, clerk of said county and of the board of
supervisors thereof, do hereby certify that I have carefully compared the foregoing copy of an order of said board with the record
thereof in my office, and that it is a true and correct transcript
thereof, and the whole of said original order; and I do further certify that the said order was made at the annual meeting of said
board held at the clerk's office in said county, on the twelfth day of
October, in the year of our Lord, one thousand eight hundred and
seventy-four.

In testimony whereof, I have hereunto set my hand, and
[L. S.]   affixed the seal of the circuit court for said county,
this twenty-sixth day of November, in the year of our
Lord, one thousand eight hundred seventy-four.
                        CUTHBERT PARKINSON,
                                    County Clerk.

In the matter of the application of J. C. Ball and forty-three others, for the erection and organization of a new township.

It appearing to the board of supervisors of Antrim county that
application has been made, and that notice thereof in writing has
been signed, posted up, and published, as in the manner required
by law, and a map having been furnished of all the townships
affected by the proposed division, and having duly considered the
matter of said application; therefore,

Resolved, That this board do order and enact that the territory
described in said application, that is to say: all that portion of
townships thirty (30) north, of ranges seven (7) and eight (8) west,
lying east of the centre of Intermediate Lake and the thread of
Intermediate River, be and the same is hereby detached from the

township of Forest Home, in said county of Antrim, and that the same be, and is hereby erected into a new township, to be called and known by the name of the "township of Kearney." The first annual meeting therein shall be held at the house of Zebediah B. Mocherman, on the first Monday of April, in the year of our Lord one thousand eight hundred and seventy-five, at nine o'clock in the forenoon, and that J. L. McKeen, J. E. Glines, and S. S. Drake, three electors of said township, shall be the persons whose duty it shall be to preside at such meeting, appoint a clerk, open and keep the polls, and exercise the same powers and duties as inspectors of election at any township meeting as the law provides.

Kearney organized.

STATE OF MICHIGAN, }
  County of Antrim, } ss.

I, Cuthbert Parkinson, clerk of the county aforesaid, and of the board of supervisors thereof, do hereby certify the foregoing to be a true copy of the original record in this office, as enacted by the board of supervisors at their meeting held at Elk Rapids, in said county, on the fourth day of January, one thousand eight hundred and seventy-five.

   In testimony whereof I have hereunto set my hand and
[L. S.] affixed the seal of the circuit court of said county at Elk
    Rapids, this eighteenth day of January, in the year one thousand eight hundred and seventy-five.

        CUTHBERT PARKINSON, *Clerk.*

BAY COUNTY.

In the matter of the application of Henry M. Smith, George Morse, Charles Carpenter, Alex. Baxter, Theodore Morse, Mortimer Noble, Rufus Morse, Jr., Charles Perry, Eben J. Church, Clayton Chatterson, Roderick McMullen, Frederick Vincent, John Mc-Mullen, George Eymer, John Beator, Niles McMullen, Rufus Morse, Sen'r.

WHEREAS, Application in writing has been made to the board of supervisors of Bay county in the State of Michigan by Henry M. Smith and sixteen others, above named freeholders of the township of Arenac, in said Bay county, for the organization or erection of the territory comprising town twenty (20) north, of range five (5) east, in said Bay county and now a part of the township of Arenac in said county, into a new township;

AND WHEREAS, It appears that notice of such application signed by the persons above named has been duly published and posted up, in the manner required by law, for four weeks immediately preceding the time of making said application, and a map of all the townships affected by the organization or erection of such new township showing the proposed alteration having been furnished to said board of supervisors; therefore,

Resolved, That the said territory described in said application is known as town (20) twenty north, of range five (5) east, in said Bay

Mason
organized.

county and now a part of said township of Arenac, be and the same is hereby erected into a new township to be called and known by the name of the township of Mason.

And be it further resolved, That the first township meeting thereof shall be held at the house of Theodore Morse in said township of Mason on Monday the fifth day of April, in the year of our Lord one thousand eight hundred and seventy-five, and Henry M. Smith, Fletcher E. Carscallen and Frederick Vincent, three electors of said township, be and they are hereby designated as the persons who shall preside at such meeting, appoint a clerk, open and keep the polls and exercise the same powers as the inspectors of election at any township meeting.

And the said Frederick Vincent is hereby appointed as the person to post the notices of such township meeting required by law.

The next township meeting to be held in the township of Arenac aforesaid shall be held at the village of Amer in said township of Arenac.

STATE OF MICHIGAN, }
  County of Bay, } ss.

I, Henry A. Braddock, clerk of said county and of the board of supervisors thereof, do hereby certify that I have carefully compared the foregoing copy of a resolution adopted by said board October fifteenth, eighteen hundred and seventy-four, with the original now of record in my office, and that it is a true transcript therefrom and of the whole therof.

In testimony whereof I have hereunto set my hand and [L. S.] affixed the seal of the circuit court for said county, at Bay City, February twenty-third, one thousand eight hundred and seventy-five.

H. A. BRADDOCK, *Clerk.*

In the matter of the application of Descum Culver, A. N. Culver, J. W. Culver, Dwight Gibbs, H. A. Wright, John Pernie, F. Beebe, W. Beebe, J. Beebe, Wm. Lacey, Aldney Rust, D. W. Rust, John F. Rust, Amasa Rust, and William Westover, for the erection of a new township.

WHEREAS, Application in writing has been made to the board of supervisors of Bay county, in the State of Michigan, by D. Culver and fourteen others above named, freeholders of the township of Clayton in said Bay county, for the organization or erection of the territory comprising town twenty (20) north, of range three (3) east, in said Bay county, and now a part of the township of Clayton in said county, into a new township;

AND WHEREAS, It appears that notice of such application, signd by the persons above named, has been duly published and posted up in the manner required by law, for four weeks immediately preceding the time of making said application, and a map of all the townships affected by the organization or erection of such new

township, showing the proposed alterations, having been furnished
to the said board of supervisors; therefore,

Resolved, That the said territory described in said application
and known as town twenty (20) north, of range three (3) east, in
said Bay county, and now a part of said township of Clayton, be
and the same is hereby erected into a new township, to be called *Moffitt organized.*
and known by the name of the township of Moffitt;

And be it further resolved, That the first annual township meeting thereof shall be held at the store of Alvin N. Culver, at Culver,
in said township of Moffitt, on Monday, the fifth day of April,
in the year of our Lord one thousand eight hundred and seventy-
five, and John Pernie, Alvin N. Culver, and John Beebe, three
electors of said township, be and they are hereby designated as the
persons who shall preside at such meeting, appoint a clerk, open
and keep the polls, and exercise the same powers as the inspectors
of election at any township meeting; and the said John Pernie is
hereby appointed as the person to post the notices of such township meeting required by law.

The next township meeting to be held in the township of Clayton, aforesaid, shall be held at the school-house in district number
one in said township of Clayton.

STATE OF MICHIGAN, }
  County of Bay, } ss.

I, Henry A. Braddock, clerk of said county and of the board of
supervisors thereof, do hereby certify that I have carefully compared the foregoing copy of a resolution of said board, adopted
October fifteen, one thousand eight hundred and seventy-four,
with the original now of record in my office, and that it is a true
transcript therefrom and of the whole thereof.

    In testimony whereof, I have hereunto set my hand and
[L. S.] affixed the seal of the circuit court for said county, at
    Bay City, February twenty-third, one thousand eight
    hundred and seventy-five.

           H. A. BRADDOCK, *Clerk.*

HOUGHTON COUNTY.

In the matter of the application of William H. Morrison and seventeen others, for the erection and organization of a new township.

It appearing to the board of supervisors that application has
been made, and that notice thereof has been signed, posted, and
published, as in the manner provided by law, and having duly considered the matter of such application, the board order and enact
that the territory described in such application, as follows, to wit:
town fifty north, of range number thirty west, and towns numbered forty-seven, forty-eight, forty-nine, and fifty north, of range
number thirty-one west, be and the same is hereby erected into a
township to be called and known by the name of the township of

Spurr. The first annual meeting thereof shall be held at the office of the Spurr Mine, on the twenty-seventh day of June, in the year of our Lord one thousand eight hundred and seventy-four, and at said meeting L. H. Cobb, John McChrystal, and James Alward, three electors of said township, shall be the persons whose duty it shall be to preside at such meeting, appoint a clerk, open and keep the polls, and exercise the same powers as the inspectors of election at any township meeting, as the law provides, and that L. H. Cobb is appointed to post the notices of said election.

STATE OF MICHIGAN, } ss.
County of Houghton,

I, Roland H. Brelsford, clerk of the county aforesaid, and of the board of supervisors of said county, do hereby certify that the foregoing is a true and correct statement of the action of said board on the matters therein contained, and that the same has been compared by me with the original act on file in my office, and that it is a true and correct transcript therefrom and of the whole of said original act, and I further certify that the foregoing order of said board was passed by them at a meeting held at the village of Houghton, in said county, on the twenty-second day of May, in the year of our Lord one thousand eight hundred and seventy-four.

In testimony whereof I have hereunto set my hand and
[L. S.]   affixed the seal of the circuit court for said county, this twelfth day of June, in the year of our Lord, one thousand eight hundred and seventy-four.
ROLAND H. BRELSFORD,
County Clerk.

In the matter of the application of James B. Smith and sixteen others, for the erection and organization of a new township.

It appearing to the board of supervisors that application has been made, and that notice thereof has been signed, posted, and published, as in the manner provided by law, and having duly considered the matter of such application, the board order and enact that the territory described in such application as follows, to-wit: township fifty-three north, of range twenty-nine west, towns fifty-one, fifty-two, and fifty-three north, of range number thirty west, and towns fifty-one, fifty-two, and fifty-three north, of range number thirty-one west, be and the same is hereby erected into a township to be called and known by the name of the township of
Arvon. The first annual meeting thereof shall be held at the office of the Huron Bay Slate Company on the twenty-seventh day of June, in the year of our Lord one thousand eight hundred and seventy-four, and at said meeting Walfred Been, John D. Williams and John Thomas, three electors of said township, shall be the persons whose duty it shall be to preside at such meeting, appoint a clerk, open and keep the polls, and exercise the same

powers as the inspectors of election at any township meeting, as the law provides, and that John Thomas is appointed to post the notices of said election.

STATE OF MICHIGAN, }
County of Houghton, } ss.

I, Roland H. Brelsford, clerk of the county aforesaid and of the board of supervisors of said county, do hereby certify that the foregoing is a true and correct statement of the action of said board on the matters therein contained, and that the same has been compared by me with the original act on file in my office, and that it is a true and correct transcript therefrom and of the whole of said original act. And I further certify that the foregoing order of said board was passed by them at a meeting held at the village of Houghton, in said county, on the twenty-second day of May, in the year of our Lord one thousand eight hundred and seventy-four, as appears by their record

[L. S.] In testimony whereof I have hereunto set my hand and affixed the seal of the circuit court for said county this twelfth day of June, in the year of our Lord one thousand eight hundred and seventy-four.

ROLAND H. BRELSFORD, *County Clerk.*

ISABELLA COUNTY.

To the Honorable Secretary of State:

At an adjourned meeting of the board of supervisors for the county of Isabella and State of Michigan, held at the village of Mt. Pleasant, in said county, on the thirteenth day of April, in the year of our Lord one thousand eight hundred and seventy, in the matter of the application of Rufus F. Glass and eleven others, for the erection and organization of a new township.

It appearing to the board of supervisors that application has been made, and that notice thereof has been duly signed, posted, and published, as is required by law, and having duly considered the matter of said application, the board order and enact that the territory described as follows, to-wit: town number sixteen (16) north, of range number five (5) west; also, section six (6), in township fifteen (15) north, of range number four (4) west, be and the same is hereby erected into a township to be called and known by the name of the township of Gilmore. The first township meeting thereof shall be held at the house of Rufus F. Glass, on north-east quarter of section twenty-four, in township sixteen north, of range five west, on Thursday, the twenty-eighth day of April, eighteen hundred and seventy, at ten o'clock A. M., and at such meeting Rufus F. Glass, Amos F. Albright, and Jesse Wood, three electors of said township, shall be the persons whose duty it shall be to preside at such meeting, appoint a clerk, open and keep the polls and exercise the same powers as inspectors of election at any township meeting as the law prescribes.

STATE OF MICHIGAN, ⎱ ss.
  County of Isabella, ⎰

I, D. E. Lyon, clerk of said county and of the board of supervisors thereof, do hereby certify the foregoing to be a true copy of the original record in this office, as enacted by said board at an adjourned meeting held on the thirteenth day of April, in the year of our Lord one thousand eight hundred and seventy.

In testimony whereof I have hereunto set my hand and
[L. S.]   affixed the seal of the circuit court at Mt. Pleasant, this thirteenth day of November, in the year of our Lord one thousand eight hundred and seventy-four.

D. E. LYON, *Clerk.*

———

At the annual meeting of the board of supervisors for the county of Isabella and State of Michigan, held at the village of Mt. Pleasant, in said county, on the fourteenth day of October, in the year of our Lord one thousand eight hundred and seventy-four, Mr. Voorhees offered the following:

Resolved by the Board of Supervisors of Isabella county, Michigan, That in the matter of the application of Wm. M. Peterson and others, for the erection and organization of a new township, that application has been signed, posted up, and published as in the manner required by law, and having duly considered the matter of said application the board orders and enacts that the territory described in said application, bounded as follows, to wit : Congressional township number fourteen (14), north of range five (5) west, in Isabella county, Michigan, be and the same is hereby erected into a township to be called and known by the name of Deerfield. The first annual township meeting thereof shall be held at the house of Joseph S. Brazee, in said township, on Monday the fifth day of April, in the year of our Lord one thousand eight hundred and seventy-five, at nine o'clock, A. M., and at said meeting William M. Peterson, Frederick M. Sanderson and Malden R. Beach, three electors of said township, shall be the persons whose duties it shall be to preside at such meeting, appoint a clerk, open and keep the pools, and exercise the same powers as the inspectors of election at any township meeting as the law requires.

[margin note:] Deerfield organized.

Mr. Bogan demanded the yeas and nays on the adoption of the above resolution.

The resolution was then adopted by yeas and nays as follows :

Yeas—Messrs. Bogan, Bown, Brodie, Broomfield, Davis, Doxsie, Estee, Fordyce, Grinnell, Mattison, Richardson and Voorhees—12.

Nays—0.

STATE OF MICHIGAN, ⎱ ss.
  County of Isabella, ⎰

I, D. E. Lyon, clerk of said county and of the board of supervisors thereof, do hereby certify the foregoing to be a true copy of the original record in this office of the resolution organizing the township of Deerfield, in said county, at a session of said board, held on the fourteenth day of October, in the year of our Lord one thousand eight hundred and seventy-four.

In witness whereof I have hereunto set my hand and
[L. S.]   affixed the seal of the circuit court, at Mt. Pleasant, this thirteenth day of November, in the year of our Lord one thousand eight hundred and seventy-four.

D. E. LYON, *Clerk.*

KALKASKA COUNTY.

In the matter of the application of Allen E. Burnham and others for the erection and organization of a new township.

It appearing to the board of supervisors that application has been made as in manner required by law, and having duly considered the matter of said application, the board order and enact that the territory described in said application, bounded as follows, to wit: All of township twenty-eight, north of range six west, be and the same is hereby erected into a township, to be called and known by the name of Cold Springs. The first township meeting Cold Springs organized. thereof shall be held at the house of A. E. Burnham, on the first Monday in April, in the year of our Lord, one thousand eight hundred and seventy-four, at the usual time of holding township meetings. At said meeting, A. E. Burnham, Andrew Croy, and W. H. Stoddard, three electors of said township, shall be the persons whose duty it shall be to preside at said meeting, appoint a clerk, open and keep the polls, exercise the same powers as the inspectors of election at any township meeting, as provided by law.

STATE OF MICHIGAN, }
  County of Kalkaska, } ss.

I, O. S. Curtis, clerk of said county and of the board of supervisors thereof, do hereby certify that I have carefully compared the foregoing copy of an order of said board with the record thereof in my office, and the same is a true copy thereof; and I do further certify that the said order was made at the annual meeting of said board, held at the court house in said county on the thirteenth day of October, in the year of our Lord one thousand eight hundred and seventy-three.

In testimony whereof, I have hereunto set my hand and
[L. S.]   affixed the seal of the circuit court for the said county, this twenty-second day of May, in the year of our Lord one thousand eight hundred and seventy-four.

O. S. CURTIS,
County Clerk.

KEWEENAW COUNTY.

SPECIAL MEETING.

Monday, March 12, 1866.

A special meeting of the board of supervisors of Keweenaw county, was held on Monday, March the twelfth, in the year of our Lord one thousand eight hundred and sixty-six, at two o'clock P. M., at the county clerk's office in Eagle River.

Meeting called per request of Samuel W. Hill, F. A. Cleveland, and John Alexander, more than two-thirds of the supervisors of the county.

Present F. A. Cleveland of Sibley, Henry Selby of Copper Harbor, Samuel W. Hill of Grant, A. C. Davis of Eagle Harbor, John Alexander of Houghton, Josiah Halls of Clifton, supervisors of the county of Keweenaw.

The meeting was called to order by John Alexander, Esq., chairman of the board.

Josiah Halls, Esq., member from Clifton, presented a petition to the board from twelve freeholders of the township of Eagle Harbor, praying that certain portions of the township of Eagle Harbor, delineated and shown by certain maps now before the board, may be erected and formed into a new township, to be known as the township of " Sherman."

On motion of Samuel W. Hill, supported by F. A. Cleveland,

Resolved, That in the matter of the application of the Central Mining Company, C. B. Petrie, Northwestern Mining Company, Pittsburgh and Boston Mining Company, Susan A. Hill, Pennsylvania Mining Company, Delaware Mining Company, Samuel W. Hill, Lawrence Madigan, Charles Kingston, Johnson Beaumont, W. L. P. Wheeler, Thomas Otis, George H. Satterlee, and Phillip R. Roberts, Jr., for the erection and organization of a new township

It appearing to the board of supervisors that application has been made, and that notice thereof has been published, signed, and posted up, as in the manner required by law, and having duly considered the matter of said application, the board,

Order and Enact, That the territory described in said application, as follows, to-wit: All that part of the township of Eagle Harbor, county of Keweenaw, and State of Michigan, which is embraced in the east fractional half of township fifty-six (56) north, the east half of township fifty-seven (57) north, the whole of section twenty-two (22), twenty-three (23), twenty-four (24), twenty-five (25), twenty-six (26), twenty-seven (27), thirty-four (34), thirty-five (35), and thirty-six (36), in township fifty-eight (58) north, all lying and being in range thirty-one (31) west; also the west fractional half of township fifty-six (56) north, of range thirty (30) west; and all fractions nineteen (19), twenty (20), twenty-one (21), twenty-eight (28), twenty-nine (29), thirty (30), thirty-one (31), thirty-two (32), thirty-three (33), in township fifty-seven (57) north, of range thirty (30) west, be and the same is hereby erected into a township to be called and known by the name of the township of Sherman. Sherman organized.

The first annual meeting thereof shall be held at the schoolhouse on the Central Mining Company's location in said new township, on the first Monday in April next, at nine A. M. to five o'clock P. M., and that at the said meeting George H. Satterlee, William Tonkin, and W. S. P. Wheeler, three electors of said township, shall be the persons whose duty it shall be to preside at such meeting, appoint a clerk, open and keep the polls, and exercise the same powers as the inspectors of election at any such township meeting as the law provides.

On motion of A. C. Davis supported by Henry Selby,

Resolved, That this meeting be adjourned without day.

JOHN VIVIAN,
Clerk of the Board.

STATE OF MICHIGAN, } ss.
County of Keweenaw, }

I, Joseph Retallack, Jr., clerk of the circuit court for said county, do hereby certify that the above and foregoing is a true and compared copy of an original entry, now on record in the office of the clerk of said county and court, and the whole of such original record.

> In testimony whereof, I have hereunto set my hand and affixed the seal of said court, at the village of Eagle
> [L. S.] River, this twenty-fourth day of February, in the year of our Lord one thousand eight hundred and seventy-five.

JOSEPH RETALLACK, JR., *Clerk.*

LAKE COUNTY.

In the matter of the application of Wm. Baker, L. M. Little, L. R. Scott, and others, for the erection and organization of a new township.

It appearing to the board of supervisors that application has been made as in the manner required by law, and having duly considered the matter of said application, the board order and enact that the territory described in said application, bounded and described as follows, to wit: All of town twenty north, of range thirteen west, be and the same is hereby erected into a township to be called and known by the name of the township of Eden. The first township meeting shall be held at the residence of William Baker, on the first Monday in April, in the year of our Lord one thousand eight hundred and seventy-five, at the usual time of holding township meetings. At said meeting Wm. Baker, U. C. Smith, and L. M. Little, three electors of said township, shall be the persons whose duty it shall be to preside at said meeting, appoint a clerk, open and keep the polls, and exercise the same powers as the inspectors of election at any Eden organized.

township meeting, as provided by law, and that Wm. Baker post
the notices of the time and place of holding said meeting.

Adopted, by yeas and nays, as follows:

Ayes—J. J. Robertson, E. R. Ottinger, A. Allen, Geo. W. Town-
send, Geo. W. Clark, I. D. Blood, Wm. Wood, Harley Hazen, and
James Blood.

Nays—None.

STATE OF MICHIGAN, } ss.
   County of Lake,

I, David A. Lathrop, clerk of said county, and of the board of
supervisors thereof, do hereby certify that I have carefully compared the foregoing copy of an order of said board with the record
thereof in my office, and the same is a true copy thereof; and I do
further certify that the said order was made at an adjourned meeting of said board, held at the court room in said county, on the
twenty-ninth day of December, in the year of our Lord, one
thousand eight hundred and seventy-four.

      In testimony whereof I have hereunto set my hand
[L. S.]   and affixed the seal of the circuit court for the said
        county this thirty-first day of December, in the year
        of our Lord one thousand eight hundred and seventy-
        four.

                    DAVID A. LATHROP,
                            County Clerk.

LEELANAW COUNTY.

STATE OF MICHIGAN, } ss.
   Leelanau county,

At the annual meeting of the board of supervisors for the
county of Leelanau, held at the county clerk's office, in the village
of Northport, on the twelfth day of October, in the year of our
Lord, one thousand eight hundred and seventy-four, the following business was transacted, to-wit:

The following petition was presented to the Board, to-wit:

*To the Board of Supervisors of the county of Leelanau and State
of Michigan:*

We, the undersigned, freeholders of the township of Centreville,
your petitioners, request and pray, that you will detach from the
township of Centreville the following territory and organize the
same into a new township, to be called and known as the township of Leland, to-wit: The fractional townships thirty (30)
and thirty-one (31) north of range twelve (12) west. A map is
herewith presented and attached, showing how the townships
will be affected and situated.

Dated Centreville, this 8th day of September, 1874.

Freeholders residing in the part to remain as Centreville:

Barney Connell, A. Mason, Jos. Ganthier, A. Schaub, T. J.
Smith, Raphael Lemoux, Thos. Horton, Frank Payette, Noel Cou-

turier, J. R. Haines, Cyrille Harper, P. O'Connell, A. Payette, Peter Payette.

Freeholders residing in the part to be set off:

C. F. Reynolds, A. Ganthier, Alex. Bush, Geo. Thompson, S. Pickard, Cornel Jones, John Dolton, J. C. Glenn, John O'Brien, G. Verfurth, J. E. Lederle, P. A. Cordes, E. A. Doty, W. W. Barton, John Porter.

The following notice was also presented to the Board, to-wit:

Notice to all whom it may concern:

Notice is hereby given, that an application will be presented to the board of supervisors of Leelanau county, Michigan, at their annual meeting to be held on the second Monday of October, one thousand eight hundred and seventy-four, praying them to detach from the township of Centreville the following territory and organize from the same into a new township, to be called and known as the township of Leland, to-wit: The fractional township thirty (30) and thirty-one (31) north of range twelve (12) west. A map showing how the township will be affected and situated will accompany the application. Leland organized.

September 8, 1874.

Signed by Barney Connell and thirteen others, freeholders that will remain in Centreville, and signed by C. F. Reynolds and fourteen others, freeholders residing in the part to be set off.

Also a map of the township of Centreville, showing the territory sought to be set off with foregoing petition, notice, and affidavit of publication of notice.

On motion, *Resolved,* That the said petition be granted, and that a township to be called Leland be erected, and to consist of the following territory, to-wit: Fractional townships thirty (30) and thirty-one (31) north, of range twelve (12) west, except that part of sections twenty-five (25) and thirty-six (36) of town thirty (30) north of range twelve (12) west, lying on the east side of Carp Lake.

On motion, John I. Miller, John Porter and G. Verfurth were appointed as Inspectors to preside at the first annual town meeting in the township to be called Leland, to be held in the village of Leland, on the first Monday in April, in the year of our Lord one thousand eight hundred and seventy-five, at the store of S. Pickard.

On motion, It was voted that the next annual meeting of the township of Centreville shall be held at the house of Urban Barnhart, on the first Monday in April, in the year of Lord one thousand eight hundred and seventy-five.

I hereby certify that the foregoing is a correct copy of the proceedings as appears upon the records now in this office.

Witness my hand and seal of office, at Northport, this sixth
[L. S.]   day of November, in the year of our Lord one thousand eight hundred and seventy-four.

A. JOHN, County Clerk.

48

MANISTEE COUNTY.

At the annual meeting of the board of supervisors for Manistee county, held at the county clerk's office in the village of Manistee, in said county on the twelfth day of October, in the year of our Lord one thousand eight hundred and sixty-eight, at ten o'clock A. M.

In the matter of Thomas N. Coply and others.

It appearing to the board of supervisors that application has been made and that notice thereof has been signed, posted up, and published as in the manner required by law, and having duly considered the matter of said application, the board order and enact that the territory described in said application, described as follows, to wit:— town twenty-four (24) north, of range thirteen (13) west, be and the same is hereby erected into a new township to be called and known by the name of Cleon. The first annual meeting thereof shall be held at the house of Thomas N. Coply, on the first Monday of April next, at ten o'clock A. M. And at said meeting M. P. Grinnell, E. A. Gilbert and Jacob Sears, three electors of said township, shall be the persons whose duty it shall be to preside at such meeting, appoint a clerk, open and keep the polls, and exercise the same powers as the inspectors of elections at any township meeting as the law provides.

Cleon
organised.

LATHROP S. ELLIS, Chairman.

JOHN M. DENNETT, *Clerk pro tem.*

STATE OF MICHIGAN, } ss.
County of Manistee, }

I, James H. Golden, clerk of the county of Manistee and of the courts thereof, do hereby certify that I have compared the foregoing copy of enactment of the board of supervisors of Manistee county with the original of record in my office, and that the same is a correct transcript therefrom and the whole of such original.

Witness my hand and the seal of the circuit court for
[L. S.]   the county of Manistee, at the city of Manistee this
fourteenth day of April, in the year of our Lord one
thousand eight hundred and seventy-five.

JAMES H. GOLDEN, Clerk.

MASON COUNTY.

At the annual meeting of the board of supervisors of Mason county, commenced and held at the court house, in the city of Ludington, the twelfth day of October, in the year of our Lord one thousand eight hundred and seventy-four, the following action was had in the matter of the new township of Eden:

To the honorable Board of Supervisors of Mason county:

Your committee appointed to examine into the matter of erecting a new township, to be called "Eden," would respectfully recom-

mend that prayer of the petitioners be granted, the same being
signed by the number of freeholders required by law, and the proper
notice having been published. We would therefore recommend the
erection of a new township, to be called Eden, from so much of the Eden organized.
present townships of Amber and Riverton as is embraced in the
territory described as township seventeen north, of range sixteen
west, and township eighteen north, of range sixteen west, of the
State of Michigan, two townships, according to the United States
survey, as shown by the map accompanying this report.

Your committee would further recommend that the first township meeting therein be held at the school-house in said township
known as the "Peter Robinson school-house," on the first Monday
of April, in the year of our Lord one thousand eight hundred and
seventy-five, and that William W. Bates, George Hall, and Cor-
nelius Hall be appointed and empowered to perform the duties
and exercise the powers of inspectors of election at such township
meeting.

Respectfully,

N. L. BIRD,
W. A. BAILEY, } *Committee.*
B. J. GOODSELL,

Which report was accepted and committee discharged, and thereupon, on motion of Supervisor Lampman, the foregoing was adopted to be and stand as the action of this board, all the members
voting therefor.

I, Charles T. Sawyer, clerk of said board of supervisors, and
clerk of the circuit court of said county, do hereby certify that I
have compared the foregoing and annexed copy from proceedings
of the said board of supervisors with the original remaining of
record in my office, and that the annexed is a true copy of said
original, and of the whole thereof.

Witness my hand and the seal of the circuit court of Ma-
[L. S.] son county, this twenty-third day of February, in the
year of our Lord one thousand eight hundred and
seventy-five.

CHARLES T. SAWYER, *Clerk.*

MECOSTA COUNTY.

In the matter of the petition of Nicholas Thieson and others, for
the erection and organization of a new township.

It appearing to the board of supervisors that application has
been made and that notice thereof has been signed, posted up, and
published, as in the manner required by law, and having duly considered the matter of said application, the board order and enact
that the territory described in said application, to-wit: Congressional township number fifteen north of range number eight
west, be and the same is hereby erected into a township, to be Martiny
called and known by the name of the township of Martiny. organized.

The first annual township meeting thereof shall be held at the
school house in district number three, in said township, on Monday, the fifth day of April, in the year of our Lord one thousand
eight hundred and seventy-five, at nine o'clock in the forenoon;
and at said meeting John Martiny, Nicholas Thieson and George
Shields, three electors of said township, shall be the persons whose
duty it shall be to preside at such meeting, appoint a clerk, open
and keep the polls, and exercise the same powers as the inspectors
of election at any township meeting, as the law provides.

STATE OF MICHIGAN, ┐ ss.
 County of Mecosta, ┘

I, Charlie Gay, clerk of the county aforesaid and of the board of
supervisors thereof, do hereby certify that I have carefully compared the foregoing copy of an order of said board with the record
thereof in my office, as clerk of said board, and the copy thereto
attached of the map or survey of the new township of Martiny, in
my office, and furnished to said board on the application for the
erection and organization of said township, and that said copies
are true copies. And I further certify that the foregoing order of
said board was passed by them at their meeting held at the city
of Big Rapids, in said county, on the twentieth day of January,
eighteen hundred and seventy-five, as appears by their record.

      In testimony whereof, I have hereunto set my hand and
[L. S.]   affixed the seal of the circuit court of said county
      this twenty-third day of January, eighteen hundred
      and seventy-five.

                              CHARLIE GAY, *County Clerk.*

MUSKEGON COUNTY.

STATE OF MICHIGAN, ┐ ss.
 Muskegon County, ┘

At a regular session of the board of supervisors for the county
of Muskegon, in the State aforesaid, commenced and held at the
court house in the city of Muskegon, in said county, on the
twelfth day of October, in the year of our Lord one thousand
eight hundred and seventy-four, afterward and the fifteenth day of
October, eighteen hundred and seventy-four, the same being one
of the days of said regular session, among other things, the following appears of record on the journal of proceedings of said
board, to wit: A petition signed by A. P. Horton and thirty-seven
others, citizens of Laketon, was presented to the board, asking said
board to divide the town aforesaid and create a new town from
that portion of said township lying south of the channel of Muskegon Lake.

A remonstrance against such division, signed by John Ruddi-
man and twenty-two others, was also presented.

On motion of Alpheus G. Smith, supported by B. F. Dow, a
committee of three members was appointed by the chair, before

which the opposing parties might appear and be heard, said committee being composed of Messrs. Heald, Marvin, and Rowe; and on the sixteenth day of said October, the said committee reported as follows, viz.: Your committee on the division of the township of Laketon, would respectfully report in favor of granting the prayer of the petitioners.

> JOSEPH HEALD,
> HORACE N. MARVIN, } *Committee.*
> MILO ROWE,

On motion of Mr. Dow, supported by Mr. Whitney, moved that the report be accepted and committee discharged. Carried.

Mr. Dow, supported by Mr. Whitney, moved the matter be postponed until the January session. The motion was voted on by townships and declared not carried.

A motion to adopt the report was made, supported, and then withdrawn, when it was again moved to postpone until the January session. Carried.

At the adjourned session held in January, eighteen hundred and seventy-five, and on the sixth day of said month, the following appears of record as aforesaid, viz.: Mr. Alpheus G. Smith presented the following:

Resolved, That the prayers of the petitioners of the township of Laketon for a division of said township, postponed from the October session, be granted, and that all that portion of said township lying south of the channel of Muskegon Lake, be and the same is hereby organized into a new township, to be known as the township of Lakeside, and that the first meeting in said new township shall be held on the first Monday of April, in the year of our Lord one thousand eight hundred and seventy-five, at the office of A. V. Mann & Co., and that John W. Moon, Asa M. Allen, and Frank H. Smith, be designated to preside at said first meeting. The first township meeting of Laketon shall be held at the office of Farr, Dutcher & Co., on the first Monday of April, in the year of our Lord one thousand eight hundred and seventy-five, and that Alfred P. Horton, Clark N. Storrs, and Joseph E. Plews, are hereby designated to preside at said first meeting. The motion was supported by Mr. McEwing, when the vote was taken by townships, and as follows, to wit:

Yeas—Dalton, Egelston, Fruitland, Fruitport, Laketon, Montague, Muskegon, Muskegon city, first ward; Muskegon city, second ward; Muskegon city, third ward; Norton, Whitehall, White River.

Nays—Blue Lake, Casinovia, Cedar Creek, Holton, Moorland, Ravenna.

Absent or not voting.—Fourth ward, city.

The resolution was declared adopted.

> STATE OF MICHIGAN,   }
> *Muskegon County, Clerk's Office,* } ss.

I, David McLaughlin, clerk of said county, do hereby certify that the above and foregoing is a true and correct copy of the action of said board of supervisors, as therein set forth. I have compared the same with the record thereof, and that it is a true transcript therefrom and of the whole thereof.

Witness my hand and seal of said county, the twenty-
[L. S.]   seventh day of January, in the year of our Lord one
thousand eight hundred and seventy-five.

DAVID McLAUGHLIN,
County Clerk.

The following resolution was presented, viz:

Resolved, That the township of Oceana, in this county, be divided in accordance with the petitions presented to this board, and that two towns be erected therefrom, viz: The township of Montague to consist of sections one, two, three, four, five, six, seven. eight, nine, ten, eleven, twelve, fifteen, sixteen, seventeen, eighteen, nineteen, fractional sections twenty, twenty-one, twenty-nine, section thirty, fractional section thirty-one, and all that part of section thirty-two lying westerly of White Lake, all in town twelve north, of range seventeen west, also the northwest fractional quarter of section six, in town eleven north, of range seventeen west; and that George E. Dowling, Joseph Heald, and Malcolm Hendrie are designated as inspectors of election at the first meeting of said township, which election shall be held on the tenth day of April, in the year of our Lord one thousand eight hundred and seventy-four, at the engine house in Montague. The other new township to be called Whitehall, and to consist of sections thirteen, fourteen, fractional section twenty-two, section twenty-three, twenty-four, fractional section twenty-five, section twenty-six, fractional section twenty-seven, twenty-eight, all that part of section thirty-two lying easterly of White Lake, fractional section thirty-three, section thirty-four, thirty-five, and fractional section thirty-six, all in township number twelve north, of range number seventeen west; and that Hiram E. Staples, Albert Mears, and Henry Slater are designated as inspectors of the first election of said township, which election shall be held on the tenth day of April next, at the Cosmopolitan Hotel, in the village of Whitehall.

A. G. SMITH.

Supported by Daniel Upton.

The motion to adopt the foregoing was voted on by townships, all voting aye, except the towns of Fruitland and Oceana voting nay, and Casinovia absent.

The resolution was declared adopted.

STATE OF MICHIGAN, }
County of Muskegon, } ss.

I, David McLaughlin, clerk of said county, do hereby certify that the above and foregoing is a true transcript of the record of the board of supervisors, on the division of the township of Oceana, and erecting therefrom the towns of Whitehall and Montague, on the twenty-fourth day of March, eighteen hundred and seventy-four, and of the whole thereof, as the same appears in my

(margin note: Montague organized.)

(margin note: Whitehall organized.)

office, in liber two of journal of proceedings of said board, at pages one hundred and sixty-six and one hundred and sixty-seven.

Witness my hand and the seal of said county, at my office
[L S.]   in the city of Muskegon, the fourth day of May, in the year of our Lord one thousand eight hundred and seventy four.

DAVID McLAUGHLIN,
County Clerk.

STATE OF MICHIGAN, }
  Muskegon County, } ss.

At a regular session of the board of supervisors for the county of Muskegon, commenced and held at the clerk's [office] of the village of Muskegon, in said county, on Monday, the eleventh day of October, in the year of our Lord one thousand eight hundred and sixty-nine; afterward, and during said session, the following appears in the journal of the proceedings of said board, to-wit:

A petition was presented for the erection of a new township, to *Fruitland organized.* be called Fruitland, out of the territory in town eleven, seventeen west, lying south of White Lake. The subject was referred to a committee consisting of Hiram S. Tyler, James P. Utter, and Israel E. Carlton.

Wednesday, October 13, 1874.

Mr. Tyler, chairman of the committee on the erection of a new town, reported as follows:

Your committeee, to whom was referred the petition of the citizens of township number eleven north, of range seventeen west, respectfully recommend the prayer of the petitioners be granted. On motion the report was accepted, and on like motion adopted.

Witness my hand and official seal, November twenty-third,
[L. S.] one thousand eight hundred and seventy-four.

DAVID McLAUGHLIN,
County Clerk.

SAGINAW COUNTY.

COURT HOUSE, SAGINAW, }
October 22, 1874. }

Tenth day of the regular session of the board of supervisors of Saginaw County.

Board met pursuant to adjournment.

Hon. John Barter in the chair.

Roll called and a quorum present.

Supervisor Roeser offered the following:

To the Honorable Board of Supervisors of Saginaw County:

GENTLEMEN:—Your committee to whom was referred the application of Colin McBratnie and eighteen others, to divide the township of Swan Creek and organize a new township out of a part of the territory thereof to be called "James," and the remonstrance against the division of said township, signed by Frank Crosby and twenty-five others, would beg leave respectfully to report that they have had the said application and remonstrance under consideration, and heard the parties interested for and against the division of said town, and would report in favor of granting the prayer of the applicants, and recommend the adoption of the following preamble and resolution, to-wit:

WHEREAS, Application signed by fourteen freeholders of the townships of Swan Creek, being town eleven north of range three east, and part of town eleven north of range four east, and part of town twelve north of range four east, has been duly presented to this board, praying to erect and provide for the organization of a new township, to be called the township of " James," to consist of the territory described as follows, viz: Commencing upon the north line of township eleven (11) north, of range three (3) east, in said township of Swan Creek, at the northwest corner of section two (2) in said township eleven (11) north of range three (3) east, running thence east on and along the north line of said sections two (2) and section one (1), in said township eleven (11), north of range three (3) east, to the northeast corner of the last named section one (1), thence north on the section line between section thirty-six (36), in township twelve (12), north of range three (3) east, and section thirty-one (31), in township twelve (12), north of range four (4) east, to the northwest corner of said last named section thirty-one (31), thence east on the north line of said section thirty-one (31) last named, to the centre of the Tittabawassee river, thence down and along the centre of said Tittabawassee river to its junction with the Shiawassee river, thence up and along the centre of said Shiawassee river to a point where the east line of township eleven (11), north of range three (3) east, crosses the said Shiawassee river, thence south on and along the said east line to the southeast corner of township eleven (11) north of range three (3) east; thence west on and along the south line of the aforesaid township to the southwest corner of section thirty-five (35) town eleven (11), north of range three (3) east ; thence north following the west line of sections thirty-five (35), twenty-six (26), twenty-three (23), fourteen (14), eleven (11), and two (2), of township eleven (11) north, of range three (3) east, to the place of beginning;

AND WHEREAS, It satisfactorily appears by the affidavits thereto attached, that notice of such application has been posted up in five of the most public places of said township for four weeks next preceding said application, and that the same has been duly published in the *Saginawian*, a public newspaper published in said county, for the period of four weeks, immediately preceding the present session of the board of supervisors of the county of Saginaw, as required by law; now therefore

Be it Resolved, By the board of supervisors of the county of Saginaw, that all that part of the township of Swan Creek as now

heretofore last organized, bounded as follows, to-wit: Commencing on the north line of township eleven (11) north, of range
three (3) east, in said township of Swan Creek, at the northwest
corner of section two (2) in said township eleven (11) north, of
range three (3) east, running thence east on and along the north
line of said section two (2), and of section one (1) in said township
eleven (11) north, of range three (3) east, to the northeast corner
of said last named section one (1); thence north on the section
line between section thirty-six (36), in township twelve (12)
north of range three (3) east, and section thirty-one (31) in township twelve (12), north of range four (4) east, to the northwest
corner of said last named section thirty-one (31); thence east on
the north line of said section thirty-one (31) last named, to the
center of the Tittabawassee river; thence down and along the
center of said Tittabawassee river to its junction with the Shiawassee river, thence up and along the center of said Shiawassee
river to a point where the east line of township eleven (11) north,
of range three (3) east, crosses the said Shiawassee river; thence
south on and along the said east line to the south-east corner of
township eleven (11) north, of range three (3) east; thence west
on and along the south line of the aforesaid township eleven (11)
north, of range three (3) east, to the south-west corner of section
thirty-five (35), township eleven (11), north of range three (3)
east; thence north following the west section line of sections thirty-
five (35), twenty-six (26), twenty-three (23), fourteen (14), eleven
(11), and two (2), in township eleven (11), north of range three
(3) east, to the place of beginning, be and the same is hereby set
off from the townships of Swan Creek, and organized into a separate township by the name of "James," and the first township   James
meeting in the said township of James shall be held at the school-   organized.
house of school district, number one (1), in said township, formerly school district number one of the township of Swan Creek;
and that the next township meeting in the township of Swan
Creek shall be held at school-house in school district number
three (3), of said township of Swan Creek.

   Resolved, That the first township meeting of the said township
of James, shall be holden on the first Monday of April next, and
that Edwin S. Dunbar, Jacob Zieroff and Joseph Egerer, be and
they are hereby appointed inspectors of said township meeting,
whose duty it shall be to preside at such meeting, appoint a clerk,
open and keep the polls, and exercise the same powers as the inspectors of election at any township meeting; that Jacob Zieroff
be and he is hereby appointed to post up notices according to law,
of the time and place of holding the first township meeting in
said new township of James, and that Reuben W. Beaman, David
A. Agnew and Aaron Burr, be and they are hereby appointed inspectors of the township meeting to be holden in the township of
Swan Creek on the first Monday in April next, for the reason that
the supervisor and clerk of said township of Swan Creek, by the
division thereof, will cease to be residents of said township, and
that David A. Agnew be and he is hereby appointed to post up no-

tices according to law of the time and place of holding such township meeting.

WM. ROESER,
MARTIN STOKER,
ISAAC SAVAGE,   } *Committee.*
WM. H. NIVER, Jr.
SAMUEL HARDER,

By Supervisor Alberti : That the report be received. Carried.

By Supervisor Haack : That the same lie upon the table and be made the special order of business at ten o'clock, A. M., to-morrow. Carried.

JOHN BARTER, *Chairman.*

FRED. B. SWEET, *Clerk.*

COURT HOUSE, SAGINAW,
        October 23, 1874.

Eleventh day of the regular session of the board of supervisors of Saginaw county.

MORNING SESSION.

Board met pursuant to adjournment.

Hon. John Barter in the chair.

Roll called and a quorum present.

The time having arrived in which the special order of business was upon the report of the committee upon organization of towns, on motion the report was taken from the table.

By Supervisor Alberti : That the report and accompanying resolution be adopted.

By Supervisor Hollon, as a substitute : That the action of the committee be indefinitely postponed.

Lost.

The question recurring, upon the motion of Supervisor Alberti, the ayes and nays being demanded, the motion was declared carried by the following vote, two-thirds of the members elect voting therefor.

Ayes—Supervisors Alberti, Andre, Brundage, Carter, Conkling, Carmer, Doyle, Dunbar, Eaton, Griggs, Haack, Harder, Hynes, Loeffler, McMullen, Miller, Moll, Nevins, Niver, Ross, Roeser, Smith, Spath, Stoker, Stark, Ward, Wiltse, Savage—28.

Nays—Supervisors Aiken, Bloedon, Hollon, Langlass, Thompson, Warner, Schaefer—7.

JOHN BARTER, *Chairman.*

FRED. B. SWEET, *Clerk.*

STATE OF MICHIGAN,
County of Saginaw, } ss.

I, Fred. B. Sweet, clerk of said county and of the circuit court thereof, do hereby certify that the foregoing is a copy of the proceedings of the board of supervisors of said county in regard to the organization of the township of James, in said county, now of record in my office; that I have carefully compared the same with the original of record, and that it is a correct transcript therefrom and of the whole thereof.

    In testimony whereof I have hereunto set my hand and [L. S.] affixed the seal of said court, at Saginaw, this first day of March, in the year of our Lord one thousand eight hundred and seventy-five.

FRED. B. SWEET, Clerk.

SANILAC COUNTY.

STATE OF MICHIGAN, ⎫ ss.
  County of Sanilac, ⎬

    At a regular session of the board of supervisors of the county of Sanilac and State of Michigan, continued and held at the court house in the village of Lexington on the sixteenth day of October, in the year of our Lord one thousand eight hundred and seventy-three.

In the matter of the application of Patrick Walsh and others for the erection and organization of a new township.

    It appearing to the board of supervisors that application has been made, and that notice thereof has been signed, posted up, and published as in the manner required by the law, and having duly considered the matter of said application, the board order and enact that the territory described in said application, described as follows, to wit: town thirteen (13) north, of range twelve (12) east, be and the same is hereby erected into a township to be called and known by the name of "Evergreen." The first annual meeting thereof Evergreen organized. shall be held at the house of John B. Proctor on section twenty-seven of said township on the first Monday of April next at nine o'clock A. M. and at said meeting William P. Hall, Patrick Walsh, and Robert Wilson, three electors of said township, shall be the persons whose duty it shall be to preside at such meeting, appoint a clerk, open and keep the polls, and exercise the same powers as the inspectors of elections at any township meeting as the law provides.

    On motion the resolution was adopted.

RUDOLPH PAPST, Clerk.

STATE OF MICHIGAN, ⎫ ss.
  Sanilac County, ⎬

    I, Rudolph Papst, clerk of said county of Sanilac, do hereby certify, that the foregoing is a true statement of the action of the board of supervisors of said county upon the organization of the township of Evergreen, as appears upon the journal of the proceedings of said board remaining in my office.

    In testimony whereof I have hereunto set my hand and [L. S.] affixed the seal of the circuit court at Lexington this seventeenth day of October, in the year of our Lord one thousand eight hundred and seventy-three.

RUDOLPH PAPST,
County Clerk.

WEXFORD COUNTY.

In the matter of the application of John W. Welton and others, for the erection and organization of a new township.

It appearing to the board of supervisors that application has been made, and that notice thereof has been signed, posted up, and published, as in the manner required by law, and having duly considered the matter of said application, the board order and enact that the territory described in said application, bounded as follows, to wit: township twenty-four (24) north, of range nine (9) west, be and the same is hereby erected into a township to be called and known by the name of the township of Liberty. The first annual township meeting thereof shall be held at the residence of John W. Welton, in said township, on the first Monday of April, in the year of our Lord, one thousand eight hundred and seventy-five, at nine o'clock in the forenoon, and that Taylor W. Gray, George W. Blue, and John W. Welton, three electors of said township, shall be the persons whose duty it shall be to preside at such meeting, appoint a clerk, open and keep the polls, and exercise the same powers as the inspectors of elections at any township meeting, as the law provides.

Liberty organized.

STATE OF MICHIGAN, } ss.
  Wexford County, }

I, H. B. Sturtevant, clerk of said county of Wexford, do hereby certify that the foregoing is a true statement of the action of the board of supervisors of said county upon the organization of the township of Liberty, as appears upon the journal of the proceedings of said board remaining in my office.

In testimony whereof I have hereunto set my hand and affixed the seal of the circuit court of Wexford county, at Sherman, this sixteenth day of October, in the year of our Lord one thousand eight hundred and seventy-four.

[L. S.]

H. B. STURTEVANT,
County Clerk.

STATE TREASURER'S ANNUAL REPORT, 1874.

———

STATE OF MICHIGAN,
STATE TREASURER'S OFFICE,,
LANSING, Sept. 30th, 1874.

To HON. JOHN J. BAGLEY, *Governor of the State of Michigan :*

SIR—In compliance with the requirements of law, I have the honor to submit herewith the annual report of this Department, for the fiscal year ending this day.

The balance of cash in the Treasury September 30,1873, was....	$854,713 44
The cash receipts for the year were........................	2,044,908 52
	$2,899,621 96
The cash payments for the year were......................	1,829,347 64
Balance September 30th, 1874...........................	$1,070,274 32

The transactions in Swamp Land Warrants were as follows:

Balance outstanding September 30th, 1873..................	$163,143 25
Swamp Land Warrants issued.............................	166,257 21
	$329,400 46
Amount Land Warrants charged...........................	201,290 81
Balance outstanding....................................	$128,109 65

The demands upon the Treasury now due and those maturing on or before January 1st, 1875, are as follows:

Past due Bonds and Coupons............................		$34,849 64
Trust Deposits due on demand...........................		2,590 35
Semi-annual Interest due November 1st, 1874.	$12,810 00	
Semi-annual Interest due January 1st, 1875........	34,054 30	
Agricultural College Interest due January 1st, 1875.	1,900 00	
University Interest due January 1st, 1875....	8,455 88	
		57,220 18
Appropriations—New Capitol..................	$131,657 61	
New Asylum for Insane..........	88,100 13	
Asylum for Insane...............	41,900 00	

Appropriations—Asylum for D., D. & B. $7,797 98
       Reform School 15,000 00
       State Prison 2,200 00
       Public School 5,000 00
       Agricultural College 5,341 13
       Normal School 5,056 73
       University Aid 7,875 00
       Geological Survey 8,000 00
       Commission on Fisheries 2,128 27
       State Board of Health 2,236 40
       Corner Stone 2,930 69
                                    $325,223 94

    Total $419,884 11

The following amounts have been received and are held in trust for the purposes named:

Sinking Fund for the purchase of Bonds $563,862 90
Canal Fund for retiring Bonds and for expenses 85,615 86
Military Fund 68,754 76
Primary School Interest Fund 85,177 39
Trust Funds received since July 1st, 1874 .... 9,153 72
Agricultural College Fund 107,879 14

                                    $920,443 77

There has been received during the year from the Treasurer of the United States $26,241 76 as five per cent of the proceeds of cash sales of Government lands lying within this State.

The total receipts from Specific Taxes were $471,263 71. Of this $22,885 75 was received for Mining Taxes from the Upper Peninsula; the remainder $448,377 96, is an amount sufficient to pay the interest on the Trust Funds and on the Bonded Debt of the State and leave $149,360 89 to be credited to the Sinking Fund.

The balance in the Canal Fund September 30th, 1873, was $79,719 04
Received from Superintendent 27,333 77

                                    $107,052 81

The payments have been:
Bonds $12,000 00
Coupons 4,199 90
Salary of Superintendent 1,750 00
Improvements 3,247 00
Expenses of Board 240 05
                                    21,436 95

    Leaving a balance of $85,615 86

This will be largely diminished by the cost of improvements now being made.

The balance in the Military Fund September 30th, 1873, was	$85,168 28	
Receipts for year under Act 16, 1862	33,382 50	
	$118,550 78	

The payments have been:

Salaries of Military officers	$1,796 03	
Soldiers' Aid, Act 115, 1873	5,000 00	
Quartermaster General's Estimates, Uniforms, etc., Act 116, 1873	43,000 00	
		49,796 03
Leaving a balance of		$68,754 75

In December, 1873, two of the $5,000,000 00 Loan Bonds, issued in 1838, were presented and paid. There are now outstanding of this class of bonds, $52,000 00, called part paid Five-Million Loan Bonds, and are adjustable at $578 57 per $1,000 00, or $30,085 64.

STATE DEBT.

The Bonded Debt of the State has been reduced during the year, by the purchase of unmatured bonds at their par value and accrued interest, to the amount of $144,000 00. To accomplish this I have, with your advice and at your earnest solicitation, made two trips to New York and other Eastern cities.

The following table shows the bonds purchased since January 1st, 1871, and the amount of interest saved thereby:

	BONDS PURCHASED.							
	Two-Million Loan, 6's, Due 1873.	Two-Million Loan, 6's, Due 1878.	Two-Million Loan, 6's, Due 1883.	Renewal Loan, 6's, Due 1873.	Canal Loan, 6's, Due 1879.	War Bounty Loan, 7's, Due 1890.	Total Am't of Bonds Purchas'd.	Total Am't of Interest Saved.
1871	$1,000 00	$1,000 00	$3,000 00		$2,000 00	$22,000 00	$29,000 00	$18,875 85
1872	145,000 00	9,000 00	5,000 00		10,000 00		169,000 00	13,855 00
1873		74,000 00	19,000 00	$39,000 00	8,000 00		140,000 00	49,985 00
1874		20,000 00	9,000 00	6,000 00	12,000 00	97,000 00	144,000 00	120,413 99
	$146,000 00	$104,000 00	$36,000 00	$45,000 00	$32,000 00	$119,000 00	$482,000 00	$202,918 85

This statement does not include $313,000 00 of Two-Million Loan Bonds paid in 1873, nor $5,892 85 of Five-Million Loan Bonds, issued in 1838 and paid in 1871 and 1873, which, added to the total amount purchased, makes a reduction in the principal of the State Debt, during the past four years, of $800,892 85.

The interest upon the State Debt for the fiscal year just closed was $95,400 91, while the interest received during the same time was

Upon Surplus Funds	$41,639 70
Past due Specific Taxes	16,397 89
Making	$58,037 59

Deducting this amount from the amount paid there is a difference of $37,-363 32, that the State paid in interest more than it received.

The funded and fundable debt of the State is as follows:

Interest-Bearing Bonds.

Sault Canal Loan Bonds, 6's, due July 1st, 1879	$61,000 00
Renewal Loan Bonds, 6's, due January 1st, 1878	105,000 00
Two-Million Loan Bonds, 6's, due January 1st, 1878	333,000 00
Two-Million Loan Bonds, 6's, due January 1st, 1883	690,000 00
War Bounty Loan Bonds, 7's, due May 1st, 1890	366,000 00
Total Interest-Bearing Bonds	$1,555,000 00

Non-Interest Bearing Bonds.

Adjusted Bonds due January 1st, 1863	$3,000 00	
War Bounty Loan Bond due January 1st, 1863	*50 00	
$52,000 00 part paid Five-Million Loan Bonds, adjustable at $578 57 per $1,000 00	30,085 64	
		33,135 64
Total Bonded Debt		$1,588,135 64

The cash in the Treasury applicable to its payment is as follows:

Sinking Fund	$563,915 93
Trust Funds received since July 1st, 1874	9,153 72
Canal Fund	85,615 86
Balance from sale of Two-Million Loan Bonds to pay adjusted and Five-Million Loan Bonds	33,135 64
	$691,821 15

Which leaves the total Bonded Debt of the State, less cash set apart for its payment, $896,314 49.

The Trust Debt of the State is composed of the following funds and amounts:

Primary School Fund	$2,157,179 53
Five per cent Primary School Fund	289,887 30
University Fund	335,287 39
Agricultural College Fund	107,879 14

*Paid October 20, 1874.

Normal School Fund	$51,038 66
Railroad and other deposits	2,590 35
	$2,943,862 37

SINKING FUND.

The credit to this fund on the Trust Fund Ledger is $1,734,785 84. The debit on the main Ledger is $1,170,869 91, which gives a net credit of $563,915 93. This amount includes * $50 for a War Loan Bond, drawn for payment January 1st, 1863, which has never been presented.

The credits to the fund during the year were:

Trust Funds	$70,983 01
Transfer from General Fund, Joint Resolution No. 7, 1869	200,000 00
Balance of Specific Taxes	149,748 47
Making the total amount of credits	$420,731 48

The charges against the fund were for:

Two-Million Loan Bonds purchased	$29,000 00
Renewal Loan Bonds purchased	6,000 00
War-Bounty Loan Bonds purchased	97,000 00
Giving a total of	$132,000 00

The transactions in this fund since its inception are as follows:

One-sixteenth Mill-tax, 8 years levied, 1861 to 1868	$111,511 06
One-eighth Mill-tax, 10 years levied, 1862 to 1871	357,256 57
Excess of taxes for interest	1,217,814 89
War expenses refunded by the United States	266,828 40
Discount on Bonds purchased	3,069 17
Trust Funds received from February 1st, 1863, to July 1st, 1874	1,734,785 84
Transferred from General Fund, Joint Resolution No. 7, 1869	200,000 00
	$3,891,265 93

Contra.

Temporary Loan Bonds	$50,000 00
Renewal Loan Bonds	111,000 00
Two-Million Loan Bonds	977,000 00
War Loan Bonds	1,249,400 00
War-Bounty Loan Bonds	940,000 00
Balance	563,865 93
	$3,891,265 93

The following table shows the condition of the Bonded Debt of the State for each year since 1835:

* Paid October 20, 1874.

45

Year.	Amount of Bonds Issued in Year.	Amount of Bonds Paid in Year.	Bonds Outstanding.
1835			
1836	$100,000 00		$100,000 00
1837	20,000 00		120,000 00
1838	5,420,000 00		5,540,000 00
1839	71,000 00		5,611,000 00
1840			5,611,000 00
1841			5,611,000 00
1842		$2,857,039 76	2,753,960 24
1843	644,045 03	4,000 00	3,394,005 27
1844	2,994 73	72,787 52	3,324,212 48
1845	380,885 66	399,299 28	3,305,798 86
1846 } *		1,015,030 35	{ 2,299,050 52
1847 }			{ 2,290,768 51
1848	345,562 92	19,798 00	2,616,533 43
1849	111,417 23	139,452 00	2,588,498 66
1850	184,709 69	243,335 48	2,529,872 87
1851	136,751 96	98,355 70	2,568,269 13
1852	65,452 74	325,871 68	2,307,850 19
1853	34,541 88	3,000 00	2,339,392 07
1854	213,809 63	21,156 00	2,531,545 70
1855	1,357,103 86	1,498,690 33	2,389,958 73
1856	56,836 98	171,859 76	2,274,935 90
1857	12,719 46	18,187 88	2,269,467 48
1858	274,000 00	205,837 81	2,337,629 67
1859	104,500 00	25,800 73	2,416,828 94
1860	6,000 00	33,486 15	2,388,842 79
1861	456,100 00	8,678 55	2,836,264 24
1862	160,200 00	15,425 69	2,981,088 55
1863	2,071,100 00	2,058,888 75	2,993,299 80
1864	801,000 00	253,150 00	3,541,149 80
1865	615,000 00	275,750 00	3,880,399 80
1866	370,700 00	271,178 55	3,979,921 25
1867		78,678 55	3,901,242 70
1868		287,164 21	3,614,078 49
1869		570,500 00	3,043,578 49
1870	15,000 00	673,550 00	2,385,028 49
1871	7,000 00	36,735 71	2,855,292 78
1872		112,000 00	2,243,292 78
1873		510,000 00	1,733,292 78
1874		145,157 14	1,588,135 64
Totals	$14,037,931 22	$12,449,795 58	

* Amount of Bonded Debt reduced in these two years.

During the past year there has been surrendered to the various townships, on the written order of their respective Boards, verified under seal by their County Clerks, Railroad Aid Bonds to the amount of $250,519 00. Below I give a detailed list of those still remaining in this office:

TOWNSHIP.	COUNTY.	RAILROAD.	AMOUNT.
Constantine	St. Joseph	Michigan Air Line	$50,000 00
Columbia	Van Buren	Kalamazoo & South Haven	20,000 00
Bangor	Van Buren	Kalamazoo & South Haven	15,000 00
Deerfield	Van Buren	Chicago & Michigan Lake Shore	28,960 00
Bingham	Clinton	Lansing, St. Johns & Mackinac	40,000 00
Greenbush	Clinton	Lansing, St. Johns & Mackinac	11,678 00
Bethany	Gratiot	Lansing, St. Johns & Mackinac	8,000 00
Newark	Gratiot	Lansing, St. Johns & Mackinac	12,000 00

TOWNSHIP.	COUNTY.	RAILROAD.	AMOUNT.
Emerson	Gratiot	Lansing, St. Johns & Mackinac	$10,000 00
North Star	Gratiot	Lansing, St. Johns & Mackinac	9,988 40
Washington	Gratiot	Lansing, St. Johns & Mackinac	8,000 00
Coe	Isabella	Lansing, St. Johns & Mackinac	15,579 00
Chippewa	Isabella	Lansing, St. Johns & Mackinac	5,613 90
Walton	Eaton	Jonesville, Marshall & Grand River	20,000 00
Lyons	Ionia	Jonesville, Marshall & Grand River	40,000 00
Douglas	Montcalm	Jonesville, Marshall & Grand River	6,400 00
Bushnell	Montcalm	Jonesville, Marshall & Grand River	11,200 00
Owosso City	Shiawassee	Owosso & Big Rapids	6,000 00
Big Rapids City	Mecosta	Owosso & Big Rapids	45,000 00
Oceana	Muskegon	Michigan Lake Shore	80,000 00
Lawrence	Van Buren	Paw Paw Valley	50,000 00
Bainbridge	Van Buren	Paw Paw Valley	15,000 00
Antwerp	Van Buren	Paw Paw Valley	30,000 00
Shiawassee	Shiawassee	East Saginaw & Ann Arbor	17,000 00
Corunna	Shiawassee	East Saginaw & Ann Arbor	14,000 00
Spaulding	Saginaw	East Saginaw & Ann Arbor	19,500 00
Bennington	Shiawassee	Toledo, Ann Arbor & Northern	10,000 00
Tallmadge	Ottawa	Grand Rapids & Lake Shore	10,000 00
Shelby	Oceana	Grand Rapids & Lake Shore	7,195 00
Lyon	Oakland	Toledo, Ypsilanti & Saginaw	15,000 00
Highland	Oakland	Toledo, Ypsilanti & Saginaw	10,000 00
Rose	Oakland	Toledo, Ypsilanti & Saginaw	10,000 00
Augusta	Washtenaw	Toledo, Ypsilanti & Saginaw	20,000 00
Superior	Washtenaw	Toledo, Ypsilanti & Saginaw	30,000 00
St. Clair	St. Clair	Michigan Air Line Extension	28,800 00
Spring Lake	Ottawa	Fruitport & Lake Shore	13,800 00
Almont	Lapeer	Romeo & Almont	45,000 00
Total			$738,214 30

The following tables show the details of revenue and expenditures for the fiscal year:

RECEIPTS.

Tax Histories and Statements	$1,649 76	
State Tax Deeds	521 25	
State Tax Lands and Bids	42,831 66	
Redemptions	26,569 94	
Delinquent Taxes	306,386 25	
Taxes on part-paid Lands	6,002 63	
		$383,962 19
Primary School Principal	$41,043 64	
" " Interest	49,162 24	
Swamp Land Principal in Warrants	166,257 21	
" " " " Cash	10,371 54	
" " Interest	3,444 92	
University Principal	4,053 36	
" Interest	7,875 46	
Agricultural College Principal	4,686 75	
" " Interest	6,879 22	
Normal School Principal	900 44	
" " Interest	1,399 63	
Asylum Principal	940 00	
" Interest	1,280 00	
State Building Principal	210 00	

State Building Interest	$238 82	
Salt Spring Principal	415 00	
" " Interest	1,171 25	
Internal Improvement Fund	50 00	
Primary School Deposits	342 50	
" " Interest Deposits	32 03	
Swamp Land Deposits	97 83	
Salt Spring Deposits	545 00	
		$301,395 84
Counties—State Tax, 1873	$621,474 37	
Tax Sales	129,637 08	
General Account	116,589 81	
Taxes and Redemptions	59,846 34	
		927,547 60
Specific Taxes—Railroad Companies	$331,787 59	
Street Railway Companies	1,160 43	
Fire Insurance "	66,583 09	
Life " "	40,690 20	
Mining, Copper and Iron Co's	22,885 75	
" Coal Companies	1 41	
Telegraph "	2,498 87	
Express "	2,230 79	
Car "	2,742 83	
Gravel Road "	192 22	
River Improvement Companies	562 04	
		471,335 22
Tolls on Sault Ste. Marie Canal		27,333 77
Interest on Bank Deposits	$41,639 70	
" " Specific Taxes	16,167 14	
" " Tax Sales	230 75	
		58,037 59
United States 5 per cent on Cash Sales of Government Lands		26,241 76
Sales of Michigan Reports	$6,030 75	
" " Compiled Laws	528 00	
" " Session "	221 75	
" " Territorial "	15 00	
" " Railroad "	3 50	
" " Joint Documents	9 00	
" " Old Furniture	101 10	
		6,909 10
Refunded County Treasurers for Insane Asylum	$463 38	
" Constitutional Commission	9 00	
" Redemption	1 00	
		473 38
Fees from Secretary of State	$809 41	
" " Auditor General—filing plats	198 00	
" " Commissioner of Land Office	2,370 52	
" " " " Swamp L'd Road Office	9 25	
" " State Treasurer	1 00	
" " Notaries Public	610 00	
" " Commissioners of Deeds	27 00	
		4,025 18

Rents from State property in Lansing	$205 00	
Peddlers' Licenses	466 04	
Hazelton Asset Lands, trespasses	1,761 86	
Secretary of Canal Board Deposit	75 00	
Penalty from Fire Insurance Company	500 00	
Swamp Land Trespass Deposit	534 00	
Primary School Land Trespass Deposit	227 20	
Escheats—Principal and interest	135 00	
Total Receipts	$2,211,165 73	

EXPENDITURES.

Bonds—Canal, 6s, due July 1, 1879	$12,000 00	
Renewal Loan, 6s, due July 1, 1878	6,000 00	
Two-Million Loan, 6s, due Jan'y 1, 1878	20,000 00	
" " 6s, due Jan'y 1, 1883	9,000 00	
War Bounty Loan, 7s, due May 1, 1890	97,000 00	
Adjusted past due	1,157 14	
		$145,157 14
Coupons—Canal	$4,199 90	
Renewal Loan	6,494 62	
Two-Million Loan	63,174 06	
War Bounty Loan	28,791 92	
War Loan	8 75	
		102,669 25
Counties—Primary School Interest Apportionment		208,935 06
Taxes collected		205,869 98
Asylum for Insane		7,876 69
Appropriations—University Aid	$27,375 00	
" Interest	38,590 00	
Agricultural College Aid	38,562 87	
" " Interest	11,896 00	
Normal School Interest	27,000 00	
State Public School	51,450 92	
State Reform School	34,400 00	
Asylum for Insane at Kalamazoo	69,700 00	
" " " " Pontiac	11,899 87	
" " Deaf, Dumb, and Bl'd	54,139 02	
State Capitol	237,299 06	
State Prison	83,000 00	
Board of Health	3,081 68	
Geological Survey	21,000 00	
State Library	2,500 00	
Teachers' Institutes	1,300 00	
Charitable, Penal, Pauper, and Reformatory Commission	2,753 41	
Fish Commission	8 145 59	
Corner Stone, New Capitol	6,515 04	
Compiling Territorial Laws	550 00	
Immigration Commission	3,210 00	
		734,368 46

Awards of Board of State Auditors—

General awards	$17,626 96	
Printing and Binding	57,589 52	
Paper and Stationery	18,973 23	
Michigan Reports	909 30	
St. Mary's Falls Ship Canal	1,252 05	
Swamp Land Road Office	978 99	
Expense of Courts	701 36	
Cost of Suits	1,680 82	
Advertising sales Forfeited Lands	295 60	
Locating Primary School Indemnity Lands	2,732 75	
Hazelton and Dewey Asset Lands	132 65	
Examining vacant State Lands	366 00	
Fugitives from justice	155 20	
House of Correction	652 95	
		$104,047 38
Swamp Land Warrants		166,257 21
Redemptions		38,190 37

Salaries—

Judges Supreme Court	$15,999 99	
Judges Circuit Courts	29,004 83	
Judge Superior Court, Detroit	1,500 00	
Elective State Officers	12,900 00	
Auditor General's Office	46,625 52	
State Land Office	13,674 30	
Secretary of State's Office	14,395 09	
State Treasurer's Office	4,238 75	
Swamp Land Road Office	4,000 00	
Insurance Commissioner's Office	2,200 00	
Supt. Public Instruction's Office	1,782 67	
State Librarian	800 00	
Officers of Insane Asylum	9,425 00	
Acting Commissioner D., D. & B. Asylum	1.000 00	
Military Officers	1,796 03	
Superintendent St. Mary's Canal	1,750 00	
State Reporter	2,100 00	
Railroad Commissioner's Clerk	1,000 00	
Attorney General's Clerk	1,083 36	
Secretary Agricultural College	916 67	
Governor's Private Secretary	866 69	
Recorder of Detroit	1,500 00	
Clerk of Supreme Court	112 50	
Immigration Commissioner	1,319 41	
		169,990 81
Coroners' Fees		1,773 84
Wolf Bounties		96 00

Expense of Courts

Expense of Courts	$1,156 21	
" " Sales	1,087 52	
" " State Reporter	207 55	
" " Inspectors of State Prison	1,010 30	
" " Trustees of Asylums	261 65	

Expense of Supervisors' Assessments	$1,396 50	
" " Suits	172 32	
		$5,292 05
Proceeds of Sales		197 43
Hazelton Asset Lands		141 14
Refunded Land Office Principal and Interest	$1,987 41	
" Bid and Interest	1,099 28	
		3,086 69
" Specific Taxes	$71 51	
" Ontonagon County Deposit	1,872 69	
" Taxes and Interest on part-paid lands	190 62	
		2,134 82
Military—Quartermaster General	$43,000 00	
" Soldiers' Aid	5,000 00	
		48,000 00
Tax Sales—Advertising	$16,764 00	
" Conducting	5,249 48	
		22,013 48
Constitutional Commission, per Diem and Mileage	$3,025 00	
" " Contingent Expenses	562 49	
		3,587 49
Legislature, per Diem and Mileage	$14,495 50	
" Contingent Expenses	595 31	
		15,090 81
Publishing Constitution	$5,325 00	
" Laws	2,640 00	
		7,965 00
Indexing Legislative Journals		200 00
Swamp Land Trespass Deposit		428 75
St. Mary's Falls Ship Canal		2,235 00
Total Expenditures		$1,995,604 85

Very respectfully,
V. P. COLLIER,
State Treasurer.

Treasurer of the State of Michigan in account with the State of Michigan.

DEBIT.

1874.

Sept. 30.   To balance Sept. 30, 1873... $854,713 44
            Receipts on account of—
              General Fund... 1,383,498 08
              Primary School Fund... 41,142 64
              Primary School Interest Fund... 49,454 44
              Swamp Land Fund... 176,772 00
              Swamp Land Interest Fund... 8,444 99
              University Fund.. 4,058 86
              University Interest Fund.. 7,875 46
              Agricultural College Fund.. 4,686 73
              Agricultural College Interest Fund... 6,879 22
              Normal School Fund.. 900 44
              Normal School Interest Fund.. 1,899 68
              Asylum Fund... 2,220 00
              State Building Fund... 623 89
              Internal Improvement Fund.. 26,291 76
              St. Mary's Falls Ship Canal Fund... 27,833 77
              Specific Taxes.. 471,885 23
              Primary School Deposits... 842 50
              Primary School Interest Deposits... 89 08
              Swamp Land Deposits... 97 83
              Salt Spring Deposits.. 545 00
              Swamp Land Trespass Deposits... 400 00
              Hazelton Asset Lands Deposits.. 1,761 86
              Secretary Board of Control St. Mary's Canal.. 75 00

                                                                                       $3,065,879 17

Ledger Balances.

DEBIT.

1874.

Sept. 30.   Cash..$1,070,274 32
            Internal Improvement Fund.. 2,408,920 95
            Sinking Fund... 1,170,869 91
            Suspense Account... 2,805 88
            Dewey Asset Lands.. 14,954 90
            Hazelton Asset Lands... 10,911 13
            Portage Lake Ship Canal Fund... 88 25

                                                                                       $4,678,824 68

Treasurer of the State of Michigan in account with the State of Michigan.

CREDIT.

1874.

Sept. 30. By paid warrants on account of—

General Fund	$596,498 81
Primary School Fund	390 00
Primary School Interest Fund	210,845 71
Swamp Land Fund	172,199 18
Swamp Land Interest Fund	290 98
University Interest Fund	88,695 84
Agricultural College Interest Fund	12,120 89
Normal School Interest Fund	27,251 88
Asylum Fund	185,783 43
State Building Fund	287,805 67
Internal Improvement Fund	1,157 14
War Fund	28,800 67
Military Fund	44,796 03
University Aid Fund	27,875 00
Soldiers' Aid Fund	5,000 00
St. Mary's Falls Ship Canal Fund	21,486 95
Primary School Deposits	430 00
Primary School Interest Deposits	82 08
Swamp Land Deposits	58 50
University Deposits	88 75
Salt Spring Deposits	545 00
Swamp Land Trespass Deposits	400 00
Ontonagon County Deposits	1,872 69
Dewey Asset Lands	8 85
Hazelton Asset Lands	265 44
Sinking Fund	182,000 00
Specific Taxes	71 51
Balance	1,070,274 82
	$3,065,879 17

Ledger Balances.

CREDIT.

1874.

Sept. 30.

General Fund	$371,048 12
Primary School Fund	2,157,179 58
Primary School Interest Fund	85,177 89
Primary School Five Per Cent Fund	298,887 80
Swamp Land Fund	193,168 07
Swamp Land Interest Fund	128,543 10
University Fund	335,297 89
University Interest Fund	64 54
Agricultural College Fund	107,879 14
Agricultural College Interest Fund	2,197 58
Normal School Fund	51,088 66
Normal School Interest Fund	8,301 48
Asylum Fund	187,798 11
State Building Fund	181,657 61
War Fund	18,973 89
St. Mary's Falls Ship Canal Fund	85,615 86
Military Fund	68,754 76
University Aid Fund	7,875 00
Treasury Notes	730 00
Michigan Central Railroad Deposits	1,897 02
Michigan Southern Railroad Deposits	147 72
St. Joseph Valley Railroad Deposits	55 00
Oakland & Ottawa Railroad Deposits	5 58
Light-House Deposits	15 00
Railroad Lands Deposits	186 00
Auditor General's Deposits	186 64
Forfeited Primary School Land Deposits	160 00
Forfeited Primary School Interest Deposits	1 83
Forfeited Swamp Land Deposits	115 56
Secretary Board of Control St. Mary's Falls Ship Canal Deposit	75 00
	$4,678,324 83

General Fund.

DEBIT.

1874.		
Sept. 80.	To paid Coupons	$69,666 65
"	Counties	218,747 67
"	Appropriations	261,915 68
"	Salaries	166,444 78
"	Awards of Board of State Auditors	98,292 84
"	Redemptions	88,196 37
"	Legislature	15,000 81
"	Constitutional Commission	3,587 49
"	Conducting and Advertising Tax Sales	22,018 48
"	Compiling Legislative Journals	200 00
"	Sundry Expenses	7,859 82
To amount Transferred to University Aid Fund		81,500 00
"	Normal School Interest Fund	17,500 00
"	Asylum Fund	155,378 89
"	State Building Fund	199,883 79
"	Military Fund	28,883 50
"	Sinking Fund	900,051 88
To balance		871,043 19
		$2,404,645 68

Primary School Fund.

DEBIT.

1874.		
Sept. 80.	To paid Warrants	$690 08
	To balance	2,187,179 50
		$2,187,589 58

Primary School Interest Fund.

DEBIT.

1874.		
Sept. 80.	To paid Apportionment to Counties	$208,985 06
"	Supervisors for Appraisals	996 06
"	Advertising Forfeited Land Sales	216 42
"	Excess of Interest refunded	406 95
"	Examining Lands	291 19
"	Error in Specific Taxes	19
' "	Sinking Fund	8 05
	To balance	85,177 89
		$296,026 82

Primary School Five Per Cent Fund.

DEBIT.

1874.		
Sept. 80.	To balance	$369,887 80
"	transfer to Swamp Land Fund	23 08
		$369,910 88

General Fund.

CREDIT.

1874.
Sept. 30. By balance Sept. 30, 1873 .... $929,548 30
　　　　　By cash for Taxes from Auditor General's Office........................... 877,959 56
　　　　　　"　"　"　"　State Land Office... 6,002 68
　　　　　　"　"　Fees.. 4,025 18
　　　　　　"　"　Interest 58,087 59
　　　　　　"　from Counties... 927,547 60
　　　　　　"　"　Purchasers of Salt Spring Lands.................................... 1,586 25
　　　　　　"　"　Peddlers for Licenses... 466 04
　　　　　　"　for Penalty from Fire Insurance Company 500 00
　　　　　　"　"　Sale of Sundries.. 6,909 10
　　　　　　"　"　refunded over-payments... 473 38
　　　　　By amount transferred from Specific Taxes 91,590 05

　　　　　　　　　　　　　　　　　　　　　　　　　　　　　　$2,404,645 68

Primary School Fund.

CREDIT.

1874.
Sept. 30. By balance Sept. 30, 1873 .... $2,116,426 89
　　　"　" cash from purchasers of Primary School Lands............................. 41,042 64
　　　"　"　Escheat Lands 100 00

　　　　　　　　　　　　　　　　　　　　　　　　　　　　　　$2,157,569 58

Primary School Interest Fund.

CREDIT.

1874.
Sept. 30. By balance Sept. 30, 1873 .... $82,815 87
　　　"　" cash from purchasers of Primary School Lands 49,874 44
　　　"　"　"　Escheat Lands.. 85 00
　　　"　"　"　trespasses.. 15 00
　　　"　"　"　rents in Lansing... 80 00
　　　" transfer from Specific Taxes, interest on Primary School Fund.................. 149,409 45
　　　"　"　"　"　"　"　on Five Per Cent Fund.................................... 14,846 56

　　　　　　　　　　　　　　　　　　　　　　　　　　　　　　$296,026 82

Primary School Five Per Cent Fund.

CREDIT.

1874.
Sept. 30. By balance Sept. 30, 1873 .... $284,771 98
　　　" amount transferred from Swamp Land Fund.................................... 5,138 40

　　　　　　　　　　　　　　　　　　　　　　　　　　　　　　$289,910 38

Swamp Land Fund.

DEBIT.

1874.
Sept. 30. To paid Land Warrants... $166,237 21
   "   "   salaries Swamp Land State Road Commissioners and Clerks.................. 4,000 00
   "   "   expenses Swamp Land State Road office............................... 978 99
   "   "   expenses collecting trespasses..................................... 28 75
   "   amount refunded to purchasers 761 86
   "   cost of suits.. 172 83
   "   amount transferred to Asylum Fund.................................... 46 15
   "   "   "   to Five Per Cent P. S. Fund.......................... 5,183 40
   "   balance... 193,168 07

                                                                    $370,551 75

Swamp Land Interest Fund.

DEBIT.

1874.
Sept. 30. To paid Supervisors' appraisals...................................... $223 33
   "   advertising Forfeited Lands.. 30 50
   "   interest refunded.. 13 10
   "   examining lands and titles.. 18 50
   "   balance.. 123,843 10

                                                                    $123,684 06

University Fund.

DEBIT.

1874.
Sept. 30. To balance... $385,237 39

                                                                    $385,237 39

University Interest Fund.

DEBIT.

1874.
Sept. 30. To paid Treasurer of University...................................... $38,590 00
   "   "   Supervisors' Appraisals.. 40 31
   "   "   advertising Forfeited Lands... 5 55
   "   balance.. 64 54

                                                                    $38,700 38

Agricultural College Fund.

DEBIT.

1874.
Sept. 30. To balance $107,879 14

                                                                    $107,879 14

Agricultural College Interest Fund.

DEBIT.

1874.
Sept. 30. To paid Treasurer of College... $11,896 00
   "   "   Supervisors' appraisals.. 65 33
   "   "   advertising Forfeited Lands... 14 85
   "   refunding Interest 145 31
   "   balance.. 2,197 56

                                                                    $14,318 47

Swamp Land Fund.

CREDIT.

1874.
Sept. 30. By balance September 30th, 1873... $193,756 67
    "   Swamp Land Warrants... 166,257 21
    "   cash for land.. 10,371 54
    "   "   "   trespasses... 184 00
    "   "   "   from Swamp Land State Road Commissioner................... 9 25
    "   transfer from P. S. Five Per Cent Fund.......................... 23 08

$370,551 75

Swamp Land Interest Fund.

CREDIT.

1874.
Sept. 30. By balance September 30th, 1873... $125,189 11
    "   received from purchasers of land................................. 3,444 92

$128,684 03

University Fund.

CREDIT.

1874.
Sept 30. By balance September 30th, 1873... $331,234 03
    "   received from purchasers of lands................................ 4,053 36

$335,287 39

University Interest Fund.

CREDIT.

1874.
Sept. 30. By balance Sept. 30, 1873... $486 95
    "   received from purchasers of land................................. 7,375 46
    "   transfer from Specific Taxes, interest on University Fund......... 30,837 97

$38,700 38

Agricultural College Fund.

CREDIT.

1874.
Sept. 30. By balance Sept. 30, 1873... $103,192 39
    "   received from purchasers of land................................. 4,686 75

$107,879 14

Agricultural College Interest Fund.

CREDIT.

1874.
Sept. 30. By balance Sept. 30, 1873... $31 60
    "   received from purchasers of lands................................ 6,879 22
    "   transfer from Specific Taxes, interest on Agricultural College Fund............ 7,407 65

$14,318 47

Normal School Fund.

DEBIT.

1874.
Sept. 30. To balance $51,063 66

$51,063 66

Normal School Interest Fund.

DEBIT.

1874.
Sept. 30. To paid Treasurer of Normal School.................................. $27,000 00
   "   "   Supervisors' appraisals.. 17 79
   "   "   advertising Forfeited Lands....................................... 8 73
   "   refunding interest... 230 36
   "   balance.. 8,301 43

$35,558 31

Asylum Fund.

DEBIT.

1874.
Sept. 30. To paid Treasurer Insane Asylum............................... $89,700 00
   "   "   "   D., D. & B. Asylum.. 58,500 00
   "   "   Commissioners Asylum at Pontiac............................ 11,899 87
   "   "   books, pictures, etc., D., D. & B. Asylum 689 02
   "   "   Supervisors' appraisals...................................... 25 13
   "   "   advertising Forfeited Lands................................ 11 01
   "   "   refunding interest... 8 40
   "   balance.. 137,798 11

$278,561 54

State Building Fund.

DEBIT.

1874.
Sept. 30. To paid Supervisors' appraisals.................................. $8 46
   "   "   advertising forfeited Lands................................... 8 15
   "   "   Contractors State Capitol.................................... 229,693 55
   "   "   Architect State Capitol....................................... 4,000 00
   "   "   Secretary Building Commissioners.......................... 1,200 00
   "   "   Assistant Superintendent State Capitol..................... 1,600 00
   "   "   Inspector State Capitol....................................... 75 00
   "   "   Commissioners' expenses..................................... 596 94
   "   "   incidental expenses... 213 57
   "   balance.. 131,557 61

$368,963 23

Internal Improvement Fund.

DEBIT.

1874.
Sept. 30. To balance Sept. 30, 1873. .... $2,484,055 57
   "   paid adjusted bonds 1,157 14

$2,485,212 71

Normal School Fund.

CREDIT.

1874.
Sept. 30. By balance Sept. 30, 1873.. $50,188 22
          " received from purchasers of land 900 44
                                                                                          —————————
                                                                                          $51,088 66
                                                                                          —————————

Normal School Interest Fund.

CREDIT.

1874.
Sept. 30. By balance September 30th, 1873... $13,607 40
          " cash from purchasers of land.. 1,899 68
          " transfer from General Fund.. 17,500 00
          "   "   " Specific Taxes, interest on Normal School Fund 3,046 13
                                                                                          —————————
                                                                                          $35,553 31
                                                                                          —————————

Asylum Fund.

CREDIT.

1874.
Sept. 30. By balance September 30th, 1873... $116,037 00
          " cash from purchasers of land.. 940 00
          "   "   "   "   for interest....................................... 1,230 00
          " transfer from Swamp Land Fund.. 46 15
          "   "   " General Fund... 155,278 89
                                                                                          —————————
                                                                                          $273,581 54
                                                                                          —————————

State Building Fund.

CREDIT.

1874.
Sept. 30. By balance September 30th, 1873... $168,956 67
          " cash from purchasers of lands.. 210 00
          "   "   "   " for interest... 238 82
          "   "   " rents in Lansing... 175 00
          " transfer from General Fund.. 199,882 79
                                                                                          —————————
                                                                                          $363,968 28
                                                                                          —————————

Internal Improvement Fund.

CREDIT.

1874.
Sept. 30. By cash from purchaser of land.. $50 00
          "   "   " United States for 5 per cent of land sales.................... 26,241 76
          " balance.. 2,408,920 95
                                                                                          —————————
                                                                                          $2,435,212 71
                                                                                          —————————

War Fund.

DEBIT.

1874.
Sept. 30. To paid coupons on War-Bounty Loan... $23,791 91
    "   "   "   " War Loan.. 8 75
    " Sinking Fund for excess of interest......................... 336 96
    " balance... 18,978 39

$43,115 31

Military Fund.

DEBIT.

1874.
Sept. 30. To paid Quartermaster General's estimates..................... $43,000 00
    "   " Salaries of Military Officers............................ 1,796 06
    " transfer to Soldiers' Aid Fund.............................. 5,000 00
    " balance 66,754 76

$113,550 79

Soldiers' Aid Fund.

DEBIT.

1874.
Sept. 30. To paid Treasurer of Soldier's Aid............................ $5,000 00

$5,000 00

University Aid Fund.

DEBIT.

1874.
Sept. 30. To paid Treasurer of University............................... $27,375 00
    " balance...... .... 7,875 00

$35,250 00

St. Mary's Falls Ship Canal Fund.

DEBIT.

1874.
Sept. 30. To paid Canal Bonds... $12,000 00
    "   " Coupons.. 4,199 90
    "   " Superintendent's Salary................................ 1,750 00
    "   " repairs on Canal....................................... 3,251 25
    "   " expenses of Canal Board............................... 235 80
    " balance.. 85,615 86

$107,052 81

Portage Lake Ship Canal Fund.

DEBIT.

1874.
Sept. 30. To balance September 30th, 1873................................... $88 25

$88 25

War Fund.
CREDIT.

1874.
Sept. 30. By balance Sept. 30, 1873 .... $17,847 14
           " Specific Taxes 25,768 18

                                                                                    $43,115 82

Military Fund.
CREDIT.

1874.
Sept. 30. By balance Sept. 30, 1874 .... $35,168 29
           " transfer from General Fund 33,382 50

                                                                                    $118,550 79

Soldiers' Aid Fund.
CREDIT.

1874.
Sept. 30. By transfer from Military Fund $5,000 00

                                                                                    $5,000 00

University Aid Fund.
CREDIT.

1874.
Sept. 30. By balance September 30th, 1873 .... $3,750 00
           " transfer from General Fund 31,500 00

                                                                                    $35,250 00

St. Mary's Falls Ship Canal Fund.
CREDIT.

1874.
Sept. 30. By balance September 30th, 1873 .... $79,719 04
           " received for Tolls 27,333 77

                                                                                    $107,052 81

Portage Lake_Ship Canal Fund.
CREDIT.

1874.
Sept. 30. By balance $38 25

                                                                                    $38 25

47

Suspense Account.

DEBIT.

1874.
Sept. 30. To balance September 30th, 1873 .... $2,305 36

$2,305 36

Specific Taxes.

DEBIT.

1874.
Sept. 30. To transfer to P. S. Interest Fund $169,736 61
  "   "   " University Interest Fund 30,337 97
  "   "   " Ag'l Coll. Interest Fund 7,467 65
  "   "   " Normal School Interest Fund 3,046 18
  "   "   " War Fund 25,768 13
  "   "   " General Fund 91,590 05
  "   "   " Sinking Fund 149,857 36
  " refunded Ætna Life Ins. Co. tax 71 51

$471,385 41

Sinking Fund.

DEBIT.

1874.
Sept. 30. To balance Sept. 30, 1873 .... $1,388,618 38
  " paid Renewal Loan Bonds 6,000 00
  "   " $2,000,000 Loan Bonds 29,000 00
  "   " War Bounty Loan Bonds 97,000 00

$1,590,618 38

Dewey Asset Lands.

DEBIT.

1874.
Sept. 30. To balance Sept. 30, 1873 .... $14,946 55
  " paid expenses for trespass 8 35

$14,954 90

Hazelton Asset Lands.

DEBIT.

1874.
Sept. 30. To balance Sept. 30, 1873 .... $12,407 54
  " refunding taxes 141 14
  " expenses of trespasses 124 30

$12,673 98

Escheats.

DEBIT.

1874.
Sept. 30. To Primary School Fund $100 00

$100 00

Suspense Account.

CREDIT.

1874.
Sept. 30. By balance_____ $2,305 88

$2,305 88

Specific Taxes.

CREDIT.

1874.
Sept. 30. By cash from railroad companies_____ $331,787 59
    " " "   street railway companies_____ 1,160 43
    " " "   fire insurance companies_____ 66,563 09
    " " "   life insurance companies_____ 40,690 20
    " " "   mining, U. P. companies_____ 22,885 75
    " " "   mining, L. P. companies_____ 1 41
    " " "   telegraph companies_____ 2,498 87
    " " "   express companies_____ 2,230 79
    " " "   car companies_____ 2,742 88
    " " "   gravel road companies_____ 192 22
    " " "   river improvement companies_____ 562 04
    " error in Primary School Interest Fund_____ 19

$471,885 41

Sinking Fund.

CREDIT.

1874.
Sept. 30. By transfer from Specific Taxes_____ $149,857 86
    "   "   General Fund_____ 200,051 83
    "   "   War Fund_____ 836 25
    " error Primary School Interest Fund_____ 3 08
    " balance_____ 1,170,869 91

$1,520,618 88

Dewey Asset Lands.

CREDIT.

1874.
Sept. 30. By balance_____ $14,954 90

$14,954 90

Hazelton Asset Lands.

CREDIT.

1874.
Sept. 30. By sale of land_____ $500 00
    " received from trespasses_____ 1,261 86
    " balance_____ 10,911 12

$12,672 98

Escheats.

CREDIT.

1874.
Sept. 30. By received on land contract_____ $100 00

$100 00

Ontonagon County Deposit.

DEBIT.

1874.
Sept. 30. To cash _____ $1,872 60

$1,872 60

Swamp Land Trespass Deposit.

DEBIT.

1874.
Sept. 30. To cash _____ $400 00

$400 00

Secretary Board of Control St. Mary's Canal.

DEBIT.

1874.
Sept. 30. To balance _____ $75 00

$75 00

Michigan Central Railroad Deposits.

DEBIT.

1874.
Sept. 30. To balance _____ $1,397 09

$1,397 09

Michigan Southern Railroad Deposits.

DEBIT.

1874.
Sept. 30. To balance _____ $147 73

$147 73

St. Joseph Valley Railroad Deposits.

DEBIT.

1874.
Sept. 30. To balance _____ $55 00

$55 00

Oakland and Ottawa Railroad Deposits.

DEBIT.

1874.
Sept. 30. To balance _____ $3 58

$3 58

Light-House Deposit.

DEBIT.

1874.
Sept. 30. To balance _____ $15 00

$15 00

Ontonagon County Deposit.
CREDIT.

1874.
Sept. 30. By balance Sept. 30, 1873... $1,872 69

$1,872 69

Swamp Land Trespass Deposit.
CREDIT.

1874.
Sept. 30. By cash.. $400 00

$400 00

Secretary Board of Control St. Mary's Canal.
CREDIT.

1874.
Sept. 30. By cash.. $75 00

$75 00

Michigan Central Railroad Deposits.
CREDIT.

1874.
Sept. 30. By balance September 30th, 1873... $1,897 02

$1,897 02

Michigan Southern Railroad Deposits.
CREDIT.

1874.
Sept. 30. By balance September 30th, 1873... $147 72

$147 72

St. Joseph Valley Railroad Deposits.
CREDIT.

1874.
Sept. 30. By balance September 30th, 1873... $55 00

$55 00

Oakland and Ottawa Railroad Deposits.
CREDIT.

1874.
Sept. 30. By balance September 30th, 1873... $8 58

$8 58

Light-House Deposit.
CREDIT.

1874.
Sept. 30. By balance September 30th, 1873... $15 00

$15 00

Auditor General's Deposit Account.
DEBIT.

1874.
Sept. 30. To balance... $186 64

$186 64

Collections from Trespassers on Railroad Lands.
DEBIT.

1874.
Sept. 30. To balance... $186 00

$186 00

Treasury Notes.
DEBIT.

1874.
Sept. 30. To balance... $730 00

$730 00

Primary School Deposits.
DEBIT.

1874.
Sept. 30. To cash... $430 00
      " balance.. 160 00

$590 00

Primary School Interest Deposits.
DEBIT.

1874.
Sept. 30. To cash... $32 03
      " balance.. 1 83

$33 86

Swamp Land Deposits.
DEBIT.

1874.
Sept. 30. To cash... $58 50
      " balance.. 115 56

$174 06

University Land Deposits.
DEBIT.

1874.
Sept. 30. To cash... $33 75

$33 75

Salt Spring Deposits.
DEBIT.

1874.
Sept. 30. To cash... $545 00

$545 00

Auditor General's Deposit Account.

CREDIT.

1874.		
Sept. 30.	By balance Sept. 30,.1873..	$186 64
		$186 64

Collections from Trespassers on Railroad Lands.

CREDIT.

1874.		
Sept. 30.	By balance Sept. 30, 1873..	$186 00
		$186 00

Treasury Notes.

CREDIT.

1874.		
Sept. 30.	By balance Sept. 30, 1873..	$730 00
		$730 00

Primary School Deposits.

CREDIT.

1874.		
Sept. 30.	By balance Sept. 30, 1874..	$247 50
	" cash..	342 50
		$590 00

Primary School Interest Deposits.

CREDIT.

1874.		
Sept. 30.	By balance Sept. 30, 1873..	$1 33
	" cash..	39 08
		$33 36

Swamp Land Deposits.

CREDIT.

1874.		
Sept. 30.	By balance September 30th, 1873..	$76 23
	" cash..	97 83
		$174 06

University Land Deposits.

CREDIT.

1874.		
Sept. 30.	By balance September 30th, 1873..	$33 75
		$33 75

Salt Spring Deposits.

CREDIT.

1874.		
Sept. 30.	By balance..	$545 00
		$545 00

BANKS IN MICHIGAN.

The annexed Tables show the Condition of the State Banks doing business in this State, as reported to the State Treasurer in the first week in July, 1874.

STATE BANKS—LIABILITIES.

NAME OF BANK.	LOCATION.	Capital.	Surplus.	Due Banks and Depositors.	Profit and Loss.	Total.
Bay City Bank	Bay City	$100,000 00	$3,000 00	$96,327 28	$2,025 00	$201,352 28
Citizens' Bank	Marquette	150,000 00	15,250 00	118,048 00	1,085 84	279,383 84
City Bank	Battle Creek	50,000 00	18,642 79	138,988 78		207,581 57
German-American Bank	Detroit	100,000 00		441,355 14	17,593 67	558,948 81
State Bank	Fenton	50,000 00	1,700 00	34,745 15	414 39	86,859 54
State Bank	Bay City	150,000 00	18,000 00	159,914 17	7,887 58	330,801 75
Jackson City Bank	Jackson	100,000 00	50,000 00	198,847 74	3,866 42	351,714 16
Jackson County Bank	Jackson	15,000 00		30,955 69	7,143 46	58,099 15
People's Bank	Manchester	50,000 00		83,611 75	366 52	88,978 27
Merchants and Miners' Bank	Calumet	25,000 00		75,496 69		100,496 69
Merchants and Manufacturers' Bank	Detroit	300,000 00		414,876 07	18,220 42	733,096 49
Mechanics' Bank	Detroit	100,000 00		373,667 27	25,075 59	498,742 86
Exchange Bank	Big Rapids	49,785 78		61,506 00	3,415 99	114,748 33
Lumbermans' State Bank	Whitehall	50,000 00		68,990 98	755 68	119,786 61
Totals		$1,239,785 78	$101,592 79	$2,247,266 66	$86,800 51	$3,725,890 80

STATE BANKS—RESOURCES.

NAME OF BANK.	LOCATION.	Loans and Discounts.	Bonds.	Cash.	Real Estate and Fixtures.	Due from Banks.	Expenses.	Overdrafts.	Total.
Bay City Bank	Bay City	$137,315 87		$15,850 92	$7,211 70	$39,893 85	$601 08	$1,479 31	$201,852 28
Citizens' Bank	Marquette	245,012 65	$1,000 00	14,119 11	1,700 00	15,472 50		1,029 58	279,383 84
City Bank	Battle Creek	167,497 66		21,848 63	1,400 00	12,550 86		3,584 42	207,581 57
German-American Bank	Detroit	298,119 05	59,944 76	119,618 27	2,050 00	80,838 94	8,744 79		558,948 81
State Bank	Fenton	58,921 54		20,087 18	778 54	2,176 81		45 02	86,859 54
State Bank	Bay City	224,858 67	5,000 00	30,587 88	2,000 00	59,089 02	1,528 00	2,848 23	330,801 75
Jackson City Bank	Jackson	258,488 65		33,206 70	10,000 00	41,729 89		3,830 42	351,714 16
Jackson County Bank	Jackson	36,288 66		11,279 88	1,250 00	3,701 89	2,984 88		58,099 15
People's Bank	Manchester	50,371 77		9,547 45	7,984 00	9,357 88	258 58	1,414 09	88,978 27
Merchants and Miners' Bank	Calumet	50,695 09		15,516 02	4,194 58	25,983 11	4,112 99		100,496 69
Merchants and Manufacturers' Bank	Detroit	567,701 25	21,900 00	41,659 98	8,745 06	98,196 25		2,602 14	733,096 49
Mechanics' Bank	Detroit	392,584 09	49,042 73	38,499 78		23,250 48	2,618 65	11,740 44	498,742 86
Exchange Bank	Big Rapids	79,478 69		7,879 39	4,608 87	6,838 28	4,619 66	2,097 44	114,748 33
Lumbermans' State Bank	Whitehall	92,904 84		5,004 43	10,068 65	9,721 75			119,786 61
Totals		$2,658,020 50	$136,787 48	$394,198 42	$56,022 87	$427,298 01	$20,858 18	$34,829 09	$3,725,890 80

The following Tables show the condition of the Savings Banks doing business in this State, as reported to the State Treasurer in the first week in October, 1874.

SAVINGS BANKS.--LIABILITIES.

NAME OF BANK.	LOCATION.	Capital.	Surplus.	Due Banks and Depositors.	Profit and Loss.	Total.
Adrian Savings Bank	Adrian	$5,000 00		$5,916 87		$10,916 87
Ann Arbor Savings Bank	Ann Arbor	50,000 00	$10,000 00	105,811 52	$2,932 91	168,244 43
Detroit Savings Bank	Detroit	200,000 00	99,700 00	1,442,219 35	24,550 22	1,766,799 57
Peoples' Savings Bank	Detroit	125,000 00		929,140 61	30,437 17	1,084,577 78
Wayne County Savings Bank	Detroit	50,000 00		1,135,695 89		1,185,695 89
Genesee County Savings Bank	Flint	50,000 00	1,000 00	90,916 99	2,758 87	144,675 86
Grand Rapids Savings Bank	Grand Rapids	100,000 00		141,762 85	8,281 40	250,044 25
Lenawee County Savings Bank	Adrian	50,000 00	8,769 55	204,644 09		273,413 64
Port Huron Savings Bank	Port Huron	75,500 00	728 88	124,098 14	12,852 99	213,179 46
Wyandotte Savings Bank	Wyandotte	50,000 00		80,978 41	3,831 06	84,809 47
Totals		**$765,500 00**	**$120,197 88**	**$4,210,684 24**	**$85,474 62**	**$5,181,856 72**

SAVINGS BANKS.—RESOURCES.

NAME OF BANK.	LOCATION.	Loans and Discounts.	Bonds.	Cash.	Real Estate and Fixtures.	Due from Banks.	Expenses.	Overdrafts.	Total.
Adrian Savings Bank	Adrian	$7,341 65		$1,410 60	$298 80	$1,595 50	$150 95	$124 87	$10,916 87
Ann Arbor Savings Bank	Ann Arbor	107,194 15	$100 00	22,291 76	2,687 84	34,968 47	795 14	277 07	168,244 43
Detroit Savings Bank	Detroit	1,029,790 55	406,761 57	78,480 98	6,749 29	238,651 90	7,880 52	584 81	1,766,799 57
Peoples' Savings Bank	Detroit	710,904 50	79,500 00	98,987 72	8,300 71	165,921 79	16,874 00	1,484 78	1,084,577 78
Wayne County Savings Bank	Detroit	827,281 95	102,000 00	242,076 75	8,045 52		11,291 67		1,185,695 89
Genesee County Savings Bank	Flint	90,569 29	25,638 11	15,131 31	285 58	12,169 44	846 63		144,675 86
Grand Rapids Savings Bank	Grand Rapids	108,616 99	89,415 58	21,742 71	4,074 85	23,599 10	2,256 85	388 72	250,044 25
Lenawee County Savings Bank	Adrian	201,473 93	90,500 00	8,567 61	1,708 00	38,441 48	2,623 77		273,413 64
Port Huron Savings Bank	Port Huron	162,718 02	16,000 00	11,785 42	1,115 22	18,402 11	3,168 69		213,179 46
Wyandotte Savings Bank	Wyandotte	56,558 82		2,229 58	6,928 36	21,158 07	539 69		84,809 47
Totals		**$3,299,464 75**	**$749,880 21**	**$502,084 24**	**$35,093 17**	**$555,202 74**	**$46,371 91**	**$2,759 70**	**$5,181,856 72**

REPORT of the condition of the Bay City Bank at Bay City, Michigan, at the close of business Monday, July 6th, A. D. 1874, made in accordance with Sections 18, 19, and 67 of the General Banking Law as amended in 1871.

RESOURCES.

Loans and Discounts	$137,315 87
Overdrafts	1,479 81
Cash Items	1,710 97
Due from Banks and Bankers	39,396 85
Real Estate	4,694 85
Revenue Stamps	70 65
Furniture and Fixtures	2,516 85
Fractional Currency	58 30
Expenses	601 08
Legal Tender and Bank Notes	14,011 00
	$20',352 23

LIABILITIES.

Capital	$100,000 00
Surplus	3,000 00
Due other Banks	1,276 24
Due Depositors	95,550 99
Profit and Loss	2,025 00
	$201,852 23

I do solemnly swear that the above statement is true, to the best of my knowledge and belief.

GEO. H. YOUNG, *Cashier.*

Subscribed and sworn to before me this 6th day of July, 1874.

W. A. YOUNG, *Notary Public.*

REPORT of the condition of the Citizens' Bank at Marquette, Michigan, at the close of business July 6, A. D. 1874, made in accordance with Sections 18, 19, and 67 of the General Banking Law as amended in 1871.

RESOURCES.

Loans and discounts	$229,720 65
Overdrafts	1,029 53
Cash Items	490 24
Due from Banks and Bankers	15,472 50
Furniture and Fixtures	1,700 00
Fractional Currency	150 07
Legal Tender and Bank Notes	13,177 00
Small Drafts of sundry Mining Companies	16,292 60
Specie	292 30
Stock and Bond Account	1,000 00
	$279,383 84

LIABILITIES.

Capital	$150,000 00
Surplus	15,250 00
Due Depositors	105,548 00
Profit and Loss	1,085 84
Dividends unpaid	7,500 00
	$279,383 84

I do solemnly swear that the above statement is true, to the best of my knowledge and belief.

J. M. WILKINSON, *Cashier.*

Subscribed and sworn to before me, this 8th day of July, 1874.

FRED. M. STEELE, *Notary Public.*

REPORT *of the condition of the City Bank of Battle Creek at Battle Creek, Michigan, at the close of business July 6th, A. D. 1874, made in accordance with Sections 18, 19, and 67, of the General Banking Law as amended in 1871.*

RESOURCES.

Loans and Discounts	$167,697 66
Overdrafts	8,584 42
Cash Items	599 30
Due from Banks and Bankers	12,550 86
Revenue Stamps	7 00
Furniture and Fixtures	2,400 00
Fractional Currency	184 33
Legal Tender and Band Notes	20,608 00
	$207,581 57

LIABILITIES.

Capital	$50,000 00
Surplus	18,642 79
Due Depositors	138,938 78
	$207,581 57

I do solemnly swear that the above statement is true, to the best of my knowledge and belief.

ROLDON P. KINGMAN, *Cashier.*

Subscribed and sworn to before me this 7th day of July, 1874.

BRAINARD T. SKINNER, *Notary Public.*

REPORT *of the condition of the Exchange Bank at Big Rapids, Michigan, at the close of business July 6th, A. D. 1874, made in accordance with Sections 18, 19, and 67 of the General Banking Law as amended in 1871.*

RESOURCES.

Loans and Discounts	$79,478 69
Overdrafts	11,740 44
Cash Items	7,873 81
Due from Banks and Bankers	4,549 58
Real Estate	4,184 81
Revenue Stamps	181 80
Furniture and Fixtures	514 06
Fractional Currency	44 28
Expenses	4,619 66
Legal Tender and Bank Notes	823 00
Exchange	1,788 75
	$114,748 83

LIABILITIES.

Capital paid in	$49,785 78
Due other Banks	14,772 44
Due Depositors	18,094 12
Profit and Loss	8,415 99
Bills re-discounted	83,780 00
	$114,748 83

I do solemnly swear that the above statement is true, to the best of my knowledge and belief.

F. FAIRMON, *Cashier.*

Subscribed and sworn to before me this 1st day of August, 1874.

F. D. BROWN, *Notary Public.*

REPORT of the condition of the German American Bank at Detroit, Michigan, at the close of business July 6th, A. D. 1874, made in accordance with the General Banking Law of Michigan.

RESOURCES.

Loans and Discounts	$298,112 05
Due from Banks and Bankers	80,883 94
Revenue Stamps	195 00
Furniture and Fixtures	2,050 00
Expenses	3,744 79
Bonds—Public	59,944 76
Cash on hand	119,418 27
	$558,848 81

LIABILITIES.

Capital	$100,000 00
Due Depositors	441,255 14
Profit and Loss, etc	17,593 67
	$558,848 81

I do solemnly swear that the above statement is true, to the best of my knowledge and belief.

H. L. KANTER, *Cashier.*

Subscribed and sworn to before me, this 9th day of July, 1874.

J. B. PADBERG, *Notary Public.*

REPORT of the condition of the Jackson City Bank at Jackson, Michigan, at the close of business July 6th, A. D. 1874, made in accordance with Sections 18, 19, and 67 of the General Banking Law as amended in 1871.

RESOURCES.

Loans and Discounts	$258,247 80
Overdrafts	8,339 42
Cash Items	8,855 05
Due from Banks and Bankers	37,769 78
Checks on other Banks	8,959 66
Banking-House, Safe, and Fixtures	10,000 00
Revenue Stamps	44 58
Premium Account	190 85
Fractional Currency	1,184 80
Legal Tender and Bank Notes	28,258 00
Coin	414 77
	$351,714 16

LIABILITIES.

Capital	$100,000 00
Surplus	50,000 00
Due other Banks	1,597 82
Due Depositors	196,449 92
Profit and Loss	8,866 42
	$351,714 16

I do solemnly swear that the above statement is true, to the best of my knowledge and belief.

BENJ. NEWKIRK, *Cashier.*

Subscribed and sworn to before me, this 15th day of July, 1874.

GILBERT R. BYRNE, *Notary Public.*

REPORT of the condition of the Jackson County Bank at Jackson, Michigan, at the close of business July 6, A. D. 1874, made in accordance with Sections 18, 19, and 67 of the General Banking Law as amended in 1871.

RESOURCES.

Loans and Discounts	$33,988 55
Stock Account	35,000 00
Due from Banks and Bankers	3,701 39
Furniture and Fixtures	1,250 00
Expenses	2,884 89
Legal Tender and Bank Notes and Cash Items	11,279 88
	$88,099 15

LIABILITIES.

Capital	$50,000 00
Due other Banks	72 98
Due Depositors	30,882 71
Profit and Loss	7,143 46
	$88,099 15

I do solemnly swear that the above statement is true, to the best of my knowledge and belief.

H. V. PERRIN, *Cashier.*

Subscribed and sworn to before me, this 8th day of July, 1874.

JAS. HAMMILL, *Notary Public.*

REPORT of the condition of the Lumberman's State Bank at Whitehall, Michigan, at the close of business July 3, A. D. 1874, made in accordance with Sections 18, 19, and 67 of the General Banking Law as amended in 1871.

RESOURCES.

Loans and Discounts	$92,904 34
Overdrafts	2,067 44
Cash Items	765 88
Due from Banks and Bankers	9,731 75
Real Estate and Banking House	8,170 00
Furniture and Fixtures	1,898 65
Fractional Currency	505 60
Legal Tender and Bank Notes	3,783 00
	$119,786 61

LIABILITIES.

Capital	$50,000 00
Due other Banks	1,116 28
Due Depositors	46,064 70
Interest and Exchange	755 63
Bills Re-disconnted	21,800 00
	$119,786 61

I do solemnly swear that the above statement is true, to the best of my knowledge and belief.

C. A. HAMMOND, *Cashier.*

Subscribed and sworn to before me, this 16th day of July, 1874.

JAS. S. GALLOWAY, *Notary Public.*

REPORT of the condition of the Mechanics' Bank at Detroit, Michigan, at the close of business Monday, July 6th, A. D. 1874, made in accordance with Sections 18, 19, and 67 of the General Banking Law as amended in 1871.

RESOURCES.

Loans and Discounts	$381,687 27
Overdrafts	2,902 14
Cash Items, Checks, etc.	17,216 19
Due from Banks and Bankers	23,250 48
Revenue Stamps	421 50
Expenses	2,613 65
Legal Tender and Bank Notes	20,962 00
Bonds	49,042 72
Suspense account	646 82
	$498,742 86

LIABILITIES.

Capital	$100,000 00
Due Depositors	373,667 27
Profit and Loss	25,075 59
	$498,742 86

I do solemnly swear that the above statement is true, to the best of my knowledge and belief.

WM. A. BUTLER, JR., *Cashier.*

Subscribed and sworn to before me this sixth day of July, 1874.

FRED E. BUTLER, *Notary Public.*

STATEMENT showing the condition of the Merchants' and Manufacturers' Bank, Detroit, on Monday the 6th day of July, 1874, as required by the Banking Law of Michigan.

RESOURCES.

Loans and Discounts	$567,701 25
Cash on hand	41,149 03
Due from Banks and Bankers	98,190 25
Revenue Stamps	511 91
Public Bonds	21,800 00
Furniture Account	8,745 06
	$738,096 49

LIABILITIES.

Capital Stock	$300,000 00
Profit and Loss	18,220 42
Deposits	414,876 07
	$738,096 49

I, Charles C. Cadman, Cashier of the above named Bank, do solemnly swear that the above statement is true, to the best of my knowlege and belief.

CHARLES C. CADMAN, *Cashier.*

Subscribed to and sworn before me, this 18th day of July, 1874.

W. H. TRAINOR,
Notary Public in and for Wayne County, Mich.

REPORT of the condition of the Merchants' and Miners' Bank at Calumet, Michigan, at the close of business July 3, A. D. 1874, made in accordance with Sections 18, 19, and 67 of the General Banking Law as amended in 1871.

RESOURCES.

Loans and Discounts	$90,695 02
Cash Items	5,806 15
Due from Banks and Bankers	25,988 11
Real Estate	3,789 80
Revenue Stamps	44 00
Furniture and Fixtures	444 75
Fractional Currency	107 87
Expenses	3,768 52
Legal Tender and Bank Notes	10,056 00
Taxes Paid	849 47
Stock Subscription, payable on call	25,000 00
	$125,499 79

LIABILITIES.

Capital	$50,000 00
Due other Banks	285 15
Due Depositors	67,947 88
Interest	4,640 15
Exchange	3,824 01
	$125,496 69

I do solemnly swear that the above statement is true, to the best of my knowledge and belief.

H. S. COLLIN, *Cashier.*

Subscribed and sworn to before me, this 8th day of July, 1874.

D. T. MACDONALD, *Notary Public.*

REPORT of the condition of the Peoples' Bank at Manchester, Michigan, at the close of business July 6th, A. D. 1874, made in accordance with Sections 18, 19, and 67 of the General Banking Law as amended in 1871.

RESOURCES.

Loans and Discounts	$60,871 77
Overdrafts	1,414 09
Cash Items	501 89
Due from Banks and Bankers	9,857 88
Real Estate	7,000 00
Revenue Stamps	46 00
Furniture and Fixtures	984 00
Fractional Currency	811 65
Expenses	253 58
Legal Tender and Bank Notes	8,788 00
	$88,978 27

LIABILITIES.

Capital	$50,000 00
Due Depositors	88,611 75
Profit and Loss	366 52
	$88,978 27

I do solemnly swear that the above statement is true, to the best of my knowledge and belief.

L. D. WATKINS, *President.*

Subscribed and sworn to before me, this 16th day of July, 1874.

S. W. CLARKSON, *Notary Public.*

REPORT *of the condition of the State Bank of Bay City, at Bay City, Michigan, at the close of business July 6, A. D. 1874, made in accordance with Sections 18, 19, and 67 of the General Banking Law as amended in 1871.*

RESOURCES.

Loans and Discounts	$224,558 07
Overdrafts	2,348 28
Cash Items	3,867 61
Due from Banks and Bankers	59,089 02
Revenue Stamps	139 17
Furniture and Fixtures	2,000 00
Fractional Currency	617 05
Expenses	1,528 00
Legal Tender and Bank Notes	30,894 00
Bonds	5,000 00
	$330,301 75

LIABILITIES.

Capital	$150,000 00
Surplus	18,000 00
Due other Banks	658 88
Due Depositors	159,280 79
Profit and Loss	8,909 07
Endorsement Account	187 76
Exchange and Interest	3,290 75
	$330,301 75

I do solemnly swear that the above statement is true, to the best of my knowledge and belief.

ORRIN BUMP, *Cashier.*

Subscribed and sworn to before me, this fourteenth day of July, 1874.

W. D. MARSH, *Notary Public.*

REPORT *of the condition of the State Bank at Fenton, Michigan, at the close of business July 6th, A. D. 1874, made in accordance with Sections 18, 19, and 67, of the General Banking Law as amended in 1871.*

RESOURCES.

Loans and Discounts	$58,921 54
Overdrafts	45 02
Cash Items	175 60
Due from Banks and Bankers	2,176 81
Revenue Stamps	4 25
Furniture and Fixtures	779 54
Fractional Currency	228 40
Legal Tender and Bank Notes	24,622 00
	$86,859 54

LIABILITIES.

Capital	$50,000 00
Surplus	1,700 00
Due other Banks—Re-discounts	3,000 00
Due Depositors	31,745 15
Profit and Loss	414 39
	$86,859 54

I do solemnly swear that the above statement is true, to the best of my knowledge and belief.

EDWIN TRUMP, *Cashier.*

Subscribed and sworn to before me, this 13th day of July, 1874.

W. P. GUEST,
Notary Public, Genesee Co., Mich.

REPORT *of the condition of the Adrian Savings Bank at Adrian, Michigan, at the commencement of business Monday, October 5th, A. D. 1874, made in accordance with Sections 18, 19,
and 67 of the General Banking Law as amended in 1871.*

RESOURCES.

Loans and Discounts	$7,343 68
Overdrafts	194 87
Cash Items—Unpaid Stock	5,000 00
Due from Banks and Bankers	1,595 50
Furniture and Fixtures	393 30
Fractional Currency	79 79
Expenses	150 95
Legal Tender and Bank Notes	1,200 00
Coin	50 90
	$15,916 87

LIABILITIES.

Capital	$10,000 00
Due Depositors	5,916 87
	$15,916 87

I do solemnly swear that the above statement is true, to the best of my knowledge and belief.

HEMAN LOOMIS, *Treasurer.*

Subscribed and sworn to before me, this 9th day of October, 1874.

A. J. COMSTOCK, *Notary Public.*

REPORT *of the condition of the Ann Arbor Savings Bank at Ann Arbor, Michigan, at the
close of business October 5th, 1874, made in accordance with Sections 18, 19, and 67 of the
General Banking Law as amended in 1871.*

RESOURCES.

Loans and discounts	$107,194 15
Overdrafts	277 07
Cash Items	31 55
Due from Banks and Bankers	$8,626 91
Revenue Stamps	68 17
Furniture and Fixtures	2,687 84
Fractional Currency	509 04
Expenses	795 14
Legal Tender and Bank Notes	21,618 00
Premium Funds	1,102 57
Bonds: U. S. 5-20 '65	100 00
Premium Account	105 74
Bills in Transit	183 25
	$168,244 48

LIABILITIES.

Capital	$50,000 00
Surplus	10,000 00
Due Depositors	105,111 52
Profit and Loss	65 97
Unpaid Dividends	200 00
Interest and Exchange	2,867 64
	$168,244 48

I do solemnly swear that the above statement is true, to the best of my knowledge and belief.

R. S. SMITH, *President.*

Subscribed and sworn to before me, this 6th day of October, 1874.

W. D. HANIMAN, *Notary Public.*

49

REPORT *of the condition of the Detroit Savings Bank at Detroit, Michigan, at the close of business Monday, October 5th, A. D. 1874, made in accordance with Sections 18, 19, and 67 of the General Banking Law as amended in 1871.*

RESOURCES.

Loans and Discounts	$1,029,790 55
Overdrafts	584 81
Cash Items, Checks on other Banks and Loans on call with Collateral	27,604 06
Due from Banks and Bankers	236,651 90
Revenue Stamps in Check Books	644 50
Furniture and Fixtures	6,740 29
Fractional Currency and Cents	2,290 85
Expenses	7,880 59
Legal Tender and Bank Notes and Gold	47,915 00

Bonds—

United States and Premium	$175,578 70	
State of Missouri	26,610 00	
Wayne County	88,000 00	
Detroit City and Paving	118,985 87	
Hargreaves Mf'g Co	26,000 00	
Hamtramck Iron Works	12,000 00	
Detroit City Railway	4,000 00	
N. Y. Central Park Fund	4,700 00	
E. Saginaw Water Bonds	18,500 00	
Hamtramck School Bonds	800 00	
Detroit & Milwaukee Railway Co	2,587 50	
		406,761 57
		$1,766,799 57

LIABILITIES.

Capital	$200,000 00
Surplus	99,706 00
Due other Banks	18,751 70
Due Depositors	1,423,467 65
Profit and Loss	24,880 22
	$1,766,799 57

I do solemnly swear that the above statement is true, to the best of my knowledge and belief.

A. H. ADAMS, *Cashier.*

Subscribed and sworn to before me, this 6th day of October, 1874.

M. T. DOW, *Notary Public, Wayne Co. Mich.*

REPORT *of the condition of the Genesee County Savings Bank at Flint, Michigan, at the close of business October 5th, A. D. 1874, made in accordance with Sections 18, 19, and 67 of the General Banking Law as amended in 1871.*

RESOURCES.

Loans and Discounts	$90,589 29
Cash Items	4,171 57
Due from Banks and Bankers	12,169 44
Revenue Stamps	58 00
Furniture and Fixtures	285 56
Fractional Currency	1,073 11
Expenses	846 68
Legal Tender and Bank Notes	9,584 00
Bonds, { City of Flint—School	14,800 00
{ Mortgages	11,358 11
Coin at par	295 18
	$144,675 86

LIABILITIES.

Capital	$50,000 00
Surplus	1,000 00
Due Depositors, { Savings	43,989 68
{ Commercial	46,977 86
Profits and Loss	2,736 87
	$144,675 86

I do solemnly swear that the above statement is true, to the best of my knowledge and belief.

IRA H. WILDER, *Cashier.*

Subscribed and sworn to before me, this fifth day of October, 1874.

A. G. BISHOP, *Notary Public.*

REPORT of the condition of the Grand Rapids Savings Bank at Grand Rapids, Michigan, at the close of business October 3, A. D. 1874, made in accordance with Sections 18, 19, and 67 of the General Banking Law as amended in 1871.

RESOURCES.

Loans and Discounts	$109,616 99
Overdrafts	338 72
Cash Items	676 82
Due from Banks and Bankers	23,599 10
Real Estate	704 22
Revenue Stamps	86 00
Furniture and Fixtures	8,870 18
Fractional Currency	261 89
Expenses	2,256 85
Legal Tender and Bank Notes	20,718 57
Bonds	12,100 00
Mortgages	71,815 58
Interest accrued	5,500 00
	$250,044 25

LIABILITIES.

Capital	$100,000 00
Due Depositors	140,710 85
Profit and Loss	8,281 40
Dividends unpaid	32 50
Bills Re-discounted	1,620 00
	$250,044 25

I do solemnly swear that the above statement is true, to the best of my knowledge and belief.

GEO. R. ALLEN, *Cashier.*

Subscribed and sworn to before me, this 5th day of October, 1874.

DANA B. SHEDD, *Notary Public.*

REPORT of the condition of the Lenawee County Savings Bank at Adrian, Michigan, at the opening of business, Monday, October 5, A. D. 1874, made in accordance with Sections 18, 19, and 67 of the General Banking Law as amended in 1871.

RESOURCES.

Loans and Discounts, viz—	
Bonds and Mortgages	$173,778 29
Bills Receivable	27,695 54
Due from Banks and Bankers	83,441 43
Furniture and Fixtures	1,708 00
Fractional Currency	102 61
Expenses	2,692 77
Legal Tender and Bank Notes	8,465 00
Bonds, { Adrian City	16,500 00
{ School	4,100 00
	$273,413 64

LIABILITIES.

Capital	$60,00 00
Surplus	8,769 55
Due other Banks	410 00
Due Depositors	204,234 09
	$273,413 64

I do solemnly swear that the above statement is true, to the best of my knowledge and belief.

W. W. BRUCE, *Cashier.*

Subscribed and sworn to before me, this 12th day of October, 1874.

L. T. ELDRIDGE, *Notary Public.*

REPORT *of the condition of the People's Savings Bank at Detroit, Michigan, at the close of business Monday, October 5, A. D. 1874, made in accordance with Sections 18, 19, and 67 of the General Banking Law as amended in 1871.*

RESOURCES.

Loans and Discounts	$710,904 59
Overdrafts	1,484 72
Due from Banks and Bankers	166,281 73
Real Estate	1,922 44
Revenue Stamps	464 06
Furniture and Fixtures	6,883 27
Fractional Currency, Nickels, etc.	1,414 27
Fractional Currency, in transit for redemption	4,943 60
Expenses, Taxes, etc.	16,574 00
Legal Tender and Bank Notes	75,360 11
Checks	16,297 71
Bonds, U. S. and Michigan	79,800 00
	$1,064,577 73

LIABILITIES.

Capital	$125,000 00
Dividends, unpaid	300 00
Due other Banks	10,271 59
Due Depositors	918,569 00
Profit and Loss	30,437 17
	$1,064,577 73

I do solemnly swear that the above statement is true, to the best of my knowledge and belief.

M. W. O'BRIEN, *Cashier*.

Subscribed and sworn to before me this seventh day of October, 1874.

L. A. SCHULTZ, *Notary Public*.

REPORT *of the condition of the Port Huron Savings Bank at Port Huron, Michigan, at the close of business October 5, A. D. 1874, made in accordance with Sections 18, 19, and 67 of the General Banking Law as amended in 1871.*

RESOURCES.

Loans and Discounts	$162,713 02
Cash Items	1,205 01
Due from Banks and Bankers	18,402 11
Revenue Stamps	96 00
Furniture and Fixtures	1,115 22
Coin	182 55
Fractional Currency, including Nickels	901 00
Expenses	3,163 00
Legal Tender and Bank Notes	10,161 00
Bonds—Port Huron City Bonds	16,000 00
	$213,179 46

LIABILITIES.

Capital (paid in)	$75,500 00
Surplus	796 32
Dividends unpaid	6 68
Due other Banks	380 72
Due Depositors	123,741 34
Profit and Loss	12,858 90
	$213,179 46

I do solemnly swear that the above statement is true, to the best of my knowledge and belief.

O. F. HARRINGTON, *Cashier*.

Subscribed and sworn to before me, this sixth day of October, 1874.

FRED A. TILDEN, *Notary Public*.

REPORT of the condition of the Wayne County Savings Bank at Detroit, Michigan, at the close of business October third, A. D. 1874, made in accordance with Sections 18, 19, and 67 of the General Banking Law as amended in 1871.

LIABILITIES.

Capital paid up	$50,000 00
Due Depositors	1,102,402 96
Interest and Premium Account	33,292 93
	$1,185,695 89

RESOURCES.

Loans secured by Bond and Mortgage on unincumbered Real Estate, (cash value over $1,275,000)	$560,417 51
Loans secured by Collaterals payable on demand (cash value over $300,000)	186,668 48
Loans secured by Collaterals (cash value over $100,000)	60,195 96
U. S. Government, Michigan, City, School, Water, and Municipal Bonds	102,000 00
Current Expense Account	11,291 67
Furniture, Safes, and Fixtures	3,045 52
Cash in vault and on deposit in Banks	242,076 75
	$1,185,695 89

I do solemnly swear that the above statement is true, to the best of my knowledge and belief.

　　　　　　　　　　　S. D. ELWOOD, *Treasurer.*

Subscribed and sworn to before me, this sixth day of October, 1874.

　　　　　　　　　　　J. S. SCHMITDIEL, *Notary Public.*

REPORT of the condition of the Wyandotte Savings Bank at Wyandotte, Michigan, at the close of business, October 5th, A. D. 1874, made in accordance with Sections 18, 19, and 67 of the General Banking Law, as amended in 1871.

RESOURCES.

Loans and Discounts	$53,558 82
Due from Banks and Bankers	21,156 07
Real Estate	5,491 68
Revenue Stamps	10 00
Furniture and Fixtures	1,836 78
Fractional Currency	116 58
Expenses	589 69
Legal Tender and Bank Notes	2,108 00
	$84,909 47

LIABILITIES.

Capital	$50,000 00
Due Depositors	31,578 41
Profit and Loss	3,331 06
Dividend Unclaimed	300 00
	$84,909 47

I do solemnly swear that the above statement is true, to the best of my knowledge and belief.

　　　　　　　　　　　W. VAN MILLER, *Cashier.*

Subscribed and sworn to before me, this 8th day of October, 1874.

　　　　　　　　　　　JNO. S. VAN ALSTYNE, *Notary Public.*

INDEX.

INDEX.

A.

PAGE.

CIVIL SUITS:
act relative to imprisonment of parties in, amended............... 187

CLEON:
township of, organized.. 338

CLERK OF THE HOUSE OF REPRESENTATIVES
to compile, index, etc., the Journal and documents of the House... 318

COAL OIL:
act to prohibit the use of any product of, for lighting passenger
cars.. 29
inspection of illuminating oils manufactured from, provided for...208–10

COIT AND CURTIS'
partition plat of lands in Grand Rapids: record of, legalized...... 145–6

COLD SPRINGS:
township of, organized.. 333

COLLECTING AGENTS
refusing to pay moneys, etc.: act providing for punishment of,
amended.. 196

COLLEGES:
land donated for the endowment of: act to provide for the selection
of, etc., amended.. 55

COMMISSIONER OF HIGHWAYS:
act relative to application of moneys by, amended................ 199
authorized to purchase the interest of any plank or toll road companies situated in their respective townships.................. 163–4
powers and duties of, defined................................80–102

COMMISSIONER OF RAILROADS:
act to provide for the appointment of, etc., amended............129–30
to be notified by railroad companies of accidents................ 80
to investigate causes of accidents on railroads.................. 80

COMMISSIONER OF STATE LAND OFFICE
authorized to cause to be examined certain forfeited and part-paid
agricultural college, salt spring, and other lands............... 132–3
authorized to convey certain lands to Joseph R. Smith........... 306–7
constituted a member of a board of control to carry out the provisions of an act relative to the examination of certain forfeited
and part-paid lands.. 132–3

COMMISSIONER, SWAMP LAND STATE ROAD:
act 51 of 1872, and act 155 of 1869, relative to the appointment of,
repealed..223, 227

COMMISSIONERS:
fish: act to establish board of, amended.....................109–10
appropriation for board of.................................. 151
fund: act to create and define the powers and duties of the board
of, amended.. 11–12
special: act authorizing circuit courts in chancery in Wayne county
to refer certain causes pending in chancery to, repealed....... 293
State swamp land: act to create board of, amended............210–11

COMMISSIONERS ON FISHERIES:
joint resolution giving construction to section 4 of act 124 of 1873,
relative to expenses incurred by board of.................... 300

F.

G.

I.

J.

54

Milton Keynes UK
Ingram Content Group UK Ltd.
UKHW010636270324
440147UK00003B/53